CW01597521

STATION CALLING COASTGUARD

By

JAMES P. FERNSIDE

NORTH YORKSHIRE
COUNTY LIBRARY
WITHDRAWN
10056 0954
CAS 25.10.05
F £26.28
BAQ 5287

authorHOUSE
1663 Liberty Drive, Suite 200
Bloomington, Indiana 47403
(800) 839-8640
www.authorhouse.com

This book is a work of fiction. Places, events, and situations in this story are purely fictional and any resemblance to actual persons, living or dead, is coincidental.

© 2004 JAMES P. FERNSIDE
All Rights Reserved.

No part of this book may be reproduced, stored in a retrieval system, or transmitted by any means without the written permission of the author.

First published by AuthorHouse 03/30/04

ISBN: 1-4184-0926-X (e)
ISBN: 1-4184-0924-3 (sc)
ISBN: 1-4184-0925-1 (dj)

Library of Congress Number: 2004091668

Printed in the United States of America
Bloomington, Indiana

This book is printed on acid-free paper.

To

Lionel and Pauline Beck

Who were there, for me, when I needed them
And to the memory of their precious daughter

Jackie.

M.D.M

Members of HM Coastguard, past and present,
in particular the Burniston, Scarborough, and Filey areas.

All those who harboured doubt.

CHAPTER ONE

'Gently now,' I whispered as I held her close. 'I know it should not have happened, but it did and we, sadly, were not in a position to do anything about it.' And that was all I was able to say, all I could think of under the circumstances.

* * *

Drug dealing: arms smuggling: suicide and murder. A unique combination to say the least, and something which even now I find difficult to believe actually happened, let alone that I was a part of it.

Despite my background and all my previous experiences, this one was, without doubt, exceptional; if only in so much that it all happened so close to home and in such a quiet, remote and most unlikely place. Not to mention that it involved a very beautiful and exceptional young woman.

However, it did happen, was all very real and all started in the middle of April last year, Thursday the 15th to be precise.

Winter was almost finished and the early spring was doing its best to regenerate everything, in preparation for the anticipated summer.

It was nine fifty five in the morning. An odd time perhaps; but then that is the way things are done in and around the department that claims to provide me with gainful employment. Punctuality is paramount. Not to me of course; but to those who have little better to do but plan their day and routine to run by the dictates of a clock. Timing is believed, though goodness knows why, to be extremely important and an essential part of the smooth running of a naval type establishment. So, at that precise moment I found myself stood in a thickly carpeted corridor, facing a polished, solid wood door.

The plaque, fixed at eye level on the highly polished surface boldly proclaimed that the occupant of the office, I was about to enter, was one Rear Admiral Sir Cecil Potts, RN Retired. Set below that, on a smaller but equally impressive brass plaque, were the instructions - Knock and Wait. So... I knocked and waited.

Seconds later the small metal rimmed circle of optic glass dulled over as an enquiring eye on the other side blocked out the light. I was being scrutinised. Satisfied, the door opened. A deadpan and lacklustre female voice said, 'Come in, you're expected. I will see if he is free.'

I dutifully followed her through the door and then hesitating watched her turn, on her regulation flat heels, and cross the outer office. Out of habit I gave her

rear view the once over before she disappeared through an adjoining door, into the inner office.

She had a neat rear end, but not my type, her being rather more than middle-aged. She was not slim but not yet excessively overweight. Her short black hair had a depth of colour and sheen that could only have come out of a bottle. She was that little bit too mature for the colour to have been natural. She wore a straight black skirt, stiff, neatly pressed, white blouse, black stockings or probably tights, there being no tell tale signs of suspenders and black flat shoes. She was dressed in exactly the same way as she had been, on each of my previous visit to this office. Her overall appearance was very precise and very military, if there is such a fashion. I guessed she was probably an ex-Wren, but her manner and attitude made it abundantly clear that the likes of me would never find out. Her personal life was probably just that, personal and of no concern to anyone else. I smiled when it crossed my mind that maybe she was more attracted to other Wrens than to men. I could have been wrong, but that was the distinct feeling that I got, but having said that, I am no expert on such matters, nor do I really care who is attracted to whom or why. The only thing I know, or care about, is what I find attractive and this one left me cold.

'He will see you now, go straight through,' said the sexless voice.

I crossed the outer office, went through the dividing door, and closed it behind me.

'Good morning Grundy, come in, and sit down,' he said indicating a vacant chair in front of his oversized desk. 'I won't keep you a moment,' as he proceeded to continue reading a sheet of paper, possibly an internal memo, which he held in his hand. I sat down and casually gazed round his immaculate office. Along with the oversized modern teak desk, on which were neatly set the obligatory accessories: blotter, freestanding calendar, clock and penholder, there was a photograph frame; it's back to me so that I still had no idea of what the picture might be, if indeed it held a picture. Everything was still in the same place and exactly as I remembered it from my last visit. There was the one single filing cabinet, a small table set against the wall and three comfortable chairs in front of the desk, one of which I now occupied. Opposite me and at the far side of the desk was a large high backed, leather covered, swivel chair in which sat the Admiral.

With the exception of the one single piece of paper in the Admirals hand, there were no other signs of an active office. This office and it's layout was definitely a far cry from my own everyday working environment, where my desk was always piled high with papers and folders and all demanding immediate attention.

As I sat, I wondered if the absence of paper, in an office, was a symbol of power and came to the conclusion that it must be, for there was no one higher or more powerful than the Rear Admiral, Retired, sitting opposite, that I was likely to come into contact with, particularly in this branch of the service. He was certainly

the top man in our set up and so much so, that a visit to this office, though essential on occasions, was rare and an infrequent occurrence.

As he read, and I presumed from the length of time it took, digested every single word on the sheet, it gave me the opportunity to study the man and contemplate on him and his position. He was the Big Man around here, the head of operations. He controlled the whole vast network of which I was but one very small part. He was answerable to no one in this office block and liased outside, directly with the Minister and goodness knows who else, that had government responsibility for our covert operations. Operations intertwined, hidden in and masked by an otherwise respectable Coastguard Service. There was, and still is, a Chief Coastguard who is in overall command and heads that part of the service that the general public are aware of and often come into contact with. No doubt the two do meet and perhaps they liased together when necessary, but their spheres of responsibility are vastly different.

As I studied the man on the opposite side of the desk, his outward appearance gave no clues as to his mood or possible present state of mind and I noted also that he hadn't physically changed very much since my last visit. He was still in his late fifties, still had a full set of naval whiskers and they, along with his hair, were the same mottled shade of grey. The pale blue, watery eyes were still the same shade of pale. The Coastguard uniform, that he proudly wore, was as immaculate as ever, supporting all the gold braid and decorations befitting a man at the top of his profession.

Office gossip and more than a few in-depth enquiries had all failed to reveal much about the man's background, or how he ended up behind this particular desk. It was obvious to all, from his title, that his background career was naval and he had done quite well for himself having ended up with the rank of Rear Admiral. Although I, along with several others, wondered if he had outlived his active role in the Navy, and not having quite reached retirement age, had been eased along sideways into the Coastguard.

Whilst I sat there and contemplated it, and not for the first time, I came to the same conclusion that he was probably never a Rear Admiral in the Navy at all, but had been promoted when moved. The Navy tend to do that with senior ranks, it having something to do with bolstering their pensions or ego or something. Anyhow they all seem to love it and will stick avidly to their titles long after they have lost their meaning and significance. The Army are almost as bad and come a close second. Thank goodness the Royal Air Force never adopted this antiquated pomposity for I would have found it annoying, if not a little embarrassing, to go round reminding people to address me as "Pilot Officer, Retired". Saying it, silently, to myself now, it sounds daft.

'You received my note?' Of course I did, I thought, otherwise I would not be here.

'Yes Sir,' I replied in anticipation of the next profound statement that would surely come my way.

'Did you clear it with AC?'

I hoped we were both on the same wavelength. That was what the note said I had to do, and don't we always? Isn't that standard procedure as laid down in 'the book'? I just love these formal, intellectual conversations. 'Yes Sir, as instructed.'

'Jolly good.'

I was not supposed to notice as he slid the tips of his fingers under the edge of his desk and pressed the hidden buzzer. Within seconds the office door opened and in marched Miss Efficiency. In one continuous movement she placed a blue folder on the desk, turned on her flat heels and walked out closing the door silently behind her. Not a word was said and during the temporary silence, I realised the reason behind the lack of paperwork on or around the Admiral's desk, it was all kept a bell push distance away in the outer office.

Ignoring me he opened the folder and removed the top sheet. He closed and placed the folder to one side and spread the single sheet out before him.

'A Coastguard Officer in one of our Northern Sectors has gone missing in rather suspicious circumstances. Our colleagues out in Region, and the local Police are not at all happy about it, and so because of that, I have decided that we will look into it, or more to the point; you will. You will carry out and make a full and in-depth investigation and report back, understand?'

'Yes Sir,' and then thinking that perhaps my answer was a bit too brief, I added, 'Was the officer on or off duty at the time of his disappearance Sir?'

'How should I know? That's for you to determine. That is why you are here and why you are being sent to find out. If I had all the answers, here now in front of me, you would be surplus to requirement. Clear everything with AC. He will be fully briefed by me this afternoon, and will be your contact.'

No change and nothing new, there.

'Anything further you require from me before you go?'

Stupid question. 'No Sir, unless that is not all of my brief?'

'From me it is. I select the operative and allocate the assignments; AC will provide the details when I have had the opportunity to brief him.'

Arse about face as usual. Does nothing change? 'Very good Sir, but if I may, can I ask what made you choose me for this particular job when there are three other capable officers in the Department? I have only recently completed an assignment and the others have not had one for quite sometime?'

'Because I select the field officers who I think are the best suited to the job I want done. If you have any objections, or no desire to accept this assignment then put your resignation in writing. If you're lucky, you will be transferred to permanent clerical duties, understand?'

'Yes Sir.'

He wasn't going to let it go at that. 'How I choose who is suitable for the work I take on, is of no concern of yours. Nor is it your place to question the rotation of assignments or the selection of partners should I consider it necessary to send officers out into the field in pairs or in teams. You just make yourself available for a meeting with AC when you will be given the relevant details. You may go.'

He pressed the unseen buzzer and Miss Efficiency appeared. So quickly did she appear that I wondered if she had been leaning against the door waiting for the call? 'Mr Grundy is leaving now, please see him out.'

Standing up and giving him a polite nod I followed Miss Efficiency out of the office. Crossing her office, I gave her a big wink, received no response, so let myself out into the corridor.

Yet again I had been to see the 'Big' man, and in the time honoured and customary shambolic manner had been given a 'job'. I would now have to wait for the meeting with AC where I would be given as much detail as was usually available and which I hoped would at least make some sense.

CHAPTER TWO

Memories of that April morning remain as clear to me now as ever they did. It started out quiet enough and weather wise was like any other early morning that frequently dominates the late Autumn, Winter and early Spring; dark, damp and miserable. I had reluctantly dragged myself out of bed having had a far from a restful night following a very strange, yet in some ways a rather pleasant, evening. Daylight was trying to edge out the darkness of the previous night and I looked at my watch to reassure myself that it was indeed time to be up and about. Satisfied that it was and having no acceptable excuse to dive back into bed I reluctantly shuffled to the door looking for the mail that I knew was there, for somewhere in my wanderings and semi-conscious state I had heard the familiar noise of the letter box flap as it was lifted, the slap of envelopes hitting the floor and the click of the cover as it returned to its original position.

Several envelopes in various sizes and colours lay scattered on the polished wood floor. I bent down to retrieve them and then pushing my hand into the small of my back forced my spine back into the upright position so that once again I was standing up reasonably straight. A flick through assured me they were all for me. Turning to retrace my steps and once again massaging the small of my back and twisting my shoulders, I felt annoyed at the discomfort and realisation of just how un-fit I really was. That's what happens, I told myself, when you spend long hours behind a desk. I remember thinking that I must do something about it. I thought about the Postman, though goodness knows why, and how fit he must be; up at the crack of dawn, come hail or shine, walking mile upon mile with a heavy bag, up and down staircases, lifts and whatever else, and still having sufficient energy to push my mail through the letter box with such force, that it passed over the door mat, and spread out all over the floor beyond it. Or was it energy? Perhaps it was anger and frustration at having to be up so early on a miserable morning. Maybe there were other and more complex reasons; anyhow who cared? Other than perhaps him. But not me. I had my own problems associated with early mornings. The thought of work, for example, or anything remotely relating to work, before at least a cup of tea and a bite to eat, created a mood of deep depression, which could last throughout the whole day.

I lent against the kitchen unit to examine more closely the mail the elusive, unseen Postman had brought? Elusive being the operative word, for in all the time I have lived in this flat I have never set eyes on him, or for that matter, was it her?

I rummaged in the drawer until I found a kitchen knife. I have never owned a letter opener but still believed that the humble envelope, no matter what it

contains has the right to be opened neatly, and if not with a letter opener, at least a clean knife. The one on the table still had congealed grease on it from the previous nights' Chinese take-away.

The previous night! The sight of that knife along with all the other discarded items of used crockery, spread carelessly on the table brought it all flooding back. I smiled to myself and shook my head. She was a strange girl that one. She danced, drank, drank some more, smoked all the time, came willingly back to the flat, ate her share of the take-away, nipped out to the all-night shop on the corner for more cigarettes... and disappeared. I waited a good twenty minutes then becoming rather concerned, went looking for her. The chap in the shop remembered her, as she was one of only two customers he had had during the previous couple of hours. He said she had come into the shop, bought cigarettes, and then used his Public Phone to order a taxi. She waited a few moments for it to arrive, then jumped in and away it went. He was sorry, but he did not hear her say where she wanted to go.

Anyway that was the previous night. Today and for the moment I was looking for a clean knife. Having found one, I turned my attention to the largest envelope, a windowed one where the address shows through from the inside.

To - The Occupier, Flat 21, Genevieve Court, 102, Londesborough Road etc. The address, at least, was correct but I didn't know anyone called Occupier. Junk mail probably but out of habit I still opened it.

Did 'The Occupier' want to test-drive the latest, state of the art, Ford Saloon or perhaps the five-door hatch back, model? Did I what? I laughed out loud; I couldn't even afford the clapped out Renault that I had, let alone buy and run a brand new Ford. The old banger may not much to look at, was far from new, but at least was paid for and could be relied upon to get me where I needed to be without draining every Service Station dry of fuel on the way. The envelope and contents were despatched to the universal filing cabinet: the waste bin.

The next one, plain envelope, neatly typed, full name, Mr M Grundy, correct postal address including postcode, everything exactly as it should be; probably a bill. What ever happened to the traditional practice of always sending bills in easy to recognise brown envelopes, something that no longer seems to apply. Now they use any type, brown, buff, or white, anything to conceal a bill and surprise the poor unsuspecting recipient.

I was wrong, for the second envelope contained an offer of Private Health Care for as little as 29p a day. It was a very impressive application form and clearly stated that no salesman would call. It even offered a free pen if I returned it within twenty-one days, and waffled on about something and about paying out twice as much, if I was buried before I died.... sorry, paid out double on death or something like that.

In the bin for who cares about things like that, when you're dead? I find it strange to be invited to pay for something now, when the beneficiary will be

an undertaker or some relative or stranger who cares little for you now and will probably care less for you when you're gone. Taking care of loved ones and perhaps making some provision for their future is fine but who have I to provide for or, for that matter, what have I got to leave them? I have no parents, a wife long gone, and no children that I know of, or are prepared to admit to. I will stick with my modest Death Benefit, that I took out years ago, when I then thought it important not to leave loved ones with your disposal costs.

Either way how would I answer and get past question three - Occupation? If I told the truth it would probably cost me twenty-nine pounds a day, not the twenty-nine pence they were suggesting. I could always declare my cover job of course, but knowing my luck, they would probably take my premiums and then wait until I was dead and not in a position to explain my circumstances, then decide I had not been truthful and refuse to pay out. Anyway why should we need these schemes? I thought we had the welfare state to provide everything through taxation, so why pay twice?

The next envelope, complete with contents was destined to go straight into the waste bin. Anything that proclaimed on the outside that the recipient had won a major prize and some immediate action was necessary was, to my mind, part of nothing more than a great con.

The BT logo, in several shades of blue, in the top left hand corner told me that the next one was definitely a phone bill. I would have to pay that one. I couldn't survive without a telephone and as far as the Department is concerned, well they insist on one. They claim they must be able to reach you at home but for security reasons neither install or pay for it. Stinks of some petty cost cutting exercise: if you ask me and so typical of the Treasury. But be that as it may, it would still have to be paid; as to be disconnected would certainly not be good form. I could see the Old Man, wheezing away in his chair, 'Tried to get hold of you last night, Grundy, but your phone was making a funny pipping sound. Telephone people said there was a fault and it has been temporarily disconnected. Get it sorted out; that call might have been urgent.' How could I possibly explain to a man on his salary, that us irks, who do all the ground work and graft in the department, have to budget very carefully to survive. There are many times when we just cannot sit down and write cheques and the annoying part is that these occasions are becoming more and more frequent.

Road Tax, was that due again already? It must be. I was holding the reminder.

What's this one? Union fees not paid, returned cheque, insufficient funds - bloody Banks. Does no one tell their computers that if they hang fire for a couple of days, salaries are due to be paid in? No they don't for they make damned good money out of bouncing cheques and causing acute embarrassment to all concerned.

The Union is just as bad and every time I have dealings with them I want to laugh for they are as false and hypocritical as you can get. As far as society knows, or cares, I am currently employed by the Coastguard Service as a Clerical Officer. I share an office with three other 'Clerical Officers' and we are based at Central Headquarters. I receive, in that capacity, the appropriate, and I hasten to add, not too generous a salary, which is paid directly into the Bank. I am required, in my gainful employment, to be a member of the appropriate Union who in turn pledge to look after me and my interests and well being, as part of my rights as an employee.

In reality and if the Union only knew it, my role within the Service is about as far removed from a Clerical Officer as one could get.

It is unfortunate, but it is the time spent on the low salaried, routine clerical work that leads to my acute lack of funding. Although, when diverted to it, I have often thought that the alternative work doesn't pay all that well either. But it does go some way towards making life a little easier. With the exception of those fortunate enough to be up near the top, no one in the Coastguard Service can be accused of being in it for the money. It is not a high profile profession, unless of course something goes tragically wrong. Then if say, someone leaves the bow doors open on a cross channel ferry and the thing comes to grief or a tanker runs aground, then for a brief period the media will raise the profile of the Service but will then drop it back into obscurity once the emergency has passed. The Coastguard Service does not spend millions on Television Advertising or often hint that they are even an Emergency Service let alone try and tell the public that their 'members' think they are the fourth one. Sadly and as result, Coastguards cannot command or even expect to get paid a salary that is anything to get excited over.

In my case, as is also the case with many of my contemporaries, we have to rely very much on the additional earning opportunities that are put our way. At least while on a 'job' the level of income does go up, if only slightly and, three cheers, the difference is tax-free. That and the opportunity to make a bob or two, out of expenses, helps. This, of course, all comes about because the, so called, 'additional jobs' do not exist. When on an official 'additional job' even I do not exist. My only open record and contract of employment describes me as 'Clerical Officer Grade 1' and as far as the big wide world and society as a whole is concerned, that is exactly what I am.

Familiarity and of course past experience told me that the last brown envelope could well be the answer to some, if not all, of my current financial problems. I sensed from the beginning what it was, so held it over to the last. The small, brown, rather insignificant envelope, with OHMS printed across the top; my name and address neatly typed on the front. Nothing on the outside indicated where it had originated. My heart rate increased very slightly as I contemplated the contents. What would it be this time? Better, I hoped, than the last one, as I

briefly reflected on the awful mess the Isle of Man 'job' had turned out to be and the monumental departmental cock-ups. That really wasn't so long ago, or it didn't seem to be so long ago. Perhaps that was due to the rapid rate at which funds just seemed to melt away while on standard 'Clerical', monthly pay.

I slit open the envelope and placed the knife back in the drawer. The contents of the brown cover were familiar and the same as always. They had never varied from the standard format in all the years I had been with the department, only the 'jobs' differed. I extracted a piece of plain, white paper totally devoid of anything except the hand written message, 'Report H.Q. Inform AC.'

The ritual could now begin. From now on there were strict rules and guidelines that had to be followed, though I often wondered why?

First, tear the sheet of paper and its envelope into pieces and destroy them. I don't have an open fire and don't like little bonfires in ashtrays, the smell of burnt paper gets everywhere and lingers on for days, so I chose plan B.

Flush it down the toilet.

Years ago, at training school, they had explained that it was perfectly acceptable to flush small objects, and in particular small torn pieces of paper, down the toilet, but only if you were satisfied that the toilet was connected to a sealed and enclosed sewer. Sound advice, especially when overseas where in some countries the sewers have a bad habit of going through the nearest wall and discharging onto the open street, but I was confident that this didn't apply here, so down the loo it all went.

That responsibility taken care of I was now free to move on to stage two, food. After all, I couldn't go to work and declare myself available for a 'job' on an empty stomach.

Shower, dress and eat were my priorities and in that order. Carefully planning so that I would have sufficient time to arrive at the office for the appointed time.

There are very rigid rules and standard practices for us minions and members of the lower echelon to adhere to and punctuality is one of the most important. No one, but no one, at least at my level dared to keep the Big Chief waiting. I had heard it rumoured that a little further up there was some flexibility and right at the very top, those who occupied similar positions to the Chief, enjoyed complete freedom to come and go as they pleased and usually did so via the Club or local Golf Course. But for the likes of me all that is on another planet and one which is occupied only by the chosen few. I exist very much on the level where one does as one is told and that includes being punctual.

I showered then decided to eat before I got dressed. Perhaps to demonstrate my flexibility when planning and to exercise what little independence I do have in my own home. There were only three pieces of bread, one of which was a crust, so the old, reliable toaster once again proved to be an essential piece of equipment

in my humble bachelor abode. A couple of slices of toast would have to suffice for now, particularly when the only alternative was a discarded aluminium Take-away tray, half full of cold rice and what ever it was that tasted so good, when warm, the night before. I would have to make time to clear all that away before I left.

CHAPTER THREE

Whether we like it or not as individuals, collectively as a Nation, high on our agenda comes National Security.

We all need it, or so we are told that we do, and they, Nations that is, need it and believe it, and accept that they could not survive without it.

Security is a well known, though rarely acknowledged, technique and tool of government and that it's history and origins, without doubt, lie somewhere around the time when men roamed in groups and it was fashionable to form up into these groups for self-preservation. The natural progression seems to have been for them to conclude how useful it would be if they could learn what was being planned and schemed by others. Those in authority must have soon learned that by having advance knowledge of a rivals plans and proposals and safeguarding their own, both before and after a skirmish, they had a very fair chance of coming out on top. Even the most primitive must have quickly learnt that it is easier to outwit an enemy armed with advanced knowledge of his intentions than it is to just stand and bash heads and hope that your side bashes more heads than they do or you have more heads to be bashed in than they have. Later as these 'smaller units' either voluntarily or from pressure of defeat, joined forces for greater self-preservation and self-gratification, so it then became country against country, with each realising the value of spying on the other, if they were to maintain the upper hand. The ever increasing demand for knowledge and intelligence, that was not readily available or willingly given, grew, until it became massive and involved National Government against Government; State against State and Nation against Nation. So from what were humble beginnings there now is a massive network of intrigue, which not only affects the whole world, but also deeply infects it. So much so that it will never be eradicated as long as someone believes that someone else knows something they aught to know and that the lack of that knowledge poses some real or imagined threat. So vast, deeply enmeshed, intertwined and overlapping has the whole thing become that present day civilisations and societies have become fractured and splintered within themselves. There now exist numerous organisations within some countries that claim to be working for the common good but who are, in actual fact, working against each other. They spy on each other; they function independently and generally cause confusion and if the governments concerned were honest, would admit that it causes no end of problems and all within the, so called, framework of the common cause. One only has to look at the USA. All the State and Federal organizations, the Bureaus, their Pentagon and it's bureaucracy and all within the United States of America. A country which is

supposed to be one nation, under one flag, with a common cause; that of security and self-preservation and yet it is criss-crossed and riddled with secret organisations all working independently of each other, whilst openly declaring that is not so and that they are for the common good. More recent examples, which are now entering the archives of modern history, are the Gestapo in Germany and the NKVD in Russia. While still in existence and still very active are those organisations within countries that find a need to have a Secret Police Service or other government sponsored departments working against and victimising its own citizens and leaders.

So it all, very much, exists and will continue to do so for as long as one government believes that it is being threatened by another, or by someone, or something. Also as long as there remains the belief that it is necessary to know what everyone else is planning or developing or there is the strong desire to outmanoeuvre or prepare to counter any moves, which might pose a threat either militarily or economically, then things will definitely not change. As long as there is someone prepared to believe that the knowledge of another's activities will give them an edge or an advantage; be that in the sphere of politics, economics, or the arena of war, then spying, intelligence gathering and covert operations will continue to be practised and not only will it all continue to survive, but also it will become more devious and subtle as modern technology develops and feeds it's needs. So called progressive nations will continue to spend vast sums of money, from however meagre their resources, in the pursuit of intelligence gathering or mounting covert operations to undermine anyone and everyone where they believe there is something, real or imagined, to be gained.

Much of this countries intelligence gathering and intelligence gatherers have tended, in the past, to have been, rather glamorised by those not directly involved in their work. Those most guilty being the fiction writers and filmmakers. While at the same time the governments of the day chose to do little or nothing to refute or dispel these myths. One cannot blame them for that, for to do so would naturally be an acknowledgement that something rather sinister might exist, and they would, naturally, rather have the general public remain ignorant. So while this popular image of the Intelligence Services being some form of gamesmanship, played out by the old public school boy network, is allowed to continue, the Government also goes to great lengths not to advertise, or let it be known, the true extent of their devious activities. The last thing they want known is some indication of the depth and scope of their 'non-existent' establishments.

Anyone who has troubled to give the matter a little thought will have quickly drawn the conclusion that in these troubled times, which unfortunately we live in, State Security is necessary; even if they are not too sure why, or if it is in the best interests of the State and it's population. At least the vast majority of intelligent people know that something goes on and as no one troubles to deny it, or offer any explanations, then they accept that it can't be all that bad. They don't

realise, as I doubt anyone does, and in that I include the Prime Minister and all the top Civil Servants, the true extent and size of all the existing, so called, Secret Service Departments, that delve into almost every aspect, and influence, all our lives both here, at home, and abroad.

Some of these numerous organisations are much closer to the surface than others and therefore tend to be known of and readily recognised. For example the Special Investigations Branches of the Customs and Excise or the Anti-Terrorist Squads or the Police Special Branch, the Investigation Branch of the Department of Trade and Industry, to name a few. Then there are the branches whose' names are well known due to their glamorisation by the fictional story tellers, the film makers and the makers of popular TV serials who all favour, for their recurring plots, the dark mysterious world of the mythical spy and espionage agent. I imagine that everyone, at sometime or another has heard of MI5 and MI6 and the James Bond image that has been built up around each one. But because no one has troubled to dispel the myths, people are happy to carry on in the belief that that is basically what it is all about. That they, the book and film characters, represent the Master Spy and who he is and how he operates and the world he lives in. How far from the truth can one get?

British Intelligence, under the umbrella of MI5 and MI6; again widely known and wrongly glamorised in fiction, is a vast and complex set-up that reaches almost beyond the bounds of the imagination let alone the realms of reality. Its web is so vast and intricate that I doubt if anyone has any concept of its overall complexity or the extent to which it reaches out and therefore influences and affects everything and everyone. A high proportion of its success, if indeed it is successful, must be credited to the fact that no one has an overall picture of the whole set-up, or the structure of all the organisations, and can therefore not betray it to any extent or do it permanent harm, should they chose to either voluntarily betray it, or be coerced into it, or if any of the organisations or sub-sections of the organisation be infiltrate from outside by undesirables or those with dubious ulterior motives; which has happened, on occasions, in the past.

What then of the other large and awesome group? Those who go towards making up, by far, the largest proportion? Those hundreds of thousands who on a daily basis; quietly collect valuable intelligence data without even realising that they are doing so? The civil servants, the form fillers in, the computer terminal operators and anyone else collecting personal details and basic information and then having done so, have no idea what happens to it or where it goes after they have finished with it?

The Dirty Tricks Departments; what about those? Sadly another fact of life that cannot be ignored and very much something that Government's are forced to support in order to maintain the grand plan. It is part of the unsavoury way in which civilisation, as we know it, is heading. The terrorist with his gun and bomb

is a growing menace and a sad fact and is probably here to stay. But I bet that every average and sane person would be pleased to see them disappear and would prefer a life without them. But if they are here to stay, then everyone would rather see everything that is humanly possible, and no matter how devious or unsavoury that might be, done to counter and eliminate them. They are a sad and sick part of our society and one that we can all do without but which can only be controlled by 'intelligence.'

So why, apart from the obvious just mentioned, or the need to smash such things as drug cartels, has this devious monster called 'Intelligence' been allowed to develop to almost unwieldy proportions and having done so absorbs increasing billions of pounds, annually, of tax payers hard earned money?

I suppose the answer could be that it was not allowed to happen, it just did and became the monster it is because it is out of control. The official answer, if there is one, must surely be along the lines of 'the necessity for survival,' but how can that be assured, despite the vastness and cost of the networks, when every other country is committed to the same thing and each has its expensive intelligence gatherers and Counter Intelligence Agencies working hard against you. Again I rather suspect that the answer might be one-upmanship; he who spends most and spreads widest, wins, and that is why the networks will continue to grow and who knows may eventually strangle themselves and just about everything else along the way. Some, like myself, are questioning the validity of it all and are rapidly coming to the conclusion that it is all a great waste of time and resources but has grown so big and become so uncontrollable that it cannot now be eliminated. I suppose it could be likened to a cancer that has spread throughout the whole of so called society and with present day knowledge, any attempt to eliminate something which has become so widespread and all embracing would only have the same results as attempting to cut out a cancer; it can be done but would result in the death of the patient. Certainly the first one brave enough to attempt it, if successful, would leave themselves weakened and wide open and very vulnerable to being gobbled up and totally destroyed by their unscrupulous neighbours.

So at the end of the day, we have all heard something and we can all claim, to varying degrees, to be knowledgeable about it; some even going so far as to claim to have a vague idea of how it all functions, or why it is even necessary. But the vast majority are quite happy to be just aware of its existence; hope it functions in the best interest of us all, but leaves them, as individuals, free to quietly get on with their lives. They simply prefer to ignore it, until perhaps, it directly or indirectly, affects them.

For many years I was just one such person. Of course, like 'Mr Average' I knew of its existence and had read a wide cross section of the available fiction, written on the subject, and along with countless others was happy to allow myself to escape into the realms of fantasy alongside James Bond, his gorgeous female

assistants, and his arch adversaries. But then, due to circumstances completely beyond my control, it became more than a curiosity to me; it became reality and dragged me in and drew me down to the very depths and having done so, has held me immersed and trapped and has exploited me ever since in the strange reality of it all.

Most minor 'Security Service Departments' - the title Secret Service - being no longer fashionable and for the present considered to be rather dated, are tucked away, for convenience, and dare I say it, for security reasons, in the least likely of places. They are often integrated into what, on the outside, seem to be a very ordinary, readily accepted, straightforward, and respectable organisations, which have a clearly understood and clearly defined, open areas of responsibility.

Ours is just one such place.

CHAPTER FOUR

It does not matter how inclement the weather or the time of year, or the amount of traffic on the roads, to estimate the time it should take to get from my home to the office, is one of the most difficult, if not near impossible tasks that I have to cope with on a daily basis. Therefore when time and punctuality are important, experience has taught me that it is necessary to ere on the generous side and to not only allow ample time but to add even more just to be on the safe side.

That morning I had been summoned to appear before the 'Big man', my Chief, our Leader, the Head of Department, which made it very important that I arrive a few minutes ahead of time as a few minutes late would not be tolerated. I hastily checked round the flat making sure everything was secure. I picked up the rubbish bag from the side of the kitchen cabinet and then letting myself out of the front door locked it behind me. I walked the ten or so yards to the lift and pressed the call button. A few seconds later the lift arrived and the doors opened. I entered the confined space and selected the button marked 'B'. It slid smoothly down three floors, indicating its progress on the illuminated number plate, then 'G' for ground level lit up. The lift continued until it came to a smooth stop at the basement level.

My car was exactly where I had left it in the basement garage, but then there was nothing unusual in that, for I was the only one who normally used it. As I walked towards it I passed and dropped my rubbish bag in the litterbin. I dug deep in my pocket and found my car keys, opened the door, got in and started up. I drove up the exit ramp and out into the weak daylight. A made a left turn at the top and immediately ran into my first obstacle, a long stream of traffic, all nose-to-tail, and all going in my direction. I sat and drummed my fingers on the steering wheel praying all the time that some caring road user would give way, and allow me to slip in.

Eventually someone did, then after much stopping and starting, waiting and edging, I finally arrived at the office. My final manoeuvre was to get off the main road and out of the main stream of traffic and turn right, through a large stone arch and into a quadrangle, which retained all the signs of having been, at one time, a large private garden. It now served as the official car park for both employees and visitors. I double checked my watch and the internal car clock and found, much to my relief that I had made it with time to spare.

Each time I enter the car park, although I hasten to add there is nothing unusual in this particular car park and there must be hundreds of thousands of a similar ones dotted about, particularly in inner cities and other densely built up

areas, I am forced to smile as I believe that in the British Private Car Park one comes face to face with the British Class System at its very best. I always feel that it is in the car park, above everywhere else, that the British display, for the rest of the world to admire, our very own unique class system. The car park is very symbolic and is used by the British to teach you, and to show you, your place. It is where you learn to know your place and exactly where you fit in to the pecking order. We do not have an open Cast System, where birth is the criteria, as practised, for example, on the Indian sub-continent. There one is actually born into a class, is tied to that class and remain in it for the rest of ones life. In Britain we have a more subtle and flexible system known as the 'Named Car Parking Space' which determines ones level of breeding or social position. Areas of parking space clearly marked out with bright wide white lines and a bold and substantial nameplate, declaring to all and sundry, to whom this exclusive parking space has been allocated. A small piece of England that is forever ones own, or until one is promoted, sacked, retired or transfers to a heavenly allocated space. But the earth bound one does not end there for it is not sufficient to be simply allocated a parking space. Spaces have to be very carefully planned, laid out, positioned, and allocated according to Seniority and Social Status. This serves several purposes, for it not only keeps those considered to be rabble separated from those who have labelled them as such. But it allows those who have kicked, cheated, and fought their way to what they believe to be seniority and superiority to dictate the allocation of other places to their family and chums and anyone else prepared to buy in. It also provides much sport and back stabbing and creeping for those further down the line as they battle for a more coveted parking space. It is also useful to the visitor who only has to note the name nearest the main entrance and the one usually under the cover to know who, currently rules the roost. The space next to him, and one removed from the door; is for number two in the pecking order, and so on. It's so simple in the well-ordered British way of doing things. It makes the insecure that little bit more secure when they know exactly where they stand. Even right down at the bottom they are secure in the knowledge of where they stand.

Being in no doubt about my own position I drove to the far corner and selected one of the unoccupied, unnamed spaces. I took care not to park in a space marked 'Visitor' otherwise later in the day the car park attendant would hound me down and ask me to move. 'Rules are rules, Sir. You do understand. Them places have been allocated to visitors and its not the first time you've done it now, Sir, is it? It's a hard life for the underpaid and under privileged, those near the bottom of the pile and the humble servants of the senior masters and nowhere is it more obvious than in the Great British Car Park.

Each time I park up and walk the maximum distance to the entrance, I smile and think to myself that the only reason that people like me, at the lower end of the pecking order, are allowed parking at all, is because if we were not, then we

might, if suitably stirred up, cause anarchy and take over their hallowed spaces. God forbid that it should happen for they wouldn't be able to handle it. Imagine the loss, the end of time-honoured traditions, and the hundreds of senior management hours dedicated to deciding who should park where.

I locked my car and looked at my watch. I had still made good time.

I should have gone straight in through the back entrance, as it was of course the quickest, but with sufficient time to spare I decided to nip the short distance down the road to the nearest Newsagents and purchase a daily paper.

I enjoy this simple exercise and the lift it gives me, for two simple reasons. Firstly, the obvious, the newspaper, and all the useless information it imparts as I vainly attempts to keep abreast of events at home and abroad. Secondly and by far the more important, the pleasure of going through the main front entrance, where at this time of day I am guaranteed to be surrounded by literally dozens of lovely female employees. Typists, secretaries, and all the other delightful young ladies, who all pursue a wide variety of responsible jobs, and who all arrive together. Most will have commuted by public transport and all will look fresh and lovely and smell delightful. Whatever the weather, they are always bright and cheerful. They all seem so desirable and immaculately turned out, and if my mingling with them and putting on my most charming smile gets me the occasional - Good Morning - or charming smile back, I am set up for the day.

The Newsagent, for some reason, never sets out his papers in exactly the same way each day. I suppose he just spreads them out as he gets them. So as usual I had to search through a random selection until I found one who's front page caught my eye and attracted my interest.

I don't consider myself to be an intellectual by any stretch of the imagination, and even less of one when it comes to reading newspapers. To start with I am not consistent in the one I take and generally go for the ones that are considered, by the self confessed, more enlightened, to be middle of the road stuff. A mixture of news, sport - although I am not an active sportsman - but do like to keep up to date with what is going on among those who are. I like general interest and even the lighter nonsense stuff and I never say no to a touch of glamour and the 'girlie' picture if it's there.

Newspaper in hand, I walked back along the street and edged into the large group of predominately gorgeous girls as they mounted the steps to the main entrance. As I went through the enormous double doors, taking hold of the edge of one of them as it was released by the person in front of me and holding it for the young lady behind, I glanced at the highly polished brass plaque mounted on the wall at the side. There glinting in the morning sunlight it proclaimed for all to see - H.M. Coastguard. Underneath and in much smaller letters it said Central Headquarters and Office of the Chief Coastguard. I remember how that had changed several times during my short stay with the firm and wondered what it might say

on the next plaque to be secured there? Then I remembered I had seen something on an internal memo that had said something about the Registered Office of the Coastguard Agency. Yet another change! The title however, or what ever the sign said, was totally irrelevant because the building still remained the same as it has always been; the head office and central administration offices; the nerve centre if you like, of the Coastguard Service. The name may have changed slightly over the years, as may the sphere of responsibility and the day to day running of the organisation. That, I feel is inevitable and is brought about by the constant need to keep abreast of modern requirements and technical improvements, but the sound principals on which the Coastguard was originally founded remain very much the same. Over the years, sections have been added, or hived off as the circumstances changed, but the prime responsibility still lies very much in Search and Rescue, Safety at Sea and Marine Pollution Control.

Over its chequered history the Coastguard Service has been under the umbrella of various military and governmental agencies. It started out life originally as a branch of the Royal Navy and was used as a recruiting ground for naval personnel in times of emergency and war. It has also been used over the years as a dumping ground for senior naval officers looking for early retirement from active duty, yet still needing to extend their working careers in less strenuous circumstances, to bolster their retirement pensions.

It has, in its time, been under the control of the Department of Trade, the Ministry of Transport, and numerous others. Now it looks like becoming the Coastguard Agency, with an independent management structure, and its own independent government budget. Despite the changes, it still functions exceptionally well, and manages to do very efficiently, what it is designated to do and most suited for.

The actual headquarters building has been in several different locations, at different times, throughout Coastguard history. It is currently housed in a large ornamental stone building which I am told is of the Victorian era and design. It is, however, typical of those found still standing close to the Canary Wharf area of London and in its own surroundings has little of architectural predominance to make it stand out from the remainder of it's neighbours, with the exception perhaps of the highly polished brass plaque on the wall and the dark blue Coastguard flag flying from an angled flag pole, above the main entrance.

There are two lifts in the main reception area and it is irrelevant which one you chose as both serve all levels and, early each morning, both is filled with the aroma and sweet smell of delightfully perfumed young ladies. Some not so young perhaps, but all still smelling wonderful. The heady aroma, which totally envelopes everything when one first enters the confines of the lift, decreases as it ascends and stops at the different floors and one or two of the occupants step out and head off to

their respective work areas. The interaction of the working day having hardly got underway at this time makes it rare for anyone to want to go down.

Finally, as the lift continued on its upward journey I was, with the exception of the lingering smell of perfume, completely alone. As I stepped out onto the top floor I glanced at my watch. I would have time for at least a quick glance through my newspaper before I had to report.

I walked along the short corridor and entered our office. Two of my colleagues, Jim and Philip were already there with newspapers spread out over desks and cigarette smoke already polluting the air. Eric, my third colleague and the forth member of our group had not yet arrived.

'Morning Mel! You look cheerful. Bet you've rode up that front lift with all the girls?' grinned Philip.

'Morning Phil! All right Jim? Yes I did but there's more to it than that. I've got a job; came through this morning.'

'Lucky sod, glad someone's getting the chance to get out of this boring hole for a while,' grumbled Jim. 'You won't know what it is yet, I suppose?'

'No. Like I said, I only got it this morning.'

'Know what?' said Jim, scowling and looking thoughtful. 'Why do we always get a chit for a job through the post, when our immediate boss is only two doors down there and the big man is on the floor below?' Beats me. If you ask me, a phone into here is all they need.'

'Ah,' uttered Phil, before I had chance to say anything. 'Goes back to the old days when boss's were miles away and us mere operatives and the back-up boys were spread out all over the place. You remember Mel? When everyone were in different offices, in different buildings and hidden away all over the place and in all sorts of obscure cubby holes. A lot probably still are but we just happen to be in this building with them. Then you know the score and the way this set-up works; more than likely no one has thought to tell anyone else that we are now under the same roof. I bet that silly bugger downstairs doesn't even know that we are sat on top of him. He probably thinks that everything is still the same as it was the last time he bothered to venture out of his office and take a look round. Anyhow, as I said, there probably are still some different sections: who knows, other than ours, in other places? That's probably why they stick with the old method. You agree Mel?'

'Never given it much thought. There's so much round here that's so bloody odd and defies all logic and common sense, that I have long since given up on it'

The arrival of Eric brought the discussion to an abrupt halt.

'Morning all,' he chirped as he breezed in.

'Morning,' from each of us in turn.

The quartet and the occupants of our particular office were now complete.

I lent back in my chair and spread my newspaper.

In this small office, were four very different people: Philip and Eric - Philip Castleton and Eric Johnson - both ex-army. While Jim Wilkinson and myself were ex-RAF. I remember when I originally joined, how it struck me as being odd, that there were no naval or ex-naval personnel in the team at the time, this being the Coastguard and being so closely associated with the sea and all that. Perhaps navel personnel are reserved for greater things. Someone somewhere would no doubt know the reasoning, if there were any, behind it all; but I didn't. The only thing we did all appear to have in common was the fact that we were all from military backgrounds, had held minor commissions and are, all unattached. I can see some of the logic behind being unattached because it would be extremely difficult to pursue our line of business with wives, lovers, or girlfriends littering the background. We needed to be free and as far detached as possible from close and intimate relationships. We had to be available to melt away without warning and spend long periods absent from base and whilst doing so not have to worry about what might be happening to loved ones in our absence. I had tried the married bit myself some years ago. It didn't work out. Looking back and with hindsight we had been on the road to disaster from the start. I was away in the services for most of the time and serving away from home, while she was at home and lonely, and liked men.

'Hey,' said Jim to no one in particular, 'Mel here has got a job, the lucky sod.'

'Anything to do with this here in the morning paper?' enquired Eric.

'I don't know, my briefing's not until later so I have no idea. Anyhow, what's that in the paper?'

I turned the pages of my paper and scanned the headlines of the numerous articles looking for clues. Eric in the meantime held his high in both hands, so that he was able to read from near the bottom of a page, 'COASTGUARD GOES MISSING OFF NORTH EAST COAST. Police say a Coastguard Officer has gone missing off the north east coast of England and the circumstances give cause for concern. A local Senior Coastguard Officer declined to give any details other than to state "It is too early to draw any conclusions."'

'Is that all it says? Typical Coastguard, that,' moaned Eric as if he expected more.

'Yes, that's all it says here. Anything in any of the other papers?'

'There is no mention of anything that I can see, in my paper,' I added.

'Nor mine,' muttered Phil.

I glanced at my watch and then at the big clock on the wall opposite, it was time I made a move. I folded and dropped the paper into the bottom desk drawer, which I reserved exclusively for newspapers and sandwiches. Reaching forward I drew the telephone towards me. Picking up the handset, I held it to my left ear

and using my right index finger pressed the internal connect button. A few seconds later the buzz of static on the line turned into a ringing tone as the connection was made. Several rings later a voice said, 'Good morning, Colonel Cruickshank's office, how can I help?'

'Hi Janet, it's me, Mel, your secret lover, is the Old Man in yet?'

'Yes he is,' replied the twenty-five, maybe twenty-six year old, tall, slim, blond, and absolutely gorgeous looking Miss Watson. I could see her in my minds eye, behind her desk and naked from the waist up with the telephone held to her ear. Why could it not have been Janet who had shared my Chinese take-away the night before, and not that odd creature, who though good looking and with a gorgeous body, had left, and done a runner on me without warning? I felt sure Janet would not do that to me. If only I could persuade her to share a take away and put it to the test. But then some women insist on remaining faithful to their husbands and I guessed Janet was one of those. Nevertheless she had been good for a very sexy kiss and cuddle at last year's Christmas office party. I supposed I should consider myself lucky, as she had made it very clear at the time that it would not have happened if we had not, by coincidence, ended up alone, and she had not had too much to drink. I don't suppose she even remembered or wondered how or why we ended up alone and away from all the others or why, I believe, she went willingly.

'Ask if he will see me; and ring me back, there's a darling,' I asked, rounding it off with a kissing sound.

'You sound very perky this morning Mel Grundy,' retorted the cool, calm Janet, 'Got a job, have we?'

Hell, was it that obvious or was she just guessing or did she already know? She probably knew: so much for the Secret Service.

'You just ask him and then ring me back, Sweetie.'

'Will do,' and the phone went dead.

As I waited, I wondered what the meeting and the job would be all about. Something interesting I hoped.

Colonel Albert Cruickshank aged sixty and the fact that he was, and for reasons known only to himself, not particularly proud of. He also believed that it was a very closely guarded secret having no idea that his wife had let it slip in a conversation with his secretary. She in turn being very loyal to him had only let it slip to a few very close associates, now everyone knew.

His wife, relations, and close friends all called him Bertie. His office staff and underlings call him, Sir, to his face and a variety of other things behind his back. He strongly believed we all had a need to maintain strict Army discipline, not the slack Naval stuff that most of his contemporaries allowed. He is ex-army and the mere fact that he resides and works in a predominantly naval establishment doesn't concern or deter him. He insists that he be treat strictly according to his rank, even

though his present 'Regiment' consisted of only one secretary, the charming Miss Watson, and four field officers, Wilkinson, Castleton, Johnson and Grundy, with perhaps a few others randomly scattered about that we don't know about.

He had suffered from a blinding flash of useless inspiration some time ago, no doubt during an out of body experience or while dreaming and wondering over the surface of a different planet, that all the names of his troops ended with O N, with the exception of Grundy. He has seriously pointed this out to me on more than one occasion. 'You are the odd one out Grundy, your name doesn't end with O N like all the others and you represent twenty five percent of my team. That's a big imbalance, twenty five percent, what,' and when I was beginning to get fed up with having this thrust at me and I dared to suggest that his name didn't end with O N either, he dismissed that as irrelevant, as the daft bugger claimed his name didn't come into the equation as he was the Officer in Charge.

Rumour has it that the originally obsession with the make up of names, and in particular their correct spelling, following, what was for him, a nasty experience in North Africa during the last war.

The story goes that during one of his campaigns, he had spent some time with an isolated group in the North African desert. On one occasion while setting up a temporary camp, a lower ranker had been ordered to find a piece of wood and to chalk the Colonel's name on it and fasten it to his tent pole. Whether the soldier had misheard his name, or did it just for mischief is not known, but the sign, when erected, read - Col A Cruckedshank. What happened to the trouper is not recorded, but it left Cruickshank with a strange obsession about names and how they can be misapplied.

'Miss Watson, if Grundy is there? Tell him to come in now please,' the intercom on her desk barked and shut off before she had time to reply. That is the Colonel, very curt and to the point every time with no wasted words or actions. What a style.

I tapped politely on his door.

'Come in..... Ah Grundy, what is it that you want man?'

Mystified and rather taken aback by the 'what is it you want man' I blurted out 'I've been notified of an assignment, Sir, a 'job' Sir.'

'Yes Grundy, I know you have. I have a memo here to that effect.'

'Yes Sir, I assumed you would have and that is why I am here now to see you sir. Following procedure, and clearing it with you before I go for my appointment with the Admiral at ten this morning.'

'Rear Admiral! Grundy,' he snapped. 'Don't give the man a rank he is not entitled to. It's not correct, and I won't permitted it, do you understand?'

'Yes Sir.'

'Report downstairs according to procedure, then clear your desk and I will see you again after my own briefing with the Rear Admiral. Meanwhile Grundy not a word to anyone: remember the name of our game - silence is security.'

I remember thinking, as I had done on previous occasions - prize twit. How could you discuss or tell anyone something you knew nothing about?

I left his office completely bemused by all his bureaucratic bullshit and walked down the corridor to the relative sanity of my own office and my three colleagues.

'How did you get on?' enquired Eric as soon as I entered.

'What do you mean, how did I get on? You've all been through the same bullshit. I did as procedure says I must. I went to see Cruickshank at the allotted time, he knows in advance that I am coming, and I tell him I have been summoned to attend on the Admiral downstairs. But he knows all about that as well, he has a memo telling him, and despite the fact that he cannot override or countermand the Admiral and his instructions, nevertheless has to give his permission for the visit. The sooner I dump my share of this paperwork on to you lot, and I get out of this madhouse, the better.'

When not on assignment the four of us share an office and perform routine clerical work associated with the day-to-day routine running of the Coastguard Service. It is rare for all four of us to be in the office at anyone time and to be all engaged on this boring routine work, but that had been the case for the last few weeks. Shortly, with a bit of luck, I would be temporarily moving out and that meant that my share of the routine work had to be divided between those who had the misfortune to be left behind.

Every Government Department has its own individual, and sometimes peculiar, method of identifying the vast range of forms and pro forma's which have to be routinely filled out and processed for it to function, it hopes, efficiently. The Coastguard is no exception. It numbers all its forms and most of its routine paperwork and prefixes them with the letters C and G. Therefore, should anyone in any department, have to make reference, for example to a CG48 the entire service knows that they are referring to a specific form designed to record Auxiliary Coastguard Watch Keeping Hours. Similarly a CG21 is used only for recording the details of an incident and is filled out by the person responsible for co-ordinating and controlling that incident.

These forms are often used as the official true and accurate record of events during Board of Trade enquiries and are often required following the loss of ships at sea and other related disasters.

Over the years, and possible throughout the existence of the Coastguard Service, every single item, as it appeared, reappeared or was reformatted, has been numbered and prefixed CG until very recently when some high ranking bright spark, probably a new comer intent on creating an impression and leaving his mark,

from the word go, invented yet another additional form that would have been quite readily recognised with a prefix of CGTS, to mean Coastguard Transport, but instead this cleaver wiz-kid, or 'thickie', depending on which way you look at it, decided to drop the CG. Now there are thousands of TS forms floating about alongside all the other long established transport forms, which are, prefixed CG81.

No one understands the reasoning behind the use of TS, but assumes that the revolutionary break from tried and tested systems can only have come from the very highest level. They say that it is the paperwork that makes the world go round? It just makes you wonder how smoothly it would all go if there were some brains at the back of it. I often wonder how some of these people get there?

Much of our routine work and responsibility is to check numbers, totals, cross-references and values, and then transfer it all into a computer terminal. From there, all the information is whizzed about and passed to other interested and I guess mostly disinterested departments for further processing or action. To say the least, it is all very boring and highly repetitive.

'There you are chaps. Three neat piles of CG's and a few TS's to get your teeth into.'

'Piss off,' moaned Jim. 'I have enough of my own to keep me stir-crazy for years without you trying to add to them.'

'It's a different story when you get a job and dump all your stuff on us. So grab hold of this lot. I have at least divided them up and sorted them out for you. The CG48s in this stack only want the hours and rates feeding into the computer; I've done the rest, the changes and updates. This one is CG81s and I've done the mileage. There's just the running times and fuel to sort out. These TS2s haven't been touched yet so you have plenty to go at there.'

'Why do they have to give us all this monotonous crap to work on? Why us?' whined Eric. 'Go on, you tell me. Surely we deserve better!'

'Obvious, my dear fellow,' replied Philip. 'First of all it is not crap to the fellow who hopes to earn a little coin out of the Coastguard for all the effort he puts in. As you know most of these forms here concern Auxiliaries who get paid peanuts relative to their commitment and efforts. So don't begrudge them the little bit they do get. Don't forget, old son, you are moaning about processing their pay in a nice warm, comfortable office when they probably earned it out in the cold and wet, and you have only to look at the recorded times to see they do a hell of a lot of it during the night. Also you get this lot to do so that your tiny brain is not overtaxed and you can stay mentally alert and fit for the 'jobs' you were supposed to be trained for, and for which you are supposedly employed and very highly paid.'

'Bull shit!' snapped Eric. 'Highly paid. You have obviously flipped and been brain-washed and sound just like the Old Man!' At which we all laughed before Philip continued with his tongue in cheek lecture. No one taking him the least bit seriously including, I believe, himself. 'Finally it's because this type of

work is all you lot are capable of and requires the minimum of effort on your part to pass it over when you get a "proper job" and can't get out quick enough.'

'OK Philip, I can understand even your bull shit with of course the exception of the overpaid bit, which I believe in your cases, but not mine, is correct, but I still think that if someone tried they could find us something a bit more stimulating than this lot.'

'Bloody hell Eric, listen to you, you spend less time in this office than any of us.'

'That's not the point, is it? We sit here for hours on end just getting bored out of our tiny minds and farting about with never ending reams of paper.'

'You fight it out amongst yourselves, chaps. It's all there and I am due downstairs at this very moment, so see you all later.'

I left them still arguing amongst themselves. Nothing would change and they knew it, but I suppose talking about it helped and letting off a little steam did no harm and was far more stimulating than actually doing the work.

CHAPTER FIVE

I was feeling very content. I had passed over, to my colleagues, all the paper work that I routinely ploughed through as a 'fill-in', and the justification for my existence, when not 'gainfully employed', as the Major often put it, on field work. I had been downstairs at the appointed hour and I was currently awaiting my second visit and briefing with Cruickshank. I also felt better for having nipped out for a bite to eat.

Living alone is not the best way, especially for me, for getting fed. Boiling an egg is a major culinary operation and I get fed up with tins of soup, where the contents have been warmed and often boiled over in the microwave. The results of my efforts then having to be eaten, more often than not, with slices of dry bread and then washed down with black coffee. Milk never lasting long enough to be anything but sour.

I can't be the only one, forced by my lack of kitchen skills, to live like this. There must be many others, especially men, who endure the same deprivations. Poor sods like me who find that a loaf of bread goes stale long before it is all eaten, and the milk goes off when all you buy it for in the first place, is to add to tea or coffee? I can't be alone in this? But then who knows? Anyhow despite all my shortcomings and inadequacies in that particular area I am really quite happy as long as I am able to grab something now and again which I feel is reasonable both in quantity and quality and also comes in at the right price.

That lunchtime it had been the pub, but I hasten to add that I am not in the habit of frequenting pubs and drinking at lunch times when working in the office. Though I do drink and very much enjoy the company that usually goes with it, possibly because, once again, it might have something to do with living alone, but I do try to confine it to the evenings. My favourite tipple, when I do indulge, is whiskey and water but I can enjoy a pint of bitter when the mood takes me. I have always tried to avoid lunch time drinking as it makes me drowsy and useless in the afternoons and it is also against my principals to drink and drive and I inevitably have to drive at sometime after lunch, if only to get home. I only went that particular day because it is convenient and I was rather limited for time.

I had also been to the bank, paying what had to be paid and making sure that I had adequate spare cash for minor contingencies, which I knew would inevitably crop up later. Before I went I took advantage of the fact that I had been allocated a 'job' and cleared out my desk and ditched all the accumulated rubbish that seems to quickly build up between times. It's almost a ritual with us and the one where we clear out all the memos and instructions, the reminder notes; all of which were very

important at the time of receipt but with the passing of time all became outdated, superseded or totally irrelevant.

I was making sure I had got rid of everything that I could safely dispense with, when the telephone rang. It took me by surprise and I think I jumped a little, the reaction making me realise just how the tension and apprehension was beginning to build. Was I that excited and did it show? I look around to see if anyone had noticed anything. No one was taking a blind bit of notice. Jim was tapping away at the Computer Keyboard. Eric was using his pen, as a pointer, to run down sheet after sheet of printed paper, obviously checking some CG or other and Phil was thumbing through and sorting a pile of papers, and possibly counting them. I don't think they had even noticed the phone ring, or if they had, there had been no reaction. As I looked from one to the other, each was engrossed in what he was doing, or more accurately was actually, sort of, semi-switched off and doing automatically what was a very routine and boring job that required very little brain power and offered almost no stimulation in return. They were applying the techniques we had all developed, to counter the lack of mental stimulation. It made the time pass quickly and helped to counter the pain and despair brought on by the sheer boredom.

The phone was still ringing. I picked it up.

'Hello.'

'Mel? Janet. He wants to see you now.'

'Thanks, Janet, I'll be along in a mo.'

I walked the short distance along the corridor. As I entered the outer office, Janet greeted me with her usual big smile, 'Go straight through. He's waiting for you and he already has someone in with him.'

'Who?'

'You will find out when you get in there.'

I knocked on the inner door before realising my knock would not be heard on the other side, so after hesitating a second I grasped the large brass handle. I opened the heavy, sound proof, dividing door and stepped into the Colonel's office. As I turned to close the door behind me, it became very obvious that he was not alone, for seated in front of his desk in one of the large leather covered chairs, was an extremely attractive girl. It was almost torture to look away from her and looking at the Old man was such a lousy alternative.

'Good afternoon Grundy, come in and sit down,' he said indicating a vacant chair.

The telephone call earlier had made me jump and caused my heart to beat faster but that was nothing compared to the way it began to pound as I glanced at the apparition in the chair beside me. My throat went dry as she turned and flashed me a lovely smile before turning back to look at the Colonel. I continued to look at her for as long as I dared and took in as much as was visible, as unfortunately, a

part of her was shielded from my direct view by the high back and side wing of the leather covered chair, which to my acute annoyance, seemed to be trying to wrap itself around her.

I desperately wanted to see more but for the time being had to be satisfied to let my imagination fill in the missing bits. One thing was obvious from the way she was sitting she was quite tall. Her hair, which as far as I could see, came down to her shoulders, was fair to blond and looked natural. She wore a white top, black skirt, and black stockings. Her face could have graced the front cover of any fashion magazine and for the few seconds I saw it full on I saw sparkling, laughing blue eyes, and a faint permanent smile. In a nutshell, very nice indeed!

I also noticed, in the brief allotted time that the white shirt appeared to be nicely filled. I also found myself wondering if the black stockings were in actual fact stockings, or tights? The Colonel interrupted and spoilt everything.

'Are you with us Grundy?'

'Yes Sir,' I replied pulling my eyes away from the girl and looking him straight in the face.

'This is Miss Huntington and she will be working alongside you. You will be working as a team on this assignment.'

I turned to face her and was met with a lovely smile. I could feel my body temperature rise. I had never worked with a female partner before. I had always worked alone in the past and up to the present had always preferred it that way. There had of course been the odd occasion when I had needed assistance or I had been assigned to provide assistance to a colleague but that is what it had been, a colleague, someone from a very familiar office down the corridor. In fact up to that moment it had never entered my head that we might have had female operatives. I had never heard mention of them nor, as I recollect, had there ever been any rumours regarding females attached to our unit. It would of course have been naive of me to think or even suggest that there are no females in our type of work but actually within our particular department, never. A very pleasant surprise, but a surprise no less. In fact when I first entered the Colonel's office my immediate thoughts and reactions were that this gorgeous creature was there simply to supply information for the briefing. Now she was to partner me. I don't think it actually sank in straight away.

I looked at the Colonel. If he was aware of the inner and uncontrollable tremble that was raking havoc with my body he was giving no indication if it. I was hard to contain myself and concentrate. Once again I turned to glance in her direction.

'Grundy.'

'Sir.'

'Are you listening?'

'Yes Sir, I was just thinking...'

'Don't think, for the moment, listen. You will have ample time to become acquainted with Miss Huntington after this briefing. So, if I can have your undivided attention, I will continue. I had a meeting with the Rear Admiral this morning and he has charged me with the responsibility of investigating an incident. An incident that the department is not at all happy about; which means that I, in turn, therefore, am not happy about, so, I am handing over the responsibility for eliminating this dissatisfaction to you two. You two will carry out a full investigation and provide me with the details and the results I require to give to the Rear Admiral.'

I couldn't help wondering how my new partner was reacting to all this, but I always found the way the Colonel rattled on and his peculiar way of putting things on these, so called, formal occasions, was not only boring, but so damned unnecessary. He always managed to make it sound like the children's game of 'pass-the-parcel'. If only he could hear himself. 'He, the Admiral, passes to me, the Colonel, the responsibility, and I take it. Then I pass it on to you because I personally can't handle it at this stage. I, of course, have to cover his back so you have to cover mine. He wants answers from me so I want them from you,' and so it goes on. The only difference between this and the kids' game of 'pass the parcel' Is that every time the music stops the parcel always seems to be squarely with us.

I looked sideways. Had she heard it all before? Either way, she was showing no outward signs of any adverse reaction. No obvious signs of boredom or disinterest. But then I hoped neither was I, for the last thing I wanted was for the Colonel to discover that inwardly I was taking the piss out of his style of briefing.

'Partner', what a thrill that word suddenly had for me. Did my partner have a first name? Of course she had. What could it possibly be? Was she as tall as I imagined? What does she really look like without half that damned chair in the way? Is she as gorgeous as she first appeared or is she even better? I wanted to stand up and move round so I could getter a better and closer look.

'As I was saying.'

Sorry Sir, has the music started again, should I be passing the parcel, I said to myself?

'There has been an incident up north which is causing the department some concern. A Coastguard Officer has gone missing in rather strange circumstances. What those circumstances were, are not at all clear at the moment, but as far as we can gather there are no obvious reasons why he should just 'go missing' and to all intents and purposes, disappear from off the face of the earth. From what we have gathered, the local Police are involved and have already made tentative enquiries into the usual domestic scenarios, debt, and the other woman theories and, as far as we know, have come up with nothing.'

'What is so unusual in that, Sir? A disappearance? People go missing all the time for perfectly good sound reasons even if those reasons should only be

known to them.' She had spoken for the first time in my presence and what a lovely, cultured, almost accent less and very sexy voice she had.

'Yes,' I found myself echoing. 'They do, all the time, Sir.'

'Miss Huntington is quite right in what she says, people do go missing all the time and for a variety of reasons. Some just don't have the courage, to face up to the wife and tell her "Look here old girl, I have had enough. I am fed up with you and our lifestyle and I'm off." Often wish I had the courage to say something similar myself.'

'What's that, Sir? You...?'

'Nothing that concerns you, Grundy! Some wishful thinking on my part, that's all.'

'Then excuse me, Sir, but I am finding this a little difficult to follow. Am I reading you correctly? You are telling us that some bloke has simply taken off, probably for some good reason and the Department intends to launch an enquiry? Hell no, Sir, more than that, the department intends a full investigation if you ask me, when it proposes to send two of us to look for him. What's the local fuzz doing in all this? Surely it's down to them? A domestic? A disappearance? It doesn't make a lot of sense to me, two people from this department to investigate a simple case of a missing person.'

'Look Grundy, before we go any further, you get this straight and understand this. Our people are not stupid. Perhaps someone higher up knows more about it than they are willing to tell us at this point in time. You well know; that as a department, we always work on a need-to-know basis and perhaps at this moment, the Rear Admiral has decided that this is all we need to know. Just sufficient to allow us to get on with, and do the job and no more. But you have my assurance, and you Grundy of all people should know, that the Department does not send out trained operatives to chase up possible domestic disputes. Do I make myself clear?'

'Yes Sir.'

He then shifted his gaze and looked directly at the delightful Miss Huntington, who in turn echoed, 'Yes Sir.'

'So, if we can move on. This Coastguard Officer has gone missing, and apparently without trace. What interested everyone locally, and by that I mean our uniform people in the immediate area and the local Police along with them, was the fact that some of his personal effects and Coastguard equipment were found in, what has been described as, an out of the way location and some distance from his home. But no one has been able to establish why they were there, or how they got there, or if indeed he himself had been there; or if he had been there, his reason for going. No one seems to know, first of all, why he had cause to go out alone. Which it is alleged that he did. Secondly, if he did have good cause to go, why did he not tell anyone? Then where did he actual go, and why? Finally, the

items found. Why those particular items, and why in that isolated location? The only other factor that maybe significant or not, is the fact that he is alleged to have taken the family pet dog along with him and the dog subsequently returned home alone, sometime later. His wife is adamant that the dog would never have left him in normal circumstances, as the animal was considered to be his dog, loyal to him, and it was believed that up to that time would never have left him.'

'What constitutes the personal effects you mentioned Sir?' I ventured as I shifted my position in order to smile at, and take yet another sideways glance at Miss H. I was looking forwards to working with this charming lady. A whole new experience, but strictly a professional one of course, I had to keep forcedly reminding myself.

'A dog lead! Not valuable in itself, but significant in as much as it has been identified as belonging to the missing mans' dog. A pair of issue Coastguard binoculars which are of top quality and expensive, a multi-channel radio receiver which, although not official issue is of the type frequently purchased privately and used by Coastguard personnel, and sadly also these days, by numerous unauthorised members of the general public, and lastly a standard issue waterproof torch. All expensive items and not the type of things to be left behind by an opportunist thief or muggers.'

'Even so Sir, should someone just want to take off, they may go to the trouble of dumping a few things and even be prepared to abandon their dog if the motivation to get away is strong enough and their irrational behaviour helps, in some way, to create a false trail or impression.'

Throughout I couldn't help thinking there was no sense of urgency in what he is saying. What had a simple disappearance to do with us: to do with two of us? It somehow didn't quite ring true. It sounded slightly false and to say the least, extremely weak. Here was I, sat in an office, in front of my chief, being forced to think about, and try and concentrate on, a man whose probable sole aim was to get away from a woman and disappear, while at the same time, sat beside me was a girl that made my heart go bump and one I couldn't wait to see more of and get the chance to chat up. Once again, I had to get a grip on myself and try and concentrate on what the Old Man was saying.

Before my brain was properly in gear my mouth was saying, 'Sir...even if it turns out to be a bit more complex than a missing person, why is it necessary to have an assistant for this investigation?'

`Who mentioned an assistant? I said nothing about any assistant. Let me remind you. I said Miss Huntington is to be your partner on this assignment.'

'Sorry Sir, partner. But partner or assistant, which she is not, it still strikes me, from what you have told us, that we are going in a bit heavy, perhaps a bit over the top, aren't we sir?'

'Not at all, Grundy! I reason, and the Rear Admiral agrees fully, that if you are to travel about in the open countryside along the East coast, snooping about and asking a lot of questions, a holiday couple or a pair of hikers, ramblers, walkers or whatever, are far better than a lone person who would probably stick out like a sore thumb, in a thinly populated area. Anyhow, you are equal partners in this investigation, which, if necessary, will allow you to go your separate ways and work independently should the circumstances dictate. Do you both understand?'

I nodded. Gosh! I thought, I have only just met the girl and he is already talking of going our separate ways. Not if I could help it, I promised myself. The thought of working close to this divine creature was too strong a magnet and the very thought of being with her much too attractive to let her escape once outside this office. None of it could start too soon for me and bugger how simple and straight forward the job might be. I dragged myself once again back to reality to hear the Colonel saying, 'You will travel from here in Coastguard uniform and use a Coastguard car. You will go to the MRCC Headquarters at Yarmouth where the Regional Controller has been advised of your visit. This will be your starting point and he will arrange your accommodation. You will be using your own names and I have arranged for identity cards to be prepared which will show you belong to an Internal Review Board. Your cover brief is; that you are to look into procedures and cost effectiveness of the whole of the Yarmouth Region. If at any time it becomes necessary for you to go further North and out of the Yarmouth Region and into the Tyne Tees Section then you will have to come back to me and I will clear it with them and issue the necessary paper work. The Regional Controller, Yarmouth is the only person there who knows that you are also looking into an internal security matter. He knows nothing else and must not be told anything else. You are to report directly back to me. The Regional Controller has been ordered, from the highest level, and through his chain of command, to give you every co-operation. Any problems from that direction and you let me know. Apart from that, you are both familiar with standard procedure for the passing of information and making reports excreta, and don't forget I need to know at all times what you are up to so keep me fully informed of your progress, whether you think it is important or not. I will decide that. Understand?'

'When are we scheduled to arrive in Yarmouth Sir?'

'Fourteen hundred tomorrow! That gives you the remainder of today and all this evening to assemble what you will need, exchange pleasantries, and prepare to travel North tomorrow morning. If there's nothing further, you may both go and get on with it.'

I rose from my chair and turned to face my new partner and for the first time and to get a real good look at her. She was stunning. She was as tall as I imagined, at least five foot ten inches, slim and from the front absolutely gorgeous with long legs, narrow hips and a tiny waist. I had been right about the crisp white

shirt… It was more than adequately filled. Laughing blue eyes and just a trace of make-up, hers was a face that just didn't need any. In a nut shell a truly lovely girl and a pleasure to look at. I was looking forward to working with this lovely lady and I hoped and prayed that the feelings were mutual, and that she was as enthusiastic as I was. This was going to be a whole new experience for me and I welcomed it with relish. I was more than ready and eager to get started and I would have to think hard to remember what the Old Man had just said. Something about a man and his dog and maybe his wife?

'Grundy, a moment before you leave.'

'Wait for me in the outer office,' I whispered, trying not to show the panic that I felt that once outside the office she might disappear and be lost forever and all because the old duffer had asked me to stay behind.

I stood and watched as she left the room closing the door behind her, the Colonel addressed me. 'Partners, Grundy, and don't you forget it. She's a first class operative and one of my best, so don't you get any bright ideas that she needs carrying. She does not need looking after. She is competent and self-sufficient and don't you forget it.'

'Where did you find her Sir?'

'That's none of your damned business, Grundy. Get along now. You have work to do, and so have I. Remember, she has direct access to me, so watch your P's and Q's.'

'Oh I will Sir, I will.'

'Remember Grundy, I am waiting for, and want, results. I want your full report on my desk as soon as possible. Is that understood? So keep your nose clean and me informed at all times.'

CHAPTER SIX

We chose the Staff Rest Room, mainly because it was close by and convenient.

Rest Rooms are provided, usually one to each floor, for those who wish to get away from their office environment during recognised break and meal times. They have always been popular places, being comfortable and quiet, and are regularly occupied by those who either wish to sit and enjoy a moment's peace or perhaps browse a newspaper or have a quiet smoke. At lunch times, however, the place can become quite lively as the girls tend to meet in large groups and chat while the men, for some reason, usually prefer to sit in smaller numbers and put the world to rights. The one we chose, at that particular moment was unoccupied: a rarity in my experience.

We sat to face each other, in two easy chairs.

'So you are Mel Grundy?' she said as she offered her hand. It was warm and smooth. 'I'm Winifred Huntington. A pleasure to formally meet you,' she laughed.

'My pleasure and nice to meet you, Winifred.' I had, at last, discovered her first name. 'A nice name, Winifred, and one that definitely suits you.'

'Oh no. No way. I don't agree with you on that one. So please, what ever you do, don't call me Winifred. I know it's my name and what I have to formally answer to. But let me explain. Oh gosh! Don't I sound silly? You must think I'm crazy. We have only just met and here am I already disputing my name. What on earth you must think of me?' she laughed.

'I am thinking just how lovely you are and I don't really care a damn about your name, what ever it is.'

'Now it's you that is being silly. Listen and just let me explain. There's not that much to it really and thinking about it, it is no big deal.'

We sat and I looked at her face, enjoying what I saw, while she began her explanation. 'If we are going to be working together please call me Fred. All my close friends and all the people who are important to me do. So please will you?'

'Of course I will. If you insist.' I immediately felt good and excited at what she had just said. If I understood correctly, I had just been invited to join her close friends and use a particular name that was obviously restricted to those she selected and chose to use it. I felt we were getting off to a very good start.

'But why Fred? You must admit it is unusual and, if you will forgive me, not exactly a girl's name. Don't tell me Daddy had this desire for a boy and a massive

train set, or some such theory, and Mummy let him down badly by bringing home a girl, saying that's all they had available in the maternity ward?'

'Hell no!' she replied with a very infectious laugh. 'Winifred is so old-fashioned in this day and age, that's all really. It was my Grandmother's name and my dad thought it would be nice if I were called after her. Why they didn't give me a more modern second name or something else to go with it, which I could have used as an alternative, I have no idea; but they didn't. So at school, after an early childhood of Winifred, I got Win or Winnie. Later, at college, the Win disappeared after I took a male part in one of those silly all girl college plays. It was one of those fun things really, but from it, and there after, all my close friends nicknamed me Fred. It just sort of stuck after that; even Dad calls me Fred. Mum doesn't of course. Christened Winifred so Winifred it will always be.'

'So do you live with your Mum and Dad?'

'No. My parents or at least Dad is, are in the Diplomatic Service and they are nearly always away somewhere. When home, for short periods, they tend to rent somewhere convenient or stay in small hotels. Dad says he will eventually retire in this Country and buy a place somewhere miles from anywhere. I don't know what Mum thinks about that. Anyhow, sometimes when they're home I stay with them for short periods but in the meantime I live alone in a flat not too far from here. Handy for the office and the daily routine stuff.'

That rather surprised me. If she lived close and worked in this office block on a fairly regular basis, why had I never seen or noticed her before? Me, Mel Grundy, the guy who considers himself an expert on beautiful birds and in particular the long-legged, non-feathered, boob-endowed type, similar to this beautiful creature, sat in front of me. I needed to know more.

'So you actually work in this particular block, do you?'

'Yes. I'm based here in the typing pool on the second floor. I also move around between other departments covering for sickness, pregnancies, holidays, and the likes. It's a useful cover because everyone gets used to me flitting about, so if I do go missing, as I will be shortly, no one pays much attention.'

'Where did the service find you then? Not in the second floor typing pool of HMCG, I'll bet?'

'No. The Navy. With Mum and Dad being away and out of this country for long periods I spent a great deal of time in Boarding School at first and then away at College, so it was almost a natural progression to go from there into the Services. I just seemed to drift towards it, although the fact that my father had been in the Navy for some years may have influenced my choice of service. I enjoyed it and was lucky and travelled quite a bit, nearly all shore-based of course, doing mainly clerical type work for the High Rankers. Then, like many others before me and some of whom I met later, I was "approached", out of the blue, and drawn into

the "Service." You must know basically how that sort of thing works. What about you? How did you start off and finally get involved, if that's the right word?"

'Me? Not much to tell there really. Similar to you in many ways I suppose. Though not quite as glamorous and no drastic name changes or getting close to any High Rankers. For me it was an ordinary school, then school on the Continent where I boarded with a local family, back to University, Air Force, and finally here.'

'Where were you at school on the continent?'

'In France, a small town not far from Dijon.'

'What was the idea behind that?'

'Parents thought it would do me some good.'

'Did it?'

'In some ways I think it did. It allowed me to at least learn another language and I loved every minute of the time I was there. I liked France and the French people and still believe the average Frenchman likes the Brits. It's the politicians who seem to dislike each other and throw political rocks back and forth across the channel, each trying to discredit the other in the process. I also find it hard to accept that some people are still prepared to claim that it has something to do with the fact that we were supposed to have saved them from the Germans in two world wars. Granted we fought on two separate occasions in their country, but each time, we were all supposed to be on the same side and I just can't see the French holding the Joan of Arc affair against us after all this time. So god knows why they do it but they do. Anyhow I personally have a lot of time for the French and admire their attitude and their way of life in general.'

'What did you read at University?'

'Psychology.'

'Where?'

'Southampton. The only place that would have me at the time.'

'So does that mean I am now working with a "shrink", as the Americans would so aptly put it?'

'No. I'm supposed to be a psychologist and as far as I know a "shrink", as you put it, is a psychiatrist and there is a big difference between the two. Psychiatrists are supposed to treat the mentally ill, whilst I, for my pains, am supposed to have made a "scientific study of human behaviour." But I will tell you one thing; having done so, I rapidly came to the conclusion that anyone who claims to know all there is to know about human behaviour, is living in Cuckoo Land.'

'And you should know, you're the expert,' she laughed.

'But enough of me! I'm an expert on nothing, as you will probably find out. But getting to the more serious stuff. I suggest that for now, and before we go any deeper into my dubious background, we should think about this assignment and draw up some sort of plan. We don't have much to go on and not long before

we have to set off and make a start and all this is so confusing and new to me. I've never worked with a girl before. In fact I'm used to working alone so this is going to take a bit of getting used to.'

'We'll get down to the serious stuff, as you put it, and work out a plan and discuss all the details just as soon as you fill me in with your age and tell me where the Mel comes from?'

'No problem! Age 39. The proper name and the correct title, Malcolm: Mally at school. Mel from a girl at University that I fancied something rotten.'

'What happened to her if you fancied her, as you put it, something rotten?'

'I married her, but she took off and left me, many years ago. The Mel just stuck. I had, after all, got so used to it and it had nothing to do with the fact, as has been suggested many times in the past, that my parents were unable to think of anything more ambitious.'

'Does it bother you a lot, the fact that you have never worked with a girl before and are going to have to now?'

'Not so far it doesn't. But then it is still rather novel. But I must admit it does feel slightly strange, but I am sure I will get used to that and I like what I have seen so far and have got some really good feeling about the future. But going back to ages; you know mine so dare I ask a delicate question and ask yours?'

'No problem as you put it. Twenty-eight. Five foot nine inches tall in stocking feet. Hair natural colour, no padding anywhere and that's all for now.'

I could see that her hair was fair, almost blond and that there were no signs of padding on the shoulders or anywhere else. All very much her own and the way a part of that pushed out the front of her shirt was a shear delight from any angle. Neat around the middle; flat stomach and the visible part of the legs a sheer delight; and the black stockings! I have always had a thing about black or blue stockings. I feel they give a girl that little something extra.

'A plan of action then,' I said as I shook my head.

'Not so quickly! Remember I have to get used to working with you. So look at it from my point of view for a moment. It was all a bit of a shock when I was summoned by the Colonel; put in a chair next to a guy that I had never seen before and told to go away and work with him. So first things first: and slowly if you don't mind, to start with. If we are going up north somewhere and for goodness knows how long there are a few things that I shall need, so I proposed to go out now and get those for starters. Whilst I am doing that it will give me chance to settle down and study my lot and think things out a bit. According to the Colonel I still have the right to pull out and decline this particular assignment.'

'Oh don't do that. Why would you want to do that? You go off and do your thing and you see things will be just fine and while you're away I will go and

collect our Identity Cards, cash and Credit Cards. Do you need anything special that I can get for you from stores?'

She thought for a moment before replying, 'No I don't think so, thanks, if you get the cards and some cash. I should have everything I need in my flat. So I will catch up with you later.'

'Where?'

'Back here but in the Canteen.'

As soon as she left it felt strange to be alone. I was excited at the prospect of working with Fred. An unusual name Fred: Winifred, Fred. I knew I would soon get used to it however unusual the name seemed at first for a beautiful, sexy, feminine, female, if there is such a thing as an exceptionally feminine female. I believed there was and I had just met her, and so for that matter who really cared about a name. Fred will do fine. Adds to the charm and mystery. I was used to it already.

Strange how for those first few moments I was at a loss as to exactly what I was supposed or intended to do. Had she already had a greater impact on me than I realised. I was happy if she had but when I thought about it I still also had some feelings of panic from when she had said that, at this point, she was not obliged to go through with it and could still pull out. She couldn't do that to me? Not now. Could she?

I pulled myself together and went to collect our ID cards. They were both there waiting so she had not pulled out so far. I forced myself to accept that this was a good sign despite the fact that it was still early days. I picked them up and carefully put them in my pocket. To loose mine would not cause me undue concern or distress but to loose hers might mean loosing her. I was being totally irrational. The only value those cards had, were to 'prove' to other people that we were from the Internal Review Board. Those and the credit cards and petty cash were nothing more than 'tools of our trade'.

Since the introduction and widespread use of Credit Cards, the service has had a financial arrangement with the Treasury so that all transactions made by agents using these cards are debited back to the appropriate Treasury account, who in turn pass it back and charge it, in our case, to the Coastguard budget. Any other minor expenses, which we are obliged to finance ourselves, we claim back at the end of the job by submitting the correct CG form. In the old days, funding was always a problem. Agents drew cash in advance and often had problems storing or handling it. They had it transferred into personal accounts and could have untold problems when they tried to draw it, especially if the ID they carried was different from that associated with the account or they were trying to use a bank branch that was not their own. Every penny had and still has, to be accounted for, so a mass of paper work and detailed records had to be kept and things got naturally messy if they got missed or went adrift. There was always hell on if claims turned

out to be wrong later. All overpayments having to be paid straight back and the chances of trying to get underpayments when the completed application had not been submitted at the correct time were virtually nil. That and everything else that goes with trying to remember details, sometimes months, after a delicate and pressurised job where the operative was glad to get out by the skin of his teeth and the last thing on his mind, at the time, being to remember his detailed costs and expenses.

Credit cards have, without doubt, made life much easier all round. Now each job is allocated its own individual account number and the boys in Finance can keep close tabs on each individual agent. Agents, for their part, are delighted with them for they definitely make life so much easier. Cash can be drawn from most cash dispensers or banks. Purchases can be made from shops and stores and any other outlet accepting credit cards with the minimum of fuss and necessity for detailed identification. It's also nice to know that all you have to do is push the credit slip into your pocket, for reference later, while someone else picks up the account each month, despite the fact that you maybe called on to explain and justify certain items or the amounts involved.

Cash, Credit cards and ID cards sorted out, I went along to stores and drew a couple of extra pairs of black socks and three new shirts, everything else I had at home. I then went up from the basement area to the canteen, to await the return of Fred. The wiggle of her bum as I had watched her leave a short while earlier still very fresh in my mind. I just hoped she would be back and all I had to do was wait.

CHAPTER SEVEN

The canteen was busy with a steady stream of people passing through. The tea was acceptable, but was typical, if there is such a thing as typical, of canteen tea, much too strong, stewed, and with far too much milk in it for my liking. Eric, my colleague in the office upstairs, loved it and drank gallons every day. The newspaper that had been left on the table contained nothing to stimulate my interest, the main contents being the same daily, boring scenario of more job losses and lay-offs. The Prime Minister had said this, or a member of the opposition said that, while a member of the Royal Family was attending this today, or were going there, or had been. Our kids were not getting educated because teachers needed more money or more money was the only answer to this and that. I put it aside and resorted to my favourite pastime, 'people watching'. I watched all the smartly turned-out young women as they drifted in and out and scrutinised all those who sat in groups chatting away and laughing. They created an atmosphere of pleasant excitement and everyone seemed so carefree, if only for the moment. I remember thinking how they all looked so damned attractive and how many would be making love to someone at some time over the next twenty-four hours; there were some very lucky men about.

I forced myself back to reality as a thought struck me. I picked up the discarded paper and scanned it closely. There it was, hidden in the centre pages, and at the bottom of the right-hand column, and where I had previously not looked or if I had it had not registered. A brief and simple statement under the heading 'Missing'. It said, 'A man has gone missing along the North East coast of England. The Police are investigating.' There was even less in this particular paper than the short statements that we had read out in the office. So in light of recent events and the happenings upstairs had it been intentionally suppressed or were the papers simply treating it as yet another missing person, and so did not consider it to be more newsworthy than to allocated only a two line announcement. I was still thinking about it and pondering on the reasoning behind the reaction, or none reaction, of the press, and the fact that the department had felt it necessary to send a team of two to investigate what appeared to be a simple disappearance, when Fred returned.

'Hi. I'm back.'

'So I see, and looking as lovely as ever.'

'Nothing's changed that I am aware of,' she replied, running her hands down her thighs as if smoothing imaginary creases out of her skirt.

'So that tells me that you must have been lovely before.'

'Thank you, kind sir,' she smiled, and holding her right index finger to the underside of her chin, bent her knees, and did a little curtsy.

'Sit down and let me get you some tea?'

'No thanks, the tea in here is dreadful, but you can get me a coffee, if you don't mind.'

I went across to the servery for two coffees, my half-consumed, unpalatable, stewed tea having long since gone cold. As I returned to the table and set down the two cups, Fred said, 'Are you ever serious? I have been watching you over there with those two girls working behind the counter. I think you must definitely be a bit of a chat-up merchant. Is a girl safe with you?'

'Oh that with those two. Only a bit of fun and they love it. But if you mean by chat-up merchant do I like girls? Then yes I do like girls and I do like chatting them up. As for being seriousness, I can be as serious as circumstances dictate, but I still consider myself as being the easy-going type in preference to the serious or the studious type. As for being safe, you can be assured you are as safe as houses with me.'

'Then we should get on fine because I like a bit of fun, and love to be chatted up. So you are free to practice all you like on me. As for being safe, I will have to give that a bit more thought. Total and complete safety could be a bit boring.'

'You're on, and thanks for the invite.'

'As long as you confine it to just chat-up.'

I sensed a warning signal in there, somewhere so having made a mental note decided to back off. I somehow felt that if I pursued it just then, it would only lead to some heavy ground rules being laid down, and perhaps insurmountable boundaries being very clearly defined. I didn't want that to happen if it could be avoided, so, for the moment, decided that a change of subject was necessary.

'Do you know the girl you spoke to when you came back into the canteen just now?'

'Yes, of course I do, that's why I spoke to her. We have worked together at various times, mainly in the typing pool, and we occasionally go out together, man hunting, and all the other things that nice girls are not supposed to do. Do you know her?'

'I've met her,' I admitted but purposely didn't add that she was the girl who had done a runner on me the previous evening.

'Never mind her. Have you made any concrete plans for us yet, or thought anymore about how we should go about this assignment?'

'Not really! I thought it best to wait until you came back, then we could perhaps work out something between us. But I have been and collected our ID and Credit Cards, and a hundred pounds each in cash: fifty in tens and fifty in fives. I've also drawn a couple of hand held radios, two spare rechargeable battery packs, and

a charger. I know there will already be a base set in the car, if we take a company car, but the hand held ones will allow us to go walk-about if we need to. I also thought that if we took my car along, we could travel as Coastguards in the official one and civilians in the other. What do you think? Does it make sense? It would after all look rather odd if two civilians, dressed in casual gear, were seen riding around the countryside in an official company car, complete with a blue light stuck on it's roof. It will also save us hassle with hire cars. So what I thought, and if you agree of course, is that you drive the company car, and I will take mine. There should be no problems parking either of them up somewhere out of sight, and then retrieving them and using them as required later, that is, if we should need either or both of them. Also if I take one of the hand held radios along with me then we will have "comms" between the two cars. If we use, say, channel Seventy-three and keep the "verbals" down to the minimum we should avoid, or at least reduce, the risk of being overheard or monitored. What do you think?'

'Sounds fine to me, so far! So I am to take the company car, and you will use yours, and we travel separately, and go firstly to Yarmouth. From there, I suppose it all depends on what we find out and how things develop?'

'That was the basic idea. What I now suggest we do and if you agree, is we go home and throw our personal things together. Compared to the weather around here, I bet it will be much colder up North, so don't forget to pack plenty of jumpers and fur-lined frillies.'

'You concern yourself with your own fur-lined frillies and let me worry about mine.'

I suddenly realised that, so far, I had taken all the initiative, as sadly I have to admit, is my style and that Fred, still a strange name for a girl but I had to confess had a certain fascination and was growing on me, showed no signs of objection. She appeared to be quite happy to let me fool myself into believing that I was doing all the thinking and forward planning. Or perhaps that was her style?

'Here, take this,' I said as I passed across the envelope that contained her ID, Credit Card and cash. 'And also this,' picking up one of the radios, from off the floor, beside me. 'I will keep the spare batteries and the charger and ensure they are all fully charged up before we leave. You aught to have this as well, you may need it.'

'What is it?' she enquired as she picked up the small white card.

'My card, then you have my address and phone number and please can I have yours in case I need to get hold of you for anything.

She reached down for her black, standard issue, handbag and took out her personal card, from one of the internal pockets, and passed it across. I glanced at it and saw, from the address, that she did indeed not live too far away from the office and it was only about thirty minutes, walking distance, away from my flat. I popped it into my top pocket.

'OK then! Unless there is anything you would like to add, I think we ought to shoot off straight away and get all our gear together. Can you give me a ring in, say, about three hours from now?'

'No problem and look forwards to it. Do you do a good chat-up line on the phone?'

'I don't know but I promise I will make a special effort just for you.'

* * *

What a smile. What a cracker. I was really looking forward to the company of this young lady and if the feelings were not mutual she had showed no outward signs of disappointment, so far. Not that I would ever dare considered myself an expert on how girls feel, or express their emotions, or how they see men. All I knew was, that I liked what I saw, and so far, as far as I could tell, all the vibes were good. There had been no evidence that I was aware of, of any emotional barriers between us. I had nothing but good feelings towards the future and the company I was about to share it with.

Having picked up all her belongings she had said, 'See you later.' and standing up, walked across the room towards the door. She gave a little wave to the girl, she had spoken to when she came in, and left.

I watched the door close behind her and sat for a few seconds, feeling very smug and very pleased with myself. I just could not believe that what had just left was to be my partner or that I was to be her partner, which ever way you looked at it. Finally, and once again, I pulled myself back to reality. I had a lot to do, dream partner or not. I gathered up the radio, the batteries and charger and all the other bits, including my new issue clothing. I left the canteen and made my way, via the back entrance, to the car park and my grubby, but reliable, Renault car, parked in the far corner.

The drive home was uneventful and despite the necessary stop for petrol, was quicker than usual.

I let myself in and as soon as I opened the door was hit by the faint, but very distinct, aroma of the stale Chinese take-away from the previous evening. That annoyed me. I thought I had adequately sprayed with air freshener before I left that morning. Either way, the smell was still there and was bloody awful. Perhaps my can of anti-pong stuff was not as good as it should be. No wonder the guy on the corner was selling the stuff cheap. Also I ought to have known, and remembered from previous experiences, and god knows I have had plenty of them, that this was one of the drawbacks, and part of the price you had to pay, for dining in, especially on highly-seasoned takeaways, who's make up includes a smell that is destined to linger forever.

I opened the window and a cold draught blew straight in, dramatically dropping the room temperature in a matter of seconds as it did so. But who cared? I had to get rid of the smell.

After a few minutes and when I thought I was about to freeze to death. The cold, the discomfort, and the traffic noises all being a bit much, I closed the window and secured it.

I crossed into the confined space that served as my kitchen, and put the kettle on. I then proceeded to move a few things about in a futile attempt to make the place look neater before going into the bedroom to retrieve my travel bag from its temporary resting place on top of the wardrobe. Placing it on the bed I started to rummage in drawers and cupboards, selecting the things I thought I might need on the trip. Casual but warm, I decided. Thick jumpers, cords, casual shirts, plenty of socks and underwear, working overalls and finally, uniform. I looked at it. Not as smart as it had once been. Of the two uniforms, that I possessed, the best one was at the cleaners, so I decided that I should go and pick it up. At the same time I could collect a pair of shoes that I currently had in for repair. I would also buy a dozen or so Mars Bars and a few cans of Coke to serve as emergency rations. In the past I have found Mars Bars to be a lifesaver, particularly when in a strange place, restricted for time, limited in the opportunity for movement and perhaps simply miles away from the nearest chippie.

On my return and laden down with my uniform, shoes, and other bits and bats, I managed, with some juggling, to manoeuvre the key into the Yale lock and eventually push the door open. The last thing I wanted to do was put a clean uniform, among all the other things, down on the floor, just to open the door. So doing a double contortionist act and taking the chance on looking rather silly to any casual observer, I eventually made it. As the bottom edge of the door slid back over the doormat, a brown envelope came into view. I pushed everything into one hand and over one arm, and stooped to pick it up. I had not been there when I went out, for had it been, I would have noticed it.

Closing the door behind me, and dropping everything onto the nearest chair, I looked at the envelope. It was a fairly common type, small, standard size, plain brown one with nothing written or printed on the outside, nor was it sealed; the flap was just tucked in. I opened it and extracted a single piece of plain white paper on which was neatly written, 'Sorry about last night, better luck with Fred.' It was not signed but I guessed who it was from and once again became very conscious of the smell in the apartment as it still stubbornly lingered from the night before. I also wondered just what, if anything, she might have said to Fred about our intimate tête-à-tête and her quick, unannounced, departure. However, whatever she might have said or did say I was not, at that moment, in a position to know or find out. Perhaps something might come out in the future. But for the moment I had other pressing things to attend to.

I placed the note and envelope on the hall table and as I did so thought how strange that girl had been and some of the strange things she said before literally running away like she did, and how now she might possibly be a friend of my new partner. I wondered if they might be two of a kind and both had strange ways of reacting to dates and men. I hoped not.

After rummaging through just about every drawer and cupboard in the flat I finally finished packing. I laid neatly to one side everything I proposed to ware the following day.

* * *

I went into the tiny area that served as my kitchen and made a hot drink.

I sat down and placed the pot on the side table. I closed my eyes to try and relax and to think a little about the future and our next possible moves.

I don't know how long I sat there thinking about various possible approaches and plans. All of which I knew, deep down, would probably not work out. For from past experience I knew we would have to take it a step at a time and see which direction each subsequent move took us; when the phone rang.

I jumped and without being fully conscious or re-oriented to my surroundings I grabbed the hand set from the cradle, which as luck would have it, was within easy reach of my chair, and snapped, 'Hello, who is it?'

'Don't shout; it's only me, Fred, and you said to ring at about this time. So in the first place that is just what I am doing and in the second I am ringing to tell you that I am hungry. Your place or mine?'

'Oh hi! Sorry I didn't mean to snap. You just woke me up. What was that you said, your place or mine? Is that right?'

'Yes, that's what I said.'

'I thought I was supposed to be the one with the chat up lines? Your place or mine baby.'

'Suit yourself. Your line or my line, your chat, my chat, it makes no difference to the fact that I am still starving. So make up your mind, is it your place or mine for food?'

'Do you have transport, a car?'

'Yes of course I do and at the moment I have two. I have the company car, remember?'

'Do you mind coming round here then?'

'Is that a subtle invitation? Is that a "Come into the parlour said the spider to the fly" or "Come upstairs and see my etchings"? If it is, then there is not much of a chat-up line in that. I thought you would be able to do better than that. OK, I will come round in the company car if that's the best you can do. If I use mine I have to pay for my own petrol.'

'No. Please don't do that. I don't want a company car seen round here. It might spoil my image and the low profile I try to maintain.'

'Sorry, I should have known better. I only brought it home tonight to save time tomorrow and I do have a garage to hide it away in so it isn't left out on the street. Do I bring anything or just my body?'

'Just bring yourself for starters. I will be waiting.'

I calculated that if she left straight away, the time it would take her to arrive would allow me ample time to shower and change. Had I suggested it the other way round, and I had gone to her place after I had showered and changed a lot of valuable time would have been lost.

Forty minutes and several squirts of deodorant, aftershave, and aerosol later, the doorbell rang, and I opened it to Fred.

'Come in, and once again, if I dare be so bold, you look lovely.'

'Now that's the type of chat-up I can't get too much of.'

She appeared taller than I remembered from a short while ago, even though she was wearing flat-heeled shoes. The uniform had gone and the tight-fitting jeans and fluffy sweater that had replaced it not only made her look taller, but also made her, in my opinion, the sexiest thing on two feet. I couldn't take my eyes away, they were completely welded onto the sweater and those thighs and if she turned round and the bum was just as captivating then I swear I would have been consumed by an overall, uncontrolled tremble. As if I was not already.

'Is everything all right with you? You sounded cross when I rang earlier.'

'Sorry about that! It was not intentional and I am certainly not cross with you now nor was I cross then. It was probably because I had almost fallen asleep and the phone made me jump.'

'Perhaps it's me who should say sorry. I didn't mean to make you jump or wake you up or anything like that.'

'Don't be daft. Why should you be sorry? You were not to know I was nearly asleep.'

'Well what ever it was and whoever's fault it was, will you settle for this as a tiny bit of compensation?' as she leaned forward and gave me a quick peck on the cheek. It sent an electric shock through my entire body and especially the important bits and I swear, had it been dark, I would have been seen to glow all over.

Desperately trying to regain control I said, 'Take a look at this,' as I handed her the piece of paper that had earlier come through the door in the brown envelope. She took it and read it; then wrinkling her forehead, looked at me with a puzzled expression and enquired, 'What's this all about?'

'I don't really know. I thought you maybe able to throw some light on it?'

'Me. Why? I don't even know who sent it. Do you?'

'Yes. It's from that girl you spoke to earlier today in the canteen.'

'Her? She was with you last night? Crafty bitch, she never said anything to me about that and she claims to be my friend and to tell me all about the men in her life.'

'Actually she did a runner on me.'

'No,' she laughed. 'Tell me about it.'

I told her everything that had happened. When I finished she laughed and said, 'Oh my god, what have I let myself in for? What have you got, or what did you do to her, that frightened her to death and made her run away like that?'

'Nothing special that I know of but perhaps my choice of spicy take-away was too much for her and she ended up having hallucinations,' I said and we both laughed.

'I bet she thought that I was chatting you up in the canteen this afternoon, and that you were my latest conquest, and that's perhaps why she wished you luck with me.'

'Well, that was very kind of her.'

'So she did a runner on you did she? It will be very interesting to hear her version of events the next time we have a little girls' get together but why bother to send a note if her only plan and intention was to escape like that? Perhaps you are a mystery man after all and I should take this as some kind of warning.'

I decided that a change of subject was diplomatically required so I began to explain my reasons for inviting her to come round to my flat as opposed to my going to hers and although, as I reeled them all off, they all sounded rather weak the final excuse for having nothing to eat in my flat sounded nothing more than totally pathetic. She, however, seemed unconcerned and raised no objections when I suggested that we should go out and dine and it would be my treat.

We agreed to use Fred's car, or she insisted that we did and she drove to a pleasant little place that I know of on the outskirts of town. We leisurely ate our fill and talked and chatted, mainly, about our-selves and what we anticipated we might encounter on our visit up North. Although neither of us really knew what to expect.

When the time came to leave the restaurant and I asked Fred if, on the way back, she would drop me off at my place. To my surprise, she genuinely appeared to be disappointed. The look on her face clearly told me that she was genuinely surprised that that was all that I had in mind. That all I was suggesting after a lovely meal was for her to drop me off and then go home. I really didn't know if she had expected to go on somewhere else, a nightclub or somewhere perhaps. But I thought I was doing the right thing as I tried to explain to her, that it was quite late and we had a lot to do and it was an early start the following day. I thought she would understand and accept my argument. She said nothing and was very quiet on the way back. When we arrived at my flat I thought I should perhaps at least try

to make amends and she willingly accepted my invitation to come in and share a nightcap.

As a pair of arms wrapped around me from behind and a soft firmness pushed against my back and perfume wafted up my nostrils, while I attempted to make coffee, it didn't take long before I completely changed my argument and suggested that it was just as easy to depart from my place, in our own cars, first thing in the morning, exchanging her car for the company car and collect her personal things on the way out of town. She was, I am pleased to say, forced, without any resistance or counter argument, to agree and so 'reluctantly' had to stay the night. She was everything I had imagined, and more beside. Ask my faithful double bed.

CHAPTER EIGHT

The following morning we were up bright and early and as there was still nothing to eat in the flat, we decided to settle for a drink and then set off straight away, grabbing a bite to eat along the way.

We dropped Fred's car off at the lock up, close to her flat, and while she changed into uniform I loaded her personal things into the company car. We arranged to stop for a bite to eat at the first Little Chef that appeared on our left hand side.

We then set out for our first port of call, Great Yarmouth via a Little Chef.

The journey North was, to say the least relatively straightforward and rather boring. We had decided to make for, and follow, the A143 and to approach the town from a south-westerly direction on the Bury St Edmunds road. As we drove along we attempted to alleviate some of the monotony by taking it in turns to lead whilst the other tucked in behind and followed at a safe distance. At one point, when I was behind Fred, without warning or calling on the radio to give me advance notice, she indicated left and swung her car off the road and onto a Service Station forecourt. I immediately followed and drew up behind her.

'You short of fuel or something?' I enquired.

'No, but a couple of gallons should cover the cost of a call of nature', she winked.

The remainder of the journey was about as eventful as the rest and apart from our prearranged stop, for coffee and toast, and yet another to attend to a call of nature we arrived in Great Yarmouth around midday and found the town, even on the approach road, to be very busy. Lunchtime is never the wisest time to arrive in a strange town and Yarmouth was certainly no exception. With Fred close in behind I drove as slowly as I dared and read every sign I could see. Eventually I found a multi-storey car park and we ran onto it and parked up side by side. I locked my car and slid into the passenger seat, of the company car, alongside Fred.

'You don't realise just how many signs there are out there until you enter a strange town and then there are millions and never the ones you want,' I moaned. 'And those amenity ones are the worst. Those brown coloured ones advertising crockery and cutlery for sale, Christmas trees and Jesus stayed here. Who cares about all that when all you want is a small convenient place to park and one where it is not all criss-crossed with yellow lines? Sea-side towns are the worst for them, they shove signs up everywhere and blather yellow paint over everything and

to hell with the poor motorist who is trying to obtain useful information while concentrating on his driving and every other road user.'

'Crockery and Jesus? What on earth are you on about?'

'You know, signs with pictures of knives and folks, a cup and saucer, a telephone handset and a petrol pump. Those signs which tell you there is crockery to be stolen up ahead, petrol available if you can afford the silly prices and a telephone so that you can moan to someone about it. Or perhaps the petrol pump symbol is really telling you that aliens are welcome. Then there are those with Christmas trees on and a country style, a tent and a caravan. What are they telling you? That you must be careful not to fall over the style when you come to pinch a Christmas tree and that you are warned, there are people intent on preventing you and they will be hiding in either a tent or a caravan.'

'You have a twisted sense of humour. So go on then, explain, in your distorted way what you meant by Jesus.'

'It's simple and for your information I don't think it has anything to do with a twisted sense of humour. Just think about it for a moment. How do you think strangers and in particular foreigners, who have had no explanation, react when they first see a picture of a bed and in particular one that looks like an old fashioned child's crib and the large letters B and B. They might think, like me; that an old fashioned crib has a religious connotation and is symbolic of Xmas and that B and B means born and bred or born and brought up.'

'But you, and they, know it doesn't.'

'It's maybe as well we all know it doesn't mean that, because if it were true then Jesus must have visited one hell of a lot of holiday towns and what about all those others with different religions? They would be totally confused and think the places specialised in the manufacture of wooden beds or something.'

'You get worse. Next you will be trying to tell me that those latest ones that have started to appear on the scene; those "Park and Ride" mean something entirely different?'

'No! They are one of the very few that are quite straightforward and easy to understand. You park up, climb, with a girl into the back seat of your car and…' I was cut short by the push on the shoulder, which squashed me against the car door.

'Now you are getting worse.'

'And damaged,' I said rubbing my shoulder.

'You'll heal and if you have finished with your in-depth analysis of road signs, can we be serious for a moment?'

'Please! Be my guest.'

'First of all we need to find something substantial to eat. Then we need to find secure overnight parking for your car and don't forget, on top of all that, that we are due at MRCC at two this afternoon.'

‘Find the MRCC first and then a Pub nearby is probably the best bet for two people in Coastguard uniform,’ I suggested.

We had no problem finding both the Coastguard Station and a suitable pub that happened to serve excellent food. We enjoyed a superb meal of scampi, chips, and side salad, washed down by two halves of shandy.

Whilst in the pub I enquired from a barman where the nearest secure overnight parking was likely to be found and he gave me the directions to another private multi-storey car park which specialised in lock-ups and over-night security. As we left and settled our bill I thanked him for his help and Fred gave him one of her sexy smiles.

‘The look on that man’s face tells me he has a thing about girls in uniform and being close to MRCC must make him a very happy man,’ she mused as we stepped outside.

‘He’s not on his own,’ I grinned. ‘Remember you don’t see yourself from behind.’

The natural wiggle of her bum as she walked, the tight black skirt and the faint outline of her knickers was enough to destroy the strongest man.

* * *

We arrived at the Coastguard Station at near enough one forty five. It was a large impressive building, which stood apart from all the others in the surrounding area. The white walls, the dark blue and white woodwork were all spotless and looked as if they had only been repainted the day before and along with everything else, within the surrounding perimeter fence, created an atmosphere of precision, neatness and correctness which is typical of the Coastguard Service.

The large sign, mounted on two posts, at the entrance displayed the impressive Coastguard Insignia and below it the words “Coastguard Maritime Rescue Co-ordination Centre”.

To anyone, with a working knowledge of the coastal Coastguard Service, that sign alone tells them that here is housed the nerve centre and Regional Headquarters of a very extensive Coastguard division and the one that extends from Norfolk in the South, along and up the coast as far as the river Tyne in the North. A very large proportion of the North Sea is covered and controlled by Yarmouth Coastguard.

We walked up to the main entrance, with Fred leading the way, and went in through the glass doors to the main reception area. A uniformed young lady, seated behind a sliding glass partition, turned, smiled and having removed a switchboard headset, slid back the glass partition and enquired, ‘Good afternoon. Welcome to Yarmouth Coastguard, can I help you?’

I remember thinking, 'anytime my dear and where does the Coastguard find such lovely girls'. She was a corker if ever I saw one. I wondered if she had been especially chosen and selected for her looks, feminine charm and personality and placed there to create a good impression to the first-time visitor and no doubt go some way to attracting them back. Not that I am suggesting that the Coastguard are not equal opportunity employers, they are, but we all know how it goes when selecting positions for people they are best suited to. One simply says to a male applicant for a similar job, 'The job is yours and part of your contract is to present yourself daily dressed in a tight skirt, fishnet stockings and suspenders and we expect you to take the hormones so that you can provide an acceptable pair of boobs within a reasonable time, say a fortnight. Although I aught to be careful here for I have come across one or two 'so called' males who might be prepared to do just that. Don't we live in a funny old world? But you know what I mean; some people are just better suited to some kind of jobs than others.

Fred produced her blue plastic warrant holder with the Coastguard crest embossed on its cover and flipped it open to reveal the two inner sections. She held it with the seam horizontal in order that the two cards it contained, showed, one above the other, and were the correct way round and readily readable by anyone looking straight at them. The top one was her official identification card. The lower one, and very similarly in appearance to the one above, indicated to all curious and interested parties that one 'Winifred Huntington' was a Senior Officer and member of the 'Coastguard Review Team'.

I held my card holder round Fred's right shoulder and smiling said, in what I hoped was my best chat-up voice, 'We have an appointment with the RC at two.'

'Yes Sir, so I understand. I was told to expect you. I will let him know that you're here. If you would care to take a seat I shouldn't keep you a moment.'

She swung round on her swivel chair and faced the telephone switchboard, replacing the headset, flicked several switches on the panel and spoke a few words into the mouthpiece. The glass screen prevented us from hearing what she actually said. She turned back towards us and opening the glass panel wider informed us, 'The Regional Controller is sending someone down to collect you shortly and apologises that you are having to wait.'

'No problem.'

I was glad of the opportunity to sit down and take the weight off my feet. As I look around I came to the conclusion that everything, including the building, was all fairly new and had been designed and constructed to the latest Coastguard specifications. Quite a contrast to some of the other Stations sited round the coastline. There they range from the very latest, like this building, which has been specifically designed for comfort and efficiency, to some very old and tastefully converted properties bought or leased from local authorities just because they

happen to be in strategic places and considered by HMCG to be the best locations for their specific purposes. One such place that came readily to mind, as I sat there waiting, was the one to be found in the lively seaside town of Scarborough in North Yorkshire. I had occasion to go there a few years ago to sort something out; a guy called Warhurst was in charge at the time and had been up to something, what I don't recall so it must have been something and nothing. Anyhow the local Coastguard Station there is housed in one of the most picturesque buildings on the entire sea front - an old Toll House to the Marine Drive, with a large round, pointed and tiled roofed tower, topped off with a large solid brass weather vane of nautical design and an archway over what is now the pavement but which was originally a Toll road. This, in it's day, effectively allowed the road to be closed and facilitated the collecting of tolls from travellers who wished to use, what was then, a private road and the only access around the foot of the substantial cliffs, which support an ancient Castle and Roman Fort, and which separated the North and South Bays. It has been very successfully converted to a Coastguard Station without effecting or destroying any of its ancient charm. It is well worth a visit when in the area. In fact the whole town is.

We had been sat there for what felt like ages. A quick look at my watch said about twenty minutes in actual fact. Fred was still sat casually thumbing through a magazine selected from a near by table. I was wondering why the delay. Who knows, I thought, perhaps they had problems and everyone was tied up with that. After all that is the prime function of a MRCC, to deal with problems.

I was still thinking about the various responsibilities of a MRCC as compared to those of a MRSC when a door opened and a shirt-sleeved officer entered and said rather flatly, 'The Regional Controller will see you both now if you would care to follow me.'

Fred laid her magazine aside and we both stood up. I winked at the girl behind the glass screen before following this guy along a short corridor and up a staircase. We arrived at a first floor office with a sign on the door that said, A.B.Tibbs. Regional Controller.

Our guide knocked and a muffled voice from within said, 'Come in.' He opened the door and having ushering us in, closed it behind us and disappeared.

Seated behind a large desk, and resplendent in full uniform, was a small chubby man with a receding hairline, made more noticeable by the lightness of the hair and the fact that it was thinning almost to the point of baldness.

He pushed back his chair and stood up, stuck out his hand and stated 'My name is Tibbs and I am the Regional Controller here.' So the sign on the door had been correct and not put there to mislead us. I took his hand, 'Good Afternoon, Sir, my name is Grundy and this is Miss Huntington.'

He looked straight at Fred and just nodded. He made no move to offer his hand. She, in turn, gave him a 'Sod you.' look and remained standing. There wasn't even the hint of a smile on her face.

'Sit down,' he snapped, and before we had time to select a chair and conform to his request, he carried on in the same curt manor, 'I don't like you people. I don't like what you do, and what is more, I don't like you in my region; so the sooner you are done and gone, the better.'

'Hang on Mr Tibbs,' I almost stammered. 'We all work for the same firm and we only have our job to do.'

'Don't give me that. It's bad enough having "Internal Review Teams" and all they stand for, but to have them as a cover for something else is diabolical and should not be allowed. This is a civilized country and we are a civilised set up so there should be no room for the likes of you.'

'You're entitled to your opinions and as far as I am concerned you are free to express them,' I snapped back as I found myself becoming a little rattled by his attitude and manner. Controller, or not, he had no right to behave like this towards us, just because we happened to have been sent or had decided, on our own initiative, to come onto his patch. 'But we have a job to do and one which your own people obviously can't do.'

I thought at that he was going to explode. 'Can't do? Can't do? If this service was given the resources it should have and was run properly, this recent incident would never have happened and there would be no need for the likes of you two and your fancy departments.'

'What do you mean, would never have happened?' butted in Fred. She also sounded rather cross and had obviously gone on the defensive.

'Cutbacks, that's what I mean. Lack of funding probably brought about by the likes of you and your infernal review boards. That man should never have been out at night alone in an isolated spot. It has always been a known and accepted fact that all coastlines can be dangerous; cliff tops at night in particular, and then without "comms" is ridiculous. It all comes down to money or the lack of it. I still maintain that with adequate budgets and resources this business up North would never have happened.'

'What exactly do you know of the events up North, Mr Tibbs?' enquired Fred in a very matter of fact way.

He looked at her and stared, completely dumfounded and surprised that a woman could ask, or would even dare to ask, intelligent questions and then to do so in a manner that fully anticipated and demanded equally intelligent answers.

'Not a great deal, in terms of detail that is, if you must know,' he mumbled. Bloody hell, I thought, now listen at him after what he has just said. 'My orders and instructions, which I am not too pleased about, are to smooth the way for you people to move freely through the Region and that it will be you, as a result, who

will come back with all the answers. What I am certainly not happy about is that I am also instructed to inform my staff that you are Internal Review. I have enough problems without my people thinking I have set you on to them and that you will be snooping about all over the place. They are already dissatisfied with recent reviews and all the cutbacks that went with them, as it is. So tell me, how am I expected to run a neat, tight ship with people like you rocking the boat all the time?'

'I am sorry you feel like that, but Miss Huntington and I do have a specific job to do and I promise we will do it with the minimum of disruption and if it will help you we can hint, without making promises, to your people here, that our review investigation might result in some improvements to their lot.'

'Tell them what you damned well like. If they have any sense, which they have, they still won't trust or believe you, not after the way the service has been decimated over the last few years. Cut upon cut, year after year and don't you dare give me any bull about improved technology making up for it all, because I am full up to here with that excuse. It takes only one five-amp fuse to blow and very large chunks of replacement technology goes straight out of the window.'

'Look Mr Tibbs, give us all the details you have and exactly what you know, then we will get out of your hair.' What little there is of it, I thought, and then glancing at Fred, noticed that she had raised her eyebrows and was smiling.

'The sooner, the better, as far as I am concerned. What do I know about it? Well you probably know as much as I do already.'

'Try me, Mr Tibbs, you tell us everything you know then we can compare notes.' As if I am going to tell you anything you stroppy old bastard, I thought.

He opened a desk drawer and withdrew a piece of paper. He laid it on the flat surface and using it as a reference began, 'A week ago today one of my Sector Officers, Philip Edison, a good, long-serving man with an excellent record, went missing just outside the boundary of his own patch. The report I have tells us that he frequently walked his dog along the cliff top paths within his own patch and did so often in his own time. That's what I mean by a good man. He would exercise his dog in his own time but whilst doing so check out his area. You know what I mean? He would check for collapsed paths, corroded cliff edges, access points blocked off, that kind of thing. All part of a Sector Officer's job to know his patch intimately. According to the report, Edison failed to return from one of these trips. His dog found it's own way home and shortly after that a search of the local area was carried out.

'By whom?'

'By our people initially, of course! We searched the cliffs in the area, both top and bottom, using all available local Auxiliary Cliff Teams. The local RNLI Inshore lifeboat was called out to search the water line. The Search and Rescue Helicopter from nearby Leconfield carried out an intensive search of the area from the air. Nothing was found so the local Police were then informed and they

started to make enquiries further inland and look at possible domestic issues. In the meantime we decided to extend our original search area to both the North and the South and fairly quickly the team who were searching to the North of the original search area, came up with some identifiable objects on the cliff top. These were found outside Edison's own patch and I am told at a much greater distance than you would expect him to walk with his dog under normal circumstances.'

'So was he actually on duty or not at the time you are talking about?'

'No, not officially.'

'What do you mean, not officially?' asked Fred.

'Well, Sector Officers work a fixed number of hours each week with days off and leave entitlements etcetera. But they can, and are, called upon to turn out at any time. The Coastguard, as you well know, cannot be confined to fixed hours and has to be available as and when required. Again as you well know we have round-the-clock coverage at all MRCC's and MRSC's and when Watch Officers are off duty they are covered by fully-trained Auxiliary Staff.'

'Yes we are familiar with all that. So what you are saying is that he was not on an official Coastguard "job" at the time. He had not been requested by Region, or anyone else that you are aware of, to turn out, or anything like that? In other words he had not informed his MRSC that he was out or had gone into someone else's patch or that he had any reason for being there, other than for personal reasons; say, for example, walking his dog?'

'Correct'

'Having found these bits and pieces; where did you say, on the cliff top? Did you extend your search any further?'

'Yes.'

'Did you find anything else?'

'No. Nothing else, apart from the personal effects, on the cliff top, there were no other things. No body. No Edison, if that's what you mean and we have found nothing since.'

'What do the Police have to say about it all?'

'I really have no idea at this stage. I have had no official reports from them but I should imagine they probably think it is a domestic problem. If you want to know what they really think you will have to ask them yourselves.'

'We will, in good time. So is that all you can tell us?'

'Yes it is, so now it is up to you to get this mess cleared up as soon as possible then perhaps London will get off my back. By the way I have arranged, as they requested, for your accommodation here in Yarmouth. How long will you be needing it?'

'I don't know but you may be assured our stay will be as short as possible,' snorted Fred.

It had now become very obvious that Fred was not at all taken up by, the delightful, Mr Tibbs. Neither was I for that matter, arrogant sod, but then I tend to take people like him in my stride and try not to let them bother me. The world is full of people who are only too ready to blame others and pass on all their own shortcomings to anyone else they come across or who just happen to be handy and not be in a position to fight back.

He pulled his telephone forward on the desktop and began to dial. 'I will get our Miss Kent. She can look after you while you are here.' When the connection was made he snapped into the mouthpiece, 'Miss Kent, step into my office please?'

Moments later the office door opened and in stepped another uniformed and extremely, good looking, young woman and this time, a redhead.

Addressing no one in particular Tibbs said, 'Miss Kent here will look after your immediate needs while you are here. If there is anything else you require, come straight back to me. Don't involve, or go through, anyone else. Do you understand.'

He stood up and offered his hand. I shook it and again he made no effort to acknowledge Fred. She just gave him the most disgusting and contemptuous look I think I had ever seen.

When we left his office and the door was securely closed behind us, one single word slipped from Fred's lips – 'Arsehole.'

I looked at Miss Kent who smiled weakly.

'You have got to get to know him. He is under a lot of pressure and strain just now and Mrs Tibbs doesn't help.'

'Under pressure,' snapped Fred, 'under pressure? Since when has pressure squeezed out manners? They are all alike these little bald headed, chauvinistic prats. Don't rock my boat he said. Don't upset my people any more than I have. Hell, they are all alike, people like him. They stand in neat lines touching their caps when all the big fat salaries and expenses are being handed out, or if there is any glory, or medals, or back slapping to be had. That's all right and of course they are all past masters at creeping around seniors or anyone they think might just be that little bit of a threat to them. On the other hand, they are equally as good at smashing down subordinates especially when ordinary work is involved, or they might be required to at least attempt to do the job they are overpaid to do. Then if there is anything slightly out of the ordinary, they can't cope, and all you get back is, "Don't rock my boat." Arseholes, people like him.'

Miss Kent looked a bit sheepish and somewhat embarrassed at Fred's outburst. Perhaps she had a soft spot for Tibbs, or was one of those people who are naturally immensely loyal to the Boss and the team as a whole. I wondered if he treated all women the same. Perhaps not, because, both Miss Kent and the young lady on reception seemed far too nice to tolerate the attitude and bad manners

he had shown towards Fred. It must have been what she represented that upset him, but then that was still no excuse for his behaviour. He, no doubt, would, if challenged, considered himself a gentleman in every way. In that case he should be prepared to behave like one.

'I agree he does come over as being a bit of a prat and could do with a few lessons in manners,' I said.

We reached the small room that served as Miss Kent's office. 'Come in,' she said cheerfully, having apparently fully recovered from her embarrassment caused by Fred's outburst. 'Would you like some tea?'

'I could murder some,' smiled Fred, who appeared to have got over her outburst. 'Men. Why the hell can't we do without them?' she added, more to the other girl than to me.

While the charming and very attractive Miss Kent made the tea, she explained that she had done as instructed and reserved two rooms for us at the local hostelry, and had booked us in initially for bed and breakfast only. She further explained that she would act as our contact, hostess, and unofficial guide. She also gave Fred a card with her phone number on so that we would have direct access to her at all times. She said that she would try and do everything to ensure we enjoyed our stay.

'That makes a pleasant change,' said Fred. 'If it were down to your boss he would have just as soon chucked us out onto the street, here and now, and have done with it.'

Miss Kent smiled and turned back to attend to the tea. Fred held up two fingers and silently mouthed, 'Two separate rooms!' To which I put a finger to my lips to silence her and stop her saying more.

When tea was over and we had chatted a good deal and exchanged a lot of pleasantries, we were much wiser as to the character and attitude behind the delightful Mr Tibbs. The story went that he had a lot of problems and none of them were of his doing, or so he claimed. Everyone was getting at him or so he said. The final straw came when he was first informed that he was to be subjected to a visit from the Internal Review Board with no further details or reasons. Because apparently prior to that there had been some internal wrangling within the Region that made him feel let down by his staff and the last thing he wanted was for it all to come out during any form of enquiry. One member of his staff, he claimed, had actually gone over his head with a request for promotion, an unprecedented move and he was certain that it would all come out and be to his overall detriment.

'So what you're saying is that the sooner we complete our business and clear out, the happier he might be?' asked Fred.

'Maybe. But you can never really tell with him. I tend to ignore him most of the time and let him get on with it.'

‘Then I think I will stay as long as possible if only to upset the old fart,’ laughed Fred.

‘He’s never really happy. His wife sees mainly to that and there are a lot of people round this Station, here in Yarmouth, that will be only too pleased and relieved when he finally retires.’

‘What’s the A.B. In his name stand for and that reminds me, if it’s not too impertinent, what’s your name? By the way I’m Fred and this character, over here, is Mel.’

‘I’m Joyce, and please call me that from now on. Miss Kent is far too formal and not at all friendly. The boss’s name is Alan. What the B stands for, no one knows. He always signs everything Alan B Tibbs.’

‘Probably Bastard, or some other suitable title.’ laughed Fred. ‘Every time I think about him it makes my blood boil and my skin creep and I just know that the less I see of him the better.’

‘I think you have already made that more than clear. Don’t you agree Joyce?’ I said. She just smiled.

She had nice legs from what I could see of them and I wouldn’t have said no to ten minutes with the boobs. What is the polite way of putting it? ‘She can park her fluffy slippers under the edge of my bed anytime she chooses.’

It was agreed that Joyce, or should I say, Joyce insisted, that she would walk us to where we were to stay. An excuse to get out, I think she said and so we all walked the few hundred yards from the Coastguard Station to the selected place. She explained that the company used it quite regularly for visitors and it turned out to be just as she had described it. It hovered somewhere between a pub and a small hotel. The adjoining rooms, which had been reserved for us, were on the first floor. They were both spacious and had the benefit of an en-suite shower and toilet.

* * *

We knew that the Coastguard Station was manned and open twenty-four hours a day, so we were able to leave the car there and come and go as we pleased. Fred had further established that Joyce Kent was not married, but lived with her boyfriend, Dave. He was used to her playing the part of the hostess and accepted it all as part of her job. She was also genuinely pleased when we invited her and Dave to join us for a meal and a few drinks that evening. We agreed to meet at seven thirty in the bar. We had to start somewhere and often the casual relaxed atmosphere with the least likely people produces some of the most useful leads.

* * *

When Joyce departed, having fussed around us like a mother hen to ensure everything satisfactory, Fred kicked off her shoes and stretched out on my bed. We had all ended up in my room, having been in Fred's first and then moving on into mine. She stretched out full length and turned on her side supporting the weight of her head on one elbow. I pulled up a large armchair and sat down. I was in the perfect position to feast my eyes on the female form reclining full length on the bed. There was one hell of a body in that dark uniform.

'She fancies you, you know.'

'Who?'

'Come on! Don't come the all innocent with me. You could see the way she kept looking at you and smiling all the time. Every chance she got she was ogling you. The same as your eyes were boring holes in her bum. There was much more to it than the friendly hostess bit. She'd have you in bed at the drop of a hat. I'm telling you… she fancies you.'

'Fancies me? Well I suppose she does. Come to think of it, what female wouldn't?' I was rather chuffed. I fancied her but had not realised it was mutual despite what I had just said. 'You're not jealous are you? You shouldn't be because you do have a slight advantage after all. You are on my bed for starters and that gives you the distinct edge over the opposition at the moment. In fact as far as I can see everything is in your favour right now.'

'What me, jealous of her, or of any other woman for that matter, and over you? Take a running jump. Take a powder. Take a good look at yourself for goodness sake. The fact that I might at the moment fancy you something rotten, and I emphasise the might, doesn't come into the equation or even into my immediate reckoning. You're nothing to look at for a start and if you take away the manners and smooth talk, there isn't very much left; is there? You might get a few brownie points for the body and maybe an extra one for the bum and important bits, but after that you're no great catch. Come to think of it, I don't know what girls see in men at all. The bit that makes us happy is ugly, and its size makes no difference. It's not fair really, all you men do is turn us on, and then take advantage of us, and we fall for it every time. No wonder we are always making a mess of our relationships, and then if that is not bad enough, we come bouncing back for more, never seem to learn from any of it and still carry on doing it all the damned time.'

'It's simple really. We put out the right vibes and you girls come running and that's just how it should be.'

'Balls! Your wife soon proved that to be totally wrong. Your vibes, as you call them, sent her running in the opposite direction. You men will never understand women because you haven't the intelligence to take it all in or even guess what we want and that's why us girls have got to battle on, hoping that one day we will succeed and guide you, so that you will finally get it all right. Then and only then, will there, at last, be genuine equality. Men will then be equal to women, and not

inferior to them as they are now. But like everything else that involves men, it will be a long slow process.'

'Do you feel better now? Now that you have battered us poor feeble men well and truly into the dirt.'

'Of course I do, silly. It's my right as it is every others girls right. Men are such stubborn naive…' She was lost for the word she needed. 'But bugger them. I love them all and can't get enough of them. It was that Tibbs that got right up my nose and made my skin crawl and almost undermined my need for the opposite sex. So you had better forgive. If you do, I will give you an extra brownie point to go with the one you already have for your important bits.'

'I agree with you over Tibbs, he is a bit of a prat, so let's forget him. We can easily work round him if we have to. But for now, what are we going to do next?'

She patted the bed and moved her entire body over to one side. 'You could come and cuddle me for starters and show me that you need to be shown the ways of the superior sex.'

I lay down besides her, having firstly, and quickly, discarded my tunic and shoes, pulled down my tie, and opened my shirt collar. She turned onto her back and raised her head so that I was able to slip my arm around her shoulders. As if as a second thought, she immediately sat up and removed her tunic. Dropping it on to the floor at the side of the bed. She settled back down, wrapping her arm across my chest.

'Here we are, on a bright and wonderful afternoon, or should I say late afternoon, laid on a bed in a strange room. Not that I have any objections to that. It feels rather nice. Don't you agree and also being paid by the Coastguard into the bargain. I didn't know they paid for such things as learning about the superiority of women.'

'Oh shut up.'

I closed my eyes and relaxed and gave in to the tongue probing my ear and the fingers finding their way inside my shirt. Now who's turning who on now, I thought? Then I remembered, that as a mere male with a lot to learn, I was not supposed to have the intelligence to work that out. Oh sod it, who cared?

'Do you realise that while it is lovely just laid here we are no further forward with our investigation than we were when the Old Man originally gave us it?' she whispered.

'I know we aren't but who cares and sod the Old Man and everyone else for that matter right now. We have only just got started and I think we ought to take some time out first to get to know each other. At least a little, don't you?'

'Mmm'

I felt the catch on my waistband release and warm fingers probe across bare skin.

'This is lesson number one. How to forget pillocks like Tibbs and the Old Man and get to know nice people better. Lesson number two is; don't just lie there, help me with your trousers or attack me, or something. Undo something. Remove something. Use your imagination. Where are all those vibes you are so proud of.'

'What's lesson number three?'

'Patience for goodness sake, you haven't completed two yet. I've still got my tie on which is not very encouraging for a start. Ease your backside up a bit or I will never get these off.'

She was, by this time, kneeling beside me, and working away enthusiastically on my trousers. I was trying to undo the buttons down the front of her shirt with my left hand, and being right handed, was not having much success. I felt my socks being pulled off and glanced to see them being shown the floor. My trousers followed, and then I was ordered to ease up yet again.

'Gosh! You can have as many brownie points for that and the other bits as you want.' Her cool fingers wrapped round what Fred called – the important bit.

Using her other hand she made short work of unfastening the buttons on my shirt, which when completed, she laid wide open. I lay with everything on full view. Fred looked and smiled before looking at her own dishevelled shirt front, with one flap still tucked into her waist band, and said, 'You're hopeless, do you know that? You look after that gorgeous thing for a minute and don't you dare let it get away. I have plans for it to earn some more brownie points.'

She stepped down from the bed and then standing beside it, took only a matter of seconds before her skirt dropped to the floor and she had stepped out of it. It was then followed, in rapid succession, by her tie, underskirt, and tights. 'Do you want to take these off or shall I?'

'Be my guest,' I gasped.

Panties joined the pile of discarded clothing. She then climbed back onto the bed and with a knee either side of me, gently settled herself down, and with a gasp of delight, managed at the same time to say, 'You could have taken your shirt off.'

'What lesson number is this?' I whispered as I reached up to hold her.

'God are you still counting? Bloody men. Who cares?'

Some time later, and when we were both aglow and very drowsy with satisfaction. All anger and resentment long forgotten, we lay full length on the bed wrapped in each other's arms.

'That was lovely, but we will have to move as I am beginning to feel a bit chilly,' she whispered, the lobe of my ear still in her mouth.

We untangled ourselves and Fred slid off the bed. She moved a couple of paces away then smiling down at me said, 'we seem to have missed a couple of lessons somewhere. But at least it's a bit different.'

'What is?'

'You are. From here you look really funny.'

'How?'

'With your shirt still on and your underpants round your ankles.'

'What about you?'

She looked down at herself and laughed. She was standing there with her shirt open all the way up the front but still fastened at the cuffs. Her bra was up under her chin where I had eased it and was still fastened at the back. 'Could be the start of a whole new fashion… the above the boob bra and open shirt front look. It only needs a pair of skimpy matching briefs and high heels to complete the outfit.'

'Never mind the briefs. I like the natural wild hairy look.'

'You would. You're the type who wouldn't care if a girl caught a chill from being over exposed. I'm going to have a shower, coming?'

'Why not? Percy can be very partial to soap suds and a good massage.'

Later, when we were both reasonably satisfied that we had each ensured that the other was exceptionally clean in all the right places, I swore that with all the care and tender effort that I had put in, Fred had the cleanest boobs in Great Yarmouth. I towelled myself down and watched her do the same. I had been right all along. There had indeed been a beautiful body in the Coastguard uniform. Coastguard work can be so rewarding.

Wrapping the towel round my middle I looked around the room until I found Fred's uniform hat and then placing it on her head, said, 'That's how all lady Coastguards should dress, everything else just spoils the overall effect.'

She laughed, and taking the hat off her head held it against her lower tummy and said, 'How would that be for an ID photograph?'

'Perfect. I'll have a full-sized one for the side of my bed and a miniature for my wallet.'

She came close, kissed me, undid the towel, and let it fall before setting her fingers to work. Satisfied with the result she hung her hat on it. 'Now I will have a dozen photos of that.'

She walked away and began picking up her cloths. 'Come on dreamer, we have a lot to do. We haven't really got our bearings yet and don't forget we are entertaining tonight and my tender skin tells me you will need a shave, and just look at the state of my uniform. I suppose it will have to be formal dress for dinner tonight?'

'I would think so. Official and all that, so must dress for the part.'

'Right. Well if that's the case I am going next door to unpack my things and at least sort out a clean shirt. If I don't see you before, I will see you downstairs in the bar at half past seven.'

As soon as she left I looked at my watch; plenty of time I thought, so stretching out on the bed I started to think.

Tibbs certainly had problems, which were nothing to do with us and had upset Fred with his attitude. I wondered if his bitchiness was because he really knew more about it than he was telling us, or that he just could not cope with his job? If so: then bollocks to him. If that's the way he wants to play it then that's all right by me. We will see if this girl, Joyce Kent, knows anything. I doubt it very much because Tibbs is supposed to be the only one, as far as we know, here in Yarmouth, who knows the true purpose of our visit and another reason why I could not understand his touchiness. After this afternoon's unpleasantness with him, I thought it was a pity we could not have bypassed MRCC Yarmouth and gone straight to Humber. But there was no way we could really do that. Tibbs was Regional Controller and as such was in overall command. It was his area in which we would probably be working. We could not go directly to Humber District because the District Controller there would have to report our arrival, and presence, back to Tibbs, and then the old proverbial would certainly hit the fan. I could hear the Old Man back in London now, shouting and red in the face, 'Grundy, we are a disciplined service and we do not go over peoples' heads nor do we bypass the command structure and although you Air Force types were always slap happy in your approach to everything and got away with it. Here you do not, and what is more, it is damned bad manners on your part into the bargain'. I could hear myself muttering my apologies as I stood in the corner with my dunce's hat on, having forfeit my sweeties, comics, and two weeks pocket money.

No, we had done the right thing by coming here first. We had to work by the rules, at least in the beginning, if we were to get off to anything like a good start. We followed the correct procedure and seen Tibbs first and he knew why we were here. Our next move was to get him to inform Humber that we were on our way to them, working on Internal Review. We should then be free to sniff about before moving on or doing whatever we decided we should do next. We could not avoid Tibbs initially, but the sooner we got away from him and his influence, the better. If we had to see him again I would do that alone and I didn't think Fred would object to that.

At some point, I must have drifted off for I was awakened, with a start, by a sharp tap on the door.

'Who is it?' I stammered.

'Me,' as she opened the door, and stuck her head round the leading edge before stepping into the room and pushing the door closed behind her.

'Hell, aren't you ready yet? It's a quarter past seven and it's a good job I changed my mind about going down stairs alone and waiting for you. But it now looks as if I will have to. Someone will have to be there to meet Joyce Kent. So get off your backside and get ready before I attack that naked body of yours and to hell with everyone and everything downstairs.'

It was then that I realised, that before climbing onto the bed, I had not even put my socks on.

'Give a chap a chance. Be a darling and go down and mutter some plausible excuses for me. Say something about having seen you in only your hat I need an extra cold shower.'

'Cut the chat and just get a move on. You can make your own excuses when you finally get there.' and as she turned to leave, she laughed and added, 'Is it really something as tiny and wrinkly as that that gets the girls going?'

CHAPTER NINE

The evening was very pleasant indeed. The meal and company were first class. Dave, Miss Kent's boyfriend, proved to be a very bright and chatty type but unfortunately knew little, if anything, of his girl friend's work. This made it rather difficult for us to use the occasion to extract much useful information from the charming Joyce. Several attempts to turn the conversation round to her working environment either got cut off by Dave who introduced a different subject or the answers she gave told us nothing. We found out that basically she worked in Central Administration, acted as a hostess to visitors, was very loyal to her boss, but shared none of his confidences nor did she appear to have any access to sensitive material. It transpired that Tibbs also had a private secretary, who was away at the moment, sick, so that accounted for why Joyce knew so little and could tell us nothing even remotely confidential, even if she had wanted to. She did however mention that on the odd occasion her boss had complained to her, at great length, about his wife's attitude and dissatisfactions with both him and his work.

It was never the less a useful exercise and I awarded myself nine out of ten for effort but scored nil for result. Come to think of it I was not really sure I expected any result. One thing I did learn, however, was a little of Fred's technique and how she posed questions and the subtle methods she so cleverly used to elicit the answers she wanted. At the end of the evening she knew more about Dave than I think he knew about himself. The more time I spent with this girl the more I grew to admire her. She was good, in more ways than one.

We bade our farewells, thanking Dave for his company and promising to see Joyce some time the following morning. At Fred's suggestion I went back through to the bar and ordered a nightcap. I asked for a large whiskey and water for me, and a large brandy with lemonade for her. I balanced the two drinks on the tray provided by the barman but then having decided that the balancing act was too much for me on top of what I had already drunk, I discarded the tray and proceeded up the stairs with a drink firmly held in each hand. When I arrived at Fred's door I tapped gently with my toe and waited. Nothing happened so I tapped once again. Still nothing. In frustration I placed one glass on the small table which was set against the wall close to the door and with my now free hand I rapped on the panel. A voice from within answered 'Come in, it's open.'

I opened the door a few inches and held it with my foot, retrieved the glass from the table, then, using my shoulder, pushed open the door and went in.

I stopped dead in my tracks, for standing there, in the middle of the room, was my Coastguard partner. She was wearing a full length, dressing gown. It had

a full skirt that touched the carpet so that it formed a circle that completely hid her feet. It tapered in at the waist and out again to the shoulders. The front was pushed forward by two large smooth breasts, nipples just showing through. I remembered those. The high collar at the back came almost up to the top of her head whilst the lapels down the front opened to form a vee, which stopped just below the point where her cleavage started. I think I have heard the colour described as Mint or Ice Green and from the sheen I guessed it was made of silk. She looked stunning. My tongue went dry and my hands shook. She raised her hat in mock salute.

'Put your eyes back in darling, surely you have seen a girl in her nightclothes before? I know you have seen one quite recently in much less, remember, the girl from this afternoon in only her shirt. Surely you haven't forgotten that already, and the shower that followed, not so soon? How much have you had to drink tonight?'

'What's with the hat?'

'Oh this!' she said once again raising it in salute. 'Sometimes a girl has to ware something so that she doesn't feel completely naked.'

She reached out and took her drink. I remained rooted to the spot.

'Sit down and stop shaking before you spill your drink down that posh uniform.'

I put my drink on the table and as casually as I could I removed my uniform jacket and draped it across the foot of the bed. I lowered myself, carefully, into the easy chair and sipped my drink. My eyes all the time glued to her divine shape. My imagination ran wild. When she moved her long legs gave the impression that she was floating or gliding across the carpet and as she twisted and turned the indent of her tummy button came and went. Her nipples tormented me. She placed her partly consumed drink on the bedside table and once again floated across the floor, this time, in my direction. My eyes never left her for a split second. A warm soft hand covered my left hand, whilst the other removed the glass from my right one. There was a mischievous sparkle in her eyes. She drifted across and placed my glass alongside hers. She floated back and took hold of both my hands. A gentle pull made it clear that I was being invited to rise up from the chair. I offered no resistance and stood up to face her. She immediately released my hands and wound both her arms around my neck. My arms automatically wrapped round her waist. As her body pressed and moulded into mine her lips brushed against mine and led into a kiss that had a passion I had only previously read about in books. We kissed until our combined breathing became heavier and deeper and then in short gasps. Throughout my hands caressed the whole of her back and buttocks. She was soft and smooth and each time I ran my hands over her perfectly shaped backside she responded by pressing her thighs tight against my ever hardening bit. She pulled gently away and released my lips and, with both my arms still around her waist, leaned the top half of her body sufficiently backwards to give herself room to undo

my tie. Once removed it was unceremoniously deposited on the floor. Then her quick agile fingers rapidly and efficiently, undid the buttons of my shirt, pulled it free from the waistband and slipped it back off and clear of my shoulders. It too would have joined the tie on the floor had it not been for the fastening at the cuffs. I tried pulling them free but they were too tight and my attempts to undo the 'inside out' buttons behind my back would have rightfully earned a place on the television show "It will be alright on the night," TV Cockups.

Fred laughed, lightly kissed me on the lips, and whispered. 'Turn round darling this is obviously woman's work.' Who was I to argue? It proved no problem for her and the shirt unceremoniously descended to floor level.

'Now sit down,' she whispered pushing me gently back towards the chair. I did as I was told, and in no time at all both shoes and socks were tossed to one side. I was gently hoisted back up on to my feet and while I loosely wrapped both hands round her waist and our foreheads touched I could feel the warmth of her through the material while both her hands went down between us and she expertly unfastened my belt, waistband and zip.

Her arms returned to wrap around my neck and we kissed passionately once again before she drew me forward so that I was able to step out of my pants. I nearly tripped and overbalanced as I kicked my underpants free. It was then my turn to ease myself back and feel for the sash of her dressing gown and draw out the single wrap over knot. The overlap fell open and I slid my arms inside and around her. She was so warm and soft. The fine material of her nightgown made her feel, for want of a better word, slippery. I was so totally absorbed in the fantastic sensations of warmth and vitality and the sheer joy created by the way she moved, that I hardly noticed, at first, that I could feel the outline of a pair of briefs. They were very skimpy but never the less there. I traced the outline. Not much more than a G string.

Hands on her shoulders and slowly over the top and the dressing gown slid to the floor. I could feel her hardened nipples against my bare chest. There was only a fraction of a millimetre of silk between us. Hands then ran down my outer thighs and nails dug in as they were drawn back up. A casual attempt to ease the smooth silk nightgown from her shoulders proved impossible. After more kissing and caressing, a whisper in my ear, informed me, 'It will have to come all the way up to come off.' At that she gently wiggled free from my grip and stepping back, reached down, grasped the hem of the gown and with one smooth, continuous, uplifting movement, drew it up and over her head. She shook her head to loosen her hair as the gown floated down to join the rest of our things, which were randomly scattered all around. She was naked except for the matching coloured G-string.

We kissed and enjoyed the closeness and exploration of smooth warm skin. She smelled absolutely gorgeous.

Jokingly I whispered, 'Your place or mine?'

'Dressed like this I am going nowhere,' she giggled, 'unless you want to. If you want to take the chance I will.'

'And do what?'

'Nip like this into your room. I'm game if you are.'

'No. I think I would rather stay here if you don't mind. Anyhow it's all right for you. You aren't completely naked, which by the way, why the briefs?'

'Because I am a girl with very high moral standards: didn't I tell you?'

'Moral standards! What's that all about?' I enquired, totally taken aback, pleasantly surprised and completely confused.

'Ah, you see you don't know everything. It's one of my fantasies. I never give myself completely, if I have time to plan it all out beforehand. I like to believe that I need to be taken against my will or at least persuaded to give in, and so it drives me absolutely mad if a man symbolically takes me by removing my panties. You see you didn't know that, did you and you think you know everything?'

'What do you mean, symbolically takes you?'

'Oh forget it and just settle for the fact that I have a thing about having my knickers taken off by a man that I want to take them off as opposed to taking them off myself.'

'But this afternoon?'

'Yes I did but you asked me to and you didn't know about my thing and I hadn't planned anything either.'

I was not sure I understood but who cared and who, under the circumstances, wanted to argue. If there had been a bloody big lock on them then I might have been tempted to go a little further into it.

'We all have and need our particular pleasures and quirks, even you, and I have already discovered one or two interesting things about you,' she said as her hands began to move around and prove it.

* * *

The following day I woke quite early with Fred snuggled up warm and cosy beside me. Some night and some girl. God knows where the briefs finally ended up or what happened to her morals after that.

Fred gently surfaced, slipped out of bed and without making any attempt to cover herself, collected all the discarded garments from the floor and began to straighten them out and lay them neatly to one side. Her only comment being, 'We can't have you looking like a rag bag this morning, can we?'

'A ragbag! A shagged bag more like it.'

'Don't be bloody crude.'

Having satisfied herself that she had collected everything and done her best to sort them out, she disappeared into the bathroom and the muffled sounds

that came through the door told me she was taking a shower. She emerged some time later wrapped in a large bath towel and a smaller one round her head. I had not moved from the warm, comfortable bed and watched fascinated as she dried her hair and then proceeded to get dressed.

It was while she flitted about that I realised, that in certain lights, and perhaps the way she twisted her body, as she moved around, the triangular patch between her legs had a very delicate tinge of ginger.

'What's all this?' she laughed as I tutted when she slipped into her underskirt. 'Am I the early morning floorshow? Come on you lazy-bones, get up, we have work to do.

I thought, Sod the job. Come here you gorgeous thing. But I knew that duty called, and my important bit, as it now appeared to be universally known, had after all, done all right for itself the night before, so a period of regeneration would do it no harm.

* * *

Outside the weather was very pleasant for the time of year and the warmth made me feel good. We had an early breakfast, carried our things down to the car, and then turned up, bright and early, at MRCC. Fred had rejected outright any suggestions that I should go there alone.

Joyce was pleased to see us and could not thank us enough for the previous evening. We spent a few moments in polite and idle chatter with her before I asked if her boss was about?

'No,' she said and went on to explain that Tibbs had rung the office, shortly after Joyce had arrived that morning, and told her that he would be away for the whole day and that she was to pass on to us, the message that he had telexed to Humber District informing them of our intended visit. The whole thing stank and it left me with the distinct impression that he had planned to stay away on purpose so as to avoid having any further direct contact with us. Fred must have felt the same as she hissed, 'Prat!' Joyce just smiled and said, 'Sorry.'

There was nothing more we could do but thank Joyce for everything and say goodbye. I retrieved my car from the secure car park and with Fred leading the way in the company car; we headed North and the Head Quarters of Humber District.

CHAPTER TEN

The journey up the east coast was not exactly boring but rather mundane and uneventful, or it was to me, and apart from one fuel stop and a bite to eat we arrived safely in Yorkshire just after mid-day.

There we were met with an entirely different attitude. Much warmer, and genuine, and far more pleasant than the reception we received at Yarmouth. The girl in the front reception office at MRSC Humber was neat, charming, and pretty. She was, I would guess, about thirty years old with a lively warm and rather sexy smile. We discovered later her name was Kathleen Bland. She lived locally and her husband was an Auxiliary in the Coastguard Service and her father flew with the local Air Sea Rescue team. Having formally identified ourselves she contacted someone, via the internal phone, and was about to explain something to us, when the door opened and into the reception area strode a tall, dark haired, clean shaven Uniformed Officer.

'Good afternoon! My name is Bob Kettleness and I am the Senior Watch Officer on duty at the moment. The DC is tied up at present so if you can put up with me, at least for a short while, I will show you around. Have either of you been here before?'

We both replied in the negative and his face lit up. 'Good, then showing you around will be a useful way to kill some time until the DC is free.'

The building itself was again fairly new and very modern in design. The ground floor, besides accommodating reception, housed a superb, though small, museum, displaying a fine collection of unused and outdated obsolete Coastguard equipment. The heavy duty line throwing equipment used in the days when it was necessary to get lines from the shore to a stranded vessel on a beach or up on the rocks, looked very formidable and bulky as it stood on display. I shuddered trying to think what it must have been like man handling all that gear to some god forsaken stretch of the coast and then having to try and work with it on a cold wet night with a gale force ten blowing. I wondering just how many accidents there had been when those using these crude, massive line-pulling rockets and their numerous accompanying boxes of heavy rope had become, because of it's unpredictable nature and the weather conditions, entangled in the thing and perhaps, as a result, received some severe injury. I could just see those massive rockets snaking out at a tremendous speed, trailing smoke, and hauling behind it masses of line which whipped in all directions posing a very real threat to anyone in the immediate vicinity. I could also imagine the frustration when having taken everything into consideration, right on the point of firing, the strong cross wind

might have dropped dramatically, if only for an instant, and so deprived the aimer of wind resistance and thereby allowing his rocket to snake out way off target. Everything would then have had to be hauled back and reset while those on the stricken vessel could only hang on and wait. A hazardous occupation for some very brave, yet no doubt astute, men. There is much to be said for the modern approach of using a Rescue Helicopter, which has gone a long way to rendering obsolete the majority of line throwing gear. As I turned away my final though was of the men on the stricken vessel itself, when that damned thing came hurtling towards them out of the dark and through the rain and sea spray. A lifeline it might have been but it looked more capable of punching a damned big hole in even the sturdiest of boats.

The second and top floor, there only being the two floors to this purpose-built station, was laid out in such a fashion that the Watch Officers, whilst seated at their Control Consoles, enjoyed a panoramic view over the whole bay and many miles of coastline beyond that. The white chalk cliffs to the North provided a perfect backdrop and I assumed was also a home to a wide variety of seagulls and other wild life. Perhaps there might even have been the odd mad Coastguard, who having succumbed to the pressures of his watch on Channel 16, had flipped and run away, had hidden himself in one of the many old caves and coves hewn out in the cliff face by the constant movement of the sea. Joking apart, the view is marvellous and would be the envy of many landlubbers.

Set out behind the Control and Monitoring Consoles are a variety of offices, which provided accommodation for the Administrative Staff and the Senior Station Staff. They also boast, in this modern station, a Press room, just to the rear, from where the media can observe the happenings and goings on in the Control Room without interfering with, or hindering, the operations in any way. There are also all the rooms that house all the electronics and the necessary hardware to run the station.

The Central Control and Monitoring Room is always a hive of activity, the pressure on Watch Keepers varying throughout a watch from busy to hectic. Search and Rescue Co-ordination requires expertise and infinite patience and believe me, these people must, and do, have it. They can handle anything from a child cut by a piece of glass on the beach several miles up or down the coast or a sea bird in distress, brought in by a well meaning Holiday Maker, to a Ferry rolling over and sinking with many hundreds of passengers on board. It is not unusual for them to be co-ordinating more than one emergency at once. A situation often requiring the services and backup of several RNLI Lifeboats, Royal Air Force Search and Rescue Helicopters and other Merchant and Naval vessels who are at sea at the time, and who are, by international law, duty bound to respond to any call for assistance.

Tugs, Salvage Vessels, and a multitude of shore-based teams and backup facilities are also utilised and all require co-ordinating to be effective. Whenever there is disaster, or emergency, or a simple call for help, anywhere along the whole of the English, Welsh, Scottish, or Northern Ireland coastlines the Coastguard will be totally committed and involved. They seldom get a mention or praise following a successful operation and very rarely is their work recognised by the general public, but believe me, very little would be done without them and their vast expertise in times of trouble.

They are the eyes and ears of the coastline and all the area covered by the sea up to an imaginary line midway between the United Kingdom coastline and any adjacent landfall. With France, Belgium, Holland, Germany, and the Scandinavian Countries to the North not being too far away from our mainland, in terms of miles out to sea, the English Channel and the North Sea might be considered to be a fairly narrow band of water. But if one then considers the distances between, say, Scotland and Greenland, Northern Ireland and Canada, Cornwall and America, the whole area mounts up to several hundred thousand square miles of seas which all need to be, and are, constantly monitored.

The English Channel and the North Sea because of their commercial relationship with the rest of the continent and there popularity as the fishing grounds of Northern Europe and, as mentioned, their physical narrowness, are one of the busiest shipping areas in the world.

If I am correct then HM Coastguard at Dover can claim to be one, if not the busiest Coastguard Stations anywhere in the UK, as they control the vast amounts of traffic that daily pass through the English Channel and which, I am reminded, is, at it's most narrow point, only twenty-one miles wide and does not ease up or slow down appreciably during the night. I shudder to think what would happen if the Dover Coastguard Station were not there or a suitable Station close by. The hundreds of ships which use the Channel daily, moving in both directions, not to mention the dozens of Ferries and other vessels which criss-cross it continuously, day and night, as they serve the cross channel ports. There are no white painted lane markings, no signposts, no traffic lights, no central reservations, or hard shoulders, only the Coastguard and the International Shipping Rules of the road. It's staggering that in terms of the overall number of users, proportionally there are far less accidents in the English Channel than there are on our motorways. You apply the brakes to a car and with a bit of luck it will stop in a relatively short distance. Where is the brake on a ship and how do you handle an object that when you stop it's engines it will continue to travel for a further three miles before it comes to a halt or that it require a half mile radius to turn round in? Fortunately the vast majority require less than that but there are those that require even more and a Lollipop Lady in a yellow waterproof would have no effect on a stream of vessels going in both directions when they are required to give way to a Ferry load

of people who wish to cross their path. Not like a gang of kids wanting to cross the road and often jumping out without warning, at a school crossing.

The North Sea is notorious for its unpredictable weather and in particular gales, and therefore witnesses more than its fair share of disasters at sea. It is also considered by many to be the worst area around the whole of the United Kingdom in which the emergency services are required to work. The Irish Sea has always had a reputation for bad seas but square mile for square mile the North Sea is by far the more evil, and mean, to those who venture out upon it. Perhaps a debatable argument depending on where you hale from but ask anyone who has experienced a good 'North-Easterly' while out there or has been on the convoy runs to Russia during the last war and hear what they have to say. But what ever their claims they will collectively tell you one thing; the sea commands great respect and will snuff out life and swallow vessels without trace and will do so without care or consideration for anyone or anything. The sea has no feelings, no emotions, and no conscience. It is simply there and has to be respected and continuously reckoned with.

Anyone hearing of a vessel putting out a SOS call or as it is now internationally known, a 'Mayday' call, should remember, it will undoubtedly be the Coastguard who pick up the call and take the first immediate action. The Submarine Service, as part of The Royal Navy has always been called the Silent Service but Her Majesty's Coastguard must come a very close second when it comes to always being there, silently listening and reacting to a call for help at split seconds notice.

* * *

No matter how many times I have entered a Control Room there has always been sufficient activity to hold my attention and to fascinate me. However, the fascination on this occasion was cut short and interrupted by the arrival of an impressive man who introduced himself as Ray Oldfield, District Controller Humber. He was of medium height, stocky without being plump, had very light grey hair that made it difficult to guess his age. He was probably in his fifties. He immediately struck us as being a very pleasant person and the complete opposite to his boss in Yarmouth. He was one of those people who immediately made you feel welcome and at ease. He ushered us into his office where formal introductions were made.

'Do you know the true purpose of our visit?' I enquired, not knowing what to expect in reply after the reception we got from Tibbs at Yarmouth.

'Yes, I believe I do. I understand you are concerned with the fact that I have lost one of my full time officers. He seems to have disappeared off the face of the earth. To be honest with you, I believe there is something fundamentally very

wrong. It is obvious that others think so too otherwise, you good people would not be here today.'

'I think you are right there. So what we propose to do Mr Oldfield is...'

'Please, call me Ray, we all work for the same firm don't we, and I feel more comfortable with Ray?'

'Yes I think we all do work for the same firm, as you put it, or I hope we do. Not unlike some we come across from time to time. So, OK Ray, as I was saying, what we propose to do is visit the wife, a Mrs Edison, I believe, and the local Police then melt away into the background and see what we can dig out from there. Do you think you could arrange for this Mrs Edison to come into here? As you will appreciate we are not yet familiar with the surrounding area and I thought, for the moment, it might be better if we saw Mrs Edison privately, so to speak, as opposed to us being seen by others visiting her. An over reaction perhaps but until we know exactly where we stand a precaution I feel aught to be taken. If that's no trouble to you?'

'No problem at all; we can send a car for her and I'm sure she will co-operate, for I am certain she wants to get to the bottom of this. She, like all of us, is hoping that he will be found alive and well, somewhere, eventually.'

'We will do our best.'

'I am sure you will. But I have a rotten feeling about it all. There is something about this affair that just doesn't ring true. People just do not disappear without trace. No notes. No plans. No hints. Someone, somewhere, usually knows something but so far, as we know, there is absolutely nothing.'

'So are you certain, in your own mind, that is what happened to this man Edison? He literally disappeared without trace? What exactly have you and your people turned up so far? Have you anything, anything at all, that might help or start the ball rolling, so to speak?'

'Hold on a moment, I have the file right here, somewhere amongst this lot.'

He rummaged through quite a substantial pile of files then extracting one of them, placed it in front of him on the desk, and opened it.

'This is the report from the Sector Officer in whose patch Edison's belongings were found. Basically what it says is that there were no traces of Edison himself. There were no signs of a struggle although the area was thickly covered with longish grass, which we all know quickly recovers after flattening, especially at this time of year. They found a dog lead, a privately owned multi-scan radio transmitter, and a service issue torch. Oh and a pair of binoculars. They were all found randomly laid in the long grass. We don't think it was a mugging or robbery or anything like that, as some very valuable equipment was left behind. The 'Scan' alone is worth a lot of money. There's a transcript of the initial interview with the wife, Mrs Edison. Here is a copy of the statement she gave to the Police.'

'Can we have a copy of all that please?' smiled Fred.

'Yes of course you can my dear; I will get Kathleen to run copies off everything. You met Kathleen on the way in no doubt. The girl in reception downstairs?'

'Yes we did' I replied, remembering the delightful creature in question.

'She will look after you while you are with us. She has already made arrangements for you to stay in that hotel down the road there. You can just see it from here,' and turning in his chair he pointed along the promenade, indicating as he did so, one of several buildings which overlooked the bay. I looked and nodded.

'We use it quite a lot for visitors. It is a good spot and very handy for us here.'

'We have two cars with us. Having no idea what to expect we came prepared to either ride round in an official car with the CG insignia on the doors or become less noticeable, we hope, in a private car. Have you any facilities for extra parking within the compound here and if so can we leave them with you until we get ourselves sorted out?'

'No problem, we have spare garage space at the back which we use for visitors. They can be locked up and will be safe and they can stay there as long as you want.'

'Good and thank you.'

'When would you like to meet and speak to Mrs Edison?'

'Just as soon as you can arrange it: sometime tomorrow would be ideal. It will then give us time to settle in here and find our way about.'

'I will get Kath to ring her and see what we can do. What about the Police?'

'Please will you give them a ring also and see if we can speak to someone. Again sometime tomorrow if possible.'

'Will do.'

'Have all your Senior Watch Officers been informed why we are here?'

'They have been informed you are here but as an Internal Review as far as they are all concerned.'

'Good, then we will dispense with any interviews with them and make out, for the benefit of all your other staff, that you have answered all our questions and that everything is satisfactory and we are pleased with the Station and that any other contact we have with you is along similar lines. If that is acceptable to you?'

'That will be perfect. They are a good bunch really and I would hate them to think they were under some sort of investigation when, in actual fact, there is basically nothing wrong with them or here.'

'There might be a lot wrong for all we know.' laughed Fred. 'But we are not here for that so you carry on just as you are.'

He laughed, 'So you suggest I carry on practising my undetected crime and devious deceit until a real Review Board comes along?'

'Something like that,' replied Fred and we all laughed. 'You keep selling the rum ration.'

'What rum? Chance would be a fine thing.'

'Ok, we will do that then. We will study your file, if we may, and then decide what to do next. In the meantime we will see you again first thing in the morning. What time do you usually start?'

'I'm usually in for eight o'clock. Will that be soon enough for you?'

'It certainly will,' smiled Fred casting a sideways glance at me. I wondered why.

Oldfield saw her smile, gave her an enquiring look, but as she said nothing further, let it pass.

'One last thing,' enquired Fred. 'That we haven't mentioned. Have you any idea why Edison was where you believed him to have been, on or before he disappeared?'

'No I'm sorry but I can't help you on that one. It's a mystery to me and to all of us that have been involved so far.'

'Have you any personal theories or thoughts on the matter that might help?' she continued.

'Sorry again, I just do not know. The Police seem to be hinting that he has done a runner, gone off somewhere, for some reason and may well be back. But I have known both of them for a long time and find it incredible that Philip would just take off without a ward to anyone.'

'Philip… That's Edison?' I enquired.

'Yes, the same.'

'Sorry, of course it is. Forgive me. I am slightly brain dead today and not thinking. It must be all this sea air or something. It will certainly make me sleep tonight.'

The way Fred raised her eyebrows and almost laughed made Oldfield look first from one and then to the other, smiling to him-self as he did so. I thought, every job has its perks and this long legged one, standing not too far away, is mine.

We left Ray Oldfield's private office and went into the main working area where he introduced us to his Watch Officers. We openly congratulated him, for their benefit on the way he ran things. While we toured round the building and went through the motions of our mini 'review' a copy of the file was prepared for us and we collected it from Reception on our way out. We assured the charming Miss Bland that we could find our way to the hotel, as we could see it quite clearly from where we stood. We collected our bags from the cars and deposited the car

keys back at reception, where Miss Bland assured us that they would be taken care of and could be retrieved at any time. We thanked her and made our way to the smart, neat, pale blue and white, seaside hotel.

* * *

On arrival we were informed that we were expected, and that rooms number seven and nine had been reserved for us on the first floor. We were also informed that the hotel was not busy at the moment, as the holiday season had not yet got underway. We were given our keys and promptly left to go in search of our rooms and carry our own bags.

'Will tonight be a waste of another room?' I tentatively enquired.

'I sincerely hope so!' came the whispered reply. 'The sea air may make you tired but it does other things to me.'

'There's no doubt about it I shall certainly have to sleep at sometime tonight.'

'We'll see.'

Both rooms were cosy, or so we assumed they both were, as we didn't even bother to look in number nine. Number seven was very comfortable and quite adequate.

Totally unabashed and as soon as we closed the door, off came the uniform jacket, the tie and white shirt, rapidly followed by skirt, underskirt and tights. A quick flick round the back, followed by shoulder straps down the arms and the bra was tossed onto a chair. She gently massaged her breasts as if they had suffered rather badly from being confined for too long.

The white briefs remained in situ as she sat down on the edge of the bed.

'Come on; don't stand around staring, get those trousers off. I need a romp and a shower before dinner.'

I loved the way sea air affected her, and so did exactly as I was told. I even remembered something about 'being a lady with etiquette' or was it 'morals and the modern miss?' or perhaps 'it's just because I like it,' as I gently removed the briefs. That was it. Something about knickers and being taken off by the man of her choice.

* * *

For a large proportion of that evening we sat in the bar, which fortunately was not busy and so we were able to discuss things without fear of being overheard. We had earlier read the copy of Ray Oldfield's reports in our room and then locked it away safely in one of the suitcases.

We decided that immediately after our interviews with Mrs Edison and the Police we would have to move further north and set up some form of a base from which to work. We decided that as far as possible that base should be flexible thus allowing us to move about without drawing too much attention to ourselves. We also came to the conclusion that it might be wisest if we dropped all identification with the Coastguard and for starter at least, moved about as two ordinary citizens. We thought early season holidaymakers would perhaps be the best approach.

After much discussion and the banding about of many ideas and suggestions it was finally decided that having dispensed with uniforms we should wear casual hiking and camping gear. We would also purchase a tent and all the camping accessories to go with it. We toyed with the idea of borrowing a mobile phone each from Humber, but then decided against it, as they can be monitored just as easily as VHF radio. We decided that if we ran into any real problems with communications we would have to deal with them as they cropped up. Initially, as we discussed it, we couldn't foresee any real problems.

We then proposed to work together as a couple - a very close couple Fred decided, but she was not at all too happy at the thought of single sleeping bags inside a canvas tent so insisted that we buy two of the type that can be zipped together to form a double one. She said she had seen something, or read something somewhere, about them, and would not consider camping unless they were included as essential equipment. It would not be much fun any other way, she insisted and I certainly had no objections.

We spent some time discussing transport. Initially I had the idea that if we were required to move around as inconspicuous as possible, then a private car was the obvious choice. We had mine but then the thought of the two of us, cooped up for long periods, in a car that would be loaded to the roof with camping gear and other supplies certainly did not appeal to either of us. Past experience had taught me that spending long hours on surveillance, cooped up in a car, can be very uncomfortable and decidedly not to be recommended. The idea of a camper came up. One of those small mobile homes that doubles for transport and a mini type of caravan. The more we discussed it, the more it appealed. We would be able, with one of those, to move around as tourists and should we be required to spend long hours watching and waiting, we could at least do so in a modicum of comfort. Furthermore, if we included camping equipment, a tent, and such like, we would be even more mobile.

In the end we decided we would obtain camping gear and hire a caravanette from a local supplier. There was bound to be one somewhere and not too far away. The decision made; we then spent some considerable time drawing up a list of everything that we thought we might need.

'You haven't included maps.' said Fred, scanning down the long list.

'You're right,' I replied. 'We won't get very far in a strange countryside without a decent map. Stick it on the list and we will see what the camping supplier has to offer. If not, a trip to the local W H Smith's should get us all we need. If the worst comes to the worst, we can always have a word with Ray Oldfield and see what he can come up with.'

'His will probably all be nautical charts unless they do keep ordinance survey stuff?'

'You could be right. We'll try and get our own first.'

We then went over the now considerable list of essentials, several times, assuring ourselves each time that there must be something we had missed. There always is, but for the moment we could not spot it.

When I decided that I had had enough planning for one day and was proposing we call it a day, Fred had other ideas. To her the day never ended until you stopped planning everything and by that she meant literally everything and you finally succumbed to sleep through sheer exhaustion. Her energy and imagination were boundless and once between the sheets she was unstoppable. Her planning and scheming were endless and from being the very calm, warm, level headed and intelligent lady that she was whilst working, she became a very sensual, sexual and extremely passionate female in bed. She was everything and more that one could wish for, but only with a man she particularly liked, as she kept reminding me. Probably still got something to do with her 'morals'. I know I found it exciting beyond belief and the more time I spent with her, the more I realised she was no ordinary person and under that cool exterior a rather special person lay hidden. Try as I did I found it impossible to put my finger on exactly what it was that made her so special. Perhaps it was the supreme confidence or the air of sincerity that she projected. She was obviously 'super intelligent', very well educated, beautifully spoken and perfectly mannered. On the other hand she was just an extremely lovely person and much too complex to even attempt to analyse or break down. What more could a man want? Maybe that was it. I know I decided I had no plans to try and change or alter anything.

CHAPTER ELEVEN

When we dragged ourselves out the following morning it was miserable and overcast. The sea was dark and looked, very cold and uninviting, a sharp contrast to the day before. But what a night it had been. Where that girl got her energy from I will never know. It must be the sea air or some other secret ingredient I knew nothing about. We had made a token effort towards formulating our future plans but once the light was turned off, all that was abandon to Fred's advances. So enthusiastic were her efforts that I wondered if she were practicing to become a world-class jockey or some sort of female impersonator specialising in mimicking a steam hammer. By the morning I was completely drained but had loved every single moment leading up to it.

Following breakfast we found ourselves, once again, and certainly not as we had pre-planned the night before, in uniform and using the company car.

Our initial plans for that morning had already backfired, which we agreed was not a very good start, and as a result we were heading North to visit Mrs Edison. As we drove through some very beautiful countryside, for which North Yorkshire is justly famous, I found myself driving with a kind of detached numbness. A feeling of not being quite with it and one that is very real but difficult to describe and I have often wondered if it is peculiar to me or if other people experience similar feelings in similar circumstances. I think Fred sensed something was not quite right because each time I glanced sideways at her she returned my look with a weak smile and said nothing. After several miles and a time span that felt like forever and the endless rustling of road maps as Fred poured over them, I found it difficult to concentrate anymore. I pulled into a small, roadside, lay bye, turned off the engine, and closed my eyes. Fred broke the silence.

'You OK? You are not looking forward to this trip for some peculiar reason, are you? Something is bugging you. I can tell.'

'Too right I'm not and the nearer we get the worse I feel.'

'Why?'

'Hard to say why! Perhaps the start of a new job and a particular aspect of that I really detest. I think right now if you were to volunteer to go on alone, I might let you. I'll get over it, I always do, but until that time, I always feel strange. It always seems to happen whenever someone goes missing, or something goes tragically wrong, all those left behind seem to hang all their hopes on you. They seem to think you have a magic wand, and all you have to do is wave it, and everything will just simply go back to normal. When it doesn't work out like that and they have to reluctantly accept that you are not a miracle worker, then they

want to blame you or feel you should in some way accept a large proportion of the blame for their misfortunes. Suddenly it then all becomes your fault. You were sent to sort it all out and restore normality, and you have not done so straight away. Why not? It's your job. What are you going to do about it? It's like a tremendous burden of responsibility where they want to heap everything onto you and something you can do nothing about and something I can do well without.'

'Do you always feel like this and anticipate the worst?'

'Yes, I am afraid I do, even though I know it is stupid and that it is a normal reaction from people who are deeply distressed and that it should in no way have an effect on me. It doesn't at the time or when it comes to the point where they actually try it on. It's before that. It's the build up to it; the anticipation of what might happen and the not knowing, that seems to bug me each time.'

'So all these feelings can be for nothing if we happen to find this missing man straight away and things sort themselves out and everyone goes back to some sort of normality. Perhaps he is already back home now and all this so far has been for nothing. Maybe the whole thing has got blown up out of all proportion and will fizzle out and amount to nothing in the end. Then what?'

'I know, and that's what makes me feel so daft about the whole thing. I know that what your saying could be right and at this stage anything is possible. But for the moment nothing can stop me feeling the way I do.'

'And I thought you were the tough guy!'

'Tough guy doesn't come into it and toughness has nothing to do with it at all. Over the years I've got used to most things, no matter how shocking or bizarre they turned out to be, but it's this particular thing about having to make first contact with someone who is very close to a supposed or potential victim. I suppose it is the thought of their grief and despair that I can't handle. None of it makes much sense really because I am sure I would have felt better about the whole thing if this Edison woman had come into the Humber Station and we had been able to interviewed her in say, Oldfield's office.'

'Don't you think you are perhaps pre-supposing and anticipating far too much. Don't you think you are building a mountain out of a molehill? Come on Mel, we know nothing about these people or their relationships. We haven't even met them as yet. This close relative, that you are so concerned about and getting all worked up over, maybe glad and relieved that her husband has gone for all we know. What if it turns out that he has simply taken off and done a runner, with another woman for example, as has already been hinted at, perhaps because he is fed up with things as they are, and sees it as a way out or his real or imagined problems, what then? What if she is glad to see the back of him?'

'I know. I know. You're quite right. I know it doesn't make much sense, but that doesn't alter the fact that I have always felt like this in similar circumstances

and it's been with me from way back and as far as I know, stems from my first job, many years ago.'

'Tell me about it. You never know, it might help.'

'One of these days when we have done everything and have nothing left or better to do I might tell you. But for now the only way to deal with it is to get on with it. It will pass. It always has in the past. How far have we still to go to this woman's?'

'A few more miles, half an hour or so should see us somewhere close.'

'We still have to find the actual place when we get there. Are you sure she knows we're coming?'

'Of course she does. Didn't you listen? When I spoke to Kathleen before we left she confirmed that this Edison woman knows we are definitely coming, and from what I gathered about the area where she lives, it shouldn't be too difficult to find. I was told it is not a large village and the layout seemed straightforward. It's past the first house on the right then turn immediately right, then first left and it's the bungalow that stands on it's own at the bottom of the lane.'

The information proved to be accurate and the directions were easy enough to follow. It took us a few minutes longer, than the original estimated half an hour from the lay-bye but that didn't matter, as no specific time for our arrival had been quoted. I now began to feel increasingly uncomfortable and did not relish the forthcoming meeting one bit.

'Well here we are,' I said as we drew up. 'I still think that it is odd that she turned down our invitation to come and meet with us at Humber.

'You mean you would have felt better about it if she had.'

'Probably. It's me and my silly feelings all being a bit unfair. I don't suppose I should expect people, in these circumstances, to come to me and who knows, perhaps she simply refused because she has not yet come to terms with what has happened. Perhaps she is still distraught. By refusing to come to us she may feel she is putting off the inevitable. On the other hand she may simply not want to become involved in anything which may reinforce her fears that something has gone badly wrong and I think I have problems.'

'Could be. But whatever her reasons, according to Ray Oldfield and much to his surprise, she flatly refused the offer of transport to Humber, but said we were welcome to visit her, here, at home.'

As we approached the house we were met on the doorstep by a very smart lady of around fifty years old. She was quite tall and very slim, almost thin. She wore smart, expensive, up to date, clothes, probably purchased from a fashionable boutique as opposed to a C & A type shop. Her hair was piled high and had obviously had a lot of time spent on it. Her complexion was very pale and the light brown of her eyes was partially obscured by large, again very fashionable, glasses. The rims

of her eyes were red and showed all the signs of recent weeping. Everything about this lady, though obviously distressed, was fashion and quality.

I felt greatly relieved when Fred had stepped out in front of me and led the way.

'Hello. Mrs Edison?' A nod and very weak smile from the lady confirmed that she was indeed the lady in question.

'My name is Winifred Huntington and this is my colleague, Mel Grundy. We are from the Coastguard Internal Enquiry Division.

'Yes, I have been expecting you. Please come in, both of you,' she said in a low weak voice which clearly indicated that she was deeply distressed.

We were lead into what was obviously the lounge and invited to sit down. Mrs Edison was not the only smart and fashionable object in the house, the whole interior of the bungalow matched. It was very tastefully and expensively furnished with everything well laid out and all very neat and tidy. Nothing appeared to be out of its place. She matched, and blended in, with her surroundings perfectly.

'Would you care for some tea? My daughter is in the kitchen and it won't take a moment.'

'Yes please, if it's no trouble. We have had quite a long ride without a break, and a cup of tea would be very welcome. What about you Mel?'

'Yes please.'

We were left alone for a few moments as she disappeared into the kitchen. I gazed around and studied the view across the fields from the window. So calm, colourful and peaceful that it made me feel as if I was almost in another world. A far cry and so different from the built up areas I was used to and had recently left.

Mrs Edison returned accompanied by an equally attractive, but much younger, version of herself who carried a tray on which the tea things were set. It was clear that she too had recently been crying, and was still very much upset.

'This is my daughter Jenny.'

We both nodded and smiled. Fred added a polite, 'Hello we are pleased to meet you.'

'Do you mind if I stay in here with Mum while you are here?'

'Not at all! Of course you can stay. Please, come and sit down. The more people we get the chance to chat with the easier things might be.'

I was still felling a bit odd inside for now there were two people pinning all their hopes on us. I was pleased that Fred was taking the initiative.

'Mrs Edison, we feel…'

'Please call me Pat.'

'Fine, Pat it is. My name is Winifred but everyone calls me Fred for short. As you already know, my partner here is Mel. We will try and be as brief as possible and not detain you a moment longer than necessary, for I know this must be a very stressful and a very trying time for you both.'

'What's happened to my Dad?' demanded Jenny as she burst into tears and began dabbing her eyes with a crumpled tissue.

Fred smiled and hesitated for a moment before she continued in a calm voice. 'At this time we know very little, in fact almost nothing but we hope we can quickly solve the mystery and get to the bottom of it and that everything will turn out to be just fine in the end.'

'Everyone seems to think he has run away, but I know he wouldn't. He wouldn't just go off and leave Mum without a word, and another thing, if he was going to run away, like they say, he wouldn't do that and leave our Skip.'

'Who is Skip?'

'Our dog,' chipped in Pat. 'Or more precisely he is my husband's dog. He has always been considered to be his dog and he has hardly eaten a thing since Philip left. I just know something has gone dreadfully wrong. The dog would never leave Philip and return home, like he did, of his own accord.'

'Would he return home alone if ordered to, say by your husband?'

'I doubt it. From what I know of him he would probably have only gone so far. He would have done as he was told initially, but then he would probably have decided that that was enough of doing as he was told and so he would have changed his mind and turned round and gone back. That would be typical of him. He is basically a good dog, but not all that obedient, if you understand me.'

I nodded. Jenny was still crying and dabbing her eyes with the tissue.

I felt at this point that I must make the effort and say something if only to ease my own feelings, 'I will try and be as brief as I can Mrs Edison; sorry, Pat, and I do apologise for the obvious distress we are causing you both.' They of course had no idea they were not alone when it came to feeling bad and I only hoped that my current discomfort was not showing. I took a deep breath. 'Please take your time, but would you be so kind as to go right back to the very beginning and tell us everything that you can remember. Who did what, and what was said. Who went where and why? Did anything strike you as odd, unusual, or completely out of character at the time? Or has anything struck you as being odd or unusual since then? Please try and remember and tell us as much as you can. Also if you have any thoughts or opinions of your own, on anything, we would appreciate that as well, and don't be afraid to add in any tittle-tattle, or chance remarks, you might have heard from other people, whether you believe them to be true or not.'

'It seems such a long time ago and yet it is only four, or is it five, days ago that it all actually happened, anyhow that doesn't matter. Philip got up at the usual time that morning. The same routine; wash, dress, check the mail and eat his breakfast. Check his "telecom pager" to make sure it is working, back the car out, check the radio telephone in the car by calling Humber, then tell them that he was leaving home to set watch at the Station; everything he has to do daily, and has done thousands of times before.'

'Was there any mail that particular morning?'

'Only a circular, as I remember, and one that went straight into the kitchen swing bin, nothing else.'

'Had he had any unusual or important mail recently. A few days before perhaps?'

'No, I don't think so because he usually brings all the mail into the kitchen to open and to read it, at the table and I don't recall seeing any or him saying anything about any. I don't think he had anything that I didn't know of. Mail is always considered to be common to both of us.'

'Any phone calls, that you know of, that distressed him or disturbed him?'

'Over the last few days, and before he went missing, we only had two calls and both those were from Jenny here.'

'No work calls?'

'No most of those come and go through the office. It is rare for them to ring here. If Philip is required outside of working hours then they page him and he will either use the car radio or ring in from here, but that isn't often.'

'What about the one, Mummy, you told me about on the day he went away?' asked Jenny.

'Oh yes, there was a call on the day he went away. It was about tea time but that was from him to me.'

'And what was that about? If I may ask?'

'Nothing really! It sometimes happens in his work. It was time for him to come home and he rang to say he would be a few minutes late, as just as he was about to leave the "lookout", someone arrived to inform him they thought a seal was stranded on some rocks a few hundred yards along the base of the cliff, and he was going to have a look. He said the chances were it was tired and had only come up onto the rocks to rest, but he would go and make sure. It has happened many times before and he is quite used to it. As it turned out he was only twenty minutes later than usual.'

'Did he seem alright in himself when he came in?'

'Yes, he muttered something about walkers and bloody seals and always when it was time to come home, never during normal shift time. He often used to moan a little bit if he was late but never seriously, and if he had to, he would go straight back out again and never give his tea or anything else a second thought.'

'So, as far as you could tell, he was his normal self?'

'Yes, he was fine: the same as usual. When I asked him if he had any plans for the evening he replied that he didn't feel like doing much, so he proposed to watch television and perhaps go down to the pub later. Very much his normal routine; television before anything else, oh except for walking our Skip, and then he still liked to go to the pub most evenings if he could.'

'Did he mention anything, that you can remember, of possible significance, say during the evening meal, or while he was watching TV. Anything which, at the time, struck you as being odd or out of the ordinary?'

'No, just idle chatter... what had I done during the day, had I remembered to do this and that. All the usual boring domestic stuff that makes for a happy household.'

'Is it a happy household Pat?' gently enquired Fred.

'Of course it is, and as far as I am concerned it always has been.'

'What do you mean by "As far as you are concerned"?' tentatively enquired Fred.

'Sorry, perhaps I didn't express myself too well. I should have said Philip and I had no problems, if that's what you meant. We had no more than the usual ups and downs that seem to go with a never-ending pile of bills and the shortage of funds to cover them. Philip would never hear of me going out to work, and looked upon the couple of hours a day that I do, down at the village shop, as something to keep me occupied now the children have grown up, more than a source of income. No, Philip and I had no problems of the type you are suggesting.'

'Were there any other types of problems you have not mentioned, at his work for example. Was he being pressured or harassed or anything?'

'No certainly not.'

'You seem sure.'

'Yes I am. If there had been any problems there, Philip would have told me, he always did.'

'So on the day in question, he came home twenty minutes late, had dinner, then what?'

'He settled down to read the evening paper and watch the television.'

'Did he do that all evening?'

'No, at about ten o'clock, which is his usual time, if he intends to go to the pub, he got up and said he was going out for a while. I thought nothing of it. He has done it often enough in the past. It is almost a habit. A few minutes later I heard him call out to the dog and then the back door close behind them. That was the last time I saw him. When it got to half past eleven and he hadn't come home, I didn't worry too much because I knew that sometimes he would stay behind for a social drink with the Pub landlord and a few of his friends. Or his pager might have been activated and he may have gone straight to the lookout or a Coastguard job. That too has happened on numerous occasions in the past, but I must admit that when that does happen, he tries to ring me and let me know, but not always. So you see I did not worry unduly, that is until about one o'clock in the morning when I heard our Skip whimpering and scratching at the back door. He was alone and had never gone off initially with Philip and then come home alone before. My first reaction was to quiz the poor dog and shout at him to tell me where Philip was until I realised

how stupid I was being, and that the poor dog couldn't tell me anything. Finally when the initial panic passed, I rang the pub, only to be told he was not there and had not been there at all that evening, and that the pub had been closed for the last hour and a half. My next reaction was to ring Humber Coastguard. They were very concerned as they assured me that no pagers had been activated that evening in this region. There were no 'jobs going on in our sector and the only transmissions they were picking up, on their radios, was general traffic from ships passing through the area. They were very kind about it and told me to try not to worry and that they would contact the Police and try to find out where he had got to. I just sat in a chair in a daze, with visions of him laid on the roadside somewhere, having been knocked down, or something. The way some people drive around in this village these days is disgusting. They have no regard for any ones safety.'

She broke off at that point and pushed up her glasses so that she was able to dab her eye with a small handkerchief before she continued. 'About an hour later I heard a car coming down the lane and I went to the front door. I didn't know what to expect, but it turned out to be a young Constable in a Police car. He told me he was responding to a report that my husband was missing and he wanted to check if he had arrived home yet. When I said he hadn't he seemed at a loss. I think he thought that Philip should have been at home. He just stood and seemed to be thinking for a few seconds, then turned away and spoke into his radio. He spoke to someone and told that Philip had not turned up at home and that he proposed to tour round the area to see if he could see him or find anything. He then assured me that everything would be all right and that if I didn't hear from them beforehand, he would come back in the morning. If, however, in the mean time, Philip did come home, would I be so kind as to ring them and let them know. His final remark, before getting back into his car and driving off, was to the effect, that missing persons usually turn up when they have had time to think things through and cool their heels, and that it was too soon to list him as a genuine missing person. Why does everyone have to automatically assume there has been some sort of domestic tiff; some upheaval that is natural and will automatically work itself out?'

'Perhaps, that is, because domestic rows are the commonest cause for people to simply walk out,' Interrupted Fred.

Pat Edison sat and thought for a brief moment before continuing. 'I sat in the chair all night and by morning I was cold and stiff and nothing had happened. Philip had not come back and the Police had not been in touch with me. I must have then nodded off because I was re-woken by the telephone ringing. It was the duty officer at Humber enquiring if I had heard anything. He said that they had been on to the local Police and that they knew nothing. What he intended to do, he said, was to turn out our local Search Team, and let them go over the patch.'

'What happened then?'

'Nothing, the first search took hours and found nothing, and a second more intensive search using more men and covering a much wider area, also turned up nothing. Finally it was decided that the Police would mount a search further inland and the coastal Search Team would carry out yet another sweep of the whole area. This time they would extend even further and use the local Inshore Lifeboat that had just returned to service after its winter withdrawal and annual overhaul. I understand also that the Search and Rescue Helicopter, which was out on a routine exercise, overheard the radio transmissions, and volunteered to over-fly the area along the coastline and also further inland. My heart missed a beat every time that big yellow helicopter flew over the house. It did this several times, and it hit me really hard when I realised that on this occasion, instead of Philip working with them, they were actually looking for him.' At this point she broke off and burst into tears and stopped talking for a few moments.

'I'm sorry,' and drawing a deep breath she continued. 'That afternoon the phone rang and the Controller at Humber said they might have some news. They said a walker, out for the day and walking just North of our area had sat on a grassy patch to eat a sandwich and had come across, what he described as, some valuable looking equipment. He was not sure how long it had been there but it looked in good condition. He had the sense, they said, to report his find to the Police. The Police were there at that moment and Humber had requested that a Coastguard Patrol from the next sector meet them at the scene. From what he had been able to gather, they had found what could be Skip's lead, Philip's multi-scan transceiver, and his hand held lamp. A search of the area had revealed no sign of Philip. At last something positive had happened, but still no Philip.' At that she began to cry once again and excused herself.

Fred reached across and placed her hand over Pat Edison's. Jenny put her hand on her mothers shoulder and both continued to quietly sob.

'We are truly sorry,' soothed Fred. 'We really are, but if there is anything else you can add. Anything else you can possibly think of to tell us?'

'I don't think so but I am getting so tired and confused. I am so weary. I think it's mainly due to lack of sleep. You have been asking me questions and the Police have been asking me the same questions, why doesn't someone do something instead of just question after question all the time? I have told everyone everything I know and despite what everyone might think, Philip and I did not fall out, there was nothing wrong between us. Please will you leave us alone now and go.'

'Yes we will,' I said as gently as I could, 'and thank you for everything. But just before we do, can you tell us what he was wearing when he went out that night? I know that is imposing on you still further at the moment, but we do need to know and it would help us tremendously if you would spare us just a few more minutes and tell us; then we will leave you in peace. I promise.'

‘I will go and make some more tea Mum,’ said Jenny as she gathered up the empty cups and placed them on the tray.

‘I am sorry. I’m fine now. I was very rude to you just then. Please forgive me. I know you are only trying to help. It’s my fault really. I am so tired and feel so helpless. I think, in my confusion, I even offered the Police to go on television and appeal to Philip to come home, but everyone said no, the least publicity at this stage, the better, they said. What was it you wanted? Oh yes, what was he wearing?’

She hesitated for a moment as if trying to unscramble it all in her mind. She was beginning to look tired and much paler than when we first met, only a short time ago.

‘At first when they asked, I said he was wearing casual jeans and a check shirt, as that’s what he had on when he was watching television. I assumed that all he would put on extra, to go to the pub, was his grey anorak, and that is what I told everyone. It was not until much later that I noticed his anorak was still hanging in the hall and I realised I must have been wrong. I knew he would not go out at this time of the year without a coat so I went into the bedroom to see which alternative he could have taken. It was then that I discovered his shirt and jeans both laid out on the bed. It was completely out of character for Philip to get changed to go to the pub for the last hour. In fact it’s not like Philip to get changed at all, once he is out of uniform. When I looked in his wardrobe, I discovered that in actual fact he had taken out and must have put on a tracksuit. His Coastguard overalls and black Coastguard anorak were also missing. When I looked, his black Coastguard gumboots were missing from the back porch. He had actually gone out dressed as he would for a search, or an exercise.’

‘Has he ever done that before?’

‘Not without telling me beforehand: no never, in all the years he has never done that without first telling me.’

‘So you find that unusual?’

‘Very and totally out of character.’

‘Have you told anyone else that you thought what he did was strange?’

‘No. All I did was tell Humber that I had been mistaken in what I told them he had gone out dressed in originally. Later I told them what was missing and said I presumed that they would be what Philip was in actual fact wearing and not what I had said earlier. I explained that, once he went out of this room, I didn’t see him again, I only heard him call the dog and close the back door, I assumed, behind him.’

‘Sorry to press you further; you have been very tolerant and patient with us, but can you tell me, did your husband always take the dog with him to the pub?’

'Oh yes, kills two birds with one stone, as he used to say. In the good weather they would set out much earlier and walk along the cliff tops before going to the pub. In bad weather, it had to be down to the pub and straight back.'

'Thank you very much Mrs Edison, you have been very kind, and we appreciate everything that you have told us. Thank you for your time, the tea, and all your trouble.'

'Please find him,' she pleaded. 'You must.'

'We will do our best. You maybe assured of that and I am sure everything will turn out just fine.'

The strange feelings of apprehension and the fear that had been churning about in my guts, before we arrived, had almost subsided. The words 'you must' and my weak and potential false promise that everything would be just fine brought it all back.

What causes me to experience these strange, and to say the least, unusual feelings is a mystery and one on which I can only speculate for a logical reason. Perhaps it is the knowledge that someone might expect more of me than I am capable of giving or providing. Perhaps I am not as cleaver as I think I am and feel threatened. Or they look upon me as the instant answer to all their problems when I know, deep down inside that I am not. Do their feelings of loss transfer over to me and stir up my own feelings of loss from experiences long forgotten and suppressed or do I simply resent their attempts to lay their problems on me when I have enough of my own. I am not aware of any of my own personal problems at a purely conscious level but who knows what is going on deep down in the subconscious.

All I know is that these very uncomfortable feelings always choose to manifest themselves at the beginning, or during, the early stages of any new assignment. They would pass. I knew they would. They always did.

CHAPTER TWELVE

We left mother and daughter standing on the doorstep, still dabbing their eyes and showing all the signs of deep distress.

'Where to now?' said Fred, who, having approached the car from the driver's side, automatically climbed in behind the wheel.

'Might as well go and see what the local fuzz have to offer. Go back into the village and try the local cop shop first. What do you say?'

We stopped in the village and asked an elderly lady who, we decided from the plastic shopping bags that she carried, looked very much as if she might be local. She was, and willingly directed us to the Police house.

As one would naturally expect of a Rural Police Officer, he was out and about on his daily business, but his good lady rang his HQ with a request that they radio him and ask him to return to his base and talk to us. When pressed as to say who we were, I told his wife to say we were investigating an insurance claim against the Gas Board. She looked at us and in particular at our uniforms, but said nothing. When Fred looked at me, slightly bemused, I reminded her that a lot of unauthorised people monitor radio conversations and non-more enthusiastically than the Police radio bands and the less people who knew of our presence, the better.

The local officer must have been close at hand as he arrived at the house in a matter of minutes. The fact that for all his trouble and prompt response he was to prove of little or no value to us didn't help.

He stated that naturally he was aware that Edison had gone missing. He had himself been initially involved. He was also aware that certain personal effects had been found. He also went too great lengths to explain that he was under direct instructions to refer all enquires, on this matter, directly to his 'boss'. He had obviously been told by his superiors to be very guarded in what he said and we could sense that he felt uncomfortable at the questions we were asking and would have preferred it if we went elsewhere. The constant referral to his superiors, even for the most minor things, and the fact that they could best answer our questions became rather annoying in the end.

'Would your boss object if you showed us on the map the exact location where the personal items were found? I chanced.

'Sorry,' came the inevitable reply. 'I was not present when the items were found and could only indicate the general area.'

'Is that a fact Constable, or are you again working under orders and not at liberty to say?' I enquired.

'Fact as it happens. I was a couple of miles away, searching in another area when the information came over my radio. It was not meant for me, I just overheard it as it was being passed to our control. I was not diverted to the scene because about the same time, I was sent to investigate a minor traffic accident in the village.'

'Nothing serious I hope?'

'No! It was just a couple of the locals who agreed to sort it out themselves. You know what I mean, no one hurt and little damage, so let the insurance sort it out.'

I nodded and was instantly reminded of my own car insurance and how little you get and the hassle that can develop the result of the most minor claim and all for the extortionate premiums you pay for the privilege.

'Thanks Constable, I understand your position,' I said out of politeness. 'We are on our way back into town now, so would you ring your Chief and ask him if he will see us when we get there? Could you arrange something for about an hour and a half from now?'

'Should be no problem. If you hang on a second, I will ring now. I would hate you to get there and find him away for the day.'

We waited the magic second, which always stretches a little beyond that one single second, to then be informed that Inspector Jablonski would see us, in his office, in about one and a half hours time.

We thanked the Constable and left. Once again Fred climbed in behind the wheel and drove as we headed back towards town and the central Police station.

* * *

On the return journey I attempted to make a few pertinent notes on the information we had gathered up to that point. The page of my notebook was still rather sparse when we arrived back in town.

'What do we know so far?' I enquired with an air of confidence.

'Not a lot,' came back an equally confident reply. 'Local copper has been gagged. Wife and daughter are mourning a missing husband and father. How does that grab you for starters?'

'Brilliant. But there may well be a very good reason why the cop has been told to keep quiet. Perhaps it makes his boss feel important. I know something you don't know type of situation; or even, in this quiet rural backdrop, gives him simply something to do. Makes him feel indispensable or something like that, who knows? As far as Mum and daughter are concerned I still can't make up my mind. The daughter seemed genuinely upset that Daddy has gone missing but left me with the distinct impression that she fully expects him to come back at anytime.

I wonder if he has done anything like this before and Wifie is too embarrassed to admit it?'

'Done like what before?'

'You know, taken off … gone on walk-about … just taken some time out for himself. Nagging wife, a secret lover, I don't know, but that sort of thing.'

'So you think he might still turn up?'

'I don't know what to think at the moment. All I do know is that it would be a shambles if you and I are now chasing all over Yorkshire while our man is in some love nest having a crafty bonk with some randy bird and intends to return back home when he gets hungry or needs a change of clothing.'

'Don't be so crude.'

'I am not being crude; well not intentionally, but what happens if it does turn out to be something along those lines?'

'Like what?'

'I give up. Drive, woman,' and with that I shoved the pad into my pocket.

'Do you know what I think?' offered Fred.

'No my dear! What do you think?'

'I think he is genuinely missing.'

'And how do you arrive at that?'

'Well, first things first! Missing or not missing we know he is not at home right now. Second, he did not go to the pub on the evening that he disappeared. Two facts for starters.'

'How do you know that for certain?'

'The wife said so, and if that is not good enough it can soon be checked out. Contact the pub. The usual routine checks, you know what I mean?'

I nodded in agreement. 'And the next reason that makes you feel so sure?'

'Who said I was sure? I am simply considering what we do, or do not know about this guy's disappearance. He did not go to the pub, yet he got changed, which he does not normally do, when all he intends to do is take his dog for a walk and visit the local pub. But why say he is going to the pub, get changed, collect the dog and then simply take off and disappear? He got changed for a very good reason and remember, after all that, the dog came back home later alone. He left no note that we are aware of, at this point. There were no phone calls to anyone, nothing; it all simply does not add up.'

'As long as that we have been told, so far, is the truth. What if there had been a phone call, to say, the wife and she can't handle it, or won't admit to it, or if there was a note that simply blew away from the scene or something like that. Maybe there is someone else somewhere who has had a phone call. Someone we, so far, know nothing about.'

'Like who?' she queried.

'I don't know, do I? If I did we could ask them and then life would become much simpler. Perhaps some dick-head with an attitude problem knows something and won't tell. You know the score, "If they can't be bothered to ask me then why should I tell them". You come across it all the time during investigations. Perhaps its someone who fancies Pat and is not going to spoil his chances by opening his mouth?'

'Pat who?'

'Pat. The wife. You haven't forgotten her name already, have you? Someone who fancies Edison's wife? Someone who may already have been knocking her off on the quiet and can't believe his luck now that the husband has gone conveniently missing.'

'You've got a vivid imagination. Do you honestly think that half the population is constantly knocking off, as you would put it, the other half? You are just not real sometimes. Do you know that?'

'You know full well what I mean. There....'

'No, I don't know what you mean. All I get is the impression that you think that everyone freely bonks everyone else, to use another of your crude expressions and that nookie is at the back of the whole thing and that is just not on and you know damned well it's not. You think he has gone off looking for a bit on the side. You suggest she is after nookie and that someone is withholding information because it might spoil his chances of getting some nookie from her. Do you want me to really believe that everyone is after "that" and nothing else? Grow up.' She was annoyed.

'Present company excepted?'

'Bastard.'

'Now who's using bad language to express her pretty self?'

'Arsehole! You know full well what I mean but if that's the way you want it you can go play with yourself.'

'Sorry.'

'Sorry. You're sorry? Too bloody late, mate. Much too late to be sorry now,' she fumed.

How the hell had this conversation deteriorate and got down to this level? She was right off course and here was I with my brain out of gear and about to screw up on the loveliest thing that had ever happened to me. I must be wired up wrong. I thanked God for the car park at the Police Station into which we had just driven and pulled up. It brought the whole stupid discussion to a very timely halt. Someone had certainly rattled her cage and that someone was me.

We got out and walked round the building and entered through the front entrance.

* * *

In all the different Police Stations that I have had occasion to visit over the years, all the front entrances and reception areas always seem to attract a certain type of clientele. We are constantly being told there is no such thing as a criminal class. If this is correct then take a look at the reception area in any busy Police Station; why in most cases are they always busy and cluttered with the less well off, the under-privileged? The dirty, scruffy people with red eyes, running noses, dirty bitten nails visible as black sore patches on the ends of dirty fingers poking out of ragged mittens. Why is the standard dress of the average visitor nearly always a dirty and often torn, anorak, dirty frayed jeans, filthy trainers, often without socks and why is this whole wardrobe topped off with a round woolly hat or a baseball cap worn the wrong way round? Why do most of the females always look as if they have been pulled backwards through a hedge? Why, too, do they often look pale and tired as if they have had neither a good meal nor a decent night's sleep in months? Why do they look so grubby, and if they display any trace of make-up, why does it never suit their complexion and always look days old? Above all else, why do these areas in Police Stations smell permanently of dirty unwashed bodies, stale tobacco smoke, alcohol, and I swear I have noticed, on more than the odd occasion, the distinct whiff of vomit. Why do most girls sit with their clothes exaggeratedly wrapped round their body and held in place by an arm across the stomach while clutching in the free hand a packet of cheap cigarettes and a disposable cigarette lighter? Why do the youths all lean against something or slouch, as if they do not have the strength to support themselves while picking their noses with one hand and holding on tightly, with the other, to dirty, tatty documents. Another very common habit, to pass time whilst waiting to 'sign the book' to prove that they have reported to the Police Station, as the court has ordered them to do at a specific time, is to constantly bite the finger nails and surrounding skin, if any remains still to be gnawed at.

As you will now realise, I am not at all taken up with the waiting and reception areas of Police Stations and whilst I have no desire to knock the less well-off from within our varied and multi-social society, I can't help noticing that these areas do attract large numbers from a certain group or class and if the majority of those that are there, are there the result of some misdemeanour or offence against the law then perhaps, I feel, that we do have the basis for a criminal type.

'Brown,' shouts the woman at the back of the glass screen. 'Sign the book then you can go.'

A tatty youth who must be proud of the name Brown by the way he manages to respond to the request, shuffles forward and with the aid of a dirty mittened hand laboriously signs his name in a book at the point where the female finger indicates.

'Same time tomorrow,' she snaps. 'Don't be late.'

There was no reaction from the Brown character; no indication that he even heard or understood, just a blank stare. As he turned to the door three other youths stopped chewing their nails, stood up and fell in behind him and they all slouched forwards. They, in turn, were closely followed by two of the girls, and before the door had closed behind them a loud chattering and general boisterousness started. Two of the youths shouted 'Pigs!' and made obscene gestures before running off down the road while the third looked aimlessly on as one of the two girls fiddled with a packet to extract, as she called it, 'a fucking fag'. Those left behind in the Station still lounged about but now they all had silly grins on their faces.

'Davis,' snapped the female.

Following the departure of the previous group there was now considerably more room to manoeuvre. I leaned forward and pressed the bell on the counter for attention. No response.

The one who answered to Davis shuffled up to the counter and without a word pushed through the slot, under the protective glass barrier, a series of grubby documents. Madam in charge proceeded to literally peel them open, then slowly and meticulously copy the information they contained on to a form.

'How old are you?' she demanded.

'Seventeen.'

'Wait there,' she snapped back at the youth.

She returned with a uniformed constable, proving to me that there was, at that particular time, more than one person residing in the building yet my ringing of the bell had, so far, still been ignored.

'How old are you?' repeated the Constable to the Davis character.

'I've told her, seventeen.'

'What year were you born?' continues the stimulating conversation and in depth line of questioning.

'Eighty-seven.'

'Where did you get this licence? From your father, older brother, who?'

'It's mine.'

'Is it? Ever look inside it son?'

'No.'

'Well you should at some time. You will find in it a date of birth that puts you around thirty, Sunshine. Go through that door, you and I have things to talk about.'

There was a loud clicking sound.

'What was that?' asked Fred, startled.

'The electric lock on the outside door so that our friend Davis there can't change his mind and consider leaving and the lock on this inside door here opening for him to go through.'

'It made me jump.'

Exit Davis. His personal aroma lingered on well after he had departed through the adjoining door.

'Can I help you, Sir?' demanded the snapdragon from behind the screen.

Indicating with my head in Fred's direction, I replied, 'we have an appointment with Inspector Jablonski. We are expected although by now we are probably late.' I just couldn't resist adding that last snippet for I was certain she had seen us and noted our uniforms the moment we entered the place. She was, in my opinion, typical of one of those supercilious civilians, who, for the most part, is out of their depth and see themselves as something they are not, and who seem to be creeping in everywhere these days.

'One moment Sir! I will let him know you are here. What name shall I say? If you will take a seat we won't keep you a moment.' Smarmy bitch.

'Coastguard,' I replied.

Neither of us moved and remained standing. I certainly did not, and expected Fred would not either, fancy a seat previously occupied by grubby and sweaty bums. I noticed also that as more visitors left the slightly sweeter the air became. It was no wonder the 'charming' lady at the back of the glass partition acted the way she did. She was being constantly gassed. Although I make no excuses for her treating everyone as if they were criminals and some form of low-life.

* * *

Once inside the Inspector's office, the atmosphere was much sweeter and I was pleased to note free of all stale odours. His offer of coffee was gratefully received. He then sat quietly while we each read a copy of the report sheets he had obtained and handed to us. There were several sheets in the folder, some submitted by different people. The one from the village Constable confirmed what he had told us. He had not been in the area when Edison's effects were found. A different Constable had made a detailed report and included a sketch of the scene and a photograph. The sketch showed that the radio and other items had been discovered in fairly long grass between a well-worn track and the actual cliff top. The Inspector had no objections to showing us the exact location on a larger map. The report also stated that the Landlord of the village pub claimed to have been behind his own bar all that evening and therefore could positive say that Edison had not visited there.

'Inspector, do you know this chap Edison, or anything about him that might throw light on his untimely disappearance?'

'We know very little apart from the obvious. We know that he is one of your chaps. We came into contact with him on joint Police Coastguard jobs. He has no form, if that's what you mean? No record. If he had he wouldn't be in the Coastguard Service, would he?'

'No Inspector, he wouldn't. But I was not thinking of a criminal record, I was thinking along the lines of his disappearance. In other words, to your knowledge has he ever gone missing before, or have the Police ever found themselves involved in his private life?'

'No we haven't.'

'So what is the Police position at the moment?'

'There is not a lot we can do right now. We have collected, as you can see from the reports, no evidence of foul play. We can only treat it as a missing persons case. You know the scenario, fellow gets fed up, for what ever reason, and walks out, when least expected, telling no one. It happens thousands of times every year throughout the country. Most return, a few don't. Some commit suicide, while some are found dead in suspicious circumstances. These we investigate, and hopefully solve. But a straightforward case of a man leaving his wife, family, and job does not warrant an initial strong reaction from us. He is an adult, not a child so I am afraid that for the moment, he is simply a missing person, big enough to look after himself. If you think we can help in any way with your enquiries, please don't hesitate to ask. We will naturally assist you in every way that we can. Tell me, as a matter of interest, why was I told that you people want this whole thing keeping quiet - you know - keep the press out of it and that kind of thing? The instructions that I received from above and which were supposed to have originated from somewhere high up among your people was that the whole thing had to be kept very much under wraps.'

'I think we are beginning to wonder about that ourselves,' smiled Fred 'But thank you inspector for your time. If there is anything we have forgotten, we will get back to you straight away.'

'You are welcome Miss. Here take my card. There is a number on it that gets you connected straight to my office and saves you having to wait while your call is routed through the main switchboard and central control.'

'Thank you again Inspector. But before we go. We may well return to the village as civilian visitors, ask your Constable there to treat us as such, if we run into him, and not acknowledge that we have met before. Can you do that for us please?'

'Consider it already done.'

We left via the front entrance that by that time smelt slightly less powerful than it did on the way in. The only occupants left in there being a young woman with a small baby in a pushchair. While we waited for the electric release lock to be activated on the door to let us through into reception and then out of the front door, we heard the girl utter, 'E's nicked me fags and Giro and I'm not leaving 'ere 'til ya nick 'im and do the bastard.' The rest after that died away as the door closed behind us and the traffic noises finally drowned it all out.

'Missing person,' grumbled Fred. 'Is that what we are supposed to believe? It's not a child that has gone missing; he's an adult so there is no problem. What now?'

'Back to the Hotel and book another night stay, for starters. Then a few more enquiries at Humber.'

'Do you intend to go into the Humber Station then?'

'I could do, it's only just along the road but I think I can get all I need just now over the phone.'

'Who's driving this time?'

'You are.'

'Why me again?'

'Because firstly, you are a good driver, and secondly I enjoy being chauffeured.'

'Do you really mean that? No you don't. You're lying. Most men think women drivers are lousy and some men, not too far away, think women are only good for nookie.'

'I don't agree.' I said hoping that here might be an opportunity to redeem myself and also the fact that what I was about to say I firmly believe so I hoped that would add to the sincerity of the statement. 'I think women fall into two distinct categories when it comes to driving. They are either very good or bloody awful. There is no in between, no middle of the road for them. You either feel safe as houses or shit yourself when you ride with them. Whereas men are all somewhere in the middle, being neither good nor bad. Police drivers are perhaps a little above average, but some of them have been known to bend a few motors when joy riding after other joy riders. Taxi and bus drivers are at the bottom of the scale, despite the fact that they all claim otherwise, but you are very good.'

'Keep creeping you idle sod. I love it; despite the fact that I now know you are only saying it so that I will drive. You would say almost anything so that you don't have to. I know you and you don't have to tell me I am a good driver, I already know that.'

'You love it? I know you do,' and I blew her a kiss and holding up my fingers and thumbs, in front of me, made nipping motions at imaginary nipples.

'One-track mind! Fasten your seat belt and let's get away from here.'

The squeeze of my knee before she slipped in the gear lever was very encouraging although I could not be sure. Had I actually been forgiven or was she working on some cleaver wind up and perhaps planning her revenge. All I knew was that I wished I had kept my mouth shut earlier. She was the last person I wanted to fall out with or get at cross-purposes with. She was too lovely for that and I had been so bloody stupid.

The atmosphere, despite my apprehension, was jovial as we drove back and we laughed and chatted about anything and everything. Twice I tried to apologise for the one-track mind and twice I was told to forget it.

Back in the Hotel, having rebooked in, Fred disappeared for a shower and, she said, to change. I removed my tunic and tie and then went to ring Humber. When I got back I showered and changed into casuals. I then collected Fred and we both went down for dinner.

CHAPTER THIRTEEN

We made our way into the lounge bar and ordered drinks. Fred had selected to wear, for that particular evening tight, thin black slacks and an equally tight black T-shirt. She look gorgeous and the contrast between her fair hair and the black of her outfit made her face look more radiant than ever. She needed and had used very little makeup and the fashionable black boots that finished off the outfit had the effect of making her look much taller than her actual height.

'Are we going to sit in here all evening?' she enquired, 'because if that is what you have in mind, I would rather like to go out for a walk and take a stroll along the seafront. It's a pleasant night, it's warm enough, and we have been sitting about, one way, or the other, for most of the day. So come on Mel, finish that drink and get up off your bum and let's go out. You can tell me all about your phone call, and what Humber had to say for themselves.'

Outdoors it was pleasant and quite warm, and as a result, a fair few people had taken advantage and were doing exactly the same as us - just strolling along the promenade at a leisurely pace. Others were browsing in the shops while a few had chosen the arcades and were feeding the hungry machines with their hard earned coppers. The voices of the different callers told us that somewhere inside some people must have been participating in the traditional seaside games of bingo and everywhere there was music and bright lights. Totally dominating the atmosphere, was the ever present, mouth watering, smell of hot-dogs and burgers and when I remarked on it to Fred she corrected me and explained that it was not actually the smell from the Burgers and Hot Dogs, although they did make a contribution, but it was in actual fact the smell of onions cooking. I didn't care, it all smelled good to me.

In contrast to the lights, noise and smell on the one side, opposite the sea and sky were very dark. The surface of the water was flat calm and the slightly undulating smooth surface reflected the multitude of coloured lights opposite.

'What a lovely evening and there are so many people about. Are you warm enough?' enquired Fred, squeezing my hand.

'Fine thanks! You?'

'Fine, but I'm glad I put a jacket on. It's still note quite T-shirt weather. Is it?'

'You can say that again and hey, just look at all those lights reflecting on the water. It's amazing and it is not often you see the sea as calm as that. I bet the tide is on the turn.'

'Talking of tides and the likes, whom did you speak to at Humber?' Inquired Fred as we slowly walked along still holding hands and enjoying the impromptu display of reflected light.

'Ray Oldfield! He was still in his office when I got through, so I spoke to him.'

'What did you ask him?'

'I told him we had been to see Pat Edison and had not learned very much. I told him of our visit to the Police Station and basically what happened there, but what I really rang for and wanted to ask him specifically, was if he had any idea if Philip Edison had ever been away from home in similar circumstances before. I asked if he had ever taken off on other occasions without saying anything, and then returned later. I asked also, if he knew of, or suspected any problems between Edison and his wife Pat. He claims there are no official records of anything of that nature. Unofficially he said that he had known the Edison's long enough, and was friendly enough with them, to be fairly certain there were no problems between husband and wife. As for the actual going away, he claimed it is totally out of character for Edison, and he was certain it had never happened before. He said that he also knew the wife well enough to be able to ask her the question directly if I thought it might help. I said to give it a try; it could do no harm and would be useful to know. I also asked him if at the same time he would mention to Mrs Edison that we were proposing to return to the area posing as tourists and should she bump into us, not to recognise us. If we should need to contact her we would do so discreetly and make all the necessary arrangements at the time. If on the other hand she needed to tell us anything, I suggested that Oldfield act as our go between. She could ring him and he could pass it on to us or make arrangements for us to meet. I also mentioned that he should warn her to be discrete and not discuss with anyone that we were still interested and proposed to stay in and around the area for the time being. Finally I asked him if he knew if Edison had used his portable radio on any occasion during the evening and night of his supposed disappearance.'

'What did he say to that?'

'He said he could not be certain on that point. Apparently their recording facility, to monitor VHF transmissions, only covers the distress frequency on channel Sixteen. They only record other channels when they specifically switch on to do so and that is usually when they have a job on. So as far as he knew on the night of Edison's disappearance there would only be channel Sixteen transmissions on the tape and again, as far as he knew, none of them were attributable to Edison. So if he transmitted on any channel other than Sixteen or the Coastguard working channel Zero, no one will have heard or monitored or logged him. No one official that is, no doubt the dozens of illegal listeners and scan users will have heard everything that night, but they are not likely to jump out of the woodwork and tell us, are they?'

'Hey! Not so fast. Listen a moment, you said no official listeners. You may be wrong. What about the Government Monitoring Stations: the ones that listen to everything? The ones most people have heard about, particularly since they had some sort of dispute with their management a while back and the media gave them rather more exposure then I bet the Government was happy about. You know, the "unofficial" official, Government listening stations. They have one or more of those places around here somewhere in Yorkshire don't they?'

'You mean that wedge shaped thing where those massive golf ball things used to be in the middle of the moors a few miles from here?'

'No silly, that's Fylingdales. That's for monitoring missiles and things that go whiz in the night. That's an RAF run place and I think the Americans have something to do with it. What I mean is, is there not a place like GCHQ Cheltenham, like they showed on telly, somewhere around here?'

'Right. I see what you mean. Keep a look out for a phone box. There is bound to be one somewhere around here.' I said as I turned in front of her to look behind. She was very close and as she looked up at me and smiled I kissed her.

'That was nice but why do we need a phone box?

'Because I have a plan.'

'Does it include me?'

'Very much so.'

'Are you sure? Didn't I tell you I don't make love in phone boxes? I'm a grown girl, in case you haven't noticed; and don't do naughty things in phone boxes any more. Anyhow, only an exhibitionist would want to do it in a glass box and I'm definitely not the type to give those sorts of public performances. Well I might be; thinking about it, if I were drunk enough.'

'We might do that after but what I am proposing right now is that we ring the Old man and ask him for the low down on this GCHQ business.'

'And I thought.... Ah well, never mind. Turn round. We passed a phone box a few minutes ago back along there.'

We retraced our steps and sure enough there was the phone box Fred had referred to, right on the corner of a block of shops and against an arcade. It was quite a squeeze, the two of us in the one box and in the confined space Fred smelt lovelier than ever. I could feel the warmth as it radiated from her. She kissed my cheek. I fished around in my pockets until I found a fifty pence piece among my loose change. I put it in the appropriate slot and dialled. It rang for ages before a voice at the other end came on.

'Hello.'

'Colonel; its Grundy.'

'Grundy, where the hell have you been? I thought I made it quite clear that I expected regular and frequent reports on your progress and current situation. Before you go any further, what is your present "sit-rep."?'

'Nothing.'

'What the hell are you ringing me for if you have nothing to report?'

'I need information and some help.'

'Carry on; what is it that you want and it had better be important ringing me at this time of night? We have only just finished dinner and I am presently entertaining guests for the evening, so I don't have time for irrelevances. So make it good and make it snappy.'

'Is there GCHQ set up in this area Sir? Here in North Yorkshire?'

'Of course there damned well is man, and you should know that. Didn't they teach you anything in training?'

'Yes sir! They taught me that if I didn't know anything or needed anything, or couldn't immediately recall anything, I had to ask. There was always someone besides me who would know. That is what I am doing now Sir, asking. Is there one, where is it, and how do I go about making contact?'

There was silence at the other end broken only by a gasping sound. Probably because I had upset him rather badly and he was, the result, at that very moment, I hoped, enjoying the delights of a cardiac arrest brought on by anger, frustration, and stress. He would have been even more distressed had he known that all the time I was patiently waiting for him to come back to me Fred was nibbling my right ear lobe and gently blowing into my ear while I, with my free hand, gently caressed the cheek of her bum and traced the outline of her briefs.

'Now listen Grundy. I am not here to lead you two by the hand. I expect all my people to be self sufficient and resourceful.'

'We are "all that" Sir and more, but I still need the information. Can you put me onto someone else who will know?'

It was then that he bit and I could hear him in the background furiously opening and closing what were probably desk drawers, and all the time huffing and puffing with the effort as he did so. I wonder how he would have reacted or what he would have said if I had put it in the way I really would have like to have done, and said to him, Oh come on you cantankerous old bastard, why don't you admit that you don't know it all off the top of your head, and you are as mad as hell that you don't have anyone close at hand to toss it over to. Admit you're normal and don't know everything despite the front you put on, and with the exception of your expertise at sleaze and deception, you probably know sod all.

'You still there, Grundy?'

'Yes, sir, I am still here.'

'You're almost sitting on it. CSOS Irton Moor.'

'CSOS Sir?'

'Yes you block head! Coastal Shipping Observation Service. It's not that secret that it cannot be easily found on a decent map. It's what goes on inside the

place that is the secret and of no concern to an outsider. Now can I get back to my dinner guests?'

'Yes Sir, but before you go; the second part of my request.'

'Good god man! Did you not hear me? I am busy. I am tied up at the moment. What is it you want?'

'How do I contact them?'

'What for?'

'Information. Part of the job, Sir.'

'I gather that you idiot! What do you specifically want from them?'

'Not over the phone Sir: if you don't mind. Can you set up a contact or something for us?' I asked, thinking to myself, now there's some of you own philosophy, you pompous old bastard, and you can shove it up your arse. Teach you to treat me like some moron.

Fred felt soft and smooth as I ran my fingertips lightly along the nick between her buttocks. She responded by lightly biting my ear lobe then thrusting the tip of her tongue deep into my ear. I stood there patiently waiting for the Old Man to say something. I had the earpiece of the telephone held in one hand against my ear and her tongue in the other. My free hand was still exploring Fred's backside when I became very conscious of another hand deep in my trouser pocket. I could feel the warmth of it through the thin material of the lining. The fingers began probing, searching, caressing. I remembered her saying something, not to long ago about not performing in a phone boxes. Well, at that moment, if she continued, she would have no choice in the matter, glass sides to the phone box or not.

'Stop it and go throw a bucket of cold water over yourself,' I whispered.

'What's that Grundy?'

'Nothing Sir, only a remark I was making to Miss Huntington.'

'Is she with you? I thought you understood that you should always use a closed call box when you ring in from outside and talk to me.'

'That's exactly what I am doing now Sir. Everything according to the rules.'

'What!' he almost shouted. 'The two of you in one call box?'

'Yes Sir, you should try it. I can highly recommend it on a cold evening.'

Silence and then a strange hissing sound: another full blown seizure perhaps.

'Leave this with me Grundy. Ring me back in an hour and make sure that if you use a phone booth, you do so alone. Understand?' A click, a buzzing sound, and he had gone.

'What did he say?'

`He says I have to ring him back and I have to do it alone, in an hour. I don't think he likes the idea of two of us in the one box.'

'The miserable old spoil sport. Perhaps he wants to chat you up. Can I have my hand back please?' as she twisted and struggled to pull her hand free of my pocket. 'You see that lady over there, she has enjoyed every minute watching you play with my bum. She didn't enjoy it half as much as I did though, you have made me go all of a tingle. I won't be able to walk straight, for absolutely ages now!'

'And I suppose I will after you have been rummaging around. In the meantime while we both stagger about, all of a tingle as you put it, how shall we kill the hour?'

'You can kiss me for starters even though she is still watching. Then you can take me for coffee. It's too nippy to persuade you to take me down onto the beach. Pity, because it's dark enough and I'm definitely in the mood. But it will save I suppose, but come on, you can still kiss me.'

I hoped the strange lady shared a little of my pleasure.

'Now take me for coffee.'

'Hang on a moment young lady. These jeans of mine were tight enough to start with, but now after all that I am in what you might call a very delicate condition. If we were to leave here now, at this very minute, the lady over there might well scream and even if she didn't there could be quite a few raised eyebrows.'

'We will have to walk in single file, with you very close up behind me.'

'Good idea but I don't think that would work. Despite what we would look like to all those people, including your lady, out there, if I were to get anywhere near you in these tight trousers, it would just make things worse. If you have no better ideas we will have to wait here for a few minutes and you can keep those wandering hands to yourself, at least until later.'

With that, she lent forward and ran the tip of her tongue across the end of my nose. 'Don't make me wait too long.'

Things, if that is what you can call them, eventually settled down, or at least one important part eventually settled down, and we were able, without embarrassment, to go to a near by Snack Bar for coffee. The lady that Fred had pointed out gave us a broad cheeky grin as we passed her. I returned the compliment with a wink and put my hand purposely on Fred's backside but didn't look round to see if she was still watching. Fred's only comment was, 'It didn't take you long to break your own rules. I hope it pops up and won't go back down, then you will have to beg me for help.'

'And would you?'

'Oh I might. Try me.'

An hour later I rang his lordship. This time from the public phone box closer to the hotel. Fred would not hear of me going alone. She said I would feel lonely and start winking at strange women.

When the phone was answered the Old man said, 'Are you alone this time Grundy?'

'Yes sir,' I lied. Then curiously enquired. 'Is there a particular reason for you to request that I am alone this time?'

'There damned well is! I want you to know that I simply do not agree with the sort of intimacy that you seem to go in for. It is not decent, it is unprofessional, and it must stop. I have my female operatives in the field to do a specific job and that certainly does not include being there for your pleasure or amusement. If Huntington makes any form of formal complaint or even hints at anything untoward, you are in very serious trouble. Do I make myself clear?'

I had held the earpiece between us and angled in such a way that Fred was able to hear everything he said, she grinned from ear to ear.

'Yes Sir: do you have the information for me Sir?'

'Yes I have. Now you just remember what I said and then take down this number.' He proceeded to dictate to me a six-figure telephone number. 'Ring this number tomorrow. Your call will be expected, and Grundy… remember, no more intimacy with that female operative or I may have to completely reappraise the whole situation.'

Fred took the hand piece from me and said, 'He will certainly remember, and good night Sir.' Without waiting for a response she put the phone back in its cradle and we both doubled up laughing.

'Thank you, young lady! Despite just putting my job on the line that little outburst might not only have been fatal for me but for the Old Man as well. I can see the headline news in tomorrow's papers. "Mystery female voice kills top Civil Servant. Bertie Bentshank, a minor Civil Servant, while zipping up his fly in a back street kiosk, suffered a fatal heart attack following a massive overdose of female insubordination."'

'Why not? And I hope the small print then goes on to read – "The Colonel, after becoming completely worked up and loosing control over the female voice and the thought of all his staff in one phone box, collapsed and died with his own important bit in his hand. His wife who had not seen it before, screamed and went into deep mourning, not for him, but for what she had missed",' giggled Fred.

When the laughter died down and after several other jokes and suggestions for his epitaphs the Old Man no longer posed a threat nor was he any longer funny, I suggested a couple of drinks before bed.

'Can we skip the drinks?'

'Why are you so bushed?'

'No, but I still have a tingle that needs attending to and these trousers and boots are so tight you won't have an easy time with them and that could cost us valuable time. OK, a couple of drinks, but you must promise to make up for any lost time.'

'I promise I will try my best.'

'I hope you do that every time.'

'I hope I do. But if the Old Man carries out his threat then this maybe my last chance to prove it.'

'Oh sod him.'

* * *

How girls can get into trousers as tight as those black things that Fred had on that evening, is a mystery to me. She promised to show me the next time she put them on and mentioned that to do so was something not unlike the position she was in just then, as I struggled to remove them.

'What on your back, and down here on the floor?'

'Yes, you lie on the floor and ease them on and up a bit at a time. You will never get them off like that, pulling from the top. They will not turn inside out or anything as simple as that. Stop kissing my tummy and concentrate. Ease them down just a bit then work on each leg in turn, do it a bit at a time.'

I had no problems with the top bit. I undid the zip and eased the waistband down under her bum. Now I was struggling and I swear the rest of the material was glued to her legs. I had had no problem with the tightly fitting T-shirt. It had been tight but elastic enough to stretched and come easily up and over her head. Now she was laid on the carpet, on her back in bra and panties with these blasted evil black pants stuck solid round her upper thighs.

'Look Fred, if you don't stop doing that, I will never get these bloody trousers off and we will be stuck here for ever. Concentrate on giving me a hand and forget that for a moment. With a bit of luck it will still be there when we get these bloody things off. It has a lot of patience and is used to waiting while I struggle.'

'I'm only doing it because I have to play with something to keep me occupied while I wait patiently to be disrobed and anyhow it feels good, all smooth and silky and ever so hard.'

'Look stop will you!'

'You're loving every pull and squeeze, go on admit it.'

'Shit now just look at what you have done.'

'Don't get cross with me. You're the one who has shot the stuff all over the place. Oh it's warm. Pass those tissues from over there. Anyhow, I think it is still ever so cute even though it's going all soft and wrinkly, and at least by the time it comes back you might have got my pants off.'

'If it comes back!'

'Oh it will, I guarantee it.'

She sat up and worked away at one trouser leg, while I worked on the other and while we struggled there was some in-depth discussion as to how it can get so big when it sets off so small, and how it gets from so soft to so hard. After that she spent more time pushing it this way and then that and stroking and squeezing it and holding it between finger and thumb and inspecting it closely than she did working on the trousers.

When they finally surrendered and were very unceremoniously thrown onto a chair, the bra and pants were no problem.

'This is the only problem we have now,' I said pointing.

'No problem, you just lie back and conserve your energy and leave this to me.'

I closed my eyes and let the tip of her tongue work wonders.

There was only one bed used that night... but boy was it used!

CHAPTER FOURTEEN

The day dawned bright and early and despite all Fred's attempts the previous evening to drain every last ounce of strength out of me, I felt remarkably fresh. I eased out of bed leaving her curled up and still asleep. I dressed and letting myself quietly out, set off for a brisk walk along the sea front. Once outside in the fresh air I was met by a fairly strong breeze coming in from the sea; strong enough to displace my hair and cause me to push my hands deep into my pockets, but apart from that it was not uncomfortable and seemed, if anything, to add to the pleasantness of the morning.

I stopped to enjoy a pot of freshly brewed tea. A large mug full of strong, sweet liquid with a touch too much milk in for my liking and always a feature of most seaside holiday places and an early morning indulgence for many visitors and locals up and about at that time. As I sat on a long wooden bench, provided for the convenience of customers and as a place to rest, or in my case, somewhere to just sit and wrap both hands round the hot mug of tea and admire the scenery and my immediate surroundings.

Spread out before me were several brightly painted wooden huts, some, due to the early hour, still shuttered up and as yet not opened up for business. They were all very similar in design with drop down or removable shutters which, despite their smallness and overall size, were so compact and, I find, inevitably crammed to the roof with a wide range of foodstuffs and assorted drinks, souvenirs and trinkets, or rock, sweets, and ice cream machines. Seek out any harbour area and sure enough there will be a 'Tea Shack', among others, somewhere close by and from very early in the morning will emit, to waft on the breeze, the aroma of bacon butty, sausages for sandwiches, beef burgers and hot dogs.

The one I chose for my early morning treat was no exception. Sizzling onions, which Fred claims are responsible for most of the aroma, mountains of bread rolls, stacks of chocolate biscuits, and other pre-packed goodies in a multitude of colourful wrappers. Tall stainless steel boilers hissing steam and radiating tremendous heat, all making a contribution to the overall attraction and attacking the taste buds, including those of the sea gulls, who perched, noisily, on the roof or clung precariously to the top rail of the nearby iron railings. A smell which, automatically affects the whole area and seems to draw people in from miles around, particularly first thing in the morning.

As I sat a young fellow appeared and set about changing one of several gas bottles that were racked up at the side of the shack. He nodded, smiled, and as he worked began to chat in a friendly, casual way. He remarked about the weather,

said he felt the wind would die down later and that he doubted if it would rain that day. I noticed and drew his attention to, the RNLI insignia on his navy blue jumper. He told me he was, and in a very modest way said, quite proud to be, a member of the local crew and added, also with pride, that recently he had been selected by his colleagues to serve as the Coxswain on the local offshore Lifeboat. At first it seemed rather odd that a chap working to change gas bottles in a 'Tea Shack' should be the Coxswain of a Lifeboat. But when I mentioned it he explained that that was very much the way things are in the RNLI. Being shore based he is always available when required and not perhaps away out at sea, as would be the case if all the Coxswain's and crews were Fisherman. He assured me it is common practice to have shore-based Lifeboat crews who are recruited not only for their capability but also their commitment and ready availability. I enjoyed the chat and said so, and felt, at least, I had learned a little of the life style of one Lifeboat Man.

I placed my empty mug on the counter and glanced at my watch. It was time I was getting back.

* * *

I went in through the main door of the Hotel and as I did so glanced into the public rooms and round the reception area. Fred was nowhere to be seen so I went up to her room to find her exactly as I had left her, still curled up tight and fast asleep. I put my hand on her shoulder and gave her a gentle shake.

'Do you propose to stay there all day, young lady? It's almost lunchtime,' I lied.

She stretched full length, rubbed her eyes with the backs of her hands, and then pushing both arms way above her head, yawned. The movement not only stretched and elongated her whole body but whilst doing so put a large proportion of her ample breasts on full display.

'Not on my own I don't. Care to join me?'

'I would love to but I have already been up a couple of hours and if you haven't forgotten, we have important work to do today, so out you get.'

'Work. Work,' she repeated. 'That's all I ever seem to hear from you. We have work to do. Let me tell you something? Normal sexy men do everything in their power to get a girl into bed; all you seem to do is try and get this one out. Well, if you want me out, pull me out!' sticking both arms out in my direction. I clasped each hand and gently pulled. With one continuous twisting motion she slid her legs from between the sheets and over the edge of the bed and as the bed covers fell away she stood up and wrapped both arms round my neck and squeezed up very close.

'You and work! "We have work to do",' she mimicked. 'Why can't you look upon me as work and do me?' Her lips pressed firmly against mine and her tongue began to wander.

Some considerable time later as we lay close together in a mass of crumpled bed linen and argued who should get out first I looked at Fred and said, 'Did you notice one of the first things you did when you first woke this morning?'

'No. What did I do? I remember you prodding me and having a crafty squeeze of my left one. Which was nice.'

'No not that! You rubbed your eyes with backs of your hands.'

'I've heard it.'

'Heard what?'

'The joke.'

'What joke?'

'You know damned well which joke. Don't try and kid me. Why do girls rub their eyes with the backs of their hands first thing in the morning? Answer; because they have no balls to scratch.'

'You have heard it then?' I said, grinning.

'Of course I have. It went all round the office months ago and who cares in any case when I have yours to scratch,' and, as she said that, I felt her nails begin to track slowly across tender skin. I pulled back sharply and pushed her away. 'Save it for later, darling, then you can scratch all you want but for now we must get up.'

We had missed breakfast, the dinning room having been cleared away ages ago, and so at a little after ten we were seated in a nearby cafe. Fred settled for a cup of coffee but I chose a bacon sandwich to go with mine. Probably a subconscious response to the earlier smells from the 'Tea Shack' or a more deep-seated need to keep up my strength. A man can burn up a lot of energy trying to persuade a girl to get out of bed whilst, at the same time, putting up little or no resistance to be being pulled in. Or was it that which took place after being pulling in which was wearing me down? A clever shrink would no doubt be able to provide some plausible explanation, but all I knew or cared about was the fact that I was in it for the sheer delight, and the fun, and that to me serious sex should always be fun.

'You had better call that number the Chief gave us yesterday and see what those people at Irton "thingy" have to say for themselves.'

'Irton Moor,' I corrected.

'Well, whatever it is, it might not be a bad idea to give them a ring about now.'

We left the cafe and walked to the nearest phone box and there I rang the number we had been given the previous evening. The other end rang several times before a strong voice snapped, 'Norton here.'

'Good morning,' I replied. 'My name is Grundy.'

'Ah yes, Mr Grundy,' he replied before I had time to add anything. 'I have been expecting your call. Your department has been in touch with us and provided all the necessary clearances. We will contact you, at your hotel, in the main bar, this lunchtime,' and with nothing further the phone went dead. I looked at the handset, scowled, and hung it up.

'What's the drill?' enquired Fred.

'I don't really know. A bloke called Morton or Norton, I think he said, says we will be contacted in the bar, back at the hotel, at lunchtime today. Nothing else. After that he rang off.'

'OK. So now I propose plan B.'

'Plan B. What is plan B?'

'Camper and camping gear: shopping time.'

The hotel receptionist proved to be more than helpful when we made enquiries about local firms who specialise in these things. She had a cousin, she told us, or someone, that owned one, or worked in one, and assured us we would get the best deal in town from them. So we went along to have a look for ourselves. The girl was right. The range was impressive and quite extensive. The one we finally selected, after much debate, was a small but compact camper and I felt confident it would suit our needs admirably. Fred was in no doubt. We worked out costs, left the length of time for hire open ended but paid for a full two weeks in advance. We filled in insurance forms and paid premiums. It came with a full tank of fuel and the agreement was that it should be returned with a full tank. If we needed to hire it for longer than the initial two weeks, all we had to do was ring in and the cost for the additional hire, up to several weeks more, would be covered by our substantial deposit. Everyone was very obliging and most helpful. We drove away having been given the directions we needed to take to find a shop that specialised in camping gear. I wondered if we were being sent to yet another cousin or friend of a friend.

'Does it matter as long as we get what we are looking for?' laughed Fred when I mentioned it.

Hiring a tent was no problem. A similar arrangement to the one we had just made for the camper… deposit, two weeks hire in advance and insurance. A very neat and smooth set-up or we could buy one outright.

'Buy one,' Insisted Fred. 'Then we don't have to concern ourselves about being over careful with it or if we should have to dump it.'

'Why should we have to dump it?' I asked, looking at the one in front of me and set out on display and thinking what a shame it would be to have to leave behind something as attractive as that.

'I don't know, do I? But for the amount involved just buy one.'

Although I must admit I was not too sure about her reasoning I decided to take her advice and so we set about selecting one for ultimate purchase. The

selection and purchase of all the other ancillary equipment proved to be more time consuming than I anticipated it would be. Partially due to the vast range available, but mainly due to Fred, who insisted that wherever possible, items for each of us should match. My protests over pure practicality were ignored and kicked well into touch.

'If we are to pose as a couple on holiday, then we match and I am very fussy who I camp with, what I wear, and how I look. Further more this is good quality gear that we are looking at, and propose buying, and will last for a long time after this job, I hope. So who knows how often I might get chance to use it in the future, so shut up and put those with the rest, over there.'

Turning to the assistant she continued, 'Do you have this type of sweater in pale blue and big enough to fit him?'

Two lightweight rucksack on aluminium frames just about completed the list and despite my comments and minor protests on the fact that we only had a small vehicle, I was once again told to keep quiet and load everything into the camper while the account was settled and the necessary receipts and guarantees obtained.

As we drove away, or more accurately, as Fred drove away and I sat securely belted up in the passenger seat, she looked at me and smiling said, 'I enjoyed that and what a choice. Now for food.'

'A good idea, I am starving,' I replied.

'Not for you, you nut. Food for camping and I suggest that I drop you off with all this camping gear, which you can sort out and unpack, while I go and find a local supermarket and stock us up with provisions for a day or two. That way you will also be around if and when that Norton fellow shows up.'

'Fine by me, but apart from unwrapping one or two items, this gear doesn't need much sorting out really.'

'Yes it does. Take all the clothing and put it all altogether in a plastic bag. The hotel should be able to provide you with one. Then, when I come back I will take it to a launderette and wash it through.'

'What's the idea of that? It's all brand new.'

'Exactly: so think about it sweetheart. Two seasoned walkers and campers all decked out in brand new gear. I thought the idea was to blend in and not to stick out like two tailor's dummies straight out of a C & A window.'

'Anything you say, boss,' I said trying not to show my admiration for her quick thinking and pure logic. She may say, what initially sounds to me like, some strange things, or things that at the time do not make instant sense, but she most certainly is not just a pretty face with a gorgeous desirable body and long legs. She is infinitely more than that and I was beginning to feel very close to her. I felt safe and very content with her. I had never worked with a female before but the more

it progressed, the more natural it began to feel and I was enjoying the feeling of having someone to share with, not to mention someone warm to cuddle.

It took longer than I expected to remove, from their respective wrappers, everything that Fred had so meticulously selected. There were bags, boxes, and plastic covers spread out all over the bed and on the floor. The small waste bin had quickly filled and it soon became necessary to stuff all the accumulated surplus wrapping and tape into one of the larger polythene bags. I also put aside one of the larger bags, which had previously held one of the two sleeping bags just purchased, to hold all those items of clothing, which Fred had suggested should be taken to the launderette.

I eventually finished and was thumbing through, and reading, selected passages from the instruction manual for the camper and the other assorted leaflets for the various other items, when Fred returned. She dropped the camper keys on the small side table and sat on the edge of the bed.

'I've parked the camper round the corner and down the side street and there is enough food in it now to see us properly fed for a day or two. What are you doing? Anything nice?'

'Reading the instructions. I thought that, as seasoned campers, we won't want to entertain the crowds on our arrival, with a display of stupidity should we not be able to open the bonnet or find a tap or light switch. Don't you agree?'

'I suppose you're right. We would look a bit daft if we had to ask someone to show us how to connect or change a gas bottle. Where is the gas bottle by the way?' she laughed.

'According to this,' I said waving the booklet. 'In a locker at the back and accessible from the outside and is there for safety or what have you. That's if there is a gas bottle in there to start with. Like I said, it is as well if we give it all a thorough going over before we set off anywhere. It might not be a bad idea if you have a quick thumb through this lot so that you are familiar with the layout and whereabouts of everything. By the way, was there anyone down in the bar, did you notice, when you came up just now?'

'I don't think so,' and she paused, screwing her eyes, to recollect. 'Not that I noticed, unless there was someone round a corner and out of sight.'

'Not to worry! I will pop down and see if that chap has turned up yet. Are you coming?'

'No, you go down and see if he's there. I will tidy up here and take this bag to the launderette. I passed one on the way back so I will see you later when I get back.'

'OK, see you,' I replied kissing her lightly on the forehead.

I went down into the bar to find it deserted. Not a single person, not even a member of staff behind the bar. I reached out and pressed the tiny bell push with the label, 'Please ring for Service'. Somewhere within I heard an almost inaudible

buzzing sound. Within a matter of seconds a smart young lady appeared and with a lovely smile enquired, 'Good afternoon Sir, can I help you?'

I turned on my own brand of charm that I reserve exclusively for the good-looking girls. This one certainly deserved it. 'Is it possible to have a coffee please?'

'Certainly sir! Is that just for one?'

Another big smile from me, 'It is unless you care to join me.'

She smiled back and looked prettier than ever. 'Sorry Sir, I have too much to do to join anyone at the moment. Perhaps the young lady staying with you might.' The smile turning into a mischievous grin as she picked up the wall mounted intercom phone and ordered, 'Coffee for one in the bar please.'

'Been busy so far this lunchtime?' I enquired as she fussed about and I felt a need to keep her engaged in conversation for as long as possible. I also liked the view she presented.

'No sir! You are my first customer this lunchtime. It is not a busy time of year but it should pick up in a week or two. I hope.'

I was about to add my feelings on the subject, not that I have any particular experience of seasonal hotel work; all I wanted to do was keep the conversation going in order to hold her there for as long as possible so that I was able to indulge in the pleasure of talking to a very pretty girl, when the bar door opened and a tall, well built, and very smartly dressed, guy entered. He glanced at me, gave me a friendly nod and smiling at the girl enquired, 'Have you a Mr Grundy, as a guest, staying here Miss? If so I would like to speak to him, if that is possible.'

'One moment Sir, I will find out.'

'No problem there sweetheart,' I interrupted and turning to the stranger, 'I am Grundy, can I help you?'

'My name is Norton, Motor Insurance Claims. Is there somewhere we might talk Sir?'

He seemed satisfied when I suggested an area away from the bar and one furnished with easy chairs and neatly tucked away in a bay window. I ordered another coffee before reluctantly leaving the charming young lady and as we settled down he casually remarked on the pleasantness of the day and in particular for the time of year. I casually showed him my ID card before he asked for it, which I assumed he would do and without deviating from our casual conversation he withdrew his from an inside pocket and held it up for my inspection. Both satisfied we continued the casual, irrelevant conversation until the coffee arrived and was handed out by the young lady.

As she bent forward to pour, I surreptitiously admired her bum and the tell tale outline of her knickers, whilst studying, at the same time, the chap sat opposite. Not an easy task, the bum kept winning. When she turned to face me and hand me my coffee cup, the deep cleavage brought everything to a standstill.

The delightful distraction, sadly, finally withdrew and disappeared out of sight.

Norton, besides being what one might describe as being thick set, did not appear so tall when sat down, but he looked fit and neatly turned out. His voice, for his size, was quiet and I detected a very slight Scots accent behind it. He reopened the conversation. 'Sorry about the insurance bit but I have used it over the years and have found it a good way to approach strangers without arousing curiosity from anyone who happens to overhear. Now Mr Grundy to the serious reasons why I am here,' he said, purposely looking about himself as if double-checking that we were not being overheard. 'It appears you have a fairly high security clearance with our Department, and I am instructed to assist you in anyway that I can. That is, up to the level of my clearance. Should you need to go beyond that, then it will have to be channelled though your Chief and mine. I'm sure you understand? I don't need to know why you want anything. That is your business, mine is to supply it, as long as it is within my terms of reference. Now how can I help you?'

'Easily I hope. Would it be possible for me to obtain a recording, that is a cassette tape recording, of all VHF and FM transmissions made in this region for a period from eight o'clock Thursday evening, the fifteenth of April last, until eight o'clock the following morning?'

'That should be no problem. Is that all you need?'

'For the moment, I think so, yes. I am collating a few items, of what I believe might be useful information, to form a picture in order to make a start on an investigation. These are still early days and as yet I have no detailed plans. There maybe other things later but for the moment that will do fine for a start.'

He produced a small note pad and pen from his inside pocket, made a note, replaced them, drained his coffee cup and put it back on it's saucer, stood up and offered his hand. We shook hands. 'You will receive your tape by special messenger early this evening. If you require anything further, you still have our contact number.'

'I have, and thank you for your cooperation.'

'My pleasure,' came the reply and almost before I realised it, he was on his way out of the bar. The coffee went on my tab.

I went back upstairs and let myself into the room. It was empty. I stretched out on the bed and began to think things through. How far had we got so far? Very difficult to tell, so what did we know? Not a lot. What do we do next? Wait for the tape was one of the conclusions I reached as I drifted off and finally fell asleep.

I regained consciousness as I became aware of someone or something touching a very intimate part of my anatomy, a pleasant sensation. I was just about to open one eye and assure myself that I had not attracted an undesirable, for I have heard that some hotels employ people of different tastes and preferences to those

which I find attractive, when a very familiar female voice quipped, 'I am pleased to see that I am not the only one who likes bed, around here.'

'Sorry,' I said lamely. 'I did not intend to doze off. It just happened, anyhow I am on the bed, not in it.'

'What's the difference? Have you ever heard me complain about being in it, or on it? Move over then you can tell me how you got on with that chap from Irton "do-dar."' That's if he came?'

She settled along side me and lightly held my hand.

'Norton himself came. He's an ordinary sort of guy. Doesn't give much away about either himself, or his set up. Just introduced himself and said he was under instructions to cooperate, within his overall sphere of responsibility.'

'So did we get anything from him or not?'

'Yes and no.'

'Yes and no! That tells me a lot. What do you mean? Yes and no.'

'Well I asked him for the tape recording and he made a note, said it would come by special delivery, and left.'

'And has it?'

'No. Not yet. Early this evening he said. That is the "no" bit to your - have we got anything.'

'So what's next?'

'To wait, I suppose. In the meantime, let's sort out this camper, read up on it and check to make sure we know where everything is, and how it all works, and also check and make sure we have got everything else we think we might need.'

By the time we were satisfied we knew more or less where everything was, how it all worked and where everything was stowed, it was time for dinner.

We were half way through our meal when the waiter came over to inform me that there was a man in reception, who would like to speak to me. I left the table and went out of the dinning room. In reception I found myself confronted by an unobtrusive fellow who politely enquired if he was addressing a Mr Grundy. When I assured him he was, he equally politely enquired if I was in a position to prove it to him. He seemed satisfied when I showed him my open wallet and warrant card. Then taking a package from his coat pocket, handed it to me, and raising a clipboard, which he had been holding in his left hand, asked me to sign, indicating the spot where I was to do so with his index finger.

'Just there Sir, if you would. Formality you understand?'

I nodded.

I took hold of the board and looking at it saw that I was signing for 'One cassette tape recording entitled, VHF Procedure for Beginners.' Without a further word he took the board back and with a nod of his head, left. Picking up the packet from the reception desk where it had been laid aside, I returned to the dinning room and sat down again at our table.

'Was that it or should I say, is that it? The tape?' asked Fred.

'Yes, it's all in there,' I replied, pointing at the packet on the table by my plate. 'Tonight's entertainment for two consenting adults.'

'Goody. I hope its really "iffy" and there are some suggestions for different positions on it that I don't already know about. That is if it is truly for an evenings entertainment and meant for adult listening only.'

'I am positive it is for adult listening only. But I doubt if you will learn anything along the lines on which you're thinking, but it might be all you get this evening.'

'In that case I can think of lots of other things I would rather do this evening than listen to a boring old tape!'

'I bet you can, but aren't you forgetting your priorities once again, my dear.'

'Remember what happened the last time you harped on about priorities and "the job" and all that who-ha?'

'Yes I do and it was all very nice, but this time, believe it or not, I am referring to "the job" as being that part of your exciting life for which you get paid.'

'I get paid for everything, absolutely everything. I'm on a salary after all, aren't you? Don't tell me you're paid by the hour, and only receive pay when actually working on the job. You are the same as me my darling, paid for twenty four hours a day, seven days a week, including sleeping time and everything else,' she laughed.

'So, you're telling me that you get paid for everything. Sleeping, eating and bonking?'

'Yes, if you like. Eh! Does that make me a lady of pleasure? No it can't do, as sleeping and eating etcetera don't happen to be part of my contract of employment so I don't have to do them, do I? So if I do, then it has to be voluntary and must be done in my break time,' she said laughing.

'Well, if my experiences are anything to go by, you take some pretty long and lovely breaks and really enjoy your well paid leisure time and you can call yourself what you like for me. A lady of leisure or pleasure! Either way you will do for me.'

'Well a girl does need her relaxation, paid or unpaid and some more than others. But we had better drop the subject for now don't you think. If anyone overhears they will think I am a nymphomaniac who not only enjoys it but needs it and gets paid for it as well.'

I whispered, 'Are you?'

She stopped eating and looked straight at me, 'Am I what?'

'A well paid nympho?'

She grinned and hissed back at me, 'No I'm bloody well not! As far as I know a nympho must have it all the time and can't control the need for it, and will go to great lengths to get it anywhere, anytime and from anyone. The only thing I have in common with a nympho, if you dare to make any comparison, is that I like it; but I can certainly control it, and am bloody fussy where I get it mate and don't you forget it.'

'Right. So from now on then, to keep the two apart, we will refer to the job as being that time during which you are under contract and we are engaged in solving a problem. The bonking will be simply bonking, paid, or otherwise and nymphomania will not be a consideration. So tonight it's the tape and the contract of employment bit.'

'Followed by a break or several breaks for whatever.'

'What if poor Percy can't take the strain?'

'He will have to be persuaded to or be prepared to have his contract of employment cancelled and be replaced.'

I gave up.

CHAPTER FIFTEEN

We both sat in the front seats of the camper, which, as Fred noted at the time we hired it, was conveniently fitted with a radio cassette player. My legs were stiff and my back ached from sitting in the cramped and confined space for so long.

'Play it again. It just doesn't make sense, does it?' she said.

She was of course right and I knew it. We had run and listened to the tape twice and it just did not make any sense at all. Twelve hours of radio transmissions condensed down into one hours' playing time, was just too much to comprehend. I think the first thing that started to dawn on me was the fact that there was so much traffic on the airwaves at any one time. The silence periods had been eliminated from the recording in order to condense the overall running time, for the tape, down to about one hour. The result was an almost continuous babble of messages going back and forth in a variety of languages, with no indication as to what channel or frequency had been used in each case. It was impossible to extract anything that we recognised or which immediately made sense.

'This is just not going to work Mel. There is just too much traffic, at any one time, to know who is talking to who or why or anything. You will have to go back to Norton and ask if it can be broken down and presented in some other, easier to understand, way.'

'Pity because I was hoping we were leaving here tomorrow and heading back north. I wish I knew if this tape would really tell us something or, at least, show us if we are on to something or if it is all a wild goose chase and there really is nothing to be found. But this lot is as clear as mud and tells us nothing.'

'Let's call it a day. I have had enough. Call Norton in the morning and see what else we can get. Come on, lock this thing up, and let's go in. I will treat you to a well deserved drink.'

The following day I rang Norton from reception and, at his request went out to a phone box and rang him again. He apologised when I finally got through to him, explaining to me that he had no idea beforehand what I might ask him. Therefore an outside phone box was more secure than the hotel switchboard, which he gathered I was going through when I used their internal phone. I told him I fully understood his concern and that to be double sure, I would avoid using direct references to anything specific as I spoke to him there and then. He said that he appreciated my extra caution. I didn't quite see the point of it all but then he was making the rules. I therefore only referred to an extension of yesterday's conversation, and that which we discussed at our last meeting. He sounded delighted.

'Too much to unravel.' he repeated as we progressed.

'Yes. Can you help and break it down?'

'Of course, that is our job. Leave it to me. We will run it through our machine. It will take about an hour and a half I guess. Same delivery method, same place and about the same time.' Then, without warning, I was left holding a telephone which had gone dead having been cut off at the other end. This man did not waste time or words.

'How did you go on?' enquired Fred as soon as I got back.

'He is not a man to mess about or waste time or bandy words, and he is ultra cautious. He seemed to know exactly what I wanted and will deliver it in an hour and a half. Do you know something Fred, he is so super efficient and so much on the ball that, I hate to say it but, it crossed my mind on the way back up here just now, that this Norton may have been taking the piss when he gave us that tape recording, knowing all the time it was probably no bloody good to us but was what we asked for.'

'Maybe, but like you say he did give you what you asked for and you know perfectly well that personal interpretations of instructions or requests are taboo and never appreciated. When asked, you give down to the last letter exactly what you are asked for. Nothing more, nothing less, you know the rules.'

'Yes, I know the rules and the form and I suppose you are right. What are you doing now?' I asked as I noticed she looked as if she was preparing to go out.

'If we have an hour, or so, to wait; then I propose going into town to pick up a few things. Coming?'

'No, not if you don't mind. I will go and run this tape through once again, unless you propose to take the camper into town?'

'No, I was going to walk. I am not going far and you can waste too much time looking for parking places. It will be much quicker on foot.'

'OK, I will have one more go at this tape, then get back in here and be ready when the delivery man comes.'

The tape finished and clicked to a stop and I was forced to admit that I was still no wiser. I still did not know what I had hoped to hear, or what the damned thing might tell me, apart from the obvious, nothing. I thought there might have been the slim chance that I might have been able to pick out if our Coastguard friend Edison had used a radio or received any messages just before he went missing. Not knowing, and therefore not being able to recognise, his voice didn't help, but I was hoping I might pick up direct references such as the use of specific call signs that might have identified him. There were none, none that is, that I could recognise from the jumbled mass, that made up the tape recording.

Back in the hotel room, I sat with the tape in my hand and racked my brain as I carefully tried to go over everything I had heard. I could recall nothing, just a mass, just a jumble and as far as I was concerned, a total waste of time. I was

still trying to convince myself that it had been a good idea asking for the tape and that we had to start somewhere, when the phone on the bedside table rang. When I answered it, it was to be told that there was a gentleman in reception asking to speak to me, could I please go down and see him.

It was a different messenger from the one the day before. As I approached him he held out a large manila envelope. 'I was told to hand this to your personally Sir.'

'No ID required, or any clip boards to be signed?' I enquired.

'No sir! No longer necessary, now that we know you. One of our men has ID you and we have your signature and a random selection of your fingerprints from the clipboard. That is all we need for our records along with the picture a colleague took of you both yesterday. It not only saves time Sir, but it makes our meetings appear all the more natural to the casual outside observer.'

'You crafty bastards,' I thought to myself, but instead replied. 'Thank you.' He smiled and leaving me holding the envelope, walked out of the front door and like his colleagues before him, disappeared.

I rushed back upstairs and once inside the room, stopped and looked very carefully at the package before I broke the seals. I have had some bad experiences with packets, or to be more precise, a particular close friend of mine had and I have heard of many others beside him. I wondered if my fingers were still sensitive but above all if I could remember the drill. I hoped I could as the slightest slip could, and in the past had, had devastating effects. I decided that this packet, about which I had no undue concern, but then neither had my friend and that is how he came to grief, would be ideal to practice on. I was alone, not pushed for time and not expecting Fred back at that moment so the opportunity was ideal.

The opportunity to practice and if I was truly honest, the opportunity to play a little, was too good to miss.

I gingerly ran my fingers over the outer wrapping, turned it over, and repeated the exercise. I could feel nothing. So I broke the seal and very carefully lifted the flap. Only the ends of a sheaf of papers were visible, so far so good. Then using my finger and thumb, I carefully drew out the thick wad of computer 'print out' sheets. This could be a dodgy time for now there was no envelope holding them tightly together. Immediately the wad was clear of the envelope I turned away and dropped onto the floor pulling my hand clear. Nothing happened. Not that I expected anything to, and the only noise in the room came from my own heavy breathing. The pages had not been holding down any form of spring-loaded device that might trigger off something else. I pulled myself back up and whilst still on my knees moved slowly round the table examining closely the edges of the pile. It had not changed shape, another telltale sign. I stood up and picking up the envelope checked to ensure that it was empty. Satisfied I tossed it on the bed. I was about to start work on the thick wad of paper when the door opened and in breezed

Fred. She placed several small plastic carrier bags and packages on the foot of the bed, unzipped her anorak, removed it, and laid it alongside the other things.

'What are you doing?'

'Checking my Parcel Bomb skills. Just messing about really.'

'Over reacting I hope or have you gone cuckoo…? Hell it's not, is it Mel? You don't think? Not for real? You're kidding. Who brought it? The same chap as yesterday?'

'No it's not a bomb, you duck egg, or it's not so far. But now look who's over-reacting, as you put it, not me, although I had every right to.'

'Look I'm sorry but when you mentioned it, for one horrible moment, I just thought…' and she let it trail off. 'But what's all that about you having every right to over-react?'

'Look just settle down and I will explain. First of all I had no reason to think it was a bomb and still don't. All I was doing was using this packet to practice on and the reason that brought it all on in the first place was the fact that I had nothing better to do and it was the actual packet as I held it that brought back the memory of a good friend that made me think about doing it. You see, ever since this friend of mine, and a damned good agent too, lost most of his fingers I have had a thing about parcels from unknown sources. Loosing fingers, though very nasty, may not in itself' be fatal, but the poisoned metal slivers that ended up in his face and neck were. Call it over reacting if you like. He didn't expect anything to happen and so didn't react, and as a result he died. I don't expect anything, but like I said there is no harm in not taking any chances and I am only practising and that way I might live a little longer. So if you don't mind I have started, so I will finish. Haven't I heard that expression used somewhere before. I seem to think that at sometime it was someone's catch phrase or some such thing. Anyhow that's not important.'

She came over and standing close beside me, whispered, 'Sorry sweetheart, don't get upset, how far have you got?'

'I am about to check if anything has been removed or inserted in the centre. The worst part is over as most letter bombs, as you well know detonate when removed from the restrictions of the envelope or outer wrapping. This is a thick wad and may still be heavy enough to hold down a snap trigger. But listen at me, lecturing you when you know all about it.'

She kissed me on the cheek, 'Keep going then. Your demonstration professor.'

I lightly ran my fingers over the surface feeling very gently for the tell tale signs, which are usually there, if anything has been inserted or removed. A typical method used in the manufacture of packet or letter bombs, as they are usually referred to, is to cut away the centre pages to form a cavity large enough to contain the explosive device. These devices are extremely difficult to manufacture so that

they lay perfectly flat, the trigger being the main problem. Therefore, no amount of skill can remove exactly the correct amount of paper without leaving some tell tale bump or hollow.

I moved my fingers lightly over the whole surface, until I satisfied myself that as far as I could tell, everything was in order. My next move was to slide the whole thing to the edge of the table and grip it firmly between finger and thumb. I then pulled the whole block gentle over the outer edge of the table until with a very gentle tilt I could secure the opposite end of the pile with my free hand. This accomplished, I turned the whole thing over and once again laid it gently on the flat surface. I then repeated the touch exercise with my fingertips over the whole of the reverse side.

'Happy?' asked Fred as I drew back and straightened up.

'Yes, I think so. As far as I can tell, it has not been interfered with, want to check it out yourself?'

'Not particularly, not if there is nothing to find and you are only playing games, but let me show you a trick I learnt. It is a speciality and favourite with us girls. You may already know it.'

'Try me. If not I am always willing to learn.'

It took her several seconds to rummage in her handbag and produce a small reel of cotton from which she broke a length of about two feet.

'You see why it is a favourite with us girls. How many men do you know who carry cotton as standard equipment? Now let's see?'

I stepped to one side and Fred took the length of cotton and holding it taught, used it to split the pile of paper about a third of the way down its thickness. She continued to move the cotton slowly from side to side in a sawing motion and very slowly and very gently made it pass through the pile of paper until having passed right through, it stopped at the fold in the computer paper at the far edge. She then reversed the movement until the cotton came back out at the point at which it first went in.

'Nothing there! Now let's try again and a bit lower down this time.'

She repeated the process until once again the cotton came free.

'That's a smashing method,' she said. 'To use on a pile of paper, such as this, or a book where the covers are stiff and finger tips might not pick out hollows and such like. You can feel and sense the slightest obstruction and as long as you don't go at it like a bull in a china shop, you shouldn't trigger anything. Anyhow, for the benefit of your exercise, I think this lot is safe, so now what after all this paranoia and your attempt to frighten me to death? When I came in and saw what you were doing you had me planning to soak it in the bath, or put it carefully back in the envelope and throw it in the sea, or take it away to some waste ground and set it on fire. I didn't realise it but just look what you have done to me, my hands are shaking like a leaf now, so let's dispense with all these dramatics and settle

down and have a look at what we have actually got here. What's the matter with you now? You're sat there looking as if you have just seen a ghost or something?'

'Sorry love! Just thinking of my pal who got in the way of one of those bloody things.'

'Were you close, was he a special pal? Did you know him well?'

'Yes, we trained together. It was a long time ago and such a long way away.'

'Your a bit of a softy deep down, aren't you?' as she wrapped her arms round mine and gave me a light kiss on the cheek.

'No. Not a softy. Well I hope not. Sentimental if you like. It's just that I just happen to like people and feel for them, particularly when things don't seem to be going right for them.'

'Then why on earth do you do this type of work if things like that get to you?'

'I don't honestly know and quite often I ask myself that very same question. I suppose it has a lot to do with my deep-seated affection for people, my misguided sense of decency and my resentment at all the evil in this rotten world. But just listen to me, it's a job that I got dragged into and I suppose I do it for the money although that is precious little. Anyhow we've had this conversation before and I seem to recollect promising you that one day if you had a week or two to spare I might attempt to tell you, but not now. Let's get on, where were we?'

She kissed me again on the cheek and whispered, 'Softy,' before reaching across and grasping the pad of computer print out sheets. 'Now, having satisfied ourselves that this lot is safe and there are no hidden nasty things in it, let's look and see that we have.'

She began to slowly turn the sheets, one by one. I looked over her shoulder studying each in turn as she did so.

From the start, it became obvious that this was a vast improvement over the previous information that we had been given on the tape recording. The layout was simple and straightforward and once we recognised the format was easy to follow. The information was laid out in columns which ran vertically and showed in chronological order from left to right, date, time, channel transmitted on, channel received on, language used, identifying call sign, transcript of message sent, and finally a transcript of any reply sent back. This was first class. If a vessel or shore station transmitted, it was identifiable by the call sign it used and the station they wished to talk to, by the call sign they called. Further down the column was a reverse of these call signs, which easily identified the reply. If the station transmitting was initiating the call and with it asking a question it appeared in the left hand column, but if it was in reply to a question already asked, then it was in the right hand transmission column. If part of any reply included a further

question, then the transmission was split into two and the appropriate parts printed side by side in their respective columns.

Although very easy to follow once one got the hang of it, after only a comparatively short period of time, running down column after column became very boring and repetitive, due to a distinct lack of stimulation, from what can only be described as very mundane and mostly routine marine radio traffic. I found myself simply reading 'message sent', 'message received' with my brain not even attempting to tie anything up other than that which was so very obvious. I never realised that there were so many bored watch keepers, who spent their evenings and a large part of the night filling the airwaves with verbal diarrhoea, an epitaph to good radio procedure and bored seamen. I also found it rather surprising to note that the print out followed faithfully what exactly had been said even down to, in many cases, dialect. I tried to concentrate and continued to read, 'Thu there 'arry?'

'I' that thee, Mick?'

'Caught owt? Ower.'

'Nowe, ower.'

'Job's knackered like I teld our lass. Knackered. Ower.'

'Right yer be. Gone me, ower.'

'What's weather for temorra?'

'Better than now I hope. Av'ny 'erd. Ower.'

'Al give Coastguard a shout an see what ees got, ower.'

'Right ya be gone me. Ower.' And so it went on page after page as bored skippers and watch keepers filled in their time.

Part way down the next page, and in the next column, and indicated as a transmission on Channel Sixteen, 'What's witha fo' Int' mornin Coastguard?'

Below that and again on Channel Sixteen, 'Station calling Coastguard, call again and identify. This is Humber Coastguard listening on Channel Sixteen. Over.'

And so it went on; page after page.

'This is going to take a long time so I suggest we settle down and start again and go through it slowly and very carefully, otherwise I have a strong feeling we, or more than likely me, will begin to miss even the obvious. So let's clear this table,' I suggested, pointing to the one set against the wall and slightly larger than the one we were using at that moment. 'Then let's get something to drink before we settle down for a long hard, dreary slog.'

The table cleared, coffee, hot milk and cups brought in from downstairs, we drew up two chairs and, sitting side by side, started once again from the beginning.

'What are we looking for and hoping to find. If that is not a silly and obvious question?' gently enquired Fred.

'It's not as silly as you think because I honestly don't know, other than that we are looking for any clues or anything that might relate to Edison. For example did he speak to anyone? Did anyone contact him? Did any other two people speak about him or make reference to him? Anything, however obscure, that passed over the air waves that night, that might give us a lead.'

'Like what?'

'Like I don't know, so please, dear lady, just read. See what you can find.'

We looked carefully at page after page. The coffee was long gone and the cups stood empty.

'Hell. How long is this going to take? Have you finished this page yet?' I said as I lent back in my chair and stretched.

'Just about! Damn it, let's stop and take a walk or a break or something before I collapse and fall asleep forever. This is never ending and so boring it's nearly driving me mad. You found anything yet?'

'If I had my darling, you would be the first to know,' and I pecked her on the cheek as she too yawned and stretched.

'Come on! Let's take that walk while we are still sane. We might then get lucky, but for the moment, we have more chance of finding a needle in a haystack.'

We walked slowly along the promenade in the fresh air. Fred insisted on a Hot Dog and not satisfied with that, then badgered me into buying her, what must have been, the largest ice cream cone I have ever seen? I settled for a humble Hot Dog with extra onions and a generous squirt of mustard sauce.

For a few glorious moments I felt like a holiday maker and wished I was, for 'the job' we were supposed to be involved in was getting me down and seemed, at that particular point, to be hopeless. We desperately needed a break, a small clue that would allow us to make some progress. Perhaps later we might get lucky. But for the moment I resolved to savour my Hot Dog.

* * *

Fred flatly refused to discuss it any further or have anything more to do with it that night as she claimed we needed a rest and were probably the victims of trying too hard and had allowed wishful thinking and over enthusiasm to over ride the necessity for diligence and patience. She claimed that bed was the best possible cure and that cuddling up to her would give me all the inspiration I needed.

I enjoyed the cuddle, had no flashes of inspiration at the time, nor did I get any clues from further close examination of the printouts later. We finally, and very reluctantly, decided that if there were any clues hidden away in there we had insufficient background knowledge to spot them. Fred insisted that it had been

worth the try, but I suspected that she only said that to be kind to me rather than to tell the truth and admit it had all been rather a waste of time.

CHAPTER SIXTEEN

We had stowed our uniforms and official clothing in the boot of my car. Then, along with the company car, had locked both vehicles away safely in the private garages attached to Humber Coastguard. We had tied up all the loose ends at the Hotel and were heading North in the hired camper. This was the first time Fred had driven it any distance and she was thoroughly enjoying the experience. She quickly familiarised herself with the layout and what the vehicle was capable of doing and the overall size seemed to present no problem.

Our initial plan, when we got there, was to blend into the local scenery as neatly as we could, as two ordinary walking, hiking, and camping-type tourists.

As we drove along I looked at Fred. She looked as gorgeous as ever despite being wrapped in clothing that was designed to almost envelop her and make her look every inch the seasoned, long distance walker. She had selected a rolled neck sweater to go with the thick cord trousers and had tied back her hair to form a small pony tail which allowed not only me, but the whole world, to see her full face and left me wondering which way I actually preferred it. As I studied her face and features, I decided that she was not perfect but by that did not mean to be unkind for she was as near perfect as I was going to get. But I believe that words like perfect and perfection can never be applied to human beings. We are all far from perfect yet each one of us has something which others will find unshakeably attractive. I don't feel comfortable with words like Animal Magnetism, Opposite Attraction, and similar expressions that one hears banded about perhaps because I don't fully understand them. A large dollop of sex appeal will do for me and Fred certainly had a very large helping of that and nothing could hide it or detract from it. Even the walking boots, that she initial turned her nose up at, and the bulky clothing she now wore and which was, without doubt, a complete contrast to the tight fitting, contour clinging trousers and Tee shirts which I had admired so much before, did nothing to detract from her overall appeal. As I looked at her, sat behind the wheel of the camper and obviously enjoying herself so much, I could not help wondering where some of the wonderful rounded, soft and tantalising, curves and bumps had disappeared to. They were still there somewhere underneath of course. Yet despite the 'somewhat padded out' appearance she still looked very attractive, exceptionally smart, and as neat as ever. The more I thought about it, the more I came to the conclusion that you could put that girl in a sack or a black plastic bin liner and she would still look devastating. Some girls naturally have it, while some sadly are not so lucky. Fred had above her fair share, and although I am sure she knew it, she never played on it or flaunted it and was never anything other than the

loveable, cuddly, and desirable Fred. Sod it; if she wasn't perfect then she came that damned close it made no difference.

I found myself comparing her with the many other women who have passed through my life, some of them only fleetingly while others have passed my way with devastating effects and have left long lasting memories and emotional scars. I thought mainly of the girls I had known who had 'it'. However, and in whichever way, you choose to define 'it'; most of them seemed to know or be very aware of the fact that they thought they had 'it' and wanted you, and everyone else to know, that they knew or thought, they had 'it' and so behaved in the way which they believed to be appropriate. They behaved like prima donnas and gave public performances where they would try, in their beliefs, to show off what they often misguidedly thought were their best attributes and which made them exceptional. Looking back I realised that many of them let themselves down very badly and were little more than bimbo's and I am now quite happy to give all those types a very wide berth. I can't handle a girl who wants the whole world to know that she considers herself to be exceptionally good looking, sexy and available. Nice to look at, good to flirt with, and at times a nice distraction and someone to be with for a limited period perhaps, but certainly not to get involved with and certainly not, in my opinion, the type to be even considered for any form of long term relationship.

There was no comparison between Fred and any of them. Fred was a natural and simply had everything and could handle it and made no effort at being anything other than her natural gorgeous self.

'Are you nodding off?' she laughed. 'Are the new big boots too heavy for macho man and making you tired? You're supposed to be the navigator, on this trip don't forget. It's a good job I have a rough idea of where we're going.'

'No, I wasn't. I was just thinking.'

'Thinking about what?'

'Nothing.'

'How can you think about nothing?'

'If you really must know I was thinking about you.'

'And were they nice thoughts? I hope so. It's an offence not to think nice things about me, particularly when in my company. Do you know that?'

'They were very nice indeed.'

'Good, shall I pull over and park up and you can tell me all about them?'

'Yes, you can if you want, but only to concentrate all of our collective thoughts on food and not just on you.'

'Spoil sport and I was hoping to hear something rather lovely when all you can think about is your stomach.'

We parked in a small lay-by that was little more than a cut out on the side of the main road and sat and devoured our simple and quickly prepared sandwiches.

'I think I am going to enjoy this camping. It's so neat and cosy in here and perfect for two people with nice thoughts and basically only one thing in mind.'

'Not so fast young lady! Sadly on this trip we have to have more than one thing in mind, but I do agree, it is very cosy in here and has great potential, but for what I think you have in mind, right now, would not be very practical. This table, for one thing, takes up most of the room and the rest of the space is littered with all our clobber.'

'You could always have me over the table.'

'I could and would very much like that but firstly I doubt if it would be strong enough to take even your delicate weight and secondly you might get crumbs, from the sandwiches, in the important bits and if that's not all, I shudder to think what passing motorist might think seeing a table used for what it was not originally designed for.'

'Sorry, just an offer, and it was there if you wanted it. Have you finished? If you have had enough, food that is then let's be off. I'll drive again and you can sit and look intelligently at the map and think of nothing until you manage to nod off.'

Ever tried thinking of nothing? It's impossible. For if there is nothing in your mind; if it is blank, then you cannot be thinking. To think, there has to be some activity in the brain and that very activity is the process of thinking. Now daydreaming is something else. That is a process of uncontrolled random thinking where the mind is not in anyway consciously controlled but is allowed to wander. I find it a very enjoyable pastime and very relaxing and an excellent way to pass the time. You can select your own subjects and if you feel a need for conversation you can also select questions and then provide the answers you want to hear.

'Nodding off again darling and so soon? Am I so uninteresting? Talk to me, for goodness sake, before I die from boredom.'

'Sorry, I don't mean to be rude. I think it's because, for the first time for so long, I feel really relaxed out here in all this open air and lovely countryside. All these rolling hills and the moors and the sea way out over there on that side. I just feel great.'

'And how much of it have you actually seen? For the last few miles you have done far more snoring than looking.'

'Sorry. Would you like me to give you a break and I will drive for a while. It would at least give you the chance to look around and admire the views. There is so much to see and it really is lovely. Pull over the first chance you get and let's change places. I promise I won't say a word if you relax and nod off. It might do you good to have a rest and a bit of a break.'

* * *

There was little traffic on the road and shortly after changing places and some small talk, Fred quietly dozed off and slept for the remainder of the journey. It was only when I pulled up outside a Pub that she shook herself awake and passed some sleepy remark about how she now understood how easy it was to drift off without realising it was happening. I smiled and climbed out from behind the wheel. My backside was numb from lack of exercise and the miles of uneven country road surfaces.

The Pub was the one we had previously noted and selected from the map and which we hoped would prove to be a convenient and potential stopping off point from where to get our bearings and then if necessary readjust and move. It was situated down and at the end of a long, lonely lane. To reach it, it had been necessary to turn off, to our right, from the main road, the road that had we followed it would have taken us through the village and further north, running roughly parallel to the coastline. We were to discover, some short time later, that the Pub, deceptive as shown on the map, was approximately half way between the main road the actual cliff top with the sea below it. When I had turned off the main road and entered the approach road to the pub it had got progressively narrower until it became almost single file. There were no houses or farm buildings beyond the outskirts of the village and the open road finally terminated in a small car park, just off to the right at the top of a gully, that we would also learn led, via a track, down to the sea. It was opposite this car park and also at the head of the gully that the large substantial and stone-built Pub, with its random selection of outbuildings, stood.

Whether the Pub had originally been built, as a Pub was very difficult to tell from the outside, some of the outbuildings had a definite farm-building look about them. But built to serve as a pub or not it all certainly looked very impressive and very much the picture post-card rural countryside hostelry. Built into its natural stone and weather-beaten walls were very old windows and doorframes, complete with stained and weather worn solid oak doors. There were large stone slates on the steep roof and tall, solid looking chimneystacks stuck up into the sky. Attached to the main building and built of matching materials and looking equally as substantial, and old, were several small outhouses and other utility constructions. They may well have been built originally as farm buildings but their present use, as we were to discover later, was mainly for storage areas and one, the most substantial, turned out to be toilets.

On the seaward side this whole group of buildings were completely surrounded by woodland that increased in density as it progressed down the sides of the gully towards the sea. On the opposite side, that is to say, on the landward side the trees had been cleared away, long ago, to accommodate the Pub, its outbuildings, a visitors' car park and a camping field that was adjacent to the Pub and across the access road from the car park. Entry to this field was through

a large farm gate to which was attached a sign which said, 'Camping. Tents and Light Tourers. No Static Caravans or Permanent Dwellings. By order of North York Moors National Park. All enquiries at the Public House'. This pleasant little camping area, which the field provided, was surrounded by a dry stonewall and screened by trees on the two sides furthest away from the road and Pub. It had its access through the afore-mentioned gate in the corner immediately to the left as one stood facing the main building.

Beyond the screen of trees which I estimated to be about thirty to forty yards deep it was possible to see fields and open ground that went all the way back to the outskirts of the village. I guessed, and a glance at the map later confirmed, that it was some half-mile, or just slightly more, away. I imagined the overall area to be a very lonely and isolated spot, especially so in winter when I guessed there would be substantial amounts of snow, laid, for long periods, on the ground and in the surrounding woodlands.

I looked over the gate into the designated camping area. At first glance it looked as if it might accommodate anything up to about fifty tents in comparative comfort and without being in any way over crowded. At that particular moment there were only three and they were all pitched under the lea of the boundary wall that backed onto the road. To the right of where I stood there was the largest of the stone built outhouses with a sign attached to one of its walls that stated 'Toilets and Fresh Drinking Water'.

Turning, Fred slipped her hand in mine and gently pulled me towards the main Pub entrance. As we made our way across the open ground and in the direction of the front door, Fred raised our two clasped hands and with a radiant smile said, 'This is because we are supposed to be lovers, remember?'

'No. Holiday makers.'

'Spoilsport. If we can't be lovers, will you settle for randy campers instead then?'

'Yes, if you promise not to tell,' I laughed.

'I promise.'

Looking at her, the smile on her face and the swept back pony tail created a very cheeky look and I don't know why, but she did seem to be taller despite the flat walking boots. However the look in her eye was enough to make me realise that I had little or no chance of influencing or altering anything she had in mind.

The narrow plastic sign mounted on the transom above the front door and main entrance, declared that one 'James Lacey was licensed to sell, for consumption on or off the premises, intoxicating liquor'. The large swinging sign above had a picture painted on either side of a large bunch of black grapes to illustrate the name of the Pub, which was simply called 'The Grapes'.

The outer door was open and fastened back while the inner one was closed; but it opened when Fred depressed the highly polished brass latch. On entering we

were immediately met by that unmistakable and unique Pub aroma that is common to all old and well established, licensed premises. A mixture of stale ale and dead tobacco smoke in about equal proportions. No amount of care and cleanliness can totally eradicate that smell and this establishment was no exception. To add to this unique, and not totally unacceptable, aroma was a whiff of a wood or peat fire and, perhaps because of the time of day, there was also drifting towards us a variety of pleasant, but indistinguishable, cooking smells from an unseen kitchen.

On looking around it was easy to see that these and many other similar smells had been soaking into the very fabric of the building for many hundreds of years. The internal floors were of well-worn stone slabs with all the walls wood panelled and the ceilings low and oak beamed. The whole interior was warmed and made very cosy by two large open fires, one in the room that served as the lounge bar and the other in the dining room. Perhaps at one time these had originally been two separate rooms but since then had had a large proportion of the dividing walls removed to, more or less, make one large fairly open area with a fireplace set in opposite corners. What now distinguished the two separate sections was the fact that to the right of the front entrance, and facing back towards it, was a well equipped bar and dispensing area. There were bench seats around the walls and freestanding copper-topped tables with upholstered stools set round them. To the left of the entrance the area was equipped with larger tables each covered with a white linen tablecloth and set out with cutlery and place settings to seat four people. At each place a high backed, highly polished, Windsor chair completed the arrangement. Everything matched and blended in perfectly with the great age, atmosphere, and surroundings.

'Seen this?' asked Fred who had drifted over towards the fireplace on the right.

'Seen what?' I asked as I moved up behind her and from a position where I could see over her shoulder, looked at a small polished copper plaque. Though now well worn from years of polishing it was still possible to read. It said, 'Originally built early Sixteenth Century. Rebuilt, on the same site, after having been intentionally set on fire by Customs men and extensively damaged, Seventeen Forty Two'.

'Can I help you?' demanded a strange voice.

'Yes' I half stammered. The sound of the voice being unexpected came as a shock and took us both completely by surprise. Quickly I recomposed myself and repeated, 'Yes' then added. 'We are looking for the Landlord.'

'He's not here. I'm his son. Can I help?'

I gave him our prepared story. I told him we were on holiday, camping, and walking the countryside and would appreciate a few days stay with our camper. He assured us, in return, that that would be no problem and that there were only a few basic and simple rules. He trotted them out and as Fred remarked later, enjoyed

every minute of playing the big boss and laying down the law in the absence of the Landlord.

"There was fresh water and toilets available for campers; we were to deposit all waste in the bins provided, dogs must be fastened up and not be allowed to roam loose. Kids can have as much fun as they like but must not be too noisy, no loud music and finally, please enjoy your stay." Added to that, and almost as an after thought, we were informed that, "the Pub and its dining room are available to campers, but please be careful and watch out for muddy boots".

Fred, very casually but obviously sarcastically, looked under the soles of both her boots then insisted I did the same. 'You now know the house rules.' she said as she held up one finger towards me.

We paid his quoted deposit and camping fee for caravanettes.

Having left the pub, but not before having been given the additional free advice, that against the outer perimeter wall, that backed on to the road, was the most sheltered place at this time of year, we backed, what was to be our home, for the next unknown number of days, alongside the end tent of those already pitched there. As soon as the engine died and we climbed out and began to look around, it became obvious that all the tents were securely fastened up and therefore probably not occupied at that particular time. After some discussion and looking at things from different angles we decided to rearrange ourselves slightly. We figured that if we left a full parking space between the last tent, and ourselves we would perhaps be that little bit more private and our conversation might not be so readily overheard. We also decided that if we backed the camper in with its rear end to the wall our side entrance would be on the side away from the nearest tent and that would also add to our privacy. A little further to walk to the toilets and gate perhaps but that was only a matter of yards and made little difference and, as I argued, we could always move later if that or anything else, proved to be inconvenient or caused any unforeseen problems.

My first task, given to me by Fred as she handed me the bottle, was to locate the fresh water and fill it. Then I was to connect and turn on the Calor gas. Check the small, but compact, two-burner stove that doubled, according to the instructions, as a heater for the whole van when required. The miniature television set and the central light were both powered by the camper battery. 'Don't forget to run the engine regularly and be aware of the dangers of flattening the battery,' the leaflet had warned.

What next? I wondered. This camping was all go. Take the wastewater container outside, place it under the wing by the back wheel, and stick the outlet pipe, from the sink, into the neck. 'Check regularly to avoid mess and unnecessary smells from overflow'. They thought of everything.

Do Romany's and gypsy men have this much fun setting up camp or are they better organised and make the women folk do it all while they play their violins and cook hedgehogs in clay? I wondered.

'Stop fiddling with that television for a moment and listen to me; we have more important things to do before that.'

'Just a second,' I said. 'I nearly had a picture then,' as I continued to rotate the ceiling-mounted control that swivelled the multi-directional aerial mounted outside on the roof.

'That's it, good, now what's that one, BBC 1? Sounds foreign. Oh Hell! It's Belgium, Dutch or German, or something. What's wrong with the BBC and good old finger mouse?'

'Sod finger mouse and listen to me. Shut that thing off. We don't need it and the whistling is driving me mad. We have far more important things to do,' Insisted Fred. So I reluctantly did as I was told.

'Now that's better, peace and quiet. I can hear myself think. Look, I suggest we have a hot drink, set out our stall so that we have room to move and know where everything is and then make up the bed ready for tonight. We can then stretch out and have a rest before you take me out to dinner and we take a look to see what the locals are like, if there are any around here that is. Tomorrow we can wander round a wider area and see what there is out there. How do you light this stove? It's OK, stay where you are I've got it. It turns this way.'

'Can I play with the telly again while you do that?'

'If you must, but remember what the man at the pub said, "Not too much noise," and that goes for me too. Telly is all right in its place but we are supposed to be on holiday and away from all that. So you get it going, if you must, then turn it off and keep me happy. There's a love.'

'OK, but I thought it might be handy to have it for the news and weather,' was my lame excuse to carry on fiddling with the thing.

'What's wrong with the radio in the cab? That's been fine so far and we have got all we wanted to know about the weather from that.'

I ignored her and continued fiddling with the tuner controls. Every time I got a decent picture it would be to find it accompanied by a foreign language. When I did manage to pick up English the picture was broken, rolled over continuously and was snowy. I had tried almost everything and was on the point of abandoning the job completely when there came, without warning, two quick and very loud bangs, like cannon shots, on the side of the van.

'Shit! What the hell was that?' I almost shouted, as I instantly pulled away, the result of an automatic reflex action, from the set, but then immediately realised that it had nothing to do with the television and turned and moved quickly to the door. I threw it wide open and jumped straight out and on doing so nearly knocked down a large rounded figure of a man who, before I had time to say anything,

blustered rather angrily, 'Sorry, didn't mean to bang so hard. Who are you and what do you think you are doing?'

I was still rather annoyed from the shock of his banging and now this guy's manner was only adding to my frustration. His very attitude and the way he stood his ground wound me up rather tighter than I would have liked and so, as a result, I found myself uncontrollably rounding on him.

'First of all, who the hell are you banging on my van like that? I demanded.

'I own this camping ground and I want to know what you're doing here in my field. You're on private property, if you hadn't noticed, and like I said, I did not mean to hit your van so hard. I am sorry about that but I still want to know who you are and what you are doing here?'

'Look here, old man,' I retorted. 'We have been to the Pub and spoke to a young fellow there; we paid him and parked where he told us to. Now as far as I am concerned that makes everything right.'

'Shit. I am sorry and I hope you will forgive me. I have had a crap day and came home to find a camper in my field that was not there this morning when I left. Never entered my head to check at home first. I wrongly assumed you were another of those who just drive in, park up, use the water, piss in the bog, dump their rubbish anywhere and then having had a lovely day out, sod off. We have had loads just recently, particularly at weekends and I thought, when I saw you that at last I had managed to catch one. Sorry, please forgive me,' and without further ado he turned away, walked round the end of the van, and off towards the gate muttering, 'Shit,' under his breath every second or third step.

'He might have had a bad day, but there was no need to take it out on us,' said Fred half laughing. 'I suppose that will be the great Mr James Lacey - the landlord with a big smile, a cheerful word and a big welcome for everyone. He has done his best to spoil our day as well as his own. I hope his food is better than his mood. Your coffee is ready.'

I stepped back into the camper and closed the door behind me.

'I know we all have our good and bad days and I am no exception, but at least I try not to take it out on complete strangers. I would have thought it would be very important for someone like him, who both directly and indirectly, takes his living from strangers, to be even more careful. Which of these is mine?' I enquired pointing to the mugs of coffee stood on the work surface.

'Either of them, they are both alike. Have you finished fiddling with that damned telly because if you have, can we now have it turned off?'

I reached across and switched the set off and watched the mass of black and white speckles disappear as the screen went dead.

'Yes, I suppose so for now. I think we must be in either a bad reception area or the aerial is too small or something. I will dig the book out and have another

go later, but for now my darling, I think I will just sit here, settle down, and enjoy this coffee.'

'It's not bad for instant, and one of the supermarket's own labels. I buy the local supermarket coffee back home but have not seen this one before.'

'I always use instant because I can't be bothered with percolators and all the messing about that goes with them.'

'Thought anymore about what we are going to do once we get settled in and now we are here?'

'I thought you had already planned our next move, dinner. But me, all I might do is take a swing at that guy if he comes back banging on our van. Anyhow before all that I thought we were making up the bed and right now I could just get my head down and sleep forever. This fresh air and that idiot have got to me. I feel whacked.'

'Come on then. Finish that drink and let's make up the bed then we can both have a snooze before we go out.'

I finished my coffee and put the mug in the tiny sink. Fred handed me hers and I placed it with mine. The sink was full.

'Roomy, these caravanettes!' I remarked, as I looked from the sink at all our stuff that was spread about. I turned to face the table. 'Right, now let's see. This table unhooks from the wall by lifting it like this… and then this single centre leg folds up underneath. Good, so you now slide yourself out of the way and then I can drop it down.'

Fred swung her legs round the end of the bench seat, stood up, and stepped behind me. The table dropped down and came to rest on two rails that ran along the front edges of the two bench seats, thus forming a level platform. The two long bench seat cushions then pulled away from the walls to meet down the centre. The two cushions which formed the back rests of the seats then folded back to lay flat and fill the gaps created when the two seat cushions were drawn together in the centre. It was all very neat and cleverly designed. We then had, what was almost, a full size double bed where the table and two bench seats had previously been. It was rather short for me and possibly for Fred also, but we would manage for a day or two.

The bed, when made up, had its head towards the bulkhead of the drivers cab and the internal window, dividing the two, lifted up and fastened to the roof, thus effectively turning the driving compartment into a temporary storage area for surplus gear. For privacy the whole van was closed off to the outside world by closely fitting curtains that completely shut out all the windows, including those in the drivers cab.

We completed the job of making up the bed by laying one of the sleeping bags, fully opened, on the base to lie on. Two pillows went against the bulkhead and the second sleeping bag over the top. Using the two zips it was possible to fasten

the two bags together by starting at the bottom centre and running both zips out to the corners and then up and along the outsides to the top. The zip could then be run back down to allow access on either side. We then had one double, though rather short, double bed, campers for the use of, as they say in best military jargon.

It didn't take long after that to stretch out and settle down and as a result the next hour or so was spent snoozing, while still fully clothed but minus boots, on top of the sleeping bags. We were disturbed only once, and that was by the arrival of a car, which drove down the lane and by the sound from it, parked up somewhere between two of the tents. Apart from that there was just peace and quiet, with the almost total silence only being disturbed by the cry of the gulls and the dull and distant pop of a tractor toiling away in some far off field.

'This will do for me.' I heard Fred mutter at one stage.

Then silence.

CHAPTER SEVENTEEN

We both slept well and after a great deal of stretching and a little cuddle, decided we were delighted with the trial run on the bed. Small but comfortable was the verdict. However, getting ready to go out posed one or two problems, as space was rather limited. It would have been better had the bed not been made up. But it was and we proposed to leave it like that, so the only solution was that we should take it in turns. One would get ready while the other stretched out on the bed and kept well out of the way. I elected to go first and while I washed and shaved, having previously waited ages for the little kettle to boil and provide hot water, Fred stretched out and promptly went to sleep again. Just before I finished I refilled the kettle and put it on the gas burner so that Fred would not have to wait for it to heat up from cold. My final act, which completed my toilet, was to comb my hair and put all my things away. I then gently woke her.

After much yawning and stretching I managed to persuade her to change places with me and I settled down on the bed and sat with my back against the bulkhead and watched. She didn't seem to mind one bit and went about it as if I did not exist. I was enjoying my camping and the view from where I sat was enchanting.

The meal that evening, in the pub, was excellent and was to be recommended to anyone. The dining area was comfortable and spacious even though, whilst we were in there, most of the tables were occupied. The pub obviously had an excellent reputation and well established clientele that was easily understandable if the quality and quantity of our meal was anything to go by. As we ate we chatted and discreetly looked about us, taking in the scenery and surreptitiously eyeing up our fellow diners. As we ate, new arrivals came in and sat down, whilst others having finished rose and went either across to the bar or left altogether.

When we finished we sat for a few minutes talking then decided to move across into the bar area. As we passed between the tables and made our way towards the bar, I realised just how busy the place really was when one considered just how far we were from a built up area and so called civilisation.

The bar area with the actual bar running the full length across the one end had an air of activity with 'relaxed cosiness', if there is such an expression? However it was, whatever the expression, warm and intimate and there were a reasonable number of customers seated round the tables and along the walls on the wall seats. There were several others standing against the bar itself. The people, their chatter, and the warmth all blended in to create a very cheerful atmosphere. On arrival at the bar I ordered a whiskey and a gin and tonic.

'Anything with the whiskey sir: ice, water?'

'Water please.'

'Certainly Sir,' replied the young lady who had just served me as she placed a water jug on the bar in front of me, handed me my change, then swiftly moved on to serve her next customer. We later found out that she was the wife of the chef, who in turn, had previously introduced himself to us as the Landlord's son. We also discovered later, that there was a Landlady, who kept in the background and there were also several locals who were employed on a casual basis. On the surface and to any casual observer, it appeared to be a thriving and successful business.

'Nice place and lovely and warm,' mused Fred. 'And that meal was first class.'

'It was very nice indeed and there was plenty of it. Makes you want do absolutely nothing, except perhaps relax, enjoy a drink and maybe, if the mood then takes me, later weigh things up a bit.'

'Weigh up what? What do you hope to weigh up and get out of here? Sounds more like you are making an excuse to do absolutely nothing and get drunk if you ask me.'

'Oh, I don't know. We might get something. If we keep our eyes and ears open and listen we might just pick up the odd snippet of value.'

'We might not as well'

The majority of the people who came in or went away all seemed to know each other. Everyone seemed to greet everyone else and the staff behind the bar addressed a very large proportion by their first names. It was all extremely friendly and I was able, with ease, to indulge in my favourite pastime - people watching.

As the evening drew on and the whiskey began to glow, the ebb and flow of customers into the bar dropped to a trickle. Of those left behind, the majority were quite content to talk and laugh, or joke, between themselves and the bar staff.

It was during this lull and relatively quiet period, but whilst the area in front of the bar happened to be still quite busy, that our casual conversation was interrupted by a young man, who having excused himself, forced a wedge between me and the chap who stood with his back to me. Naturally, I shifted my position and moved closer to Fred so that he was able to get in behind me. He ordered a pint of bitter and a pint of cider. When served, he said simply, 'Thanks' and left to return to his seat and the company of a young lady who, picking up the pint of cider, proceeded to devour it at a rapid rate. I had previously noticed them, or more accurately her, for not only was she quite attractive, but her voice had begun to rise and attract, not only me but also others as the effects of the cider took hold. The tighter she got, the louder she became, and the very distinct West Country accent became more pronounced. Later, this couple were to be the first people we got into conversation with. It came about when the girl came up to the bar clasping two empty pint glasses. She was noticeably unsteady on her feet. She smiled and said,

'Your van in the field next to our tent?' Saw you'd come in when we came back at teatime. Staying long?'

This led on to the usual general and polite conversation and then before long we were being introduced to her partner and invited to join them and sit at their table. That girl could talk. We had only been with them for a short time, when already we had their life history and were through telling them almost all of ours. They were not married. Both were self-employed and were able to take time off to suit themselves and this they did, and spent it camping. This area of Yorkshire being a particular favourite of theirs and a place they regularly visited.

We were very guarded as to what we told them and naturally mentioned nothing of our true reasons for being there. We stuck to holidays and camping as the purpose for our visit. We led them to believe, as indeed was true, that this was our first visit to Yorkshire. We were not married, but shared a flat in London and both worked, in different departments, for the Civil Service. When pressed on the subject, Fred lied and claimed that it was the Inland Revenue Branch of the Civil Service.

Shortly after, the bar bell rang and last orders were called.

We started to assemble our odds and ends and put on our coats in readiness to leave, when we were stopped by our newfound acquaintances. Francis, who was now well away on the cider, informed us that time was called only for the benefit of casual visitors, not for locals and guests like ourselves who could enjoy at least another hour or so. So taking her at her word we settled back down again and established that it was my turn to buy a round of drinks. I approached the bar and was promptly served without question. We were also told that this was fairly standard practice in most rural areas and made a pleasant change to the more rigid rules that were usually applied in the town centre establishments.

When it finally came round to 'Can we have your glasses now please' we realised that quite a few had stayed behind and as we left, having accepted an invitation for coffee with our new found friends, I noticed there was still no real effort being made to shut up shop.

The coffee was hot and strong and when I casually made reference to the amount of Brandy it contained, having accepted the offer of a drop of brandy 'to make you sleep', we were jokingly informed that we would need all the brandy we could get if we required to sleep through all the noise there was around the field at night.

I looked at Fred and she took it up.

'What, from all the people at turning out time from the pub?' she enquired.

'Yes, that and all the other racket,' retorted the boy friend, Wesley who was also rapidly folding due to the amassed alcohol surging round in his system. 'Some nights you would think they are building a motorway through here.'

'Don't talk daft. It's not as bad as all that otherwise we wouldn't stay here,' chipped in Francis 'But we do get a lot of tramping about and car doors banging and I must admit that sometimes it does go on until late into the night.'

'Me, talk daft. What about the other night?' snapped Francis.

'What about the other night? It's like the Landlord said, the tide was right so a few of them, all the worse for drink, decided to take a boat out and do a bit of fishing and they made a bit of noise. No harm in that and that is why some of the locals keep that boat round at the back of the Pub.'

'I don't know how many that pissy little boat is supposed to hold or how long fishing trips are supposed to last but it sounded to me as if the whole Pub was taking it in turns to go out in the damned thing. There were people munching about nearly all the bloody night and loud voices and loads of car doors banging. Every time I nodded off something woke me up. It felt as if it went on all night. I might be exaggerating a bit but it just seemed like that to me. You would think that after getting pissed all evening they would want to go home and get to bloody bed like the rest of us.'

The conversation began to dry up as the, almost neat, brandy with coffee flavouring began to have its effect. We managed to take our leave and tramped the twenty to thirty yards or so, to our own tiny accommodation.

After wobbling about quite a bit and much fumbling and rummaging through pockets, Fred finally found the keys. She struggled with the lock and eventually opened and slid back, the side door. I reached in and gingerly felt up and down the doorpost until I located the internal light switch and the single low voltage strip light came on. In contrast to the almost total darkness outside the light was almost blinding and had the effect of making our living space look even smaller than it really was. The bed, in the made-up state, taking up by far the largest proportion of the available space or was it me, and the effects of the drink, that made it just feel like that, perhaps not. I was not at all sure.

'What are you looking for, Mel?'

'The torch; I need to take a walk across the field before I turn in.'

'Good idea and very important right now: I'll come with you. I put the torches up there somewhere in that locker. No, Mel, the one next to it. Found it? You're drunk.'

'Yes. No,' I replied as I extracted a torch from its storage place.

'What do you mean, Yes-No? You must be drunk.'

'Yes to the torch: and no to me being drunk. A little mellow perhaps, if you like.'

'Drunk will do for me. Give me the torch. I said give it, not drop it. You are drunk.'

It was very quiet and dark outside as we staggered the short distance across the field to the toilet block. A light breeze was blowing making it feel chilly and

that had a very bad effect on a body full of booze. Above the rustle of the leaves in the trees all around us I could hear, from somewhere beyond the Pub, the murmur of the rolling sea. The night sky was dark with no visible moon, and it's black velvet mass above only being broken by the odd star. All in all it was a dark, chilly night.

On the return journey we had reached about the halfway point when Fred stopped, turned off the torch, touched my sleeve and whispered, 'Shh'!

I stopped and listened, rocking gently on my feet. 'Nothing,' I whispered.

'Exactly and not what we were led to believe it would be by those two in the tent a short while ago.'

'Oh, come on, forget all that, its time we were in bed before I fall down and freeze to death out here.'

We had almost reached the van when Fred, once again, tugged my sleeve, cupped her hand behind her ear and nodded towards the tent occupied by our 'friends'. Just audible above the noise of the breeze as it passed through the trees and flapped the tent canvas was, just discernible, two similar, yet uniquely different, sounds that could only come from people in deep sound sleep. How peaceful and content it all sounded, that deep, brandy-induced, relaxed, human sleep. Snoring is the technical term that I believe is normally applied to it.

We tiptoed the remainder of the way trying not to make a sound before letting ourselves in. I lit the gas ring to take the chill out of the night air. Then despite the overall effects of the drink and the confined space we managed to remove boots, trousers, and jumpers. The main light was turned over to torchlight and the gas ring extinguished. Then following some manoeuvring and minor readjustments we made it into the sleeping bag without any real problems.

'Here take your jumper.'

'What do I need that for?' demanded Fred.

'Stick it in bed with you. There is nothing better than a warm jumper when you get out on a cold morning.'

'Who says I'm getting out in the morning? If I like it, I might stay here forever or at least until the afternoon when it might be a bit warmer.'

'Can I join you?'

'Only if you're warm and cuddly and are prepared to get up and make the tea. Now kiss me before I fall asleep without my good night kiss.'

It was not a passionate kiss, more like one of those that brings to a happy conclusion the end of a wonderful day.

Fred eased over gently and pushed her back against my chest. We both raised our knees and lay as if Fred was sat on my knee, seconds later we were both lost to the world.

CHAPTER EIGHTEEN

We were up the following morning bright and early and I felt rested despite all the booze from the night before and the fact that as we shifted about in our sleep the bed turned out to be slightly short for my height and meant that most of the time I had to sleep with my legs drawn up. Fred apparently had no objections and simply curled up as close to me as she could get.

A quick wash and tidy round, the bed broken down and the table re-instated, we had beans on toast for breakfast and having washed up after it, we were ready to venture out and investigate our local surroundings in some detail.

The map showed the Pub to be located at the head of a ravine that must have been eroded back from the coastline, over the centuries, by the stream that flowed off the land and descended down, over rocks, to sea level. That same stream still flowed through the woods and around the back, and to the North side, of the Pub. It flowed flat and calm as it twisted its way behind the buildings but within a few yards from that point the streambed narrowed and the rush of the water increased. This must have had the effect, over the years, of cutting into the surrounding rock and the result was a series of fast flowing mini-waterfalls. In a matter of only a few hundred yards this cascade of water found its way down to sea level where once again it spread out and slowed down as it finally fanned out and ran over smooth rock, shale and sand into the sea. The shingle and the accompanying line of dead and rotting weed, left behind by the tide, showed that a large part of this natural gully was flooded twice a day, at high tide, with seawater.

The cliffs along that stretch of coastline varied in height but were in the region of some two hundred feet high, perhaps even more in odd places. The mouth of the ravine was only about fifty yards wide at the most and had very steep, wooded and scrub covered, sides. From where the stream started it's fall and descent towards the sea and the mouth of the ravine would be no more than a quarter of a mile in total. To get down from the top onto the shingle beach below, it was necessary to use a well worn path which ran from the open space in front of the pub down along the southern sloping side of the ravine to the bottom. It was this path or track that enabled one, providing they were fairly fit, to descend relatively easily from pub height to sea level. It was not, however, a gradual descent, and varied from stretches that were almost flat to those which were steep in places. It proved to be much easier to descend than to climb back up, especially the steep parts. It showed some signs of having been maintained and repaired, presumably by the National Parks people or some other conservation organizations, in order that visitors and locals alike could have reasonable access to the beach.

There was also, according to the map, and which proved on investigation, to be fairly easy to find, a path or track that ran parallel with the cliff top. This allowed walkers and hikers to follow the coastline without having to descend down one side of the ravine and then climb up the other, which would have been an almost physical impossibility, as they followed the North to South route along the cliff top. In other words this track ran along the cliff top, coming up from the South, until it reached the Southern edge of the ravine, there it turned inland and followed the high ground and wound its way through the woods until it broke out at the side of the car park opposite the pub. To proceed North from there it was necessary to walk round the edge of the car park, cross the lane and then go behind the pub. Once round the back of the pub the track re-entered the woods and followed the ravine along it's Northern high bank until it once again came out on the cliff top. The stream being crossed by a substantial wooden bridge which not only served as a crossing point to get from one side to the other but afforded a wonderful viewing platform from which to observe the stream as it cascaded over the rocks down towards the open sea. Standing on the bridge the tree covered slopes on either side of the ravine formed a large V-shape down which, when one stood and looked, the sea gave the impression that it came half way up to meet the sky which filled the whole of the top half. On a clear day it was possible to see twelve to fifteen miles out to sea; the distance of the sky line relative to the height of the bridge above sea level.

Having crossed the bridge, the track had slightly less of an incline than it's counter part on the Southern side due to the lie and formation of the land. It broke out of the woodland onto a grassy open space before turning and continuing north and judging by the overall condition of the track, which was well worn, it was very popular.

Of all the different places we went to on that first day we both agreed that the track down to the beach, whilst not being difficult to follow still needed to be negotiated with care, but was never the less the most picturesque and from a purely visual point of view, the prettiest. Parts were quite steep and the hike back up, when we returned, was hard going. One could understand and appreciate the wisdom of the specially erected, short stretches of rough hand rail and the randomly spaced tree trunks which had been felled and fashioned into bench type seats and set at various points, as convenient resting places, along the route.

The shingle beach was just that. Predominantly shingle mixed with some sand that ran in from the sea and ended in almost a straight line where it met with the scrub-covered rocks. Through the middle of it all ran the stream.

A line of weed and flotsam, well up the shingle, indicated the average height at high water and showed how much of the area was regularly covered by the sea during normal tides. It didn't take much to work out that, at high water, well over half of the ravine would be completely flooded, while at low water, it

would be possible to walk round the flanks of the cliff edges and proceed along the base of the cliff to either the North or South. How far one would get after that would depend on several variables. In other words it would depend on ones own rate of progress over the rocks and shale. Another and far more important factor would be the time and speed and height of the incoming tides. Without sound local knowledge it would be very foolish to venture far. Anyone not familiar with the area and know the escape routes and how to avoid being trapped or cut off by the tide could end up in big trouble.

A stroll of a few hundred yards in either direction along the base of the cliffs revealed nothing. Not that we really expected to find anything. We only went as part of our plan to familiarise ourselves with the overall area. We did however note the usual flotsam and jetsam wedged between the rocks and which is a common phenomenon and can be found along almost every coastline throughout the world. At least the non-degradable plastic bags, washing up liquid bottles and the multi-coloured nylon fishing net, that seems to get everywhere, might not have been there a few years ago. What did we do, I wondered, before the discovery of plastic or the development of the disgusting habit of throwing almost everything into the sea in the misguided belief that it will break up and disappear?

When we travelled North along the base of the cliff, we stopped at the point, which, according to our map, was the place directly below where Philip Edison was last supposed to have been. Obviously, we did not expect to find anything down there as the whole area would have been very carefully searched after Edison's disappearance and since then, of course, it had been covered several times, in fact twice daily, by each incoming tide. It was, however, sufficient for us to note that if he had gone over the edge at low water, he would most certainly have fallen some two hundred feet and landed on exposed rock below, or if at high water, or for that matter anything up to four hours before or after high water, he would have gone straight into the sea. We noted that the tide line was at least a meter up the cliff face and that reinforced our suspicion that the ravine, even on an average tide, would be well flooded. Also we calculated that at the same time, the depth at the cliff bottom might still not have been sufficient to save someone from hitting the submerged rocks should they fall from a height of two hundred feet. We also spent some time clambering over the rocks and through the weed in an attempt to satisfy ourselves that, had someone landed in the sea at high tide or less and miraculously survived there were no easy 'walk outs', that we could find, in the immediate area. A 'walk out' being an access point from the top of the cliff down to the beach which is know to, and used by, locals, anglers, walkers and, of course, Coastguards, to escape incoming tides and avoid being cut off. We came to the conclusion that anyone cut off in that area would be extremely lucky to get out if not spotted in time, from above.

We retraced our steps and returned to the cove. After several stops and short rests, my excuse being to admire the view, we finally made it back up the steep track and went directly into the pub for a well-earned drink and bar lunch.

* * *

During the afternoon we extended our trek and went along the track that went behind the pub and crossed the bridge and then went north. At the top we stopped at the spot, marked on our map that indicated, where the personal effects belonging to Edison had been found. It was an open, grass-covered patch between the actual track, and the cliff edge, an area, roughly circular and some twenty to twenty-five feet in diameter. If we stood in the middle and looked around we could see for some distance along the track in either direction. Then with our backs to the sea, we could see into the woods. Our range of vision being some what limited by the dense trees and the undergrowth. Looking the direct opposite way we could see for several miles out to sea.

We moved as close to the edge of the cliff as was considered safe and looked down but the angle was such that it was not possible to see the base of the actual cliff below. Neither was it possible to see the entrance to the cove from there, the bushes between the grassy patch and the top of the cove side obscuring everything. We could see it was a very secluded and perfect place to sit and picnic but decided it was not much of a vantage point from which to observe anything.

'Nor to hide from anything,' observed Fred as we discussed it.

'You're right. Even if it was very dark and you chose to just stand here. You would hardly be hiding. The undergrowth over there would be a much better place to go for that. So would you come here to just meet someone perhaps? You might, but it's a very lonely and isolated spot and a long way to come, late at night, just to meet someone. A woman not used to that sort of thing may find it a bit much, if a woman was involved. But I would have thought that out here, in a remote country area such as this, to meet discreetly would be possible and more practical much closer to civilisation. So why come all the way out here, at night, for anything? I have a feeling there's more to it than a simple amorous rendezvous, or the meeting of just two good friends, but what exactly I don't know. However hanging around here all day isn't going to tell us, so let's call it a day and head back.'

We decided to spend some time around the camper, behaving, as far as we knew how to, as typical holidaymakers and campers. We fussed about and re-arranged things. We went on short walks round the immediate area, just nosing about, and it was whilst doing that that we decided to venture a little further and visit the local village. It would be better than doing what we were doing and would be an ideal opportunity to purchase a few bare necessities to keep us going, as Fred put it.

We were sitting in a small cafe come tearoom, when we decided it might not be a bad idea if we found a phone box and rang the Colonel. It was some time since we had last reported, but even now we had no real reason to do so as we had little, if anything, to report.

'You ring him Fred, your feminine charm might stop him dropping down on us from a great height when we haven't much to tell him.'

'OK I'll give it my best shot. I don't mind living dangerously when it's all for a good cause,' she laughed and leaving her shopping on the seat beside me, went out to the phone box, which we had discovered on enquiry, was a couple of hundred yards down the road and sited outside the village Post Office. She seems to be away for a long time, or longer than I would have thought necessary for a single phone call. On her return, she looked remarkably cheerful, where I had expected nothing but doom and gloom.

'You look pleased with yourself, has the Old Man given you a promotion or salary increase or extra leave or something?'

'Oh, that old pratt. No, I've been talking to a friend of mine that I haven't spoken to or seen in ages.'

'I thought you went to talk to the Old Man?'

'Yes I did and he's as foul as his backside because we have nothing to report, so I thought I would ring my friend and cheer myself up a bit.'

'What did you find out then, anything?'

'Yes, my friend's sister has just had a baby girl and it weighed eight pounds.'

'No. Not that. Don't misunderstand me. I am of course pleased for your friend and her sister. But what had the Old Man to say? That's what I want to know.'

'He prattled on about the time we were taking, department budgets, costs and no results. I'm sure you have heard it all before many times, it's like a well-worn record when he gets going. In the end, I just shut off, stood there, and let him waffle on. When he finished I said, "Yes Sir. Very good Sir, will ring as soon as we have something," and hung up. What does he think we are?' Bloody magicians!'

'I wonder if there is anything to be gained by ringing Oldfield at Humber, do you think he might have something that might help us? Some recent development perhaps?'

'I don't really know but if you decide to, then it's your turn to do it. One call to the Old Man is more than enough for me for one day. Although I suppose ringing Oldfield is all right. The phone is just down there and easy to find,' and pointing in the general direction of the Post Office, continued, 'Get me another coffee if you're going to shoot off and leave me, there's a darling.'

I strolled down the street admiring the view. I was particularly impressed by the neatness and how pretty everything looked. Most of it looked antiquated

and old and very original and gave the impression that nothing had changed for centuries. Things had of course and I knew that. The people were modern and their clothing was in line with the latest fashions. Also one had only to observe the yellow lines, strung out like parallel strings of bright yellow spaghetti along almost every single inch of road and street. The very modern petrol station with the latest pumps and plastic decor along with the masses of overhead wires and cables that criss-crossed everything. Then the TV aerials on ever roof top and the Satellite dishes dotted about and all desecrating the natural charm. All that and plenty more told you that the village had not failed in it's efforts to keep abreast of modern technology and that a large proportion belonged to the present if only in their communication and television viewing habits. It was the buildings themselves where time had stood still and which attracted me the most. The solid structures, which had, more or less, remained unaltered since the time of their construction and which time seemed to have passed by and thankfully leaving them unmolested. No matter in which direction I looked, I could see another perfect picture for the front of a Country Calendar or the top of a Chocolate Box.

I stopped and looked about me. It was wonderful to see so many buildings that, despite the ravishing of time, still managed to maintain much of their original charm. It was obvious that the people who lived in them took pride in their maintenance. The whole place had a unique charm and personality all it's own. It was very much the type of place city dwellers dream of retiring to, though very few, thankfully, ever do, otherwise this rather special and picturesque villages and many others like it would be full to overflowing; would be ruined beyond recognition by those with little understanding of village life or the desire to learn and conform to it. No village can survive the pressures put upon it by outsiders who bring with them the need to widen roads and accesses to property, to build double garages, patios, and conservatories and dig up vast tracts in which to sink swimming pools or build tennis courts. All of which does nothing to improve the village, puts up property prices and drives out the locals, who born and bred there, do not earn sufficient to be able to afford to buy.

Later when we became more familiar to the locals and they seemed to accepted us as harmless tourists, there only to spend our money and then move on, some opened up to us and chatted quite amicably about the village, the local inhabitants, some of their hopes, aspirations, disappointments and down right prejudices and hostilities. On the other hand, as we expected, many others remained tight-lipped and had all on to be polite or even force themselves to pass the time of day with us. From those who chose to speak openly we quickly gathered that many rural communities complain bitterly of the proportion of property still being snapped up by outsiders, or by 'Immies' or 'Wessies' as they refer to them, and then they are left standing, unoccupied, for most of the year and used only as holiday accommodation or as long term retirement investments, all of which when finally

taken up and occupied are done so by people with little, or no, spending power to add to the local economy. Apparently the latter, with a lot of spare time on their hands then tend to form themselves into organisations and pressure groups with the sole aim of influencing village life to their added advantage. I could understand and see that causing a lot of problems and causing a fair amount of ill feeling among the village elders who's families went back generations.

I made my call and then adopting the same casual stroll, retraced my steps back to the tearoom where I found Fred, as I had left her, but with a fresh cup of coffee. She greeted me with, 'Any luck?'

'No nothing new.'

'OK, if there is nothing else you want to do, let's finish up here. We can then call at the bread shop before it closes and then make our way back and call it a day. We have walked some miles if you think about it and I am all in and have had enough.'

Like most north country seaside villages, a large proportion of the village economy revolves around its immediate agricultural surroundings but the heart of the village revolves around its shops and the likes and they are usually to be found strung out along just one, or perhaps two, of the main streets which run through the centre of the village. The cottage industries, on the other hand, which also play a vital part in their overall survival; the blacksmith's forge and farm implement repair shops, the village joiner, builder, dry stone-wall erecter and fence post maker's saw mill, are nearly always set back from the main thorough fare and are usually to be found just off the main streets, often hidden away down little back allies or tucked away down narrow lanes. These in their turn are surrounded by an infinite variety and wide range of differently designed and constructed houses and cottages. These not only house the local population but often provide temporary accommodation for a large number of visitors, desirable and often encouraged to come to the area because they are short stay residents, bring in ready cash and naturally bolster the economy. The remainder, shut up for most of the year, simply stand there and cause ill feeling. However, one way or another the whole conglomerate goes towards making up the present day, modern, village. This one, as I observed, was no exception.

The number of cars dotted about was a sure sign that in this day and age the present generation of inhabitants were more travelled and used to getting about than their ancestors were ever likely to have been. The number of well kept cottages, some with letting signs in their windows indicated clearly that although no longer totally self-sufficient as a closed community, some at least were doing quite well. It was difficult to pick out from these which, hidden behind their closed doors and lace curtains, were the houses of the, so called, 'Immies'.

The shops were numerous, mixed and varied. There were again those with an all year round trade and catering mainly for the needs of the locals, and

hopefully enjoying a boost from visitors during the summer. On the other hand there were those who catered specifically for the visitor. One such shop that I noticed, was geared up to specialise in the sale of souvenirs, aimed specifically at the visitor, and which, at the moment, was closed and displayed a sign which stated 'Open Easter Bank Holiday'. Another that had all the trappings of a cafe, displayed no such sign, but its very appearance showed it to be well maintained, but at the same time, obviously well and truly closed up for the winter.

The cafe or tearoom we had just left must have been one of the lucky ones which attracted sufficient trade for it to be able to stay open all the year round.

We went into the baker's shop, which was only a couple of doors down the street, and on the same side as the cafe. I noticed in there a small area to the rear that had been set out with four oblong tables each with four chairs standing neatly on top. Dividing this area off and separating it from the remainder of the shop was a partition about four feet high, a light frame construction draped with a curtain. I stood close to this partition and casually looked over at the piled up furniture, while Fred looked into the window display at the food on offer, when a middle aged, rather red faced lady in a white overall and apron, entered the shop from a door at the rear, behind the counter, and said, 'The cafe is closed and we only have left what you can see in the window.'

'Fine,' answered Fred. 'I will have those four bread rolls and those two pieces of pie please.'

'Apple. There's only apple left. All the rest have gone'.

'Fine.'

Without another word the lady, proceeded to wrap the bread rolls and pie in thin tissue paper and placing them on the counter in front of Fred, took the offered five pound note and then turned round to the till and punched the keys. When the drawer opened she selected the change and turning back offered it to Fred. At the same time she looked directly at me and said, 'We don't open the tea room until the summer proper.'

'Oh I see,' I replied somewhat taken aback. 'We have just come from along the road where we have had a nice cup of coffee.'

'You would have. She only manages to keep that place open because she doesn't have to.'

'I'm sorry. She doesn't have to? I don't follow you.'

'Just what I said: she doesn't have to. Plenty of money she has. Husband has his own business and she lets out a couple of cottages in the summer and just does that to keep herself busy and find out everyone's business. She would be better off staying indoors and looking after her kids. She doesn't care about them or that shop or the "High Class Tea Room" as she calls it and it doesn't matter to her if she makes no money, her husband keeps her anyway. If you ask me she is like the rest of them round here who haven't been around for more than two

minutes. She does it just to upset everyone and chat up all the men and anyone else who goes in to collect and swap tittle-tattle. It would be a different tale if she were like me and had to make her business pay, to survive. Ruins the village her and her kind; the same as that "Miss Fancy Pants" across the road there. There's another, just as bad and there's plenty more of 'em round 'ere.'

We both turned and looked in the direction she had indicated. There was a clothing shop opposite. 'Clutterbox' said the multi-coloured sign running the full length of the shop front. 'Ladies and Children's Quality Clothes'.

'You mean that shop across there? "Clutterbox" on the other side?' I enquired.

'Yes. Miss Fancy Pants. Now there's a wrong one if ever I saw one. Her husband is supposed to be a builder. Pots of money, big house up there on the edge of the village, they have. Always entertaining and living it up they are. She opened up that shop opposite, to give her something to do, or that's what she claims. Not to make a living like some of us has to. Put the old lady at the other end of the village, out of business she did and she had been there years and years and needed it to make her living, she did. This one even has a woman in to help her. Goes in every afternoon so the other one can go out shopping in town; or so she says. Amazes me how many different cars pick her up and supposedly takes her shopping. I have never known so many men being interested in taking one woman shopping. There's something wrong and it 'ain't right if you ask me. She never goes to Church or the Community Centre either or goes anywhere decent like that. Not the type we need round here.'

'You say she runs a shop when she has no need to, and then employs a woman to look after it just so that she can go shopping with lots of men? Luck lady,' declared Fred.

I am sure that the look she got back was meant to burn her to a cinder right there on the spot, but fortunately, and naturally, it didn't. Then, to what had already been maliciously said, was viciously added by the lady, 'It just 'ain't right if you ask me. She is a wrong 'un through and through. You mark my words. Anyhow she will be stuck for all her shopping trips now, with all her fancy men, until she gets someone else that is.'

'Why's that?' I ventured out of pure curiosity.

'Well, if what they say is right, and I don't listen to gossip you understand, the woman who helps her in the afternoons has lost her husband. He just up and disappeared one night without telling anyone. Most people round here seem to think he has run away. Maybe it has something to do with the two of 'em and what they get up to over there. All the men in and out and respectable people like me trying to get on with me work and ignore it. All I'm doing is just trying to live a decent life and make an honest living.'

'You think this "helper" woman's problems may have something to do with what goes on over there?' enquired Fred before looking straight at me.

'Maybe. She's as bad as that Fancy Pants with the men and he probably found out and left her. They are as thick as thieves across there and always laughing and joking together and showing off and flaunting themselves in front of men.'

'Who exactly were big buddies? Fancy Pants, as you call her, and the other woman's husband. Is that what you mean?'

'No, the two women! Always performing for the men, any man. But I must admit, because I do try and mind my own business you understand, she has lots of men who come to the shop that I don't see. So for all I know, her husband might have come to the shop.'

'As a visitor to the women or as a customer?'

'Hardly a customer! To a woman's shop! No, more than likely to pick up his wife from work or what ever. I don't know because like I said I mind my own business and don't spend all day watching other people misbehave. You used to see him about a lot in the village though. He was one of those "Lifeguards" that wonder about on the cliff tops and never seem to do much else other than go in the pub or drive round in that fancy blue van. He might have come to the shop when his wife was not there, I don't know. But if you ask me, it's all-wrong somehow,' and then she threw in for good measure and with obvious disgust, 'You don't turn a sign round on a shop door to say, "Closed" every time a male traveller comes in. She does it all the time. Will there be anything else? I am busy and want to get closed up for the day.'

'No thank you,' muttered Fred who sounded disappointed that the conversation had come to an end. Never the less, reeling from the onslaught, we stepped outside and walked several yards along the pavement before Fred almost exploded. 'What do you make of that lot? For someone who minds her own business and sees nothing, do you think she was trying to tell us something?'

I could not help laughing, 'Perhaps she is jealous that no male reps turn her "Open" sign round for her and then tries to do battle with her over a sack of flour and punch holes in her dough nut! All I know is, -"It just 'ain't right and a non-church goer at that."'

'You know the other woman she was referring to and the husband who is a "Lifeguard"?'

'Yes, of course, I know what you are getting at. Pat Edison. She told us herself that she worked for a couple of hours in the afternoon in the village and that her husband was not too pleased about it. The woman in the bread shop referred to her as - the wife of a Lifeguard. Is she mistaken and I bet she is? I bet she means Coastguard.'

'I wonder if our Mrs Edison has been up to something, or if she is innocently employed to cover for the boss lady's loose living. Is it all legitimate and nothing

but bitchiness on the part of Mrs Bun the Baker, with the un-punched dough nut, back there?'

Fred thought for a moment. 'Perhaps a visit to that fashion shop might be in order? Not now but perhaps tomorrow. If all tongues wag like Mrs Bun and we can encourage it and collect something from it, and then sort out fact from fiction, a grand tour of all the village shops and the local pub maybe all we need.'

'You could be right. But, for the moment, let's bomb back to the camper and see what tonight has to offer.'

'Thinking about tonight already. Randy sod. Don't tell me that all that talk about Miss Fancy Pants flaunting herself and turning signs round and men calling on her. Not to mention the possibility of a shop full of frilly knickers has got you going. Or is it Mrs Bun and her un-punched doughnut?'

'No, don't be daft. You must be the randy one if you are thinking like that. What I meant was let's see what tonight brings by way of a visit to our local, back at camp. I think we should try and be a bit friendlier there. Mix more. Buy a few drinks perhaps, get everyone going, get in among them, loosen tongues, and see just what we can glean. You know what I mean. We may, without realising it, be surrounded by talkative locals like our Mrs Bun back there.'

'Yes dear, I know exactly what you mean but after achieving all that will you promise to try and loosen my tongue a little later. I got nothing last night remember, rolled up tight in that sleeping bag with no room to move, although it was lovely and cosy wasn't it? I think I am slowly beginning to like camping and who knows if there is an improvement tonight, I might want to do it more often and I know you simply love it already.'

'How's that?'

'Well we haven't been here two minutes and you are already making reference to "our local."'

CHAPTER NINETEEN

We had, yet again, another first class evening meal in the pub and having, as we thought, perhaps overstayed our welcome in the dinning room, retired to the lounge bar. There were a surprising number of people dotted about, the volume having increased steadily while we were relaxing over our meal. The time was nine thirty according to the bar clock. I smiled and gave a little wave to our next-door neighbours who I noticed were seated over in the far corner.

Fred ordered the drinks and I paid, then, as we turned away, drinks in hand, our friends of the previous evening beckoned us over to join them.

'Do we go?' I whispered.

'Why not,' Fred muttered. 'It might be difficult not to and at least over there gives us a good vantage point from which to look around the room and observe as well as providing us with someone to talk to. Although they are not locals and perhaps sitting with them won't do much for your plan. But it's up to you.'

'I'll follow you.'

Once seated the topic of conversation immediately centred round where we had all spent the day. We also discussed proposals and possibilities for the following and subsequent days. Fred was very good at fabricating our side of the plans as she went along and was purposely vague about most things. Eventually the conversation got round to the people in the bar. We found out that our friends had been on the camp site for over two weeks and had, more or less, as they put it "sussed out" who might be locals and who were very probably visitors.

'That couple over there... never seen them before tonight.' said Francis pointing out and describing a young couple standing near the bar. 'When we first came here we sat in here and did exactly what we are doing now, playing a sort of game - trying to guess who were locals and who were visitors or strangers - when Wesley decided, "It's no problem. You can pick them out just by listening," and when I said what the hell do you mean, he said, "Just listen to the bar staff," and then I realised what he meant, and it's easy after that. It doesn't matter how they dress, or who they happen to be with, if you listen to what the bar staff say, it's a dead give away. If you are a stranger and they do not know you, they will invariably address you as "Sir" or in some other formal way, but they are always exceptionally polite. If you are known, they are friendly and casual and will address you by name. In the two weeks we have been here, we have graduated from "Sir" to "Hello you two" or as the Landlord now calls Wesley, "Mate" or "What can I get you two happy campers?" and such like. Just try it. Look, just watch these two fella's that have just come in.'

Sure enough, she was right. 'Good evening, Gentleman, and what is your pleasure?' greeted the Landlord. Then, while proceeding to pull two pints of beer to fill the order, turned his head to one side and said to a man standing further down the bar, 'Hang on John, you can see I am serving, you won't die of bloody thirst so just wait a minute.'

'He's serving two strangers and making a local wait,' whispered Wesley.

From there it turned into quite a game, with each of us trying to guess, as we worked our way round the room, who was a local and who was probably a visitor. Or who was a visitor but had been there long enough to be shown a degree of familiarity. Our guesses either being confirmed or dismissed as each one of them approached the bar and placed their order. Some we could not hear, particularly if at the time, the level of conversation, in the lounge, was rather high or if there happened to be a minor rush to the bar for service. The bar maid was the least help as she tended to be rather withdrawn and treated everyone with the same formality and the same degree of politeness.

'Except those two young fellows at the end of the bar,' corrected Wesley. 'They are obviously locals and it is difficult to tell if they are chatting her up or she is chatting them up.'

Of all those in the bar some were obvious strangers, and we could tell before they even went to the bar, by the way they looked around when they came in or politely enquired of anyone standing close, where the 'Ladies' was. An enquiry for the toilet was a dead give away to the fact that they had never been in the place before. They all became, unknown to them participants in a light-hearted game as far as Francis and Wesley were concerned. They, of course, along with everyone else did not realise or know that we were interested for entirely different reasons.

Some time later, as the evening progressed, and during a sudden lull, caused by the fact that quite a few more had left than had come in, Fred suggested we try and guess what the locals did by way of a living; what might their occupations might be?

This we quickly realised was not very successful. Those we thought were obvious. For example the ones dressed in fishermen's clothing, in deck boots, denim trousers, smock tops and sweat rags neatly tied round their necks. They were, without a doubt, Fishermen or, closely associated with the fishing industry. Perhaps being lumpers or filleters or any one of a variety of occupations surrounding any busy fishing port. Net menders perhaps and they were treated as locals by the staff and in the majority of cases, they were addressed and called by their first or nickname. But they were not all locals as it turned out. Most of them lived in the thriving fishing port to the north and then whenever circumstance permitted, would travel south in a variety of cars and vans to visit this pub and enjoy what they considered to be a quiet drink. Later we established that at least two or three

of them did actually live in the village and they travelled north on a daily basis, in turn, to earn their living.

It was also too easy to assume that everyone who had a weather beaten face and did not ware deck boots was a farm worker. That was wrong because it did not take into account the 'dressed up' fisherman, the forestry workers, milkmen, postman and so on, all where equally smartly turned out and sported the same red, weather beaten, features which gave away nothing of their individual occupations. All it told us was the fact that, they all braved the elements on a daily and probably all year round, basis.

Even so, whilst sitting and chatting away, and whilst being discreet, for we had no desire to make anyone aware in the bar that we were talking about them, it gave us a wonderful opportunity to study at close quarters, all those around us. Perhaps it would prove to be of some value in the future. Who knew?

'Did you see that?' said Francis at one point.

'See what?'

'That stocky guy in the, none too white, jumper over there. He's a local. We have seen him around in the village, and up to two nights ago he has been in here every night. He usually stands and talks with those fishing lads, over there. He seems to know them all pretty well. Well, just now, when you were all busy talking, he walked up to the bar and the Landlord leaned over, very close to him, and said something. I couldn't hear what but I did hear what he said back. He said quite clearly, "Up you," and he said it nastily.'

'Who the Landlord?' asked Wesley.

'No, that bloke in the mucky jumper, who has just walked out, he said "Up you" to the Landlord and he sounded cross. Then he turned and just walked out. Didn't you notice how all those lads over there went quiet for a second and all stood and said nothing? A few days ago they were all big buddies and falling all over him.'

'Something has obviously happened. Perhaps between them or just the bloke and the Landlord. If he's a local, it could be anything,' I suggested.

'Yes, but it's not the first time he's had a go like that,' added Francis. 'Last week, if you remember Wes, we heard him and the Landlord having a real dingdong row. Remember, all the colourful language, by the side of his van out in the car park. Don't you remember, we distinctly heard the Landlord say, "If you don't knock it off now, I will bloody shop you" or something like that and we wondered then what it was all about, and our friend who has just gone out, replied, if I remember rightly, "You are in it too deep to split on anyone, so belt up and piss off." Don't you remember Wes? They both went quite when we walked past? They just stared at us and then the guy in the jumper got in the van and shot off down the lane like a loony out of hell. It was that day, when we heard later, that he had gone out of the end of the lane and pranged into the side of another car. You remember,

they were talking about it in here and someone was telling us that not only had he bumped into this other guy, but that he got out of his van and was going to hit him over it. The Police were called but apparently did nothing about it. He's probably the local nutter.'

'Sounds very much as if he is,' said Fred. 'To run into someone and then hit them is not exactly rational behaviour is it? He must have been well wound up and really full of hell.'

'Or something else!'

'Something else! What do you mean, something else, like what?'

'I don't know. Just guessing: booze, wacky backy or maybe both. There's that much crap about these days, he could be full of almost anything,' said Wes.

'And I suppose we could speculate on that subject as long as we like and still never really know. Same again? It's my round.'

I gave my order to the Landlord and as he was pulling the drinks; I said, as casually as I could, 'Having a spot of bother with the local natives?' and I nodded towards the door.

'No not really! He's just a local shit head that gets out of line now and again and has to be jumped on so that he remembers his place. He's been bother on and off since he moved into the village and I just have to show him who's the boss around here.'

'Oh, so he is not really a local, born and bred then?'

'No. He moved here a year or two back and set himself up in the village with a young lass he brought along with him.'

'What does he do for a living round here. Anything?'

'You'd have to ask him that. Lives in a biggish cottage, always seems to have plenty of money. She spends most of her time pregnant and shells out kids on a fairly regular basis.'

'Sounds like an active sort of man.'

'Randy bastard, if you ask me and as for her? Well she's such a rough little bitch, that one. Both need to be kept at arms length.'

'You don't seem to like them very much.'

'It's not that. He's been winding me up a bit lately and I had the feeling he was looking for trouble tonight when he came in, so I pissed him off quick before he got chance to get going.'

I didn't get the chance to find out more as our conversation came to an abrupt end when he turned and said to a young lady standing close by, 'Same again Joyce. Nice to see you both: your Mum any better?'

I carried our drinks back to the table and sat down. I didn't mention my conversation at the bar. I could always tell Fred later.

We continued in our vain attempts to categorize people as they came in and out of the bar. It did not come to very much after that and in the end the general

conversation drifted round to other things and the evening slowly slipped by as we all mellowed from the effects of alcohol.

On our way back to the camping field, Fred insisted that it was our turn to provide a nightcap, so all four of us rounded off the evening sat in our van. Fred produced four mugs of coffee laced with brandy, which she purposely bought at the bar before we left. But this time with not quite as much brandy in the drink as the night before. I can drink brandy in coffee at anytime, but I prefer more coffee than brandy. On the previous evening I am sure our friends tried the reverse and as a result had successfully served more brandy than coffee.

The first chance I got, I again brought up the subject of the stocky guy in the, none too clean jumper, in the bar, and his exchange with the Landlord.

'He's always hanging around somewhere round here,' muttered Francis after I mentioned that it was the first time I had seen him.

'You see him a lot, round and about, then?' I asked.

'You will see him about all over the place and at all different times of the day and night,' said Wes. 'The other night I got up for a tiddle and I saw him walking past the pub and going off down the track towards the beach. That would be three o'clock in the morning. He has a van that is nearly always in this car park. A battered old thing it is. I saw him the other day, as well, with a gun under his arm and two rabbits over his shoulder. I have seen him go into the woods with a couple of dogs on another occasion. Before that, I saw him throw a sack full of something, into the back if his van and drive off. Once he had some plastic fish boxes and some of those curved pot shaped things they use to catch things in. Or what ever they do with them. Odd times we have seen him and some other blokes from the pub, lug that boat, the one that is at the back of the pub, all the way down to the bottom and leave it on the rocks, for a couple of days or so. His van is usually on the car park all the time then. So I suppose he must be going out fishing or something. Fishing must be profitable, or should I say, it would have to be, to get me to go out there all night long, like he does. He must catch quite a bit because, you remember Fran, he was up and down all night last week, loading things into his van, before he finally drove off and we got some peace.'

'What things?' I enquired. 'Fish boxes and the likes?'

'Oh I don't know. We only heard most of it, and on the odd couple of times we did look out, you could only just see the van and him with the back doors open. But, it was too dark to see what he was doing really. He was either putting something in or taking something out. I don't know.'

'How many trips do you think he made altogether then that night?'

'Five, six, I don't really know. He would set off down to the beach and then come back, then disappear again and perhaps come back in half an hour or so. We didn't take much notice. We were just pissed off at the noise and the fact we

couldn't get any sleep. Our tent doesn't keep out much and when you are used to the quiet, the slightest noise seems to screw you up.'

When our company finally left, and we were tucked up tight in our sleeping bag, Fred whispered, 'What do you think? A local poacher, or local bum: a Jack of all trades, a bit here a bit there? What do you make of it?'

'Could be. A bit of fishing or pot setting, rabbits and a gun, a bit of poaching, dogs for poaching. It's possible that's all he is. By the way I didn't get a chance to tell you before, but the Landlord told me earlier that this guy lives in a fairly big cottage in the village. He always has plenty of money, has a rough wife and a string of kids. Can he support that lot on the earnings of a casual poacher and don't forget he also run's a van. A bit of a battered one, according to our friends next door. But he still has the cost of running it.'

'He might be doing that with the help of the DHSS. They are very generous when it comes to a string of kids. You know their philosophy, "You breed 'em: we keep 'em". On the other hand he maybe one of those odd types you hear of now and again, who win, or get left, large sums of money. They then move into the country to "get away from it all" and do their own thing. Do you think he is worth looking at a bit closer? The "plenty of money" bit intrigues me.'

'Maybe. There might be something in it and it sounds a bit of a funny going on and we haven't got much else, have we? That reminds me, The Old Man is expecting another call from us tomorrow. It would be nice to have something to report, if only to keep him quiet and get him off our backs for a while.'

'Ok, let's go into the village tomorrow and sniff around there a bit. At the same time I could go and have a closer look at Miss Fancy Pants, or what ever they call her, and her little set up.'

All agreed we settled down for the night. Well hardly settled.

Making love in a camper, and in particular with an active girl like Fred is one hell of an experience. I shudder to think what a casual observer, stood close by on the outside, would have made of it. Under normal circumstances the slightest movement inside the van caused it to rock on its springs and I am sure that at one point the additional gyrations from her enthusiasm almost vibrated it off the ground and into orbit.

Later, after much pulling and tugging and general rearrangement the sleeping bag was re-zipped up.

As we cuddled up close and settled down I closed my eyes and instantly and very vividly recalled the tantalising sight of Fred, dressed only in a long woolly jumper and stretched out on top of a sleeping bag.

'It's too damned cold to take it off' she had complaint. Apart from that there had been no other complaints on either side.

CHAPTER TWENTY

The following morning we set out early and having planned it that way started the day with a leisurely stroll around the countryside before ending up outside the village dress shop. The shop itself was very attractive and unusual in its outward design and appearance. The frontage was made up of a very large bow window, divided up into small square glass panes. Into these, a random selection, of crown glass, or as they are often refer to, bull glass, or bottle bottom glass panes, had been introduced and set in. Most of the woodwork was painted dark green and the entrance, which was to the left of the main window, was recessed and stood back from the front. The overall impression was that of a Victorian shop or something that had survived from around the Charles Dickens days.

The window display was very professional and all the items offered for sale were of an excellent quality and design, with prices to match. My first impressions were that a shop offering goods of this quality was somewhat out of place in a small village. It would, in my opinion, have been more in keeping with the higher-class areas that are to be found in most of the larger towns. However it happened to be where it was, and whether it was viable as a business proposition, or not, in that particular location was very difficult to tell.

We stood and both admired the fine display and Fred enthused over almost every item on show. At one point I thought, from the way she was talking, she was seriously contemplating buying up the entire stock and when I tried to reminded her that we were on expenses she remained undeterred, pointing out that she had her own personal credit card tucked away specifically for just such occasions.

A tiny bell, suspended on a spring, above the door gave a tinkle, and announced our entry. Having closed the door behind me I turned and was met by an astonishing display and variety of female attire which spanned the whole age range from adult, through teenage to children and, from what I could see, on down to tiny tots. Every square inch had been taken up to display the goods for sale. They were on racks and on mannequin models. They were also mounted on specially constructed displays that raised them up until they almost touched the ceiling. There were illuminated display shelves and counters with innumerable spotlights strategically placed to light the whole interior. Every last space appeared to have been cleverly utilised to display, to its best advantage, a tremendous range of female attire. Fred's eyes were everywhere trying to absorb everything at once. She was in a whirl and grinned with sheer delight at the abundance of elegance and choice.

From somewhere behind the folds and mass of clothing there emerged, as if from nowhere, a very tall, very slim, elegant and immaculately turned out lady, who I would have guessed was in her late forties, or early fifties. Everything about her, the way she moved, the way she held herself, was all class and quality. The natural smile was only temporarily dislodged while she enquired if she could help.

'I would just like to browse for a moment if I may,' replied Fred.

'But of course, my pleasure, please feel free. I was just having a break, so if you will excuse me I will go back and finish my cup of tea. Don't hesitate to give me a shout if there is anything I can do to assist.' She disappeared back from where she originally appeared and we were once again alone and surrounded by the magnificent display of female finery. I have never really been one for browsing round shops and definitely not round ladies clothes shops, so I very quickly became bored and found myself spending much of my time looking through the shop window into the village street and the surrounding area outside. As I did so Fred became more and more absorbed and excited as she rummaged. Fingering this, standing back from that, holding this dress in front of her and then quickly following it with a skirt. There was no doubt she was having the time of her life and I began to wonder if I would ever be able to prise her away.

'What do you think of this?' she enquired, standing before me with one hand pressed to her stomach to prevent a multi-coloured skirt from dropping to the floor. 'Isn't it gorgeous? Is it too long? What do you think?'

Bless her for she was not to know that it all left me cold. I have never been able to understand how a girl can clasp, with one hand, an item of clothing up in front of her and make some sort of valid judgment as to its suitability, let alone expect someone else to do so. All I can say is that women must have terrific powers of imagination particularly when it comes to selecting clothes and items to wear.

'It looks very nice' I muttered, trying to show an enthusiasm that really wasn't there.

'Nice? It's lovely, absolutely fabulous, and all you can do is stand there and say "nice".'

'No. It really is lovely and I think it suits you.' What else could I say? It was an item of multi-coloured clothing, held by a flat hand against her chest. Before making a decision was I supposed to take into account the bizarre effect of the trousers and large hiking boots showing below? I could only say what I thought she wanted to hear.

'I'm not sure now, you don't like it, do you?'

'Yes I do, honest, Fred, but I am the last person you should be asking. I prefer to consider myself as an expert on their removal and not on the selection or choice of item in the first place.'

She smiled. 'You stick with what you are expert at darling, and you will do for me. I've gone off it anyhow. I think I much prefer this one.'

So it went on for five, ten, fifteen minutes. I lost track of time. Dashing from here to there. Holding this up front, admiring that at arm's length, looking at this in the mirror, a screwed up expression on her face and a not so sure comments about that one, then a smile at the sight of something else, and often a low, almost imperceptible whistle when the price tag was consulted. I gathered things were dear.

'Our Miss Fancy Pants is a little dear on some of her items,' whispered Fred very quietly into my ear and then followed it up with a light peck on my cheek.

I noticed a couple of items had, never-the-less, found their way on to the counter top as if singled out for special attention.

'Everything all right?' came an unexpected enquiry from the lady who had silently returned.

'Yes. Fine thank you. Is there any chance I might try on these two items?'

'There certainly is. If you will follow me, the changing and fitting rooms are through here in the rear.'

I had been alone for only a matter of minutes when, without warning, I suppose because at the time I had my back to it, the door opened and the bell tinkled, and who should barge in but our 'poacher' friend, the guy in the same dirty white jumper. We had christened him the Poacher as a quick and ready way to identify him. At the same time the shop lady came from behind wherever she had been secreted, and before he even had time to open his mouth, she glanced quickly at me, and then addressed the new arrival, saying in a very sharp and stern tone of voice, 'I have told you before not to come in here when I have customers. In fact I have even asked you not to come here at all but you don't take any notice.'

He looked squarely at me and grinned. Goodness knows what was going through his mind. Perhaps he thought that I was the customer and the only one in the shop. Perhaps he expected the 'Closed' sign to be in place in the window.

'Don't matter to me who the hell you got in here or what you want. What I have to say is important. Tell your husband we have some gear to move and move fast. Things round here aren't too healthy right now, see.'

'That might not be convenient, or possible, because he is away for the next day or so.'

'That's not my problem. You get him back. You get hold of him and tell him quick.' And turning, he left just as noisily as he had arrived.

'A very nasty man! I am sorry about that. I have told him time and again not to come into my shop. Whatever arrangements he has with my husband are of no concern of mine and I wish he would not use me or try to involve me.'

'He works for your husband, does he?' I casually enquired.

'No, he is not employed by my husband, if that is what you mean? He is nothing more than a common lay-about but calls himself a "jobber", what ever that is supposed to means.'

'A jobber?'

'Yes. That's what he says but he really does mainly labouring work, when he works. He also messes about doing things like welding metal bits, repairing, or so he claims, cars. He buys and sells, fishes and poaches. I think if you can name it he will try and claim he can do it and I think that's what he means when he calls himself a jobber. He messes about with anything. Whether he can do it right or not I don't know but I doubt it. You only have to look at the man.' I nodded, she continued, 'I don't like the man and I certainly object and dislike him coming in here, and particularly when he brings that horrible young woman he lives with. She handles and touches everything while their totally obnoxious children run riot rubbing their grubby, sticky hands over everything. I think the biggest insult is when she selects something totally inappropriate and he produces large bundles of dirty notes and contemptuously throws them on my counter and says, "Keep the change and buy your-self something decent". He thinks he is being funny, I think he is loathsome, ignorant and ill-mannered, nothing more than an uneducated oaf. He causes nothing but ill feeling in the village and no one, that I know, likes him and everyone is curious to know where he gets all his money. I keep asking my husband to tell him not to come into the shop but it doesn't seem to make any difference and every time he or one of his family come in I always feel the need to spray the shop with air freshener. He is a horrible man. But just listen to me. I am dreadfully sorry. You must forgive me, as I know it has nothing to do with you. It's him, he makes me so angry that I could scream.'

'Please can I have these?' asked Fred, who had returned from the rear of the shop during the minor outburst. Just how much she had overheard, I didn't know, but the expression on her face showed that she had heard enough to gather there was no love lost between the proprietor and the Poacher.

As we left with Fred grinning and clutching her new purchases, the shop lady, who must have been more upset than she showed, followed us to the door and after a weak 'Goodbye' closed it behind us. She then turned the 'Open' sign over so that it read 'Closed. Back in five minutes'.

We walked along the street towards the village Post Office, which also doubled as a newsagents and stationers, and there I remembered, that on the previous day, I had been unable to find a pen that had obviously been misplaced. It would, no doubt, turn up later, when least expected, but in the meantime I was short of and needed a pen. 'I'm going to pop in here and buy a couple of cheap biros until mine decides to turn up. Coming?'

'Why not?'

The Post Office was only small and the few people who happened to be in at the time, made it appear quite busy and it was, as a result, difficult to move around. It was made even more inconvenient for me as I had no idea of the layout and therefore no idea of which direction to head in order to find the location of the pens and biros. There seemed to be children everywhere and they were literally into everything. They were opening boxes and pulling out the contents. Toy cars were being run back and forth on the floor, coloured crayons cascaded all over the place. Once examined, each item was quickly discarded as their tiny eyes saw something else as yet not plundered or ripped out of its box. They were a group of kids who were obviously out of control and were just being a damned nuisance. The pillaging continued unabated.

'You going to be all bloody day in here? Don't know why you have to come on a day when it's full of senile old sods with nowt better to do than shuffle about for a few manky quid.' I looked behind me and saw standing outside, the poacher. I thought I had recognised the voice.

'Piss off and wait outside and sort them bloody kids out. Different bloody story, i'nt it, when you want bloody money.'

I looked back into the shop and in the direction of the female voice that had answered the outburst and saw, at the head of the postal counter queue, a gangly and skinny woman of about five foot four inches tall. I guessed she was in her late twenties but her overall appearance and haggardness made it difficult to accurately judge. She was probably nowhere near as old as she looked. She had an overall air of scruffiness about her and was definitely not as clean as she might have been. The grubby, food stained, tee shirt did nothing to enhance here appearance. The large tattoo on her upper arm and the purple streaks in her untidy hair blended well with the nicotine-stained top lip and fingers. The jeans were torn and also grubby and the outline and movement of tiny boobs that only just managed to push out the front of the discoloured tee shirt displayed the absence of a bra. Not exactly a well turned-out young lady who took pride in her appearance.

She was laboriously counting out the ten pound notes, which had been passed to her under the glass security partition, in a slow, deliberate and exaggerated way which gave me the impression that her brain was not working anywhere near a normal speed.

'You get them kids in the van while I count this lot to make sure these sods aren't robbing me. This bugger back here thinks I'm a wanker and bloody thick and can't count.'

The middle aged man behind the partition replied, 'There is no need for that remark young lady. You will find the money is correct, so if you will move to one side I can serve the next person.'

'Sod off. Let 'em wait. I'll move when I've done.'

'You having bother up there?' drawled the Poacher.

'Nothing I can't fucking handle and the bloody state you're in you couldn't find yer bloody dick. So piss off out and take the kids out wiv ya.'

Eventually the mayhem subsided following several half hearted and hysterical attempts to round up the kids and wrestle them away from the displays. They randomly discarded everything they had picked up and finished with, while they clung to that which they intended to keep, paid for or not. Eventually the whole tribe - for that was the only way to describe them - departed and a relatively peaceful atmosphere descended over the shop.

'How that lot can draw all that money is beyond me? I worked all my life and all I have to show for it is a pension while that young article has done nothing but breed kids and comes in here with I don't know how many books and draws literally hundreds,' bitterly complained a very charming elderly lady who had been standing patiently throughout the whole fiasco.

'Not hundreds, Mrs Williams' corrected the postmaster. 'But nevertheless, I agree, a rather substantial amount when one considers that neither of them has any desire to work and beside the money they also get allowances to cover their poll tax and rent.'

'Well I stood and saw you count out more than a hundred,' protested Mrs Williams. 'Nearly two hundred and that's a lot of money every week and to think most of that will end up as drink and down there necks, if I am not mistaken, or up in smoke. Little ones won't see much of it either way.'

'Unfortunately what they do with it is none of our concern,' admonished the man behind the glass screen. 'But I agree, something is wrong somewhere.'

'Well it's far more than people like them deserve. No wonder the country's in the mess its in,' and still muttering to herself, and rightfully so, a disgruntled Mrs Williams slowly made her way to the door and out on to the street to continue on her way.

'What I find difficult to understand,' added a young woman, who up to that point had been standing patently waiting her turn to be served, and minding her own business, 'Is that they get away with it all. You name it and they get it. Handout upon handout and have you noticed how they always know their "rights".'

'They are part of a new class within modern society. They are known as "well paid, professional layabouts". Not the unemployed but the "unemployable". Those with no intention of working because they can get more than they need from the state and thereby make a good living out of being unemployed. Then if they do need that bit extra they do a bit of work on the side. Cash in the hand, they call it,' someone added. 'Their profession is to make a damned good living out of not working and a lot of them are getting away with it.'

'Them two certainly do,' replied the young woman. 'I wish I didn't have to work and could afford to go out every night and booze and smoke and bet and use wacky backy or whatever it is that those two seem to be always on. If it's not that

then it's pills or something. He was high just now and she is always at the Doctors demanding prescriptions for Ativan and Methadone because, she says, she can't cope and then she is always balling and screaming that she has to go into town to collect them because the local chemist never stocks any since he was broken into and burgled not long ago. I know because I have been in and heard her and then him. How does he drives that van the state he gets into. Look at both of them today, on a different planet the pair of them. It's the kids I feel sorry for, poor little things, growing up with those two and in those conditions. Yet they continue to produce them. That's all them types seem to be able to do. Breed kids and demand their rights. It isn't right and something should be done about it!'

There was no reply: perhaps because no one had an answer. But I think we were all aware that it is becoming more and more of a social and economic problem. I suppose it is always easy to blame someone else when the true blame really lays with each and every one of us for not taking responsibility for ourselves. It's funny how we always expect someone else to sort out all our problems. We think that if we vote in an election then that is the end of our responsibilities. It is then down to the politicians to sort it all out.

I paid for my two cheap biros and as I stepped outside I immediately felt a sense of relief. There had certainly been an atmosphere of dissatisfaction and tension inside that little Post Office and all caused by the presence and attitude of only two, not very nice, people.

'Gosh, I certainly would not like those two as my next door neighbours!' smiled Fred. 'I suppose in a small community like this, they must cause quite a stir. Did you notice how everyone was hostile towards them? They probably get everyone's back up at some time, in one way or another. I have to admit that my first impressions of them are not very good. She strikes me as being the perfect slag and he looks evil and definitely not a nice person to mix with.'

'Here's the Phone Box, shall we ring the Old Man while we're here? At least it will keep all the agro together for today.'

We both squeezed into the confined space. I inserted a coin, pressed the appropriate buttons, and waited. 'Hello. Janet? Mel Grundy here, is Cruickshank available?' There was a click, followed by another, then, 'Grundy, glad you rang,' the almost pleasant voice on the line taking me completely by surprise. 'Get in touch with Oldfield just as soon as you can, they have found a body. I can't tell you anymore at the moment because that is all I know. I have just been informed, so you get in touch with him directly and find out what it is all about. What have you to report?'

'Not a great deal, Sir.' I reluctantly had to confess. 'We are following several leads of course,' I lied. 'But this is a small and close community and on the surface there does not seem to be anything untoward. However, we are discreetly

making enquiries and as soon as there in anything significant to report, I will come straight back to you Sir.'

'Good. Make sure you do. Well get on with it. You now have Oldfield to contact, have you not?'

'Yes, Sir! Goodbye for now Sir.'

I replaced the receiver and rummaged in my pocket for another coin.

'What was that all about?' demanded Fred. 'Did I hear him say they have found a body? Where?'

'Yes, but I don't know where,' I replied. 'We have to contact Oldfield straight away to find out the details.'

When I got through to Humber, receptionist Kathleen Bland sounded genuinely pleased to hear from us and insisted on questioning me in an attempt to find out if we were enjoying ourselves and if we liked camping and if the weather was nice and so on. When I finally persuaded her to put us through to Oldfield it turned out that he was not there and Bob Kettleness, the Senior Watch Officer answered his phone. He sounded genuinely disappointed when I told him that I felt he could not help and that I needed to speak directly to Oldfield. He told me that Oldfield was with the local Police and he had no idea when he would be back. He then suggested that if it was very important, it might be possible to contact him on his mobile radio, but that would only work if Oldfield happened to be in his car with it switched on. After much persuasion, I managed to get him to accept that it was only necessary for him to leave a message for Oldfield, telling him that I would be in touch again later, in the meantime there was no need for anyone to concern themselves further. When I finally hung up, I dug in my pocket for yet another coin, and then lifting the hand set, dialled another number.

'Good afternoon, North Yorkshire Police, how can I help you?' enquired the voice.

I told the lady who I was and who I wished to speak to. I was then immediately connected to the appropriate office, only to be informed, by a secretary, that Chief Inspector Jablonski was not available. He was out of the office and not expected to be back that day and his assistant, DC Ellis, was currently tied up with the Coastguard. I explained that it was the Coastguard that I was actually trying to contact and believing that he would probably be with the Chief Inspector had asked for him in the first place. So would DC Ellis please have a word with me?

'Ellis.'

'Good afternoon Mr Ellis, could I please speak to Ray Oldfield?'

'Who's calling?'

'Mel Grundy! Coastguard.'

'Oh Mr Grundy, good afternoon Sir. One moment please.'

'Good afternoon Mr Grundy, Oldfield, how can I help you?'

'Quite simply, I hope. I am ringing you because I understand a body has been found. I'm sorry to contact you where you are now and be a nuisance to you, but I would appreciate it if you can tell me what you know?'

'There's not a great deal to tell at the moment. A body has been washed up about four miles South of your present location, but before you ask it is not Edison. This one is assumed to be that of a Merchant Seaman, from what he was wearing. He had no identification on him and he has been in the water quite some time but has not deteriorated sufficiently to be un-identifiable. His clothing, in no way, compares with what we believe Edison was wearing when he went missing. I am with the Police now, as you are well aware, discussing it.'

'Who knows of this find, this body being picked up… so far?'

'We do, of course, and the Police and, as far as I know, you are the only others. Hold the line a moment.' A few seconds later and he was back on the phone. In between times I took advantage of the wait and pecked Fred a couple of times on the cheek. 'Sorry about that but according to DC Ellis, there has been a press release to the effect that a body has been found on the beach, and that Police enquiries continue.'

'Pity. It may of course have nothing whatsoever to do with what we are interested in, but you never know. It might have been better to keep it under wraps, if we could have done, for the time being.'

'Yes, I see what you mean and as I was saying earlier to Mr Ellis, according to our calculations, for a body to end up where it was found, indicates that it went into the water at some point to the North and that puts it very much in your general direction. Just hold the line again for a moment, will you?'

I smiled at Fred and winked. Before she could say anything, I held my finger to my lips to indicate that I wanted her to remain silent. I did it in order to try and hear any background conversation that might have come through the jumble of noises, I could already hear, on the other end of the line. What I was hearing was, in fact, unintelligible and then it went silent and static filled the system.

After a brief pause Oldfield came back on, 'Sorry to keep you waiting. I have discussed it with DC Ellis and although he can do nothing about the press release that has already gone out, we can, if it will help, leave it at that. In other words the press will only know that a body has been found and that the Police are making further enquiries. We will make no further comments and stall them with a promise that they shall be the first to get to know any future developments. The local press can be a pain in the arse at times, but they can also be very cooperative when we want them to be. OK?'

'That's better than nothing I suppose. The whole thing might amount to nothing more than a wild goose chase and prove to be irrelevant. That is if finding a body is ever irrelevant. But you know what I mean? I am speaking specifically from the point of view of our current investigation and I have the feeling that for

the moment it might be for the best if we can keep a low profile on it. By the way, does Mrs Edison know anything about it yet?'

'Not from us, but I don't know about the Police… No not from the Police either I'm being told.'

'Do you think it might be a good idea to give her a call and tell her. I would hate for her to come across some vague announcement in the local press, simply stating that an unidentified body had been washed ashore, or whatever they choose to print. I think it is only common decency that she should be told and assured it is not her husband and it should come from someone like you. You might ask her, at the same time, if she will be discreet and say nothing should the press try and put two and two together and start hounding her. Ask her to deny everything and make no statements. It may well work to our advantage if people are given no details and are left to assume and speculate. It might make someone nervous and we may just get lucky and stumble onto it. Goodness knows we need every little help we can get and, god knows, we have precious little just now.'

'Leave it with me. I will attend to it right away.'

'Thanks and my kind regards to DC Ellis. I will be in touch with you later.' I hung up and Fred and I spilled out onto the pavement.

'Did you catch all that?'

'Yes I think so. Basically they have got a body, but it is not Edison?'

'That's what the man said. A body of a Seaman, they think, but definitely not Edison.'

'Do you think it's significant?'

'I really don't know, but we seem to know so little about anything at the moment. Perhaps we are clutching at straws. We can only be patient and see what develops.'

'Do you think it was wise to tell people like Oldfield and the old man for that matter that we are not getting very far. Should we not be keeping things like that to ourselves?'

'I suppose so. But it is the truth and can't do us any harm at the moment and I don't care what they might think of us, or our abilities. In fact, with a bit of luck, they may feel sorry for us and try and help us that little bit more.'

'You would be so lucky. Pity we did not find out about that body sooner.'

'Why?'

'Well at least then, we could have arranged to have a D notice issued on it.'

'Yes I suppose we could but it's a bit too late for that now.'

CHAPTER TWENTY-ONE

We were strolling round the village holding hands and idly looking in all the shops and casually wandering up and down the side lanes and narrow alleyways.

'Can I make a suggestion?' asked Fred.

'Of course you can. Is it serious or saucy?'

'Serious, so just listen. I feel we should, in some way, widen our horizons and look further afield. I have a strange feeling that we are not getting very far simply wandering round the village or sitting in the pub. Not that I don't enjoy doing both, but we seem to be getting nowhere fast. What do you say if we come back this evening and try something a bit different? For example why don't we visit that other pub here in the village and keep our eyes and ears open in there. You never know we might get lucky as they say, if there is such a thing as luck in our line of work but at least it's somewhere different.'

'Sounds a good idea to me but isn't it a bit of a contradiction. First of all you suggest that we are not getting anywhere just sitting about in pubs and then suggest we try another one. As I say that's fine with me. I don't mind sitting about in pubs and don't see why we should not give it a whirl.'

'I really meant wandering round the village doesn't seem to be getting us very far. I just felt we should try and plan things a bit better and suggested the pub here in the village for starters and don't forget we also discussed looking closer at the Poacher. When are we going to fit that in and how are we going to do it? Although, after this afternoons episode in the Post Office, we do know a little bit more about him.'

'I agree there and you are right about just wandering around the village. So we will do that but before we do let's go back and get something to eat.'

* * *

Early that evening we returned to the village.

The pub went under the name of 'The Dog and Gun' and from the outside was very similar in many ways to the one down the lane adjoining the campsite. It was perhaps not quite so old, in terms of years, but was very similar in appearance. It's internal decor, the beamed ceilings and polished wood panelled walls excreta, together with the fine collection of antique knickknacks, served to remind everyone who ventured in, that the pub had been in existence for a great number of years. This antiquity blended well with the furniture and upholstery despite the fact that they were relatively modern. I was to note later that the toilet facilities were also

very modern having no doubt been added on and refurbished from time to time and not hidden away in some out house, as was the case down the lane. There was a great deal of evidence to suggest that a lot of effort had been put into the place to make it comfortable, whilst tasteful maintaining a balance between the modern aspects and its antiquity. A sharp contrast to The Grapes that appeared to have stood still in time and sadly lacked anything remotely connected with the twenty-first century.

We entered to find the place deserted, with the exception of a bored barman who looked up and sighed at our arrival. As we approached the bar he laid aside a newspaper that he had evidently been reading. He took his time serving a whiskey and a gin and tonic, all as if the effort of getting going was a bit too much. He said very little and was more than happy, having completed the chore of serving us, to return to his paper.

Once settled by the open fireplace, Fred moved close and whispered, 'Seen that paper he's reading?' nodding back towards to bar.

I looked across and there, blazoned along the top of the newspaper that the barman held, was the headline, "BODY FOUND ON BEACH".

'Excuse me,' I said in a raised voice towards him. He looked up and if the look on his face was anything to go by he was not happy at being disturbed. 'Where is the nearest place I can buy a newspaper at this time of day?'

'Out front, turn left, they're open 'till nine.'

'Thank you' and turning back to Fred, said in a normal voice, 'I won't be a sec.'

On my return, I laid the paper on the table and there across the top of the front page, in large black capitals, exactly as we had already seen in the barman's copy, was the headline "BODY FOUND ON BEACH". It was big and bold and despite the fact that we would rather it had not been there I couldn't blame the newspaper for exploiting a situation that would obviously sell them papers. That and of course it is not every day, that a body gets washed up on the beach and provides a good headline. However, whatever the initial impact they hoped their headline would create, it rather fizzled out when all they had to follow it was a few words, which stated, "A body has been found on a local beach. Police are investigating and at this time, no further details have been released. When our correspondent contacted the Coastguard there was no one available to comment".

'At least everyone will now know a body has been found. A pity it had to get into the paper,' commented Fred as she turned the pages and glanced at the other headlines.

'Come on drink up. That barman is obviously not in a talkative mood and would probably be happier without us. So if that then leaves only the two of us in here, we are not going to learn very much from each other and it's still daylight so let's go for a walk. We can always come back here later.'

We drank up and left the barman to his paper. Outside we turned down the first lane that we came to and had hardly gone five hundred yards, when Fred exclaimed, 'Just look over there! A van and a very familiar one at that, so the Poacher must live somewhere round here?'

'Unless he's visiting.'

We casually walked past and carried on down the lane to where it eventually ended at a farm gate. We turned round and retraced our steps crossing to the other side to make our walk appear as casual as possible. When we returned to the main road, we continued, still holding hands, until we reached the next side turning. Much to our pleasant surprise, this narrow lane opened up into a kind of village-square that had all the features necessary to make a perfect picture for a chocolate box cover.

It had a closely cropped grassed plot in the centre, a preserved, though I noticed, not working, water pump, a horse trough, seats and small memorial to those who died in the world wars. Next to it, as is often to be found in coastal villages, a memorial to those Merchant Seamen who also lost their lives at sea, both at home and abroad. It always strikes me as strange how these memorials inevitably seem to end abruptly when all the available space for the display of names, has been used up. I felt certain there must have been many others who had lost their lives at sea since 1948, which happened to be the date of the last entry on the slab we stood in front of. I wondered if perhaps the fashion for war memorials and memorials in general had died out. A pity, for I feel sure that living relatives would prefer to see their loved ones remembered, as opposed to simply seeing recorded those who were long gone, with no one left behind to really remember them.

We stood for a moment and read the names. I secretly believed I did it just to make sure I was not listed. I do the same with death notices in the newspaper, to re-assure myself that I am still alive. I wonder how many other people do the same?

Satisfied I was not listed, we sat on one of the seats, to admire the view and enjoy the atmosphere and feelings of tranquillity. It was hard to believe, surrounded by all the peace and quiet that we were so close to the main road. It was a truly lovely setting and made one feel good.

'What are you thinking?' enquired Fred, squeezing my hand.

'I was thinking how I could sit here forever. It's so peaceful, even though surrounded by all those houses over there. I wonder if they appreciate how lucky they are, and how much I envy them.'

'Probably not and I bet it's a rather different story in the winter, with all the snow and cold.'

'I think I would take my chances. Particularly if there was no need to get out and about, no need to have to go to work and things like that when it was cold.'

'I see what you mean, but I think it might be a little too quiet for me. For a few weeks perhaps, OK. Maybe even a few months but certainly not anything permanent. Perhaps when I am old and past it I might think differently, but for the moment it's a bit too quiet for me.'

We continued to sit and soak up the atmosphere. Fred finally broke the silence, 'I think it is fairly safe for us to assume that the Poacher lives in that cottage where his van was parked outside. We know it is his van and you can see that the stonewall has been roughly knocked down so he can park it off the road and then the rest of the garden is certainly in keeping with them. Did you see it? It was like a rubbish tip. Kids broken toys everywhere and a broken pushchair with its wheel missing and the old washing machine dumped on its side and rusting. The greenhouse had hardly any glass in it and a ground floor window in the house was broken and there was a dirt nylon curtain flapping through it. It all fits in neatly with the behaviour we witnessed in the Post Office earlier today. No wonder the locals are not impressed with them. The cottage itself is quite big and must be worth quite a bit in terms of property, but it's all so sadly neglected, and the state of that garden, when all the rest in the area are so neat and tidy. I think we can safely say he lives there.'

'He gives me the impression of being the type of person who has a shotgun and no licence, and that the van will not be taxed or insured. Come to think of it, I don't remember seeing a tax disc in it, but then I didn't look that close. I don't suppose he will bother about a driver's licence either and I bet their names crop up with monotonous regularity at Parish Council Meetings and the likes.'

'I bet it does but come on. We can't stay here forever; it's getting a bit chilly. It's time we went back to the pub.'

I don't know how long we had been away from the pub, an hour perhaps, but during that time business had not picked up very much. In the bar, beside our-selves, were just two other blokes sitting and quietly chatting behind partly consumed pints of beer. The suits they wore and the briefcases suggesting they were either professional types or reps, salesmen or perhaps just dressed up office bods. If there was anyone through in the other bar they were very quiet and it was impossible for us to see anything from where we stood. The barman, as enthusiastic as ever, laid his paper to one side before sliding off his stool to serve us.

We resumed our original seats and looked at each other. It was so quiet that anything said, in a normal tone of voice would easily have been overheard by everyone and this was well illustrated by the fact that despite the whispering we could clearly hear the conversation from the table across the room. Fred being obviously well aware of all this decided, for reasons known only to herself, to poke fun at me. 'Are you going to take me to bed early tonight dear? Because if you are please promise that afterwards you won't make me stand naked in the corner

all night.' She raised her glass adding, 'Do you know, another of these and I'm anyone's?'

The two at the table stopped talking and the barman looked up. I replied, taking her up and as usual enjoying the fun of this kind of thing, 'Does your husband know you give it away for a couple of gins?'

'Gin has nothing to do with it. I give it away, because it's mine and is free to anyone I fancy. The gin is a bonus and might add to the fun but that's all,' she laughed.

'Shut up you fool,' I whispered, 'I like people to think I can afford to pay for it. Get the Gin down your neck. You know it melts knicker elastic.' At which we both laughed out loud, attracting more attention.

A group of people came in through the door and turned to look in our direction to see what all the laughter was about. The other two, who had long since stopped talking, continued to look across. We abruptly stopped laughing and just sat and looked at each other as if everything was normal and nothing had happened. Under cover of the table Fred slipped her hand onto my inner thigh just above my knee and gently rubbed. I returned the compliment by gently rubbing hers. The two guys opposite could obviously see this and stared fascinated, until another group came in and blocked their view.

'It's getting busier,' observed Fred as she twisted to get a better look at the latest arrivals, the movement causing my hand to slide much higher up her leg. I gentle massaged the fabric. She turned back to face me and with a grin on her face, was about to say something when a loud gruff voice, raised and almost shouting, came from somewhere over the other side and from within the other bar. Everyone on our side stopped talking.

'Eh you! I'm talking to you. Yes you. How many times do I have to ask? Where's Harold?' the voice bellowed.

'Upstairs like I said,' replied the barman, addressing his remarks through an opening into the other bar.

'Well get the bugger down here, now, fast! I want to talk to him.'

'That sounds very much like our friend - the Poacher,' whispered Fred.

'It does,' I whispered back, 'and you don't have to be able to see him to tell that. He's an aggressive, noisy, bastard, isn't he?'

Harold, whom we took to be the Landlord, when the barman stated that he was upstairs, must have entered the other bar through another, unseen, door. The Poacher, almost shouting said, 'Come here you! I want you now, outside!'

'Stay here Fred,' I hissed, 'this might be interesting. I am going to slip out and see if I can see anything.'

Fortunately for me, it was now fairly dark and I could only just make out the poacher's van. Where he had chosen to park it allowed me to hide myself round a convenient corner, and be close enough to hear all their conversation. The two of

them stood at the rear of the van with the doors open and what I heard was more than interesting. The Landlord spoke first, 'Look here Johnson I've already told you I am not taking all that bloody lot. In fact I am not taking any of it. I don't want it, and that's final.'

'You don't want it? What the hell's up with ya?'

'Look Mick, you are as high as a sodding kite, off your bloody trolley and not thinking straight. Have you seen tonight's paper? It's now all getting beyond a bloody joke. No one paid much attention at first when that Coastguard bloke went missing, but now there's a body come up, we will probably have the bloody Police crawling all over the sodding place again.'

'So what!'

'So what? You bloody dick head. Use your bloody loaf, buying this stuff is doggy enough at any time, but now it's time to call it squits and knock it off!'

'How do you mean - knock it off? It was all right before and the price has always suited you all right! Made a sodding fortune you have and with me taking all the fucking risks! You miserable tight bastard!'

'Risk? What about when all this stuff is sitting in my bloody cellar? Aren't I taking any bloody risks? Don't I have to store the bloody stuff.'

'Are you buggery. You just shove it in another bloody bottle and sell it to your bloody punters. You don't store the bloody stuff.'

'That's only when there are just one or two bottles but look at this lot. How many have you got there, forty, fifty? Piss off. I'm not taking that lot and what about paying for it? Unless you're giving it away or giving credit, and knowing you there's no bloody chance of that, where do you think I am going to get enough for all this bloody lot?'

'You're sodding loaded! All bloody Landlords are sodding loaded! Hit the fucking till. Anyhow, all I know is that I want rid of this lot, all of it and now!'

'Go sell it to your bloody mate down the road at the Grapes then. You're always telling me what a good guy he is, and your special chum who sees you alright when you are a bit short, well go see your chum now! Sell him it. Let him hit his bloody till.'

'He's the bloody same as you, shit scared. What's up with you all? Find a body, they do, down the road and you all shit yourselves. It's got nowt to do with anybody round here and the bloody fuzz, round here, are too fucking thick to work anything out anyway.'

'What makes you so sure there is nothing to work out? How do you know it has nothing to do with anyone round here? How do I know it has nothing to do with you or any of your bloody cronies for that matter? You're probably in it up to your bloody eye balls somewhere.'

'Because I know different, that's why. So just what are you getting at? You're just gobbing off. Do you know that? Well shut it! You know fuck all. So do you want this stuff or not?'

'How many more times? I have just bloody told you! No I do not! It's all getting too sodding dodgy. Sorry Mick, maybe later, but leave it for now, there's a good lad. I am just not interested at the moment and that's it. Finished.'

'Up you! I need cash and I need it now. This stuff has to be paid for in the first place you know? They don't just give me the bloody stuff.'

'Listen Mick, I have already told you, count me out. This lot's your bloody problem, not mine.'

I heard footsteps and assumed the Landlord had walked away, presumably towards the rear of the pub. When I could no longer hear his footfalls I further assumed that he had disappeared inside through a back door. The rear doors and the drivers side door of the van all slammed shut. The poacher was cross. The engine started up, and there was a squeal of tyres as he accelerated and left the car park at break neck speed. It was fortunate that no one was approaching at the time or passing in the opposite direction, as a collision would have been unavoidable.

I left my hiding place and returned to the pub where I found Fred in deep conversation with another couple. As I approached, Fred said, 'This is my husband,' and then she added, 'Had you left it in the car dear?'

'No,' I replied taking up her lead, 'I have searched everywhere. I can't have lost it, it's sure to turn up somewhere.'

'I have just been saying to these two good people, the length of time you have been away, you must have dismantled the car, piece by piece and then put it back together again.'

'Almost,' I laughed.

'Was it anything important?' enquired the strange lady.

'No,' I replied, racking my brains for a plausible answer for my supposed searching. If I said something like 'My cigarette lighter,' someone might have offered me a light and I don't smoke. Then came a flash of inspiration. 'I wanted to ring a friend and realised I had mislaid his card with the number on it and thought I might have left it in my car.' That seemed to satisfy them, and they let it drop. Looking straight at Fred, I continued, 'Are you going to stay here with these good people while I go back and see if I left it in the camper? I did promise to ring tonight and they will be waiting.' I hoped I sounded convincing.

'I think I aught to come with you dear. There are, one or two bits I need to do, and I can get on with them while you are phoning. So please excuse us. It has been nice talking to you and perhaps we might bump into each other again some time. Bye for now.'

'Who were they?' I enquired as soon as we were outside.

'Just customers! They came in and struck up a casual conversation with me, probably because I was sat there alone. Seems everyone is talking about the body on the beach and the performance in the other bar but they don't seem to have much idea what it was all about. That woman is convinced that the body is the same man who went missing a while back, meaning Edison, and that everyone was wrong when they said he had left his wife and run away. They seemed almost disappointed that it might all now have been a simple accident, with no romance or intrigue attached to it. But more to the point, how did you get along.'

'OK, but first of all; that was good thinking on your part about the car. My mind went blank for the moment and I could hardly admit I had been outside eaves dropping, now could I?' I said laughing.

'Come on then, tell all.'

'Our friend the poacher has a name; Mick Johnson, and from what I gathered, he is trying to sell booze to the Landlord who, for some reason, is scared out of his wits, and won't touch it at any price. From what I overheard, there has obviously been some dealings in the past, but only in small quantities. Maybe on a regular basis as well, I don't know. However there is no doubt that it is spirits that is involved, as I overheard Johnson, the poacher, say "You only have to put it in another bottle and sell it to your punters." The Landlord agreed, but said that in this case there were too many bottles involved. Even if he wanted them, he said, which he was adamant that he did not, he could not finance the deal. The amount of cash involved was too much or so he was claiming. I got the impression that all deals were and had been for cash up front. Johnson, the poacher, was rattled and seemed desperate to off load the whole lot there and then, if he had his way. He nearly exploded when the Landlord told him to take the whole lot down the road and sell it to The Grapes. There's no doubt there is wheeling and dealing going on and probably has been going on, on a fairly regular basis but now, for some reason, things are not quite as they should be. I got the distinct impression that one or more of them are more than a little on edge. I would say they are running scared and it's my guess that it has something to do with the fact that a body has been found.'

'So you think this … who?'

'The Poacher! Mick Johnson, you mean?'

'This Mick Johnson is selling booze? Nothing unusual in that, is there? It's the sort of thing that goes on all the time and by the wagonload in the big cities. There have always been wheeler-dealers in spirits, particularly in pubs and clubs. That and a lot of other stuff to go with it and very much a part of pub life I would have thought.'

'I know, but what surprises me was the amount involved here. This is no big city and as far as we know there are only two pubs and no clubs and I heard one of them mention forty to fifty bottles. That's not just a bit on the side. That's a consignment. I can understand the odd bottle here and there to beat the taxman.

But what he was offering was large scale. So first of all, ask your-self where is it all coming from and why suddenly should something, that appears to have gone smoothly in the past, now throws everyone into a panic. I think the fictitious phone call we invented, back there, in the pub, should become a real one to DC Ellis to check with him and see if there have been any large scale spirit thefts anywhere round here or perhaps a bit further afield, recently.'

We had, by this time, almost reached the end of the lane leading back to the campsite.

'Can you see what I see over there?' pointed Fred.

'Yes. If I am not mistaken that's Johnson's van. I wonder what he is up to down here. Probably taken the other guy's advice and has come to try to offload a van full of booze. Let's go in and see if he is about.'

We went into the Pub, ordered a drink and stood at the bar and looked round. Neither Johnson, or for that matter, the Landlord, were anywhere to be seen. I looked at Fred and shrugged. There was nothing we could do, so we stood and chatted until our drinks were finished then having decided not to buy another, we left somewhat disappointed.

* * *

The van was still there as we crossed to the camping field. I opened the gate and we passed through and as I turned to secure it Fred said, 'you go on ahead; I am just popping in here for a tiddle. You can be putting the kettle on.'

I crossed the field leaving Fred walking in the direction of the loo. I let myself in and did as instructed. The kettle had just begun to sing as it built up to boil, when the door opened and in she climbed.

'What do you make of this?' she enquired, offering me an empty bottle.

'What's that all about and where did you get it? What are you telling me?'

'I found this outside the loo. I went to throw some tissues into the wheelie bin by the toilet and I noticed a black plastic sack down the side. It had split and this is one of the bottles that poked out. There were quite a few others, all similar, but I just picked up this one as I thought you might find it interesting. They have all been bagged up separately and put to one side for some reason because the wheelie bin is not full. It is only just over half full and there are already loads of other empty bottles in there. There was plenty of room for the sack and more besides. My guess is that these bottles have been put to one side for a reason. I had a sniff in this one, as I walked back across the field, and I am sure there's been vodka in it. I can't make out the label, can you?' as she passed the bottle over to me to look at.

I agreed that it was more than likely that it had contained vodka but the overall appearance of the label told me nothing. I checked the base and around

the neck and shoulders and they told me nothing either, there being only a few numbers moulded into the glass. I went back to the label for past experience has taught me that many foreign manufacturers and exporters quite often include in the wording of their labels, small print in English, such as "Made in..." or "Product of...", "Imported, Bottled and distributed by .....for.....etc.". But I had no such luck with this one. This bottle could have come from anywhere as far as I was concerned and was probably never intended for the U/K market.

'Right young lady! I think it might be a good idea if we go back out and have a closer look at these bottles and at the same time scout around and see if we can find Johnson, or the Landlord, or anyone else for that matter. I am curious to find out, if we can, why the Poachers' van is there and why he doesn't appear to be in the pub.'

CHAPTER TWENTY-TWO

At Fred's suggestion I carried one of the small rucksacks into which I had loaded a couple of torches, the radios, in case we split up and needed to communicate, a flask of tea quickly made from the kettle that had just boiled and not been used, and a couple of spare jumpers, in case we stayed out late and it got colder. I collected our own rubbish and the plan was to put it in the bin as an excuse for going there. I don't suppose we really needed an excuse to go to the rubbish bin but should we accidentally stumble upon someone else then I argued, with myself, that it would look better if we were actually disposing of something. The time of night might arouse some suspicion but we would have to take a chance on that.

It was not there. Fred pointed at the spot and there was no black plastic bag. It had been moved and in a very short period of time. The wheelie bin was in the same place, she said, and the only difference now was no black bag. A quick look inside the bin confirmed that the bag had not been deposited in there and that the contents were the same and it was still only about half full. We looked around and found nothing. There was no trace of any black plastic bag or any other bag for that matter or any foreign looking bottles. What ever had been there had all obviously been removed in the short time between Fred finding the bottle and our return back to the scene. I deposited our rubbish in the bin and let the lid drop.

'Someone has been and moved them,' said Fred, stating the obvious as we moved away and walked slowly towards the gate. 'Now who, or why, would anyone want to do that? They were there as obvious rubbish, now they have gone. Rubbish does not move of it's own accord so why should someone want to move it?'

'You tell me. You saw them. Was there a lot, was it a big bag, or a smallish one?'

'Like I told you before, there were quite a few bottles and the bag was a black plastic rubbish bag. It was full and tied at the top. But it had a split in it and that's how I got the bottle. If the sack had been put in the wheelie bin it was big enough to almost fill it. That's how big it was.'

'So you think someone has changed their mind, decided they were not rubbish and so, as late as this, have moved them?'

'Something like that! Perhaps someone has decided they don't want the likes of them to be found in the rubbish. I wonder if it has anything to do with what you overheard earlier? The Landlord and the Poacher arguing outside the pub. Is everyone "running scared"? Is it the Poacher, or what ever you call him, Johnson, trying to get rid of dodgy goods as he is worried about something and was the

Landlord refusing because, he too, is scared. Remember, you said, the Landlord up the road told this Johnson to bring his stuff down here. Perhaps he did and this has caused some sort of panic at this end and resulted in an attempt to get rid of some sort of evidence, in other words, foreign spirit bottles. Johnson's van is over there now. Has that got anything to do with these bottles being moved, do you think?'

'Let's go and have a look. But before we do, let's have a really good look around here to make sure no one has simply moved them and dumped them round a corner and we have missed them.'

Moving as quietly as possible we looked round every corner and searched among the various outbuildings. We found nothing.

'Nothing here.' whispered Fred. 'Let's take a close look at the van. What do you think?'

'Wait a minute. It's a bit too light at the moment. There is too much moon for one thing and that floodlight in the car park doesn't help. If we can see it from here, then anyone in it will be able to see us if we just walk up to it. Although at this distance you can't tell if there is anyone actually sat in the cab. So I suggest we work our way round into those woods behind and use them as cover. At least from over there we will be closer to it and should also be able to see across to the pub as well. So if from here we set off along the lane, as if heading towards the village, anyone looking our way will assume we are doing just that. We can then cut off into the woods and double back.'

Once out of sight of the pub and the car park, we climbed over the dry stonewall and made our way back through the bracken and undergrowth.

It always makes me smile when I find myself going through virgin undergrowth, areas where there are no worn paths or tracks to follow, as I am always reminded of the numerous occasions where I have read in books that one or more of the characters, "Moves speedily through the undergrowth without making a sound and comes up on his unsuspecting victim and grabs him from behind." What a load of rubbish. It doesn't matter how slowly you move or how carefully you tread, you make some noise with nearly every step that you take. The undergrowth is inevitably brittle and it will snap and crack under the pressure of your weight and things like branches that you can't help disturbing will rustle and all these sounds are always amplified and are much louder at night. Even on this occasion, when there was a fairly strong breeze stirring the leaves and whistling through the branches of the trees, it was still impossible to move quietly or remain undetected from someone close by and blessed with normal hearing.

However we still proceeded with caution making as little noise as we could and hoping that, what inevitably there was, would perhaps be drowned out and dissipated by the wind. It seemed to take us ages to work our way round to the rear of the car park and because the ground beyond it was on a slight slope there were many places where it was possible for us to see clear across to the opposite

side of the ravine. We avoided these open spaces, not wanting to expose ourselves to anyone who may have been looking in the opposite direction.

We moved around and tried out several different vantage points before we finally decided that a large rock with two substantial trees close by, on the edge of a small clearing, not only gave us the best cover but the maximum field of vision. If we sat behind the rock we were completely out of sight from the car park and the road and would only be seen if someone approached quite close from the rear. Standing, we could rest our arms on the top of the rock and have an excellent view with only our heads and shoulders exposed and therefore visible from below. The trees offered us near perfect cover as they were wide enough to stand up behind.

The wind had risen since we first set out. Now all we could hear above it, was the distant sound of the waves breaking onto the shingle beach and although we knew that was some distance away, the wind blowing from that direction, carried the sound much clearer and made the sea appear to be much closer than it really was. I leant against the rock and looked around searching for any movement or signs of activity. Fred, crouching down beside me, proceeded to fill the two flask tops with tea from the thermos. She passed one up to me and I sipped it as I continued to survey the area.

Time passed and I began stamping my feet to keep warm. Using a torch I ducked down and looked at my watch, to my surprise I discovered we had only been there for about twenty minutes. Time was passing very slowly and up to then there had been no signs of activity either around the pub or the van.

'It's going to be a long night at this rate,' I whispered.

'And a cold one! I'm frozen already,' replied Fred, who shivered visibly and reached for the rucksack to pull out her spare jumper.

'Huddled up down there isn't going to help. Stand up and stretch your legs, move about, get the circulation going a bit.'

She stood up and handed her anorak to me to hold. She then proceeded to pull on the jumper and then putting her anorak back on zipped it to the top and pushed her hands deep into the pockets. She visibly shivered. 'Cuddle me,' she pleaded, letting her full body weight rest against mine, pressing me against the rock. I unzipped the front of my anorak and she came in close and wrapped both arms round my waist inside my coat. I took hold of the edges and wrapped them as far round her as they would stretch. Then by shuffling our feet, we rotated ourselves, so that Fred ended up with her back to the rock and I ended up with my chin on her shoulder. That way I was able to continue to look out over the area we were supposedly covering.

We continued to stand there, for what felt like a very long time, the only pleasure being the warmth of Fred's cheek against mine. Suddenly she bodily stiffened, and then barely audibly whispered, 'Hear that?'

I was poised to ask what, when I too heard a noise coming from somewhere. Where exactly, was hard to determine and the wind didn't help. Then it came again, only this time louder and closer. It was the sound of someone walking, the sound of foot falls coming from somewhere over to my right. We automatically released each and dropped down behind the rock. As I struggled to zip up my anorak Fred slowly raised up, I whispered, 'See anything?'

'Not yet, but it's coming closer.'

I drew the zip up tight under my chin and raised myself up alongside Fred. There was no doubt then that someone was approaching from the right. Finally a man emerged and came into view, from the track that led down to the beach.

'It's our friend the Poacher,' whispered Fred, 'and coming up from the beach. I wonder what he has been up to at this time of night and alone?'

'He may not be alone but with a bit of luck, we may soon find out.'

We stood and watched while he made straight for the car park and his van. He proceeded to open the back of the van and extract a large cardboard box which by the effortless ease with which he handled it, did not appear to be very heavy, relative to its overall size. He closed the van doors, picked up the box, and set off back in the direction from which he came, towards the beach.

Everything was once again quiet, with only the wind and the sea crashing somewhere in the distance and it was the wind that was preventing a build up of cloud. Cloud, which had it occurred, would have obscured the moon, and greatly reduced our range of vision. As it was, there was sufficient light to see what was going on, over a large area in front of us, despite the dark shadows. I ducked down into one such shadow and again using the torch, shielded in my hand, looked at my watch. Then having made a mental note of the time continued to watch and wait. Some ten minutes later, there was the sound of footsteps once again, only this time they were much slower, almost a plod. He, or who ever else it might be, was on his way back up the hill.

Once again the Poacher came into view and he was again carrying a box, only this time it was a much smaller one, and from the way he handled it, much heavier than the one we had seen him take down earlier. He stopped and put the box on the ground. He took a large handkerchief from his pocket and wiped his brow. He then began to look round as we both instinctively ducked behind the rock. In the crouched position, and sheltered from his view, I moved sideways to the nearest tree. Once behind, I slowly stood up and peering round it was able to observe him. He was still looking about himself and probably getting his breath back at the same time and, I hoped, was totally oblivious to the fact that he was being watched. He picked up the box and continued towards the car park. As he reached his van he once again placed the box on the ground and opened the back doors. He then withdrew another box of a similar size to the one we had seen him carry down towards the beach, on his first trip, and placing it on the ground picked

up the smaller one and slid it into the van. Closing the doors he then picked up the larger box and proceeded once again to go towards the beach. I ducked down and in a whisper, told Fred everything I had seen.

'What do you think might be in them?' she asked.

'I don't know. They obviously weigh differently. The larger of the two appears to be the lightest for some unknown reason. But what ever it is, I intend to find out. I don't think he has locked the van, so as soon as he is well out of sight, I am going down to have a look. Pass me one of the radios. Set them on number one, then all you have to do is watch out for him coming back and as soon as he comes into sight, press the transmit button twice. Don't say anything over the radio unless it is a dire emergency. I will hear the two clicks you make, on my set, and that will be all I need.'

She turned on the radios before passing me one. Then pressed the talk button twice in quick succession on hers. Mine clicked twice; they were both working.

I waited a few more minutes to let him get well clear and as Fred took up her position behind the tree I set out down the hill towards the track. I tried to remain concealed from the Pub, but, apart from the wind, everything appeared to be still and quiet in that direction. There were no lights showing that I could see, and no signs of life. I was nevertheless cautious, stooping low and moving as fast as I could whist making every effort to be as quiet as possible. I reached the entrance to the car park, stopped, and had a quick look round. I could see, nor hear, nothing, so I walked in a straight line up to the van, turned the handle, and pulled open the door. What happened next and at that precise moment, I shall never forget.

The door swung wide and a large black mass snarled and leapt out at me. My heart stopped or I thought it had, as I smelt it's foul breath and felt its hot saliva splash my face. I leapt back at the speed of lightning. Thank God the thing was securely tethered and could do no more than stick its head out into the open and snap and snarl and tug at it's leash as it made frantic efforts to get at me. Thank goodness also for the survival instinct, for I swear it was by pure instinct, fuelled by possible sheer terror that made me immediately slam the van door shut. I scrabbled about on the ground, in blind panic, trying to find the radio that I had dropped. Finding it, I charged towards the boundary wall, went over the top in one smooth roll and ended up in a heap on the other side. The breath knocked out of me, and my heart beating fit to burst, I lay there.

The dog was still barking and despite being enclosed in the van, was making a frightful noise. I eased myself up and looked over the wall. No lights had come on in the Pub, but a light was shining from one of the tents in the field opposite. The dog, fortunately, then quietened and stopped barking. I decided it was time to beat a hasty retreat. So once again stooping low I moved as fast as I could into the undergrowth and made my way back to our hiding place. Taking no

chances, Fred had ducked down behind the rock when she heard my approach. I slumped down beside her.

'What on earth happened down there?'

'There's a bloody big dog in that sodding van and I thought the thing had got me. Thank god it was fastened up otherwise goodness knows what would have been happening to me now. The bloody thing never made a single sound as I went up to the door; it just leapt out at me when I opened it. Made me nearly mess myself and I'm still shaking. Did you hear it up here?'

'I certainly did and thought everyone else must have done but all I saw was you running and one light from one of the tents. The wind was probably in our favour. Thank goodness.'

'You can say that again and I saw the light in the tent but are you sure there was nothing else?'

'Positive, as far as I could see. There was nothing from the pub if that's what you mean?'

'Good. That was lucky. My heart is still beating fifty to the dozen.'

'What do we do now?' she enquired as she stood up and resumed her watch.

'Not a lot! Keep watching I suppose unless you want to go down there and have a go at the van.'

Instead of a reaction there was silence for a few seconds before she whispered, 'He's back with one of the smaller boxes.' I stood up beside her.

Still in a whisper I said, 'The van is a waste of time with that damned dog in it so what do you feel about my following him back down, if he goes back down, and trying to see what's he's up to down there. We could still use the same system as before with the radios only this time you could give me two clicks each time he either comes out of the track or sets off back down and only call in a dire emergency.'

'OK by me but are you sure you don't want me to go? You've hardly got your breath back.'

'I'll be fine. Look he is on his way now so get up behind that tree and remember to give me two clicks when he gets to the track and two more each time he comes and goes.'

'Then you be careful.'

'After that bloody dog, I will be ultra-careful. I have no intention of entertaining anymore dogs to a game of snap, snarl and eat me up if you can.'

I left the shelter of the rock and set off down the slope, moving as did so, to my right, to join up with the track somewhere further down the ravine. I was extra cautious this time and very careful to make as little noise as possible. I was very conscious of the fact that I might stumble across anyone or anything, at any time, and so had to be prepared to dive for cover at a split seconds notice.

I joined the track having cautiously looked and listened in both directions at a point not too far from the bottom and where I recognised it from our previous visit. I edged forward straining for the slightest sound and being conscious of the radio in my hand that might signal at anytime the movement of the Poacher, noticed also how the sound of the breakers on the shingle beach was getting much louder. I was approaching the last bend before it broke out onto the beach. I eased forward. My radio went "click, click" and I jumped. Where the hell did that put him? At the top of the ravine and going away from me, good. Thank goodness for that, at least he would not have heard the radio but had anyone else? Was he alone? Was I alone? Were any of us alone? I toyed with the idea of turning off the radio but then decided against it when I realised that it was important that I had a rough idea of where the only one I presently knew about, was. I edged further down the track and had gone perhaps some eight to ten yards, when I thought I heard voices. Was I mistaken; was it the wind? No. It came again and more clearly this time. There were at least two people talking some distance away. It was time to get off and into the thick undergrowth. I made sure I was well concealed and could not be seen from the track in either direction. The voices continued to drift towards me and I then knew there were at least two others, beside myself and the Poacher and of course Fred out and about that night.

Two clicks. The Poacher was on his way back down. Now I had something else to worry about. I decided to move through the undergrowth away from the track and towards the beach. Fortunately the vegetation was thick and covered quite a large area on that side of the ravine. Progress was slow as I felt it necessary to stops every couple of yards or so and listen. The voices, still coming from the same direction, grew louder, but remained unintelligible to me. Then I heard footsteps approaching from somewhere behind and to my right. I stopped and remained perfectly still behind a particularly thick clump of bushes. I saw Johnson approached and pass quite close by without even a glance in my direction. He continued on, down the track until he disappeared from sight, round the bend. I resumed my descent towards the beach, keeping myself well concealed in the process.

I moved from one patch, through a less dense area, to the next, stopping and listening for several seconds each time to make sure it was safe to move on. Finally I came to the edge of the undergrowth, which by then was totally devoid of trees, and consisted mainly of thick brush and bracken. It was necessary to lie on my stomach if I intended to remain concealed. Slowly, I raised my head and peered through a gap. I could see the whole beach spread out in front of me.

There were four men in total, Johnson and three others and they were standing a few yards inland from the water's edge. Close by were several cardboard boxes. Three were of the type we had seen Johnson carrying down the hill from

his van and standing next to them were two of the smaller ones we had seen him carrying back up, in the opposite direction.

Pulled up, and clear out of the water and sat firmly on the beach, was a small rowing boat. Two of the men stood close by it, both smoking and looking in the direction of the other two. They were waving their arms about and gesticulating in order to emphasise what they were saying. The wind caused the volume of their conversation to rise and fall, but I still managed to make out sufficient, to get the general gist of the discussion. I heard the stranger complaining. 'You take all night, where is help?'

'Like I told you, help is not here tonight, only me. You give me a hand if you want to be away in such a fucking big hurry,' snapped back Johnson.

'I bring, you pay, you move. I stay here only.' retorted the other in the same strong foreign accent. It was obvious that at least he was not English. The other two said nothing.

'One more trip and you can all piss off!' snapped Johnson as he bent down to pick up one of the smaller boxes. He then turned and made his way towards the track. I dropped down and kept very still as he passed.

When Johnson had departed, the remainder muttered something between themselves, in their own language, shuffled about on the beach in an agitated manner, then eventually went to their boat and began to manhandle it towards the waters edge. The tide must have fallen away since they originally beached it so it took some effort to push it across the shingle and position it so that the bow was in the water. They then proceeded to load up the boat with the large boxes that Johnson had laboriously transported down the track. I took advantage of the fact that they were all occupied and were making plenty of noise as they chatted and disturbed the shingle under their feet and moved some ten yards or more so that I was further away from the track and at the same time had a much wider view of the open sea. Sure enough, as I had half expected, there was a trawler anchored about a quarter of a mile out. She showed no navigation lights. It was just too dark to make out any detail and I had no binoculars with me. But it was easy, from the silhouette against the night sky, to work out that she was of continental design.

The radio clicked twice. That was Johnson on his way up. All I could do was watch and wait. All that remained on the beach were the three men and one of the smaller boxes, waiting, I assumed, for Johnson to collect.

After a short while, the radio clicked again telling me Johnson was on his way back down. A further delay, and a couple more cigarettes lit and smoked by the men on the beach, and once again Johnson appeared. He set down the box he had brought with him and, straightening up, reached into an inside pocket and withdrew, what looked like, a small package or a large wallet. From my position, Johnson had his back to me and so I was unable to see exactly what he was doing but a few moments later he moved a little to one side and I could see the other man

and he looked to be counting, what I suspected were bank notes - money. When he finished he nodded as if satisfied. He deposited the bundle in the back pocket of his trousers, shook hands with Johnson and turned and made his way straight towards the small boat. One of the others picked up the box and followed him; the third one shuffled along behind. Johnson stood and watched as they manhandle the boat into the water. They climbed aboard and setting a pair of oars, began to row gently out to sea. When several yards out and putting distance between themselves and the shore Johnson bellowed, 'Thieving bastards!' The man in the stern raised his arm in a wave without even turning round. Johnson picked up the last remaining box and promptly set off up the hill. I gave him a good head start then broke my cover and proceeded to make my way cautiously up the track behind him, keeping, what I hoped was, a safe distance between us.

I worked my way cautiously round each bend as the track wound its way up the hill, all the time straining for any noise. Suddenly I realised I was more than half way up, and that being the case, Johnson should have passed in front of Fred by that time, but the radio had not clicked. That meant he must have either slowed up considerably or stopped completely to take a rest or something and was now somewhere between Fred and myself. I moved very slowly and very cautiously round the next bend. Nothing. The area was empty with nothing to be seen but the natural surroundings. The clicks would surely come at anytime now. In the meantime I cautiously approached the next bend and there he was not thirty yards in front of me and I had almost walked into him. He was sitting on one of the log benches with the box on his knee. I froze for a second before very slowly side stepping towards the undergrowth. I fumbled behind my back to turn off my radio. Fortunately he had neither seen nor heard me and I blessed the wind that was creating the background noise as he continued to rummage through the contents of the box. Almost frozen to the spot and hardly daring to breath I stared at him but nothing in his manner changed and he continued poking about, totally absorbed. I side stepped again, waited a split second, and then took another slow motion step. All it needed then was for a twig to snap underfoot and I would be in trouble. But nothing happened, no sharp cracks or any disturbance that would have signalled my presence. After an eternity, I slowly lowered myself to the ground and lay very still in the undergrowth. I listened and the wonderful wind was the only noise I could hear. Slowly I lifted my head and looked in his direction. He was standing and folding down the flaps of the box. He picked it up and continued his climb up the hill totally oblivious of the scare he had just given me. I waited and tried to breath easier while giving him ample opportunity to get well ahead of me.

I turned the radio back on and resolved to stay exactly where I was until the clicks told me he had reached the top. When they came the feelings of relief almost overwhelmed me. I know we can all make mistakes, but what had just happened

was stupid and broke one of the major rules of surveillance; never ignore cover, if it's there use it. At least I had got away with it and was free to feel a bloody fool.

My breathing had settled back to normal, but I was still perspiring. The wind helped a little, cooling my face but my body, under the layers of clothing, remained hot and sticky. I reached the point where it was necessary to leave the track, and cut through the woods to the left, to make my way back to where I had left Fred.

* * *

'That took some time. I've been stuck here, half frozen to death with little else to do but signal you each time he came past. Where have you been?'

'You've done a great job and sorry it's taken so long but without you and the signals it would have taken I damned sight longer and I would probably have been in a hell of a mess.'

I eased myself up and peered over the rock and looked down into the Car Park below, it was empty.

'Where is he now?'

'He came up for the last time and stuck a box he was carrying into the back of the van and then drove off down the lane towards the village. What happened with you down there?'

'I'll tell you all about it later, but for now I would like to try and follow him, if we can.'

'Follow him. How and where? We don't know where he's gone other than down that lane towards the village and we don't have transport other than the camper and we can't just jump in that, particularly at this time of night. What about all those in the tents?'

'You're right, but I thought it would be very handy to know if he went anywhere other than straight home.'

'In that case we can at least check that out. We can leg it down to the village and check out his house assuming he hasn't been anywhere else before we get there. So come on, grab the gear; the walk should at least warm me up. I am frozen.'

'Lucky you! I am steaming after that climb and the shock I got.'

'What shock? Is there something you aught to be telling me?'

'Later! It's nothing that can't wait for now.'

Having grabbed our gear we left the wood and set off at a brisk pace along the lane towards the village. It was getting late and I was beginning to feel a bit weary as I settled down from the jolt that Johnson had given me.

As we trudged along at a fairly brisk pace I recounted, at Fred's insistence, everything that had happened and exactly what I had seen and overheard down the

ravine. When I mentioned almost falling over Johnson, she laughed and said, 'you poor dear. I bet that gave you a fright and that makes two in one night. Not bad when prior to that, we had nothing.'

After a short silence she added. 'It all stinks of smuggling, doesn't it? But smuggling what?'

'Oh, he's smuggling all right. No doubt of that. I saw as much. I saw the exchange of boxes and probably some cash settlement and then them rowing off into the dark and a boat, without lights dodging off out there. If that's not smuggling I would like to know what is.'

'I would like to know what was in those boxes.'

'So would I despite the failed attempt and my brush with that bloody dog. Let's hope we get lucky down in the village.'

'Our Mr Johnson, the Poacher, has turned out to be a very interesting man and I feel that now, at long last, something is beginning to develop and there might well be the chance that all this is somehow tied in with the Edison affair.'

'I hope so and that this lot is just not some red herring or something. Now that would really piss me off if we were flying round in the middle of the night like blue arsed flies and for nothing.'

By this time we had reached the village.

CHAPTER TWENTY-THREE

We had planned to go directly to Johnson's house, or more accurately to the house where we had seen his van parked previously. In my mind there was little doubt, if the state of the property was anything to go by, that that was where he probably lived. So on entering the village, we walked the short distance up the main street, before turning off down the side lane. When we arrived the house was in total darkness with everything quiet and still and the space where Johnson had previously parked his van, was empty and there were no signs of it in the immediate vicinity. Either he had not returned home, or he had, but before doing so, had left his van parked somewhere else. Or this was not his house and he was somewhere entirely different.

'Now what?' Fred whispered.

'I don't know. I'm sure this is his house and this is where we could expect to find his van, but now? I don't know. Is he still out and about in the village? If so we haven't seen or heard anything of him and at this time of night you would be able to hear a motor at some distance. Should we look around, do you think? Do you think he might have parked up somewhere else and then walked home although I can't see him doing that if his load has any value, can you? I bet he has gone somewhere to deliver those boxes. But where?'

'Unless he has actually parked his van somewhere so as not to disturb his neighbours at this time of night.'

'Johnson! Do you really think he is the type who would care a damn about his neighbours or if he was disturbing them? Not him.'

'I suppose your right. But not if he didn't want to disturb them because of what he has been up to. But look! I know it might be a waste of time, but let's walk along the main street and have a quick look down some of the side lanes. You never know, he may have parked up somewhere for entirely different reasons and at least we will feel better if we have at least tried.'

'OK, a quick walk up the road on the one side and back down on the other, then, if nothing, back home and bed.'

One thing about most small villages and that is, they don't bother too much about street lighting. A couple of overhead lamps attached to telegraph poles down the main street often appears to be sufficient to satisfy their requirements and this village was no exception. The severely restricted lighting however, on this occasion, worked to our advantage when we needed to snoop around in relative safety but worked against us when we needed to see any distance, as in this case down the side lanes. Therefore when looking for Johnson's van we were obliged

to go down each lane in turn and walk some distance to make sure it was not there. Torches were of course out of the question as flashing lights other than down at the pavement at that time of night would have been sure to attract unwanted attention.

As we approached the far end of the village and had found nothing, I whispered. 'This is a bit of a waste of time. We have covered almost half the village and just look how long it has taken us. The only good thing is the fact that while we have been looking, we know that Johnson has not come back or passed us, because if he had, we would have either seen or heard him.' I turned down the next lane and peered into the darkness. Fred rushed after me and grabbed my sleeve.

'What's the matter?'

'Shh. Did you hear that?'

'Hear what?'

'I thought I heard a dog bark.'

'I didn't and I've had enough of dogs in any case for one night. But are you sure? I would have thought it unusual for a dog to bark on a quiet dark night like this.'

'Quiet and listen. There was definitely a dog somewhere and I heard it bark.'

'Then why have we not heard it again? Dogs don't usually bark only once at night or at any other time for that matter?'

'I don't know, do I? Anyhow, why all the silly questions? A dog barked and that's all I know.'

'Because I think it is unusual, that's all. A dog usually has a reason to bark. Correct me if I am wrong, but I thought dogs are more than likely to bark, and to do so at night, when they are disturbed and then to carry on barking until the disturbance goes away or they are ordered to shut up.'

'Yes, but so what?'

'Well that one barked only the once. You heard it, I didn't and it has not barked again.'

'Meaning what?'

'That it was perhaps disturbed in the first place and then quickly silenced. In other words there could well be someone out now, with a dog, and both within earshot. Johnson had a dog with him in the back of his van tonight and it nearly took a big lump out of me, remember, but then it went quiet after I slammed the door,' I said, shivering at the memory.

She put her hand on my arm and this time we both heard it, a single woof in the otherwise relative peace of the night. 'There it goes again. Did you hear it? It sounds to be coming from over that way,' she indicated by pointing towards the end of a lane that ran off into the darkness on the opposite side. 'Shall we go look?'

'Yes, but take it easy. Remember that bloody thing of Johnson's.'

We crossed over and as the lane took us away from the main street so it got progressively darker until it was almost inky black. We walked in the middle of the road until the houses on either side petered out and we were left, almost tiptoeing in a tree lined lane. We had neither seen nor heard anything.

'Is that a light over there?' whispered Fred.

I could just make out her outstretched arm in the dark and the direction in which it pointed, she was right. There was a faint light barely visible through the trees. The movement of the branches made it appear to flicker and it was often blocked out completely as the night wind gusted, but there was no doubt about it, there was a light of some kind and it had come just at the point where I was beginning to believe it was all a waste of time. Now I was still not sure because even at this point people had every right to have lights switched on in their homes, day and night, and may choose, or need to do so for a multitude of reasons, and they are also quite entitled to have dogs that bark during the night and that they may also do so for any number of reason. It could all be so innocent and have a perfectly logical explanation.

'It's probably nothing. But seeing as we have come this far we might as well take a look… Wait! Where's it gone?'

The light had disappeared leaving only blackness and us, stood, in the middle of the road.

'Probably turned off,' said Fred, 'but come on; it came from just down here.'

It was almost impossible to make out anything, at any great distance. We had a low wall on the left with, I assumed, open fields beyond it. To the right was a low wall with trees behind and only darkness behind that and up ahead. We followed the tree line. Some hundred yards or so along the lane the low stone wall suddenly rose up at right angles to become a solid, purpose built, eight foot high, boundary wall.

'I bet there's a house behind there and through those trees and that's where the light came from.'

'Look there's an opening or gateway there.'

It was then, as I looked at Fred and where she was pointing, that I realised that not only could I see her outline for the first time since we had left the main street and it's limited overhead lighting, but I could also see, some distance ahead, the opening she referred to, in the wall. It was getting lighter, either because the dawn was approaching or because cloud that had previously blocked out the moon had broken. However, whatever the reason it was now possible to make out solid objects and features that were silhouetted against the still fairly dark sky.

We moved over to the side and approached the opening in the high wall. Through it we could make out, from it's basic silhouette, a substantial detached

house standing in its own grounds and completely surrounded by an eight-foot high wall. From what I could further make out, surrounding that, there was nothing but open countryside and fields stretching out in every direction until finally they disappeared into the darkness.

'I wonder if it will be daylight soon? We can certainly see a lot more now than we could when we left the village.' I whispered. 'It would be nice to know the time but it's a bit too dodgy to shine a light to find out. Can you hear anything?'

'No, can you?'

'No.'

I looked behind me and could now just make out the skyline.

'If there was a light, then it must have come from in there and the dog bark,' whispered Fred, nodding towards the house. 'Let's take a peep in the grounds seeing as we have come all this way and there doesn't appear to be anywhere else.'

The boundary wall was built of solid stone and was considerably higher than the average man was tall, and I assumed surrounded the whole house and garden. To get in and see more we had little alternative but to go in by the opening that was now in front of us.

We walked towards the wide entrance where I noted that on either side there were large solid wooden gates used to close off a drive that stretched beyond. The gates were wide open and fastened back. We stopped on the threshold and listened, we could hear nothing.

'Let's go in,' whispered Fred as she set off to lead the way.

Two or three yards inside the gates we stopped again. We could still see nothing except the drive ahead and that was bordered on both sides by some type of, six-foot tall, evergreen shrubs. To continue would have made us very vulnerable and easy to spot by anyone looking that way or coming away from the house. I decided to use this natural barrier, on either side, to our own advantage, so tugging on Fred's sleeve, I parted and pushed between two shrubs and we went behind them. Fortunately the ground felt firm underfoot and so I hoped would not show any footprints. Fred, who was now leading, suddenly stopped and pointed. When I came up close behind her I could see, over her shoulder, a patch of artificial light. Fred gently tugged at my sleeve and moved forward. I followed her through a narrow gap between two of the bushes. There we crossed the drive and went behind the others on the opposite side. We made our way, once again, towards the house until we saw through a space, that we were now adjacent to the source of the light. It was an overhead porch light, and it illuminated the front entrance. The front door to the house was wide open. We could see a second light inside which illuminated a hallway.

Standing with a dressing gown wrapped tightly round her, and with matching furry slippers on her feet, was none other than Miss Fancy Pants from

the village high street shop. We happened to be close enough to see that the look on her face, told us that she was not pleased. She was standing on the step alone and glowering in the general direction of a garage, which had been built and was attached to the end of the building. It had a large up and over door, which was open. There was no light showing from within but standing on the gravel before it, was Johnson's van.

At that moment Johnson himself emerged from the dark interior of the garage and into the ring of light from the porch. He addressed a remark to the lady on the doorstep. 'You sure I can't come in, some of this stuff is too valuable to leave in a bloody garage.'

'You certainly cannot come in. I have told you before, you should never come to this house, especially when you know my husband is away and I have told you not to come to the shop either, but you take no notice. You just put what ever it is in the garage and go, understand?'

'Look Missis, it's not my fault your husband is away, them lads down the road don't give a shit about that. They have a delivery to make and they make it, it's up to us to sort out this end. By the way, you sorted out that other gear in the shop yet?'

'That's got nothing to do with you either, that's my husband's business.'

'It's got everything to bloody do with me. It's part of our deal. Anyhow he better be back before bloody Sunday, we've got a fishing trip organised for then. So don't you go sticking your fucking oar into that either.'

'You disgust me, do you know that? Just hurry up. I'm freezing to death stood here. You know you had no right coming here and dragging me out of bed like this.'

'Dragging ya in would have been more like it.'

'Fff.' she hissed and he laughed.

'One of these days and you'd love it but not tonight darling. Too much to do and got to get back. Might have had time if you had shown up quicker. So where were you? You certainly took your bloody time, didn't ya? But you can piss off now, I'm finished here, but I'm still not happy leaving this stuff in there. Sure I can't put it i'nt house?'

'Positive and lock that garage door.'

'Don't you worry about that. Do you think I am bloody stupid or something? I'll make sure it's all well fastened up.'

He reached up and pulled down the overhead door, and having turned the key, rattled the handle several times to make sure it was secure. He then walked the short distance between himself and Miss Fancy Pants and handed her the keys. She almost snatched them from him and as she did do, he reached out with his free hand, and roughly squeezed one of her breasts. She immediately recoiled and with

a full circular swing of her arm, slapped the side of his face. He just laughed and said, 'One of these days…Best fuck you'll ever have.'

'Never, you dirty bastard,' she spat at him. 'Now get out of here, or I will call the Police.'

'With that lot in the garage: I bet you will. Piss off, snotty bitch,' and still laughing he climbed into his van, did a tight turn, and drove off down the drive and out through the gates. His headlights indicated that he turned left at the end and headed back towards the village.

Miss Fancy Pants turned to re-enter the house and as she did so she released the dressing gown that she had been clutching tightly round her. It fell loosely into its normal hanging position and the bright light from inside the hall silhouetted her body through the thin fabric.

'Bet that has just made your day?' whispered Fred.

'Not bad.' I replied.

The door closed behind her and the outside porch light went out. Shortly after that the internal hall light also went out, leaving the whole house in darkness. I closed my eyes to adjust to the darkness and had just reopened them when an upstairs window lit up. Thin, semi-transparent curtains were drawn across it, and as we both looked in the direction of the window, there was a silhouette, caused by what was, unmistakably, Miss Fancy Pants with the internal light behind her. She slid her dressing gown off and let it fall to the floor.

'A peep show for you darling,' giggled Fred, then gasped, 'See that? I thought she said her husband was away, you heard her.'

I grinned and continued to watch as a second silhouette took her in its arms before seconds later the light went out.

'I don't think she has any plans to bother about us tonight. Some lady; there ought to be more like her about.'

Fred slapped my backside with the flat of her hand. 'Remember what you are here for lover boy. Come on; let's have a closer look at that garage before it gets light. Just settle down and watch out for alarms. I don't want you to break any beams or sensors and set off any bells or floodlight this whole place. But if we do accidentally trigger something and all hell breaks loose, be prepared to leg it and fast.'

'By the time she lifted lover boy off and got up and dressed we would be miles away.' I laughed only to receive another playful blow.

There were no visible signs of alarms but then there wouldn't be if the installer had done his work properly. So we made a very cautious approach straight up to the garage door. Fortunately nothing happened. As expected the door did not give as I pulled on it. It was securely locked, for we had stood and watched Johnson do it and then give Fancy Pants the key. I looked back up at the bedroom window; the one from which we had probably seen the original light. I smiled. Any

actual "fancy pants" she might have had on, were probably now somewhere on the floor of that bedroom.

'Go down that side and see if there are any windows.'

Fred led the way and I followed. 'There are two windows and a door and you won't believe it but this door is not locked,' announced Fred as she struggled to pull it open. We eased ourselves in through the partially open door that, although not locked, had creaked on rusty hinges through lack of use before sticking fast. I was more than pleased at this bit of luck.

The narrow beam from Fred's torch located recognisable boxes neatly stacked against the back wall. They were the same ones we had seen Johnson humping up the hill a short while ago. On closer inspection we saw that the labels on the outside of the boxes were very similar, though much larger in size, to the label on the bottle Fred had retrieved from the black plastic bag outside the camp toilet block. I picked up a box. It was quite heavy and I noticed that it was securely sealed up. I shook it and by the feel and re-action I got from it, was convinced it contained bottles. Although they did not rattle, as they were probably packed with cardboard divisions to reduce the risk of breakage I could feel the sensation that a bottle of liquid makes when shaken in a box. The weight was about right for a dozen, or so, bottles of liquid in a standard packing case. 'Booze no doubt, and with the same label as the one on the bottle you found.'

'I agree', whispered Fred, 'But look around, there is no where near as much as I thought there would have been.'

'What makes you say that?'

'Well, just stop and think for a moment. Smuggling is a high risk and costly business and I find it hard to accept that a trawler would put in to the bay tonight, and take all the risk of coming ashore, to sell only half a dozen, or so, boxes of booze. There's little or no value in that. If Johnson manages to get ten pounds a time for each one that he sells, he would make very little relative to all the risk he, and everyone else, has taken and I doubt if he would get as much as ten pounds for foreign stuff. If he worked at it alone he could possibly be just thick enough, to be happy with the little he would make, but we now have reason to believe Fancy Pants' husband is in some way involved, not to mention the three men from the trawler and a skipper and god knows who else on board who would all want a cut out of it.'

'Just a minute', I interrupted. 'That reminds me; these are all sealed. Where is the box that was open? When I stumbled on Johnson he had a box open and was rummaging about in it and I don't remember seeing or hearing the sound of any bottles then.'

'Open?'

'Yes, remember I told you that when I nearly fell over Johnson and he nearly caught me out by sitting down half way up the track on his last trip, he had

one of the boxes open and was examining the contents. Look and see if it's here. Look for one that shows signs of having been opened.'

We found it at the bottom under two of the sealed ones. I moved it out and placed it to one side. Sure enough there was evidence that it had been opened for the sealing tape was slit. I lifted and folded back the flaps. 'There's your answer.' I said triumphantly. 'That's what makes the trip worthwhile. The hard stuff.'

'Hard stuff?' enquired Fred, reaching in and taking out a flat rectangular package about the size of a videocassette tape, which was wrapped in polythene and brown parcel tape. 'This is hard and solid all right. I bet we are looking at something very much like cannabis.'

'Probably slate cannabis, judging by the fact that it is so hard and solid.' I suggested as I sniffed the package but recognised nothing through the plastic smell.

'This one is softer,' she said, 'and is probably the real hard stuff. This is powder and if all these others are all drugs of some description then I shudder to think what this single box alone and it's contents are worth on the open market. More than enough to keep everyone in this deal very happy indeed I should think. Let's not hang around here any longer. This has now got very serious and we have seen all there is to see in here so let's put it all back exactly as we found it and clear out.'

I felt elated although I had no idea how all this related to Edison, if indeed it did.

'At last we now have something to get our teeth into and which might lead somewhere,' I enthused. 'It has been a long night and I am ready for some sleep. Fancy Pants is probably already in the land of nod and god knows where Johnson has gone; home probably.'

'Or at least if not in the land of nod, as you put it, winding up on some very serious bonking and I don't give a damn for Johnson,' laughed Fred.

We put everything back exactly as we had found it and left the garage, carefully closing the side door behind us. We retreated from the garden the same way we entered and once outside the gates set off at a brisk pace back towards the campsite.

'It won't be long before it's light now,' Fred said wearily as we finally reached the van and let ourselves in. She looked at her watch. 'Have we really been out all night?'

'I don't know what your watch says but according to the sky over there, we have.'

The door closed, I said, 'Will you make a hot drink? I have one last job I would like to do before we turn in. I want to soak the label from the bottle you found and send it off to the Old Man for identification. It will boost him up no end and make him feel important and might also make him think we are doing

something positive. On the other hand, knowing it's origin might actually tell us something.'

Fred made a drink and I fiddled with the bottle; the sink was hardly big enough to submerge the whole bottle so I had to constantly pour hot water over it using a pot.

'Pity I couldn't identify that trawler that anchored off here tonight but then I suppose that's the whole idea; they don't want to be identified. It was definitely a continental design though; I am pretty sure of that.'

I laid the label, once it came free, out on a tea towel to dry and not long afterwards, with our coffee pots washed out ready for later, we finally crawled into our sleeping bag for a few, much needed, hours of sleep.

I settled down; closed my eyes and tried to relax. I was beat. It had been a long day and an even longer night. Warm fingers began to slowly roam.

'Sleep,' I said.

'I a sec! I am just checking to make sure it is still there and the dog didn't get it.'

'It's there all right, but in a much reduced and relaxed state at the moment.'

I let my fingers slide across a warm soft tummy.

'Mine's still there too, but tired and dry,' then turning to kiss me fully on the lips, whispered, 'Come and see me later when I have had some sleep and hedge hog has woken up.'

Seconds later we were both sound asleep.

CHAPTER TWENTY-FOUR

The arrival of the local Corporation cleansing truck finally woke us at about midday as they clanged and banged and made a dreadful noise with, what I presumed was, the large Wheelie bin outside the toilet block. But the length of time they were there and judging by all the shouting, they were obviously collecting more than just one bin. I groaned and hissed, 'Noisy buggers.'

'Forget them… Now who's a big boy?' as a warm hand gently rubbed and squeezed.

'Only because I need to go to the loo.'

'Sadly, so do I. Well, never mind, there is bound to be another time,' as she gave another squeeze and then let go.

We dressed, let ourselves out, and went off towards the toilet.

On the way back I suggested that the first thing I should do was go into the village and ring the Old Man and give him our report and post off the label from the bottle. Fred in the meantime, I suggested further, could prepare some lunch.

'There's not much left out of which to make a decent meal so I suggest we both go into the village, ring the Old Man and then find something to eat there.'

That decided we walked to the village and made straight for the phone box. It took some time to get through and when we did the Old Man sounded very grumpy.

'Smuggling?' he said in disbelief.

'Yes Sir,' I politely replied. 'We have definite evidence of smuggling… Yes, that's what I said sir. We believe booze and drugs… No Sir, spirits, and illegal drugs… Yes, and I am sending you a label for identification, from a bottle…Yes I will send it through the usual PO Box …No sir, we don't know if it is tied in with Edison or not… That's what we intend to do sir… No we don't think it is a good idea to hand it straight over to the police or anyone else… Well what happens then if they are in on it and there is a tie up with Edison, it rather makes our being here a waste of time… Sorry sir… Yes sir I will ring again as you request.'

'What's biting him?' said Fred when I rang off.

'God knows. Do you know, Fred, sometimes I wonder about him. I'm sure he thought I was only talking about a few bottles of beer and a jar of aspirin. Then when he finally latched on to what I was trying to tell him and how it might not all tie in he was all for turning out the cavalry. Inform the local Police, send for Customs and Excise, inform Fishery Protection, shadow every boat in the North Sea. Seal off the whole area.'

'He always does that if he thinks you might know a little bit more about something, than he does or if you're planning something and don't want to discuss it with him. I have learned from bitter experience and so now find it easier, when dealing with him, if you turn everything round and put it to him in question form.'

'How do you mean?' I asked.

'Well, for example, take the label. You could have said or should have said, "Sir, I have found a label, do you think it would be good idea to send it to you for identification?" He would jump at that and immediately say, "Yes" as that would be his decision. Or you could have said "We have found some bottles with liquid in them and some parcels with funny smelling powder in them, what do you think they might be, Sir, could it be spirits and illegal drugs?" and so on. Nudging him a bit when he is slow to latch on. He falls for it every time.'

'With you perhaps; but knowing my luck, he would argue with me and try and tell me it was something entirely different from what I knew I had found.'

'Well he should be happy, the miserable old sod. We have at least had something concrete to report this time. I think we should forget him for the moment and have something to eat and then work out the rest of our plans for today.'

'Just before we do, let's just take a look down here,' I suggested as we stopped and stood at the intersection of the main street and the side lane that we believed led to Johnson's house.

Casually, we slowly walked down the lane and noted that Johnson's van was parked in his garden.

'Probably still in bed after last night spent humping those boxes back and forth. Which reminds me, we never managed to establish what was in those larger boxes that he carried down to the beach. Obviously part of the pay-off, but what would be in them that would be of value to foreigners?'

'I don't know,' said Fred. 'But like you say, they were part of the deal and so were obviously of some value to someone. Anyhow his van is there and so presumably is he. So apart from that, what has coming down here proved? Let's forget Johnson and his van for the moment and go to the cafe and get something to eat. I might function a bit better on a full tummy.'

We sat in the cafe and the good lady had taken our order, when Fred remarked, 'I see Fancy Pants, opposite, has managed to open despite last night's ordeal and orgy.'

I laughed and we chatted until the food arrived. It was more than welcome. I hadn't realised how hungry I was.

I was concentrating on my plate and not taking particular notice of anything else and so failed to see that something had attracted Fred's attention. 'You wait here, I won't be long,' she said, and before I had time to ask her what it was all about, she had walked out. I watched, through the window, and saw her

cross the street. It was then that I noticed the delivery van outside the dress shop on the opposite side of the road. A deliveryman was carrying into the shop a large cardboard box identical to the one we had seen Johnson take down to the beach the night before. I watched Fred disappeared into the shop.

Some ten minutes later she re-emerged and came back.

'What have you got there?' I enquired, looking at one of "Fancy Pants" customised plastic carriers that she carried.

'Well, I was obliged to buy something as an excuse to go in there wasn't I, and it's only a scarf? But what is more important; is what I managed to find out. I walked in and started looking around. At the same time the deliveryman was carrying in those big boxes and piling them in the middle of the shop. She was standing there with, what looked like, a delivery note and was checking them off. When the man had finished, and she had signed for them, he remarked on the number of boxes in the consignment and she replied by saying that her husband orders them in such large quantities to sell them at an open market. To which the driver commented that, he would have thought that, jeans of that quality would not be the type to be found in a market. She countered by saying that it was nothing to do with her; she just orders them, as requested, for her husband. So there you are, now we know, part payment is made in top quality jeans. Hubby is using the shop to purchase jeans in quantity. Clever?'

'So, if you are right, then that ties in both her and the husband. With her, perhaps, only indirectly involved as far as we know.'

'We know that Johnson is a bit thick; so that may mean that our builder friend, because that is who her husband is, as you remember we were told by that woman in the shop down there, could be Mr Big with Johnson only doing most of the graft, and taking most of the risk. As for Miss Fancy Pants, you are right, she is either a part of it, or is being used by the husband. It would be interesting to know how they distribute all the stuff they get and how often they get it. I know we are principally here to find out what happened to Philip Edison but perhaps his disappearance fits in somewhere with this lot. We don't know as yet, but it could well be connected and I think we should check it out. I suggest we stick with it, for now at least, and see where it takes us.'

'Yes, I agree and for the moment we will still send off that bottle label and then I suggest we go back and get our heads down for another couple of hours. I'm still whacked. Bye-the-way are you still hungry; you shot off before you had finished? Damn! Blast!'

'What's the matter?'

'I forgot to bring that bloody label. It's still in the camper. Damn!'

'Never mind. Just hang on a moment while I finish this then grab a few things for later.'

We trudged along the lane, back to the camper, after having bought several item to replenish our food stocks and half a dozen large envelopes and stamps from the Post Office.

As soon as we got back I took the bottle label and placed it inside one of the envelopes along with a plain piece of paper on which I had printed, "O in C – Grundy. As per our telephone conversation". Standard practice and all that it took to ensure that it got delivered to the right place. Receiver and sender being all that is required, according to laid down procedure, to ensure internal identification. The address on the envelope could hardly be simpler either; "The Managing Director, PO Box… London". The mail, as it arrives at the PO box being picked up at regular intervals during the day, by special courier, and taken directly to the department. All I had to do then was make another journey to the village post box and post it. Fred suggested that she stay behind to tidy up. "It doesn't take two to post a letter" I think she said at the time, or words to that effect.

When I got back, she was curled up in the sleeping bag and breathing deeply. I tried not to disturb her and having removed my jumper and trousers, did my utmost to slide in beside her without waking her. It was only when I was in and moved close, that I realised she still had a jumper on, but apart from that, was completely naked from the waist down. A little exploration discovered that there was nothing but two luscious bare boobs under the jumper. She moaned and rolled over, pulling as she did so, at my underpants.

'You can get rid of those for a start and then love me. The fires burning and only needs gently poking.'

I did as instructed and it was some time later that we both sighed deeply and fell asleep.

As we woke, or more accurately as one of us woke and disturbed the other, there was more kissing and cuddling and a great deal of resistance towards being the first one to get out of bed. In the end I was forced to make the first move, as I could no longer stand the tickling. I stretched and smiled at Fred who sat, knees drawn up to her chest, completely wrapped in the sleeping bag.

'You've got a lovely bum,' she said making a whistling sound as she drew in breath.

'What is it about a bum that fascinates girls? I enquired casually.

'I don't know. I just like them but I think I read somewhere, in one of those all enlightening women's magazines, that it is all about pumping power, the power of the thrust in lovemaking. But for me, I have always been interested in bums even long before I knew anything about humpy pumpy and I simply don't like men with saggy bums.'

I shaved, got dressed, and sat on the end of the bed. Fred had not moved.

'Come on lazy bones, out of bed. It's you're turn to be studied at close quarters. So out you get and let's see the shape of your lovely bum and the interesting saggy bits.'

'There's nothing on me that sags that isn't meant to sag and what's more, there is nothing on me that stands up and then immediately dies after a one-off performance, so remember that before you even open your mouth and say something you might regret.' She then stepped out of bed, turned her back on me and deliberately bent down to pick up something from the floor. 'How's that for saggy bits?' she said as she grinned at me through her legs which were slightly apart and as a result, displayed her breasts to perfection. I lent forward and using the backs of my fingers, gave her a quick flick on the cheek of her bum.

'Dressed, you prick teaser, before you find yourself with another hard guided muscle to soften.'

'Be quick then, I'm getting backache bending over like this, and I am not too warm either.'

I did my best and once again was more than content to die a little after the one-off performance.

'Now who's the one with a soft dangly bit, yet again?' she grinned.

She finally managed to get dressed, then between us we made a brave attempt to tidy up.

'I know we did a fair amount of walking both yesterday, today and last night or whenever, but I would like, if we can, to go up and round to where Edison was last supposed to have been. We could perhaps do that before we go into the Pub tonight. If you don't fancy it, or can't see the point in both of us going, you can wait here until I get back, or you can meet me in the Pub if you prefer.'

'No way; that sounds awful, going into the Pub on my own if I don't have to. I will come with you, you might, after all, need protection,' she laughed. 'You never know, Miss Fancy Pants may be out on the prowl looking for a new man to devour if her husband is still away.'

'Why? Do you think she has something to do with it?'

'No silly! Not like that. I was only joking. If she's been through all the eligible men in the village she maybe out on the prowl for something new. It's a joke - silly! Men, Fancy pants. Fancy pants, men. Oh forget it.'

* * *

We set off and went round the rear of the pub and across the wooden bridge, which spanned the stream. We made our way along the track in the Northerly direction.

'Strange about that bag of bottles going missing like that,' reflected Fred as we trudged steadily along.

'No not really! Now that we know more about them, and what is going on round here, you can understand them taking precautions and ensuring that strange bottles don't get mixed in with the general rubbish. They have probably been taken away and dumped somewhere so that then if found they couldn't be traced back. Or they might even go to the trouble of soaking off the labels and burning them. Then the bottles need only to be broken and mixed in with the ordinary refuse and disposed of in the normal way. They just need to take a little trouble to make sure they don't get caught, that's all. Those bottles you found may well have ended up in the big wheelie bin and been taken away on that wagon, for all we know. With or without labels.'

After a steady uphill trek we reached the grassy spot where it was alleged that Edison had been on the night of his disappearance, and what I had theorised before we set out, proved to be correct. He would have had, from that point, as we would have had in the same place, had it still been there, a perfect view of the trawler that had been anchored just offshore the other night. However, I was now able to establish that he would not have been able to see the small boat up on the beach, but he would have seen it being rowed from the trawler up to the point where it disappeared from view below the cliff. He would also have been able to see it on its return.

'I wondered if anything was going on that night and if Edison either knew about it, or simply stumbled across it by accident? What, if anything, did he see from up here and why up here? Why did he choose to come up here, why this particular spot. There are still a lot of unanswered questions and a lot that does not quite make sense.'

* * *

The visit to the pub that evening yielded little of any value but we enjoyed the break. When the opportunity arose, I mentioned to the Landlord about hearing a dog bark during the night, but of course, did not tell him it was barking at me or that it frightened the life out of me. He said he heard nothing, but if he had, he wouldn't have taken much notice as there are often people about with dogs during the night, poachers mainly, rabbiting and going after the occasional deer. He advised me to ignore it in future. I assured him I would.

We ended the evening playing dominoes with some locals who, as time went by, became quite friendly towards us. The odd treat that I paid for undoubtedly helped that. However, before we started, the house rules were spelt out for us in a firm but friendly manor.

'We play for fun. We don't play for money or for drinks, although some of the young ones in here do. We buys our own drinks and plays round once, after one of us chips out. My shuffle and this young lady's down.'

There being no pressure or real incentive to win I enjoyed the opportunity to relax in good company and to chat about almost everything and anything and yet nothing in particular, whilst still swapping from subject to subject and often with us all trying to talk at the same time.

There was one minor incident that caused Fred and I to exchange glances. We had been playing for sometime when someone, I don't recall who, called a temporary halt to the game for a visit to the loo and the bar. As I rose and reached across to pick up Fred's glass, one of the players said, 'If that's vodka you're drinking Miss, ask him for some of the special stuff he keeps under the counter.' He then half turned in his seat and, in a raised voice, called across to the Landlord, 'Give this lass some of that vodka you've got down there underneath.'

The Landlord looked visibly rattled and snapped back, 'Shut up Lionel, you don't know what you're on about. You always talk a load of crap when you have had a drink.'

'Sorry, I didn't mean no harm, only thinking of the lady.'

'Well, don't think, just get on with your game.'

'Gin for the lady isn't it Sir?' he said to me, emphasising the word Gin.

'Yes please, and another whiskey in this one.'

'Don't take any notice of old Lionel over there. He comes out with all sorts of things when he gets drink in him. Thinks he is being funny, nice chap otherwise.'

I sat down and picked up my dominoes ready to resume the game. If this Lionel was, as he seemed to be, a little naive and very talkative when mellow with drink, I thought about raising the subject of the newspaper announcement - that a body had been found - but I changed my mind. If he failed to respond in the right way, we would only draw un-necessary attention to ourselves, and I wanted to maintain the casual visitor image as far as I could, so I decided to let it drop.

We left a little after midnight and although the evening had been very pleasant and we had been made very welcome, we had learnt very little from it.

There was no sign of Johnson or his van and by one o'clock in the morning, there was nothing but silence, broken only by the breeze through the trees and the distant crash of the sea. Everywhere was in total darkness.

* * *

The following day nothing happened. No vans, no Johnson, no strangers, even the village itself seemed quieter than usual. I don't know what I expected to happen, but what ever it was, it didn't.

Our friends, in the next tent, began the day by packing their belongings and then came to say goodbye. By lunchtime they had gone. That left an even bigger space between our van and the next tent along. In the end, after idling the

whole morning away, it had to be the inevitable trek into the village to ring the Old Man.

We both squeezed into the phone box.

'Good afternoon Grundy! That label is from a bottle of Polish vodka. It is manufactured in Poland but is mainly done so specifically, for the countries export market, so the chances of it coming directly from there are remote. Customs and Excise tell me there is, at this time, a particular surge and that large quantities of spirits and other illegal merchandise is currently coming out of Holland. We are all aware, or we should be, that a large proportion of all illegal drugs that reach this country do so via Holland, so the two maybe tied up in some way. The trawler you spoke of may well be Dutch. As I said, Customs have been informed, as per the information exchange agreement, but I have requested they confine themselves to surveillance at sea and keep well away from you until they hear directly from you, through me. I have also arranged it so that sometime tomorrow someone from the Anti-Terrorist Squad will contact you. Their operative will have your description and will make the necessary contact, understand?'

'Yes Sir: but why the Anti-Terrorist Squad at this point? All we have so far, is a missing man and some evidence of drug and alcohol smuggling, hardly enough to get the Anti-Terrorist mob all excited. Customs and Excise I could understand but why the heavy mob?'

'Listen Grundy, you let me worry about who fits in where and why, you have your working brief and you will be further updated by their contact man. If you have anything further to report, ring me,' and he hung up.

'So the Old Man seems to think the Dutch are in some way involved, fair enough but he now thinks we need the Anti-Terrorist squad in with us. If you ask me he has finally flipped. He hasn't proved anything and like us, at this time, can only hazard a guess. I hate guessing, they have been known to be seriously wrong and particularly when it is that old buzzard who is doing the guessing,' scowled Fred. 'Facts are what we need right now, not guesses.'

After that we felt there was not much else we could do for the moment. We discussed various options and not very much emerged. Finally Fred came up with the suggestion, 'Do you fancy a run round the countryside in the van. We really haven't seen very much of the wider area since we arrived.'

'That's not a bad idea and why not. Let's do just that. Have a run round and see what is out there, just waiting for us, in the big wide world.'

CHAPTER TWENTY-FIVE

The next morning we were up bright and early. The day was fine and sunny with a slight breeze that helped what little cloud there was, to pass overhead at a leisurely pace and carry away with it any rain there might have been. All in all, a perfect day for walking and so we decided to do just that.

We made our way down the lane, which was now becoming very familiar to us, and entered the village. Once there we, almost automatically, sidetracked and went down the side lane past Johnson's house; there was no van outside that morning. We retraced our steps and came back to the main road and then passing Fancy Pants shop, along with all the others, some open for business, some not, we turned down the lane at the far end of the village. Then much further along the road, than it had seemed in the dark the night before, we once again came to the large detached house, built on the road side and surrounded by a high stone wall. As we approached and looked through the open gate, we could detect no signs of life. The builder's house was quiet and very still with an atmosphere of being lived in, but uninhabited, at that moment. We moved on.

We had now become very familiar with the overall layout of the village and knew where most of the side lanes and turn offs would eventually lead to, so choosing one of the few remaining ones, which we had, as yet, not ventured along, we set off to investigate.

The unfamiliar lane was fairly typical, and in general followed a very similar layout, to most of the others, with an assortment of houses and cottages stretched out along either side. As these dwellings diminished, the thoroughfare turned into a country lane, with a dry stonewall on either side. As we walked along, with the road ahead disappearing into the distance, we could see the open fields and I noted that scattered throughout them, was the odd farmhouse and outbuildings. What traffic we saw; either in the distance or close at hand as it passed us in both directions, was nearly all associated with farming and farm work. During our brief walk, at least two tractors and several Land Rovers, some with trailers attached, passed us as they went about their business. Often the driver would give us a cheerful nod or wave as he passed by.

A study of our map showed that if we took a right turn at the next intersection, we would join another country lane which, a short distance along, at a further intersection off to the right, would take us back to the village, passing as we did so, in front of the builder's home and in the opposite direction to which we had approached it before.

The round trip, of approximately two miles, made for a very pleasant walk, and apart from having to take precautions and stand back on the grass verge, as traffic passed, was uneventful.

When we arrived back in the village we walked along the main street to the general store and purchased several daily papers. Armed with these, we headed straight for The Dog and Gun, which, due to coincidence and not planned timing, had just opened for the lunch time session.

I got a couple of drinks from the bar and we sat by the fire to read the papers. As we sat, a steady stream of people came in and by noon the bar was quite busy.

'I should go and order now if we are going to have something to eat in here, otherwise we will be waiting ages if most of these people have the same idea,' suggested Fred. Shortly after, our meal arrived and so, for the time being, papers were folded and put out of the way.

'It would be lovely to go to a first class restaurant and order a really gorgeous meal,' sighed Fred as she looked at her plate and then across at mine after the waitress had withdrawn.

'I suppose it would and yet I am quite happy with Pub Grub. This sort of thing will do for me anytime. I have never been one for the fancy food and all the fuss that goes with restaurants. But we can try and do something about it, just for you if that's what you would like, as a special treat.'

'I'm not complaining. I don't mind fast food and this sort of thing, but I simply adore to eat-out and in style. To dress up and everything. Go in a taxi and drink lots of lovely expensive wine.'

'I'm not a great lover of wine either,' I had to admit. Then added, 'Hell! Listen at me; I sound like the perfect gourmets' kill joy. I bet you think I am a complete waist of time and a hopeless bore. Don't you?'

'You're terrible! But you're not a bore; just sad and a complete let down when it comes to food and treating a girl. Sorry I even mentioned it. So forget all about it; forget the restaurant, the gorgeous food, the wonderful wine, the lovely evening; forget everything,' she sighed. 'It's good old egg and chips and a pint of beer from now on for this poor soul, and it looks as if I will have to get myself another man if I want a decent meal. I wonder if there is anyone in here who wants a girl in exchange for a few glasses of decent wine?' she added as she twisted round on her seat and looked about her.

'I promise I could honestly make an exception in your case, if pushed hard enough. If you really insist and it is really important to you, I think I might just manage to forfeit the egg and chips, at least for the odd once.'

'I do insist, and you're on. I will show you what a wonderful experience a really good meal can be. Both during and after.'

'In the meantime, are you ready for another drink to go with your chips?'

'Yes please, the same again.'

There were several people stood round the bar and I had to wait patiently for my turn to be served. As I stood and watched the barmaid who did wonders for me as she reached and stretched in her tight fitting tee shirt, a strange voice came from over my left shoulder and said simply, 'Excuse me.'

I half turned to look at the chap, who was standing close beside me, and who, as I did so, continued to say, 'When you took your hand out of your pocket just now this fell onto the floor.'

I looked at his outstretched hand and held between two extended fingers was a plastic credit card.

'I don't think it's mine.'

'Oh yes it is, old chap. I saw you drop it. Here take it.'

'Thank you very much. I won't get very far without that, will I?' I said with a half laugh as I took it from him. I glanced at it, as I knew it was not mine because I don't keep loose credit cards in my back pocket. Never the less it had my name impressed on it. I casually slipped it into my pocket and said, 'Thank you for that. You have saved me no end of problems, can I buy you a drink?'

'No thanks! I am going as soon as I have finished this one. I have to meet someone. Some other time perhaps.'

'Cheers,' I replied before turning back to the bar and giving the girl my order and offered once again to buy the guy a drink - he again refused - I paid for the drinks and went back to re-join Fred.

'Drink up. The guy going out of the door over there has just handed me a credit card. He's the contact we've been expecting.'

'Where's he going now?' enquired Fred.

'He didn't say. But he will have worked out something no doubt. He has made his initial contact but no more, so the next move is still his. How he goes about it or where he does it is up to him. No doubt we will probably bump into him again soon, possibly somewhere outside or away from here. That's why I thought it was perhaps a good idea to leave now, so come on, drink up.'

When we left the pub, he was outside. He was standing by the entrance to the car park, or to be more precise, he was lent against a low wall at the side of the entrance and was studying a map. We walked past and as he looked up I casually nodded. He made no sign of recognition or acknowledgement; so we carried on walking. He had let us pass him by and had done nothing.

'What now?' Fred enquired.

'I don't know; perhaps he is not happy with things as they are. All we can do is carry on along here and leave it up to him. Perhaps he doesn't intend to pursue it at all today. Maybe he will wait until tomorrow, who knows?'

We walked at a leisurely pace and had covered perhaps a quarter of a mile or more. I know we had left the village and were on a stretch of road that, apart

from us, was deserted. I was beginning to wonder if he had decided not to make any further move at this time, when a car came along the road and approached us from behind. It drew up along side and the driver, who was also the contact, leaned across the passenger seat and said, 'Hop in and let me give you both a lift.'

I looked at Fred and smiled as I nodded towards the car. Then I opened the rear door and she climbed in; I followed and closed the door behind me. Once underway he said, 'We will go a couple of miles along this road, find a quiet spot, park up, and talk.'

For the remainder of the short journey we travelled in silence. When a convenient lay-bye appeared on the left hand side of the road our driver pulled on to it and stopped the engine. He turned in his seat to face us and said, 'Pleasure to meet you Mr Grundy, Miss Huntington. My name is Eddie Scott. I'm with the Anti-Terrorist Squad,' and holding up his official identity card, continued, 'Please, both of you, call me Eddie.'

'I am Mel and the better looking one is Winifred, but she prefers, and tells me and everyone else that she will only answer to, Fred.'

'Then Fred it is, and how lovely to meet you. Now let me fill you in as to the reasons for my being here.

'Please do. We are fascinated to know why your people have been sent,' said Fred with more than a touch of sarcasm in her voice.

If he noticed it, he chose to ignore it and carried on, 'Some time ago our people came across a consignment of arms and ammunition during a raid on a house in Birmingham, which was known, or thought to be, by the opposition, as a "safe house" and the headquarters of a local IRA cell. During this investigation it was noted that one of the ammunition boxes must have got damaged at some time and had been repaired in a crude and make-shift way. Our forensic boys were taking everything apart, as is their speciality, in an attempt to try and establish where the stuff originated from, or if it had already been used in any illegal activities excreta. You know the drill. Well, when they pulled this damaged box apart, it had been repaired with a piece of rough wood with some stencilled writing on it. Further investigation showed it to be a piece of wood from a fish box, of the type used by fishing boats, to hold and land fish in. The lettering on it formed part of the name of a fish-selling agency. This agency was eventually tracked down to Whitby, here in North Yorkshire. From there on these lads came up against a brick wall, for it was your boys, the Coastguard, who quickly pointed out that fish boxes in all different conditions and states of repair are found washed up all along the coastline. Although this particular fish box may have started life in Whitby, it could have come from almost anywhere round the entire East Coast, or even been picked up way out at sea. So you see that angle drew a complete blank. Then, out of the blue, as it were, you two good people are sent and are working not too far from Whitby and discover smuggling. Bells start to ring in high places and my people

become all excited. They want to know what this smuggling is all about, who is doing it and what and where it is going on and so they send me. All cleared and agreed through your people, you understand.'

'Oh we understand alright.' snapped Fred. 'It's good of them to send someone from a different firm to sort us out. Makes us feel kind of appreciated and more than capable.'

'I agree with Fred to a certain extent and I don't understand what all the enthusiasm is about as we don't have a great deal. All we have so far is proof that there is, and probably has been in the past, some smuggling going on in this neck of the woods and that we witnessed some of it the other night. It involved a man called Mick Johnson who on the surface of it appears to be, and to all intents and purposes is, a thick lay-about character and a person not too well liked by his neighbours. We actually saw him take delivery of several cases of what we believe to be, Polish vodka, and a substantial amount of unknown drugs. Although we think that part of the haul included slate cannabis, there was also powder with it as well. We also believe he exchanged all this for cash and good quality denim jeans. The latest delivery, if it is a part of an ongoing operation, is stored in the house of a local builder on the outskirts of the village. We also have reason to believe that this builder is involved, as is also his wife, who has a shop in the village and which we believe, is being used to purchase the jeans. How they distribute the stuff remains a mystery so far and is something we have still to established but we do know that foreign vodka has, in the past, been retailed through at least the two local Pubs, one in the village and the other further out towards the cliff top. That is basically it so far and we thought we were doing a good job until you were dumped on us. Now I am beginning to wonder. By the way, now that you are here, where do you propose to stay?'

'I've already booked in at the Dog and Gun, where I met up with you. Where are you two located? Locally I assume.'

'We are on a walking holiday and as part of our cover we have hired a Caravanette which at the moment is parked in a field attached to a Pub called The Grapes. The Pub itself is close to a ravine and it was via this ravine that we saw the smuggled goods being brought ashore.'

'Is it a well secluded spot, then?'

'Very secluded, and well out of the village. Some of the locals, if chitchat and gossip are anything to go by, are well aware that there are some dubious comings and goings. I wouldn't be surprised if there hasn't been similar activity, in one form or another, going on around there for generations and it is now all part of a well established, and accepted local custom. I should imagine that in the old days such things as Gunpowder, rum and tobacco and many other illegal things have all seen their way up that ravine; anything to avoid duty and make a quick profit.

There is nothing new in smuggling and throughout history this part of the coast has been renowned for it.'

'What cover are you going to use?' asked Fred.

'Farm and Agricultural Insurance! A cover I have used very successfully before and one that is ideal when working in sparsely populated areas. I have brought a brief case full of insurance literature and I have already given the Landlord at the Pub one of my cards and asked him if he will put it about that I am available and open for business.'

'What happens if you get any?'

'No problem! I tell the client that I have to pass it on to head office as it is outside my range. They are not to know, unless they should all get their heads together and that is highly unlikely, that everything is out of my range; although over the years it is surprising how much I have picked up and can talk fairly knowledgeable about. So anything I am obliged to deal with, to avoid blowing my cover, my people see is passed on to a legitimate company and everyone, hopefully, is then happy. Come to think of it, I should be in line for some commission for one or two bits and bats in the past.'

'We may be able to use you right away,' said Fred who then explained to me later, when we were alone, that she had said that primarily to establish that he was there to help us and to dispel any ideas he may have had that he was going to use us, in any way, to further his own ends or that he might have had plans to take over from us. 'You can start by trying to interest our Builder friend in some insurance. We need to get as close to him as possible, as indeed we do with all of them. We need to know a lot more about him, his wife, and this character Johnson. At the moment we have reason to believe he is away and don't know if his actual whereabouts and the reason he is away, are significant.'

'Fine by me! Just point me in his direction and then if there is anything I can do to help further don't hesitate to ask. I will have to do something or find some excuse to establish my credibility and justify my being in the area.'

'Mel. If Eddie were to go to the Builders house tonight and find him at home he could always spin him some yarn about getting his name out of the Yellow Pages, providing someone checks first to make sure he is in there, and offer special rates for new farm buildings or some such plausible story. If he's not at home then he may find out, from his wife, when he is due back or even get lucky enough to find out exactly where he is now. Also it would be useful to know a bit more about the fishing trip. Remember what we heard Johnson say to the Builder's wife outside her house: "He'd better be back for Sunday, we have a fishing trip organised". That tells me they have something special planned for Sunday because I can't see a fairly affluent Builder going anywhere with a yob like Johnson for recreation or pleasure. So I think it would help if we could find out a bit more.'

'No problem, I can do that for you,' he said consulting his watch. 'If I were to check out the Yellow Pages or think of some other excuse and then go at about six thirty this evening, do you think the wife will be at home?'

'I should think so. From what we have seen so far she closes her shop fairly early. It still being early in the tourist season there are not many visitors about for her to stay open late for.'

'Fine,' I interrupted. 'If we go back now, we can show you the house where they live, then you can drop us off and we will walk back and meet up with you later in the Pub. If we leave now the Pub should still be open when we all get back.'

Eddie started the engine, then turning the car round, headed back towards the village. As we approached I directed him to turn left into the same lane we had walked down earlier. I then directed him first right and then, at the next junction, right again. I showed him the house as we approached and he slowed down as we passed. The gates were closed. I then asked him to stop just beyond and out of sight of the actual house, and let us out. I told him to go to the end of the lane and turn right, he would then be back on the main village street, and we would catch up with him, and see him, back at the Pub.

When we arrived back we saw that Eddies' car was already parked up in the Car Park and when we went inside he was in the Bar and half way down his first pint. As we approached the bar Eddie opened the conversation, by saying, with a broad smile on his face, 'Lost any more credit cards lately my friend?'

'Not since the last one you found, I hope, thank you. Can I offer you that drink now?'

I ordered the drinks and while we waited we passed the time of day chatting, as any strangers might, following their first meeting. When they arrived we all moved casually to a vacant table and sat down.

'Time at the Bar please, Ladies and Gentlemen.' came a bellow from somewhere over in that direction. 'Can we have your glasses please?'

'We only just made it. I didn't realise it was so late,' remarked Fred.

As we sat, doing our best to oblige and drink off, who should walk through the door but Johnson?

'See who I see?' I said, touching Fred's sleeve.

'Yes I do.'

'Who's he?' enquired Eddie.

'That one is Mick Johnson, our Smuggler or the Poacher as we named him before we knew his real name. The guy we told you about with the battered van and the one who carried and transported all the gear the other night. He is the one who took it all to the Builder's house and locked it in the garage.'

'Rough looking character,' remarked Eddie.

Johnson went straight up to the Bar to be greeted by the Landlord, who informed him. 'We are closed. Open again tea time.'

'I'm not bothered about that. I came to see if you want any gear?'

'No I do not, and you damn well know I don't and you know why. So don't come here bothering me again, and tell whoever it is that keeps ringing here for you, that I am not your bloody keeper or private secretary. So when I say to them, "I don't know where you are". I damned well mean I don't know where you are and what's more when I ask them who's ringing I don't want a load of verbal abuse, understand? This is the last time. You tell whoever it is, no more. This is the last one. You are to ring this number.' He handed him a piece of paper that he picked up from the shelf at the back of the bar.

'Change that for the phone then,' demanded Johnson, holding out a coin. With a look of disgust the Landlord took it and delving in the till, produced the necessary change. Johnson picking up the coins from the bar top, then shuffled his way towards the Payphone that was located in a recess to the left hand side of the Bar.

'Quick, come with me,' said Eddie taking hold of Fred by the arm and pulling her towards the payphone.

Standing about six feet away from the Public Payphone was a Gaming Machine. Eddie pushed a coin in the slot and proceeded to play the machine while Fred stood watching him from the side he had guided her to and which then placed her between the machine and Johnson. Johnson finished his call and hung up. He then walked straight out through the front door. Eddie continued to play the machine until the money ran out, then both he and Fred returned to the table.

'Can we have your glasses now please, it's getting late and I am shutting shop. My lunch is getting cold.'

I looked at Fred, 'What did he have to say?'

'Not a great deal, unfortunately. When we got there he was already talking to someone so I didn't hear him ask for anyone by name, then he said, "Where, the welcome at nine, when, tonight, bloody hell, OK nine o'clock", or words very similar to that, then he hung up and walked out.'

'The welcome at nine! Could that mean a Pub or Cafe or Snack Bar type place or perhaps even some sort of Club?' mused Eddie. 'Sounds a bit like a Salvation Army set up or a Seaman's Refuge to me; The Welcome Mission to Deep Sea Mariners, or something like that.'

'Wait here a moment while I take these glasses back to the bar and ask the Landlord if he can throw any light on it.' I crossed to the bar and put our empty glasses alongside all the others waiting to be washed.

'Excuse me, but is there a Pub or Club or eating house round here called "The Welcome"?'

'Not round here, only place I know of which is called the Welcome is the Welcome Inn at Whitby. It's a pub. Why?'

'I saw it advertised somewhere and it referred to good company and good food,' I lied.

'Then it won't be the Welcome in Whitby. It's a riverside pub used mainly by local fishing folks and it's doubtful if they do food. More of an ale house and whore house, if you ask me.'

'Thanks anyway! I guess I better go back to the Guide Book and pick somewhere else.'

Fred and Eddie were standing by the door. I joined them and we all went outside together.

'Find out anything?' enquired Fred as we stood on the pavement.

'It's a Pub apparently, on the riverside, in Whitby. So if the meeting, or whatever it is, is at nine o'clock tonight how about an evening trip to Whitby?'

'How do we know he is going to Whitby and even if he does, he might be going there for anyone of a hundred perfectly innocent reasons. How do we know it has anything to do with us?' replied Fred.

'We don't but it has something to do with Johnson and he is our only lead at the moment and so if we don't go and take the chance then we won't find out, will we and let's be honest we don't have anything else right now, do we?'

'I agree with Mel.' At which Fred gave him a "who asked you look".

'Listen,' I said. 'This is what I propose. We go to Whitby in our Camper and Eddie, you go separately in your car.'

'How far is it and where do we meet when we get there?' enquired Eddie.

'It's only a few miles up the coast. It's a small commercial port split down the middle by a river, if the map is anything to go by; that is. So to locate a Pub on the riverside should not take long. When we get there we will meet up outside the local Police Station.'

'The Police Station?' asked Eddie looking rather surprised at my choice of rendezvous.

'Yes, outside the Police Station. They are a great favourite of mine. Every town has a Police Station and usually only one. They are more often than not very easy to find and if you should need to ask directions you do not arouse any suspicions and all the locals know exactly where it is, so you don't waste time chasing about and having to ask more than once.'

'Right,' said Eddie. 'Outside Whitby Police Station at eight tonight: that then gives us an hour to find the Pub. See you both later,' and he walked away.

We went back to our Camper.

CHAPTER TWENTY-SIX

We arrived in Whitby a few minutes before eight o'clock having, much to our surprise, calculated the time to get there fairly accurately and when we enquired we were directed to the Police Station by a friendly local. There happened to be a Public Car Park close by and so we had no problems parking and we had time to make our way from there across and up the slight incline, to the Police Station. As we walked along I enquired from a gentleman, who was walking a dog towards us, if he could direct us to the Welcome Inn. We were instructed to go to the end of the road we presently stood in, and then that would lead us down to the River and the Harbour area. If we then turned left and followed the road, which ran parallel to the side of the river, we would eventually come to the Welcome Inn, which happened to be, according to him, the third Public House along.

Eddie Scott arrived a few minutes later and as we all stood outside the Police Station I told him that we had a rough idea of which direction to go in.

The Harbour at Whitby is on the estuary of the river Esk, which flows through the middle of the town and effectively cuts in two. The two halves are joined, at two separate points, by bridges. One, a swing bridge, which can be opened as and when required, to allow shipping to pass further up the river. The second is a permanent structure and spans the river much higher up and is at the point where the river begins to cease to be navigable for anything but very small boats. There is a road running parallel to the river bank on the North side and, part of which, also serves as a quay and provides mooring spaces for a wide variety of sea-going vessels. The South bank, and more so on the lower reaches, is for the most part lined with buildings that actually reach down to the water's edge at high tide. Therefore, as a result of this, most of the harbour activities are centred on the Northern side of the river.

The Welcome Inn was not difficult to find, for having followed the directions we had been given, we took the road down the hill until it opened out on to the river side, then turning left, we walked along the quayside, passed the first two pubs, and all the fish filleting sheds and storage houses until we reached an open area which was the location of the ice house; a large, tall structure used to produce ice in large commercial quantities for the fishing trawlers. Directly opposite and across the road was the Welcome Inn. The period facade, with a central doorway and large bow windows on either side, gave the appearance of a building that had stood on the same site, unaltered, for many years.

Once inside we found ourselves in one large room with a central semi-circular bar. A door on either side of the bar had signs on them that indicated

Ladies and Gents toilets respectively. There were several solid cast iron tables in the centre with wooden polished stools set round them. The walls were close-planked to a height of approximately five feet. Partitions of the same construction had been added to form a series of cubicles all round the outer walls. In each of these spaces stood a large oblong iron table with one or perhaps two stools placed before it. The three sides of each cubicle had bench seats attached. All the timberwork was very dark and naturally stained from many years of constant use and wear and tear. The ceiling was supported by large solid wooden beams, perhaps originally obtained from the old timber boat yards or washed up on the beach from wrecks, and the decorations which created the intimate, and perhaps slightly oppressive atmosphere, were all of a nautical nature. There were knickknacks and curios; old large brass navigation lamps, a couple of large old sailing ships' wheels, brass portholes, old navigation charts and a large collection of sepia photographs of people and events long gone.

The Pub was very busy and most of the tables were occupied by what I could only describe as, sea-going types. There was a predominance of woolly jumpers and round woolly hats. Some had donkey jackets or tartan thermal shirts on and nearly all were wearing sea boots. Dotted about were a few females but the clientele was predominantly male. To round things off, the whole atmosphere was heavy with smoke and the distinct aroma of the sea with a strong fishy smell thrown in. Most of the language was quite ripe, too.

After a few minutes we managed to get served and holding our drinks we stood with our backs to the bar, and looked around. 'People watching' Is my expression for it. Some short time later a table close by became vacant so we made our move and sat down. From this position, between us, we could observe all the cubicles, or we could, after some rearranging and quite a bit of shuffling by Fred so that she had, what she claimed to be, a much better view.

'We look a bit conspicuous sitting here in the middle of all this lot don't you think?' queried Fred after a few minutes, 'I would feel much happier if we could get into one of those side alcoves.'

'I don't think we are so conspicuous; look about you. No one is taking the slightest bit of notice of us and apart from when we came in no one has even given us a second glance. I know we are sitting here hoping that Johnson will be turning up at about nine o'clock but he doesn't know us, and even if he remembers us from the previous Pubs or the local shops, so what? People go from Pub to Pub; isn't he doing exactly that? So why shouldn't we? What do you think, Eddie?'

'We're not so bad here. We can always move later if we get chance or we have to. Let's just hang on and hope that one of those tables becomes vacant, if that's what you want Fred. Let's just see what develops.' That decided, we settled down to chat and wait.

'By the way, Eddie, you haven't mentioned the Builder. Did you go there this teatime?' asked Fred.

'Yes, I did as a matter of fact.'

'And how did you get on?'

'Apart from noticing the fact that she is a very smart, good looking lady, not very much I'm afraid. She was not interested in anything I had to say and it was plain she has nothing to do with her husband's business as she couldn't or wouldn't answer the simplest questions. She virtually told me to go away and come back again when he was at home; told me he was away at the moment and made it very clear that I was being nothing but a nuisance to her. She was agitated all the time and kept looking at her watch; so much so that when I tried to make light conversation and introduce the subject of fishing all I managed to get was a vague reference to the fact that her husband sometimes went fishing and what was that to do with Building Insurance? I tried the line about Personal Insurance, Personal Accident, perhaps while fishing, and what type of fishing did he go in for, freshwater or sea angling, and where did he go? Was it dangerous or risky? I expressed my own keen interest in the sport, but all I got was, "I am sorry, I can't help you. You really must go, I am expecting someone at any time and don't have the time to talk to you", and then to my surprise, she added with a very sexy smile, "Any other time and I would love to chat with you, but now you must go". The next thing I know I am stood on the doorstep with the door closed in front of me. So we are not a great deal wiser in that direction.'

Several drinks later and what must have taken us well past nine o'clock, Fred nodded towards the door and in a lowered voice whispered, 'He's here.'

I glanced sideways and saw him immediately. He walked across the room and up to the bar, passing behind where I sat. He didn't even give us a cursory glance. He ordered a pint of beer and stood looking about the room, then eased his way towards one of the alcoves and enquired, of the two men sitting there, if the seat was taken. When told it was not he sat down, promptly produced a newspaper, and began to read it. The other two continued their conversation, totally ignoring him. He read and we watched, but nothing happened. We ordered more drinks and Fred went to the loo and we rearrange the stools slightly when she came back so we each had a better view of him. Our conversation, in the meantime, revolved round a discussion on the virtue of a young woman, who was behaving in a very unladylike manner, with three men. All four of them were obviously very drunk and enjoying the performance.

Meanwhile the two men, in the same alcove as Johnson, drank up and without a word to anyone, stood up and left. Immediately two others, from a nearby table, moved to the one occupied by Johnson, and sat in the vacant places. Neither one spoke to Johnson and apart from a cursory glance at them, he carried on reading his newspaper. The other two struck up a conversation between themselves,

ignoring Johnson. A few minutes later another man, who had just entered the Pub, went up to their table and said quite loudly, 'Room for a little 'en in here?'

The two moved round and he slid in beside them. Johnson laid his paper on the table and angrily demanded, 'Where the hell you been? I haven't got all bloody night to sit here waiting for you.'

'Got away as soon as I could, didn't I?' replied the latecomer.

'Nine o'clock you said. You should get a fucking watch?'

On the arrival of the fourth man the other two had stopped talking. Now one of them said, 'Shut up the bloody pair of you and listen.'

Johnson put his newspaper on the seat beside him and they all leaned slightly forward, towards the centre of the table, and from that point their level of conversation dropped so that it was impossible for us to catch even a single word.

'Damn!' cursed Eddie, 'Can't hear a bloody word they are saying.'

At that same moment, almost as if pre-planned, but we knew of course that it was not, a group of five or six men, who were recent arrivals, positioned themselves between us and Johnson's group. We could now see nothing, let alone hear anything.

'If we can't hear what they are saying, then at least, I think I will try and get a photograph, if that's possible with all this lot about,' grumbled Eddie. 'I can then check if any of these boys are in any of our photographic records.'

'You can't take photographs in here. There's not enough light and you certainly won't get away with letting off a flash,' laughed Fred.

'I will with this baby,' he replied, producing a small black plastic camera. 'With this and the special film that goes with it, no flash is required and it will take recognisable pictures in almost any light. A useful little gadget and looks like an ordinary inexpensive camera. Can we move round a bit so that I will be facing them even though we can't see them at the moment?'

I became rather agitated as time passed for we could still neither hear nor see them and I was inwardly, and very tempted outwardly, to curse the group in front of us, when with loud 'Goodbyes' to the bar staff, they place their empty glasses on the bar and left.

We could now, at last, see them again and they were still deeply engrossed in conversation. Before anyone could move and fill the space in front of us, Eddie took his pictures. He did it by simply pointing the camera in their direction and pressing the shutter release while the camera was still on the table. He then equally unobtrusively picked it up and slid it into his pocket. Shortly after that, two of the men in Johnson's group got up and walked towards the toilet.

'Time for a visit to the Gents,' I said quickly to Eddie, who immediately got up and together we followed them in. Once inside we stood politely doing what gentlemen do. As we had entered the other two were talking but stopped as soon as

they saw us. As they prepared to leave one said, 'Er, nobody's said 'owt about tide. What's times top of flood on seventh?'

'About five 'int morning, give or take a bit either way,' was the reply.

'So, he's on about hour afore that then?' as the door closed behind them.

I looked and smiled at Eddie. When we returned to the table I must have still been grinning.

'What are you so cheerful about?' mused Fred. 'Been looking sideways in there have you?'

'I didn't look, but I don't know if he did. Anyhow, where's Johnson?'

'He left as soon as you two went into the loo and the other two, who went in there before you, have also gone straight out. The other one, the fourth one has gone to sit over there and is talking with the chap next to him. They are both getting ready to go now.'

'Any point in following any of them?' enquired Eddie.

'Well, I don't fancy staying in here longer than we have to,' said Fred, 'and they may just lead us somewhere. Let's take the change and see what happens.'

We stepped out into the open. The last two to leave were some distance up ahead, so we turned to follow them. There were no signs of any of the others. Of the two up ahead, the one who was not part of the original four, raised his arm in a farewell salute, and turned off into a side street and disappeared from view. We decided we could ignore him. That left only the one so we continued to follow him. He stopped outside a Taxi Office, rummaged in his pockets, looking for, I assumed, money before he eventually went inside. We had, by that time, almost caught up with him. Fred quickly said, 'I hope there is a Hospital in this town. Will one of you find out where it is and pick me up there?' as she disappeared into the Taxi Office.

The Hospital was not far from the Police Station so Fred did not have long to wait before I arrived at the main entrance, in our Camper and picked her up. She climbed in, shut the door, and secured the seat belt.

'As I followed him into the Taxi Office I was surprised to see one of the other four already sat in there waiting. But there was no sign of Johnson or the fourth man. I told the girl I wanted to go to the hospital and then I sat down to wait. All I managed to hear was the girl in the Taxi Office say, over her radio, to one of the cabs, was that she had a job from the office for two to go to "Middle Walk". She then requested a second cab to come to the office for a fare to the Hospital. That was for me. When the first cab arrived the two men went out together and I assumed they were both going to Middle Walk, wherever that is. The next car to arrive was for me and brought me here to the Hospital. Where's Eddie?'

'He set off back to the Dog and Gun. He and I looked around on our way back to the Car Park but we saw no one. So there was no point in him hanging around any longer. But back to what you were saying. You say a "Middle Walk"

was mentioned? Well I think I might just know how to find out where that is. Down here we passed an illuminated Tourist Map. Let's go see what it can tell us.'

I drew up alongside the map and we both got out. It was a large one and took in the whole of Whitby. A small illuminated bulb set into the map face, at a position along the side of the river, had a label attached that said, 'You are here'. The buttons arranged along the bottom edge each had a name below them and were listed, left to right, in alphabetical order. I scanned along the line and came to a label that stated 'Hospital'. I pressed the button and a light came on close to the 'You are here' light. I saw the Car Park we had previously parked on. Fred, in the meantime working in the opposite direction, pressed the button for the Police Station. It too was close to the Hospital. We could now relate to the map and the layout to our present position. Indicating with my finger I said to Fred, 'Here is the road where the Welcome Pub is. The Taxi Office is somewhere here and I bet this Middle Walk is a street or somewhere far enough out of the centre of the town to warrant a taxi ride.'

'Look, it's here,' exclaimed Fred, pointing to a button with the label 'Middle Walk'. She pressed it and a tiny light winked towards the top right hand corner of the map. We both looked up and read the label simultaneously, 'Middle Walk Estate.' and with that particular section of the map showing numerous interlocking roads typical of a modern housing estate.

'Not much chance there. I bet there will be hundreds of houses all looking very similar and telling us absolutely nothing,' she said, sounding disappointed.

'I have no idea what I hoped we would find,' I said. 'But it was worth a try. Never mind. Press "Harbour Master's Office". I've seen a button for that along here somewhere.'

Fred found it first and the appropriate little bulb lit up. Looking away from the map and pointing, I said, 'Some-where just over there and not too far away. I wonder if they have Tide Tables on display outside. Some Harbour Offices do and some don't.'

'What do you want that for?'

'Just an idea! Remember the guys in the toilet? One of them mentioned tide times and I thought we could check it out.'

We found out that at Whitby, they don't. They displayed the times of High and Low Water only on a daily bases. Again it had been worth a try and we lost nothing from it as the Harbour Master's Office was on our way out of town.

The drive back to camp in the dark was uneventful with the roads, at that time of night and on that particular occasion, very quiet.

'Do we have any of that whiskey left?' I asked as we drove along.

'Yes, it's in the top back locker up on the right.'

'Good, I just feel like a decent drink when we get back. All that shandy back there has done nothing but fill me up with gas.'

'You should have let me drive. I don't mind not drinking and I can manage quite well on soft drinks all night, if I have to. I was surprised when you went for the shandy and decided to drive.'

'It's a good job I did otherwise you would have had to walk all the way back from the Hospital. Eddie doesn't seem to bother too much, does he? Although I noticed that he got a pint shandy to start with but after that it was straight pints.'

We parked up and climbed into the back. Fred began searching in one of the lockers and I thought she was looking for the whiskey, but instead she turned and offered me a small blue booklet.

'I bet you forgot about these. We bought them when we were selecting the maps.' I took hold of the booklet and immediately recognised it as a set of Tide Tables. 'Here's your whiskey,' she said. I took the bottle and stood it on the table and went back to the tables.

The seventh of next month, the seventh of this month having already passed, gave High Water at Whitby for the early hours of that morning as four fifty a.m., for Scarborough, two minutes past five, and Bridlington twenty one minutes past five.

'The tides along this coast setting North to South creates a difference of twelve minutes between Whitby and Scarborough, so for a point somewhere in between it works out at near enough to five in the morning. They have arranged for an hour before High Water so we are looking at four in the morning of the seventh. Daylight is just after six and, according to these tables there will be no moon. I think we might be onto something there.'

CHAPTER TWENTY-SEVEN

The next day was warm and sunny and once again we went into the village but this time, primarily, to buy provisions. We were discussing progress and what we were supposed to be doing and really what little information we had and naturally whilst doing so the subject relating to the tide times and the Whitby trip came up again.

Fred was saying, 'we don't have very much really, do we? We have a possible time and date that you and Eddie overheard and four men huddled together in a Pub where we assume they were making some sort of arrangements. Then out of them we only know one and then not all that much about him and on top of that, two others that took a taxi to a place called Middle Walk.'

'You could be wrong there, Fred. Four men with two known to us, or about to be made known to us: just look over there, what do you see?'

'Only the Coastguard Land Rover parked outside the Post Office; we've seen it out and about all week. There is nothing unusual in that.'

'I know, but wait until you see who comes out of the Post Office and gets in it.'

A middle aged, average sized, male, dressed in the uniform of an Auxiliary Coastguard, came out of the Post office, opened the passenger door of the Land Rover and climbed in.

'Don't you recognise him? I will swear that he was one of the four in the Welcome pub last night.'

'Are you sure? He's a Coastguard.'

'So what? There's one way to find out. Come on, let's walk past and turn straight round and walk back. We should, with a bit of luck, get a good look at him.'

'Too late they are pulling off.'

'Sod it. But never mind. If they are on watch then at some time they will end up at the Coastguard lookout. All we have to do is walk along the cliff top and visit the Coastguard Station. Come on, if we set off now and leg it we should be there before they change the watch over at one o'clock.'

'Are you still sure about him? I didn't think any of them looked like a Coastguard.'

'Enough to want to go and take a closer look and anyhow what does a Coastguard look like out of uniform?'

'Which one do you think he is?'

'The one who when they moved round ended up sat next to Johnson, in the Pub. The one with the donkey jacket on.'

'Well, if it is him, he was one of those in the Taxi Office when I went in last night. But somehow he looks different.'

'That's probably the uniform. Last night, remember, he was wearing a donkey jacket and a round woolly hat. In fact you stand a much better chance of recognising him than me. You saw him in the Taxi Office, so let's go pick up the binoculars and do our walking, bird watching and hiking routine, and head towards the Coastguard Station.'

It was a good walk from the Camper along the cliff paths to the Coastguard Station, not to mention the distance from the village back to the Camper in the first place, but we got there about mid-day.

From the outside the place appeared to be deserted and apart from the Land Rover and a private car parked alongside it, there were no signs of life. We went some way past and selected a patch of soft green grass to sit on. I opened out the map and studied it. Fred, using the glasses, looked out to sea, observing distant shipping. There was no sign of movement around the Coastguard Station until just before one o'clock, the usual time for watch change when a uniformed figure appeared through one of the doors in the building. He proceeded to unlocking the private car and then spent a few minutes, loading his personal effects into it, before getting in, and driving away.

'You were right,' said Fred excitedly and with the binoculars still held up to her eyes. 'He was one of those in the Taxi Office last night. I am sure of it now. Now for a name! We ring Ray Oldfield at Humber and he should be able to tell us who was on watch here this morning.'

We trudged all the way back to the village to ring Oldfield from there.

'We should be fit after all this walking, but I'm not. My legs are ready to drop off,' I moaned.

* * *

I was glad when we got back to the village, because for some reason, my legs really did ache. Fred suggested that it might be from stretching out on the grass that, she claimed, was still a little damp; there having been hardly sufficient decent weather, of recent times, to dry it out properly.

'You go and order some coffee or something while I ring Oldfield,' I suggested.

I managed to get through straight away and apart from a short delay while he put the phone down to go and get his file, I managed to join Fred in the Cafe just before she started her second cup of coffee.

‘What could he tell us?’ were her first words before I even had time to sit down.

‘Wait a moment. First of all I am hungry. Do you fancy Soup and a Roll or something like that?’

‘Yes. What a good idea. Soup will be fine. It is a bit chilly and is definitely not as warm now as it was first thing this morning.’

We ordered soup and there was a further delay while plates with rolls and butter were put out on the table.

‘Come on, tell me, what did he say?’

‘I asked him who was on watch this morning and he checked with the Watch Officer and informed me that it was a guy named Raines. Full title Ronald Raines, but known locally and to his colleagues as Ron or Ronny Raines and guess what? He lives in Middle Walk, Whitby, and has been an Auxiliary on this patch for just over four years.’

‘That’s interesting and mixing with the likes of Johnson.’

‘There’s a bit more. According to his record he came over here from Ireland where he claims he was working for a good number of years. He brought back an Irish wife and as far as Oldfield knows, there are no children.’

‘Brilliant. Two down and two to go, as they say in sporting circles,’ laughed Fred.

‘So we know this man Raines is from Middle Walk. I wonder if the other guy who went with him in the taxi is also from Middle Walk or if he was just visiting?’

‘Eat before your soup gets cold.’

Conversation stooped for a few minutes while we concentrated on the soup and fresh bread rolls.

‘That soup was lovely and just what I needed.’

‘Yes, it was. Have you had sufficient?’

‘Yes thanks.’

‘OK. Now you just stay here for a moment and finish your coffee or something, while I pop up the road and buy one or two bits that we need. I know it’s a bit of a bind buying bread rolls and things like that two or three times a week but, at least that way, they don’t go stale and get wasted.

A short while later we were heading back for the campsite.

‘As soon as we get back I’m going to relax and after this mornings success, indulge myself in nothingness for at least an hour.’

‘That’s a damned good idea.’

Lovely warm flesh, roving female hands and soft sensuous lips are not my idea of nothingness and complete rest but, I must admit, it comes a very close second and at least I did eventually get, what I call, some proper rest. I think Fred

did also, but how much I wasn't quite sure because once I closed my eyes I went out like a light and when I woke she was up and about.

'Come on lazy bones; time to rise and shine. I have been up ages.'

She was standing in front of the tiny work surface chopping salad. She wore only a tee shirt and tiny pink briefs so I just lay there and admired the view as she worked away.

'Salad for tea! OK with you?

'Fine. Anything.'

'Well get up and fix the table so we have somewhere to sit.'

'Bugger the table, just put yourself in a bread roll and I will have you for tea.'

'Then what will you do for your after hours nookie, if you have eaten me? Look, stop messing about and put the table up or you might find your important bits covered in mustard and in my Hot Dog sandwich.'

'Then what will you do for nookie?'

'We girls have our methods.'

'I know you have, but at least mine doesn't need batteries.'

'Nor do some of ours, but enough of that for now. That's better, now put these plates and pots on the table while I make the tea or would you prefer coffee?'

'Either, I am not fussy. You as you are will do.'

* * *

Washed and fed we once again wound our way along the lane towards the village. It was dark, although it was still only early evening.

'I think we ought to contact Bertie Cruickshank, give him an update and ask him if he can get us a complete run down on this Raines. He is after all an Auxiliary Coastguard, and you know how the Department has to know everything there is to know about it's own people. Raines will be no exception and there might be something interesting. A full address in Whitby, for example, might be of use to us.'

'We can't do much now, can we? Its Saturday don't forget, and tomorrow we said we would do a stake out on Johnson and the Builder and see what, their fishing trip was all about. Are we going to use Eddie on that?'

'Why not? He's here and if he is willing, an extra body could be useful. We are all supposed to be all working together or so we've been told. Let's see what he has to say, that's if he's back. I was surprised, this lunch time, when they said, at the Pub, he was away all day.'

'They probably think he is out selling his Insurance.'

We arrived at the Pub to find he was back and he greeted us with a wave as soon as we went in.

'Been back long?' enquired Fred as we settled down.

'No. Not long. I had one or two odds and ends to tidy up from another job and I was supposed to be working with a colleague on something else, when I got side tracked and sent here. So I had to sort that out. But now everything is neat and tidy and, by the way, I managed to get those photographs that I took. I'll nip upstairs in a moment and get them.'

'They came out OK then?' enquired Fred.

'Yes, fine and I have had several prints run off. I will show you.'

'Great and we think we have identified another one of them,' said Fred, who then proceeded to tell Eddie everything we had gathered, so far, about Raines.

'Good. You can't beat a name and it's even better with a picture. I think I ought to run him through our records; see if we have anything on the name,' suggested Eddie. 'It can't do any harm.'

We both nodded in agreement. The more we can turn up on any of them the better, I thought.

'Wait here while I go to my room and get the pictures. They are quite good considering the circumstances in which they were taken.'

He returned a few minutes later with a large manila envelope from which he produced several glossy photographs. There appeared to be dozens of them, which surprised me, because I thought, that at the time, he had only taken one or two. The first one he selected to show us was about ten by eight inches in size and showed a very large area of the Pub's interior with Johnson and his cronies occupying only a small area near the centre.

'That's the original picture and is the result of the wide-angled lens fitted in the camera. The advantage of that type of lens is that it allows you to do what I did and place the camera casually on the table, press the shutter release and capture a wide area. This second picture,' as he selected a second ten by eight, 'has been blown up to give us more of what we want.'

The quality of the second picture remained surprisingly good considering the lighting conditions under which it had been taken. All four men in the picture were clearly visible and readily recognisable.

'That's Johnson,' said Fred, 'and the one sitting next to him, we now know, is Raines and that one there, next to Raines, is the one who went off with him in the same taxi. This one at the end is the one who disappeared along with Johnson.'

'These may also be useful,' added Eddie as he produced several smaller sized pictures. These were further blow-ups of the main picture but had been masked out to show each individual separately; the other three having been obliterated from the picture completely.

'They have lost some of the quality of the original and are a bit grainy at this magnification but at least we now have individual pictures which might be useful. The worst one is of, what did you call him, Raines, as it shows only part profile. As you can see a small part of his face is blocked out by Johnson. But that is not really important as we have already identified him, or should I say, you have.'

'That's a really good selection of pictures and all from just one negative.' mused Fred as she slid them about on the tabletop with her fingertips.

'In actual fact there are twelve altogether. Two sets of six, one for me, and one for you two, each of two large pictures and four small ones. It does look a lot when you see them spread out over the table like this, doesn't it? Oh! By the way and before I forget, my people have had a close look at them and can tell us nothing. We apparently have no pictorial records on any of them and we have no written records or files on Johnson and I don't know, as yet of course, if we have anything on Raines.'

'We propose asking our people, the first chance we get, and particularly now that we have identified Raines. But it's Saturday night and unless it was a dire emergency we can't do much by way of routine enquiry before Monday. But more important, for the time being, we have to sort out what we are going to do about tomorrow.'

'Are you coming with us or do you propose we do this one alone?' enquired Fred of Eddie.

'Yes, of course I will come, if you can use me. That's what I am here for. What's your plan?'

Fred smiled at me. 'Yes, what's the plan, Mel?'

It was obviously down to me. I thought for a moment.

'Fishermen are notorious for going off fishing at all different times of the day and night. It seems to make no difference whether they do it for a living or for pleasure; they still go at different times and in all weathers. We overheard Johnson make a particular reference to Sunday. He said nothing about Saturday night but how early on Sunday morning they propose to go we simply don't know. So I think we could be looking at a time from somewhere around five o'clock in the morning onward. Also we have no idea where they intend to go. From that, all I can suggest is that we stake out both Johnson's house and the Builder's and hope they don't leave earlier than we anticipate. You talked with the Builder's wife, Eddie, did she give you any leads or mention any times?'

'No. Like I mentioned before. When I tried to talk to her of my interest in fishing she showed no interest at all, saying she knew nothing about it and only said that sometimes her husband went fishing on Sundays. Nothing more. She wanted me to go at the time; she wanted rid of me and kept looking at her watch the whole time.'

'Right, so are we all agreed, is five o'clock early enough?' Both nodded so I continued. 'We, that is Fred and I, can park the Camper somewhere out of site in the village and then, without much difficulty, stake out Johnson's house. Now if you, Eddie, can stake out the Builder. We cover both starting points.'

'No problem! Leave that to me. Now what about comms?'

'We have two hand-held Coastguard radios. We can use those on one of the lesser-used channels.' I suggested.

'I have some cheap Citizens Band radios. You know the type? They are sold in pairs, cost only a few quid, are meant mainly for kids and are all on the same single fixed frequency. They are quite handy and I have used them quite a few times in the past. The beauty of them is that the frequency is so low and the range is limited to about a mile, so no one bothers to monitor them and even if they did, they would have to be within the mile radius to pick them up. We can use them if you like and keep your radios as back-up and to be used only in an emergency if we get out of effective range with my Mickey mouse ones.'

'Sounds good! Let's do that. Now what about call signs?'

'I would think Eddie, E for Echo, and you Mel, M for Mike.' suggested Fred.

'Agreed, Echo and Mike. We will set up the stakeouts at five in the morning and do a quick radio check that will also serve to establish that we are in position. So for now I suggest another drink then call it a day. If we have an early start I will need an early night.'

'The radios?' asked Eddie. 'If you wait a moment I will get you one of mine from upstairs then I will walk down the lane with you and collect one of yours.'

* * *

Some time later, having finally kicked Eddie out and seen him off on his return journey back to the village, I set the alarm for four o'clock and we settled down for a short nap before the proposed early morning start.

'It's a good job we managed a couple of hours this afternoon.' I said.

'Mmm.' Was all I heard as she slid her hand under my tee shirt and slowly stroked my chest with the palm of her hand. The tip of her tongue gently worked its way round my ear.

'Yes, wasn't it? Let's do it again.'

'The stakeout is at five o'clock. If I don't get some sleep I will never make it.'

'Yes you will. I will see you are up and out there on time. But I have plans for getting something else up right now. So don't just lie there. Show a bit of passion for a girl who needs a little loving.'

One of my last thoughts before she finally let me drift off to sleep was, am I really so weak-willed or am I just putty in the hands of this girl. Either way it was now up to her to see that I was woken in the morning.

CHAPTER TWENTY-EIGHT

We left the van neatly tucked away around a corner and within easy reaching distance. We then selected a secluded position from where we could clearly see Johnson's house and his van parked in the garden. I was still half asleep and really not with it. Fred seemed bright enough.

There was a strong wind blowing in from the sea and it was cold. After a few minutes of stamping her feet and rubbing gloved hands, Fred asked, 'what time is it?

I took out my flash light and carefully illuminated my watch. 'About two minutes to five.'

'I hope this is not going to be a long drawn out job. This cold is getting through to me already and we have only been here for two minutes. Better give Eddie a call and see if he has made it.'

I took the small radio out of my pocket, pulled out the telescopic aerial, and switched on.

'Echo...Mike...over.'

No reply. I waited another couple of minutes then tried again. 'Echo... Mike...over.'

'Mike...Echo...loud and clear...over.'

'Loud and clear with me...listening...out.'

'I hope this isn't going to take long,' she moaned yet again. 'There isn't even a light on in the house that I can see.'

The next half hour was one of the longest I think I have ever experienced. The wind was biting and stung our faces and made my nose run almost uncontrollably. I was also still very tired and as I looked at Fred, she had her hands thrust deep into her pockets and stamped her feet continuously in an attempt to keep the circulation going.

'Go back to the van Fred. This is stupid. Nothing is happening and it doesn't need two of us to watch over there and if you are going to drive you will do it much better if you're warm.'

'Thanks sweetie! If nothing happens in a short while I will come back and relieve you.' Then having said that she gave me a peck on the cheek, with cold lips, and disappeared round the corner to make her way back to the Camper.

A further half an hour slowly passed and I was wondering just how long it might be before Fred came to relieve me, because by then, I was almost frozen stiff. I continued to move round in a small tight circle, stamping my feet and glancing at the house each time I faced that way, when I was brought to a halt, and I must

admit taken somewhat by surprise, when a light over the door of Johnson's house came on and in the darkness I had got used to, seemed to flood-light the whole area. I stopped stamping and stepped quickly back into the shadows. I peered out at the activity that began to unfold up ahead. The front door opened and he stepped out into the light. He was wrapped in heavy waterproofs. He had a small bag in one hand and several long fishing rods in the other. He laid these aside and opened the rear door of his van. He returned to his front door and disappeared into the house. A moment later he re-emerged with a large fishing box over his shoulder and loaded it into the van. Then picking up his rods and the small bag loaded those into the back and secured the doors. As he once again went back to the house, this time to close the door, I lifted the small radio to my mouth and pressed the transmit button, 'Echo…Mike…movement here…over.'

Johnson, by this time, having climbed into the van and started the engine, turned on his lights and backed the van out into the lane. I did a rapid retreat into the shadows and then as quickly as my stiff legs would allow, headed back towards our van. As I opened the door and climbed in I was lightly gasping for breath. The cold and the long period of inactivity had really got to me.

'Johnson is on the move. Start up and move out to the end. Give him plenty of time to get in front and keep your fingers crossed that he goes to the Builders.'

At the end of the lane Fred, not wanting to disturb the neighbourhood at this early hour, turned off the engine thus depriving us of the much needed warmth from the heater. Less than two minutes later.

'Mike…Echo…movement here, van approaching.' Then after only a few more minutes, 'Van turned into Builders.'

I looked and smiled at Fred. We sat and waited, the Radio in my hand remained silent.

'Do you want a cup of tea?' asked Fred, as she passed me the flask.

'I would love one, but not just now. Sods law says that if I do, something will happen and we will either miss it or something.'

We continued to wait and as we did so I slowly began to warm up.

'Mike…Echo…Range Rover leaving, headed your way. Johnson and one other in it…over.'

'Roger…Will pick it up as it passes and follow.'

A few moments later a large dark grey Range Rover passed by and continued on down the road. I made a mental note of the registration number and saw at the same time that Johnson was in the passenger seat. Fred started up and slipped the engine into gear and then having allowed the Range Rover time to get some distance beyond us, switched on the lights and pulled out. A few minutes later and we could see their rear lights up in the distance ahead and kept, what we thought was, a healthy gap between us.

'Echo…Mike…you following…over.'

'Roger…behind you…out.'

'Don't get too close Fred. In the dark, if we can see them, then they can certainly see us. We don't want them to realise they are being followed and if they have done this sort of thing before and they have always been the only vehicle on the road at this time in the morning then us behind will certainly attract their attention. Then if Eddie catches us up and we are all going the same way god knows what they will think.'

'Yes boss, never done it before boss, never would have worked that out for myself boss, thanks for the tip boss.'

'Shut up and drive,' I laughed. 'At least it's getting a bit warmer. Is that heater turned up full?'

We had no idea where they were going so we could only settled down to follow wherever they led.

'I hope, if the roads improve, he doesn't go too fast in that Range Rover otherwise we will not be able to keep up. Eddie might in his car but we would have no chance in this thing.'

'No, these things are not exactly made for rally driving, are they?'

The roads became busier as dawn broke and in addition the fact that we were now following them along major roads, meant that we were obliged to drive closer to avoid loosing them. Along the minor roads it had been easy as we had only them in front of us and we could clearly see their lights up ahead. There, when the distance between us varied, it was not so important, but now when we were in traffic and side lights were being turned off as the day brightened, it became more important that we did not let them get out of our sight. Also if they were suspicious of us then this is where they could loose us. It was time for a change.

'Echo…Mike…Pull round. All yours for the next mile or two…over.'

'Roger…will be with you in a few minutes…out.'

We drove on keeping a careful eye on our friends up front then Fred, glancing in her wing mirror, said, 'Here he comes,' just before Eddie cruised past on the outside, waved and pulled in front of us.

'All mine…out.'

I pressed the radio transmit button twice in acknowledgment, as Fred eased up a little thus allowing us to drop back. The gap between Eddie up front and us quickly filled with other road users all heading in the same direction. From there on we would have to rely on Eddie to let us know of any major route changes.

'Time to have a go at that flask now,' I said as we relaxed a little. 'Although that heater has done a good job and I feel OK now I could still do with getting rid of the fur in my mouth.'

'Have you any idea where we are now?' enquired Fred.

'Yes, just here,' I said, pointing to the map on my knee. 'We picked up the Pickering road someway back, and if they keep going in the same direction, we will shortly pick up the A64 and the Malton Bypass.'

Things worked out exactly as I predicted and we were travelling at a steady pace West towards the A64 when, without warning, we got a bit of a scare. I had just finished the half cup of tea that I had managed to pour, despite the motion of the van, and was carefully packing away the flask when I heard our call sign over the radio, followed by a badly broken message. The transmission was very weak and faint. I picked up the radio and transmitted, 'Echo…Mike…say again. You are badly broken and weak…over.'

The reply was barely audible, 'you too are very weak. Close up and call again.'

'Damn it Fred, we have fallen too far behind. There's a limited range on these things and we are losing it. Step on it and close the gap between us. If we loose Eddie we are lost and knackered.'

'We still have our own and if we loose it on that thing then surely Eddie will realise and will use ours. We are only using his low powered ones as we agreed there was less chance of being overheard on them by the so call modern crooks who will listen to everything if they need to and the enthusiasts who can be a damned nuisance. So turn ours on just in case and hang on while I catch him up and keep your fingers crossed he hasn't turned off or stopped or anything.'

Fred accelerated and overtook one or two other vehicles and then a few minutes later I called Eddie again and to my relief a much clearer and louder reply came back.

'You are loud and clear…last message reads, have turned right on to bypass signposted York, Tadcaster, Leeds. Dual carriageway, target now accelerating, close up and maintain…over.'

'Roger…will do' I replied. Then turning to Fred, said, 'we had better step on it a bit. If that Range Rover pulls away on the dual carriageway and Eddie stays with him we might lose contact again.'

'OK. Hold tight and I will do my best.'

By this time we were leaving the Pickering road and running onto the dual carriageway and bypass of the A64. Fred experienced no problems making up some of the ground between us and we were discussing whether we had done enough, to effectively close the gap, when Eddie informed us, 'Mike…Echo…End of dual carriageway, traffic slowing, still on A64…over.'

'Roger…We are right behind you. Do you want us to relieve you…over.'

'Negative…All the traffic going in same direction, no problem. Stand by.'

Within a very short time he was back on the air without using any call signs; 'Immediate...Target indicating right, two miles past end of dual carriageway, minor road, sign posted Kinder Hall...over.'

'Roger...Right two miles, Kinder Hall...over.'

'Affirmative...Am right behind him...Only him and me now; will pull back after turn off. You take it...over.'

'Roger...Right behind you...out.'

Then, turning to Fred, I said, 'Did you get that?'

'Yes. Keep an eye out for the sign...Forget it, I can see it now, there it is. Not much traffic going in that direction at the moment. Here we go.'

Fred indicated right and drew into the middle of the road, waited for a break in the oncoming flow of traffic then turned right and entered a minor country road. About half a mile along this road we passed, and waved to, Eddie, who had pulled off the road into a convenient lay-bye and was waiting for us to pass. As we rounded the next bend Eddie dropped out of sight. Some distance up ahead, as Fred accelerated to close the gap, the Range Rover came into view. There was no other traffic on the road.

The next traffic sign told us we were approaching a T-junction and that we had to 'Give Way'. Kinder Hall was to the left and the village of Nutring was on the right.

We could see across the open fields and saw that the Range Rover had turned left.

'He is heading towards the Hall. Stay with him but don't get too close.'

'Why?' said Fred whilst pointing, 'the sign up there says all visitors are welcome and that's what we are, simple Sunday morning visitors.'

So, to all intents and purposes, as casual visitors out on an early Sunday morning, we followed the Range Rover into the grounds of the Hall and the signs which directed us to a large, fenced off, area designated for Car Parking. I was surprised to note that, despite the early hour, the grounds were open and there were maybe a couple of dozen cars and assorted vans already parked up. We took our time, allowing the Range Rover to select his spot and park up first. We were then able to manoeuvre so that we ended up with the maximum distance between us. As we were doing so I remembered Eddie who was, I presumed, still parked in the lay-bye and patiently waiting to hear from us.

'Echo...Mike...End of lane, turn left, enter grounds of Hall. Target in Car Park...over.'

'On my way...out.'

Not long after and while we were still sat watching the Range Rover, Eddie drove in and parked some distance away from us. He immediately got out of his car and walked off back towards the entrance. While he was away the Builder and Johnson emerged from their vehicle and, carrying large fishing boxes and several

rods, passed through a gap in the boundary fence and made their way towards a very large lake that was clearly visible from where we were sitting.

'Let's climb into the back. We should be able to see just as much from there and it will be more comfortable,' suggested Fred.

Fred put the kettle on and I sat watching our intrepid fishermen. The door opened and Eddie stuck his nose in.

'Come in and close the door before we lose all the heat and freeze to death. Would you like some coffee?' enquired Fred.

'I could murder some thanks. What's happening with those two, Mel?'

'At the moment they are walking along the lakeside just over there. Hell! I hope they haven't really come just to go fishing, but at the moment it looks very much as if they have. I can just hear the Old Man, "You what? Grundy, spent all day watching two men fishing and travelled how far for the privilege?" Yet you know there's something not quite right about all this though. The two players in this scenario are as different as chalk and cheese and would certainly not mix casually and definitely not socially and no matter how strong the common bond of fishing, I doubt that also and yet here they are. Pass me one of those pots, please Fred, I'm ready for a decent warm drink.'

I continued with the surveillance while Fred fussed about before finally sitting down to idly thumbed through a glossy magazine she had picked up on one of our shopping expeditions.

Eddie, who was alongside me and also looking out through the window, said, 'When we came in I went back and read that information board on the wall by the entrance and it seems this place, or should I say more politely, this Stately Home, is quite old and was built way back. The present family bought it, from the family who originally built it, and re-named it Kinder Hall. There is some strong Irish connection, the Kinders having made their fortune during the potato famine over there and then on their return to this country, the first Lord Kinder, bought this place and settled here. It's still in the family to this day, but is now owned by English Heritage who has it open to the public. It doesn't say much about the present family. Two brothers, the eldest has something to do with the legal profession whilst the youngest is involved in car hire, what ever that means. The grounds are open all year round, the house in Summer, and the lake is available for fishing either with a yearly licence or a daily ticket purchased from the water bailiff.'

'Pity the house isn't open,' Interrupted Fred, 'I would have loved to have gone and had a look round. My Mum used to say, when I was a little girl, that if, while you strolled round a Stately Home, you half closed your eyes you could imagine it was yours and what it was like to live there. Good old Mum; she had a vivid imagination, and still has.'

'No chance of that: even if it had been open. You're here on a job and not to wonder round stately homes and the likes.'

'You could always come back in your own time,' suggested Eddie.

'Listen you two,' I interrupted, 'they have stopped and are setting up on the far side of the lake. Fred, pass me the glasses please. They're in that cupboard just above you.'

She dug them out and passed them across. I focused on Johnson and the Builder. 'Now let's have a closer look at what they are up to... From what I can see I think they are actually going to fish. They have set out all their gear and now they are baiting their lines and look as if they are preparing to cast.'

I continued to watch through the glasses. 'Now Johnson is settling down on his canvas stool and opening a flask, while the Builder is prating about with an umbrella. The whole bloody scene is typical Sunday morning where thousands of blokes from all over the country will be sitting round hundreds of lakes, relaxing and getting away from it all. Wasting hours and not caring a damn if they catch anything or not and here am I ogling two of them through binoculars. I am beginning to wonder what the hell we're doing here.'

Fred came across and knelt on the seat beside me, peering out of the window she said, 'Is that them over there?' pointing in their direction.

'Yes. The Builder is on this side and Johnson is the furthest away. That's Johnson who has just stood up.'

'What's he doing?'

'Something with one of the fishing lines.'

'What are these other people doing over here?' she asked as she indicated further along the shoreline, at a point below us.

'The same: them and all the others. They are all doing the same, just fishing, some standing, some sat down, but all doing the same, fishing.'

'Give me the glasses and you take a rest.'

She took hold of the binoculars and began re-focusing them.

'Move out of the way then I can lean in that corner.'

I moved to sit on one of the side seats and looked around, 'Is there anything to look at or read around here?'

'Only my magazine or yesterday's paper under that cushion,' replied Fred without lowering the glasses.

'There's that little kiosk by the gate,' said Eddie. 'They may sell newspapers. I'll pop out and see if they are open and get something if you like.'

'No. You stay here, Eddie, thanks; I could do with a leg stretch so I'll have a walk over and see what I can find.'

They had just opened the kiosk and were preparing for the days trading. A woman was hanging display racks on the outside and arranging the counter. They were rather limited in what they had on offer but I managed to select, from what

there was, a couple of thickish newspapers, with colour supplements. At least, I thought, they would help to pass some of the time from what looked like a rather futile and wasted trip.

'Anything happened?' I asked as I entered the Camper and offered one of the newspapers to Eddie.

'Nothing. No change, no movement. They are still there just as they were.'

'They must be mad. It's freezing cold out there. You still OK Fred?'

'I'm fine. You read your paper. I will let you know when I need a break.'

I settled down and before long, found myself half reading and half nodding off. I don't know how long it lasted but I remember I felt very warm and content as I drifted somewhere between the half waking state and sleep.

'Hey, fella's,' called Fred. 'That's unusual.'

The shattered silence jerked me awake and I shook my head to get rid of the fuzziness.

'What is it Fred?'

'I'm not sure. There is something going on over there. Our two have not moved and to all intents and purposes, they appear to be just idling their time away fishing. Nothing unusual in that, granted, and the other groups and individuals dotted about are doing exactly the same. There are also a few people walking casually round the edge of the lake and I have noticed the odd one passing the occasional comment to those sat or stood fishing. As I said, nothing unusual in any of that, until I saw one person, a man, who walked along the side of the lake and totally ignored everyone else, until he reached Johnson. There he stopped and talked to both of them at length. I swear I saw Johnson give him something out of his fishing box. Anyhow, this man, this person, then retraced his steps back along the water's edge and because my attention had been drawn to him, I watched him all the way back. He has just come straight into the Car Park, got in a car and driven off and that's not all. There were also two youths fishing together about half way between us and Johnson and while I was watching them, one of them left his mate and went alone to talk to our two. Nothing wrong in that, perhaps just talking shop, but on his return the pair of them hastily gathered up their gear and returned to the Car Park and have also driven away.'

All the time Fred was talking she continued to watch through the glasses. 'There… It's happening again now. A bloke who has, up to now, been fishing alone has left his rod on its rest and ignoring everyone else has gone straight up to Johnson. The Builder is digging in his box and is now handing something to this guy. Damn! He has moved and has blocked my view. The three of them are obviously in deep conversation. He is turning and walking away now. There he goes, past the first man fishing - he hasn't even looked at him - past the next pair - not even a nod. He's just walking along and ignoring everyone else.' Then after

a short pause, 'He's collecting his gear… He's moving off now and heading this way.'

Eddie and I both knelt beside Fred and followed her pointing finger. 'Which one, Fred? Where is he now?' I said as I looked out over the lake.

She stabbed the air with her finger. 'There, that one there, walking this way with the long dark green waterproof coat.'

'You keep watching. I am going to take a closer look at him. Coming, Eddie?'

We left the van and strolled over towards where I thought this guy, who was still heading in our direction, would come into the Car Park. We judged it just right and almost collided with him in the narrow entrance.

'Morning,' I said casually. 'Much doing out there this morning?'

'Eh, what d'ya mean?'

'Fish biting this morning: anything about?' asked Eddie.

'Dunno… Yes,' came the semi-unintelligible reply. However, during this short and strange exchange, I had ample time to study this youth, for that was all he was, a scruffy youth, complete with skinhead haircut and tattoos all over his forehead, neck, and hands. He carried a selection of fishing gear and wore a badly worn and shabby, long waxed waterproof jacket. We lent on the fence and watched him. He approached a battered old Vauxhall car, opened the boot, and roughly dumped his gear in. It was then that I noticed someone was already sitting in the driver's seat: a second youth who we had not seen before and who immediately started the engine, billowing clouds of smoke from the exhaust. I took the pad from my pocket and wrote, 'Two youths, Kinder Hall, dark red Vauxhall' and included the registration number along with the date and time. After they left the Car Park we returned to the van.

'That scruff had a chauffeur.'

'What do you mean?' demanded Fred with a look of surprise.

'You know the one we went to intercept? He was a proper yob and the amazing thing was, that when Eddie asked him the simple question, "Much doing out there?" he twitched and gave the impression he didn't even understand the question or even have the slightest inkling as to what he meant. Any fisherman, even the slowest, would know instantly what that meant, but not our brain-box. He's no fisherman and even more interesting, is that while he was out there, supposedly fishing, he had a mate sitting in a car waiting for him.'

'Perhaps because he has no Driving Licence or something like that,' suggested Eddie with a smile.

'Probably and it wouldn't surprise me if the other driver didn't have one either, or Road Tax, or Insurance for that matter. The car might even be stolen. They certainly look the types, if you know what I mean and certainly not the type

I would expect to see fishing early on Sunday morning; nor would I certainly not expect to find one of them fishing while the other sat in a car and waited.'

'Let me give you a break Fred and you rest for a while,' suggested Eddie.

She turned from her kneeling position and handed the glasses over to him. Then standing up and stretching, she enquired, 'Coffee all round?'

I continued to look out of the window, observing the overall scene, as I sipped my coffee. Fred read for a while and then fell asleep. Eddie continued to watch. An hour or more passed with no one speaking. Eventually I broke the silence.

'Anything happening, Eddie?'

'Not a thing! They haven't moved in the past hour. They haven't even got up off their backsides to tend to their gear. No one has approached them and with the exception of one couple, who just walked past and didn't stop, nothing.'

'Do you want a break? I will take over from you, for a while, if you like?'

'No, it's OK Mel. I'm fine.'

I sat back down again and started to read and soon drifted off into the twilight zone thinking how boring surveillance work can be. I must have fallen deeply asleep as I jumped at my rude awakening.

'What's the matter?' I demanded before my brain was back in gear and before I became fully conscious and aware of my surroundings. Fred was still sitting opposite and although her eyes were open, she too had a look of not fully understanding what was going on around her.

'There's a group of them down there,' said Eddie. 'Four of them have turned up together and they all made straight for Johnson. Both Johnson and the Builder are up on their feet... One is pushing Johnson and Johnson has raised his fist... He is going to hit him... No, wait a minute, one of them is handing the Builder something... Now they are all walking away... Johnson is gesticulating and shouting something after them... I would love to know what is being said down there. Johnson and Co are still standing and watching the others as they head back this way.'

'Time for one of us to take another walk, don't you think?'

I picked up my coat and having put it on, stepped out of the van. It was still very chilly outside so I zipped it up, shivering at the same time.

This time I chose a second exit from the car park as this would allow me to cut across some open ground that lay beyond it and fall in behind the returning group. I was then able, without drawing undue attention to myself, to follow them back. They were all busy talking and didn't even notice me but unfortunately I was just too far behind to hear what was actually being said, but was never the less able to study them from a distance and at least observe where they went.

They were all youths, in their teens or early twenties, and certainly not fishermen. They had no gear with them or any protective clothing. One was unshaven with his face completely covered in an untrimmed and matted beard. Another a skin-head was also unshaven; the third had his hair in the teddy boy style of the fifties and a goatee beard, while the fourth had his hair long on the top and shaved round the sides so that he looked like a coconut which had gone badly wrong. Their clothing was tasteless yet I noticed some of it was nevertheless expensive. One of them was wearing a leather bomber jacket that must have cost a fortune if bought and not stolen, but then he augmented it with combat trousers and Doc Martin boots. The other three had adopted similar styles. A mixture of very expensive items balanced out with cheap rubbish that is usually associated with and readily available from, Sunday markets. One had on a pair of beautiful black leather trousers that simply oozed quality, while at the same time his anorak had a large rent in it, running almost its full length down the back. The remainder followed similar fashion trends, expensive jackets or quality trousers and I also noticed, as one lifted his hand to push back his hair, all his fingers supported large expensive, chunky gold rings.

As they made their way along the path there was a lot of laughing and pushing and general tomfoolery. I followed them into the Car Park, changing my direction once inside, but still making sure I could clearly see where they were going and what they were doing. They wove their way through the parked cars, which had increased in number quite considerably since we had arrived earlier but then I was not surprised as it was now, after all, about noon.

The four youths gathered round a car and stood waiting to get in. The youth with the coconut hairstyle opened the driver's door and released the other door locks for the remainder to climb in. A few seconds later they drove away leaving me to jot down all the usual information, date, time, number and description of persons, location etc. The description of the car read - "expensive pillar-box red Mercedes."

I returned to our van and related to Fred and Eddie everything I had seen.

'Anything further on the lake side with the other two?'

'No. Nothing since you left. They have settled down again and have not moved. No one has approached them either.'

'Give me the glasses and let me take my turn.'

I positioned myself, as comfortably as I could, but soon found, to my discomfort and annoyance, that if I took the weight off the glasses by resting my elbows on the window-sill, the glass of the window created a mirrored effect and I could see nothing. There was no alternative but to pull back from the window and support the full weight of the binoculars with both hands. I knew they would soon become heavy and was amazed that the other two had stuck at it for so long.

* * *

Time passed slowly. No one approached Johnson and the few people actually walking round the lake just passed by. The afternoon dragged on with both Fred and Eddie each taking another turn with the glasses.

About four o'clock Eddie, who was on watch at the time, broke the silence when he stated, 'I think they are beginning to pack up… Yes they are. They are gathering their things together and preparing to move. When they leave, are we going to follow them?'

'In the van you mean? Yes, I definitely think we should. It's only teatime and I would hate them to divert or stop off somewhere else and us miss it. If we do the same as this morning and use the car for at least the first legs and only use this more conspicuous Camper in the middle, I see no problems.'

'Right,' said Eddie. 'I will get my stuff together and go now before they get back here. I will pull in behind them and follow them out and you two try and remember not to get too far behind this time. Those little radios have such a limited range and I thought we had lost it at one point this morning.'

'So did we but they are nevertheless a very handy piece of equipment and work well and you would have to almost drive past someone with a monitor, to be picked up by them and that reminds me. If they are short range and of a fixed frequency, there really is no need to use call signs. After all, call signs are to identify individuals when there are numerous people using the same frequency. We could just use the single letters E and M or nothing at all. What do you say Eddie?'

'I agree. I suppose you're right. E and M should do fine. So let's do that then. See you both later.'

'And another thing just before you shoot off. If it all goes pear shaped with the comms don't forget we can always fall back on our Coastguard radios although I would rather not unless we really have to.'

'OK, see you.'

He left and went off towards his own car. We quickly stowed the few things we had about and then climbed into the cab and awaited our turn to leave. Not long after, we saw the Range Rover depart and Eddie called, 'E to M, on my way.'

I clicked the transmit button twice so Eddie knew we had heard him. We waited a few more minutes to let them get clear and then, with Fred once again driving, we pulled out and headed towards the A64.

'Back by the same route?' enquired Fred.

'I would assume so, unless we hear anything to the contrary from Eddie.'

'So what do you think of it all then? A smart way of distributing drugs if you ask me,' smiled Fred. 'Two innocent men out for a days fishing, sitting quietly at the side of a lake, with a very convenient Car Park close at hand. You realise,

of course, that we have no actual proof that they were distributing drugs and have only assumed so from what little we have seen and suspect.'

'True but to start with, that is not our worry. It's up to the Drug Squad to sort that side out. We have established the method or one of the methods of delivery and now a possible location for the distribution. The onus of proof now rests with them, but I will bet my last fiver, that if you could get into one of those fishing tackle boxes, it would reek of the stuff and I bet that Merc, that I saw those youths climb into, was well and truly loaded with the stuff. So as far as I am concerned we have had a good day and I also have a very strange feeling that all this and Edison somehow fit in.'

'Let's hope so, otherwise we have gone well out on a limb and the Old Man will not be too pleased about that and the time we have spent on it so far today.'

'Oh I think, either way, he will be. The very fact that he will have something to give to the Drug Squad or Customs and Excise, will make his day. Also remind me in the morning, will you Fred, that I must still have a word with him about Raines.'

'M…E. On dual carriageway, heading back, increasing speed, don't fall behind.'

'Roger.'

We joined the dual carriageway and as we did so, Fred was able to pick up speed and hopefully maintain a reasonable gap between us. The miles slipped by.

'M…E. Leaving bypass, left onto Pickering road.'

'Roger.' Then turning to Fred, 'Seems we are heading back home, so far so good.'

'M…E. Traffic slowing, ready to take over?'

'On our way.'

'There he is, up front,' Indicated Fred. 'And there is Eddie, two cars behind him. I will pass this blue one, in front and then drop in behind them.'

It was not easy, on the minor roads, to pass saloon cars in a van the size of ours. We had the power, albeit only just, but the overall size was restricting. Fred drew up close to the blue saloon car in front a couple of times, but on each occasion had to drop back because of oncoming traffic. She was about to make her third attempt when the driver in front, very conveniently for us, decided to turn left. He turned off and disappeared at the next intersection. Eddie was now in front of us. I picked up the radio.

'E… M. When you are ready.' At which he acknowledged by raising his left hand in a mock salute. Fred replied with a flash of our headlights. Eddie slowed down, pulled well over, and we passed him easily. I gave him a wave as we went by and he then fell back as we settled down to tail the Range Rover. There were, at that point, only two cars in front and between us. The trip, up to then, had been

fairly uneventful and had followed, in the reverse direction, the same route that we had taken earlier that morning and while Fred pulled over to allow up and coming traffic to overtake we made sure the Range Rover did not get too far in front. That was until we were approaching a roundabout and where, much to my surprise, all the other cars in front of us turned either left or right and left only us and the Range Rover going forward. Within no time at all we were hard up behind him.

'I don't like this,' said Fred, decelerating. 'And there's nothing behind us at the moment to overtake.'

'Just drop back, that's all you can do.'

'Hang on, he's turning left into that Filling Station.'

'Keep going.' Then picking up the radio. 'E… M. He has pulled into garage, left through roundabout. We have been obliged to pass.'

'Roger: got that. I will pick him up.'

I pressed twice in acknowledgement as we proceeded to motor on ahead for several miles.

'See anything of him back there?' I enquired.

'Not a thing: shall I pull in and wait?'

'Not yet,' as I picked up the radio. 'E… M. You OK?'

'Fine. I'm right behind him. Where are you?'

'Up front somewhere, with no sign of you. Propose to stay on same return route unless you advise otherwise. Might not look good if we try and pull in behind you.' Two clicks came through on my radio. 'Keep going Fred. We will at least be the first home for tea if nothing else.'

The rest of the journey back to the village was pleasant, but again uneventful, and not hearing anything from Eddie we could only assume that he was experiencing similar and was somewhere behind.

We eventually arrived at, and turned into, the lane that led back to the campsite. Fred pulled onto the grass verge at the side of the road and we waited. Some short time later the Range Rover passed the end of the intersection and headed towards the far end of the village. To be closely and quickly followed by Eddie.

'M… E. Stopping in village, target turning left. Will wait return of second target.'

I clicked twice and we all waited.

Some ten minutes later… 'M… E. Second target heading for his own nest; see you in your watering hole tonight.' I acknowledged with the usual two clicks.

'Home young Miss. It's all over bar the shouting and I don't know about you but I'm starving. It's been a long day and we haven't exactly had a lot to eat. Have we?'

'We'll find something to put us on until the Pub opens. Right now a hot shower would be more welcome than food.'

We parked the van and I took forty winks, while Fred did, whatever she did, while I slept.

CHAPTER TWENTY-NINE

Later that evening, when we were all seated round a dining table in The Grapes, Eddie having joined us earlier, our conversation naturally drifted towards the events of the day. We were able to talk relatively freely as the nearby tables were all empty and over the background noise, which was there but not annoying, we could not hear any of the conversation from the other tables, at the far end of the room, which were occupied, so we assumed they could not overhear us. Never the less, as a double precaution, we kept the conversation low and fairly light and made no direct references to anything specific or mentioned anyone by name.

'I don't think it takes much intelligence to work out what they were up to today, does it?' asked Eddie.

'No,' replied Fred. 'But you must admit it is an ingenious way they have of distributing their gear. I often wondered how these people did it and no doubt there are hundreds of other different ways, but that one today I thought was ingenious and so innocent looking. I have heard of Night Club Bouncers passing it on the doors of course and we hear of school kids getting hold of it and sharing it with their classmates. We also hear, all the time, of dealers passing it out at Rave Parties and on street corners and the likes. But they all can and no doubt do, attract a fair amount of unwanted attention unless they are extremely cautious and very, very subtle. But today's method, as I see it, can only be described as "cool man"; to use what I think is the right expression among today's with its.'

'Listen at her. Gear, with its and cool man. Sorry you were saying?'

'Well that's what they say, isn't it? Anyhow as I was saying to all the uninitiated as well as the likes of you: I know how it comes into the country now, or at least I now know of one of the ways it comes in, and I now know how the dealers and users, at the end of the chain, get their supplies. I appreciate that compared to the ship loads, which we all know are discovered fairly regularly, what we have seen so far is only a drop in the ocean… I saw you.'

'What?'

'Raise your eyebrows. I know what I said: drop in the ocean, the sea, Johnson and down the ravine and all that. I realise the pun or what ever you want to call it. But nevertheless there must be tremendous profits to be made by those who do it, even on the small scale we saw. I wonder if today they off loaded everything we saw hidden away the other night, in the Builder's garage?'

'I don't know. But what we saw in that cardboard box they could easily carry between them in those large fishing tackle boxes. They're big enough and our man and his mate, the Builder are two strapping lads. But today I got the feeling

they didn't have sufficient customers to off load a great deal. I know we were a fair distance away and didn't see everything close up, but all the time I was watching I never saw anyone approach with a bag or any sort of holdall so, what ever was handed out was in small quantities and went straight into pockets. I reckon that today they might have brought a fair amount back with them.'

'How often do you think they go?'

'I don't know but I guess they have to go regularly, otherwise how will their customers know when they will be there and available to do business. If their visits are few and far between or random, then their buyers will quickly get confused and feel let down and not be happy to make wasted journeys. In other words they will not be considered as regular, reliable suppliers and that, I imagine, is what users and dealers must have. I wouldn't be surprised if the whole operation isn't worked as regularly as a Sunday market and if that is the case, then I don't think they will be too concerned if they haven't off-loaded everything today. There's always next week, or what ever their regular trading days are but I feel pretty sure that for it to work supplies must be regular and reliable. But on the other hand I don't, for one moment, think their suppliers deliver on a regular basis. That would probably be much too risky. Supplies to them will be much less frequent. But if the quantity is sufficient then they will absorb the fluctuations and be able to smooth out the flow.'

'How do you think they arrange for their supplies to be brought in?'

'They no doubt, have a way of communicating when they are in the market to buy, or the seller lets them know when he has merchandise for sale. For all we know, some of those unintelligible messages on those computer printouts we looked at may well contain pre-arranged passwords or codes concerning that last shipment. It's simple enough to do and proven time and again by the amount of codes we, for example, use in the course of our work. Granted we all know that codes can be cracked and that it is relatively easy to do so, but only if the code is being used regularly, but no one can crack a code that is used only once. So therefore if the next code to be used is passed on verbally at the time of the last delivery or when first contact is made, cracking it is virtually impossible, if there are any brains behind it. Then if that's the case, then who knows, for example, what was arranged the other night, down on the beach when the last drop was made or what was arranged in some other way before hand? Simple codes are very effective if used only the once.'

'Aren't we the clever one then. Codes for this and codes for that. Go on, give us an example Mr Code Man,' taunted Fred. 'If you are so sure, then give us a simple one that you think we can't crack. It's you and I, Eddie, against the brain box here, what do you say?'

'Suits me,' he laughed and leaning forward added in a whisper, 'It might be as well if we drop the serious stuff now that these two are about to settle down on this next table and the place is beginning to fill up.'

I look around. He was right. It was becoming busy.

'Just like that, off the top of my head. I know I'm good, but even something fairly simple could take me some time, you carry on talking while I think. Are you sure you want to do this?'

'Yes,' they both chorused.

While they chatted away I could only think of the rather complex systems that I had been required to learn and use, many years ago. Off the top of my head I couldn't readily recall anything simple that I thought would suitably impress them. Also I had to take into account the fact that, I had no idea of their own existing knowledge of codes and knowing Fred that might well be quite extensive. The more I thought about it the more I wished I had not raised the subject or accepted the silly challenge in the first place, but I had.

'Pen and paper please,' I demanded knowing that each would be carrying both items as routine and that also included myself, but the request for one of them to supply it added, I hoped, to the drama.

I took the pen and pad that Eddie offered and removed a single sheet. I gave him his pad back and then turning away from them used the table next to me on which to rest as I wrote a series of letters and numbers. I then tore the paper into two equal pieces and turning back to my original position, facing them both, I handed the first piece to Fred.

'That is your code, and for the benefit of this demonstration is supposed to be memorised and known only to you.'

Handing Eddie the second piece of paper I said, 'This is the message you are sending to Fred.'

Both looked at their respective pieces of paper and then at each other's.

'What does that mean to you Fred?' I asked.

'Nothing! All it has printed on here is the word - WHITBREADS.'

'What does yours say Eddie?'

'Nothing! Only a series of numbers.'

'Read them out and you standby Fred, for here comes your coded message.'

'034134279937 - that's all,' he said.

'Pass it over to Fred. There's your message Fred. What does it say?'

'I don't know.'

'Oh come on Fred; stop playing the thickie. How can you claim not to know when you have the code? Number your code word from one to zero, left to right, then decode that group of numbers.'

She sat and looked at it for a moment then produced her own pen and wrote the letters below the numbers. A smile began to spread across her face as she said, 'But I am.'

'I know you are. But you see how simple it is, and yet it would be so difficult for anyone without the code word.'

'But anyone skilled in deciphering, would crack that in no time at all. Messages based on that one simple word wouldn't last two minutes,' said Eddie.

'I know that. But two things have to be considered. One, if it is only used once and then discarded, it is of little value to anyone who troubles to decode it other than to give them the one off, or perhaps tell them something that is history, it having already happened. It is of no value, or use, to decipher any future intelligence if it is not going to be used again, so a lot of effort has gone into preparing for something that is just not going to happen. Secondly, you have to remember that here we are dealing with only simple codes which was the original idea of this bit of fun. But even so, let's see what can happen if we plus it up a little and move only slightly away from basics. The one I have just shown you, is based on, the one ten-letter word. Now consider what would happen if we used say… ten words each made up of ten letters, and all different. I know what you are going to say, it could still be cracked, and you would of course be right but what if we further complicate it by introducing a special formula to determine the order in which the ten words are used, it can then become very complex. For example, if the order in which the words are to be used, is determined by the recipient's birthday, and remember, that would be something known only to him and the sender, things can become even more complex whilst the basic code remains relatively simple and easy to apply. To illustrate, if the recipient's birthday is the 13th May 1935, the order in which the words would be used becomes… 13051935. Number one word is used first, then word three, then word ten, then five and so on. When those eight selections from the birthday sequence have been used up they can always be reversed, 53915031. Almost infinite, well not quite, but still one hell of a lot of combinations can be achieved by using, in a predetermined order, the recipients birthday, forward and reverse. Then there is his mother's birthday, used both ways, his father's, brother's, sisters, and so on including even the family dog. As you see, it now becomes somewhat more complex and if used sparingly, is very effective. Anyhow I am no cipher expert and in the past have only used what was given to me and left the worry of their security up to those who devised them. You asked me for a simple example and I have given you one. To the bar now and it's not my round.'

'Do you remember the great classic they used for demonstration purposes at training school?' asked Fred.

'Hey! Wait a minute. I thought you knew nothing about this sort of thing?'

'Who said I didn't?' she laughed. 'I did do some training for this job as well, you know.'

'Go on Fred, you were saying?' said Eddie.

'Well when I was there, in the not too dim and distant past, they told us of the classic that was used by intelligence services throughout the world for years. It was a method that was considered to be near fool proof and it was of course until the opposition caught either the sender or the recipient using it and then the whole thing was compromised and could become a complete shambles after that. If one side was ignorant of the fact that his fellow conspirator had been busted then what happened and often did, as much on our side as anyone else's, the organisation was either busted wide open, smashed and eliminated or it could be subtly infiltrated and fed duff and misleading information. In fact the opposition, on either side, could often use it undetected and rake havoc for years and could go on doing so until they too were busted or the whole set up outlived it's basic usefulness.'

'I bet you are referring to the double book method?' I said.

'The what?' Eddie asked.

'The double book method,' repeated Fred. 'Yes, that's the one. If only agents didn't get caught then the double book method was good, but once caught, it went completely into reverse. The method itself is straightforward and is where two identical books are purchased and sender and recipient have one each. After that messages are passed using numbers as their basis. There are various methods but a popular one was to designate the first group of numbers as being a page, the second group the paragraph down that page, the third the line and the forth or final group the word along the line from the left. Time consuming to prepare and also to decipher, but without the basic reference books near impossible to crack. That is until someone within the network got busted and the opposition got its hands on the book. First thing the cipher boys and not, of course, forgetting the far more intelligent cipher girls, would do and might still do, although I think the method is now well outdated, is look for books. Any odd book or a piece of literature out of character with its owner would be a dead give away. But any and all books would be seized. After that it was a slow and careful slog to work through them until a match was made with previously intercepted numerical data. You can then imagine what happened when the guy on the receiving end, having no idea his colleague had been nabbed, continue to send valuable material and act upon any instructions received, as long as they appeared and he believed them to be, genuine.'

'What a mess,' laughed Eddie.

'It often was and mega problems developed on all sides. I bet that for years MI6 was a complete shambles as they stumbled on believing everything was fine and that they were safe and for all we know might still be doing the same,' laughed Fred before adding. 'Despite the influx of cleaver women and so called progress and modern technology.'

'It must have been a bit like that German Enigma thing they invented during the war?' suggested Eddie. 'That was supposed to be the cleverest thing in it's day, for cipher sending, but failed miserably once they lost one. If I remember rightly we got hold of one, from somewhere in Poland or the likes of there and then some code books or something from a submarine, and then unbeknown to them we calmly sat back and listened to it chattering away for most of the war.'

'Same sort of thing I suppose,' said Fred. 'But is any of it so cleaver? The Germans used a sophisticated machine that failed on a minor error. They lost one. The book method failed when people were arrested in possession of books. Even Mel's example, however complex you choose to make it and the fact that it relies, to a very large extent, on memory, all sounds good on the surface, but it can be tortured out of an individual. Then don't forget, that although methods of passing information become more complex all the time but so do the methods of countering and cracking them. It's tit for tat all the way; it's all a big game and will continue to be one just as long as someone believes it is necessary to spy on someone else or try and find out something that he or she is not supposed to know.'

'It keeps a lot of people employed and a lot more paranoid people happy,' I suggested.

'Who's for a drink?' asked Eddie.

After that the subject died and with little else to do, for the time being, left us to settle down to an evenings relaxation.

We drank rather more than our fair share of alcohol and as a result completely relaxed and tended to laugh a lot and became somewhat giddy over almost anything.

'What are you doing now?' enquired Eddie of Fred.

'I am sending him a secret message,' as she passed a piece of paper over to me.

I took it and looked at it –'02342789' - and then I thought about it for a moment; to make sure I had worked it out correctly. 'That's nice,' I said in reply. 'Especially as I thought someone said all this stuff was very boring?'

'No it's not really. Well yes, it is boring. Well you know what I mean even if I don't. It's the message I am on about. You know I don't mean it, but it is all I could manage to work out with the booze swilling about in my brain. Don't you think I am a clever girl, even if I am a bit drunk?'

By this time Eddie had de-ciphered it and immediately burst out laughing. 'I think she is right. Spot on old girl.'

'Thanks pal,' I retorted, and grabbing hold of the pad was determined to try and top it. I thought for a few seconds, then said, 'OK, the pair of you, try this... 459856.'

They both sat quiet and pondered through their individual, drink induced, haze. Eventually Fred blurted out, 'this is a load of rubbish, Grundy. It doesn't make sense. Does it Eddie? You're drunk. What on earth does TBDABR mean?'

'Nothing!' I grinned, feeling very smug with myself, 'unless you know the correct code word? That's what it's all about.'

'Which is?' They both demanded in unison.

'Try TOPMACHINE for starters,' I replied with a very supercilious grin. 'It's all about knowing which code word to use. Remember I told you it can be made very complex in a very simple way.'

'That's cheating!'

'No it's not. It's called codes. It's called me being cleaver and you being drunk. Now, one last attempt, just to show you how good I am, and then we abandon it, all right? I've had too much to drink as well. OK?'

'Go ahead, bighead. One last one and I will show you that you maybe drunk but I'm not.'

I thought for a moment and then said, 'This is what you are, a 1234567890 and your occupation is 9234587.'

'Which code do I use for this one? Don't look at me like that. You think I'm too drunk.'

'Drunk or not, I can see you are finally getting it and you now see that without the right word, you can do nothing. Try SEDUCTRESS as your master code word for this one and remember that this is definitely the last one. As I told you, I've had far too much to drink to think of any more tonight. But at least you get the idea of how simple codes can be and how effective, for short term use.'

'Or something like that,' she said.

'Or something like that,' I echoed.

The effects of the drink increased and the conversation, as a result, deteriorated proportionally.

Following a long pause Fred slurred, 'I don't think you are very clever at all. If that's the best you can do, it stinks. Seductress, who me? Never. I wouldn't know where to start. Professional virgin. That's more like it. Anyhow that's what my mother thinks I am or I think my mother thinks, or something like that and who am I to challenge what Mumsie thinks or you two drunken bums, for that matter?'

'What are you twittering on about now?'

'I don't know. But it all sounds good to me.'

The evening progressed a little further and definitely deteriorated until finally I reached the stage where I could take no more. All I wanted to do was curl up in a corner and sleep.

Eventually I got my chance and remembered little else until the following morning.

CHAPTER THIRTY

'You were useless last night. You were so drunk that any attempts at being a seductress, as you called me in one of your silly numbers games was a total waste of time. Do you know you fell down twice while trying to get into bed, and then when you finally made it, you proceeded to snore all night long. In the end I had to lay there all woozy and mellow until I finally fell asleep. Which I must admit didn't take long.'

'Did Eddie get back all right?'

'I don't know. We left him staggering up the road with his head and shoulders moving faster than his feet. If he didn't fall flat on his face, then he made it. If not he probably slept in a ditch. He was worse than you. Men!'

'It's all right for you. You look OK and are much too cheerful. How come I feel as if someone has been sitting on my head all-night? Hot black coffee is what I need, or at least that will do for starters.'

'I'm fine. I'm one of those lucky ones who don't suffer from hangovers, no matter how drunk I get, and I was reasonably drunk last night for a change. So you were not on your own in that.'

'That's why I didn't feel lonely last night then?'

'What are you talking about now?'

'Nothing, forget about it, only a joke; "feel lonely", feel Fred, feel anyone, get it? Oh never mind. Any coffee over there?'

I sat and Fred watched me for a few moments while the coffee did it's best to unscramble my brain and slowly clear my head.

'What have we got on for today? Did we plan anything?' I moaned.

'A report to the Old Man and a run down on Raines.'

'Oh yes, I remember that. God, I can't face the Old Man today; my brains are scrambled enough without his verbal battering to add to the agony.'

'I'll go and ring him if you like, while you rest your poor fuddled head. The walk in the fresh air will do me good.'

'Bless you. You're a darling. Sometimes.'

'No I am not. It's only because you are worse than useless, in the state you're in and I don't want you to cock things up. So get your head back down and for goodness sake, try and sleep it off.'

I took no further persuading and stretched out, full length, across the warm sleeping bag. I must have drifted off almost immediately. How long I slept I don't know. All I do know; is that I was woken by Fred opening the door and letting herself back into the van.

'How are you feeling now?' she enquired.

'Much better, thanks: the extra sleep was what I needed. How did you go on?'

'Fine and I've brought something back for lunch, so if you can drag yourself out, we can eat.'

'How did you get on with the Old Man?'

'Fine, like I said, but food first. Then I will tell you all about that.'

I got up, dressed, and moved to the van door. 'I need to go across there.'

'Good! While you are over there get some more water for the coffee and go now if you are going so that I can set this table.'

With food inside of me, and several cups of strong black coffee, I was more or less back to my old self and eager to know what the Old Man had had to say.

'First, I gave him my report and an A to Z of yesterday, and all the build-up that went into it. He just listened and much to my surprise, said nothing until I had finished. Then he said he would inform the Drug Squad and I agreed with him but asked him to tell them to hold back so that they wouldn't jeopardize any of our plans. He agreed and said that he would tell them now so they could get their act together but to wait for clearance to move from us. He seemed all right about that particularly when I reminded him yet again, this place is rather quiet, and the last thing we want is for it to be cluttered up with strangers, even though they may all claim to be campers or holidaymakers or what ever. To my surprise he agreed with just about everything.'

'Just like that?'

'Well almost! But then, I did put most of it to him in question form and let him make the final decisions for me.'

'What do you mean?'

'Well, for example, what I said was, "It's very quiet here at the moment as you already know, how do you think the locals would react if an unusual number of strangers suddenly turned up. Do you think it might jeopardize what we are attempting to do?" He fell for it and he decided not to let the Drug Squad in at this time. I have told you before, if you want anything, let the Old Man make the suggestions and decisions, you just pose what you want, as a question.'

'Good old female logic! What about Raines?'

'It has nothing to do with female logic. It's called survival. Know your enemy and how to deal with him. Knowing people and how to use them, that's all and I know him and what he's like and so do you.'

'And Raines?' I repeated.

'We have to ring again tomorrow about him.'

'Tomorrow?'

'That's what the man said.'

'OK. Did you see anything of Eddie while you were in the village?'

'No, but then I didn't actually go looking for him. I looked in the car park and his car wasn't there but that doesn't mean anything. He may still be in bed and sleeping off last night and his car might be anywhere. What are we doing next? I wondered if we might pick up something of value from a visit to the Coastguard Station down the road. So far we have avoided it, but it came to me while I was walking back down the lane, we might pick up something there. Anyhow I think it might be worth a try and the walk will certainly do you good - blow off all those cobwebs from last night and help work the alcohol out of your blood stream. Come on! Get ready and let's go.'

I enjoyed the walk along the cliff top. It was again a fine day and no doubt would have been a warm one had the strong breeze, blowing in from the sea, dropped. However, we were well wrapped up against the chill and looked every inch the all weather, intrepid walker.

As we approached the Station, it once again had that same silent, unoccupied atmosphere about it. There were no signs of life and even the Coastguard Land rover, parked alongside, looked as if it too, had been left there and abandon as an additional blot on the otherwise natural and unspoiled countryside.

We opened the gate and entered the fenced off enclosure surrounding the building. Everything was neat and tidy and all the paintwork was bright and had a new and freshly applied look to it. The building, which was square and two stories high, was built of red brick with solid wooden doors painted in the traditional dark blue. A concrete staircase built into the side of the building lead directly to a door that allowed access onto its first floor level. The ground floor had obviously been designated for the storage of essential equipment and to raise the first floor operational area. This was confirmed by the fact that the windows at ground floor level were of frosted glass and covered with protective wire grills. The first floor had one large clear glass window running the full length of the seaward side and then two others running half way back along the two adjacent sides. They were angled, slopping inward towards their bottom edges, to help shield them against rain and bad weather. In addition each window was fitted with large window wiper, which could be used in bad weather, to remove excess water and thus help maintain a clear view out to sea and some distance to either side. All the window frames and surrounding woodwork were painted white, which contrasted nicely with the dark blue paint of the remainder and the red brick of the actual building.

The sign at the bottom of the staircase said – 'H.M. Coastguard. No unauthorised persons beyond this point. Official business only.'

We climbed the steps and, at the top, were confronted by a blue painted door on which another large sign said – 'H.M. Coastguard. Enter. If the Station is unmanned and there is an emergency, dial 999 and ask for the Coastguard.' A small

box, painted bright yellow and mounted on the wall, to the side of the door had inscribed on it the words – 'Emergency Telephone - Dial 999.'

I knocked, and opened the door, and we both stepped inside.

The room, or operations area, was large and well lit through the wide expanse of clear glass, which in turn provided a panoramic view out to sea. The two windows in the adjacent sidewalls allowed for good clear unobstructed observation to the North and South along the cliff tops.

There was a long desk, running the full length of the front wall, just below windowsill height. This work surface being supported by drawer units with gaps between, to form knee holes and each of these had a swivel chair pushed into it. On the desktop were all the items of equipment required by a working Coastguard Station in order for it to function efficiently. There were telephones, a fax machine, an answer-phone, numerous manuals, and information files neatly arranged in racks, a wind speed indicator, and a large digital clock. There were VHF and FM radio transmitters and receivers, multi-channel digital scanners and a variety of other essential items, including the, all important, daily log book into which is meticulously entered the day's business of the station. The remainder of the office area was furnished with additional desks, a display case, filing cabinets, a photocopier and a large chart table with charting instruments neatly laid out on it. The doors leading off, I assumed, led to storage areas, kitchens and toilets; these stations having to be fairly self-sufficient and self-contained. Particularly when long continuous watches are required, for example during bad weather or when long protracted search and rescue operation are in progress.

As we entered, we were prevented from going far by a counter type arrangement with a lift up flap built into one end. This was to create a barrier between the official occupants and any visitors.

'Good afternoon, can I help you?' greeted the occupant of one of the chairs before the main console. A multi-channel scan receiver chatted away in the background.

There was no one else in the room and the man who greeted us wore the uniform of a Coastguard Sector Officer and would therefore be the senior man in the area. He and Edison, who was also a Sector Officer, must have shared the duties of running the sector, supplementing it with Auxiliary Coastguard cover as and when necessary; something which is standard practice throughout the service. He was a middle aged, dark haired man, going grey at the sides, moustached and from his manner, a rather curt individual; or that was the first impression he gave me.

'Good afternoon,' replied Fred. 'We're holidaying in the area and were planning to walk along the beach and would like to know if you have the times of the tides for the next few days. We have already looked along the beach below the

cliff and although it appears to be quite rocky, we thought it might make a change to tramp about along there; if only to see how far we can get.'

'You holiday makers never cease to amaze me. What fun is there in clambering over a load of rocks?'

I felt like saying 'Up yours!' but instead, with supreme control, I managed to answer, 'We just thought it might make a change. Something different.'

'Suit yourselves. I can give you the times of High Water but don't come hollering for me if you slip and break an ankle down there.'

He tore a sheet of paper from a pad and after consulting a set of tide tables, wrote several times on it. Fred and I just looked at each other, neither of us quite sure what to make of him.

'There you are. It starts from today and covers the next five days, is that enough?'

I forced a polite, 'Yes, thank you.'

'Do many people slip and break things around here then?' ventured Fred.

'Some of them rocks are slippery, being covered twice a day by the sea. You get weed and all sorts of marine life on them and if you are not careful who knows what can happen.'

'We heard in the village the other day, that fairly recently, someone had slipped on these rocks and drowned.'

'That's a matter of opinion. Someone did drown recently and that's common knowledge, but I am not at liberty to discuss it any further at the moment, as it's still under investigation.'

'I understand,' said Fred. 'It's just that people were talking about it and we, naturally, were curious.'

'You will hear many stories round here. My advise is to take it all with a pinch of salt and just enjoy yourselves climbing over the rocks, or going wherever you want to go. If you do decide to go clambering about down there, either pop in and tell me, or give me a ring. It will save me from worrying about whether you have decided to go or not, or if I see you going myself or hear of you going from someone else, if you have got back safely. I have a bit more to do than worry about holiday makers getting stuck or lost.'

'We will certainly do that, and thanks for your time,' I replied with effort as I turned to leave, Fred following close behind.

We left the compound, making sure to close the gate behind us.

Once out of earshot, Fred burst out, 'He's not very nice, the supercilious sod. A bit of a waste of space if you ask me and I certainly couldn't work with him.'

'He might be OK when you get to know him. It might be just one of those days, although I am not defending him and come to think of it, after all, he has recently lost his partner in rather curious circumstances and he doesn't know that

we know something about it. His routine and workload may well, as a result of all that, gone to pot and increased dramatically, and that in itself could well have upset him.'

'Upset him. He's the type who is permanently upset. Don't make excuses for him. He is just not a very nice man, so let's leave it at that.'

'If you say so! However we didn't get much out of him, did we? Although I must admit, we didn't try very hard. Best thing is to forget him for the moment. He is probably a bit too close to things for us to reveal ourselves or ask too many loaded questions just yet. So, following that very successful visit, what do you propose we do now?'

'I don't know. What say we just follow this track and see where it takes us? We have nothing better to do for the moment until we hear from the Old man about Raines and it's a lovely day. Who knows it might help us to think of something useful and we can't just stand here with him, in there, probably watching.'

We set off along the cliff top in the Southerly direction.

Some distance down the track and out of sight of the Coastguard Station, we climbed over a stile that had been purposely built into the fence, and followed the footpath that ran along the edge of a field. At the far end another stile, built into a dry stonewall, enabled us to climb over and follow the track, which now took us into the woods. We tramped on for at least a mile enjoying all the sounds and smells of the woodland.

In those surroundings where it was so peaceful it made me feel that I was a million miles away from everywhere. The trees sheltered us from the wind and the smell of bracken, wild garlic and leaf mould, which was all around us, made for a different world and the hundreds of different sounds made by all the insects and wild life, added to my intense pleasure.

Some distance along, the trees and undergrowth began to thin out and become less dense. Finally the path broke out, at right angles, onto a much wider mud track. Two deep ruts in this track showed evidence of wheeled vehicles passing along it in both directions, and at fairly frequent intervals, judging by the fact that the grass was worn completely off and the bare earth showed through. It was a track that effectively split the natural woodland, which grew on the one side, the seaward side, from the manmade forest on the opposite side.

The forest trees grew right up to the edge of the track and were evenly spaced and close together. They were predominantly spruce, if my early botanical education served me rightly. Anyhow they looked like very large, tall, Christmas trees, covered in pine needles as apposed to flat leaves that grow on other types. They were all uniform in their appearance and rather monotonous; a dull dark green colour, and if they had any charm at all, then it came from their own peculiar, and very pleasant smell. Their aroma always reminds me of pine disinfectant, a strange, yet to me, an attractive smell.

'Let's have a look at the map and see just where we have got ourselves.'

Fred spread the map out and sitting on the grassy bank, pointed and said, 'There's the Coastguard Lookout and here is the track we took across the field and into these woods. This dotted line is the path we followed through the wood and here is the track we are on now. So we are just about here.' She then pointed towards the dense trees, and continued, 'this is Forestry, and according to the map, forms part of the Duchy of Lancaster Estate. Lancaster! I know we have walked a long way but surely we have not walked half way across the country and ended up in Lancashire?' she laughed.

'No. You daft brush! Wasn't it during the "Wars of the Roses", if I remember rightly, where Yorkshire lost the final battle, and that's why Lancashire ended up with most of the land. Or it could have been the other way round for all I know. Don't ask me how, or why. History is not one of my strongest subjects. I only know, from looking at maps, that the Duchy of Lancaster Estate covers vast areas of North Yorkshire and this must be part of it. It probably has more to do with the fact that the Crown owns the land here and the Queen is the Duke of Lancaster or something like that. Ask me something I know something about and not who may, or may not, own all these bloody trees.'

'So, whoever owns them, does not alter the fact that we must go that way if we want to make our way back in the general direction of the village.'

'If you say so and at least it should be a bit easier walking along this track, than it was on that narrow path through the woods, back there.'

We set off along, what turned out to be, a long straight, and if you took away the distractions created by the pleasant sounds and smells, a rather boring and monotonous track. Just two deep ruts, running in a straight line, with a ridge of grass covered earth along the centre. It looked as if it might all have been carved out intentionally, in the beginning, in order to created a division between the manmade forest, on the one side, and the natural woodland on the other. It was probably some form of specific boundary and access track.

We trudged on for a while without saying a great deal, perhaps because we were both enjoying the peace and quiet. Fred walked in one rut, while I walked along side her in the other. At least now we were walking side-by-side and no longer in single file, as we had been obliged to do for the last few miles as we passed through the woodland.

The forest was dense, the trees growing so close, that the upper branches blocked out almost all the natural light and prevented much of it from reaching ground level. So much so that, very little survived and grew at ground level, and what did manage to hold on in there, only grew to a height of about two feet and was mainly a tangled mass of briars and weeds. The lack of light made it almost totally black in the inner depths, and definitely restricted the distance that one could clearly see into it.

'I bet you could easily loose yourself in there,' suggested Fred.

'I bet you could and more so at night or in the dark. To stand any chance at all, you would need a map and compass; definitely a compass, as I should imagine that without one you would simple go round in circles. The map you might manage without, but with one, you would have the added advantage of finding the nearest Fire Break and from it the shortest way out.'

'Fire Break?'

'Yes. On the map, if you remember, when we looked at it back there, it showed the forest area divided up into neat, almost square sections. Look here,' I said, pulling the map out from my pocket. 'You see those lines there. Well, they are Fire Breaks. They are gaps deliberately left between the trees when the forest is planted, to help prevent the spread of fire. I don't know how effective they are, but at least because they are like tracks, they can be used for access. So if you are lost you can use them as a way of finding your way out. Forestry workers, I understand, use them all the time, for access.'

'I bet it's spooky in there at night.'

'I bet it is. It looks ominous enough in daylight, so it must be worse in the dark.'

'Can you hear that?'

'Yes, it sounds like a vehicle of some kind, coming from somewhere and coming closer.'

As the noise got louder we realised it was in actual fact coming from behind so we stopped and both turned round. A Land rover was approaching along the track. It's wheels fitting neatly into the two ruts. We stepped to either side to let it pass. As it did so, the driver, who was on my side, waved out of the open window, and called out a cheerful, 'Good afternoon, lovely day.'

'Yes it is,' I replied.

There were two people in the cab and as they went slowly by I saw that painted on the door panel of the vehicle was some form of crest and the words "Duchy of Lancaster Estate. Works Department." Having past they drove on at a steady ten to fifteen miles an hour until eventually they went out of sight. We fell in side by side and carried on walking. Once again peace and tranquillity reigned.

A short distance further along, a new sound, previously unheard by us, disturbed the silence and filtered through the trees towards us.

'What on earth is that?' asked Fred, stopping to listen.

I turned my head from side to side to pick up the new sound and assess, if I could, the direction from which it came. It rose and fell at irregular intervals. It also stopped and started and was at times much louder than others.

'A mechanical saw, probably a chain saw. It must be someone in there cutting timber somewhere.'

The sound got louder as we continued on down the track until we reached a point where I felt we should have been able to reach out and almost touch them, but we couldn't see anything.

'Where are they?' enquired Fred. 'It sounds to be coming from very close over that way. Let's go across there and look.'

A few yards further along and where there was another Fire Break running off at right angles to the track we were on, we turned off, followed recently made tyre tracks and went towards where we thought the sound was coming from. Several yards down, the tyre tracks turned sharp right, into what was yet another Fire Break. We followed this one, and once round the corner, came upon the sight and sound we were looking for. Off to one side of the break a small clearing had been created, which was littered with freshly cut logs and long, stripped, tree trunks. Among all the clutter, was a make shift trestle, on which one man held a tree trunk, while a second man, using a hand held chain saw, cut off logs. Sawdust was flying everywhere, and the air was thick with dust and that wonderful pine disinfectant smell. A third man was dragging discarded branches and scrub, and making a pile of them, to one side. The Land rover, which had passed us not long before, was parked on the track close by.

No one heard our approach, for not only was the chain saw making a high pitched whine as it cut through the green timber, but each of the men was wearing ear protectors; those earphone look-alikes which are designed to block out sound, and protect the wearers' hearing.

We stood at the edge of the clearing and watched with interest. No one took any notice of us as they were totally unaware of our presence. When finally the last log dropped to the ground, the man holding the remaining stump tossed it onto the pile and the chain saw shut off. The man holding it, having cut the motor, laid it on the ground, and removing his ear protectors, declared in a loud voice, 'I need a piss.' Fred coughed and all three turned round simultaneously to face us.

'Sorry Miss, I didn't know you were there. Is there anything we can do for you good people?'

'No thanks! We were just curious and came to watch. Please don't let me stop you doing what you need to do.'

The man grinned sheepishly and disappeared into the undergrowth and was quickly lost from sight.

'We passed you two coming up the track,' said the man standing by the Land rover.

'Yes, that's right. We're out for a walk. We're camping in the village and tramping all round the countryside. Can I be nosy and ask you what you are doing?'

'We're doing nothing now my dear. We're finished for today, but what we have been doing is more or less the same as we do everyday. Mostly cutting down

mature timber that is ready for use and for sale, or like today, we have been cutting up timber, which is either diseased, or stunted and not fit for anything but fire logs. Sometimes we might get a few fence posts out of them if we're lucky.'

'Do you work here all the time then?'

'No love! Not just here. We move all over the estate, cutting down, chopping up, replanting, clearing brush, clearing fire breaks and what ever else needs doing.'

'So you are always roaming around then?'

'Well, not exactly roaming. We work from the Estate Office for this area, if you can call it an office. It's more like a wood cabin, but the Foreman likes to call it his office.'

'Where is that then?' asked Fred. 'Is it near here?'

'No love! It's a few miles up the road from here. Just off the Whitby road. There's a lane with a big gate at the bottom and a sign on it and a track which leads to the main saw mill and the office.'

'That's fascinating, and how many of you work in here?'

'There are twelve of us in this area, but not many of 'em work,' Interrupted the man who had returned from the undergrowth, looking very much relieved.

'He calls himself our charge-hand,' said one of the others.

'Please to meet you,' said Fred. 'Twelve, you said and all doing the same as this?'

'More or less! Working in gangs of three or four mostly, unless we have a really big job on, but mostly it's doing much the same as we have been doing here. There is also a permanent gang of wood cutters based at the saw mill up the road.'

'What happens to all this then?' asked Fred waving her arm towards the freshly cut timber logs.

'Nothing for now! As we're finished here for today and we're going. But later it will all be collected up and taken to the sawmill yard. So if you would care to squeeze in the back,' he said, nodding towards to Land rover. 'We will be only too pleased to give you a lift. We will be dropping off one of these lads in the village if that will do for you. Then me-lado over there is making for Whitby. You are welcome to the lift if you are going our way.'

'Very kind of you! But no thank you. We are out for the walk and are quite happy to tramp back to the village on foot. Which one of you lives in the village?'

'Me,' said the one over by the Land rover. 'I do. Why?'

'No real reason, but if you live in the village and should bump into us either in the Grapes or the Dog and Gun come up and make yourself known. We would love to buy you a pint and chat to you some more about forestry work, it fascinates me.'

‘I might just take you up on that, free beer sounds good,’ he said laughing. ‘But it won’t be i’nt Grapes. Can’t stand the prat who has it.’

‘Well, we go in both, so why not try your luck in the Dog and Gun.’

‘Never can tell, might just see you in there,’ he replied as he climbed into the Land rover and the other two followed him.

‘Nice talking to you,’ said the charge hand. ‘Have a nice walk, might see you around and, by the way, how come he is the only one to get an invite from a pretty thing like you?’

‘Perhaps it’s because he’s the best looking,’ laughed Fred. ‘Anyhow nice talking to you all.’

We stood and waved as they drove away. I realised I had said very little during the time we were there. Funny how all the men love to talk to the girls.

We continued on towards the village.

‘I have not seen any of them before and in particular the one who lives in the village,’ commented Fred.

‘No, come to think of it, neither have I, now that you mention it. Perhaps he is not a regular drinker, or perhaps he has been in the Dog and Gun and we have simply not noticed, or we have missed him. But from what he said we are not likely to have seen him in the Grapes.’

We left the forest track and wound our way along the paths and lanes, until eventually we joined the main road about half a mile South of the village.

‘I really enjoyed that walk through all those woods and lanes. The countryside round here is really something. However, I will be glad when we get back. I could eat a horse, or some other such delicacy, I’m starving.’

‘I’m sure we can find something, we usually do, which will keep us going until we go to the Dog and Gun then you can have your horse, if they serve it.’

‘Of the two I actually prefer the Grapes for the food.’

‘So do I sweetie, but don’t forget, we have to go there and meet Eddie. We have plans to make.’

CHAPTER THIRTY-ONE

It was eight thirty that evening when we finally arrived at the Dog and Gun, the inevitable having happened when we got back from our long hike. We had a bite to eat, and coupled with the warmth of the caravanette, simply nodded off.

Later we both admitted to feeling much better for the sleep but then had to rush to make up for time lost. After a quick wash and tidy round we headed for the village.

The pub was busy so we had to thread our way through the crowd and did so without taking much notice of anyone around us. I ordered drinks, and having paid for them, turned towards Fred just as Eddie approached us from the opposite direction.

'Hi! Nice to see you both! You're a bit late. I thought perhaps you had decided to give it a miss tonight.' Then turning to the bar, requested from the barmaid, 'Two pints of bitter please.' Looking back at us he continued, 'Have you got yours?' I raised the glass in my hand so that he could see it. 'Good, then come over here. There is someone I would like you to meet.'

He threaded his way through the crowd and we followed him to a table in the corner. Already seated there was a very smartly dressed young man and as we approached Eddie handed him one of the pint glasses. Then addressing the stranger, said, 'this is the couple I was telling you about, and who I met a couple of days ago and who are on holiday here.'

The room was busy but the people close by very kindly shuffled round to make sufficient space for Fred and I to squeeze in. Once seated, Eddie continued, 'Fred and Mel, I would like you to meet Len.'

Without attempting to stand up, I reached across and offered my hand to the stranger. He took it and we both said, more or less simultaneously, 'Hi.' Then when he shook Fred's hand she gave him one of her sexy smiles and said, 'Three men in my life now. How lucky can a girl get?' and everyone laughed.

'So you know Eddie, do you?' I enquired of the stranger.

'No! Not really. I only met him this afternoon. I booked in then later, down here in the bar, got into conversation with him. I invited him again to have a drink with me this evening but he explained that he had promised to meet you two, but even so, he said, I was more than welcome to tag along, if I wanted. So, here I am and I hope you have no objections?'

'Of course not! As Eddie told you, we are on holiday and met him in here and from there have spent some of our evenings together. What brings you to this neck of the woods, as they say?'

'I'm an Agricultural Rep, selling mainly seed and fertilizer and I'm here to try and drum up some business in the area. I booked in this lunchtime and got into conversation with this guy quite by accident. Like all reps, where talk is the main tool of our trade, we like to chat and meet people so we seemed to hit it off. It breaks the monotony when you are away from home, and in strange surroundings. But as I said I hope you two don't mind my being here tonight. If you do, please say so and I will disappear and try and find some other equally lovely girl who might want to chat me up.'

'Don't be silly,' said Fred, 'and deprive me of the company of a man. How could you be so cruel?'

We all laughed. Fred was obviously taken with our new acquaintance and one had only to glance across at his face to tell he was well and truly smitten by her.

'Do you two propose eating?' enquired Eddie.

'We do indeed, eventually. We've walked miles today and are starving; well he is,' said Fred, inclining her head towards me. 'Got to keep your strength up, haven't we darling?' and then leaning towards me, gave me a peck on the cheek and as she pulled away I felt the warmth from the tip of her tongue as it lightly touch my ear lobe followed by her cool breath as she gently blew on it.

'If I can make a suggestion,' said Len the newcomer. 'Why don't we all eat together and let it be my treat, by way of compensation for being the new boy and the intruder. I am sure my expense account will stand it, at least on this occasion.'

Then looking round, and craning his neck, he continued, 'How do you go about getting food in here?'

'When it is so busy, the best bet is to go to the bar and book a table,' suggested Eddie. 'But you all stay here and I will go and find out what the drill is.'

He promptly got up and made his way to the bar. He returned a few minutes later with a tray, laden with drinks and slid it onto the table. He picked up the empties and headed once again back to the bar. On his return he sat down and said, 'that has sorted that out. They will give us a shout when there is a vacant table. In the meantime it's down the hatch with this lot.'

He picked up his drink and took a mouthful then looking directly at me said, 'you've been very quiet so far tonight Mel.'

Before I could answer, Fred cut in, 'He's almost asleep, aren't you darling? All that walking has near killed him.'

'No, I'm fine really and I'm sorry. I didn't mean to be rude, but I suppose Fred is right. I could close my eyes and go to sleep right here. The fresh air has

knocked me out. Forgive me,' I said, shifting my position and shaking myself to force away the waves of tiredness that were sweeping over me.

After that I forced myself to be more attentive and seemed to brighten up as we laughed and passed the time with light conversation and more than a smattering of wit. Although I must admit my input was considerably less than that of the others.

Len was explaining the advantages of fresh manure over the artificial or the dried variety, with a great deal of innuendo and humour when Fred, looking towards the bar pointed a finger at herself, and interrupted saying, 'I think our table is ready,' and wrapping both arms round one of mine said, 'Come on lazy bones, you will feel much better when you have eaten.'

I allowed myself to be led away towards the dinning area. Once seated, Len announced, 'Order what you want. Wine everyone: the tabs on me. So order just whatever takes your fancy.'

We studied the menu and gave the order to the waitress, laughing and joking between ourselves as we do so.

The food was good, although the menu was not as varied as that in the Grapes. But as far as Pub Grub goes, it was more than acceptable. The wine was also mediocre with regards to quality, but still went down well.

I felt better and much of my tiredness had passed, but unfortunately the wine and the drink began to have an adverse effect and I began to feel woozy.

The girl came to clear away the table.

'Is it alright if we stay here for a while?' Eddie asked the young lady.

'I don't see why not sir,' she replied. 'It's gone quiet now, and meals are over for tonight, and even if they were not, there are still plenty of other tables we could use.'

'Bless you sweetheart,' said Len slipping a five-pound note in her apron pocket. 'That food was excellent and the waitress superb and if you do need this table, just give us a nod and we will move straight away.'

'Thank you sir, but I don't think we will. Anyhow two of you are residents, so that gives you some priority, should anyone say anything.'

When she finally left us, I said, 'More drinks folks? I believe it's my turn.'

No one contradicted me so I went to the bar and got another round and as I sat down again, Eddie said, 'Good, now that it's quiet in here and we are well away from everyone else, we can talk.'

'Talk?' declared Fred. 'Haven't we been doing that all evening?'

'Yes we have,' replied Eddie. 'But listen; this is serious. Len and I go back a way. We have worked together before, and this fertilizer story is exactly what it is, a load of fertilizer, it's a cover. Len is Drug Squad and he knows all about you two. He was briefed before he arrived, but go on Len, you explain.'

Len looked round to make sure no one was within ear shot before he lent forward in his seat and began, 'Apparently your people, the Coastguard, informed my people, that you might be onto something important here; something that could be more than just of interest to us. But I was also told that what you have discovered is only a small part of what you were actually looking into. I was also told that I had to keep away until we heard from your people that we were free and clear to move in. What I want to know is, are we free to come in now?'

I felt a sudden surge of anger. After everything we had agreed with the Old man here we were with a bloke who was formally introducing himself and saying that he had been instructed to keep away. Yet at this moment we were with him and having this conversation. I couldn't believe it.

'Then why the hell are you here now if you were told to wait and keep away?'

'I just thought I would come along and introduce myself, and let you know I am around.'

'Well you have! So now I suggest you clear off at the first opportunity and do as you were told to do in the first place, and wait until invited. What are you trying to do, blow the whole bloody job for us? These people we are dealing with and the local population, are not bloody stupid. Don't think, for one minute, we are all sat here unnoticed.'

I was so angry I stood up and made straight for the Gent's toilet. I needed to get away and simmer down.

'That was a bit heavy Mel,' said Eddie, as he opened the toilet door and saw that I was in there alone.

'Who the hell is this guy? No offer of ID and with some story about fertilizer and a load of other shit. Did he ID to you?'

'He didn't have to Mel. I already know him from way back.'

'And can you be certain he still works for the same firm, the same set up? No you bloody can't. You have just taken him at face value. Get rid of him. Let him sell his sodding fertilizer somewhere else.'

'You're upset, aren't you old son?'

'Yes I bloody am. He was told to back off, to wait until he got the nod from us. The man is incredible. I get put on a job and every other bugger wants to home in on it. They're like a load of wasps round a bloody jam pot.'

'Does that include me?'

'No! You know what I mean. I'm pleased you're here and you have been invaluable to us. You have done everything I have asked you to do. You have not interfered, but this prat sweeps in like a white tornado. The next thing we know, the place will be crawling with all his bloody cronies who will be happy to settle for a few cannabis tabs and no sodding arrests and then they will march out again with drums banging and flags flying and shouting the odds about how good they are. We

are not here for their bloody glory or their sodding drugs, important though they might be. They're only coincidental to our main objective - which could be murder - and God knows what else. We tell that prat nothing and I hope you've not told him anything already, until the right time. For now, we get rid of him; he goes.'

'As you say.'

'I do say and I'm going to have a short sharp word with him right now.'

We went back into the bar and to our table, and found the drugs man deep in conversation with Fred.

'Excuse me, but if I can pull this girl away, I would like a word with her in private.'

I took Fred, who gave me a rather odd look, gently by the arm and led her some distance away and out of earshot of the others.

'Fred I am not happy about this guy. I haven't time to explain now, but he just drifts in, having openly admitted to disobeying orders and not doing as he was told. He is of no value to us at the moment and will only clutter up our scene and with the tactics he has used so far, perhaps cause us major problems. He has to go. Have you told him anything that he doesn't already know?'

'Of course not! What do you take me for? All he was interested in was trying to chat me up and I strung him along for the hell of it. He's rather a nice guy really but your the boss.'

'Nice or not, he has to go and go now.'

'OK, I can see your point. As you say, we are in danger of becoming rather a large group in a very small place, I must admit. Who tells him?'

'I do.'

We returned to the table and sat down.

'I have just had a word with my partner and we have briefly discussed our present position.'

'Good, and what do you propose we do then?' enthused the Drug Squad man.

'First of all you, Len, you will melt away. Drop right back into the background. So much so that you will leave the area straight away and wait in the wings, as you were originally instructed, until you hear from us.'

'And in the meantime, what do you propose to do?'

The cheeky sod! Just listen to the man, I thought but said, 'I propose to bid you good night. To thank you for your company and for the meal and I hope to see you soon. In the meantime I am going to call it a day. It's been a long one for us and we are tired. You coming now Fred, or are you staying on for a while?'

'I'm coming with you. You're not the only one who is worn out after all that walking. Good night Len. Thanks for everything. See you in the morning Eddie.'

She pecked each of them, in turn, on the cheek and we left.

When we were safely outside she tugged my sleeve and demanded, 'what was all that about and what was it about him that upset you so much back there Mel?'

'I don't know really. I suppose it was the blatant cheek and un-professionalism of it all, if I can use such a word. The fact that this guy just appeared, uninvited and after all the Old Man said. He didn't ID or approach us in the correct way. Eddie just accepted him from their past dealings, which may be fair enough to him, but not good enough as far as I'm concerned. When you rang Cruickshank, you said that he would inform the Drug Squad that we were currently in the area, but then they were to stay out of it until they heard from us. Correct?'

'Yes, that's right. I pointed out to him the needed to keep a low profile at the moment.'

'Precisely. So what's this guy doing showing up here and now? If he's one of those types who goes in like a bloody bull in a china shop or simply can't follow orders, then he could be dangerous, and we can manage without him. I don't like it Fred, and the sooner he clears off the better for me.'

'Are you going to mention any of it to the Old Man?'

'Of course! We must. He needs to know that his orders are not being carried out, which is the most important. But also it will give him the opportunity and one that he loves so much, to throw shit in the fan, for the benefit of his illustrious colleagues, that he loves and envies so much. Also I have to ring him, in any case, about that business with Raines so I can mention it then.'

When we arrived back at the van I was still annoyed but had settled down considerably.

'Cheeky bastard,' was my final remark to bring the subject to a close.

We cuddled up close and in only a matter of seconds, we were fast asleep. It had been yet another long day.

CHAPTER THIRTY-TWO

I woke to the sound of heavy rain battering down on the roof. On the flat, thin metal, it was almost deafening and seemed to pound away incessantly. As I lay there I realised that it was the first time it had really rained hard since we arrived. Fred groaned and pulled the sleeping bag tight up under her chin.

'I suppose in a way we have been lucky with the weather.'

'Mmm,' as she snuggled down deeper.

The thought of all that wet outside was having a thoroughly demoralising effect on both of us. We knew we would have to get up, but the desire to do so at that precise moment was at an all time low.

'I suppose we should make some sort of effort to contact Eddie,' I said.

Instead of a reply she slid down below the top edge of the sleeping bag and cuddled up closer.

'If only to find out if the drugs man has taken the hint and cleared out, and also we have to ring the Old Man today… Do you think I should apologise to Eddie for slinging his pal out?' I continued.

'No, why should you,' said a muffled voice. 'You were right and Eddie should understand.'

There is something rather pleasant about being wrapped up warm, in a small caravanette, when it is raining hard outside. One of the last things on your mind is the desire to get up. Hands wander and sensations heighten, or they do when Fred's hands begin to roam.

'Who's a big boy?' she cooed as she fondled and stroked. 'Who cares a damn about the Old Man, Eddie, that Len or the weather?'

Who indeed! I thought.

The rain continued to bounce on the roof. The wind howled and gusted and having temporarily abandoned all thoughts of getting up, we shut ourselves off from it all and rocked the van in our own special way.

An hour or so later I woke. The rain had stopped, but when I drew the curtain to one side and wiped the condensation from off the window with my fingertips, and peered outside, it was to look out onto a very sad scene; everywhere was very wet, dull, damp, and miserable.

'If we don't make a move soon, we will be here all day,' I complained as I slid back down into the warmth and comfort of the sleeping bag.

'Suits me,' sighed Fred as her hand once again slowly wandered. 'Oh you poor thing, all soft and floppy. Was I too much for you? Oh no, there's my boy, rising once again to the occasion.'

I found it really hard to concentrate. 'Look Fred, much as I like it, we really should be getting up.'

'That's exactly what I had in mind, and so far he's doing alright.'

It was almost lunchtime before we finally made the supreme effort and dragged ourselves out of bed and to face, what was still, a dull and miserable day.

'We will eat in the village. Ring the Old Man and then see what's with Eddie.'

'What ever you say lover,' she said as she wrapped her arms around my waist from behind and ran the tip of her tongue across my shoulders. Her hand slid down my stomach and her fingers gently tousled the hairs.

'I wish it would rain again.'

'Why? It rained enough last night to last us a lifetime.'

'Then we would have to go back to bed and this time you could make love to me.'

'Why? Didn't I make love to you last time?'

'You didn't do too badly. But I did most and anyhow, in this bad weather, you need all the practice you can get.'

'This conversation is beyond me. I always understood that the weather had nothing to do with it and that the more practice you got, the worse you became, until finally you were worn out and finished. Unless of course you were a duck, then perhaps the weather might have helped.'

'Well if that's true, you have no time to waste. Kiss me before you're finished for good.'

I turned to face her and she came close and we kissed tenderly. Her hand slowly slid between us and wandered south. The kiss slowly became passionate as I lowered her back onto the bed. When we finally came up for air and I stood up and looked down at her she whispered, 'Nice.'

'It may eventually wear out, or what ever is supposed to happen to it. But for now, please can we save a little bit for later?'

She reached up and gave one last gentle squeeze to a very sensitive area. 'Save as much of that for me as you can and promise me we can have an early night.'

'Jee-wizz.'

'Go on.'

'I will. But for now let's settle for up, dressed and a cup of tea, and then dig out those oilskins. Something tells me we are going to need them.'

Some time later we walked along the lane, wrapped from head to foot in oilskins, and holding hands like two young lovers. Despite the dampness and the dullness of the day, I felt good and each time I glanced at Fred, who seemed quite content to walk along saying very little, she smiled, winked, and blew me a kiss. At that moment I could not think of anywhere else that I would rather have been.

Two people in a phone box can be quite a squeeze at the best of times, as we already knew, but when the two in question are clothed in bulky oilskins, space is, without doubt, at a premium. The windows very quickly steamed up and there was much manoeuvring and twisting in order to operate the telephone. The biggest challenge was to work my way through the cumbersome waterproofs to reach my inner pockets and find the necessary change for the call.

When we finally made contact there was a slight delay while the internal lines were connected. Instead of the usual feelings of frustration we took full advantage of this and passed the time gently kissing. The condensation on the windows provided adequate shielding from any prying eyes on the outside. When the connection was finally made, the Old Man sounded almost pleasant. It was however, not to last long.

'How's it going up there Grundy? If your interested the weather down here is dashed awful; storms everywhere, playing havoc with my golf and no damned chance of getting into the garden.'

'We're fine Sir. Thank you. It has rained a bit up here last night and today, but apart from that, we have only one minor hiccup to report. A Drug Squad bloke turned up on the scene yesterday and this has annoyed me intensively as I understood you to say, that you would hold them off for the time being. Have you changed your mind on that, sir?'

'Yes I did, and no, I have not changed my mind,' he almost shouted. 'Someone has simply turned up you say? Without warning? I don't know what the hell they think they are playing at. They were told categorically by me to await instructions. Bloody idiots, no wonder they can't catch any of the so-called big fish if they can't even accept, and act upon, a simple, straightforward request. Leave this with me. I will get onto it straight away and get to the bottom of this shambles and blatant disregard for my orders and you maybe assured it will be attended to immediately.'

'Thank you sir; that would be appreciated.'

'Have you anything further for me Grundy? As if you haven't already given me enough. What about progress?'

'Nothing to report there Sir. But there is one other thing. Do you have the report on the Raines character for me?'

'Yes, of course I do. I have it in front of me. Are you ready to take it down?'

'One moment sir; I will get something to write with.'

I twisted round to face Fred who, in turn, proceeded to twist and wriggle, and grin all the time, as she attempted to retrieve a pen and note pad from somewhere deep down in an inside pocket.

'What's going on there, Grundy? Where the hell are you? What's all that background noise? Are you in a phone booth and have you got that woman in

there with you again? Damn it man; I am seriously thinking about reviewing your situation. Perhaps it would be better if I withdrew her from this case altogether and sent another field man to work with you or left you there to work on your own.'

'That just would not work, sir. You can't do that,' I blurted out in panic; knowing full well he could and would, and might do so on nothing more than a whim, if I had caught him on one of his really bad days.

'If you withdrew my partner at this point in time, sir, I would have no cover what-so-ever, and two men, or for that matter, one man on his own, would look highly suspicious wandering around when we have gone to a lot of trouble to cultivate a couple; and as such have been seen in the area. Another thing, sir, how would I explain her sudden disappearance and the appearance of another bloke to take her place or how could I make up for what she already knows or the detailed planning that has gone into the part she is going to play?' I wondered if he knew we were sharing a caravanette? Hell, what would he do if he knew what had happened only a short while back. I broke out in a sweat.

The panic just would not subside and was made all the worse by the fact that he remained quiet and said nothing. In sheer desperation I found myself adding, 'I need her, sir. I need her to get into places only a woman can penetrate. Believe me, sir, what we are doing at this moment is very delicate and can only be handled by a woman. She is very much a part of our cover and very necessary for the success of the job.'

My heart pounded as I desperately hoped he would not ask for a detailed explanation to back my reasons and my story. I just preyed I sounded convincing. I could do no more, so I held my breath and hoped for the best.

'You had better be right Grundy, for if I thought for one moment you were not giving the whole one hundred percent, that I expect from my people, or if there is any hint of tom-foolery I will have you two replaced immediately and worry about the consequences of my actions later. So you just make sure you two know exactly what you are doing or it could quite easily be a permanent desk job for you both. Understand?'

'Yes sir, I do understand. We both understand, sir, and you may be assured we are not being irresponsible or in anyway shirking our responsibilities.'

Fred looked in amazement and wrinkling her brow. She whispered, 'Tell him to piss off.'

I slapped my hand over the mouthpiece. 'Shut up or you will only make things worse.'

I desperately had to get him off the subject and get rid of him as soon as possible, if I could, so I blurted out the first thing that came into my mind.

'What about Raines, sir? It is very important I find out as mush about him as possible and as soon as I can.'

'What about him? Oh yes. But you remember what I have just told you, are you ready?'

I snatched the pad and pen. 'Yes.'

'First name Ronald; also known as Ron or Ronny. Aged forty-two. Address; Four, Long Rope, Middle Walk, Whitby. Four years, seven months an Auxiliary. Trade; Builder's Labourer. British by birth. Lived and worked as a builder's labourer in Northern Ireland up to four years ago. Married an Irish girl, name of Bridgett, brought her back to the mainland with him. No children. Well liked. Good Coastguard. Is that all you require?'

'Yes sir! Fine sir. If that's all you have? Thank you sir. We will be in touch. Thank you again sir,' and I hung up before there was any chance he could return to the original subject, and start winging again at what we were doing, or how we were going about it, and in particular why there were two of us in the phone box.

'Miserable old sod! I suppose I am expected to stand out here in the rain? What does he think we get up to in a phone box anyhow?' muttered Fred as we spilt out into the cool air. 'If his mind is running riot over a phone box, he would probably have had a heart attack if he had known what went on in the van this morning. I can't imagine him ever doing anything natural, or human, and I certainly can't imagine that old battle-axe he's married to, doing anything, other than lording it over the Bridge Club, or the Cross Stitch Circle. I bet she has never had a feel in a phone box and I bet she thinks an orgasm is a group of women who come together and plan a Ban the Bomb march, poor old cow.'

'Now don't get bitchy.'

'He's enough to make anyone bitchy. He's sat in his warm office with probably little to do but contemplate his extended lunch break with one of his government cronies. The best of everything, all on expenses, while it is the likes of you and I that do all the rough work, and suffer the discomforts. Oh how I hate rain and in particular these horrible oilskins. They do nothing for me.'

'Oh I don't know. Girls in oilskins! It has its possibilities. I have never had a girl in just oilskins. The mind boggles.'

She jokingly made to kick my shins, missing intentionally. 'Well you can count this girl out straight away. They're uncomfortable enough with loads of clothing on underneath. Against bare flesh they would be a complete turn off for me. So right now you can forget any plans that might be rushing around in your tiny mind to have my bare bum rub against rough oil skin.'

'According to the Old Man, it is more than my jobs worth to even think about anything remotely resembling anything like that right now. So voluptuous boobs in oilskins are definitely out, remember. Thoughts of even sharing a phone box place me under threat of a desk job at this point in time.'

'Now that's a different matter.'

'What is?'

'A desk job! Forget the oilskins, you can have me over a desk, in a nice big warm office, anytime you like.'

'Then we would certainly both be for the high jump.'

'There you go again.'

'What?'

'Not satisfied with just the desk. Now you are suggesting a high jump over one. Now my mind boggles.'

I slapped her backside and she laughed.

'Listen and be serious. Can we perhaps concentrate on this bloody awful weather, this rotten job and anything else that seems to be getting forgotten while your mind has you spread out in oilskins high up over some desk or other.'

'Spoil sport! The Old Man's got to you good and proper this time, hasn't he?'

'No, not really but he can be such a prat... Well I suppose he has in a way, but if I can just get you to concentrate for a minute then I might survive.'

'I'm listening, if I must. Go on high jumper, what's bothering you now?'

'I'm still not happy about that Drug Squad chap. I hope the Old Man gets him and any back up team he might have in the vicinity to pull right back and out of the way.'

'Oh he will. Be assured of that. You know the Old Man. If he thinks he has been over ridden, or ignored, heads will definitely roll.'

'And that might include mine. He still surprises me at some of the things he does and the way he reacts, and I thought I knew him better than that. He has always been a cantankerous old bugger with plenty of weird ideas. But this thing about phone boxes is something new and has got me beat. Do you know, I actually panicked when he ranted on about it and thought for one horrible moment, we had blown it, and he was going to give us both the chop and then when you said, "Tell him to piss off," and I thought he might have heard you, I really flipped.'

'Blown it! It's just him who is a miserable old sod. An early night or, for that matter, a bonk in a phone box or even the thought of a bonk in a phone box and, do you know what; it would probably kill him. Thinking about it, perhaps at some time, in the past, he has had a nasty experience in a phone box. Perhaps a girl friend or even a boy friend pinched his chewing gum or stopped him looking at the phone book or worse than that, cut him off in mid-sentence or something equally dreadful,' at which we both laughed.

'Perhaps he or she pinched his ten pence.'

'Or perhaps he caught something nasty,' Fred added. 'Perhaps there was a dirty picture or something obscene written in the phone book or the speaking clock told him to sod off. But to hell with him: let's settle down and forget all about him for now and let's get somewhere out of this horrible weather and find something to eat. Come on. The cafe is just up here.'

'That sounds like a damned good idea.'

We sat down at a table in the cafe, having discarded our heavy oilskin coats and dumping them, unceremoniously, onto the floor. It felt much warmer in doors than usual. Perhaps due to the weather and the fact that it was cold outside. It was still raining steadily and the chill on the outside, against the contrast of the warmth inside, caused all the windows to steam up. This had the overall effect of making the place seem much smaller than it really was, and with it, somehow more cosy and private. We could certainly not see what was happening outside.

We were the only customers.

Having served us the lady who owned the cafe had disappeared into the rear but not before telling us to be sure to give her a shout if we required anything further.

As we ate, our conversation started out fairly light, but as usual, as we progressed, we moved on to discuss progress and plans but, at the same time, remained conscious of the fact that the proprietor may not be too far away and could be "ear-wigging".

'You know how little things seem to flit into your mind as you walk along, or you aren't thinking, or doing anything, in particular? Well a moment ago while that woman was setting the table and bringing in the food and I was thinking about nothing special when it suddenly struck me how useful, but at the same time, how limiting those photographs are, that Eddie took.'

'What ever made you think of that and what do you mean, useful but limiting?' asked Fred, who obviously did not understand what I was getting at.

'Well, it's very useful to have the pictures, I admit. But only to us because we can't very well go round sticking them under peoples noses and asking, "Who's that?" Now can we? That's what I mean when I say they are somewhat limiting.'

'You mean we have pictures but could do with someone putting some names to them? We need both, pictures and names. Is that what you are getting at?'

'Precisely. It would help. Don't you think?'

'There could be a way round that. I'm not too sure how, at the moment, or even if my idea would work.'

'Go on; surprise me. Any spurts of inspiration or for that matter, anything to get the taste of the Old Man out of my mouth would be more than welcome right now.'

'Well, I just thought. What if we bought a camera and went round taking photographs of literally everything. Well everything within reason I mean, but making sure that most of the pictures included the local inhabitants as the main subject. If challenged we could always use the excuse that we are doing some sort of project on village life, the inhabitants and local architecture, or some such story. If we then just happen to catch certain people in our pictures, then that would

be sheer coincidence. After that if we then took a selection and fabricated some excuse to show them around. Perhaps while asking about the history of a certain building or a place and then casually asking if certain persons were known to be a local or were visitors or recent arrivals or what have you. You know the type of thing. A build up to names and things like that and connections, whereabouts and anything else useful. I don't know exactly how we could work it, or even if it would work at all, but it is something that just crossed my mind.'

'That's not a bad idea. Doesn't have to be time consuming particularly if we fit it in with everything else as we move about. But processing might be a big problem. The Post Office or some other place I have seen in the village does one of those twenty four hour processing deals, for holiday snaps, during the summer period but I doubt if any of them will be doing one at this time of year.'

'I bet there's a Chemist, or some photographic shop, in Whitby that certainly does. Why don't we go and find out. We would have to go to Whitby to buy a decent camera in any case… Now what are you laughing at? Have I said something funny?'

'It's the Old Man again. I can't get away from him… "A camera Grundy. You bought a camera. It cost how much? Did no one ever tell you that cameras are standard equipment and can be drawn from stores? You can get yourself into a phone box with a woman, but you can't remember that we have a complete range of all types of camera for use out in the field. Make sure the one you bought gets put into stores when you get back and next time make sure you attend to small details like that, otherwise you will end up paying for your negligence out of your own pocket."'

'You've certainly got a thing about the Old Man today, haven't you? Sod Him. He sits at the back of a desk with nothing better to do than criticise. We do our best and no one is perfect. We didn't bring a camera and now we need one and that's that. So what?'

'Whitby it is then. At least if we go and have a look, we can see what's available and talk it through a bit more and make sure it is a sound idea before we actually commit ourselves.'

* * *

Our meal over, we trudged back along the lane to the campsite. The rain, if anything, was coming down harder. We hardly spoke a word to each other and kept our heads down to prevent the rain from blowing directly into our faces. It was certainly a miserable day and I hoped it was knocking hell out of the Old Mans' garden.

Wet clothing is not the easiest of things to cope with in a limited space so in the end we had no choice but to bundle up our wet oilskins and lay them, on newspaper, down on the floor.

'Can't have them things hung up, dripping all over the place,' complained Fred. 'It's miserable enough in here today as it is, without damp clothes hung about everywhere.'

So with Fred driving, we pulled out of the field and in a steady downpour, headed along the road North to Whitby.

The trip was miserable with visibility limited to forward vision through the space on the windscreen created by the window wipers. However, as we approached the town, the rain eased off, until by the time we had made our way through the town centre and parked on the large car park beside the river, it had stopped. It remained grey and overcast but at least for the moment, the rain had eased off. A strong breeze blew inland, up the river estuary, from the sea making it feel much colder than perhaps it really was.

'Thank goodness we don't have to get into those wet oilskins and let's hope the rain holds off long enough for us to do what we came here for and then get back.'

We locked the van and headed back towards the centre of the town. Once we reached the main shopping thoroughfare we quickly came upon a camera shop. They even offered a twenty-four hour processing service; that is if the sign outside was anything to go by.

'Are you much of a photographer?' I enquired as we browsed in the shop window.

'Not bad! At least I think I have progressed a bit beyond the "point and press" stage. My holiday snaps are usually clear and I don't often cut off heads and feet. What about you?'

'Very much the amateur I'm afraid.'

Fred moved up close and in a lowered voice said, 'what was all that about? You know as well as I do that we were trained in all aspects of photography, or at least I was.'

'So was I, but I was just making polite conversation while those people went past.'

Several more people passed, going about their business, as we stood looking in the window. I continued in a similar vein, 'Probably still safest with a point and press. Photography was something I never really seemed to get into.' Which was very true of my younger days. 'I always found it too expensive, as a hobby.'

'My dad was always very interested, and originally taught me much of what I know. Expense never really came into it because he took care of all that and I know we spent many happy hours taking and processing pictures.'

'Smashing! Shall we go in and see what they have to offer inside. The sign there says we are welcome to go in and browse.'

I held the door for Fred and then followed her through. The shop was devoid of customers. Perhaps because of the weather, the economic climate or the time of day or even just pure co-incidence.

Once inside we were surrounded by literally hundreds of different cameras, telescopes, camcorders, videos, televisions and an infinite range of accessories and processing equipment.'

'Good afternoon, can I help you?' enquired a very smart young man with a smile on his face that anticipated a large sale and with it all the answers to their cash flow and financial problems.

'I hope so, but perhaps a little later. For the moment we would like to browse around, if we may?'

'Certainly sir! Help yourself and give me a call if you require any further assistance.'

He then retreated a short distance and stood behind a small counter with his back to a glass covered wall display unit. From there he had a clear view of the shop and us as well.

I drifted in one direction while Fred went the other: the overhead video camera recording our every move.

The range was fantastic and totally confusing. I really did not know what I was looking at or for that matter what I was looking for. Perhaps in a situation like that, there was, after all, something to be said for going to our supply stores. At least there you stated your requirements and then took the camera and film issued to you and the end results were usually satisfactory. Here, I had to admit that, it was very much down to Fred and what I hoped, was her superior knowledge. To me they were cameras. Granted different sizes and shapes, but nevertheless to my untrained eye, simply cameras. The prices too were staggering. Two cameras, which looked very similar to me, varied in price by several hundred pounds. I realise that appearance has little or nothing to do with cost, and that it was the mechanical, electrical and technical specifications that counted for everything. I put down the one that currently baffled me and moved on.

Having worked my way round and still not really knowing what I was looking for, I came up alongside Fred who was holding a very small camera body which had a large lens attached to the front. The whole think looked ugly and disproportionate.

'Is that what we need?' I asked. 'I am totally lost, so I am relying on you, and what your Dad taught you.'

'It's gorgeous is this one. I'd love it, but it's far too expensive and far superior to anything that we need,' she explained as she carefully put it back on the display shelf. 'What we need is something more like this.'

I looked at the one she had picked up, but then without further comment, she apparently changed her mind and put it back and moved on.

'That's the one. That one there, perfect,' she said as she pointed rather excitedly at a rather bulky object sat in the midst of all the others in the window display. Then turning towards the young man who had not moved the whole time we had been in the shop, 'Can we have a look at that one please?'

'Certainly Madam,' as he moved forward to verify the one she pointed to. 'If you will step over here to the counter, I have one right here that you can look at.'

He bent down and from under his counter produced a large box that he then proceeded to open. He removed the packing and plastic wrapping and eventually handed a rather bulky object across to Fred.

'Just what we need: a Polaroid. Versatile, no skill to operate and will produce pictures good enough for our requirements, but above all else the pictures are instant and so there is no waiting for processing. We will take this one. Will you accept a credit card?'

So after all that, our problems, regarding processing, were solved in an instant.

The transaction complete, we left the shop with me carrying two plastic carrier bags. One contained the repacked camera, the other ten packs of films. The shop assistant had been a little surprised when Fred enquired about spare film and when she had not been particularly enthralled, or interested, when he pointed out the fact that the camera came ready equipped with a free film. The ten extra, that we had just purchased, were his entire stock. However, I think we made his day when he added it all up and made out the receipt and guarantee.

As we made our way back to the van I was curious to know, 'Why so much film? Ten seems rather a lot don't you think?'

'No. Not really. There are only ten exposures on each film and we don't want to be running back and forth all the time buying more film. It would be annoying to run out at a time when we most needed it. It looks a lot because the cassettes themselves are bulky, but really we haven't got that many.'

We sat in the van and I unpacked the box. I looked at the camera while Fred read the simple instructions. The free film that came with the camera was in a separate box, so having removed it from its outer wrapping, I loaded it into the camera, taking it a step at a time as Fred read out the instructions. I then inserted the batteries.

'Is that it?' I asked as I replaced the battery cover.

'Yes, that's it. According to this you are ready to go now. So let's nip outside and you can take a picture of me so that we know everything is working OK.'

So with Fred standing by the open van door, I lifted the camera up to eye level and remembering the instructions on how to take a picture, I pressed the exposure button. There was a flash and a motorised whirring sound from within. In a remarkably short period of time a fully developed glossy photograph popped out of an aperture in the front of the camera. I pulled it free and handed it to Fred. She took it, looked at it, and smiled.

'What about a picture without the flash? Less attention later on and all that,' I asked.

'You just press that single lever on the side, the second one in. If you depress the outer one, it triggers both, and you get a picture taken with the flash.'

'Go on then, you take my picture this time,' I said handing her the camera.

She handed me the result.

'It's very quick. I wonder what the quality of picture will be like inside, without the flash. I suppose the only way to find out is to give it a try.'

'Quick, you take another picture of me, out here, standing further back and without the flash, and then let's get back inside. It may not be raining now but it's still too cold to be standing about, posing for pictures.'

We examined the three pictures as they lay side by side on the table. Each was clear and the colouring remarkably good. Naturally the two taken using the flash was slightly better than the other.

'At least mine is as good as yours, so that takes good care of the skilled element,' I boasted.

'Yes. The whole thing is simple, straightforward and just what we need. These pictures show that if there is a reasonable amount of light outside, it works well without a flash. Come on: let's try just one inside the van here and then we can get warmed up a bit. I don't know about you, but I'm cold. The sooner we get back on the road with the heater going full blast, the better.'

The picture I took of Fred inside the van turned out well and showed us that we could get reasonable results in mediocre, to poor lighting conditions, without the use of the flash.

The fifth and final shot, which she took of me and despite the fact that the one I took of her was supposed to be the last, and using the flash inside the van, proved the camera worked well at close quarters. But then I suppose that was one of the things it was designed to do.

* * *

The return journey was a bit brighter: the rain clouds having passed over, but the surrounding countryside still looked very damp and miserable, following its soaking from the prolonged downpour.

'I hope this wind keeps up, and dries things out overnight and that it stays fine tomorrow, otherwise it is going to be pretty miserable and darned uncomfortable tomorrow night.'

When she said that I checked the date on the dial of my watch as if to reassure myself that Fred had got the day right. She had. Today was the fifth; tomorrow the sixth and the early hours of tomorrow night would be the seventh.

I had the feeling that we had a lot to do in preparation for the seventh, and yet at this point, we hadn't a clue what was likely to happen, or what we were preparing for, or even what we could expect.

'I feel a bit useless when all we can do is let it develop and only play it by ear, so to speak,' I said as we discussed it.

'But that is really all we can do.'

'True,' I had to agree.

We arrived back in the village and as we passed along the main street, Fred flicked the indicator switch and moved over into the centre of the road.

'Where are we going now?'

'I am going to park over here,' she pointed, 'and pop in and buy two Cornish pasties for tea and fill this thing up with petrol at the same time before we go back to camp.'

We were on the forecourt of the village Service Station and I was holding the nozzle of the pump in the filler cap and at the same time keeping one eye on the pump dial. As this did not require my constant attention I was able to glance casually up and down the main street. Among other things, I noticed a dark green Land rover parked outside "Fancy Pants" dress shop and immediately began wondering if it was the same one, that we had seen, in the forest the previous day; when a girl, who I instantly recognised as Edison's daughter, Jenny, came out of the nearby shop and climbed into it. As she closed the door, her mother, Pat Edison, came out of the same shop and began banging, rather viciously, on the side window.

'What's the matter?' asked Fred who's attention had been attracted when I stopped the fuel pump and stood on my tip toes, with the nozzle dripping, to gain maximum viewing height.

'Over there,' I said, nodding my head. 'Pat Edison looks to be having some sort of a difference of opinion with her daughter.'

As I spoke, the driver's side of the Land rover opened and a stranger stepped out onto the road. He was dressed in a similar manner to the guys we had seen in the woods, but I was not close enough to know if he was, in actual fact, one of them. He walked round the front end, passed the bonnet, and pushed his way between Pat Edison, and the side of the vehicle. She immediately started pounding her fists on his shoulders and chest while he just stood there and did nothing to retaliate or defend himself.

'Here, quick, take a picture,' said Fred as she thrust the camera at me.

I grabbed it, looked at the pump in my hand and not knowing quite what to do with it, stuck it back in the filler nozzle and then stepped forward for a better view. By the time I was ready to take a picture Fred had jumped out of the van and was off along the road at a half run, fast walk, in their direction. I took a picture and hoped for the best. I had no idea if it would come out, as I had only had time to lift the body of the camera up to the front of my face and press the shutter release. Pat Edison had continued to pound her victim and only stopped when she saw Fred draw level with them. Then Fred, having passed behind them, slipped round the first corner she came to and disappeared out of sight.

I stood waiting for the possible chance to take another picture.

'You having trouble with that pump Sir?' said the attendant, who had appeared from nowhere and was now standing behind me. 'Just that it stopped registering on the machine in the office and you haven't turned the pump off.'

'Sorry. I broke off to take a picture of my misses sprinting up the street. It's a new camera, that we've just bought, and I'm playing about with it. The misses running like that, just looked funny, so I took a picture,' and I held the camera forward so he could see it, and then reaching in through the open window, lowered it onto the seat.

I indicated with my head towards the Land rover and the shop, 'Seems there's a bit of a battle going on up there at the minute.'

The garage attendant looked along the street. 'Oh, them lot. They've got problems. He was knocking her off first and now he's knocking the daughter off and the mother doesn't like it.'

'Interesting. They call her Edison, don't they and if I am not mistaken he's…? Damn, I should know his name. I've heard it often enough but for the moment it escapes me,' I ventured hoping the remark sounded sufficiently innocent and casual that he would supply the missing information but I might just as well have asked a direct question for all the good it did me.

'Nowt to do with nobody! Minds my own business, I do and so should everyone else. Ya can get enough bother of your own without sticking ya nose in other folkses,' came the reply as he started to walk away, adding as he went, 'If you've finished with that pump, hang it up and come in the office and settle up. Then I can get away.'

Disappointed at what I thought would have worked like a charm I finished filling the tank and replaced the pump nozzle and filler cap. Then I walked into the office to "settle up" as he had put it.

'My credit card OK?' I said coldly.

'Suppose so. Don't like 'em myself, but you have to accept them these days 'cos no one carries any money any more.'

He picked up my card and turned it over several times, obviously trying to demonstrate to me that he knew exactly what he was looking at.

'Do you know that bloke up the street with the Land rover then?' he demanded, much to my surprise, as he fiddled with my card, and his machine.

If it was no business of mine why was he now pursuing the subject I wondered; my turn to answer questions perhaps? This might just be the time to be diplomatic and careful in what I said.

'No I don't think so. At first I thought I did,' I said. 'But now I am not too sure.'

'Then why all the interested in his name then if you are not even sure you recognise him?'

'I really don't know. No particular reason. Perhaps if I had recognised his name it might have rung a bell. I had more or less asked you before I realised I had done so. You know how it is when you think you know someone, you ask before you realise you perhaps don't know them,' I lied, shrugging my shoulders as if I couldn't care less.

To my surprise, as he handed me my credit card back, he said, 'Bad news that one, ever since he came here. Works as a Park Ranger or something like that. Name of Simpson, or Sumption, or something like that: sure he is not a friend of yours?'

'Positive. Don't know the name,' I quickly assured him, before adding. 'What do you mean, a Park Ranger or something like that?'

'Well, it says something like that on the side of his Land rover, which he is always running around the village in and leaves parked all the time outside his house.'

'He lives locally then?' I ventured.

'Couple of miles out of the village; small house, on it's own. Some say it belongs to Parks, others say North York Moors or something like that.'

I took the chance and decided to push the issue that little bit further. 'And you say he's bad news? In what way bad news?'

'He bothers with women he shouldn't do. Thinks because he is on his own with no permanent woman in that house of his, he can share everyone else's.'

At that point, when what could have developed, from there, into a rather interesting and informative conversation, sadly came to an abrupt end as a customer entered the office to pay for fuel. I knew there was going to be no more when the proprietor said to me, 'Thank you sir, please call again,' and handed me my receipt.

'Thank you,' I replied and with my credit card and receipt, left the office and returned to our van. As I did so I looked back up the street. The Land rover had gone and Fred was on her way back towards the garage forecourt. She said nothing as we both climbed into the van and she drove away. A couple of hundred yards

down the road she turned off the road and into the pub car park and stopped. As soon as the engine died I said, 'Well I wonder what all that was about? What did you make of it? Was he one of those we saw in the woods?'

'No. But shut up and listen for a moment. As I went towards them, Pat Edison was crying and thumping him, and as I went past I heard her say, "Bastard, you bastard, how can you."'

'Did she see you?'

'No, I don't think so. She might have been aware of someone passing by; but she had her back to me and was busy shouting and waving her arms about and crying and so I doubt she even looked in my direction. She was far too busy to bother about me. Anyhow as I passed she said bastard several times and was very upset. When I went round the corner I stopped to try and listen and I heard her say, "Not satisfied with me, you bastard, now it's my daughter. She's a married woman and you're not going to ruin her life as well, you pig". All he said was "Piss off. I'll do as I bloody please." Then I heard him, but couldn't see him, get back into the Land rover and drive away. When I looked round the corner she had gone back into the shop and so I came back to the van.'

'While you were up there did you happen to see anything painted or attached to the side door panel of the Land rover, a name or something like that?'

'Yes. It said, "National Parks" and "Park Ranger" with some sort of crest. I saw that clear enough.'

'That's magic. Now you just sit here quiet and wait for a moment.'

'Why? Where are you going?'

'To the phone, to ring that Inspector at the cop shop, and hopefully find out who owns that Land rover, or more accurate to find out, who drives it, as we already know who owns it: the parks people. Just wait here and look at the picture I took. If I'm lucky, I might just catch him before he goes off for the day.'

I walked to the phone box, dialled, and waited. When he came on the line, I said, 'Excuse me Inspector, Grundy from the Coastguard, I need some information about a Park Ranger, lives a couple of miles outside the village and goes by the name of Sumption or Simpson, can you tell me anything?'

'We know him well sir, provides us with some of our light entertainment with all the domestic scrapes he keeps getting himself into. Ever since he came to this area, he has been involved with one woman or another and, while doing so, has upset a lot of husbands and boyfriends. Of recent times he has been seen going around with a young lass who is supposed to be married, and lives out of the village. No doubt we will hear of it shortly after her husband finds out. Anyhow, what you want know is this; his name is, in actual fact, Scampton, Alf Scampton. He lives in a small cottage at Wood End. A detached place that stands on its own, with a bit of land. He is the local Park Ranger and works for the National Parks people.'

I thanked him, assured him that we were making good progress and promised to keep him up to date. I then walked back to Fred who had been sat patiently waiting in the van.

'Any luck?'

'Yes. I got the Ranger's name and address. That is apparently what he is, a Park Ranger working for the National Park and it also appears that he loves the ladies, anybody's lady, and doesn't much care if anyone gets in the way or gets hurt in the process.'

'Well I am please you managed to find out all that, because I didn't get chance to finish my story before you dashed off.'

'What do you mean, there's more?'

'Well you were in such a rush to shoot off that you didn't give me time to finish properly.'

'So there is more?'

'Yes, there is. The guy with the Land rover, the Park Ranger as you now call him, the one that Pat Edison was trying to beat to death back there, was one of our four friends in Whitby. He was one of the four in the Welcome Inn that night.'

'Are you positive?'

'Of course I am. I'm not daft, or blind, and why should I fib?'

'Sorry. I didn't mean it like that. It came as a bit of a surprise, particularly when you didn't tell me in the first place or I didn't recognise him from the picture I took of them at that distance. Let's hope he didn't recognise you.'

'Why should he? He was busy and not looking my way and even if he did see me, this is such a small place, where everyone sees everyone else so often, that eventually no one takes much notice.'

'I hope you're right. Anyhow, if the worst comes to the worst and he did recognise you or remember you, there is nothing we can do about it. As you say we've been around here long enough now for most people to have seen us out and about. So now let's go back to camp and get ourselves sorted out and ready for tonight. We have, at least, had a very interesting afternoon and must have made a little progress even if, at the moment, nothing fits into any semblance of a plan.'

'This morning was not too bad either.'

'Sexy beast.'

She grinned, 'Yes and you loved ever minute of it.'

CHAPTER THIRTY-THREE

It was still cold, but at least it was dry as we walked into the village and as we entered the pub the bright lights and warmth, that immediately enveloped us, were in sharp contrast to the cold and dark of the outside.

'That's better,' exclaimed Fred as she pulled off her gloves and stuffed them into a pocket. Then unzipping her anorak she proceeded to unwind and pull the scarf from around her neck. 'A pleasant evening in here is just what the doctor ordered after the cold and damp of today. Something to squeeze out the damp and stimulate my tired blood is definitely a number one priority.'

'If that's not a scientific diagnosis then it sounds like party time to me,' I said. 'I can see someone will have to keep an eye on you tonight.' I recalled that that was not the first time she had hinted at relaxing a little and enjoying a 'good drink', as she put it.

'A bit busier than usual tonight,' remarked Fred, 'and look there's Eddie over there.' Indicating, as she said so, towards a side table where Eddie sat, oblivious to his surroundings, with his head deep in a newspaper.

'You go over and join him while I get the drinks,' I suggested.

'Make mine a large gin and tonic. I can still feel the cold attacking the body beautiful and covering it with goose pimples.'

When I joined them and set our drinks down on the table, they did a little shuffle so that sufficient space was created for me to sit down. Fred removed the bag, which held the Polaroid camera, from the table and placed it on the floor between her feet. We had discussed earlier and at some length the for and against the carrying of the camera and decided, or Fred had, as she claimed that she was the one who would carry it, that it might be as well if we did so on every possible occasion. Otherwise, she argued, what was the point in getting it. So, the decision having been made, a large, floppy casual shoulder bag had been selected for that purpose.

'Busy tonight,' I observed as I settled down and looked around.

'Some darts match or other, from what I can gather,' said Eddie. 'That's why there is a large party over there in that corner.'

I turned to look and could see above were the group were standing a ceiling mounted floodlight, which sent a strong beam towards one wall. From where I sat I could not see an actual dartboard, but there was no doubt there would be one on the wall somewhere.

'Much to tell me?' enquired Eddie.

'Lots. We have had a lovely day in Whitby, despite all the rain,' said Fred. 'But that can wait,' she added as she inclined her head towards the strangers sitting beside her and smiled.

'Excuse me love. Are you using that ashtray? They seem to have taken them all over there for the darts,' said a young woman on an adjoining table.

'No. Please help yourself,' I said, picking up and handing her the ashtray from our table. 'Who are they playing tonight?'

'I don't know love, some Whitby pub? Ere, George,' she said turning away. 'Who are they playing tonight?'

The man sitting next to her, who must have been George, lent forward and replied, 'I think its Coach House, bloody noisy lot, who ever they are.'

'Thanks,' I said, turning back to face Fred and Eddie.

Being conscious of the fact that we were well within earshot of several people, we chatted between ourselves keeping the conversation light and the subject matter general and for the most part totally irrelevant to anything. We listened to Fred debate, mainly with herself, the difficulties of preparing a decent meal in a caravan and Eddie expounding his theories on the financial deals being offered towards the purchase of new cars and almost convincing everyone in the process that it was all a great con.

'I will go to the bar and get some more drinks,' I offered as Fred put her empty glass on the table and very pointedly nodded at it.

'My turn,' Interrupted Eddie.

'No, you stay where you are. I can get out of here much easier than you. But if it bothers you, you can pay,' I laughed.

I crossed the room and stood at the bar. It had come to my turn to be served and I had just given my order to the barmaid when a voice from behind my right ear said, 'Mine's a pint.'

I half turned to look into a face, that I instantly recognised as belonging to one of the group of men we had come across in the woods, cutting logs.

'With pleasure! Add another pint of bitter to that order please, Miss.' I said to the barmaid and then turning back to him, 'Is this your local then?'

'Well it is when I come out for a drink. But I don't come out all that often since I got my ulcer. But I like to come in here for the darts if I can.'

'Should I be buying you beer then, if you have an ulcer?'

'I'm OK as long as I watch it. Anyhow free ones don't count. I always reckon that them ones do nobody any harm, the free ones.'

'You play for this team?'

'Twenty-odd years… Where are you sitting?' he asked as I handed him a pint.

'Over there,' I pointed. 'Catch you before we go.'

'You will, I owe you one.'

'No you don't, otherwise that one will not be a free one and will knock hell out of your ulcer,' I grinned before turning and leaving him stood by the bar.

'Who was that you were talking to?' Eddie casually enquired as I sat down.

'A nice guy that we met, out in the woods, when we were out walking the other day. He was cutting wood with a group of others. Apparently he lives local and plays darts here for the pub team.'

'What do you think of that?' demanded Fred, completely changing the subject and pushing a Polaroid picture of Eddie under my nose. 'I have been showing Eddie the new camera that you bought for me this afternoon and showing him how good it is without a flash.'

'It's very good,' said Eddie, 'You're a lucky girl and you couldn't get a more handsome model to photograph than me.'

'It probably won't work again after that,' I joked. 'A face like yours has probably screwed up all the gubbings inside and from now on everything will come out all green or blue or some other horrible mess.'

'You leave him alone. He likes my camera and I think it's a good picture. Better than those you took this afternoon.'

'It's all in the subject matter,' claimed Eddie, holding up his picture. Which I had to admit was remarkably good considering the surroundings in which it had been taken.

The lady, sat beside him, had obviously been taking it all in and strained her neck to get a better look. Eddie half turned, holding up his picture for her inspection.

'I think it's lovely, and if I was thirty years younger would be after you to buy me a brown ale.'

'What you on about Ada?' demanded her partner on her opposite side.

'Nothing,' she chided, 'nothing to do with you. You sup your pint. I'm talking to this young man.'

Fred leaned over and pressing her lips close to my ear, whispered, 'Seen who's just come in?'

I swung round on my stool and as I did so I clearly saw the character Raines striding across the floor with a woman close on his heels. As he got abreast of us he half turned, and addressing his remark to her, said, 'What you want to drink?'

She replied, in the strongest Irish accent that I think I have ever heard, 'Jesus. You know what I bloodty drink. Have you got that many bloodty women that you forget what each of 'em drinks now? I'm your bloodty wife remember, the one dat drinks the bloodty lager and lime in points.'

Eddie may have noticed, but I don't think anyone else did, or if they did, they showed no recognisable signs of interest, but while Raines was talking, or

discussing or whatever he was doing, with his wife, Fred took their picture. She then held the camera below the lip of the tabletop while she removed the exposed photograph from the front. Having done so she casually dropped everything into her bag.

We watched as Raines got their drinks and then he went to join the group around the dartboard while she went and sat, some distance away, with a group of other women and, by the way they all greeted her and behaved, it was obvious that they all knew each other.

'Don't we know that girl in that group? I have only just noticed her, that one there, sitting with her back towards us,' I asked.

'Which one?' enquired Fred leaning forward in order to get a clearer view of them, 'where?'

'The one in the middle with her back to us in the silver coloured anorak.'

'I don't know. Wait until she turns and I can get a better look.'

We watched and waited, saying nothing.

'She is not going to move, is she?' complained Fred, shifting her position. 'Sod's Law isn't it? When you want someone to do something or expect them, to do something, they don't. Hang on. I know what I can do and I need to go to the loo in any case.' So, standing up she picked up her bag and wiggled past everyone to weave her way through the throng to the ladies' loo.

'While there is room for me to get out I will go and get another round of drinks,' said Eddie.

'Take it easy old man. I am not used to drinking at this rate and Fred has had quite a few and I would like us both to be able to stand up at closing time.'

'OK, but let me get them anyway. We can always make them last.'

While he was away Fred returned and noting that he was missing looked about her. I said, 'He has gone to the bar for some more drink. Give him a moment and he will be back. Any joy?' nodding my head backwards in the direction from which she had just come.

'Yes. It's Jenny; what do you call her? I don't know her married name, but Edison's daughter, who we saw this afternoon. I think the Park Ranger is somewhere over there in the far corner by the dartboard. Anyhow I got her picture. Do you know, waving that camera about, I feel like David Bailey. The only difference is, that in my case, no one is taking any notice of me, thank goodness.'

Eddie returned and we were in the process of rearranging ourselves when from somewhere behind me and coming from not too far away, a voice said, loud and clear.

'Piss off!'

'No, you piss off!' replied a familiar female voice. 'I paid the other night. Mine's a soddin pint. No bloody halves ya' tight sod.'

I did not need to turn round and look to know that Johnson and his charming wife had just entered the pub. I heard the camera whir and knew they had been captured on film. When I did twist round it was to see her go and join the same group that Jenny and Raines' wife were both in. Johnson went straight to the bar, pushed in, and demanded in a voice that could be heard across the room, 'Two pints of bloody bitter and not that shit from there, this, out of this bloody pump, here.'

When served he pushed his way towards his wife and standing in front of her thrust forward one of the glasses and bellowed, 'Make it last, yer paying for yer own from now on in.'

In an equally loud, antagonistic and gruff voice she replied, 'Tight arsehole!'

He simply laughed and pushed his way towards the dartboard area. Once in the middle of the group and obviously for the benefit of as many as possible, he raised his voice even louder, and remarked, 'Still dicking that bit over there, Alf?'

Immediately there was a scuffle but from where I sat I could hear more than I could see. Seconds later and above the melee the Landlord's voice came across loud and clear, 'Knock it off, the pair of you, or you are both out, and will stay out, and you can cut that language now or you are out in any case.'

Johnson laughed and said, 'Take no bloody notice of him Alf, he's only jealous.'

'Enough. That's your last warning.'

Johnson seemed determined, despite the threats, to have the last word, 'Go wash glasses and water your bloody beer.'

Looking back at Fred I said, 'There is no doubt now that the Park Ranger is in then and is obviously the Alf character.'

Throughout Eddie had sat there looking totally bemused along with the majority of the others in the bar. He realised from our remarks that we knew something he didn't and that we were not saying too much because of the close proximity of the people on either side of us. Fred held here finger to her lips, as a precaution, in case he might have been tempted to ask questions.

A few moments later, when things had settled down and the bar seemed to be back to normal, Fred said, 'Don't turn round but there's the Park Ranger chap taking a drink across to Jenny. He must have already been in, before we arrived and was either stood or sat where we couldn't see him or maybe he came through from the other side.'

As she spoke she casually took a picture of them both.

We continued to pass the time steadily drinking and chatting and occupied ourselves further by watching the comings and goings in the bar. The couple to my right eventually left and as they did so handed back the ashtray they had borrowed. Unfortunately, as they did so their places were immediately taken over by two

other strangers who had been standing close by. We tried, among all the other things, to show some interest in the game of darts but we were really too far away to see much or understand exactly what was going on.

'Oy, pillock! How's about a drink over here?' bellowed a familiar female voice.

'Johnson's misses?' I said.

'How did you guess?' laughed Fred.

'Get your own, bitch. I'm bloody skint.'

'I've told you Johnson,' Interrupted the Landlord.

'Tell her. She's the one doing all the shouting, not me. I'm trying to play a game of bloody darts over here, against all this heap of crap.'

I swivelled round on my stool to get the best view I could. I didn't want to miss this if I could help it. But to my surprise Johnson's wife said nothing. She calmly got up from her seat and went to the far end of the bar, there, without a word, she handed her glass over to be filled. While she stood and waited, the much taller stranger standing at her side bent his knees in order to bring his lips into line with her ear and whispered something. She looked at him and laughed, then with her drink slopping over the edge of the glass and all over her hand she returned to her table and sat down. Once seated and satisfied she had managed to flick most of the spilt beer from her hand onto the carpet, she leaned over to Raines' wife and whispered in her ear. Raines' wife Bridgett, as we knew her to be called from the information supplied by the Old man, turned and looked across the room towards the bar and at the chap who was still stood there. He nodded his head, in the way a person does if they want someone to come over to join them and she nodded back in reply.

'Something going on over there by the looks of it,' suggested Fred as the camera went click and the man at the bar was captured on film for posterity.

'Could be. Keep an eye on them while I nip to the gents.'

'Why?'

'Because I need to.'

When I returned Fred said, with more than a touch of disappointment, 'He's gone… left.'

'Who?'

'The one at the bar! He finished his drink and left. She is still sat over there.'

Nothing further seemed to be happening as I sat down and I began to wonder if what we had seen was nothing more than casual familiarity between two people who happen to know each other. She remained seated and chatted away with the others before she eventually stood up and made her way across to the Ladies. A few moments later she emerged, but instead of making her way back to

the table, she went towards the outer door. As she passed close by our table, I heard the camera go click as Fred took a picture.

As the processed picture and the camera dropped into Fred's bag, she leaned close to me and in a barely audible whisper suggested, 'Is it time for you to take a little walk in the fresh air? Good idea, don't you think?'

Without saying anything, I stood up and casually walked towards the outer door. As I did so I imagined every one was watching me, but in reality, I bet no more than a smattering of people took any notice and of those who did, my reason for leaving would not be obvious to them or cause them any concern.

It was dark outside. I moved quickly away from the beam of light shining through the glass panel in the front door, and the pool of light cast by the overhead illuminated sign. Once round the nearest corner, I was in the car park and in almost complete darkness. I listened, but could hear nothing except the wind blowing through a nearby clump of trees. The same wind that kept the dense rain clouds moving and blocked out the moon. I strained to catch the slightest sound but all that came to me was the noise I made, with my own feet, as I slightly shifted my position.

I inched forward, moving slowly and progressing very cautiously round each car as I came to it. I took extreme care not to let myself get too close or touch any of them in case of car alarms. I was prepared to curse loudly and pretend to trip over something and thereby declare my rights to be there should I accidentally stumble upon something or be taken by surprise.

I moved some distance through the car park, managed to avoid bumping into anything, but saw or heard nothing. My eyes had adjusted, as best they could, to the darkness and I could now make out the silhouettes of many of the solid objects. I went a little further but then began to wonder if I had chosen the wrong direction and that the woman, as she left, had in fact, gone the other way. I stopped again and listened, and was just about to retrace my steps and change direction, when, barely audible above the sound of the wind, I heard, what I believed to be, a snatch of a female voice. I did not catch any actual words but the voice was definitely female.

I cautiously eased forward round the back of the next parked car. Then there came to me a sharp clear "Shh" sound.

'What's the matter with ya? Ya jumpy. It's the wind or something. There's no one here.'

Silence again for a few seconds as I stood routed to the spot.

'Come on, kiss me again,' whispered the Irish voice, clearly audible on this occasion.

I eased forward as I tried to orientate myself and determine the precise direction from which the sound had come. At the same time I prepared to reveal

myself, if necessary, and make a lot of noise and act in a stupid drunken manner to hopefully cover and excuse my presence should I accidentally give myself away.

'Quiet, there's someone coming,' whispered the male voice.

'I hear nothing. It's you that's jumpy this time.'

'Shut up.'

He was right, there was someone coming. I could quite clearly hear something myself and I knew it wasn't me. I stood very still. The noise increased as it came closer; until I could clearly hear footsteps as someone walked between the cars and across the car park. The shuffling suddenly stopped and then a few moments later, a car door slammed, an engine fired, lights came on and a car pulled out of the car park. As it turned towards the entrance the headlights swept across everything in a wide arc. I ducked down and watched as Johnson's van was illuminated, along with all the other vehicles in the vicinity. It was not too far from where I was standing and there were maybe, at a guess, six or seven cars between it and me. I saw little else after that as I ducked down further in an attempt to avoid the full beams as they passed over me. When darkness returned I could see nothing in my immediate surroundings except a mass of coloured lights, which registered in my brain from the collapse of my retina; a temporary, though annoying few seconds of blindness following the strong glare of light.

I guessed the couple must be somewhere in front of me, but where: three, four or maybe five cars away? Perhaps by Johnson's van. I really couldn't be sure, as I had seen nothing of them in the short stab of light from the car headlights. That was probably because they too, no doubt, had dodged out of the direct glare as quickly and instinctively as I had. I stood with my eyes closed tight and cursed the bright dancing lights for not subsiding as quickly as I wanted them to and all the time hoped that in my earlier enthusiasm, I had not got too close for comfort. Then I heard the female voice once again. I guessed about five cars distant. I held my breath and with my eyes now wide open I tried to force them to focus in the darkness. I felt I might be a bit too close for comfort.

'Jesus Christ yer hard!'

I heard him laugh lightly before he replied, 'And ready for it.'

'To be sure I bloody know dat with this lovely ting in my hand. Oh shit der's someone else coming now,' and as her curse drifted off into the wind, the darkness was once again shattered by headlights.

This time it was from a car swinging off the road and entering the car park. I quickly closed my eyes to prevent a repetition of last time and simultaneously dropped down out of sight to avoid detection. I assumed the other two somewhere out there in front of me, and for slightly different reasons, did the same. As I waited for the bright light to extinguish I found myself smiling as I imagined them both bent down and trying to balance with knickers and trousers down around their ankles.

When the darkness once again returned and all was relatively peaceful, except for the wind, the female voice was the first to say something. 'Where's Johnson's bloody van?'

'Over that way.'

'Well come on then; lets try dat. It's a bloody waste of time here.'

I stood and listened as their footsteps moved away and the noise, from the crunching of the gravel underfoot, diminished. I waited a few moments and then, when I thought it was safe, I tiptoed in the direction where I now knew Johnson's van was parked. As I cautiously approached I heard the sound of the van door open and a lowered, and now familiar, female voice say, 'I know he does not always lock it up now, and when he comes to the pub he leaves da dog to look after da kids at home.'

Shortly after that there came a faint metallic creaking sound, which I assumed came from the van as it gave way to the weight of the two of them as they climbed in, and then that was followed by the creak of a door closing behind them.

Once again I moved forward and rounding the rear of the next car. From there I could just make out, and recognise the shape of Johnson's van. I listened but heard nothing.

Satisfied, for the moment at least, that I felt I knew why they had chosen Johnson's van, I decided to withdraw. It was obvious, unless I was badly mistaken, that they would be preoccupied with each other for some time, and that as a result I was not about to learn anything of further value to us. I turned and quietly retraced my footsteps back to the pub door.

Once inside the light almost blinded me yet again and I had to hesitate for a moment to adjust. It was becoming a habit and one that I decided I did not appreciate, as not only was it annoying but the inability to focus properly had made my head ache. I was still blinking when I sat down.

'Where have you been?' asked Fred with an air of innocence and aimed at those sat within earshot.

'I just popped outside for a breath of fresh air. I didn't feel too good for a moment just then. Perhaps something I ate or the smoke in here. The beer's OK, I think, so what it is I just don't know. But I feel better now,' I lied.

'Before you settle down you are just in time to come with me for some drinks. It's my round,' said Fred, standing up and pulling at my hand.

She had obviously made the move on purpose but for what reason I had no idea so turning to follow her I said, 'Yes, Oh great white mistress. Your slave does as you command and especially when you are paying. Mine's a double.'

As we crossed the room, Fred enquired, 'Anything?'

'Yes. They are having it away in Johnson's van.'

'What, the two of them?'

'Yes of course, I can't see her going to all that trouble to be out there doing it on her own!'

'You know what I mean, Raines wife and that guy who was standing here at the bar? Them two?'

'Yes. They are both in the back of Johnson's van now, making sweet music, or they were when I came back in just now.'

'Lucky girl! No one ever had me in the back of a van.'

I gave her rear a sharp slap and said, 'Go across and ask Johnson if you can go next. He might be taking bookings.'

* * *

Eventually the darts were over and sandwiches were being passed around for distribution between the players and their supporters. A few from each of the teams had left as soon as the game was over, while of those who remained were now either stood against the bar, or had moved over to pull up stools and sit nearer the centre of the room with the women folk.

Johnson had drawn up a stool and was sat opposite his wife and while the remainder of the group all talked across each other or in some cases over each other, the pair of them continuously bickered and sniped, throwing insults back and forth and all in sufficient volume for the entire pub to hear. Scampton, the Park Ranger, took a drink over to Jenny, and sitting down beside her, kissed her full on the lips. Johnson stopped in mid sentence and turning his attention on Scampton, raised his voice even louder, as if what he was saying was definitely intended for the whole bar, and sniped, 'Be getting his end away tonight he will,' and laughing out loud, followed it up with, 'Into something a bit younger these days aren't ya?'

Further abuse or follow up, if there was going to be any, was instantly cut short by the verbal admonishment and foul looks from behind the bar.

Raines remained standing with his back against the bar and a drink in his hand. Whilst most laughed or passed a remark at Johnson's statement he said nothing and just stood passively surveying the whole room.

While this was taking place Fred casually changed the film cassette in the camera and stuffing all the wrapping paper and empty cartridge into her bag lowered the whole lot onto the floor at the side of the table.

The Forestry Worker, for whom I had earlier bought a drink, came up to our table and pulling up a vacant stool, settled down beside us.

'You on holiday then?' he enquired, looking at each of us in turn.

'Yes,' said Fred and I, almost together.

'And what about you?' he enquired of Eddie.

'No. I am a rep currently working this area. I am not lucky enough to be on holiday.'

'You all friends then?'

'Well yes and no! We didn't know each other before we came here, but since then we have met up and have spent some time in each others company, mainly here in the pub.'

He seemed satisfied with our explanation and did not pursue the subject further.

'We lost, they won, but then we always do,' he said.

'Oh, the darts you mean. You lost you say? I'm sorry about that,' said Fred. 'Why do you always seem to loose?'

'Simple. Useless players. Useless captain. Not a bit like it was in the old days, when everyone played to win. Back then if you were beaten, you were beaten fair and square and by better players than you and you accepted it. Him at the bar, he's supposed to be captain, doesn't even live in the village. Doesn't give a damn. Comes in here, gets pissed then drives home and can't play darts to save his life. The fat one over there,' Indicating Johnson. 'No better and an ignorant sod. Slut of a wife. Them two alone, just being in here, puts a damper on everything. He can throw very fair darts, I will give him that, but we could do without his mouth and we would all be much happier if he would leave her at home.'

'What about your colleague over there with the young lady in the silver grey coat? Is he in your team?'

'Who? Him there?' Indicating with a nod of his head, towards Scampton.

'Yes. Doesn't he work with you as well as play darts in your team?'

'Hell no! I'm Forestry: he's Parks. Big difference. He's nowt but a nuisance round us he is; works for a different set up altogether, he does. Shouldn't come into the forest unless he needs to buy something for Parks and then he should go to the office, but he's there all the damn time. Drives round where he shouldn't and asks no one. Our boss complains but says nowt about it to his boss and that one there takes no notice of him. Thinks he owns the damned place, way he behaves sometimes. About time somebody sorted him out if you ask me. You see he's Parks and we're Duchy and we are nowt to do with him and he should keep away from us. Parks and Duchy aren't the same and don't mix and never will.'

'Duchy?'

'Yes Duchy; that's us and he is Parks and works for the County Council. We are Forestry, which round here, is all owned by the Duchy of Lancaster, so we are Duchy. Like I said, he has nothing to do with us, and us nothing to do with him, but you try and tell that arrogant sod.'

'So he's a bit of a nuisance then?'

'More than that, like I said, he drives up and down as if he is some sort of big boss around her. He is always in the woods scrounging and begging or nicking timber. He digs and takes leaf mould, without asking, when he shouldn't. Probably sells it for gardens or something. He must do something like that, the amount he

takes. What's more; only the other day we heard that some people had complained that he had stopped them going through somewhere, when it is not down to him to do that. No, he's certainly no friend of mine or is he of any of the lads I work with. We've no time for the likes of him and his kind.'

Fred nudged me and jerking her head in the direction of the door, drew my attention to the fact that Raines wife had just come back in and was walking across the room. She went straight up to the bar and ordered a drink. When served the Park Ranger tossed some money onto the bar, and picking up their glasses they then both took their drinks and went and sat down with the others. They joined in the conversation as if they had been there all the time and that nothing out of the ordinary had happened. There was no sign of the guy she originally left to meet outside.

'What do you make of all that?' said Fred.

'Make of what my dear?' answered the Forestry Man.

'Nothing!' said Fred, who obviously on the spur of the moment had forgotten the Forestry Man was still sitting there, but quickly recovered and changed the subject by adding. 'Whose turn is it to get the drinks this time and get this gentleman one at the same time?'

'Not me love, Ta. I have to watch my drinking, as I explained to this chap here earlier.'

'The free ones don't count if I remember rightly?' I reminded him, and we both laughed.

CHAPTER THIRTY-FOUR

In line with the arrangements we made before we parted the previous evening, Eddie came to our caravanette the following morning, for the express purpose of discussing and planning our next moves. We all felt fairly confident that something significant would happen on the night of Wednesday the sixth or the early hours of Thursday the seventh. With a bit of careful thought and planning, we felt, we just might be lucky and come up with something of significance and value.

'We are all agreed then that we expect something, or more to the point, someone to land something ashore here, in the cove, in the early hours of Thursday. In which case, we need to stake out the spot well in advance and allow ourselves sufficient time to do it, without arousing any suspicions among the locals. With there being only the three of us, we will have to split up and each take a vantage point and simply stay out of sight and watch them. We can use your radios Eddie, if that's OK by you and with them all being on the same fixed frequency and short range, if we keep usage down to bare essentials, we should reduce the risk of detection. Do you both agree so far?' Fred and Eddie both said nothing but nodded their agreement.

I unfolded and spread the map out on the table and as we all leaned forward for a closer look, Eddie said, 'You know the area better than me. Where do you think the best vantage points are?'

'One on either side and one down at the bottom should give the best coverage,' suggested Fred. 'If one of us goes to the North and gets well out of sight on the cliff top, near where Edison's gear was found, they should have a clear view of anything approaching the coast from the seaward side. One down the bottom of the ravine, hidden in the scrub, which is fairly thick and should offer good cover, will be able to observe what, if anything, goes on, down there on the beach. Then one to act as an anchorman, hidden somewhere at the top of the ravine, on the other side of the Car Park I suggest, away from the road. From there, who ever it is, can keep an eye on all comings and goings, again if there are any, in that area. Don't forget, it is one thing to know what is happening down on the beach; but it is essential that we know what is happening regarding comings and goings up at the top. Anything that happens down there has to start and finish either at the top of here,' pointing at the map, 'or out at sea. We cover the seaward side from up here, the beach from somewhere down here and the top from here.'

'So who does what and goes where?' I enquired.

'I'm the least familiar with the whole area,' said Eddie. 'So stick me up top there, out of the way, and you two choose between here and here.'

'Ok with you Fred?'

'Yes, fine! Where do you want me?'

'Will you do the Car Park end and I will go down and look after the beach. That's if everyone agrees?'

I was glad they did and raised no major objections for although I did not, for one single moment, doubt Fred's competence, I felt much happier at the thought of her well hidden in the woods behind the Car Park and as far away as possible from anyone prowling about and possibly up to no good in the dark.

'What about some extra help?' Eddie suggested. 'Some unknown bodies in some unmarked cars parked at the end of the lane for example, or in the village? If we want, it can easily be arranged.'

'I am sure it could, but I don't think it would help,' replied Fred. 'If these people have done this sort of thing before, and I am pretty sure they have, and on more than one occasion, then they would expect everything to appear normal and that, I imagine, includes for there to be no one else but them around at that time of night. If suddenly, on this particular night, there are cars running around the village and surrounding districts, or for that matter, cars simply parked in places where they are not usually found, I should think they would immediately smell a rat and probably call the whole thing off. I am just trying to think it through like I feel they might, and I know that if I was onto something risky the slightest thing out of place and I would back off straight away and call it all off.'

'I agree and think it is very much down to the three of us so let's work it out on that basis,' I suggested. 'Firstly, we will need to know who is coming and going in the main group, and what sort of back up, or support they have. That is if there is a group or for that matter if there is any back up. For all we know it might only be a simple, one man, operation when it comes down to it, but from what we have gathered we suspect a group, but we don't know that for certain. That will be down to you Fred.'

'OK. I should be able to do that, no problem, from somewhere where we were the other night behind that big rock. Leave that one with me.'

'Should be as good a place as any, if you are happy with it? It's a good vantage point and you will be able to see the lane leading to the Car Park, the Car Park itself, the Pub and also the start of the track down to the beach and at least you will be in the safest place.'

'Chauvinist pig! The safest place: what are you saying? I will not be safe and be frightened, anywhere else, out there all alone in the dark? Who the hell do you think I am? Some prissy miss frightened of the dark?'

'OK, back off dragon lady, I'm sorry. I know you are capable of looking after yourself, and I didn't mean anything by what I said.'

I had lied of course and knew very well I had lied and shuddered at the thought of anything nasty happening to that girl. She was also right of course, I am an old fashioned chauvinist pig, always have been and always will be. Anyhow how could I help my feeling towards her?

'Knock it off you two,' Interrupted Eddie. 'You sound like a couple of lovesick school kids. Let's establish, here and now, that she is a big girl and can look after herself, even behind the bike sheds.'

'Look, I'm sorry. I didn't mean to suggest anything. You go where you want and Eddie and I will go where you decide to send us.'

'Now this is daft and getting us nowhere fast! OK, I'm sorry also. Perhaps it was me and I over-reacted. We only need one chief on this job, so come on, Mel it's your plan. So what's next? I go into the woods, OK, so what happens then?'

'Well, as long as you're sure you're happy; you stake out the Car Park and I will toss a coin with Eddie for who goes up and who goes down.'

'Are you deaf, daft or just plain stupid?' snapped Fred. 'You're making the decisions therefore for God's sake make them. This, toss you for this, toss you for that, is getting us nowhere fast. I go into the woods at the back of the Car Park, with a radio and note comings and goings and tell you two. Now who goes to the cliff top?'

'I will,' said Eddie, 'as originally agreed.'

'OK, I will take the bottom. Everyone happy and agreed so far?'

No one commented while Fred tutted and shook her head from side to side; so I continued, 'We will get ourselves into position at least two hours before we expect anything to start. I figure this is necessary because we don't want there to be any signs of activity on our part, should any of their people happen to turn up early, or for that matter, already be hanging around in the area; say in the Pub. Let's face it, we don't know at this point in time, how, or if, the Pub is involved, or if they do meet early for these operations, or turn up as a group or casually come together as individuals and at different times. They may even have their own lookout strategically placed well in advance for all we know.'

'Can we not get into position from any other angle, apart from the top of the ravine here?' suggested Eddie as he firstly looked at, and then pointed to, the map.

'We could go North along the main road here and approach your position by coming back South along the cliff top path,' said Fred as she traced the coastline with her finger. 'But I need to be around here somewhere so I can easily reach my position by setting off from here and simply ducking down behind the wall and skirting the Car Park. The only way Mel can get to the bottom of the ravine is by the direct route, down the path, or by going the way he went the last time, and that is diagonally through the undergrowth on the South side of the ravine here. Either way, we have to more or less approach it from this general direction. So I think we

have no choice but to make an early start and be prepared for a long wait to get any results.'

I agreed and Eddie said nothing.

'Right, so now let's consider what we need to take? Obviously a radio each and checks can made before we leave. We use the same call signs we used last time for identification purposes. Then we should perhaps take a bit of something to eat and definitely a flask each. We must also get well wrapped up, for I have a feeling that it will be a long cold night. You take the glasses with you Eddie, as you will be the furthest away and will probably have more use for them than us.'

'Thanks, but I have my own.'

'Fine. In that case you take ours Fred.'

'Eddie, you mentioned that your radios have detachable ear pieces, am I right?' asked Fred.

'Yes, they have both a single ear piece attachment and an ear piece with mike attached, so that you can leave the radio in its carrying case attached to your belt or slung round your neck, or in your pocket, and just press the button on the microphone to transmit. Do you want me to bring them along?'

'It might be as well for I was just thinking; what would happen if someone, for some reason, came very close to you or where you were hiding and in the dead quiet, your radio started squawking. You would be in the proverbial and very deeply.'

'You're right Fred,' said Eddie. 'A radio belting out would certainly drop you in it. I'll bring them along. That also reminds me of something else regarding the radios that might be important now you mention blown cover. If we transmit when we are out there and don't get an immediate reply, we must remember not to pursue the issue and carry on repeat calling. We have already agreed that there maybe the slight chance that someone might be close enough to hear, but more important, it may not be convenient to reply, because to open your mouth would give yourself away, even if you whispered. So can we agree that if you get no reply to your call, accept there is probably good reason for it, and leave it a reasonable length of time before calling again? Let's say anything up to as much as three or four minutes might be well worth considering. Finally, if you are in a tight spot and calling to answer would only add to your problems, press the transmit button rapidly three times, that will indicate – Wait. If however you require immediate assistance, then press rapidly more than six times. Do we agree?'

'Yes,' we said together.

'Good, so I will bring the radios and attachments,' reaffirmed Eddie, 'and my own bits and bats and I can probably get hold of a sandwich or something, in the Pub, for later.'

'No, forget that. I will sort out the food side of things,' said Fred.

'Is that it then? OK, so finally, where exactly, and at what time do you propose we meet up before we set off?'

'Fred and I will meet you, some time close to eight o'clock, in the Pub.'

'Right, I will go and get my gear together and see you down here about eight.'

'Are you going to come in your car?'

'Why? I can if you want.'

'Well I was thinking. If you brought your car, you could park it here alongside us, somewhere tight up under the wall, out of the way, or at least sufficiently so that in order to see it from the road, it would be necessary to climb part way up the wall and look over the top. Anyone looking through the gate would not see it as it would be blocked off from view by our van. Then if we should need a vehicle later on, it would be more convenient and less conspicuous on the road than our big van.'

'I agree; it's a good idea. So we will do that. I will bring the car with me but for now, if there is nothing else, I will leave you two to get ready and see you in the Pub around eight o'clock. I will give you time to get in first and get yourselves a drink then I will come in. It should look a bit more casual and less of a planned thing if we do it that way, although I don't know why I am worrying about it really, because I think that by now we have been seen around together often enough for no ones suspicions to be unduly aroused. I don't think anyone will bother if we meet in the Pub, and eat together; do you? Then when the Pub closes, we can come back here for a night cap, kill some time and get our stuff together and then set off from here; about what time do you think? Half past one, two o'clock?'

'I reckon about two in the morning. From what we know or assume, they have planned their operation to start an hour before High Water. We calculate that to be at four in the morning, as high water, according to the way I worked it from the tide tables, is at five. So I reckon we need to be in position by two. After that, all I hope is that it stays fine.'

'You and me both, as the last thing I want, is for us to all be out there in the pouring rain,' said Eddie as he stood up and prepared to leave. 'See you both in the Pub just after eight. So long for now.'

The door closed behind him.

'Put the kettle on Mel and then move out of the way so that I can see what we have to make into sandwiches for tonight, otherwise it is up to the village for you.'

'Why the kettle? You're not making flasks up so soon are you?'

'No, of course not silly! I just need a drink now, but I can at least be getting the things together for the sandwiches later.'

I sat at the table and studied the map while Fred went through the cupboards and produced a variety of tins, containing goodness knows what, then bread, butter

and a range of other bits and bats. I concentrated on the map and tried to see if there was any better way we could deploy ourselves, but as always it is one thing looking at a map and another the reality of the terrain actually out there. In the end I decided we were better off sticking with what we were familiar with and not making any last minute changes. I folded the map and put it to one side.

By this time Fred was, more or less, confining her activities to one small area so I began rummaging through my gear, selecting the warmest clothing that I could find, for I knew there might well be a long, chilly night ahead.

'I am going to wear everything I can lay my hands on,' said Fred over her shoulder. 'Because I think that not only will it be cold out there tonight but if we are going to be more or less confined to one spot for any length of time, then it will play havoc with the circulation and I always find it harder to concentrate when I am bodily cold. Also if it's very cold one small flask each won't help much. Which reminds me, shall I put some booze in them?'

'That's a good idea. At least if we are destined to eventually freeze to death it will be nice to do so under the influence,' I laughed.

Whilst poking around in the small cupboards and lockers, looking for anything that I thought might come in useful, I came across a pack of playing cards that I had not seen before.

'Whom do these belong to?' I enquired, as I continued to search in the cupboard while holding out my right hand and the cards.

'Are they yours?' asked Fred.

'No.'

'Then they must be mine.'

'Cards?'

'Yes, I often carry a pack around when I'm on assignment and I got those a while back when I was in the village. They help to break the monotony sometimes. I am a dab hand at patience and it often makes a change from reading, especially if there is no radio or television handy.'

'How come I haven't seen them before?'

'Either because you haven't looked in there since I got them or I have not been sufficiently bored to need to use cards to occupy myself. Do you play?'

'No. Not seriously. I tend to get bored with the majority of card games. I tend to see them as a valuable waste of brain power that serves no useful purpose, and all that jazz.'

'Oh, I love to play and to play to win, but not for money or high stakes or anything serious like that. In fact I don't gamble much at all. But I do play a mean game for Matches or Smarties and I have been tempted in the past to cheat a little to win the odd extra toffee.'

She placed two mugs of freshly made tea on the table and sat down opposite me, 'What did you do with those cards?'

'I put them back where I found them.'

'What time is it now?' she enquired as she consulted her watch. 'Come on, we have plenty of time, so get them out again and I will show you how quickly I can win this box of matches off you,' reaching, as she said so, for the box of matches from beside the cooker. 'I go wild and mean when matches are up for grabs.'

I reached for the cards while Fred divided the matches into two equal piles. Then having removed the cards from the box I placed the pile in the middle of the table.

'OK pardner, whadda we play in this 'ere joint?' Which came out sounding nothing like the American Wild West accent that I had tried to emulate.

Laughing, Fred attempted her version of a Bar Room drawl, 'It's good to tell you are no bar room bum, otherwise pardner you would know, that there is only one game a high class Moll like me can play, for high stakes like matches, in a bar room like this and that is Pontoon. I trust you know how to play Pontoon, pardner?' Then in her normal voice she added, 'because I don't know how to play Poker or what ever it was those cowboys were supposed to play. So it will have to be Pontoon or nothing. You do play?'

'Yes. I have been know to play the game on very rare occasions.' Which was only true of recent times. During my days as a Serviceman, I had, on numerous occasions, ended a very long, hard session of Pontoon with my barrack room pals, minus all my pay and that weeks free issue of cigarettes, and had to borrow to survive to the next pay day.

'Prepare to be beaten and made matchless,' she challenged.

An original concept and a new slant on a very old game, I thought. Matchless? I don't think I could recall having been made matchless before. Cashless. Cigarette-less. Yes. But matchless, no, I don't think so. Perhaps this would be the experience to complete my education and make me truly a man of the gambling world. I didn't know at the time what a pleasant surprise I was in for and what being matchless, in Fred's terms, really meant.

I was to quickly find out.

We played the standard game, as I knew it. The Bank changing hands with each Pontoon and the matches passing back and forth as the amount staked and the individual wins and losses, dictated.

'There you are, you're broke again,' said Fred, for the second time as she sat back and beamed with satisfaction and gloated over the pile of matches heaped up in front of her.

'That's the second time you have lost everything to me. The first time I felt sorry for you, as I knew you were up against a superior player but this time you've had it. I am not going to lend you anything anymore. You will have to declare yourself bankrupt and turn all your assets into matches and pay off all your debts

to me. You owe me twenty-two matches and from what I have seen, your whole assets are not worth that much, so you are well and truly wiped out. You're dead pardner.'

'Sad. Perhaps if it had been a different game?'

'Playing with what? You have no stake. You're broke. I hold all the matches. You're wiped out, Grundy. Skint. Broke. Finished. Gamblers Anonymous is all that is left for you.'

'I could give you my I.O.U.'

'Backed by what? You have nothing. You don't even own a single tube of Smarties or a packet of Chocolate Drops or anything else worth gambling for.'

'There must be something. I have some loose change.'

'I don't gamble for money. Cash is strictly for spending. So you can spend that on me later.'

'So that's it. I'm ruined, finished, and will never be able to hold my head up in public ever again or sit down to another respectable game of cards. Ruined by a scheming female who robbed me, not only of all my strength, my virginity and my dignity, but now all my matches, and having thrown me deeply into debt, will now not give me one last chance to redeem myself.'

'Right first time, although I would challenge the virginity bit. But either way, that's it.'

'Not one last tiny chance,' I pleaded.

'Be very careful because if you push your luck too much, I might just take you up and ruin you completely.'

'Oh, yes please.'

'Right. If that's the way you want it. You have asked for it. One last chance. No more. My game. My rules. My stakes. Yes or No?'

'What's the game?'

'Yes or No?'

'I've no option have I? I face ruin and must go the way of all compulsive gamblers and say, yes. Do your worst wench.'

'Oh, I intend to.'

She drew the loose cards towards her and faced them up before tapping them into a neat block. She looked across at me with a mischievous look and a grin that made me more than a little apprehensive of what was to come.

'For this game, rule one, you sit on the floor.'

'On the floor? Why the floor?'

'My rules. No argument. The floor.'

We sat facing each other with legs stretched out in front and running parallel. There was not a great deal of room but in the small space between us Fred laid the pack of cards, face down, on the carpet.

'Cut once,' she instructed. 'Go on, anywhere you like. Split the pack in two and put the bottom half on top of all the others.'

When I had done so Fred reached over and picked up the whole pack. I watched closely waiting for what was to come next. She dealt three cards, all face down: one in front of herself, one in front of me, and a third to one side. The pack, still face down, she returned to the centre. I reached for my card.

'No. Not yet. Leave it. This one comes first,' as she reached out for the odd one set on the side and turned it over. 'It is the colour of this card that is important, not the suit or the value. We turn our cards over and try and match them for colour. The odd one out loses.'

'So that one there,' I said, pointing, 'is a red card. If you have a red card and I have black one, I lose, right?'

'Right.'

'But what if all three cards are red? Is that it, null and void?'

'No. If all cards are the same colour then their value comes into play. That odd one, there, would be the losing card. Let's have a trial run and I will show you what I mean and then it will all make more sense. Turn your card over.'

I did, and so did she.

'There you are. That one is red, yours is red. Mine is black. I lose. OK so far?'

'Yes.'

'Now let me sort out some cards to show you what happens when they are all the same colour.'

She picked up the pack and the loose ones we had just used and, rummaging through, selected three cards and placed them face down. Again there was one in front of each of us and one just to the side.

'Now suppose we had just been dealt these cards, this is what happens,' and reaching to the side she turned over the odd one, which this time was black. She turned over her own, which was also black and pointed to mine, 'Turn yours over.'

I did and it too, was black. So far so good: all three black.

'All black therefore all void on colour, there not being an odd one, so we look at face value. In this case, that one there is a seven, mine is a ten and yours is a two. You loose because ten is nearer seven than two. Two is the odd one out, being furthest away.'

'Ok, I follow that but what happens if that card was, say, a five and I had a six, and you had a four?'

'If they were all the same colour, then that would have to be void, because neither would be far enough away to be odd. So all you would do in that case, is pick up the cards, put them at the bottom of the pack and re-deal.'

'So who deals in the first place?'

'It doesn't matter when there are only two playing. With more players, the winner would claim his or her prize and then deal. But in this case, me, because it's my game and you're broke, remember?'

'What's this game of yours called, if it has a name?'

'Yes. It's called Odds and Evens, Highs and Lows, and it is played extensively and exclusively by very nice people.'

'Deal me in then.'

'Right, you social climber, but don't forget, still my game, my rules, and you will quickly find out what all that means, as we go along.'

I thought at that point that all she meant was that she intended to remain the dealer. I was wrong, there was much more to it than that.

Three cards were dealt and the rest of the pack placed to one side. The odd card was turned over. I remembered the rules… colour comes first. It was red. Fred turned hers over. It too was red.

'If mine is black, I loose?'

'You sure do.'

It turned out to be red.

'Ah, ah.'

'Not so fast: let's just see. The card there is a red Jack. Yours is a red eight and poor little me is left with a sad little red two. OK big boy, so you win this one, beginners luck. What would you like as your prize, my left or right shoe? You can only have one.'

'A shoe! You mean one of your trainers; one you are actually wearing?' I said, half in disbelief and half in amazement and all with a strong feeling of excitement running through me. The game definitely had potential and was certainly different from anything I anticipated and nothing like the one we had previously played and which had cost me so many matches. The stakes had apparently changed quite dramatically and already I was apparently winning and being offered a shoe as my prize.

'That's what I said.'

'I will have the right one please.'

She unlaced her right trainer, pulled it off, and handed it to me. As I took it she smiled and said, 'Make the most of it, it is all you are going to get.'

She picked up the pack of cards and placing the three exposed ones on the bottom of the pack, dealt three more, face down.

The odd one this time, was black. Fred turned over hers, and it too was black. Mine was red.

'What did I tell you. The shoe was just beginners luck. Your jumper please.'

'My jumper; that's not fair, all I got was this trainer.'

'You're broke; remember. Lost all your matches. My game, my rules, your jumper.'

I began to get the feeling that there might be an element of, not only biased and perhaps slightly unfairness about this game, but that there was definitely something tantalising and rather exciting. I arched forward and grasped the waistband of my jumper. Fred put her hand on my shoulder, to stop me.

'My game, my rules, remember darling. Normally when you win, you nominate your prize, and then you collect it. The exception being, that you cannot demand anything that necessitates the removal of something else to get at it. You understand what I mean? You cannot ask for a sock, for example, until you have won the shoe. But this is my game, and for this game only, I have altered the rules slightly to deter you from gambling forever. So in this particular game, if you win, you get what you are given. You cannot select. On the other hand, if I win, I will nominate what I want from you, and will take it. So lean forward, so that I can have my jumper, there's a good boy.'

I had a single shoe on the floor beside me. She had my jumper.

'Would it make you fell any better if you dealt the cards?' she mocked, offering me the pack.

'No, you seem very capable. I will let you know if I would like a change. That's if it is in your rules?'

'It might be, but you will soon find out when you ask.'

Two reds and a black this time: so without batting an eyelid, she took my T-shirt.

'Learnt your lesson over gambling yet?'

'Learning,' I grinned.

Two reds and a black again: I got the other trainer casually tossed over to me.

Three blacks, two sevens and a four. I got a sock.

Two reds and a black again: I got the other sock.

Another deal, and three more cards were turned face up.

'Mine this time,' beamed Fred. 'What shall I have this time?'

'You will have to have a shoe and like it. Everything else means taking something else off first. Hard luck sweetheart. Your rules, remember?'

'The game's not over yet,' she smiled as she slowly untied my shoe. 'There's a long way to go before I'm beaten and I can always change the rules again, if it suits me.'

Three blacks and much to my surprise they were four, five, and six. The first null and void game: no problem, just start again.

Three more blacks which cost me a sock, as the value of my card was the furthest away from the spare.

'Why not the other shoe?'

‘The sock! It’s bare flesh that I’m after.’

The next deal was equally as unsuccessful for me and cost me my other shoe, but then my luck changed.

‘Two reds and a black,’ I gloated. ‘What trinket would madam care to dispense with and toss my way, this time?’

I got a sweet smile and a jumper. That meant it would have be, the T-shirt or jeans next.

It wasn’t, it was my other sock that went. Only my trousers and underpants were left. Things were not going my way, or were they?

A two for Fred, an eight and a ten, and all black cards, assured me of yet another prize. Would it be her T-shirt or the jeans that joined my meagre pile of trophies?

‘Do I have a choice?’ I asked meekly.

‘No you don’t. But if you had, which one would you take?’

‘The T-shirt; bare flesh and all that, remember?’

She smiled and standing up and with slow deliberate movements casually dropped her jeans. Finally stepping out of them she said, ‘Still my game, still my rules,’ and dropped them over my head and sat down again.

She certainly knew how to play this game and I could hardly contain myself as I waited for the next deal.

My odd black card looked very lonely against the other two reds, and naturally cost me my trousers.

At this stage I suppose I should have been apprehensive, or at least a little bit concerned, but I wasn’t. In actual fact, I was enjoying every single minute of it all.

My luck returned when, from three more black cards, I drew a three. Fred an eight, and the odd card, when turned over, turned out to be a five. If I had had a choice at that stage, I would have gone for the panties, but I was once again reminded that I was not making the rules, and would have to settle for the T-shirt. The decision made, it was removed and casually tossed in my direction.

I needed just one more win to even things up. I needed two outright wins to be the overall winner.

Fred dealt me a card, then one to her-self, and a third, which she laid to one side. The pack was carefully placed in the centre. She reached out and slowly turned over the odd card… a red Jack.

‘Go on, yours next,’ she said with a mischievous grin.

‘Your rules again I suppose,’ I said smiling.

‘Right every time! My rules.’

I turned over my card… It was red and an eight. Good, I thought because if Fred has a red, at least an eight is very close to the Jack.

She half lifted the card, curving it slightly in the middle, so that she was able to see it, but I was not.

'Stand up,' she said triumphantly. 'This will teach you to gamble.'

As I slowly got up I said, 'I bet you're cheating me, let me have a look at that card.'

'No. My rules, remember?' as she leant across and grasping hold of each side of my underpants, tugged a little at a time, using alternate hands to slowly ease them down. She was very close, and from her kneeling position looked up at me as I looked down into her mischievous eyes. They sparkled as she ran the tip of her tongue round the inside edge of her lips before whispering, 'I win.' Then dropping her chin she shot forward and kissed me and then with the tip of her tongue traced an excruciatingly delightful track along the length of the most sensitive part imaginable.

'Now who's a big boy? Who has just learnt a valuable lesson and is now standing very proud the result of it?'

She raised herself up and wrapping her arms around my neck and pressing very close, whispered in my ear, 'Game over. There are no more rules.'

The bra and panties soon joined the rest of the discarded clothing littering the floor and both arrived there without the turn of a single card.

* * *

Passions eventually subsided and as we came up for air we realised that time was catching up on us, and that we still had some other rather important things to do.

Whilst dressing and sorting out my belongings, I noticed the cards were still scattered and lay as we had finished with them. Fred's last card was as she had left it; isolated from the others and still face down. Curiosity got the better of me and a strange inner compulsion left me with a desperate need to know what it was. Something drew me towards it and I just could not resist. I reached down and turned it over. It was red. I could hardly believe it, red, the same as the other two. I let it drop and reached out and taking hold, gently drew her very close to me and with a long gentle kiss, muttered, 'It was red, you cheated.'

'Look again, lover,' she whispered.

I retrieved the fallen card and looked again, it was a nine.

'Damn, a nine.'

'See,' she said, digging her nails into my buttock.

We laughed and kissed, 'You cured now?'

'Definitely. Lend me a box of matches and I will prove it. I will never be able to look upon the humble match or a pack of playing cards in quite the same light ever again.'

'You put those matches back in the matchbox and put them where they belong. They're all mine and live beside the cooker.'

I picked up my jumper and while I struggled to get it over my head, casually enquired, 'Can I ask where you learnt and mastered that particular game of cards?'

'No you can't, but even you must admit, it is a good way to pass the time. We found it useful when we played it at college, particularly when funds were low, and we couldn't afford other things. It's a game that any number of players can play. You just vary the rules a little, to suit the circumstances. If an odd number play, there is no need for the odd card to be places to one side. The only snag is that when a few play, there are quite a few void hands, but then the game lasts longer. So it all depends on what you want out of it. Bare flesh is the name of the game. When I was younger and again in college and where we tended to play the game in groups, we had one golden rule. You were a complete looser and dropped out when you got down to just panties or underpants. After all we were very well brought up young ladies in those days and very civilized in such matters. Boobs for the boys were OK but nothing more.'

'Oh yes, very civilized and what did the girls get?'

'A good snog with the guy of their choice and no more.'

'Oh yes. All very civilized, I can tell. Are you ready yet? It is almost eight o'clock and we should be out and away from here by now.'

'You go if you want, if you're ready. Then at least one of us will be on time. I still have to attend to one or two bits and bats. I still need to comb my hair and go to the loo before I'm ready to go anywhere. I will see you across in the Pub.'

'Will you be OK?'

'Of course I will, silly. If I am to spend all night, tonight, hidden alone in the woods out there, I am sure I can find my way across a field to a Pub. Go and get yourself a drink and wait for me. At least I will get things done much faster with you out of my way.'

'See you in the Pub then,' I said as I stepped outside and closed the door behind me.

I headed across the field towards the gate and the general direction of the Pub. As I walked through the grass, I looked up at the sky and wondered what tomorrow would bring? Would there be more time for cards and lots of red nines? Beaten by a nine and with incredible results. I felt that from now on the Nine of Hearts would have a whole different meaning for me and would remain emblazoned on my heart for the rest of my entire worthless life. My imagination ran riot and I couldn't and didn't want to stop it. Among the multitude and jumble of images that danced before me, I could see myself fully clothed and slowly turning over a

red card, and saying in a very suave manner, to an already totally naked Fred, 'My rules this time darling, my rules. Undress me.'

The vision of her, so gorgeous and desirable and so clear in my minds eye, as I tramped across that field in a semi trance, began to blur and go all distorted and out of focus; only to reshape and reappear, as a clear picture of a very large Joker Card. As the image before my minds eye grew larger and the colours brighter, somewhere in the background and down in the depths of my subconscious mind, I could hear the seductive voice of Fred, whispering, 'Dream on darling. With that card; chance would indeed be a fine thing.'

I pushed open the pub door.

CHAPTER THIRTY-FIVE

Having rid myself of all the tantalizing daydreams and visions of Fred and dragging myself back to reality I closed the Pub door behind me. A quick glance at the wall clock told me it was a little after eight and although there were a few people in the bar, it was not quite as busy as I had expected it to be at that time. Maybe things would improve as the evening wore on. However, the fact that at this time, it was relatively quiet allowed me to choose a seat which I considered would be in a good location to observe the whole bar area and note the comings and goings of the clientele and staff.

I sat with a drink and while relaxing and enjoying the welcome warmth from the open fire looked around. Of those in the bar there was no one that I instantly recognised as being part of the group we were becoming familiar with. There were one or two that I recognised from previous visits and there was a couple I had seen before in the other Pub and one guy I had definitely seen about in the village. Of the remainder, two other couples and three single males, I had seen around at various times and I assumed to be locals while the other eight or nine were complete strangers and unknown to me. They all looked very ordinary and none of them had that furtive look about them. What ever a furtive look is supposed to look like? I was forced to smile to myself at the thought and began to wonder what the true definition of furtive might be. Was it men in Trilby hats, pulled down low on foreheads; cigarettes dropping from the corners of mean looking mouths; long overcoats; white topped shoes; black shirts; hand painted ties? That was it, I decided; or was it? Should the modern day furtive type be very smart in a well tailored suit and only give himself away by the tell tale gun holster creating a bulge under the left arm pit or the violin case propped against the bar. Or should he be the same but appear to be out of place because he carried a slim black briefcase possibly loaded with the tools of his trade? In that case what about the complete scruff with the possibility of a saw off shotgun hidden under his long dirty raincoat? Sadly if all those different types were possibilities I was out of luck this evening for no one remotely resembled any of those. They make it all so damned easy in films and books while all my lot looked so ordinary and perfectly innocent.

As I sat, lost in a world of my own, the door opened twice and on each occasion more strangers arrived. It opened for the third time or perhaps it was the fourth, I hadn't really been taking that much notice as I had long since surrendered to the heat of the fire and had been engrossed in my dogged, dreamlike determination to work out how to identify and pick out the baddies.

Sleep continued to tug at my brain, and I was doing little to prevent it, for I was increasingly enjoying the pleasures of drifting in and out of semi-consciousness and indulging in all the fantasy that went with it. Soon thoughts of baddies were overtaken by thought of Fred and the things she had done or might do and I was quite happy to stay right where I was forever. Sadly, delightful though that might be, it was not to last, for each time just when things were reaching a climax and the pleasure was at it's height, it would be rudely interrupted and I would immediately be thrown back into consciousness by the violent spasmodic jerking of my head as it fell to one side or lolled forward and my chin hit my chest. When this happened, which was extremely annoying and seemed to happen all too frequently, I would jerk upright and attempt a semi focused look around the room before once again allowing my eyes to close down yet again.

I was somewhere beyond the realms of reality and enjoying a particularly pleasant episode, where a strong theme of red and black playing cards seemed to be dominating the sexual sensations, when my head fell forward with an unusually heavy wrench. I sat bolt upright and shuffled in my seat, forcing my eyes to open and at the same time desperately trying to get them to focus and my brain back into gear, when I became aware of the door opening and someone coming through it. It was Fred and the sight of her jerked me willingly back reality. There she was: tall, slim and despite the chunky clothing, looking gorgeous and very sexy. As she walked across the room towards me I shuffled in my seat to ease my aching bum. Then it hit me, what exactly it was about her that made her so alluring and such a very vibrant, desirable, and sexy female. It was her walk; the way she carried herself and the way she moved.

Most girls carry themselves well and appear to do so quite naturally and without any effort, but odd ones seem to spontaneously exaggerate it without even being aware that they are doing so. The result can be, and is, absolutely devastating to the majority of normal, natural, rampant male observers, of which I confess to be one such creature, and an avid observer of the female form. If viewing the female form and the way it moves is an art form; then I am an artist or is it a voyeur? Anyhow, that wonderful way some girls have of walking, a technique where they place one foot directly in front of the other, thus causing their hips and thighs to twist and gyrate in a very sexy tantalizing manner. They look as if they are walking on an imaginary tightrope that might be a strand of barbed wire or have been covered with a mixture of slippery grease and broken glass.

I have no idea if they consciously know they move like that or if they have any idea of the sensations they cause whilst doing it, or, if they are aware, then do they do it naturally or have they learnt the art and perhaps consciously practice doing it? All I know is, that it makes them move, in this case across a room, in a very special and extremely attractive way.

A quick glance around, having torn my eyes away, confirmed that I was not the only one to appreciate that particular entrance. The scowls and looks of scorn on the faces of some of the women told me they too had noticed it.

Eat your heart out fella's, I thought. Not too long ago this gorgeous creature beat me at a very interesting game of cards.

Fully awake I smiled as she came up to the table.

'Hi!'

'Hi!' she replied, looking at my almost a full glass. Then, without another word, she changed direction and headed off towards the bar. She was even more tantalizing from behind and I watched her every move as she stood shifting her weight from one foot to the other and moving the rest of her body as she fidgeted slightly while stood against the bar. I noticed also that I was not alone and that the same view was being carefully studied and appreciated by all those males who could do so, and get away with it. Those who felt they could not, because of the company they were in, settled for the quick surreptitious glance whenever the opportunity presented itself or they thought they might get away with it.

She walked back, set her glass down on the table, kissed me on the cheek, and sat down beside me. I was not sure, but I could have sworn that the general level of conversation rose slightly after she sat down and the distraction she had caused, receded.

She took a sip of her drink before enquiring, 'Anyone in that we know?'

'Not in the true sense of those we're interested in. There are a few dotted around that I have seen about before. But I don't think there is anyone in that we are specifically looking for. But it's early yet. It's only twenty five past eight by my watch,' I said, double-checking with the clock on the wall.

'I noticed a few cars in the Car Park as I came across, but none that I recognised.'

'Do you know, when I came across I never looked.'

'Slipping darling. Good job you have me to take good care of you and look out for you.'

'And me. I am on the look out for you all the time. Even now,' said Eddie, who having just come in, came straight across and must have heard Fred's last remark. 'Drink everyone?'

I covered the top of my glass, using my flat hand, and shook my head.

Fred smiled, 'Not for me thanks Eddie. Just got mine.'

'Back in a tick,' he said as he turned on his heels and went to the bar. When he returned he put his glass on the table and pulled up a stool and sat down beside us.

'I put the car where we suggested and all my gear is in the boot. Before I left the village I checked out Johnson's house and his van was missing. It was not

in the village Pub Car Park, nor is it in the Car Park down here either. I checked both as I came past. No other vehicles, or anyone else, that I recognised either.'

'Fred checked out the Car Park as she came across and there was no one in then, that she recognised. Nor is there anyone in here that we readily recognise as being of special interest.'

'The waiting begins,' sighed Fred. 'But at least the surroundings are nice and I have the company of two gorgeous men to help pass the time. I hope we are going to eat soon; I am starving after what he put me through earlier.'

'Oh, and what was that, if one can diplomatically ask?' said Eddie, grinning.

'A very heavy game of cards, if you must know and for very high stakes,' I got in quickly before Fred could answer; for I thought she just might decide to be mischievous and elaborate. 'And what's more, I lost a whole half box of matches in the process and she was so mean that she wouldn't lend me any of them back so that I could carry on playing.'

'That is mean,' laughed Eddie. 'And so you are you telling me she ended up with all the matches and would not lend you a single one? Now that is very mean.'

'Very. But she's like that when we play cards.' And that is all you are going to find out, I thought, as I winked at Fred who smiled mischievously back.

'It was the Nine of Hearts that really got him and killed him in the end,' she said as she squeezed my knee under the table.

'Food then,' I suggested, hoping to get off the subject before Eddie had time to latch on and perhaps pursue the significance of the Nine of Hearts.

We moved across into the dinning area and sat down. Eddie handed the menu over to Fred and began, 'As it's going to be a long night, I fancy something substantial and filling; especially as it feels such a hell of a long time since I last ate.'

'I managed to find enough to make us all a sandwich before we set off and there are heaps for us to take with us. So you don't have to over stuff yourself now,' replied Fred without lifting her eyes from the menu.

We placed our order and chatted while we waited: most of it being irrelevant and for the benefit of our fellow diners. The food, excellent as always, was polished off in no time. We declined coffee and returned to the bar area. We were lucky for despite it having become quite busy we were able to find a vacant table.

'That worked out just right,' said Fred, as she began to push aside the empties.

An added bonus, that we did not fully appreciate until we sat down, was the fact that the table was fairly central and thus allowed us to have an almost perfect, all round, view of the Pub. I collected the empties and took them to the bar, where I ordered drinks.

On my return Fred observed, 'As far as I can see not much has changed while we were eating and no one, that we know, has turned up in the meantime.'

I looked around as I handed out the drinks and lowered myself onto a stool. People stood or sat in groups or were in couples. There were one or two single men up by the bar.

We laughed and chatted and kept a careful eye on the comings and goings of those around us. There was a steady stream of new arrivals and those who, for reasons known only to themselves, decided to leave. At one time new arrivals outstripped leavers and so the bar became much busier and all of them and unbeknown to them, were carefully scrutinised as, we hoped, we gave the impression of minding our own business. It was during this time and through our casual conversation that we discovered that Eddie was married and that his wife knew all about the complexities of his occupation, having been involved herself at one time, and therefore tolerating and understanding fully his long absences from home. All his close friends and relations believed, and accepted, that he made his living as an Insurance Broker and at one stage, funded and encouraged by his department, he had even taken a course in the principals of Insurance, so that he could maintain his cover if questioned closely.

He had, he told us, actually been offered commission when once cornered and left with no choice but to pursue an enquiry. Apparently something had happened and he could not wriggle out of it, so he passed it onto a legitimate broker who accepted it and offered to pay a commission.

'I might even take it up as a full time occupation, sometime in the future, if ever I have to leave this business,' he said quite seriously. 'I have long had visions of making early morning calls on households where I would be greeted warmly and enthusiastically by ladies in nothing but dressing gowns and see-through night gowns. You know how it is? The bored housewife: Husband gone to the office. Come in for coffee. Let's talk it over in comfort and all that. Insurance could be exciting? But knowing my luck, I would get all the old biddies, who all look like dried prunes and who wanted to seriously claim for their silicone implants which had finally slipped down and caused their feet to blow up and become enormous. Or their cat has gone missing and was last seen as part of someone's fur coat, or something equally disastrous. I can see it now, I would get all those who's husbands could not manage it and one look at them would tell me why.'

Fred laughed. 'Don't be despondent and so negative. You could always specialize. What about young women who needed to insure their sex drive or the shape of their legs or think about it; the size of there boobs. You could investigate their needs or claims and check them out and see if it was all accurate and true.'

Without showing any obvious signs of emotion or enthusiasm, Eddie said, very seriously, 'Do you think there is such a policy and that I would stand a chance? They do say you can insure anything, if you can afford the premium.

Perhaps I could waive my commission and offer special discounts to attract more business. If ever you hear of a company covering this sort of thing you promise you will let me know straight away?'

Fred was almost beside herself at Eddie's seriousness and through her laughter, promised, 'I certainly will, just for you Eddie.'

'And will you promise that all my clients will be just like you?'

'I will do my best, but can't make any firm promises just now.'

'Yes. Firmness. That's something else I could cover.'

We carried on with much of it along the same vein and we all laughed. I began to feel that some of it had a direct bearing on the fact that a certain amount of tension and apprehension was beginning to build within us. I know that was true in my case but I said nothing to the others and assumed they felt the same and based the assumption on the fact that we were indulging in increased frivolity and often slightly exaggerated laughter. Certainly much of what was being said was funny but sometimes the reaction was a little excessive.

'Last orders at the bar, Ladies and Gentleman please, thank you.'

'Well! What now? So far it has been rather a waste of time. No one has turned up here. In fact nothing has happened at all. Has it?' remarked Fred.

'Did you really expect them to?' I remarked, making rather a pathetic excuse to cover my own disappointment. Had I been honest with myself I was not really too sure how I felt at the way things had gone thus far. All I knew was that we had become increasingly nervous and edgy and all apparently for nothing.

'They have probably met up somewhere else and might well be planning their next moves right now, or they may not have even met up at all. Or if they are going to then perhaps later, as there's still a few hours to go before high water, so all we can do is go back to the van and wait until things quieten off round here, then move into our pre-arranged positions and be ready at the time we originally said.'

But instead we sat in the Pub, making no attempt to leave, for as long as we were allowed, mainly to kill time. When we finally left, we were among the last to go and it was approaching midnight.

'I wasn't sure if he was going to serve after time tonight, but having done so it has at least helped to pass some of the time and might also have told us something.'

'Like what?' Eddie asked.

'Well it struck me, that if the Landlord, or any of his close associates, are involved in any way, they may have wanted an early turn out so that the customers had every chance to be out of the way and well clear of the pub before now.'

'He may still be involved, despite carrying on tonight. For all we know, part of his cover may well be to act normally. If it is standard practice round here to go beyond closing time on a fairly regular basis, then to cut off dead on time

tonight, just might have attracted some unwanted attention or comment,' observed Fred.

'Perhaps your right.'

* * *

We sat in the van and talked while Fred made coffee. Eddie had collected his things from the back of his car and now placing the radios on the table, proceeded to arrange and sort them out.

'I have made sure that each one has a fully charged battery attached, so there will be no need to carry a spare. The amount of use we are likely to put them to, they will last at least eighteen hours. The headband slips over your head like this so that the earpiece sits over your left ear,' as he demonstrated by slipping on one of the headpieces. 'This mouth piece then twists round so that it comes to within about an inch of your mouth.' Again he demonstrated, twisting the arm that attached the mouthpiece to the earpiece so that both were aligned in the correct position. 'When the radio is on, you pick up and hear, anything transmitted on this frequency; providing of course you are in range. When you need to talk, you simply squeeze the mouth piece between your finger and thumb, top to bottom, like this and pass your message.'

He then proceeded to switch on all three sets and then placing the ear piece of each set, in turn, to his ear, depressed the transmit buttons on the mouth pieces, to satisfy himself that each one was working. Leaning one against the bulkhead of the van, he turned off the other two and laid them aside on the table.

'No need for individual radio checks now; they are all working.'

'Why leave that one stood there?' enquired Fred, pointing to the one leaning against the partition.

'Only that should anyone, by sheer chance, be using that particular fixed channel tonight, then we will pick them up on that set. I've disconnected the earpiece for now, so that the internal speaker is working and we will be able to hear it as we sit here; should anyone transmit. It's a long shot and the chances of it happening, I know, are very slim, but it might be worth the effort. It would be useful to know if anyone else is using this frequency, because if they are, not only would we hear them but later on they would be able to hear us and we don't want that, do we?'

'As we have now eliminated the need for radio checks, I suggest that when we each arrive on sight and we are set up and in position, we let the others know by clicking the transmit button, in the same way that we would do to acknowledge the end of a message received. But in this case I suggest we do it this way; I reckon you, Eddie, have the furthest to go, so once you are in position, give us a few minutes to ensure we are properly set up, then, you depress your button twice in

quick succession. Fred and I should pick that up and from that know you're settled in. If I am, at that time, in my position, I will send out two pairs of clicks, so you both know that I am set up and ready. If we don't send until properly in place, the others will know we are not ready. By that time you, Fred, should be set up and in your place and can acknowledge the fact by depressing three pairs of clicks. Don't anyone send until they are happy with where they are and have settled down to wait and of course are ready to receive. No verbal transmission at first. We have already agreed that there is always a slim chance that we might be monitored, so we must keep it all to the very minimum. No complex call signs as in standard practice. There are only three of us so Foxtrot, Mike and Echo should be enough. No excess and pass only cold hard facts, no explanations and try to avoid asking for repeats.'

Fred looked at Eddie then burst out laughing and gave me a mock salute, 'Yes Teacher, Captain, Sir. Three bags full Sir,' and turning to Eddie, 'You would think we had never been taught anything,' then back at me, 'We know the drill, sweetie.'

'Yes I know you do. I was just checking to make sure I could remember it,' I lied, and we all laughed.

Fred filled the flasks, including the extra one brought in by Eddie and handed out the packs of sandwiches. 'Anyone want a sandwich now, before we go?' she asked.

'Not for me, Ta,' I replied while Eddie shook his head and declined.

We each proceeded to don our outer protective gear.

I was a bit annoyed that my oilskins were so bright. They were ideal for all weathers and good protection against the cold but being a semi-luminous yellow made them highly unsuitable for blending in with a predominately green background, so weather or no weather, I was unable to wear them. Therefore should it rain heavily during the night I would inevitably end up rather wet. But at least the waterproof leggings that I proposed to use, as an alternative, and which had originally been bought for walking, would afford some protection for my legs and lower half. For my top, I would have to make do with two T-shirts, an extra thick jumper, and my dark anorak.

I zipped my anorak up to my nose, and eased my arms into the shoulder straps of my small hiking rucksack. I adjusted each straps until it sat comfortably over the extra layers of clothing. Next I slid a radio into my left hand pocket and brought the wire up across my left breast and donned the headset. Once in place and with the mouthpiece suitably adjusted, I topped off the whole lot with my round woolly cap. I finally put on my gloves and pressed the transmit button on the radio mouthpiece with my gloved hand. I heard the click in the earpiece and knew the radio was turned on and working and that I could operate it satisfactorily with a gloved hand.

'What was that?' said Fred with a startled expression.

'Sorry. That was me testing my radio, proves at least, yours is working.'

'So is mine,' echoed Eddie who had picked up the same click in his earpiece. 'Next time, will you do us all a favour and give us some warning before doing that.'

'I said I'm sorry. But at least it shows everything works. The next time we hear something it should be to let each other know that we are in position and ready to go. Everyone ready?'

'Ready,' said Fred, 'Just my gloves.'

A nod from Eddie confirmed that he was also ready.

'OK, you go first Eddie. Turn out the light Fred and then give it a minute, so that we adjust to the darkness outside. Anyone now looking in this direction and seeing the light go out, will, I hope, assume we have turned in for the night.'

We stood in the darkened interior of the van and apart from the rustling of clothing, as we each fidgeted, we made no sound. After a few moments the silence was broken as Eddie whispered, 'See you later,' and quietly opening the door he let himself out. He closed it behind him and slipped away into the night.

Fred touched my sleeve and then her fingers crept down until she held my hand. Her whole body weight pressed gently against mine as she whispered, 'Hold me.'

I half turned and we wrapped our arms around each other and stood silently in the dark. It was then that I realised just how much stress had slowly built up inside me. Up to that moment, no doubt because we had all been fairly busy and had covered our feelings with light-hearted chitchat, I had not been aware of it. But now as I stood in the darkness and could feel Fred very close, I was experiencing a great deal of tension, and a fair amount of apprehension. They were all feelings I have experienced many times before and all whilst waiting for the unknown. Feelings I have always kept very much to myself and feelings I have not talked about or even remotely felt ashamed of. Fortunately, from past experience, I knew they would all quickly melt away just as soon as I needed all my wits about me and things began to happen. But now I realised, and for the very first time, perhaps because I was holding Fred so close and had time to dwell on it, that maybe I was not alone with my feelings and that Fred was perhaps now experiencing very similar. We said nothing. We just stood and held each other and I know it made me feel a damned sight better. I hoped it had a similar effect on her.

'Time for you to go sweetie: Eddie should be well along the track by now,' she whispered, easing herself free. I leaned forward, without thinking, to give her a peck on the lips and almost ended up with my mouthpiece stuck up my nose.

'Save it for later when you are not all wired up for sound,' she said, gently pushing me away.

I re-adjusted the mike and opening the van door, stepped outside.

It was cold and there was a gentle North Easterly breeze blowing: the type that readily goes through you. It was strong enough to rustle the leaves in the surrounding trees, and therefore, at that time, for once was working to our advantage. It would help cover the noise we would unavoidably make as we moved about in the undergrowth and darkness. Apart from the wind there was silence; I could see no lights from any of the tents or the pub buildings. I half crouched and made my way quickly across the field to the gate. I remember thinking how one inevitably crouches when crossing open ground in the dark. As if the stooped profile helps to make you invisible, when in actual fact if you crawled across open ground, you would still be visible to anyone standing erect and looking in your direction, unless of course you were heavily camouflaged and kept very low to the ground and moved very slowly, yet we all do it; we stoop down. Perhaps we subconsciously have a need to; to at least attempt to be small and thereby kid ourselves that we might, by doing so, become in some way invisible.

I reached the gate and stopped. I looked over and scanned the general layout paying particular attention to the Pub and it's surrounding area. I could not see or hear anything, only the wind in the trees. I opened the gate just wide enough to pass through and pulling on it, closed it behind me. I made the short dash across the road into the Car Park and dropped down behind the boundary wall. I was now out of sight of the Pub and all its surrounding buildings. I could, perhaps, be seen from within the Car Park, but a quick look round told me that it was empty at that moment. Ducking down behind the wall, I moved swiftly to the corner of the Car Park furthest away from the Pub. I raised my head just above the top and looked about. Still nothing. I could just make out the top of our van some distance away, on my left, above the top of the campsite boundary wall. Visibility was good. Dark enough for good cover, yet with sufficient light to be able to make out large objects at a fair distance. Everything so far, was in our favour.

Satisfied that all was clear, I hauled myself over the top of the wall and dropped down into the bracken on the other side. I was now in the woods and fairly well concealed, so as long as I was careful to keep the noise of my movements down to the minimum, I was able to move about reasonably freely.

I headed in the direction of the cliff top on the South side of the ravine. I knew that if I did, I would come upon the cliff top track that ran round its outer edge. In less than five minutes I found it, stopped and listened. Listening for what, I thought; I really did not know, but nevertheless I thought the precaution was necessary. I crossed the track and entered the wood on its opposite side. Having only travelled a few feet further, the ground began to slope sharply and fall away. Following the incline I began to ease my way down the steep side of the ravine. I made a point of not going straight down, but to go at an angle and bear to my right, in order, I hoped, to come out somewhere close to the shore line.

The noise of the sea breaking over the pebbles on the beach got progressively louder as I worked my way downhill, until eventually even the noise of the wind was drowned out by the crashing of the waves.

The undergrowth began to thin as I slowly eased forward. When I had gone what I thought was a safe distance, I stopped again and listened. I strained my ears and standing very still listened for what seemed ages. In fact it was just long enough for me to satisfy myself that all the sounds I was hearing were the natural sounds of the woodland and made only by nature, not man, and that all the shadows that seemed to be constantly moving were, in actual fact, just what they were, shadows. From where I now stood, I could see through the gaps in the undergrowth and just make out the opposite side of the ravine. The tops of the trees on the upper slopes were clearly visible and outlined against the night sky. Eddie would, if he were in position, be somewhere up there. Fred would have left by now and was probably already settled down and watching.

I suddenly felt very lonely, but failed to understand why. I enjoy my own company as a rule and have always preferred to work alone, but even then, as I quickly thought about it, I had to admit that at times I had experienced twinges of loneliness. I decided that this was definitely not the time to dwell on my inner most feelings, or for that matter anything else not directly concerned with the job in hand, so I quickly dismissed them all and carried on.

To my right the sea was breaking onto the beach and the iridescence from the water, as it flowed back and forth across the shale, helped to increase the illumination in an area that would otherwise be very dark; the steep, tree covered, sides of the ravine blocking out a large proportion of what little light there might otherwise have been reflected down from the clouds above. The waves, as they broke, progressively ran that inch or two further up the beach. I remembered that at that particular time the tide was still rising and would continue to do so, for quite some time.

When I looked to my left I found it was difficult to make out any detail. The trees forming a very solid backdrop and their density aggravated, even further, on this occasion, by the light reflected up from the sea. I had to study hard to work out exactly where the path, coming down from the Pub, actually broke out onto the beach.

I looked all around taking in as many features as the reduced light permitted and at the same time took stock of my immediate surroundings and present position. I soon realised that where I was standing was far from ideal. If the tide continued to rise, as I knew it would, then by the time I expected some action, the tide line would have flooded passed me. I would be safe, as far as height above it and possible prying eyes were concerned, as there was plenty of scrub in which to conceal myself, but from this position, to observe the beach above the high water line, I would be forced to look inland, with my back facing the open sea

and peer into the darkness of the woods. What I needed was to be further inland, further up the ravine and at a point somewhere above the high tide line and as near as possible to the place where the track opened out onto the beach. I would be better placed, I decided, with the action between the sea and myself. From where I stood I could not readily pick out where I thought that might be so I decided to shift my position and scout around further inland. I crept quietly and slowly towards where I believed the track came down onto the beach, listening all the time for any unfamiliar sounds that would alert me and tell me I was not alone.

The vegetation and undergrowth thinned out close to where the track left the woods and opened up onto the actual beach and this presented a problem. I discovered that when I was far enough back to be completely concealed from the path, my view of the beach area became restricted and I felt it was important that I should be able to observe as much of that as possible. I was therefore obliged to shift my position several times and this often entailed retracing my steps and stopping frequently to check my field of vision as I found, to my annoyance that often as one improved the other deteriorated. Finally I found a place that I thought was about the best I could expect, under the circumstances, for my purposes. To improve on it would need daylight and that was out of the question. Where I selected I would, at least, be able to sit down, as there was a convenient boulder close by. There was also a large tree that I could easily hide behind and the thick dense clump of brush and undergrowth between there and the beach that could not be bettered. As this was now the chosen spot I began to check it out in detail. When seated I could, by stretching my neck and peering through the undergrowth, get a reasonable view of most of the beach. The rock was almost flat on the top and should not to be too uncomfortable. If I needed to stretch my legs or shift my position I only had to slid off it and lower myself deeper into the scrub. From there I could move sideways in either direction and despite the fact that movement was somewhat restricted it would allow me to get a better view of either the path or the beach in turn should circumstances demand it. I also found that I could crawl the short distance back and get myself up behind the tree from where I had an excellent view in all directions. The only drawback to that being, that it left me exposed from the waist up to anyone positioned anywhere where the tree was not directly in line between them and me. I did not dismiss the idea of using it altogether as I could not predetermine the development of events and the view from behind the tree would be by far the best of them all, if not the safest.

Reasonably satisfied I settled down on the rock to wait. I took off my pack and began to rummage through it's contents when I suddenly became concerned with time, for having been on the move for what then felt like an eternity, I had lost all track of it. I could not see my watch in the darkness so I unzipped my anorak and pushed my left arm inside. Taking my pocket torch, I circled the watch face to shield it, and turned on the light… Two-forty. It had taken me much longer than I

expected and yet thankfully I was still well in hand for the calculated rendezvous time. I wondered how Eddie was getting on. He should have made good progress as most of his journey was along well-worn tracks. Granted he had further to go than me, but the going was easier and he had set out before me. Anyhow, my immediate worry was my circumstances not Eddie's. He could look after himself.

With nothing to do but wait, time began to drag. I had looked at my watch twice and checked all my equipment yet again, and still only ten minutes had lapsed. I also made a mental note that the next time I bought a new watch to remember to get one of those that automatically illuminate when the button on the side is depressed. I was surprised I had not thought of that before and how useful and almost essential it was in these circumstances, when I remembered how I had dropped and broken my last one and how I had dug this one out and how it had been a raffle prize that I had won in an Christmas draw somewhere. The Office or was it the local Pub, I couldn't quite remember; however still no contact with Eddie. I began to wonder why: probably because I had nothing better to do?

I decided against spreading out my gear just in case and for some unexpected reason, I needed to move my position quickly. Who knows what might happen I thought, as I lowered my bag to the ground. I didn't have all that much to spread out in any case as I hadn't brought a great deal, but for the moment I settled for the rucksack on the ground by the side of the rock and within easy reach. Other odds and ends, such as my torch, I left where they were, in my pockets.

Time dragged.

* * *

Two or three times I thought I heard something stir close by and tensed up so that all my senses became needle sharp and focused on what I imagined I had heard. Each time it proved to be nothing. Some small wild animal perhaps going about its nocturnal business, but more than likely just the wind in the trees and undergrowth playing tricks on me or some silly seagull that couldn't be bothered to settle down for the night. Funny birds, seagulls, I thought, as I distinctly heard one call from somewhere in the distance. One of the very few species of birds that remain equally active throughout the day and night and fly about and behave as if it is at all times broad daylight.

I became increasingly concerned for Eddie. Possibly as the result of boredom, or nervous tension from the waiting, or from some unrecognised fear of the unknown that was equally derived from my imagination and it's distorted belief in what was to come.

Since my arrival, which the ache in my backside from the hard rock told me was ages ago, I had heard nothing from him. Fred, I was not so concerned about for I knew she would not acknowledge her position until she heard first from

Eddie. Where was he? I tried to calculate how long I thought it should take him to reach his designated spot and no mater how I worked at it, I came up with the same conclusion; he should already be there. He should be well established by now and should have signalled to us to confirm it. I knew that time becomes distorted when one is tense, isolated and, like me now, lacking in stimulation. I tried to reason against all that, but my conclusions always returned to the same solution and basic question… where was he? What if he had slipped and fallen, knocked himself out, been hit over the head and Fred and I knew nothing about it. What if something had gone wrong and Fred was now in trouble. My imagination began to run riot. What time was it? Where was my torch? Stop; I thought. Stop and get a grip on yourself before you loose it altogether and your ability to apply simple logic freezes up, along with your body. That was it; it was dark, cold, windy, and lonely in that ravine and the waiting was getting through to me; that was all. I forced myself to stand up, stretched and raised and lowered my feet alternately as if marching slowly on the spot to improve the circulation.

Click – Click! I jumped a mile and cursing, screamed silently, 'Bloody hell man… don't blow my bloody brains out.'

The surge of relief that swept from the very top of my head to the tip of my toes was unbelievable. Good old Eddie, he was all right and I was not alone anymore. All my doubts and concerns for him vanished in that instant and I felt good. The human mind plays all sorts of tricks on the unwary and unprepared. What was building up to becoming a major crisis only a few minutes ago, was all swept away in an instant and everything reverted back to normal and once again there was a kind of peace where everything made sense once again.

Fred would have heard the clicks at the same time and I wondered if she too was feeling the same sense of relief that I felt.

In the heat of the moment and the confusion, I almost forgot it was now my turn to signal and let them know that I was in position and ready and that all was well at my end. I felt a little ashamed at my feelings of panic and my unjustified reactions but I instantly dismissed them knowing that they were my secret and would forever remain so. Everything was fine now and I was in complete control, so I clasped the mouthpiece of my radio and pressed. Click, click, pause, click, click.

In reply I heard, loud and clear in my earpiece… Click, click, pause, click, click, pause, click, click.

That was Fred and she was OK. We were now all set. Suddenly everything seemed to be going like clockwork and the timing of it all was perfect. I stretched and flexed my body once more to improve the circulation and relive the stiffness and at the same time heighten my senses as I strained to pick up the slightest noise. Nothing; then suddenly there came a strong need to relieve myself, no doubt the direct result of relaxing from the recent self- inflicted tension. I got up and moved

behind the tree and after much pulling and tugging at my bulky clothing, managed to complete the necessary. No sooner had I rearranged myself and settled back down, than I developed a raging thirst and I needed a drink. I decided that would have to wait, for sod's law said that something would happen if I relaxed any more and lowered my present level of alertness and concentration.

Eventually I had to stand up. I could hardly believe it, but despite the cold, I was dozing off. I stretched. I was once again cold and now very stiff, and I was hungry. Sod's law or no sod's law, I needed a drink and something to eat and the length of time I had been sat there I could have walked up to the top of the ravine and back again, to get a retched drink; anyhow that's what it felt like to me. So I reached for my rucksack and flicking back the flap, extracted the pack of sandwiches that Fred had so meticulously prepared for each of us. I took the top one and in silence slowly ate, and listened... there was nothing.

I looked towards the shoreline, closed my eyes, and then re-opened them in the hope of getting a better focus as I concentrated on the water line and where the waves were running up to. Was what I was actually seeing, true or was I deluding myself? Had the tide actually stopped rising? It was very difficult to tell because every now and again, an odd wave seemed to come higher than the rest, giving the illusion that it was still flooding. The more I stared and concentrated, using certain larger pebbles on the beach as markers, the more convinced I became that the tide had, in actual fact, stopped rising, and was on the point of turning. Further more, I suddenly realised, as I shifted my gaze, that I could now distinguish features at greater distances, and more clearly than I could only a short while before. I realized then that it was beginning to get light and that the dawn was breaking. I noticed also that the wind had eased off and things were much quieter. I was very cold and stiff.

For the first time I could now see my watch without the torch. Five-fifteen in the morning, dawn breaking and nothing but that strange stillness that greets every tide change.

I felt totally deflated. Nothing had happened. I stood up and stretched. Then depressing the transmit button of my radio said, 'Foxtrot, Mike, anything?'

'Mike, Foxtrot, nothing,' replied Fred.

'Echo, Mike, anything?'

'Mike, Echo, nothing,' from Eddie.

So that was it. Dawn was upon us and the tide was well on the turn. We had convinced ourselves that something would happen on this particular night and would do so around an hour before high tide. That high tide was now long past and it would soon be daylight. Somewhere down the line we had got it horribly wrong. I was not a happy man.

'Foxtrot, Echo, Mike, Abort. Return to base,' I said into my mouthpiece, with a sense of total hopelessness and defeat. I felt completely dejected and well pissed off.

Two clicks. Closely followed by two more. They had both heard my call and like me, were calling it a day. It no doubt had been an equally long and disappointing night for them too.

I slung my rucksack over my shoulder and twisted the radio mouthpiece up and away from my face, then pushing myself forward on very stiff and reluctant legs, I broke cover and made my way up the main track, heading back towards the camping field and the anticipated comfort of our van.

Despite my extreme disappointment I remembered to exercise some caution as I passed the front of the Pub, but apart from that, I wandered wearily back, literally forcing my reluctant legs to carry me. As I anticipated, Fred had already returned and despite all her discomfort, had managed to open some tins of soup and was warming them. As I opened the door the smell almost overpowered me.

'Soup. Just what I need after that bloody shambles.'

'What we all need, but you can still wait a few minutes for Eddie and while you're waiting, don't leave your things scattered all over the place. Put them up in the front with mine. You are not the only one who has had a rotten night, you know. There were three of us out there, remember?'

I felt it best to say nothing, as it was obvious by her manner and the tone of her voice, that she too had not found it a pleasant experience. So perhaps after all, I was not alone with my lousy feelings. By the time I had sorted out most of my things and stowed them away, Eddie came in.

'Well that was truly a sodding waste of time,' were his opening remarks, as he slumped down on the side bench seat.

'Come in. Take your things off and sit down at the table,' curtly commanded Fred. 'When we get some soup inside us, we can talk. Mel, you get up and get some mugs ready for coffee. There's whiskey in that cupboard.'

Eddie said nothing, took off his outer clothing and along with his other personal effects, took them outside and locked them in the boot of his car.

We were seated at the table and the effect of the hot soup was beginning to raise our spirits. Any uneaten sandwiches from our pack ups and the extra Fred had made up and we had left before we set out were quickly devoured along with numerous additional thick slices of fresh bread from an uncut loaf.

'Well, what happened?' I said as I sat back and wrapped my hands round my coffee pot.

'You tell me. As you know, I was the last to leave,' said Fred. 'You were both out there longer than me. I locked up, went straight across the Car Park, which was empty, and over the wall. I stayed behind the wall from where I could see the

approach road and where I also hoped I would be close enough to perhaps overhear any conversation that might drift my way, from anyone who came into the actual Car Park or for that matter from anyone in the surrounding area. I seemed to be there for hours before the clicks came through to let me know you two were in position and then I just waited and waited. No one came, nothing. There was no activity round the Pub. No one came up or down the lane, simply nothing. I just leaned against the wall and slowly froze, until you finally called Mel. Then I came back to the van. I saw nothing and heard nothing all the time I was out there. What about you two?'

'When I left, I made it as far as the gate and was about to go through to make my way behind the Pub, when someone came out of a back door and started moving about. I ducked back out of sight and went into the toilet block. I stood and waited there until it went quiet and I was sure it was clear to come out and set off again. I got through the gate this time and I was about to go round the corner of one of the outbuildings, when I got a strong whiff of tobacco smoke. When I carefully peered round the corner someone, I don't know who was standing in an open doorway smoking a pipe and a dog was sniffing round in the yard. I thought for the moment that I'd had it and was rapidly trying to think of an excuse for being there should the dog suddenly show an interest in me, when the bloke called it over. They both went in leaving the door open, even though it was a cold night. I stood for ages not daring to go past the open door in case I attracted the dog's attention and it came flying out. When I finally picked up courage, I went past very gingerly and fortunately all was quiet. Once clear I moved fairly rapidly and got across the bridge then I made my way along the track to the top of the cliff. I must have been very tense and on a knife-edge, because, twice on the way up I froze when I thought I heard something, which was only the wind or something flitting about in the trees. When I got to the top, I selected a spot from where I could see most of the entrance to the ravine, and also out to sea. There's quite a good view from up there, but then, like you Fred, I stood watching, and waiting until I slowly froze. I don't suppose you had any more success at your end Mel?'

'Nothing. It took me a fair while to find a good spot, but then like you two, I just got colder and colder. I spooked myself a couple of times when the wind played tricks and made me jump, but apart from that, nothing. I could hardly believe my eyes when I realised the tide had turned and it was beginning to get daylight. In the end there was nothing for it but to call you two and then knock off.'

'My biggest problem was that I drank all my coffee rather quickly and then with the cold, I found myself soon busting to go to the loo,' said Fred.

'I poisoned a few wild flowers and some healthy bracken behind a big tree, myself,' Eddie admitted.

'Oh well, if its confession time, so did I,' said Fred with a laugh.

'Gosh, the heat in here is beginning to get to me now,' I said, as I reached forward and slid my empty mug onto the table. 'I think we are all agreed that tonight has been a total waste of time, so for now let's get our heads down and catch a few hours sleep, then we can have another, fuller, debrief. Though God knows what good that will do us, in light of what has happened, or more to the point, not happened, tonight.'

I kicked my boots off as blankets were handed out. Fred grabbed the sleeping bag and completely wrapping up in it, curled up to make a large quilted ball. Eddie and I wedged into convenient corners.

We all slept soundly and for all we cared, the cold wind outside could howl and do its damnedest, as nothing was going to have an effect on us for some considerable time to come.

CHAPTER THIRTY-SIX

We were a sorry sight when we finally emerged; dishevelled, bleary eyed and with unkempt hair all over the place. I think we were all stiff and, to say the least, I was totally demoralised.

Fred, bless her, was the first to rally round and having bullied us into folding and stowing away the blankets had, in the meantime, produced a large plate of sandwiches.

'Sandwiches. My favourite food,' I yawned.

'Shut up and eat them. If you can do any better then get on with it. I am doing my best with what we have.'

'I think your sandwiches are wonderful Fred,' said Eddie, as he started on his second.

'Creep,' I muttered.

'Stop winging and move up,' said Fred, as she pushed me sideways along the seat so that she could sit down.

We sat there and despite earlier comments, silently devoured every single sandwich as if we had not eaten for months.

'I was ready for that,' I admitted, 'And if you will excuse me Fred I am now going to take a walk across the field.'

As I returned I passed Fred, about half way across the field, as she embarked on a similar expedition and found Eddie fussing around his car.

Fred returned and then Eddie ambled off towards the toilet. When he came back he and I sat on either side of the table while Fred handed out pots of coffee.

'What a night and what a complete shambles it all turned out to be,' I said. 'I was so confident that everything would just fall into place and then what happened? No one showed up. I have been thinking; the total absence of any form of activity what so ever, tends to tell me that the whole thing was called off well in advance. I don't think it was a last minute decision or anything like that, on their part. That is if there ever was anything planned by anyone, except us, for last night.'

'How do you know? Just tell me how you arrive at that informed and carefully calculated piece of inside information,' demanded Fred, as she continued to tidy up. 'Pass me those dirty plates and things if you have finished with them please. You are speculating and you know as well as I do, that won't help solve any problems. We simply do not know why there was no activity, or why nothing happened, last night. We may find out later, if we are lucky or if ever we get that far, but for the moment we know nothing. The only thing we can be sure of right

now, is the fact that, we will have to report to the Old man today and you know that he will be chomping at the bit and eagerly awaiting a full report on the outcome of last nights venture and he will, without doubt, be expecting a success story.'

'We could always send Eddie,' I suggested with a grin. 'But whoever reports; what can we tell him? Only the truth: nothing happened. As you rightly say, he will be waiting for our report which he will already have assumed will have solved whatever problems it was supposed to solve last night. But he is going to be as disappointed as we are and will have no choice but to accept it, however hard he may find it, that nothing happened.'

'Look. Let's try and be serious. To start with, forget all the silly suggestions about Eddie making reports on our behalf. It's bad enough having no success and nothing to report without being frivolous about it. So seeing as I have to clear up in here and make our future plans; me being the duty slave, skivvy, chef, domestic and forward planner, the reporting is all down to you lover. You're the brave one. So wrap up warm and I will be waiting for you when you get back.'

'I will give you a lift into the village old man. I need to make my report to our people and then I think a shower and some more sleep is the order of the day for me. When do you suggest we meet up again? In between times it might give us all a better chance to think things through and see if we slipped up somewhere last night.'

'Better make it sometime later tonight up at the Dog and Gun and if you are ready to go now, I will accept the ride up the road. The sooner I get it over with, the better.'

'I don't envy you. Things are much simpler for me; all I have to do is report back to my people and tell them that you have had no success and made no progress and that all I can do is wait until you do.'

'You and I work for the wrong firm, don't we Mel? It should be us hiding behind this guy instead of the other way round.'

'Our turn will come,' I laughed.

Eddie drew up and dropped me off outside the phone box and then disappeared along the main street, heading in the direction of the Pub. I experienced little difficulty getting through to the Old man and wondered if perhaps that was because he was waiting for us to report our success and had cleared all the channels to facilitate it. I dismissed the idea. It could only be coincidence. After all he had much more to think about and concern himself with, than us, as we were only one of many in a complex and multi-functional organisation. Perhaps it only came as a surprise, because in reality, I was subconsciously hoping for delays in getting through to prolong the moment of truth. When those delays did not materialise I, for some very obscure reason, began to think it had all been planned, and done so simply to add to my agony. I was right in one sense, and wrong in the other. It obviously had not been planned to add to my agony. But he was, as it turned

out, when I did get through, very busy and the fact that I had got through with minimum delay somehow caught him off guard and appeared to irritate him and to such an extent that I became a victim of his frustration and as such had to be dealt with quickly and then dismissed; leaving him free to deal with his more pressing responsibilities.

'Make it quick Grundy. I have an important meeting and can't be delayed talking to you all day. What have you to report?'

'Nothing.'

'Nothing,' he snapped, and from the severity of the reply I could imagine his face going all red with frustration.

'That's what I said Sir, nothing. We staked the place out and waited all night, but nothing happened. No one turned up. Nothing.'

'Nothing,' he repeated in disbelief. 'Your cover's been blown; you know that? Are those Customs people still in the area? They should not be. If you hear of anything you let me know straight away.'

'Not that I am aware of, sir but if they are then they are keeping well out of our way.'

'You need a complete re-think Grundy. Come back to me when you have some concrete and feasible proposals that stand some chance of success,' and he rang off. End of debrief: end of my report.

I walked slowly down the lane thinking over what the Old man had said regarding blown cover. Was he right, had someone become suspicious? Have we been around too long? Is someone concerned about our presence? Were we that obvious? Have we been asking too many questions? Has Eddie or that other silly bugger, Len, cocked it up for us? I turned it over and over in my mind. I asked myself a million questions. But nothing came of it or inspired me into thinking I had found a solution. I was tired and thoroughly deflated.

I opened the van door and let myself in. Without removing my coat, I sat down.

'What's the matter? You look just about all in.'

'It's something the Old man said that has worried me a bit and had me thinking as I came back down the lane.'

'Why? What has he had to say for himself?'

'Very little really! Firstly, it threw me, the speed with which I got through; which I know it shouldn't, but it did and secondly he was pushed for time and wanted to be away to some important meeting or other. Also for some reason he didn't quite react in the way I expected him to, when I told him nothing had happened. Although, thinking about it now, I must admit I don't know how I expected him to react. Perhaps I expected him to blow his top completely and he didn't. All he basically said was, "Your cover has been blown. Have a re-think and

come back when you get your act together," or words to that effect. I think it must be me. I am so damned tired I'm just not thinking straight at the moment.'

'That's a load of rubbish to start with: our cover blown. How does he know? Did he tell you? Does he know something we don't? Did he tell you anything?'

'No.'

'Well you can't just sit there and tell me, that he would say that, if he knew it to be true. He would have told you how he knew, and where he got his information from.'

'Would he? You know he doesn't always tell us everything that he knows,' I said wearily. 'You know his silly theories on "need to know" and all that.'

'Oh come on Mel, use your noddle. If I thought for one moment that he knew something relevant and was withholding it, so that we got nowhere or were left here like stuffed dummies. I would pack up here and now and go back and tell him to shove the whole damned lot up his big fat what's it. Take your coat off. I will make a cup of coffee and we will sit down and work this thing through, a step at a time. Just forget the Old man for a moment and we will work this out.'

While Fred made the coffee, I sat and thought. It's amazing how when logical answers, to immediate problems, are not readily available, the mind quickly drifts to the ridiculous and often totally bizarre. I found myself contemplating and speculating on various preposterous propositions including the installation and a need to search for, hidden bugs or other secret listening devices planted in and around the van. I thought Len might have been one of "them" and had passed on information; despite the fact that it was highly unlikely as he had gone before we gathered our latest, if somewhat now rather useless, intelligence. I imagined that everyone in the local pubs and shops could lip read and that they all belonged to one massive organisation and left little notes everywhere for everyone else, but us, to read.

'I thought we were going to talk this thing through?' said Fred.

'We are.'

'Then wake up! Here is your coffee and do take your coat off, it's warm in here and you look ridiculous and can't be comfortable sat like that.'

I removed my anorak and pushed it through into the front.

'Right. Now let's consider and think carefully through what we know. What are, if any, the cold hard facts?'

'First of all we definitely know that no bugger turned up last night, as we expected them to do and that is cold hard fact number one.'

'But we do not know why they didn't turn up, only that they did not.'

'Right.'

'I know it is not always wise or even cleaver to speculate too much, but with what little we have to go on at the moment, I feel speculation is all we have to rely on right now. So let's consider ourselves first of all. Are we at fault? Is it

our fault? Have we slipped up in any way? Have we been over confident? Has our presence had an effect and alerted them somehow, or put them off in any way? Have we done or said something that to us may have appeared quite innocent, but to them proved to be highly suspicious, or give them some sort of clue? Have we talked to the wrong people without realising it? We believe they are playing a highly suspect and dangerous game, so therefore they are not fools. They are going to take a lot of precautions despite the fact that they may have got away with it many times in the past and local gossip may well be used, by them, as a useful form of intelligence gathering. They may well use local gossip as a means of sounding out the levels of activity of say, the Police or the Coastguard and allow that to have an influence on there decisions. There may be only one or two of them directly involved in the actual operation, but the local community here is a very close knit one and although the majority of them may not be directly involved, or even remotely connected, they may be aware that something goes on. This is not uncommon in rural villages and probably applies here and maybe more so due to the locality on the coast and the historical background of this village. My guess is that they all turn a blind eye to whatever suits them the result of generations of dodgy dealings and above all else they will remain loyal to each other and tight-lipped despite what happens. An innocent chance remark, made by one local, within earshot of another maybe all that it takes to start the ball rolling.'

'Like what?'

'Well who knows? I am only speculating. Perhaps something along the lines of - "Nice couple those two in that white caravanette. Yes they are but she seems a bit nosy to me, always asking questions about people and things that, if you ask me, is no concern of hers. That's right, he was doing the same thing the other day and they are always in that phone box, hardly ever got used until they came. Must spend a fortune on telephone calls, and where to and why? The odd one is OK but they are always squeezed in there together, up to no good if you ask me. Doesn't seem right to me" - and so on. "Always sat with that so called Insurance Man in the Pub; some Insurance Man if you ask me. Has he been to see you? No, and he hasn't been to see anyone that I know of." Our very presence, here in this camping field and so close to the ravine, maybe sufficient to put them off. Perhaps we should consider relocating and move away. Have we simply been here too long? Does just our very presence make them suspicious and uncomfortable?'

'Do you think that would be sufficient to actually make them abandon everything?'

'Who knows how these people think or react. They are not used to strangers outside the holiday season and I have no doubt that they would rather do without visitor's altogether if they could survive economically without them. While we have been here has anyone said anything, that you have actually heard, that might

give us a clue that they were not satisfied with our explanations and alleged reasons for being here and that we could actually have spooked them?'

'Not that I am aware of! People have shown interest in us, I assumed, because of the smallness of the community and their natural friendliness, or because they believe we have money to spend. There is, as you say, a need for tolerance towards visitors and holidaymakers and their economy no doubt needs us. But as far as I can tell they have been satisfied with any explanations we have offered and they haven't asked too many questions about us. Or if they have, then they haven't asked them of us.'

'As far as we know and, as you say, certainly not of us,' emphasised Fred.

'As far as we know. So let's see if we can break it down a bit further. Let's consider here. Where we are now, this Campsite and the Pub. We came and booked in, claiming to be holidaymakers on a walking holiday and had randomly chosen this area. I think we made sure we looked the part and we have certainly done a lot of walking and been seen to be doing a lot of walking. I don't know of anywhere, that we have been, that may have struck the locals as being odd or so unusual as to arouse their suspicions.'

'What about last night? I wonder if by sheer chance someone saw us moving about in the dark. Remember Eddie nearly bumped into someone behind the Pub and we have only his word for it that he was not seen. What if he was?'

'But he assured us he was not seen by anyone and don't forget how late it was by then. Would anyone who saw him, or any of us for that matter, have had the time or the means to call it all off at that late hour and at such short notice?'

'If they were in telephone or radio contact with the Pub, or if someone, after seeing Eddie, or anyone of us for that matter, left the Pub and went and warned the others. I know we saw no one and he told us that no one saw him, but what if they did and he or us were allowed to carry on without challenge, so as not to arouse our suspicions and alert us to the fact that we had been sussed. Suppose they were and have been all the time, watching us as part of their security.

'There is always that possibility and you could well be right, but as far as Eddie is concerned, I don't think he is the type to lie or say he had not been seen, if there was the slightest chance that he had been.'

'Can you be sure? Can you be one hundred per cent sure?' said Fred as she tilted her head to one side and raised her eyebrows. 'Think about it; would it not be easier for him to say he had not been seen, than to admit he had and as a result, blown it for us? After all it is our job and not his.'

'I know it is and I am not trying to defend him, but he also has a lot at stake don't forget and even so, do you think that as a result of that, they would still cancel at such short notice?'

'Of course they would. Haven't we already agreed that they are not stupid? They must make contingency plans, the same as we do.'

'OK then. Let's put Eddie to one side for the moment. Can you think of anyone or anything around here, within this immediate area, that could be significant or might have had a direct influence on last night's outcome?'

Fred thought for a moment then said slowly, 'Nothing that readily comes to mind at this point. But we can't afford to dismiss the Pub altogether either. Someone stood behind a darkened window, for example, can see a long way, particularly with decent binoculars and why should they not post look outs?'

'So what about further afield? What about in the village itself? We have sniffed around the Builders, Johnson's, Fancy Pants shop, and several other shops and what have you, down in the village. There was also that occasion when I spoke to the guy in the garage and he more or less told me to mind my own business. It could have happened there. He might have something to do with them; even be directly involved?'

'A strong possibility, I admit. Garage, transport, and all that? Come to think of it, he maybe even related to someone of significance and passes on information gathered at the garage without being directly involved. In fact we could go on for ever, for let's face it, we don't know who is related to who round here and you know what it can be like in a small close knit community. What exactly did he say when you spoke to him?'

'I don't remember the exact conversation, but when I saw the Park Ranger with Pat Edison in the street, I asked him who he was and he, the garage man, was a bit surprised that I should be interested. But then thinking about it, I got the impression that his attitude was more to do with his dislike or disapproval of the Ranger and not exactly anything to do with my actual question. I suppose later he could have made some remark to another customer, or a member of his family, or to someone who, in turn, might have passed it on to someone else. You know the sort of thing - "that Ranger been performing in the main street again, it's disgusting the way he goes on, even the visitors are beginning to notice. Only this afternoon those two, who's in that caravan thing down the road, were showing a keen interest and wanted to know what it was all about".'

'That may well be true, but what has the Ranger's behaviour with Pat Edison in the main street, to do with what we might suspect someone round here to be up to? Unless you mean Pat Edison?' enquired Fred with a frown.

'I don't know, but I thought we were speculating on reasons why nothing developed last night. I wonder if the Builder or Johnson were aware that we followed them the other Sunday? Is that where we slipped up? What about the pub in Whitby or you going into that taxi office?'

'I think we did the job well enough for them to have no idea that we were attempting to get anywhere near them. I doubt very much the possibility that any

of them are trained agents, or anything like that, which would make them notice such things. They would probably assume coincidence if they did notice us and I still doubt if they would cancel last night even on such a coincidence,' she re-affirmed.

'I suppose you're right. All the other places we have been to, we have done so, very much as visitors and if anything, that has been a large part of our problem. Because we have been obliged to be so casual and laid back we have not been able to ask enough people, enough direct or indirect questions. I think that so far, if anything, we have played it cooler than cool and not made any obvious blunders that I am aware of, or for that matter, done anything to attract undue attention. But let's go back to Pat Edison for a moment. Do you think she has anything very significant to do with all this?'

'Regarding last night specifically or the job as a whole?'

'Either.'

'Now there is a strong possibility! If I could see her clearly and recognise her, as I went up the street, when she was fighting with the Ranger, then she would have been able to see me. Unless she was too preoccupied and didn't even notice I was there. But let's assume she did. She is, or has been, very close to the Ranger and she is the only one in this area, with the obvious exceptions of Eddie and that Len bloke that you blew out that knows we are investigating her husband's disappearance. So if her husband's disappearance is in any way connected with what is going on round here and we suspect it might be, then we may have a big loop hole there.'

'So there is her?' I said. 'Then among the other unknowns, you didn't mention, the local copper and I am not too happy about the visit to Whitby; but there again, if they had had a drink or two then we probably got away with that. Then there is that Len which once again brings us back to Eddie. We still can't afford to ignore Eddie, even though deep down I feel he is sound, and above suspicion at the moment.'

'I think you are perhaps being a bit mean towards him and you are over-reacting. If you want to attach any sort of blame onto Eddie then I think you are doing so looking more for excuses and just someone to blame for our lack of success, more than sticking to facts that you can prove. He is, after all, Anti-terrorist and all that stands for and he is here for a very good sound reason. His people also have a vested interest in what is going on. I know that so far, we have been doing most of the work and Eddie has just been sitting on the fence, so to speak, and reaping what little benefits there have been. But if there were anything at all dodgy about him, or the activities of his department, the Old Man would surely have let us know. If you had been working directly for Eddie last night and had blown your cover, would you have told him?'

'Yes of course I would. But that is not my point. I am not looking for excuses or anyone to blame for anything that has happened or not happened so far. We were speculating; remember? Considering all the possibilities. Trying to find reasons.'

'Yes, OK! So if you had blown your cover you would have told him and so would I; and I believe, so would he. He is sound and after all if we cannot trust our own team then we are becoming paranoid and it is time we all packed up. Something happened last night and at this particular point in time, we don't know what. This is, unfortunately, not an open investigation. We can't bring people in for questioning, or insist they produce alibis or account for their movements. So we have to settle for what we have and what we know; which is very little and guess the rest.'

'So we keep Eddie in with us?'

'Yes of course we do and carry on as if nothing has happened,' Insisted Fred.

'Then let's go back to the other unknown. Do you think the village Bobby has a part in all this?'

'Probably. As village Bobby, with little to do but nosy around and keep his ear to the ground, he probably knows everything that goes on. But knowing is one thing. It is what he does about it, that is the big question and my guess is that, in his case, he does nothing. Let's face it, he is stationed way out in the country, he has to live and work with these people and counter the pressures they could bring to bear on him and his family if it suited them. Not to mention any threats to his personal survival from within the Police Force itself, if he persists in stirring up hornets nests and finding unnecessary work. That, I should imagine, is probably his biggest headache. Nick the odd poacher, motorist or unwary holiday maker keeps his superiors and everyone else happy, but apart from that, I should imagine that all his efforts go towards keeping his nose clean while he enjoys the quiet life and waits for promotion, or eventual retirement with a big fat pension.'

'Yes and I've also come across many coppers who freely talk. In fact there aren't many who don't, particularly when pissed and suitably goaded. A bored, village one, maybe just what our friends need.'

'Perhaps and some day we might find out. On the other hand we may never know.'

'What about the Whitby trip? I know it is easy to say nothing probably happened if they were worse the ware for drink, but were they? Perhaps their business to them was as serious as ours is to us and they were stone cold sober and, don't forget, we didn't see them drink all that much. So if that was the case then we can't ignore the fact that we were all in the same Pub, at the same time, and later you even went into that taxi office and followed a couple of them.'

‘We were just ordinary people in a crowd. We didn’t have bones through our noses or axes embedded in our heads. You don’t even have purple hair, or anything else to make you stand out and be remembered in a crowd. We were everyday punters in a Pub. I was just another customer in a taxi office.’

‘But I would remember a gorgeous creature like you, with or without a bone through your nose. Blokes notice boobs and good looking girls even in a big crowd.’

‘Yes, but so what? Hardly the boobs in what I was wearing that night and I know I was not the only girl in that Pub during the whole of that evening or any other evening for that matter. I suspect that they would remember good-looking girls for far more obvious reasons than to remember just one who happened to accidentally cross their path on the one odd occasion. Seeing a girl in a Pub and then a Taxi Office hardly amounts to being followed by her. You might become suspicious if the same girl kept turning up, time and again, everywhere you went, but not on a one off in Whitby. By the way, thanks for the good-looking girl bit but remember that I don’t quite see it like that. As far as I am concerned I was just another female in Whitby that night and I don’t think I stand out and definitely not when dressed in this hiking stuff and I certainly didn’t give them the wink, which girls can easily do if they want to attract attention to themselves. In fact I don’t think any of us appeared out of place. Perhaps your bias and don’t quite see it like that?’

‘I am, I suppose, and to me you would stand out anywhere, but that still does not alter the fact that I still don’t know what to make of any of it. It is all so bloody frustrating. We seem to have done everything right and still nothing has happened and we have got nowhere. It looks as if I have failed miserably, so now it is all down to you sweetheart,’ I laughed.

‘Thanks a bundle and who loves you? What do you think I can do about it?’

‘Perhaps you should dig out your crystal ball. The one you have hidden away somewhere and not told me about.’

‘I wish I had one. Not that I believe in them, but right now, I agree that anything that could give us the smallest glimmer of hope would be useful. But seriously Mel, what did we actually expect to happen last night?’

‘In a nutshell, I think we expected someone, with something, to come ashore at about an hour before high tide and what ever it was, would involve Raines, Johnson, Scampton, the unnamed Fisherman and anyone else that we didn’t know about at that point in time.’

‘Right, that being so, did we expected who ever it was, or what ever it was, that was supposed to be coming ashore; to do so by boat.’

‘Yes, I think so. But you know all that, so just what are you getting at?’ I replied.

'Just this! How would you stop a boat coming ashore if you had to cancel the job? Remember, we saw and heard nothing. Eddie, remember also was on the cliff top and could see a good distance out to sea, despite the dark, and he said he saw nothing. You saw nothing and I certainly didn't.'

'Radio?'

'Yes of course: by Radio. So where is that computer print out?'

'That won't tell us anything. It's way out of date to start with.'

'I know it is. But the name of the guy we need to contact is with it. An up to date print out, of the last two days, up to six o'clock this morning, might well give us something.'

I stood up and search through one of the lockers where I knew I had put it for safekeeping. Pulling out several folders that we had managed to accumulate since we set out on this job, I selected the thickest that held the computer print out and several other relevant pieces of paper.

'Here it is. A guy named Norton and here is the phone number.'

'That's it then; our next move. Coats on and down to the village!'

'Does it take two of us to ring this guy?'

'No. But I just thought that if you were going into the village, as I have decided you are. I will come with you. I need to buy a few things to re-stock up. We ate nearly everything last night and early this morning. But I can go on my own and do both jobs, if you like.'

'If you don't mind because I'm shot and as you say, it doesn't take two of us to make a phone call and at least then, if I am left here alone and quiet, I can think things through and perhaps come up with something positive while you are away. On the other hand if you wait until I have been to the loo I will come with you.'

'No you stay where you are and rest your weary legs. When it comes to shopping I am better off on my own. You don't know what you're doing and just get in the way and it might give me a little time to think things out for myself.'

Well wrapped up, she set out for the village. I closed my eyes; decided she was not peeved that I had let her go alone and I started to think.

* * *

The noise of the van door opening, on Fred's return, woke me.

'I bet you have been asleep all the time I have been away,' she grinned.

'No. Not all the time. But I must admit, most of it,' I confessed. 'You know what it is like when you are alone and it is warm and cosy.'

'No I don't. There's a cold wind blowing out there and it's not at all warm and these shopping bags are heavy.'

'Any success with Norton?'

'Yes. It will be delivered by hand later this evening to the Dog and Gun, no thanks to you. Have you come up with any future plans yet or have you simply slept all this time?'

'No. But I obviously needed the sleep and should now be able to think more clearly.'

'Some excuse. I will believe you where millions wouldn't. Especially if you now get up off your bum and make me a pot of coffee. There's a new jar in that bag there.'

* * *

Later that evening we sat in the lounge of the Dog and Gun. Eddie had joined us earlier and the three of us had eaten together. We discussed with Eddie most of what we had talked about earlier, omitting only the parts where we had discussed him. We made no mention either of the fact that we were expecting a visit, that evening, from Norton or one of his people.

'Excuse me,' said Fred as she stood up and squeezed behind my stool, 'But nature calls. I will bring some drinks with me on my way back, same again for all of us?'

We both nodded.

'I have been in touch with my people,' said Eddie, 'And my instructions remain the same; to continue to give you all the support and cooperation that I can.'

'Were they disappointed that we came up with nothing last night?'

'If they were: then they said nothing. Just said for me to carry on working with you.'

Fred returned and once again squeezed behind me and sat down. I noticed she was holding her coat tightly wrapped across her front and that she was holding it in place with one arm.

'I thought you were bringing drinks?' said Eddie. 'Shall I go?'

'Yes please if you don't mind. Sorry about that.'

He got up and made his way to the bar.

'Are you alright?' I said, looking at the way she held herself.

'Yes, fine. It's just that I have a big envelope inside my coat. That's why I couldn't carry drinks. A girl passed it to me, just now, in the loo.'

'In the loo?'

'Yes, while I was in there, this girl came in and said "Miss Huntington? Mr Norton's compliments" and handed me this envelope and walked out. I put it inside my coat and had to hold it like this with my arm, to stop it slipping down. I will be fine as long as I sit here, but I didn't want to return from the loo brandishing a large brown envelope, for the benefit of all these people sat round here.'

‘We had better make this one our last,’ I said to Eddie when he returned and sat down. ‘Despite all the rest and sleep I have had already since last night, I could still use an early night.’

A few minutes later Eddie excused himself and headed for the toilet, I followed him.

‘We need to go Eddie. Fred has just picked up some information that we need to study in private. It’s in a large envelope under her coat, so we will be leaving as soon as I go back to the table.’

‘OK, see you back there.’

I returned to our table and reaching over for my anorak put it on. Standing with my back to the room I said to Fred, ‘Give the envelope to me,’ and taking it from her I tucked it into the waistband of my trousers and zipped up the front of my anorak. Fred quickly finished her drink and was zipping up her anorak when Eddie returned.

‘We will see you sometime tomorrow Eddie, Goodnight.’

We left him to finish his drink.

We didn’t talk much as we walked down the lane. It was still cold and windy so as soon as we arrived back, I lit the cooker to help warm up the inside of the van as quickly as possible.

‘Don’t start messing with that envelope now. Make up the bed while I make a drink, then we can both look at it together.’

I dropped the table and adjusted the cushions to form the base for the bed and then having spread the sleeping bag, I puffed up the pillows and set them in their place.

Fred handed me a mug of coffee and sitting herself down on the edge of the bed said, ‘Now let’s see what we have in here.’

The packet was large but fairly thin and was now slightly curved from where it had been wrapped round my middle. Once opened, I drew out the familiar computer print out sheets. We started from the top, and with each of us running a finger down an opposite edge, worked our way through the list of entries. We progressed from one page to the next, turning the zigzag folds carefully as we went.

The first few pages yielded nothing: just a list of common everyday transmissions passing from one vessel to another. Navigation warnings, weather forecasts, port information, and chit chat between friendly skippers.

Suddenly Fred stopped, ‘There’s a bit I have been looking for,’ and turning round grasped a felt tipped pen from the work surface. Pulling off the top with her teeth, she inscribed a large circle round one group of printed words. ‘Now keep going. There maybe more.’

We reached the bottom of the last sheet and had found no further causes to make any more marks.

'Go back to the beginning and let's go through it again but a bit slower this time. I am sure there should be something else. More than I have already seen.'

We repeated the process and once again I found myself reading dreary, repetitive stuff that after only a short time began to fail to register in my tired and bored brain.

'There it is! I bet you a million that's it,' and once again with the marker pen she circled a particular group of words. Up to then I had seen nothing that attracted my attention.

'A simple code and right there! Now keep going until we get to the end once again and I am sure I have got it all.'

When we finally reached the end she said, 'Now go back to that first mark I made, which is near the end… There… They are our transmissions. That first entry there, is you asking Eddie and me if we have seen anything. There is our answer and there is your final transmission - "back to base". Now I knew that if there were going to be anything it would have to be before that entry. If you look closely, everything else is routine, standard stuff and rather boring. Call signs, questions, answers, everything you would expect on a day to day basis except this,' and she pointed to the circle towards the middle of the string of printed sheets.

I looked closely and was immediately convinced she was onto something. The time of the transmission was Three Thirty-two, on the afternoon before. There were no call signs to identify the sender or the recipient. It was a single message sent from a shore station. It read – 'Big boy this is little boy. Baby is crying tonight. Will baby-sit twenty-first, same time.'

'That has to be it. It's a form of code. It can't be anything else. There are no call signs, no acknowledgement. Check out all the rest; they all balance out one with the other. This one doesn't. It's on it's own; is on marine band and according to strength and direction, was transmitted from a shore base. All the rest of the stuff on these sheets is pretty straightforward with the vast majority of transmits being plain English and answered. That one,' she said, stabbing with her finger, 'there, is the only exception out of the whole lot. The big question is, do we go for it?'

'Why not? It looks good to me despite the fact that at the moment I can only guess at it's meaning and I have to admit there certainly doesn't look to be anything else among this little lot that is going to tell us anything in any case.'

'There is little doubt in my mind and I think we would be very foolish to ignore it. So let's clear all this paper away for now and climb into bed where it's bound to be a lot warmer and then we can talk about it some more from there.'

For the first time, in a long time, I felt a strange sense of achievement although why, I had no idea because we hadn't actually discovered the crown jewels or a bottomless pot of gold. In fact all we had was a vacant transcript of a message that we maybe able to manipulate to suit our purposes. On the other hand perhaps this was, after all this time, the break through we had been hoping for.

Lucky maybe? Who knows? But whatever, we deserved something after all the frustration we had experienced to date, be it luck or not.

'We may at last be getting somewhere,' sighed Fred, as she drew the cover tight round her neck and pushed back against me.

We both lay facing the same direction with my knees drawn up under Fred so that she was sat on my knee. My right arm was draped round her and my hand gently cupped her left breast. It was soft and she was warm and cuddly.

'Fancy a day or two living in a tent?' I whispered.

'Right now sleep is all I fancy despite all I said about discussing things further in bed. Tell me all about it in the morning.'

CHAPTER THIRTY-SEVEN

'Who had the nerve to suggested something about camping last night? Have you seen the weather out there this morning? It's literally belting down. The heavens have opened,' stammered Fred as she dropped back down and snuggled deeply into the sleeping bag. I'm staying here until at least things improve out there and you are going to cuddle me until they do.'

I jumped and shivered as she cupped my important bits and not from excitement but from the simple fact that her hand was freezing and it instantly made me draw up tight.

'I'm not the only one who doesn't like the cold and all that rain out there, by the feel of things,' she whispered.

'I agree,' I said, brushing my fingertips across and round one of her nipples. 'Something here tells me I am not the only one affected by the cold this morning.'

'Sorry darling,' as she gave one final squeeze and withdrew her hand.

Now it was my turn to be sorry for she had chosen to pull away just as her hand had started to warm and generate some of the nicer sensations that go with it. Spoilt right on the point of becoming very pleasant. Her hand slid up and came to rest on my chest.

'Now what's all this you were on about last night? Something, you said, about camping? I thought that was what we are doing right now or were you referring to the tent. Because if you were, are you really serious, particularly in this weather? Just stick your head up there and have a look at it.'

'I just thought that if our conclusions, from the computer print outs, are correct, and the job has now been postponed until the Twenty-first, it might be a good idea if we were to pull out of here and leave this area altogether. That way, if our presence has aroused any suspicions, it might help to alleviate them if we clear out. We could move further along the coast, either to the North or the South for a few miles and lie low there for a day or two. Then if we go so far as to collect my car, we can travel about in a vehicle and one that has not been seen in or around this area. Nearer the Twenty-first, we could then come back and perhaps discreetly set up a camp somewhere out of the way, using the tent. I am not suggesting a long stay or anything like that, perhaps a couple of nights at the outside, around the time of the anticipated second stake out. It was just a thought.'

'What about Eddie?'

'That's up to him. But there is nothing to stop him doing the same. He could always take off for a couple of days, perhaps making out that he is working

further afield. He could still maintain a base at the Pub but, as I say, that would be up to him. He can simply stay here if he wants. We can put it to him and see how he feels.'

'I hope he feels as good as you do right now,' she whispered as she nibbled my ear and closed her fingers tighter round my, now hardened, "important bit" and then gently stoked it.

'Rising to the occasion nicely darling? Is it the rain out there this morning or the thought of a wild night under canvas that's doing it? Or is it simply your naturally high blood pressure first thing in the morning? Or perhaps it's me that has some magic effect on you? It must be, see how he jumps when I do that.'

'Who cares?' I replied, as I reached across her body and gently rolled her over and eased her up on top. 'If you want it then you can work for it.'

She worked.

* * *

'God, I hope camping is this much fun!' she gasped as her body stopped shuddering and she finally collapsed on top of me.

'We will have to make sure it is. One thing though, a tent should not rock quite as much as you have just made this van gyrate. The springs on this thing must be just about knackered.'

'I didn't do that. It was the wind.'

'Was it? I have never known the wind to gust like that before and get faster and faster as it did just then. I thought it was you and your thunder thighs.'

'Wrong. If it had really been me who wanted to make this van rock just now, it would have been broken in bits and you would be stone cold dead and not just laid there all soft and limp with a smug grin spread across your face.'

'I suppose you are now going to try and tell me that the wind has dropped?'

'Yes.'

I nipped the cheeks of her bum with both hands.

'More!' she laughed as she bit my earlobe quite viscously. 'You never know I might be into having my bum nipped, that and all sorts of other kinky things.'

'Well you just let me know when you are ready to indulge and I will make sure I have pen and paper at the ready.'

'Pen and paper! What for?'

'To draw diagrams and make notes for future reference, or to keep for when I write my book on the kinky sexual preferences of unusual women, what else?'

'You're mad! I don't know about your other unusual women, as you call them but who needs diagrams and reference notes when you have a grand master of the art of kink and an experienced teacher to fall back on, like me?'

'Please Miss, when can I join your Master Class?'

'As soon as you like but you must remember to bring your own important bit with you.'

'What? The Whip?'

'Yes, if that's what you call it. I have a slightly different name for it.'

'And what might that be? If one is permitted to ask before enrolling in this master class.'

'Well it's like this,' she said, adopting an air of mock seriousness, 'Ever since I became curious about this particular piece of male anatomy I have studied it in practice and theory and part of the theory included terms to describe it; labels it has been given, past and present for example. The names girls privately give to it along with those they use in polite company. So as you will realise I have heard it called many things and I have seen many labels attached to it. But the one I think I like the best is a name I first heard shortly after I joined the Wrens. All the girls seemed to use it quite openly after that; because Wrens in general are very open; particularly between themselves when describing their love of men and it so tickled my imagination that I too began to use it and have continued to do so ever since. I can still see the face of the girl now, in the barrack room, the very first time I ever heard it. She was explaining, to a very captive audience, her experience out on a date, one night. It was a first date and he had tried and failed, to get her drunk. Everyone laughed as she explained how she had gone along with the idea in order to keep him happy but was getting more and more annoyed as he staggered everywhere and tried his best to make love to her. One of the other girls chipped in and wanted to know, "Was he very amorous?" "Amorous," replied the girl who was telling the story, "I hadn't been with him in the back of the car for five minutes before he popped his "giggly pin" into my hand and said, "Pop that where it can do most good," and she added, "All I wanted to do was drop it on the floor and stamp on it" and we all fell about laughing. But that was it; from then on it has been a "giggly pin" ever since.'

'I think I am going to enjoy your classes, particularly when we get round to the practical bits.'

'That's enough for today. Just look!' as she pushed down the cover, 'All it is doing is getting you all excited and we have work to do today, rain or no rain.'

We laughed and kissed until eventually someone insisted and forcedly suggested that it was time to get up.

Fred jumped up first and made a dash for the cooker where she lit both gas rings, putting the kettle on one.

'Come on, it's not as bad as you think out here,' as she turned to face me, completely naked and with her hands resting lightly on the top of her head. Then without removing them, she looked down at herself and gently twisted the top half of her body from side to side as she continued, 'At least the interesting parts on a girl are fairly evenly spread, and are fairly substantial. They are not all bunched together and concentrated down there and they don't shrivel up when not in use, or when it is too cold for them to dangle free. Just look at yours. It is no wonder you don't often see pictures of naked men. There is nothing of interest to see. Just a shrivelled up pink thing.'

'And what would you do without that shrivelled up pink thing?'

'That's a different story and will be fully discussed in one of my other lectures.'

We finally dressed and drew back the curtains and stowed away the bed.

* * *

The remainder of the day, weather wise, was miserable. It rained almost incessantly and there was a heavy mist for much of the time and despite the fact that we thought we ought to be doing something more constructive, we just lounged around and killed the time reading and eating until eventually the daylight failed and a miserable evening set in.

'What a rotten day and I suppose we should be making tracks towards the village, although I could think of much better things to do right now.'

'If it is still raining, I refuse to go anywhere. You can go off by yourself and tell Eddie our plans.'

'It's cleared up a bit and at least its no longer raining,' I said, feeling much relieved as I rubbed at the condensation and peered out of the window. I was not sure if Fred was being serious when she said she did not want to go out. I know I certainly did not fancy it and even less so to go down to the village on my own. A nights boozing with Eddie would be all right in it-self. A touch of the boys together is something I can enjoy. But I much preferred Fred's company and felt very reluctant to have to get all wrapped up just to go out on a cold, damp, and thoroughly miserable night.

'I will come if you promise that it will be fine all the way there and back,' she pouted.

'I can't promise that now, can I? But I could promise something rather nice when we get back.'

'Yes you can and you must.'

'Now who's talking a load of rubbish?'

'I am, and doesn't it make a pleasant change. Come on, put your coat on, and pass mine. If the look on your face is anything to go by you will never make it on your own.'

Following a miserable trek, where we were obliged to continuously step from side to side and stagger along, in order to avoid the puddles which were everywhere, we made slow progress along the lane until finally the warmth and comfort of the Pub was achieved and very much appreciated.

As far as I could see Eddie was not there when we arrived, but I was not concerned for I knew he would turn up eventually.

'If only in time for bed,' was the way Fred put it.

He did as expected and well before bedtime as it happened.

'Hi you two. How's this weather suiting you hardy campers?'

'Hello Eddie! The weather is just fine; for ducks, and I will have you know that I only came out tonight because he has promised me that it would stay fine.'

'As Fred says, we are coping just fine and have enjoyed every minute of our stay, but the weather can do what it likes from now on because tonight is our last,' I said mainly for the benefit of everyone in the immediate vicinity and there were quite a few, who had turned to face in our direction as Eddie walked up. He looked rather surprised.

'Let's all sit down over there for a minute and you can tell me all about it. Is this the end of your holiday or are you just moving on?'

'Moving on. We still have some holiday left.'

We talked between ourselves and then when the opportunity arose we told him what we had found and extracted from the computer print outs and he seemed genuinely please.

'I've given myself a headache today trying to figure out a way in which we could calculate or anticipate their next move. The thought of having to go right back to square one really pissed me off. Sorry Fred, but you know what I mean?'

'That's OK Eddie,' said Fred. 'Mel and I felt very much the same way about it until we discovered what we hope is going to be something useful. Since then we have discussed it and have decided to move out of the area for a few days. Where exactly, we have not yet decided but we propose to move somewhere along the coast. We figured that if we moved completely out of this immediate area, then any suspicions surrounding our presence would be alleviated. We have a tent and all the equipment with us so we propose to disappear for a while and then return nearer the Twenty-first and using the tent, stay hidden and completely out of sight from here and the local population.

'How are you going to travel around? Still use the camper?'

'Only to live in: to sleep in at night I mean. We have a car garaged not too far away and we thought about changing over. That way if we needed to get close: say to pass through this way, we would at least be doing so in a strange vehicle,

and hopefully it would be less conspicuous than the camper. I know that we have already considered coming back the next time in secret, but we will still need some form of transport between then and now and a strange car is probably the best we have. I can't see us being very effective or covering any great distances, should we need to, if we are obliged to walk everywhere.'

'Unless you use public transport.'

'Use the bus? We might even have to consider that when the time comes, although from what I have seen it is almost non-existent round here.'

'How will we keep in touch?'

'There are several ways that we have discussed to do that,' said Fred. 'If you choose to stay here at the Pub, I can ring you posing as a secretary or business contact or something like that and ask to speak to you about Insurance. Or we could ring the phone box in the village at a set and pre-arranged time, although that might attract some attention. We could ring here and pass you a number that we could set up, for you to ring back on. That would then allow you to go away from here and find a more secure phone to use, such as the phone box or where ever you think fit. Alternatively, we could even leave one of our radios with you, and then we could set up a listening watch for a pre-arranged time, say on the hour, and listen for up to one minute after. A radio will plug into the dashboard socket on your car, so there would be no battery recharging problems. We can easily work out something.'

'Sounds fine to me; what do you think suits you best? I think I will stay here for the moment. It presents no problems for me to go missing for long periods and then to keep coming back. It only looks as if I am working further afield. At least that's what I tell them and if I remain at the Pub, we will at least have an anchorman in the village. That is if you don't think it would be better if I cleared out as well? By the way, would it be of any value to you if you were to hang on to my short-range radios? If you do, then should you have a need for them you will already have them and they won't be of much use to me until such times as you return.'

'Yes we will, if you don't mind, they might be useful,' I said.

'Fine, so now let me make a note of that date and the times,' as he rummaged through his pockets until he produced a small note pad, 'And we had better arrange a time now, if we can, for our next contact.'

'If we are correct and interpret that radio message correctly, we expect that they will make their next attempt on the Twenty-first. I have checked the times and high water is at Four-twenty Eight on that day, the early tide that is. So an hour before makes it around Three-thirty in the morning. Also, there is no moon on that night, exactly the same as the other night. So how about the Eighteenth for our next contact? Two full days before. That should give us plenty of time to prepare and arrange things.'

'What time and how?'

'I will ring you here, at the Pub, at Eight o'clock in the evening of the Eighteenth, posing as your secretary. It should be safe enough,' decided Fred.

'OK, that's settled then. Eight o'clock on the Eighteenth.'

'So let's have a few farewell drinks in here and say our goodbyes to the staff and any locals we have been on nodding terms with. Then go down to the Grapes before closing time and do the same. Let as many people know as possible that we are going.'

We left the table and moved back to the bar area and stood in a small group chatting. When the opportunity presented itself, we thanked the Landlord for his hospitality and informed him that we were moving on.

'Surprised you stayed as long as you did. Not much to do round here. Too quiet and now that the weather has turned that can't help things too much.'

'That's what we liked about it,' said Fred. 'The quiet and the fact that we are close to the surrounding countryside and neighbouring towns, yet far enough away from everything for it to be peaceful and the weather doesn't really bother us all that much. Anyhow we have decided to travel further afield but we have enjoyed it so much here that we intend to come back this way on our way home. We still have a few days left before we are due back at work. So we hope we might see you then.'

'I shall miss you both,' said Eddie. 'It has been great having someone to talk to in the evenings. In my job I spend so much of my spare time on my own that your company has made a pleasant change.'

'We have certainly enjoyed your company too and hope to see you again if you are still here when we come back.'

The conversation continued along similar lines until several people had been made well aware that we were leaving.

We made a big show of shaking hands with Eddie and Fred even treated him to a big kiss. We also waved and called out loud goodbyes, in the general direction of the bar. Eddie insisted on coming outside with us to say his final farewell.

'To give you the radios out of the boot of my car in actual fact,' he whispered under his breath.

Taking them, Fred managed to secrete them in her bag, and with a final handshake, Eddie went back into the Pub. We made our way down the lane, once again dodging the puddles that by then had begun to drain away, and went into the Grapes. We went straight up to the bar and then remained standing there with our drinks. We put ourselves out to be sociable and drew as many people as we could into our conversation, making it clear to them all that we had decided to move on. Before we left we bought all the staff a drink, thanked them for their kindness and as a final gesture shook hands with as many as we dared before it reached the point where it was in danger of becoming over demonstrative.

* * *

Early the following morning we stowed everything neatly away: went across to the Pub to see if there was any outstanding site rent due and bade a final farewell to the Landlord, assuring him that we would be back, on our way home. We were, in turn, assured that we would be very welcome.

'Where to now?' enquired Fred some half an hour later as she drove down the lane towards the village.

'First things first! Fuel and a sit-rep to the Old Man, my favourite occupation and then we will think of somewhere nice to go and make love tonight.'

I left Fred on the garage forecourt to fuel up the camper, while I walked the short distance to the phone box. When I finally got through to the Old Man, his lordship was as pleasant as usual.

'What have you got for me this time Grundy? Some vast improvement on the last occasion, I hope.'

'A sit-rep Sir.'

'A what?'

'A sit-rep Sir,' I repeated.

'Don't you me a Situation Report?'

'That's what I said Sir, a sit-rep.'

'I hate people who clip and chop words. Why can't you say exactly what you mean? Well what is it?'

I gave him a complete rundown and whilst I was in the process, Fred drew up in the van and parked outside the phone box.

'So what do you propose to do with the next few days?' and before I had time to answer he continued, 'I suggest you report back here to Headquarters and we will see if the department can find you both something constructive to do. By the way, is that woman in the phone box with you?'

'No Sir, she is waiting outside. Shall I call her?'

'No, you will not. It is still beyond my comprehension why you two have this desperate need to both cram into a single phone box at every given opportunity.'

'You should try it Sir. But I think I have already suggested that. Please excuse me a moment Sir. I have just had a thought and need to consult with my partner,' and without waiting for his reply, I laid the handset on the side and, leaving the phone box, side stepped across the pavement to the open window of the camper and Fred.

'Do you have any outstanding leave owing to you at the moment?' I asked her.

'Yes. Why?'

'Fancy taking some of your leave now and sharing it with me?'

'Yes, but what…'

'Back in a moment,' and I quickly returned to the phone box and picked up the handset.

'You still there, Sir?'

'Of course I am. Where have you been?'

'Just checking.'

'Just checking what, for God's sake man?'

'With my partner, Sir, I needed information from her, Sir. We both have leave due to us and propose, as there is no pressure on either of us at the moment, to take the next few days off as leave.'

'You need permission for that and require to give advance notice. You have to file requests and fill in the necessary forms. You are both fully aware of that; it is departmental procedure. You are required to consult the leave clerk before any leave can be even considered let alone sanctioned.'

'Yes Sir, we are aware of all that. But I am sure you can take care of it for us on this occasion. We are only requesting a short period Sir. It would be a waste of time for us to make our way back to London and then have to return all the way back up North later. The fuel costs alone hardly make it worth while for the few days.'

Got you, I thought. Mention money and costs and he folds. There was a moment's silence, no doubt while he worked in his own form of logic to assess my argument, or more to the point, the costs against savings of what I was proposing. It would not take him long to convince himself that it would be cheaper to pay for leave, which is owing, than to pay for travelling time and then still have to pay for leave at a later date.

'You make sure you submit all the correct paper work when you get back and see it comes directly to me and do not attempt to claim any expenses or offset any costs while you are on leave. Do you understand?'

Bollocks! I thought. But instead I said, 'Yes Sir, I fully understand.'

'Take your leave then and don't forget to get in touch immediately you get back on the job,' and the phone, with its customary precision, went dead. I hung up and leaving the phone box, walked round the van and climbed in beside Fred.

'What now?' she enquired.

'You are, from this moment, officially on leave and all your expenses are suspended from now on and that is official from the Old man himself.'

'What on earth for? Has he flipped or something, or has the company been privatised, or gone bankrupt in our absence? Perhaps we have, at last, been taken over by a foreign power and in future will be paid in subsistence vouchers or join "Boff" and his Barclay Card.'

'No. Nothing like that: although what you are suggesting could have happened and would not surprise me in the least, if it has. The fact is, you, or should I say we, are now both on leave for the next few days.'

'Honest: on leave? Free to do what we want?'

'Yes, I have arranged it with the Old Man. A little moral blackmail, you might say, where he thinks he is saving money on his precious budget by allowing us leave. We are, as you rightly say, free for the foreseeable future.'

'Good,' and slipping the engine into gear she eased away from the kerb and headed out of the village.

'Coming?' she enquired a few moments later.

'Do I have a choice?'

'Yes you do. If you want, I can stop here and now, and you can get out and I will pick you up on my way back. But right now, I am heading for the best hotel and the warmest bath I can find and you are welcome to join me if only to scrub my back. So do I stop or are you coming with me?'

'I'm with you my darling,' I replied. 'If only as your back scrubber.' And I could see it all so vividly as I let my head fall back onto the headrest and closed my eyes. I began to daydream of a hot bath and a large warm bed and everything else that might go with it.

I decided, at that point, that I honestly did not really care a damn about which direction we were heading in, I was quite happy to sit there and be taken.

CHAPTER THIRTY-EIGHT

The following few days were some of the most enjoyable I think I have ever spent and were made all the more so by the fact that I sat back and let Fred make all the major decisions. She selected the Hotel where we stayed and booked us in as man and wife – 'I think we know each other well enough by now, for that' - was her excuse. We dined out where she chose and visited places of particular interest to her. During the evenings we frequented local Night Clubs and often stayed until the early hours of the morning. We certainly lived it up and not once during the whole time was, 'The Job' ever mentioned. Fred went shopping and spent a fortune, or I thought it was a fortune, on clothes and then proceeded to take a great deal of pleasure in sexily removing them or encouraging me to do so. We went to bed at what ever time suited us, taught each other a few tricks, or to be more precise, I think I learned far more than I taught, for Fred showed no surprise, only enjoyment in everything we did. We rose at whatever time took our fancy. The bath took a tremendous hammering, not only for what it was originally designed for, but for the more exciting things we devised while trying to economise on water and share the soap.

There was no doubt about it we had a wonderful time. But then all good things have to come to an end, or so some lousy killjoy decided at some time. No doubt, some poor, sad, sick intellectual that obviously had never had the pleasure of sharing a bath with someone like Fred.

On the last day, we were laid side by side in the oversized bed. It was sometime around mid morning and we were contemplating, without much enthusiasm, the necessity of getting up. We had never had this problem when the reverse was the order of the day and it was time to go to bed.

'Is it really time to go back to work already? What a horrible thought. I've almost forgotten where we were and what we planned to do. Didn't we say something about we should arrange to pick up your car and find somewhere to garage the van? Also I think we promised to ring Eddie tomorrow night. Gosh, it all seems to have come round so soon.'

Suddenly, a lot of the magic of the last few days just melted away as we found ourselves dumped back in the real world.

'Do you think we will get a chance to do this again?' I asked hopefully.

'Only if you want to: it depends on you. You may not want to know me the next time.'

It hit me like a blow from a sledgehammer. Bloody women. What a stupid and unexpected thing to say. How their logic works, is beyond me. They get these

silly notions that, if they let go for just a moment and be their true selves, then no one will want to know them after that.

She must have seen the look on my face. 'Get up, silly. You know full well it all depends on how much leave I have left, or for that matter, how much you have and then whether you can persuade me or not.'

'In that case you had better kiss me now, just in case you have none left or I can't persuade you.'

I turned and embraced her and was determined to make it last as long as possible. When our lips finally parted I kissed her lightly on the end of her chin. 'Lower,' she whispered.

I kissed her again gently on the neck, just below her chin.

'Lower.'

I kissed her upper chest.

'Lower.'

I kissed between her breasts.

'To the left.'

I kissed her nipple that was all taught and enlarged.

'Now the one on the right.'

I kissed the other nipple.

'Now lower.'

I kissed her stomach and slowly ran my tongue round her navel.

'Lower.'

I tracked back and forth just above the hairline.

'Lower, lower... Ah... that's right, kiss me just there.'

We eventually got up and while Fred went and showered, I gathered my things together and began to pack. Then whilst I showered, Fred packed her belongings and tidied round. When I came out of the bathroom, she was every bit the Fred she had been before our break. Jeans, trainers, and chunky jumper with hair tied neatly back. Gone was the long flowing hair, the long legs and split skirts and figure revealing tops. I sighed. At least I had had the pleasure of seeing another side of her and enjoyed every single inch of it. I would have to make do with that for now but with a bit of luck, who knows what the future might hold.

I was downstairs and sat in the hotel lounge, when Fred came in and joined me.

'I have settled up and ordered coffee to be served in here,' she said.

'Good. How much do I owe you?' I asked, very conscious of the fact that the company would not, on this occasion, be picking up the bill.

'Nothing. My treat. You can pay next time round and then we will stay twice as long.'

So there was to be another time. That definitely made me feel good; never the less I said, 'Are you sure about that? Our stay here can not have been cheap.'

'I'm positive. I chose the place and it was all my idea, remember? So I don't want to hear any more about it or you will spoil a good thing.'

'OK, if you say so. But are you sure you're sure?'

'Yes. Didn't I just say that?'

'OK. But I might have to think about it a bit more, later. In the meantime come and sit down.'

'Have you found anywhere or decided where you think we should stay, when we get back, yet?'

Looking back at the map, which I had spread out over the table, I replied, 'If you look here, there are several possibilities in the general area. We don't want to be too far away because of distance and difficulty of travelling and yet, on other hand, we don't want to be too close so that we get noticed by the whole village as soon as we turn up.'

'What about one of these two?' said Fred, pointing to two different 'marked' camping-sites, 'they are both a fair distance outside the village and look as if they might be handy near the roadside.'

'A bit too handy, so near the road, do you think?'

'Maybe, but a lot will depend on the layout and how busy the site is when we get there. But I can see your point. If we turn up with two vehicles and find the field empty, but for us that could be a problem. That is if we are still thinking of taking both the van and your car? Also we know that Johnson goes or has been to Whitby and he and the builder have both been to Kinder Hall and both ways they pass that site. Then there is the Parks bloke and goodness knows where he gets to.'

'What about this one then?' I said, pointing to a third site, some distance further away. 'Not only is it further inland, but also it is certainly off the main road. If you look here at the map, this green patch suggests that there are some trees between the actual camp and this road so it might be fairly well sheltered. I suggest we take a look at that one first. We can always move on and look somewhere else if we have to.'

'I suppose so and if it proves to be suitable we can use the van as a base and then use either your car or walk to get in and out of the village over here. It's not all that far.'

'Hard to tell from this map so we won't know for sure until we actually get there and have a look. So let's make for this place first and then work out what it has to offer against what we need.'

'Have we got everything together for camping?'

'Yes, I think so.'

'Are you sure, because if we do propose to spend some time, in the near future, in a tent, then we will need a good supply of tins and convenience food. Anything and everything, that can be eaten quickly and if necessary cold. But

leave that to me. I'll attend to provisions. I know we still have a few bits left in the van that we can use, but I will check up on that. You make sure we have everything else.'

'I don't see us being out there and holed up in a tent for very long and we should surely be able to get back to the van for a half decent meal, or a quick wash, if we need one.'

'I hope so. But that aside, I think it is probably more important that what ever we do, we see that we keep warm.'

'I agree. Anyhow, do you think I should ring Humber before we go and collect my car or should we just turn up on their doorstep to collect it?'

'Just drop in on them should be all right. From what they said, as long as it is during normal office hours there will be someone about to sort things out for us.'

So it was decided and the map was stowed away and our bags gathered up.

We reluctantly left the Hotel, taking away some very fond memories. We did the essential shopping according to Fred's dictates and then headed for Humber.

On arrival, we were received like long lost cousins. Where had we been? What had we seen? Why did we need the car? Where were we leaving the camper? Where were we going next? I felt a little guilty at all the lies we so easily trotted out in answer to the barrage of questions, yet surprised myself how simple it was, to tell them. After all I had done it often enough in the past, and so too probably, had Fred. We needed the car, we said, so that we could travel further afield, a half truth, and the camper was proving to be too big to take down some of the narrow lanes that we found so attractive, another half-truth. Fred even produced some of our Polaroid pictures and showed them round so that they could all see where we had been. Good lass, I thought, and not realising until I saw them all together just how many she had taken and the variety and diversity of subjects she had covered. Some I couldn't even remembered her actually taking. Anyhow, everything went well. We eventually got away and promised that we would call in and say goodbye before we left for home at the end of our "break".

'How much more holiday do you both have?' asked receptionist Miss Bland, or Kathleen as she kept insisting we call her, as she thought up and asked yet another question.

We looked at each other. Thankfully Fred's quick thinking once again saved the day.

'We are not sure. There was some mix up with the leave quota. I might have more than I originally thought and Mel is not at all sure about his. But they are sorting it all out at HQ and when we think the time is right, we might just ring in and ask. In the meantime, we are just taking it on a daily basis and simply

enjoying ourselves. We are leisurely travelling round the countryside and just pleasing ourselves what we do.'

'If I can help in any way; sorting things out for you or anything like that, please let me know,' volunteered Kathleen. 'I am sure Mr Oldfield wouldn't mind.'

'That's very kind of you. We might just ask you to do that if we don't get any sense out of them.'

Shortly after and when we were outside and alone in the Car Park, and I was rummaging in the boot of my car, Fred said, 'It seems so unfair lying to our own people and especially to a nice girl like Kathleen.'

'I know, but that's the way the cookie crumbles. Security is important, and we don't know who knows who, or what, or who is related to whom, or is friends with A, B, or C, or anything, do we? It's all very sad but necessary.'

'I suppose you're right. But we seem to have to tell an awful lot of lies in this retched business, don't we?' Like when you tell me you love me, and all the time you are doing nothing but fibbing to me.'

'Sod off Winifred Do-Dar and pass me that radio and enough about lies and loving you. As far as I am concerned the two go well together and if you can be serious for a second, are you sure you are happy to follow me if I take the map?'

'Yes of course. You know I am not too happy driving and looking at a map at the same time. It makes me dizzy so if you don't mind I will follow you. Which radio do you want? One of Eddies or one of ours?'

'One of Eddies please. That's one of ours. Oh shit…'

'Language. What's the matter now?'

'We should have given Eddie one of our radios. We agreed we would use it for comms between us and charge it from the cigarette lighter socket in the car.'

'Not initially! We didn't say that at all. I am to ring him, remember? All it means is that we forgot about it at the time, but if we decide to use our radios, then we will have to arrange some means of getting one to him.'

'All right, but for now give me one of Eddies and you stick the other in the cab with you. Disconnect the ear piece then you will be able to hear through the speaker.'

I sat in the car and started the engine. It fired at the second attempt, which rather surprised me, after having been stood for so long. I picked up the radio and turned up the volume.

'You receiving me over there Big Girl? Over.'

'I will receive you anytime Big Boy, over.'

'OK, follow me Big Girl, out.'

I pulled out of the Car Park and Fred fell in behind me, once again we were heading north.

* * *

I suppose the drive could have been described as mildly interesting due to the magnificent scenery but apart from that it was dull and uneventful. In fact sometimes I found it rather boring without Fred to chat to but, at least, with there being little traffic on the road we were able to make good time. Each time I glanced in my rear view mirror, Fred was somewhere behind and on several occasions, when she drew up quite close, I raised my hand, and she flashed her headlights in reply.

I had no problems locating the camping site and it proved to be much bigger than the impression created from map and there were trees between the camp site and the nearest main road, quite a large clump of them. On the actual approach, there were no obvious visual signs of a caravan park, except for an erected sign at the end of the lane that lead directly into it. The trees were no doubt, part of the original planning permission to hide the site from the road or reduce its visual impact on the rural landscape. Most of the enclosed area, when we got there, was for static caravans with an area set aside for mobile homes, and an entirely separate field for tents. Among the few permanent buildings there was a little shop and a Reception Office and I also noticed a toilet and shower block and a compound that contained gas cylinders. Some distance away there was a separate, designated, play area for children. It was all very neat but also very quiet. There was an almost abandoned atmosphere about the place.

I drew up in the open space in front of the building marked - OFFICE - and Fred pulled in behind me. I got out and walked towards the door. Before I reached it, I stopped.

'Is something wrong?' said Fred through the open van window.

I pointed to the little note pinned on the door, "Back in an hour", it said.

'I wonder how long that's been there?' I said as I looked about me, 'There is no one about. It's all very quiet. Too quiet; the place has an abandoned feel to it.'

'Never mind. Climb in beside me and have a drink of coffee,' Fred said, showing me a flask through the open window. 'We can wait a few minutes and see if anyone shows up.'

Somewhere in the distance we could hear the sound of farm machinery and a few moments later, and about the time I was half way through my coffee, a tractor, pulling a large grass cutting machine, appeared from somewhere behind the office building. It stopped as it drew alongside us and a big, well built, weather beaten, outdoor type climbed out of the cab and approached the van.

'Sorry about that! Saw you coming up the lane. The wife is out and I am trying to get all the grass cut before the season starts proper. When we get going there is always someone about. But you know how it is, when it's quiet. The wife

likes to get out a bit herself when she can, as she will be pretty well tied up most of the summer. Can I help you?'

'Yes, we would like to book in for a day or two if that's possible. We are touring in the area and thought it would be very nice and convenient to make our base here.'

'You two together?'

'Yes.'

'Whose is the car then?'

'It's ours. You see we park up the camper to live in and use the car to travel around. It's less bulky, cheaper to run and easier to get round the narrow lanes.'

He looked past me at Fred. 'She drive this thing about all the time then?'

'No, only today! We take it in turns usually.'

'Bit big for a girl, isn't it?'

'My usual and full time job is to drive Earth Movers and JCB's on motorway construction jobs,' snapped Fred.

His expression remained unmoved. He neither looked surprised or amused or impressed.

'Nowt to do with me, I suppose, what women get up to these days. Just seems strange that's all. See that opening there?' he said, pointing in the direction we were facing. 'Go through there and park anywhere in that field that suits you. It's for camper vans and mobiles through there. The wife will be along to see you when she gets back.'

'Can I park the car alongside the camper?' I asked.

'Can for me son. It should be all right but the wife will sort it all out later. She will tell you all you need to know. I must get on and get this grass cut while it's still dry and daylight. Bungs everything up when it's wet, treads in everywhere and the wife plays hell,' and without a further word he climbed back onto his tractor, closed the flimsy door, and disappeared round the corner.

'I bet you didn't know it bungs everything up when it's wet,' laughed Fred.

'No I didn't. But you heard what the man said? "The wife will sort you out later". But in the meantime I suggest you drive though that opening and I will follow you. And try not to knock the gatepost down with your Earth Mover.' At which I got a shove in the middle of the back as I turned to climb out.

We selected the corner nearest the entrance and parked the car alongside the van. Then having checked to make sure there was nothing in it that we immediately required, I locked it up.

We were in the process of setting up home, so to speak, when a female version of the tractor driver came round the corner. Even the 'wellies' she was wearing were identical to his. The only give away, that she was in fact female, was the very large chest in front and the long straggly hair that protruded from below

a large brimmed and unusual straw hat with some dead looking artificial flowers strewn all round it.

'He said you'd come. Well your welcome as long as you don't churn up all the grass while it is still wet and soft underfoot with these here vans and things. Straight in and out if you must move. Showers and toilets over there. Hot water only at teatime, until the Season gets going. If you want ow't from the shop, or gas, come to the Office. You get clean water and empty waste by the Toilet Block. If I'm not there and you wants me, you goes looking for him. But don't be bothering him too much he's busy. If you knows now how long you're staying you pays me in advance, if you don't then you pays me a deposit now and then for each night in advance.'

Fred handed over the required deposit. 'Could I have a receipt please?'

'Right now! Why? Don't you trust me?'

'Of course I do,' replied Fred, defensively, 'it's not that, I do trust you, but if I have a receipt I can claim back my expenses.'

'Expenses! Is he that tight he makes you account for everything you spend, does he? He wouldn't me I can tell you.'

'Oh forget it. It's not that important.'

'Tight sod! Wouldn't do for me, he wouldn't,' she muttered as she waddled off in the direction of the Office.

'You have just acquired a new name darling - tight sod,' giggled Fred, 'although I don't agree with her totally. Funny old crow. Did you see the hat and I wonder what her rules are for rocking the van at night?'

'There are bound to be some - Nookie must be booked in advance at the Office - Wellies must be worn at all times to prevent damp grass getting in it - and they are probably only just two of many but I bet that they appear well up on the list.' We both saw the funny side of it and laughed. So much so that we did not hear our genial host return until she stuck her head round the door and said, 'Here you are dear and mind you don't loose it,' and sticking out her large, work worn, hand offered Fred, what was obviously, a receipt. 'And before I forgets, we don't allow loud music or any tomfoolery in the field. Noise to be kept down to nothing after dark. Enjoy yourself,' as she withdrew the head, hat and dead flowers and disappeared from view.

Fred had to press her hand hard over her mouth, to prevent herself from bursting.

'I told you, no hanky panky in the field, especially after dark and now you know, but if you do it and do it to music, then you will get more than grass cuttings stuck in it and should you get caught at it, you will be liable for immediate expulsion.' as the tears streamed down her face. 'How long have we been here?' she spluttered. 'An hour or so and already I dare not go across there for a wee.'

'I wonder if she puts on Jackboots and patrols the perimeter at night,' I ventured, 'or who mans the machine gun posts and operates the search lights?'

'She probably makes him do it while she is in charge and mans the switchboard in the Guardroom. But joking apart Mel, I hope we are free to come and go as we please. It might be a nuisance if she is clocking and checking our every move.'

'We will have to see about that, but for the moment I am looking forward to this. The total isolation and complete peace and quiet of this place, especially when he knocks off on that tractor, should be nothing short of magic. Do you realise that unless we go in the car and are prepared to travel a bit, there is nowhere, close at hand, to visit. The village over there is out for us, as you know, so we must steer clear of it and the alternatives from here, don't appear to add up to much.'

'There must be somewhere that we can nip out to, a Pub or something not too far away, unless you really want to stay right here all evening and do nothing.'

'I just thought it would make a great change and it should only be for this one evening, but if that doesn't suit you, then we can always head inland and look for something. I agree, there will be something, somewhere, and we can always go in the car and look for it, if you want.'

'No, you are right. A quiet evening here would make a very pleasant change and I have decided; that is what we will do.'

'OK, fine! So that sorted, you hang on here. I will go and see if Madam Sin has any canned booze or anything like that in that shop of hers. Do we still have some whiskey tucked away somewhere?'

'We have both whiskey and brandy up there in the cupboard. I got some a bit back and so if you can get some lemonade and perhaps something to read and if there are any, bring me some crisps; no bring me a box of chocolates as a special treat. I might as well spoil myself, if I am to stay in. Shall I dig out the cards?'

'If you want.'

The shop door was locked when I tried it so I moved the few feet along the front of the building to the office door… It opened.

'Oh it's you, come in and close the door quick, you're letting all the heat out and this gas is not cheap you know,' she said pointing a finger at a Calor Gas Heater that stood in the middle of the room and which was turned up to full. Not only was it radiating an unbelievable amount of heat but it was also drying up all the oxygen in the process and also doing so, to such an extent, that I found that within seconds it was becoming difficult to breath properly.

'Do you have anything to drink? Are you licensed to sell booze?' I enquired as my eyes began to smart from the gas fumes and the peculiar smell of the bottled gas hit and began to irritate, my nose.

'Why? Are you some sort of Official Licensing Man, or something?'

'No I'm not. All I wanted to know was, do you have any cans of beer?'

'Only from last year. Everything we have left is from last year; he hasn't bought in for this year, yet. Come through here and have a look for yourself. We will have more stuff in when the Season starts,' as she got up and crossed over to open an adjoining door which allowed us both to pass through into the part of the building that served as a shop and where, thankfully, the atmosphere was cooler and fresher.

'He doesn't keep much out of Season, says it's good money tied up doing nothing, but you can have what you want out of what there is.'

I looked around at the almost empty shelves. It was all rather untidy, with what little there was, scattered about with little, or no, semblance of organisation. It looked more like an abandoned jumble sale, than a working shop.

'I was looking for canned beer and perhaps lemonade, if you have it?'

'Plenty of pop, keep it in for the kids but the little beggars didn't buy much of it last year,' she said as she wiped, what must have been, at least six months dust from around the neck of a one and a half litre, plastic bottle of lemonade.

'As you can see he hasn't got round to cleaning up in here yet,' as she picked up and thrust forward, two, four packs of ale. One was beer and the other lager. 'That's all we got. Anything else?'

'Anything to read?'

'Like what?'

'Papers, magazines?'

'No.'

'Have you any chocolates that might still be fit to eat?'

'They would be fit to eat if we had any, but I ate all we had left, last Christmas. He will be getting some more later.'

'When the Season starts,' I prompted.

'That's right. But we have some boiled sweets over here. They are usually alright until they go sticky, or if you want there's a couple of Mars bars, that's if you want sweet things.'

I decided to take a chance on the Mars bars; they were just within their sell-by date. 'OK I will take those with the beer and lemonade. How much do I owe you?'

'Bring them through here,' as she disappeared back into the Office leaving me to carry everything.

She then produced, after much searching, an equally dusty, soft backed book from a desk drawer and opening it, remarked, 'All prices should be in here,' and thumbing through and turning the pages meticulously she jotted down some figures on a scrap piece of paper. After a few moments and some additional page turning, she returned the book to the drawer. She then took the piece of paper and began to add up the figures, muttering to herself as she did so.

'Mars bars, two of them, pop, beer, no… one beer, one lager, wasn't it? That's why the prices here are different.'

From where I stood I could see what she had written, so I was able to add up the figures at the same time as she did. We both reached the same grand total. I took a note from my pocket and offered it. She took it and laid it on the desktop. She opened one of the other drawers in the desk and from it produced a small cash box and then a key from in the corner of the same drawer. The box was carefully opened to reveal several pieces of paper, a selection of keys and a few coins.

The change was carefully extracted, counted, and laid out on the desktop. Eventually, satisfied that there was no more loose change in the box, she closed the lid and exclaimed, 'I don't seem to have enough change. But then I suppose that doesn't matter; this will be near enough, as prices have bound to have gone up since last Season.'

I was so taken aback and lost for words that all I could manage to gasp was, 'A lot depends on the Season round here, I see!'

She completely missed the point of my sarcasm and continued to treat my remark as if it was a rational statement of fact.

'Not as much as it did when we were just farming: and before we stated this caravan thing. The Season was really important then.'

I was still dumb founded but managed to pick up what had been offered to me by way of change and mutter my thanks, although God knows what I had to be thankful for, and left. I could hardly contain myself as I returned to the camper.

'Oh lovely, pressies,' enthused Fred as I set my purchases down on the table and she reached forward to see what I had brought.

'You will not believe this,' I burst out. 'You don't get discount for cash or for old stock round here. You have to pay more for inflation and towards the all important - season.'

'Season?'

'Yes, the bloody Season,' I repeated and then told her exactly what had happened in the so called shop, where I was nearly gassed and felt as if I had been robbed and she laughed so much, she had to sit down and "cross my legs before I have an accident".

'Times is hard dear,' she mimicked. 'It's the Season and all that you know, but we country folks still knows just how to stitch you townies.'

'Round here things must only devalue for just so long, then with the change of Season, must become instant antiques and as a result, appreciate in value. Judging by the dust on these, they must now be classed as seasonally seasoned, very desirable and much sort after as expensive memorabilia.'

'They are classed as something and as you rightly say, it obviously has an awful lot to do with the all important, mythical Season that we are rapidly becoming acquainted with. Crack that, and you crack the local economy. Open

a Mars bar quickly and then if it is not fit to eat, she can have the damned thing straight back before it deteriorates any further and goes up in price.'

Fred tore away the wrapper of the one nearest to her.

'This one looks fine and unaffected by the season as far as I can tell.'

She tore the corner off the other.

'This one is OK too. You didn't bring me any chocolates, or are they too badly affected by the Season?'

'Very much so! They didn't make it past Christmas. The old bag claims to have knocked them all off herself.'

'Well if this is it for our party tonight, you had better nip back and pick up another couple of Mars bars, they at least seem to be alright.'

I tramped the short distance back to the shop. I assumed the door would still be locked so I went straight to the Office door. This time it too was locked and pinned to a cross rail, and well below eye level, was a note that informed all interested parties and me in particular at that time, that it was indeed closed and would not be re-opened until nine o'clock the following morning. Any emergency, and we were to contact the house at the end of the lane. I went back to the van.

'Nothing left or can you not afford the new seasonally adjusted prices?' jibed Fred.

'Neither. They are shut and she has gone until tomorrow morning or so the note says. In the meantime if you have an emergency, you must report to the big house. I assume by that, they mean the one we passed as we entered the lane to come along here.'

'The one on the left?'

'Must be that one, there was no other that I saw so I assume they must live there.'

'That's good. I had a strange feeling at first, that they may have lived somewhere on the camp and been snooping around all the time.'

'Probably do…' I replied and Fred anticipating the remainder of the sentence, chorused with me, … 'in the Season.'

'Well let's see what we can do with these poor Mars bars.'

Producing a knife and plate, she sliced them up and arranged them in a neat circular pattern around the plate. Then with a damp cloth she carefully wiped all the beer-can tops and the lemonade bottle.

'All we need now, for a quiet evening, is the television. By the way you might have noticed that they had no papers or magazines; thank goodness, as they would probably have been months old and cost well over full price. I wonder if this thing works around here or if the reception is still as bad as ever?' I said as I stood up and looked at the TV.

I switched it on and waited for it to "warm up". It was the first time I had done so since I originally tried to tune it in, when we first got the camper. The

screen lit up, but then to my complete surprise, with very little adjustment, I got a perfect picture and crystal clear sound. As I went through the different channels, each proved to be as good as the last and I was well satisfied.

'Might make a pleasant change,' said Fred. 'I have not seen television for absolutely ages nor have you since we have been together. Pity we don't have a TV Times or something like that, to find out what is on.'

'What is on? Round here!' I joked. 'All you're likely to get, if it's typical of round here, is last years seasonal repeats at an inflated price. Which reminds me. How do you suppose we go on for a license for this thing?'

'Why? I don't know. Have you got one?'

'No, unless it's covered in the hire of this thing.'

'Well if you don't know, I should forget about it then. You can't do anything about it now and then again, why should you?'

Later, at Fred's suggestion, I made up the bed. She, in the meantime, made some sandwiches and then propping ourselves in opposite corners we created sufficient space, between us, for all the food and goodies to be placed within easy reach. After that we settled down for an evening of television. When the late night film ended and I turned it off, I gathered all our empties together.

'I will go and dump this lot before we turn in and call at the loo at the same time.'

'I think I will come with you. It's dark out there and all that talk earlier of guards and the Gestapo patrolling about, has made me nervous,' she laughed.

As we approached the toilet block, I noted there was a single, high-powered, light in a fitting high up on the wall. This had the effect of lighting up all the immediate surrounding area. Another light shinning out through the toilet block windows told us that there was also a light on inside.

We both approached the same door, which according to the sign above it, indicated that it was for Ladies.

'Gents must be round the other side somewhere,' I stated. 'Too far to go on a cold night,' so we both went through the same door.

'Looking round as we came across just now, I couldn't see any other lights on in any of the other caravans, so we are probably the only ones here tonight.'

'No you are not and the Gents Toilet, for you, is round the other side. If my husband can use it, so can you,' boomed a strange and very cross female voice from behind one of the closed cubicle doors.

I put my fingers to my lips and grinning at Fred, tip toed out. I waited outside, getting as far away as possible from the direct ring of light.

When Fred came out, I whispered, 'She still in there?'

'She must be, if she hasn't come out.'

'Not while I have been stood here.'

‘Come on then, quick. Let’s get back before she does.’ and with me holding onto Fred’s wrist we hurried towards our van.

‘I feel better for that,’ claimed Fred as she clambered back inside and I hesitated and didn’t follow. ‘Where are you going now?’

‘For a wee! I got thrown out back there, remember.’

I went a few yards along the boundary wall and after one final look round to make sure I was not being observed, watered the vegetation growing at the base of it.

Back inside the van Fred was almost ready to climb into bed. I quickly caught up with her and as I turned off the light and we snuggled down for the night and indulged in our goodnight kiss, Fred drew her head away and as I moved forward for more she whispered, ‘Good night fellow inmate. You have just ended your first day in Stalag, Luftwaffe Two or whatever camp we are incarcerated in for the duration of this Season.’

CHAPTER THIRTY-NINE

We woke early the next morning to the sound of a tractor which, from the volume of noise that filtered our way, was working somewhere over towards the far end of the campsite. Our realization, from last nights' experience in the toilet, that we were not in actual fact the only residents on the site was further confirmed by the fact that on two separate occasions we heard voices and were aware of people passing to and fro.

As we laid, snuggled up in bed, and listened we heard at least one car engine start up not too far away. We could also hear, because of the time of day and the stillness that went with it, cars passing along the approach road. Also we could hear other vehicles, although not as clearly, passing along the road that passed the end of the lane that led up to the actual camp site. Later we discovered that, from where we were, we could not see them due to a natural barrier, created by the trees, set between the campsite and the main road.

When Fred opened the door she found two young children half cowered behind the wall and just inside the entrance to our compound. 'Hello you two,' she said cheerfully.

The two youngsters did not respond, they just giggled and then ducked round the corner and ran away. As they did so, we heard one say, 'It's a woman, let's go tell our Mam.'

Turning to me Fred said, 'I don't think the place is teeming, but at least we are not alone. I will be back in a moment,' and she stepped out of the van and walked away.

On her return she said that she had seen one or two people around, at least, a couple of the caravans, and that the water in the Toilet Block was cold. The, so-called, shop and office, had a - Back in Ten Minutes - notice pinned on one of the doors. All in all, she said, she had come to the conclusion that it was a pretty isolated place and could be ideal for what we required.

After a makeshift breakfast we cleared away and then once again spread out the map on the table.

'This is the most direct route to the village,' I indicated, 'and this minor road, that goes round the back from here, comes out at the side of the Garage. Therefore there are two different ways in and out of the village from here. That might be handy.'

'Does this one,' enquired Fred, pointing to the more major of the two alternatives, 'pass the Builder's house? It's somewhere near here. No, sorry, it's

here. You would have to detour along this way, wouldn't you, if you wanted to pass the Builder's on the way into the village? His house is here.'

'Yes, that's right.'

'Good. It would be unfortunate if we were to pass their house and either him or his wife, Fancy Pants, see us when we have supposedly left and moved on.'

'I think it's important that we stay out of the village altogether, don't you, and definitely avoid the Builders house if at all possible. We have no reason to go there, anyway, for the moment. In fact I suggest we confine ourselves very much to this campsite, as we have no idea who we might bump into or pass along that road at the end there. All we need for the moment is a phone to ring Eddie tonight. He should, if he's remembered, be expecting us to call at around eight.'

'Right: so first things first. I suggest a leisurely stroll round the camp to get the layout of the place and find the whereabouts of the nearest telephone. There is bound to be one somewhere. Coming?'

'Yes, pass my coat. At least it's dry outside today and a bit warmer than it has been for the last few days. Perhaps the weather has finally decided to pick up.'

We set off in an anti-clockwise direction. Why I don't really know but I think it was perhaps because that way took us directly away from the entrance to the camp and the shop area and from where we could hear voices at the time. The camp was neatly set out and all the caravans looked to be in a good state of repair. Most were empty and showed all the signs of having been shut up for the winter. Those with cars parked outside, which were few and far between, had a more lived-in look about them and the frilly net curtains draped across the windows and which were a common feature of most of them, allowed the occupants to look out, while at the same time block prying eyes from the outside looking in. At one point we heard low-level music from either a radio or television as we passed one of the vans. Others, with their doors open, or with personal effects out on the grass before them, were obviously occupied. We received the odd "Good Morning" from those persons pottering about outside and accidentally overheard a string of obscenities from a man who with his head under the bonnet of a car was obviously oblivious and unaware that we had passed close by.

As we slowly walked along the noise of the tractor, which had been chugging away in the background, grew louder. We also noticed that the amount of wet, cut grass that stuck to the soles of our boots progressively got thicker.

'I wonder if he goes round later and collects all this messy stuff up?' remarked Fred as she attempted to scrape off a large accumulation from under one foot. 'Or does he leave it and let it dry out and blow away?'

'I don't really know. But if that area, back across there, is anything to go by, that which, as you can see, has already been cut, then it looks as if it has been collected up.'

'Yes it has! And look over there,' exclaimed Fred as she pointed to a large pile of grass clippings neatly piled up in a corner. 'That's all been collected up from somewhere. Perhaps his cutter thingy, which he is using now, doesn't have a collector and he does that separately, with another thing later.'

'Probably when the early morning dew has dried off or when some of the damp has dried out of the grass itself and it is much easier to handle. He then, probably, collects it and dumps it with the rest over there. But if the smell round here is anything to go by, then he has just been round and cut this lot.'

'Yes the smell of the new cut grass is lovely. I can remember it from being a little girl when my dad cut the lawn using one of those cutters with a roller on the back, the type that you had to push. Now he uses one of those new petrol things and all you can smell is the engine. Mum hates it so much that she closes all the windows when he mows the lawn. Talking of Mum; I wonder what she would think if she could see me now; walking round a field, holding hands with a lovely man and with my feet all covered in grass clippings and dressed like this. She knows I am presently working away, but thinks that I have a regular, respectable office job. She knows also that I move around all over the place as part of my job so to keep her happy, if I am working in a particular place for any length of time, I send her a couple of postcards. But when I am on the move, as we are now, she has to make do with the odd phone call and only then if I can fit it in. Poor Mum, all those lies I have to tell her and I wouldn't dare let her know about you, or she would have me married and settled down in less than a week, but enough of Mum. Look! That is what we're looking for at the moment. Over there.'

We had walked the entire perimeter of the campsite and were approaching the main entrance and the group of small buildings, which provided the, so-called, services for the camp. Against the back wall of the building that served as the camp office and shop, was a single telephone booth. As we reached it Fred opened the door and lifted the receiver putting it to her ear. 'It's working and no wonder we did not see it before, when it is tucked away round here at the back.'

'I thought there was likely to be a phone somewhere, because of the telegraph poles which run along the length of the lane and end up here at the corner of the office. At first, when I saw them and where they led, I had a horrible feeling that it might be just a private line and that we would have to get permission from the Dragon Lady to use the office phone and then only in dire emergencies. Well now we know we can ring Eddie at Eight tonight and the little PH on the map, which indicates a public phone, is correct after all.'

We strolled round the building, which was still closed, despite the fact that the ten minutes stated on the note had long since elapsed. As we made our

way back to where we were parked, Fred remarked, 'You know we decided that we would stay away from the village and not wander down the approach lanes and things like that, well, what is to stop us getting in the car and heading in the opposite direction, away from the village? There is nothing much that we can do now until tonight, when I have to ring Eddie. So let's go the other way and see if we can find at least a decent meal. That stay in the Hotel has spoilt me and I just adore it when someone else cooks my food, serves it up to me, and then comes along and clears away all the mess when I have finished.'

After that there was no argument, as she had obviously made up her mind and so we went inland and covered quite a few miles as we drove around, taking in all the 'sights', as the Americans would say. We went through villages and down narrow lanes and alleyways, wandered round Novelty and Craft shops, found a perfect little restaurant and had a thoroughly enjoyable afternoon.

Early that evening, as we returned to the campsite and I pulled up alongside our camper, Fred got out of the car, stretched to her full height, obviously to rid herself of the stiffness from sitting and the lack of fresh air, and simultaneously yawning, drawled, 'We should do that more often. I have enjoyed this afternoon as much and if not more, than anything we have done since we set out together. Kettle on, I am nipping to you know where.'

Some time later and at the point where I was on the verge of slipping from a light doze into a deep sleep; a state brought about by a combination of warmth, fresh air and boring television, Fred shook my arm and said, 'Come on Mel, it's nearly time to go and ring Eddie. When we do, what do we need to tell him?'

I shook my head and sat upright and arched my shoulders. 'First of all we have to arrange a convenient meeting so that we can give him one of our radios. Look.' I said, changing my mind. 'Before we tell him anything, the best thing is to just arrange a meeting. I know that originally, we said we would try and avoid meetings if we could, but the slip up over the radio, alters things slightly. So what say, we just give him the map reference and ask him to come out here to us?'

'When?'

'Might as well make it later tonight, if he agrees. See what he says when you get through and then take it from there. I'll walk round with you, so if you will pass my boots across from the side of your seat.'

It was very dark outside and the only guide to the exact location of the phone box came from a small single bulb set in the roof of the booth and which cast a weak circle of light all around it. Out of habit and I assumed, still to the Old Mans' disgust, had he known anything about it, we both squeezed into the confined space. Fred inserted a coin and dialled. Within a matter of seconds, I could hear it ringing at the other end.

'Good evening! Could I speak to Eddie Scott please? I understand he is one of your guests,' asked Fred when the ringing tone stopped.

There was a pause, where she winked at me and smiled, before she continued, 'His secretary, and he's expecting the call. Yes I will wait. Thank you.'

A further pause during which time I enjoyed a long, gentle kiss as Fred held the hand set away from her face.

'Hello! Eddie? Fred... Yes I know, we forgot. Listen Eddie can we meet...? Now... Good... Write down this reference.' She then read out the six-figure number we had calculated and taken from the map and which she had carefully jotted down onto a piece of paper. 'I will wait for you. It's about four miles and shouldn't take long. The actual name of the place is Roman Caravan Park. See you, bye,' and she hung up.

'He's on his way,' as she pushed open the door and stepped back outside.

'He shouldn't be too long so we might as well wait for him back in the van, at least it's warmer in there than it is out here just now. It's got chilly again since it got dark.'

I filled and put on the kettle and Fred prepared a drink. I then slid back the curtain from the window on the side facing the direction of the approach road.

'Can you see anything from here?' enquired Fred.

'No, not really, but at least in the darkness I should be able to see the headlights from anything coming down the approach road.'

I sat and waited; finished my coffee and still no one came along the lane that I could see. Time passed until eventually it was long after the time I calculated it should have taken Eddie to reach us.

'Where on earth is he? I wonder if he has got lost or missed the turning or something,' suggested Fred. 'Just check that reference again and make sure I gave it to him correctly.'

I checked and came up with the same coordinates that Fred had written down and passed on.

'You were right there. So there should be no problems unless the silly bugger hasn't got a map. But he will have and if he hasn't, then he would have said so to you at the time.'

'Do you think I should go and ring him again. He's had time to walk here by now, and all I can think of is that I either read them out wrongly to him, or he wrote them down wrong. In which case I would think he would quickly realise and go back to the Pub.'

We went back out to the phone box, but stopped on the way as we noticed car lights approaching. We waited, but the car, on turning into the camp, passed us and went down between two rows of caravans and out of sight. We heard its engine stop, followed quickly by a return to complete darkness, as its lights went out. We continued towards the phone box.

Fred went through the same enquiry procedure as before, ending with, 'Thank you, good night.'

‘The girl, who just answered, said she was the same girl I spoke to the first time I rang. She distinctly remembers that after my call Eddie put on his coat and left the Pub only a few minutes after I rang off. She is certain he has not come back as she thinks she would have seen him. So I wonder where he is?’

‘Short of breaking down, I have no idea and I don’t think it would be wise for us to go looking because sod’s law say’s that if we do our paths will cross. All we can do, for now, is sit tight and wait.’

We sat and waited, drank more coffee, became more agitated and increasingly concerned. ‘Where the hell is he? It’s after eleven, he could have crawled on his hands and knees and still have been here by now.’

‘How much longer do we give him?’

‘I don’t know. It’s too late to ring the Pub again and we can’t afford to keep on doing that in any case, as it is bound to draw unwanted attention. I suppose all we can do is give it a bit longer and if then he hasn’t shown up, then we will have to call it a day, abandon the job, and try again tomorrow. If only we had remembered to give him one of the radios in the first place, we could then, at least, have tried calling him on the hour.’

‘Well we didn’t and there’s nothing we can do about that, so forget it. And what is more, don’t let’s just sit here doing nothing, let’s start to get ready to turn in for the night,’ as she stood up and moved across the van.

‘Hold it! I thought I saw a light just then, across there… Yes I did! There it is again. There’s something coming up the lane. Hell, I hope it’s him. I’m going out to see.’

As I turned out of the entrance to the field, in which we were parked, a car turned into the main entrance and, as it did so, its headlights fully illuminated me. They flashed twice and went out. Then out of the blackness that immediately followed, a familiar voice said, ‘Sorry I’m late. I have had a spot of bother.’

‘We thought you’d got lost. Take your car through that opening. We are parked round to the left,’ and as he drew forwards I turned and retraced my steps.

Eddie parked his car alongside mine and as he climbed into the van Fred grabbed him and wrapping her arms round his neck hugged him with an obvious display of relief. ‘We were worried. They said that you had left immediately after I rang and that was hours ago.’

‘I did but I ran into a minor problem.’

‘Come in and sit down. You can tell us all about it, while I make a hot drink. Do you want another Mel?’

‘Yes please. What happened?’

‘I was followed.’

‘Followed?’

‘Yes. Followed but first things first. Thanks Fred,’ taking hold of the pot of coffee that she held out towards him. ‘After you left for your break, I started

going out and about for the whole day, sometimes staying away until well into the evening. When anyone said anything or passed any remarks, I said I was travelling further afield, but liked where I was staying so kept it as my base. When in the Pub itself, I kept my ear to the ground, but nothing happened, or so I thought, up until tonight that is. Now I realise of course that there were signs but prior to that I did not think much about it. But a couple of nights ago I was sat in the bar having a drink and chatting to the barmaid, when in came Johnson. He was stoned out of his tiny mind and could hardly stand up. The barmaid called upstairs and the Landlord came down to deal with him. But to cut a long story short, it was what Johnson said when they were arguing. At the time I didn't take much notice of it, but to continue; he said something to the effect that, "You will serve all these arseholes, these bloody toffee nosed gits. Ask him where he gets all his bloody money from," and he waved his arm in a circle towards the main group standing in the bar. At which a well dressed guy, who I discovered later was the Builder, that being the first time I had seen him close to and obviously not knowing who he was, came across and hissed in his ear, "That's enough for now. Shut up and piss off Johnson before someone gets cross."

"No you piss off," replied Johnson and then swinging round and almost falling down, addressed the entire bar as he continued, "Gets all his 'effin money from me. I'm the one who keeps him, and that snotty nosed tart of 'is. Without me he's shit." Then without warning he turned to me and said, "What are you grinning at. What do you find so bloody funny? You can 'eff off as well. You can't move round this bloody place as long as there's 'effin strangers like you sniffing about. So why don't you piss off as well and let us get on with our business." Eventually the Landlord and the Builder literally threw him out with the threat that they would send for the Police if he returned that night. That was the end of it, as far as I was concerned, until tonight. Up until then I had dismissed it all as a load of verbal rubbish from a drunk, but then tonight.'

'What happened tonight?' said Fred.

'Well you rang and asked me to meet you. As soon as I checked the map and discovered I was looking for a campsite, I got my coat and went out to my car. As I drove out of the Car Park another car fell in behind me and followed me. At first I didn't take much notice of it. But when I turned into that narrow lane that runs along the side of the Service Station, it followed. I still didn't bother too much because out in rural areas, people have to travel for a drink and have every right to do so. I argued with myself that the guy behind me had as much right to be on that road as I had. He couldn't overtake as the lane was narrow and so he was obliged to follow me. All this time I fully expected him, at any time, to turn off at one of several side turnings, but he didn't. He stayed at a fixed distance behind me, even when I turned left into the wider road and where he could have passed at any time, and where I was intentionally not going very fast, but he didn't. He just

stayed there. If his intention was to follow me then he was a complete amateur at the job because when I decided he had become a positive nuisance, I pulled into one of those lay-byes, where they dump salt and road chippings, and he pulled in and stopped in front of me. I sat there and waited and so did he. In the end I started up and pulled out and the silly sod fell in behind me. I went fast and then slowed down, so did he, so now I was in no doubt about his intentions and amateur or not, he was definitely following me. When I arrived close to here, I ignored the turn off and carried straight on down the main road. I then drove as fast as I dared on these strange and narrow roads for about three quarters of an hour and he still stayed with me. In the end I waited for a convenient place and when it came I pulled off the road and onto a Pub Car Park. I thought at least I would have a look at this creep if nothing else. He followed me into the Car Park. I locked the car and went into the Pub. Fortunately there were only a few people in there so I got served straight away. No one followed me inside, so when I finished my drink, which was only half a beer, I went back outside, having by this time, made up my mind to approach him and ask if he was in the habit of following innocent people who were simply out for the evening and here to meet a friend for a quiet drink. When I got back outside and into the Car Park, he had gone. There was only my car and three others that were already there when I pulled in. I sat in the car for a while and waited. Still nothing happened. When I felt certain that he must have gone, or moved off somewhere out of sight, I decided it might be safer not to go back to the village at all tonight. So I got back out of the car and went back into the Pub and rang the Grapes to tell them I was staying with a friend and would not be requiring breakfast in the morning. It was then that the girl, at the Grapes, told me you had rung a second time and I said I would contact you. I then drove slowly back this way watching my rear view mirror and looking into every intersection and lay-bye to make sure that my "friend" was not hidden and waiting somewhere. I saw no one and so satisfied that no one was following me, I eventually arrived back here. So here I am.'

'You can stay here with us tonight. That presents no problem. But what do you think tonight's episode, with the guy in the car, was really all about? Do you think someone knows something, or have you been mistaken for someone else? Have you been chatting up someone you shouldn't, or is someone edgy and uncomfortable about the fact that you are a stranger and so decided to see where you go when you go out? Another Insurance Agent perhaps or someone expecting you to visit his Missis while he is out?'

'Mel,' said Fred.

'Well! You know what I mean.'

'I don't know Mel. But why follow me for whatever reason? Where did they think I would lead them and who ever it was, didn't know what they were doing, that's for certain, by the way that guy went about actually following me tonight.

It couldn't have been more obvious if he had stuck a sign on his front windscreen saying - "Following you. Lead on!" – It was definitely not a professional job.'

'Coincidence, a warning, or just some silly game?'

'Not coincidence because of the route I took and the total distance I travelled. Remember, I covered a hell of a lot of miles before I finally pulled into that Pub Car Park. If it were a game, then why not follow me into the Pub for a drink? He mimicked everything else that I did. I know there are some strange people about, but why this guy, and why pick on me, and why tonight? Unless the man is a complete nutter he must have thought that I was going to lead him somewhere or to someone. Yet he didn't come into the pub to see if there was a someone.'

'What about a warning?'

'A warning about what? If there was meant to be a message then he certainly did not covey one that I saw.'

'Could he have overheard something in the pub, on the phone perhaps?'

'Oh come on Mel, you of all people should know that when answering the telephone you never repeat anything said to you if there might be a third party within earshot. If you are not sure what has been said, you ask the sender to repeat the message while you stay shtumm. You know the drill as well as I do; credit me with a bit of savvy.'

'Yes, sorry. What about extensions? Could anyone have listened in upstairs?'

'They could have, I suppose. But if they did and from that, set that tail on me, they chose a complete waste of space, to do it and learned nothing from it.'

'If they did listen in and they do have the map co-ordinates of this place and then sent their man to follow you, rubbish though he was, then that may be telling us that they are getting better organised and know something. That being so, I wonder how they will react, after tonight's disaster, when he reports back and tells them that you went miles, led him nowhere and came nowhere near here? They may well send someone to these co-ordinates to do another check.'

'If that's the case, what do think we should do now?' asked Fred.

'Eddie stays here tonight then returns to the Grapes tomorrow to confirm his night out and visit to his friend in the Pub. We move away from here, first thing in the morning.'

'I'm sorry about that folks. Seems I have caused you some problems.'

'It's not your fault Eddie. But if there are going to be some problems then we might just have learnt something. But I think it's a necessary precaution. If they, who ever they are, are on to us, in any way and they do have the map reference, it is as well that we move and are gone from here when they get here, if only to be one-step ahead. It's all part of the game.'

CHAPTER FORTY

The following day, Eddie got up and left the campsite for the village early, planning on his return, to inform the Pub Staff and anyone else who happened to be around, what a great time he had had with his friend the night before and how he had been so drunk that he had been obliged to stay the night. We remembered this time, just before he left, to give him a radio and arranged to listen, if convenient, on the hour and up to one minute past. We also selected, from the map, another campsite that was not too far away so that Eddie knew where we proposed to go, before he left. Fortunately, there were several Caravan and Camping Sites, dotted along that particular stretch of the East Coast, so selecting another, at a reasonable distance from the village, was no real problem.

Unless anything unexpected cropped up in the meantime, we finally arranged that we would all meet up at the proposed new location even, we decided, if it proved to be unsatisfactory when we got there. We would still use it as a meeting point and meet up on the day before the proposed stake out.

As a further precaution, we decided to eliminate the need to pass phone numbers over the radio, or even by telephone, by giving each of the common ones, which we thought we might need to use in the near future, a label. We agreed that the Dog and Gun should be phone "one", the village call box, "two" and the Grapes, "three". Our new proposed campsite telephone number would be known as "four". Fred having already looked it up in the phone book and then ringing to ask if they were open to take campers and thus confirming that it was the correct number for the site.

As soon as Eddie left, we started to get our things together and prepared to move out.

'Do me a favour Fred, you go and settle up with the dragon. I'm afraid if she were to mention inflation or the impending Season just once more, I might strangle her or something and what ever you do, don't let her pull any fast ones on you.'

I had everything stowed away and both the van and car turned round and ready to go when she returned.

'How did you get on with the Lady Mud Wrestler?'

'No problem! I told her that our reason for leaving was that my Mum was not very well and we were going home. It works every time, she was full of understanding and sympathy. Are we all ready to go?'

We travelled in a two-vehicle convoy on to the next Camp Site, which was less than two miles away and not only was it about the same distance from

the village as the last one but was also fairly secluded and, the result of careful landscaping, well hidden from the nearest main road. Apart from some minor differences in the approach to it, the layout of the main entrance and of course the different name of the site, it was almost identical to the last one. But then many caravan sites are very similar with their office, shop, gas store, toilets, showers and phone boxes; two this time and both to prove later to have different phone numbers to the one Fred had taken from the phone book and Eddie had copied down. That one later proved to be their office number and used by them for reservations and business. At first glance this new campsite was at least comparable in size with the previous one and the establishment was again very much the same, as far as terms, rules and regulations were concerned, although it was in the overall control of a much younger lady.

'There is not much competition along this coast,' mused Fred, having paid a deposit and been directed to the space reserved specifically for mobile homes. 'It costs just the same to stay here as back there along the road.'

We parked and I connected the gas and wastewater container. Spare gear was once again taken out of the body of the van and stowed in the driver's cab.

Checking my watch, I found it was almost Twelve o'clock, mid-day, so taking the radio I switched it on.

'What are you doing?' enquired Fred.

'Going to pass Eddie the new phone number.'

'Have you got it?'

'Yes. When I went across to the Toilet I nipped into both boxes and wrote them down. I can pass him at least one of them for now. It's also a good opportunity to see it our comms are working.'

'And a hopeless contradiction of all our security arrangements. That brilliant idea of numbering phone numbers and all the effort you put into it, didn't last long.'

'What makes you say that?'

'Simple. You said we wouldn't pass telephone numbers over the airwaves. We will give them a code number. Now on our very first transmission you are going to pass a full number. So much for anyone overhearing or listening in.'

'We don't have much choice do we, if we want Eddie to have the number? We are only passing a number, not an address or any other clues to its location.'

'And what damned difference does that make to anyone with an iota of common sense. Have you never heard of, or used, directory enquiries? A phone number is as good as a name and address to anyone determined enough to find out.'

'I know that. So, tell me, do I pass it or not?'

'I suppose you must; if you want him to have it right now.'

I held up my watch and counted down the seconds. Straight on the hour I called, 'Echo, Mike, over'.

'Wait one, traffic,' came the instant reply that both pleased me and surprised me. I think at first I didn't think he would be listening, but when he was, and then came back so quickly, it caught me completely off guard.

'What did he say?'

'Wait one. He is obviously in his car and driving. At least he is receiving me and has remembered to switch the thing on.'

'Mike, Echo, go,' squawked the radio in my hand.

'Echo, Mike… Change and correction to number four… Now reads…' and I passed the amended number.

'Roger, got that, listening, out.'

I had nothing further to add and neither, apparently, had Eddie as I timed it with my watch to make sure a full two minutes had passed before switching off the radio and laying it aside. I beamed at Fred, 'Well at least something has worked without a hitch.'

'Despite passing a complete phone number, I am very pleased for you. Now let's see if your legs still work. Take this container and go and find some fresh water. Then I suppose a tour of the camp aught to be the order of the day?'

It is only when you move from camp-site to camp-site rather quickly, as we had just done, that you realise just how similar they all are. All the amenities and facilities are generally grouped somewhere near the entrance and are probably there to minimise the distance for pipe and drain laying or some other such consideration. But it is all as if someone, long ago, planned out the very first campsite and since then everyone else has copied it without even a thought of innovation or deviation. Perhaps Caravanners belong to a peculiar group of people who don't like, or can't handle, change and differences. It's all as if no matter where they choose to go they expect to find everything in exactly the same place and that is the reason for the conformity, at least, in site layouts. As I wandered round on that afternoon, I smiled to myself as I wondered if this peculiar group of people, not that for one single moment did I suspect, or accuse, any one of them of being peculiar in any accepted way, really did have an influence on any of this, apart from accepting it. The Caravans all neatly laid out in straight lines and all painted in similar pastel shades, grass all neatly cut and cars parked alongside. I just could not help myself pondering the subject and I found it very amusing as, in my twisted way, I attempted to rationalise the obscure necessity for similarity in Caravan Sites. Not that I had any extensive knowledge; but that did not stop me. Was it? I wondered, down to the fact that no matter how dark it gets at night, or how drunk they, as individuals, get, they can, by habit, familiarity, and instinct, find the exact location of everything on this site and every other. As I looked about

there were even signs of recent grass cutting and a large pile of clippings in a corner, not too far away. The uniformity was unbelievable.

Pointing at the pile as we passed, Fred said jokingly, 'that reminds me of somewhere else I have been recently. But at least here it is not all sticking to the soles of my boots.'

I laughed and muttered, 'God I hope they have no inflation problems here or are using last years prices.'

'What's that?'

'Nothing. Just thinking aloud and remarking how much these places are all so much alike.'

We toured round the site and on our return once again dug out and consulted, the map. We then determined from it, which lane led where, and also where exactly we were in relation to the village and everything else that might be relevant.

'Look here,' said Fred pointing at the map. 'If I am not mistaken, this is a path or some sort of right of way across this particular area here and it ties up here with this other path that runs north to south along the cliff top. If we use that, assuming we can get through and I don't see why not as it is clearly shown on this map, we can get to the cliff top without the need to go anywhere near the village and we only need to cross the main road once… here,' she pointed. 'Let's make up a flask and go and have a look. I know it's a good walk, but we have time and nothing planned for the rest of today and I have a feeling that it may prove useful in the future. It's a round-a-bout route I know, but at least by going along it, we can get to the ravine without going anywhere near the village and I think that could be important and useful.'

The next couple of hours, or so, were soon taken up tramping through fields and along narrow tracks and pathways. We stopped at least twice for a rest and a hot drink and on more than one occasion hesitated for a few minutes to consult the map. I had taken the radio with me, but despite my careful timing it remained silent for the whole minute past each of the full hours I tuned in to.

When we got back to the van we were both tired, yet pleasantly invigorated from all the exercise. Two cans of soup and a large tin of potatoes, along with half a loaf of bread, soon disappeared. The next I knew was that Fred was prodding me and shaking me out of my doze.

'Come on, Eight o'clock; radio watch before you fall asleep,' as she passed the radio across the table.

I switched it on and consulted my watch. It was two minutes to eight. I set it down to wait and closed my eyes. That, coupled with the fact that I was not expecting anything, left me to doze off again. The radio made me jump.

'What was that?' gasped Fred, who must also have nodded off and therefore jumped in turn at the sudden noise.

'The radio… Listen… It will go again.'

'Mike, Echo, over.'

'Echo, Mike, go.'

'Ring Two, in five minutes, over.'

'Roger, out,' I replied before looking at Fred. 'Damn and just when I was settling down. I hope what he wants is important.'

'I need the loo, so I will ring him if you like. You stay here and rest you poor tired, whatever it is, that needs resting the most.'

I must have drifted off again immediately Fred left. I had no idea how long she had been away, when the door flew open and with an air of urgency, she said, 'Come on. Wake up, we have a problem.'

'What sort of problem?'

'Someone has blasted Eddie's car with a shotgun!'

'His car! What about Eddie and with a shotgun? Shit! Tell me about it.'

'That's what he said. He is OK. He will give us all the details later. But for now, he is catching the Eight-thirty bus from the village through to Whitby. He intends to get off two stops out of the village and wants us to pick him up. In the meantime we are to keep the radio on all the time.'

'If this is trouble: or the start of trouble. Then we had better split up. No point in everyone rushing headlong into it. You stay here. I will take the car and go and pick Eddie up. It may all be a storm in a teacup but until we find out we will take no chances. Shotguns, under any circumstances, are bad news. I will also take one of Eddie's radios with me so that I can talk independently to you, if necessary.'

'As long as you are in range,' she added. 'Don't forget you have only about a mile or so on one of those things.'

'Yes I know, but I don't anticipate going all that far, do I? You keep our radio and one of Eddie's, then, at least you can talk to both of us, if you need to. Any other way would mean that one of us would be left in the dark as far as comms are concerned. I won't be too long. The second bus stop can't be that far along the road, so if I set off now, I should be there in plenty of time and waiting.'

I drove along the Whitby road, having joined it from a side road that lead back to the camp. As I drove North, I kept a wary eye out for the bus stops. I had noticed that they were not always clearly marked in the open countryside because those who use them, passengers and drivers alike, all seem to know where they are and don't need signs to remind them.

The first one was easy to find. The sign was clear and nailed firmly to a telegraph pole. Part of the grass verge had been dug out and surfaced to make a lay-bye and suitable stopping place. There was also a wooden rubbish bin that is, usually, a further indication of a stopping place.

About a mile and a half further along a similar set up indicated another bus stop. Although on this occasion there was no actual sign, only the remnants of a battered and broken timetable hanging off the telegraph pole.

The road, at that point, was narrow and so I was obliged to pull off onto the small lay-bye in order to minimise the space I occupied. I pulled as far as I could up to the far end. I switched on my hazard lights, released the bonnet catch, and got out. I lifted the bonnet to give the impression of a problem and an excuse for being parked there.

Eventually I heard the noise of a bus as it slowly approached and its engine sound progressively increased as it made its way round the twists and turns of the narrow country road. As it drew level, the driver made no attempt to pull in to the lay-bye, but stopped in the road and opened the door to let off two men, who from their appearance, both looked as if they were farm workers. The driver, addressing each in turn by his first name, bade them good night and they each nodded and waved back in reply.

'See you half seven in the morning,' was his parting shot as the doors closed and the bus began to pull off. There was no Eddie. Was it the correct bus I wondered? Had I got the right stop? I began to panic a little as I looked at each window, along its full length and at the occupants behind them, as the bus slowly moved away. Eddie was there all right; sitting two windows forward from the back. He was looking my way and I knew he must have seen me. All he did was raise his eyebrows and carry on looking in my direction. He had seen me; I was positive. I must have got the stop wrong, yet I was sure that this one was the second one out of the village and the one Fred told me to go to. She had definitely said that Eddie was going to get off the bus at the second stop out of the village and I was at the second stop now. There was nothing for it, I closed the bonnet, got in the car and pulled out onto the road and set off to catch up with the bus and then follow it.

Each time it stopped I drew in behind it and waited, but Eddie did not get off at any of the subsequent stops. Eventually, after a good half hours' drive, we pulled into Whitby itself and the bus made its way through the town to the Bus Station. I was unable to follow it all the way as part was reserved and restricted to buses only, so I parked as close as I could and sat watching the station exit. Eventually Eddie emerged carrying two large holdalls and, without even looking in my direction, walked directly across the square and into the Railway Station. I knew something was wrong, but could do nothing, so I remained where I was and waited.

As if from nowhere a young lad of fourteen or perhaps fifteen years of age came up to the window and tapped on it. As I wound it down he said, 'The man in the Railway Station says you are to wait' and he walked off, away from the station.

Ten minutes later Eddie emerged and walked straight towards the car. I opened the door and he threw his holdalls into the rear seat then climbed in beside me.

'No rush! The bastard's gone' he said.

'Well, what the hell was that all about?' I demanded.

'Right. If you sit here for a minute and listen, I will tell you. Earlier tonight I was sitting in the bar of the Dog and Gun having a quiet drink and reading my paper when, somewhere outside, there was an almighty bang and, along with everyone else, I dashed outside to see what it was all about and there, just inside the Car Park, was my car with the two side windows blown in and the door panels peppered with buck shot. In the dust, on the bonnet, someone had written, "Piss off shit-head". There was no sign of anyone who might have done it. I insisted that the Police were sent for and when the Village Bobby finally turned up all he could suggest was that perhaps it might be better if I leave, "for my own good seeing as someone seemed to have it in for me", was the way he put it. He rattled on about it being his opinion that it was not safe for me to stay as things were. When I pressed him about the ownership of the shotgun and the severity of the offence surrounding it's use, he had the nerve to say that he knew of no one in the village with a shotgun. That was a load of bullshit, if ever I heard any and I would have been more inclined to believe him if he had said that it could be almost anyone in the district as most people in a village and out in the country, own shotguns. Anyhow the message was clear, both from the shooter and the law and so, left with little or no choice, I put on a big display of indignation and had a lot to say to all and sundry about the matter as I packed. I also let it be known that I was not going to stick around when there was a lunatic at large and that I proposed getting the bus to Whitby and a train home from there. The law, if that's what you can call him, insisted I leave the car although it was in no fit state to be driven in any case and said it would be garaged over the road in the Service Station and would remain there until he completed his enquiries. My initial plan was to go up the road towards Whitby for a couple of miles or so and then meet up with you and that's the message I gave Fred. But when I got on the bus a bloke, a stranger to me, but known to the bus driver, said to the driver, through his side window, "I want to know if that pratt gets off this bus anywhere between here and Whitby. Watch and see that he goes into the station". So you see, after that, I had no alternative but to stay on the bus. When it arrived in Whitby the bus driver followed me into the Railway Station and hung around until it was time for him to leave and take his bus back to wherever. It was only when I saw him pull out of the bus station and drive off, that I came across to you.'

'"Piss off shit-head", scratched on the car bonnet. A touch of the Johnson's, do you think?'

'Could be, he's mad enough and thick enough, but so might be any number of others, back there, in that village. Someone obviously wanted me out, but who and for what reason, I have no idea.'

'Well, they have achieved their purpose, so far, or think they have and if it was part of some complicated or carefully calculated plan it may well have boosted their confidence. Let's hope so, for over-confidence often leads to mistakes and we need them, who ever they are, to make as many mistakes as possible. On the other hand I would hate to think they have actually caught on to us, know who we are and know what we might be up to and believe we are getting close to them. So, for the moment, let's hope it is only brain-dead Johnson, or someone like him, who has got it all out of proportion and really knows nothing.'

'Where is Fred now? Will she not be worried? I thought you might have brought her with you.'

'No, I left her as anchorman. She will be listening. Give her a call. If we are within range she will get us.'

Eddie picked up my radio; or more accurately his own that was on loan to me, from the dash and opening the window, for better communications, tilted his head so that the aerial of the handset stuck out through the opening.

'Foxtrot. Echo. Over.'

There was no reply. Fred was not receiving, or if she was, we in turn were not picking up her reply. It often happens when working at the extreme ranges of handsets.

Eddie of course realised this also, so waited a few minutes and then tried again but still there was nothing.

'I will leave it for another couple of miles and then try again. This thing is probably well out of range here.

We drove on in silence for five or ten minutes, perhaps longer, then, winding down the side window once again, Eddie called.

'Foxtrot. Echo. Over.'

'Echo... Foxtrot... You are very faint but readable... Over.'

'On our way home, out.'

The receiver clicked twice so we knew Fred had received and understood us. I felt much better, for I knew, despite what she might say, she would have been concerned at the length of time I had been away.

We finally arrived back on the camp site and as I pulled in alongside the van the door opened and a familiar voice said, 'Enjoyed your trip?'

'Yes thanks,' I replied. 'And for my trouble we have acquired ourselves a permanent lodger,' Indicating Eddie.

'Is there a phone close by?' asked Eddie.

'Yes. Over there: by that light. It's round the back.'

'Good. If you will just give me a minute, I am going to ring one of our guys so that he can come in, as soon as possible, hopefully tomorrow, posing as an Insurance Agent investigating the damage to my car. He can ask a lot of prying and embarrassing questions and may just be able to pick up something of value to us.'

'Wait a minute Eddie. Don't let's overload the job with additional labour at this stage for goodness sake.'

'That was not the idea. My plan was for him to come in, be indignant and what have you, about gunshots damage to a car that his company has insured and at the same time perhaps pickup something of value; a one off. He can then disappear again into the background. All Insurance Companies have investigators, so his presence should not arouse any suspicion, or draw any attention to us. To do nothing might have an adverse affect. Might give the impression I am scared or have something to hide.'

'OK, as long as he doesn't get in our way.'

While Eddie went to make his phone call I related to Fred everything that had happened. As I finished I said, 'What do you make of it all?'

'The same as you! They might have rumbled Eddie, but I doubt it. More likely it is Johnson or someone like him, drunk, and expressing his dislike for strangers. A bit strange and stupid of that Policeman to say he knew of no one with a shotgun. Makes you wonder if he is involved in some way or just thinks everyone is thick like himself?'

'It does, doesn't it? He is probably used to going round making silly statements and having no one with enough brains or inclination to challenge him. But I can't see that, they are not all thick in that village. There is something about that copper that I am not too happy about.'

'Mel, before Eddie comes back, give me a hand to split these sleeping bags. I know he's not daft, but I think I will feel more comfortable if we split them up while he's not here. I promise I will make up for it later.'

I was naturally disappointed but fully understood her feelings. We had just finished and Fred was closing the bench seat where the bedding was kept, when Eddie returned. 'That's better. I needed that, but in all the excitement I never got round to it and I have also made my call, so that is taken care of. Look I am sorry about all this inconvenience.'

'No, you look,' replied Fred. 'There are no problems over anything unless we make one. We will be a bit limited for space, but we will work round it somehow. I'm going to make a sandwich for us all, that is if you two will move up there, out of my way and you Mel, dig out what is left of the booze. There are a couple of cans and some whiskey up there, and half a bottle of lemonade. We will worry about the small details and sleeping arrangements later.'

We ate and drank all that we had left over and as we did so, Eddie found it highly amusing when I told him about the old dear back at the other camp and her seasonal inflation and adjustments to the cost of 'out of date' cans of booze.

'Is that it? No more? Is it all finished?' As I tipped up the bottle and let the last drip of whiskey fall into my empty glass.

'For tonight, it is. You have had enough. There's another full bottle but it stays where it is. We keep that for later. We might need it for more practical reasons. So now, for the moment, what is more important, is that we need to sort out who is going to sleep where.'

With the table down and fixed in place, the two separate sleeping bags were laid out. Everything else, that was soft and flexible, was spread out evenly on the floor, to make a base for Eddie. We had two spare blankets in the van, to which I added the blanket from the boot of my car. Eddie had a car blanket of his own that he had stuffed into one of his holdalls, when he emptied his car, before leaving it behind. He looked comfortable enough and claimed he was fine.

It seemed so strange, after what I had been used to, to sit and watch Fred removed only her boots and loosen her hair. Having done so, she smiled and slid down into her own, now single, sleeping bag. I followed suit and feeling distinctly uncomfortable in all the extra clothing, knew I was about to miss the wonderful closeness and warmth of Fred. But things being the way they were, we had no option but to compromise. All that came my way that night and sadly for the next few nights, was, a light kiss and the tip of a warm tongue on the end of my nose.

Out of the darkness Eddie muttered, 'It's been a hell of a day; roll on tomorrow, when something really exciting might happen. Good night all.'

'Good night,' we chorused.

CHAPTER FORTY-ONE

I spent a very uncomfortable night trussed up in that single sleeping bag, almost fully clothed. There was hardly room to move. I slept fitfully, then woke and dozed and then I suppose slept some more, until eventually it was morning and I reluctantly shook myself back to reality. I decided that a single sleeping bag, with a fully clothed body inside, is not the best place to spend a night. My stirring woke the others and, before long we were all stretching, yawning and, to varying degrees, complaining.

'If you two get up now and go outside, I might have room to move around in here. So go to the loo or see if you can find some milk for breakfast, or something,' yawned Fred.

I worked my way out of the bag, fighting against the friction of my clothing and the unbelievable number of twists and turns that had worked their way into my underwear and the lining of the sleeping bag. Eventually, free of all quilting I found my boots and put them on. When I stood up and opened the van door, the blast of cold, fresh air that hit me made me realise just how warm and stuffy it had become in the confined space.

'Give me a second and I will join you,' said Eddie.

'While you two make up your minds who is doing what, will you please close that door. I'm freezing to death in here,' moaned Fred.

Eddie and I tramped slowly across the damp grass towards the toilet block. The ground was wet from the heavy overnight dew. The clouds were high and moving fairly rapidly across the sky, despite the fact that there was little breeze to be felt at ground level. The air was thin and the light weak, as is often the case just after dawn. Somewhere in the distance could be heard the noise, that continually breaks the silence of the countryside these days, of a tractor engine. The best thing about that particular day was the fact that, so far, it was chilly but not too cold and it was fine and dry.

On the way back we passed Fred, carrying her toilet bag and towel and leisurely strolling towards the toilet block. As we drew level she enquired. 'Did you get any milk?'

'No the shop is shut.'

'It will have to be black then and dry cornflakes, if you want them. Put the kettle on when you get back.'

About an hour later and breakfast over. No one having chosen cornflakes, we cleared away. Shortly after that we sat round the table and spread the map out in front of us. We discussed and debated our plans and possible moves for the day.

'This is the area we need to concentrate on, the same as last time,' I said pointing to the wooded area surrounding the ravine. 'To get there and avoid the village altogether, we will have to circumnavigate it. Good word that, circumnavigate. Go round it, is more like it, in this direction preferably. We could go by a Southern route, if we need to, but this Northerly one is the shortest, seeing as we are here now. So let's work out how we get from here to somewhere there,' pointing to the campsite first and then the ravine. 'We can work our way along this track, cross the main road here, then take this track, which follows this wall and crosses these fields to here and then follow it until it reaches the cliff-top path just about here.'

As I traced it on the map Eddie lent forward and followed my finger.

'If these paths are open and just not lines, drawn on the map. Because you know what farmers are like? They will pinch every bit of land they can get away with.'

'They are open as far as here because Mel and I went yesterday and we had no problems,' confirmed Fred.

'Good, so if the rest is blocked off, then from there, all we might have to do is climb a few walls and walk along the edge of a few ploughed fields. With the map we can always argue our right of way if anyone stops and challenges us.'

'I don't think we will have any problems,' replied Fred. 'Because if it was open as far as here then the chances are it will be open for the rest of the way. It certainly will along here as this path along the cliff top is a recognised and clearly marked, tourist track.'

'So on reaching here,' I said. 'If we then go in this direction and work our way along the cliff top we will come to the point where Edison's radio and things were found and finally end up here at the top of the ravine somewhere about where you set watch last time Eddie. The woods look as if they will be fairly thick just there and according to the map, stretch a couple of hundred yards or more inland back from the coast. My original thought was that we could make our way there today and set up a base camp in those woods and possibly work from there.'

'Are you proposing that we stay out in the open for two whole nights?' asked Eddie.

'No. Not exactly! We have a tent, which at a push, will accommodate the three of us and I thought that if we take sufficient pre-packed food, sandwiches and so on, along with us, we would then only need a stove, which we have, to boil water. You will see, that this stream, that ends up in the ravine, flows through the woods here, so we should have no problems finding fresh water.'

'And to powder my nose?' said Fred.

'You will just have to keep one eye out for passers-bye and the other for nettles.'

'You have sufficient camping gear for the three of us?' asked Eddie.

'Only the bare essentials but it will be more than adequate for a couple of days. There's a good tent, which was bought originally for two, but will take three, in the short term, with care and a bit of planning. We have sleeping bags and blankets, a stove, pans and water bottle. It's only going to be for a couple of nights and for one of those we won't need a tent to sleep in because we will be staking out the ravine and, if the worst comes to the worst, we can work out some form of shift system for sleeping. All the clothes we will need, we can carry on our backs along with the other equipment. We should only need the odd spare jumper and waterproofs. Split the load between the three of us and we should have no trouble. How do you two feel? Anyone any other ideas or suggestions?'

'It's better than going straight into the village and announcing to the whole world that we intend to hide in the woods tomorrow night,' laughed Eddie.

'It is not all that far to go and we have all day to do it in. Let's hope it doesn't rain, that's all. What about you, Fred? Have you anything to say? Anything to add from your point of view?'

'No. I suppose I don't mind sharing my life with the creepy crawlies and earwigs for a couple of nights.'

'Are you a creepy crawly, Mel?' asked Eddie, looking at me and smiling, 'Or are you an earwig?'

Fred, jokingly sideswiped him and, laughing, said, 'I can handle you two. It's the little tiny ones I don't like. The ones you don't see or feel until they bite.'

'Well, shall we make tracks and get ready to leave, or not?'

'I suppose so, as no one else seems to have come up with any better alternatives old man, lead on.'

'Right. So if we assemble all our gear now and set out as soon as possible, we should leave ourselves with sufficient time to change our minds and location or make any additional contingency plans should the original proposal not work out as we anticipate.'

'As we anticipate? As you anticipate. Your plan and your proposals so far, don't forget darling.'

'OK, OK, but you know what I mean. It is one thing when you are sat here looking at a map and a much different story when you arrive on scene and I just feel it would be better if we had as much time as possible to make changes.'

'From what to what exactly?'

'Oh, come on, I don't know. Let's wait and see what happens when we get into the woods. What's the matter with you all of a sudden? Not happy about something, because if not, say something now.'

'I'm fine, but the thought of nettles and crawling things doesn't help.'

The next hour or so was rather hectic. Fred cheered up some what as she attempted to put everything she could lay her hands on between slices of bread and then pile, what she thought we might need by the way of food, on to the work

surface. In the meantime I squeezed back and forth, past her, to get in and out of the different lockers, trying to remember exactly where we had stowed everything and trying not to forget any of the essentials.

We chatted freely as we worked at our different tasks, perhaps to release some of the tension.

'You like pickle, Eddie?'

'Yes.'

'On everything?'

'Yes.'

'Good.'

'Have you seen the spare container of gas for this portable stove?'

'No, you put it away.'

'No I didn't.'

'Yes you did. Have you tried up there? No, there to the left.'

'How did you know it was there if you haven't seen it?'

'Just remembered you putting it there, didn't I?'

I gently tapped her bum.

'Don't take the matches away yet. I need them for the stove. I still have to fill these flasks.'

Eddie was probably the wisest, for he had taken his holdalls outside and was neatly packing, into just one of them, everything he thought he might need.

'Have you got all your things together?' enquired Fred.

'Almost' I replied.

'Then be a good boy and take them outside over there with Eddie. I will then have some room to work in here. I still have to start on my bits and pieces. Take all this food away from here and put it somewhere safe.'

I carefully carried and piled, everything she had indicated onto the boot lid of my car and then taking one of the frame rucksacks, assembled it and laid it aside ready for her to use. As I assembled the other, Eddie asked, 'Where did you get those?'

'Bought them at the same time as the tent and all the other equipment.'

'Did you plan to go camping right from the beginning then?'

'No. We planned nothing specific. We had no idea what to expect or what might develop when we got here. I remember thinking, at the time we bought it, that we might be over-indulging as Fred had already made it quite clear that she was rather reluctant to go camping, especially in a tent, for pleasure.'

'You're right there,' came a female voice from somewhere within the van.

* * *

Finally we each had our own pack: Fred and I a rucksack each and Eddie his holdall. We each carried our personal things and had shared out the remainder. I had the tent and groundsheet slung under my frame. Fred took most of the bedding, which was bulky but fairly light and Eddie had carefully packed the radios, torches and stove and so on into his holdall. We had shared out the tinned food that was the single, most heavy item, of all our stores. Fortunately, as Fred pointed out, most of it was only going in one direction.

We checked to make certain everything was secure. Satisfied I hoisted my pack onto my back and was surprised how little it seemed to weigh, at first, relative to its overall size. Later it was to get, not uncomfortably heavy, but a burden and nuisance that I would be glad to unload.

'Not too bad for a couple of miles or so,' I said as I settled it down onto my shoulders. 'We don't have to rush and we can stop as often as we want. Will you be all right with that holdall Eddie?' I then enquired as I had visions of him constantly swinging it against his legs, due to it's bulk and then having to changing it, every few yards, from one hand to the other, after only the first half mile or so when it began to get heavy.

'No problem! These handles are long enough for me to put my arms through, like this, and then the bag effectively becomes a pack on my back. I bought those two holdalls specifically with this in mind after an experience, a while back, when I had to carry a heavy load for miles in a very small, short-handled holdall. My arms ended up eighteen inches longer and the sides of my legs were scuffed red raw from catching into the damned thing. I swore then it would never happen again, if I could help it. So I bought these two and have used them ever since. It's surprising how much they hold and they can be carried in the normal manner or they sling on your back like this, no problem.'

I felt relieved, for again I had had visions of being obliged to offer to exchange packs with him, after a mile or so and I didn't relish the thought of a holdall banging into my legs either.

We set out and fell into a single file along the roadside with Fred leading the way. The map stuck out of her pocket.

'Keep up, you there behind. On my expeditions stragglers will be shot and their bodies thrown to the crocodiles or given over to the native women,' she laughed.

At least one of us was in a fairly cheerful mood.

At the end of the lane, leading away from the campsite, we turned right and followed the road, walking comfortably on the grass verge, for about a quarter of a mile. No traffic passed us in either direction.

'We need to climb over this style and take that path,' said Fred, pointing with her outstretched arm over the adjacent wall.

For most of the way the path clung to the wall side and passed through several fields. I noticed that each field was different in so much that there was either a wire fence enclosing the path or a rough natural hedge doing the same. Some had no barrier at all which meant that a short side step would have taken us off the path and straight into the ploughed field. Here was obviously a farmer, who was determined on this occasion, to get the maximum yield from his field. At one point the path took a sharp left hand turn to make a detour round a complete field. In another place the track, open on both sides, went diagonally from corner to corner across the middle of the field. When we reached this particular one Fred observed, 'From my Girl Guide days I remember this field is always the one normally reserved for the Bull.'

We all stopped and looked round as if we genuinely expected to see a bull, scraping the earth with its front hoof and preparing to charge. The field was empty.

'Probably somewhere else chatting up the cows' suggested Eddie.

The path came to a temporary halt up against a dry stonewall, into which individual stones had been arranged, during its construction, to make it relatively easy to climb over.

We stopped for a moment and Fred, extracting the map from her pocket, consulted it before stating, 'If I remember rightly, this brings us up to the main road we have to cross.'

'You're right,' said Eddie who, standing on one of the lower protruding stones, was able to see over the top of the wall and observe what lay beyond.

Returning to the map Fred instructed, 'we go over here, onto the side of the road, and turn left. There is another track marked on the right hand side a short distance further along. This road is the main Whitby road, so no lingering you two once we are over.'

'Yes, Great White Hunter and leader and devourer of brave men,' I said shaking her pack.

'Don't be silly. This is one place we don't want to be seen and must cross over quickly. There's no point in creeping around the countryside trying to keep out of sight and then advertising our presence out on the open road.'

'How far do you reckon we have to go?'

'About two hundred yards or so; I don't really know. It's difficult to tell accurately from the map but it is not that far.'

'Is it worth taking the trouble of going over the wall and along the roadside one at a time, or do you think that is being a bit too over-cautious? After all there hasn't been a single vehicle pass along this road in all the time we have been stood here.'

'Let's just climb over the wall as we are. We are hikers out for the day, remember,' said Eddie, who was, by this time, half way up the wall and looking along an empty road.

Fred followed and was next to climb over. I took up the rear. We moved, once again, in single file along the edge of the road and some three hundred yards further along it, found the style we were looking for. This time it was a wooden one, constructed into a boundary fence, which gave access to a similar track and not unlike, the one we had just left. It followed the side of a dry stonewall.

Fred was, once again, in the lead and we had gone about fifty yards along this stretch when the first car of the day came into view along the main road. It was heading north and therefore the wall was between it, and us as it approached. The chances of anyone seeing us, as they passed, was very remote and even if they did happen to be looking specifically in our direction, at the time, they would have been rapidly moving away from us and would therefore have had to purposely turn round to observe us for any length of time; something that would have been very difficult for a single driver to do and still concentrate on his driving.

The car disappeared into the distance and we trudged on.

Fred decided to call a short halt.

Directly ahead, we could see clearly the point where the skyline appeared to meet the sea. But we were on a slight incline that made it difficult to judge exactly how far we still had to go to reach the cliff top.

'We should come to the cliff path quite soon now,' said Fred. 'I suggest that when we do, we don't linger on it any longer than necessary. It's a popular tourist walk and we could bump into anyone at any time.'

We sat with our backs to the wall and enjoyed the welcome break before setting out once again. Shortly after that we broke out on to the cliff-top track. Turning south we passed the point where we believed Philip Edison had been, at some time, on the night of his disappearance. We saw no one, the noisy seagulls, circling and swooping above, being our only companions.

'So far, so good! Now let's get off this track and into these woods and let's hope we can find a suitable site and set up camp.'

I took the lead on this occasion, not because I was more competent, but because I happened to be the first one over the wire fence and Fred and Eddie had followed close behind. Not too deep into the wood and yet an adequate distance from the track to be out of sight from anyone passing along it, we came to a small clearing.

'Rest time,' I said, slipping off my pack and lowering it to the ground. I sat down on the grass. 'Pass the map across so that I can take a peak at it for a moment, please Fred.'

I spread it on the grass, then pointing, said, 'we are somewhere about here. The nearest point to the stream, if there is one, is over there so we need to be moving over in that direction.'

Both Fred and Eddie looked in the direction I indicated but, like myself, could see nothing but trees and undergrowth.

'You two rest here for a moment while I go take a look,' volunteered Eddie.

He disappeared out of sight but was back in less than two minutes.

'Just over there,' he pointed. 'There is a small shallow hollow which is perfect to set up camp in, and running close by is the stream which flows in that direction towards the ravine.'

Eddie picked up his bag and Fred and I, our rucksacks. Eddie led the way to this second clearing and it was exactly as he said, perfect for our requirements. A slight depression in the ground sloping off to one side and then a small stream, not too far away, flowing in the same direction.

'No drainage problems; well in from the track and out of sight and earshot from anyone walking along it. You would have to come over the fence and into the wood and right up to this spot before you realised it was there,' commented Eddie.

'Fine. I just wish it were that little bit warmer. It's ok when you are on the move but sitting about here might get a bit uncomfortable. This breeze is rather chilly but I suppose we will survive for a couple of days. At least I remembered to bring the bottle of whisky,' grumbled Fred.

'OK Fred, you stay here for the moment with all our gear and make yourself useful while Eddie and I go and take a look around.'

I picked up the map.

'Why don't you stay and I will go take a look around.'

'Yes, OK. Fine by me, here's the map.'

'Don't be silly. All I was doing was making sure I had not been relegated to duty slave. Off you go and don't be long.'

I turned to Eddie. 'We know the cliff top is that way. This stream must be this thin blue line marked here and goes, according to this map, towards the ravine and joins the main stream here, so let's follow it this way to start with.'

We discovered that the stream went more or less in a straight line to the edge of the ravine where it then tumbled in a series of miniature waterfalls down the steep incline of the ravine side. The side of the ravine at this point was not a sheer drop but was angled at about forty-five degrees. It could, if necessary, have been negotiated with difficulty, but I believed it would have been near impossible in wet weather without the aid of ropes, as the grass and earth would then become too slippery to obtain secure footholds. The slope however, though steep, supported a wide variety of large trees and other dense vegetation and the whole lot seemed

to be evenly spread over the entire ravine side. The undergrowth was sufficiently dense and more than adequate to allow a person to conceal themselves without the slightest difficulty.

'Good cover all the way down,' observed Eddie. 'I can't see the bottom from here but through there you can just see the track that goes down the side and round the back of the Pub. That's the way I went up to the top and back the other night.'

'It's a bit steep just here but let's carefully work our way down and see just where this tiny stream crosses that path. You never know, it might be a useful route to use if we have cause to come back up from the bottom and make for the camp, in a hurry.'

The water from the stream ran through a series of cracks and over the rocks until it reached the side of the track. It then flowed downhill running parallel with the track for a few feet before entering a man-made gully, which took it across the track, to then exit on the other side and carry on down and out of our sight heading towards the main stream or onto the pebbles somewhere above the high water line down on the beach.

We stood and watched the stream for a few moments as it flowed and disappeared out of sight. There was no one about and nothing to be heard but the natural sounds of the water and the surrounding woodland.

'I don't fancy climbing all that way back up to get back to camp, do you? Let's take the longer and I hope, the easier way.'

We followed the track back up, along the side of the ravine, round the corner at the top and back deeper into the wood, climbing over the fence at a point close to our original point of entry. We almost came upon Fred before realising she was there which proved the excellence of our choice of sight.

'Enjoy the walk? I could hear you coming long before I saw you, which gave me plenty of warning, and should be very useful to us if anyone should choose to stray our way.'

'The walk was just fine, thank you. We found out that this little stream goes more or less in a straight line from here and crosses the track, about half way down, which leads to the rear of the Pub. It's steep from here and not easy to climb but could be used in an emergency.'

'While you have been away I have found a good spot for a loo.'

'Good. Where's that?'

'I'm not telling. You go and find your own, mine's Ladies only.'

'Right. No doubt when the necessity arises, we will each find our own, but for the moment, let's go and see what's in that direction.'

'Fields. According to the map. If I remember rightly,' said Fred.

'Good. But let's check and see how far these woods actually stretch back that way and if there are any natural barriers or hidden fences that might present problems in the dark.'

'Why? Who is going to go that way in the dark?'

'We are, if we have to. We want to know how to get in and out of these woods in as many different directions as possible.'

'Can I come with you this time?'

'Of course you can. You go with Mel this time and I will stay and unpack,' suggested Eddie. 'I might even go and hang a GENTS sign on a suitable bush, while you two are out of the way.'

Fred and I, with our backs to the ravine, set out in a Northerly direction and headed towards where we eventually expected to find fields. The woodland was fairly level and there were no paths or worn tracks traversing through it, or any other evidence, for that matter, of humans tramping about on a habitual or regular basis.

'With perhaps the exception of the odd poacher, I bet no one ever comes into these woods year in, year out,' I observed.

Several hundred yards along, the woodland stopped abruptly and we came to the edge of a ploughed field. The boundary was a post and barbed wire fence.

'Nasty, if you ran into this in the pitch dark, but no problems, if you know it is there. From what I can see it also looks as if it runs the full length along this side of the wood. I can't see any point in following it, can you?'

'No. Not really. As you say, it runs as far as you can see in both directions and it probably runs even further than that and stretches all the way along between where the woodland meets with the fields.'

'Let's go back. I am hungry and could murder one of your sandwiches. It seems forever since we last ate.'

'It is!'

When we got back, Eddie had a few things spread out and was still unpacking his holdall. There was a small pan of boiling water, on the stove.

'I hope you don't mind me delving into your pack, but I just fancied a hot drink and thought you might also. That tea in the flask will probably be stewed by now. Care to join me?'

'Yes please.'

I devoured a large corned beef sandwich in no time flat. The tea was the best I have ever tasted, even though we were obliged to use tinned milk. While we ate, I told him about the wire fence that bordered the fields.

'How high is it?' asked Eddie using his head to nod in the direction from which we had returned.

'Three foot; three foot six. No problem unless you run headlong into it by accident.'

‘As long as we know it is there.’

‘Don’t you think we should be thinking about putting up the tent. It’s getting a bit chilly sat out here in the open,’ shivered Fred.

‘I thought we ought to wait a little longer, until at least nearer dark, in case we had to move in a hurry, but I think we are safe enough here now. Apart from that odd car back there on the main road, we haven’t seen a single sole since we left the Camper. We may get the odd dog walker out, later in the evening, after tea and maybe the poachers at night, but I think we are still safe enough here. Anyhow, we have not had that tent out of its bag since we bought it, so it’s as well if we get it out and sort out all the bits and pieces, while there is plenty of daylight left and we can see what we are doing to sort it out.’

Erecting the tent was simplicity itself; the result of some very clever design work. The aluminium poles that made up the frame would only fit one way and, once erected, the outer cover was draped over it and secured down and in place with pegs. Four guy ropes from the top corners held the whole thing down and ensured that the wind did not carry it all away. Next a ground sheet was laid inside and secured. An inner lining, which I would best describe as a large fabric box, was suspended from the main frame using small hooks and fabric ties. The tent walls and top had effectively two skins; an inner and an outer, with air trapped between for insulation. According to the instruction leaflet the whole thing was completely windproof and waterproof and access to the interior was gained through the circular holes, one in the inner, and one in the outer layers. Each was sealed up tight by a zip that ran for more than three quarters of the way round its circumference.

I was pleasantly surprised by the overall size in relation to its weight and once erected there was ample room for three persons to lie down and still have sufficient room left to store all the gear towards one end. It was described, in the literature, as being for two persons and that was the reason we bought it. But for the short term it would certainly take three with no problem and we agreed, that if used by just two people, for any length of time the suggested, optional extra, of a zip-on front canopy and additional poles with a curtain wall, would definitely not be a ‘must’ as the brochure hinted.

‘A bit overloaded perhaps for three,’ said Fred. ‘But for now, who cares? It’s warm, dry and not for ever.’

‘Who’s going for the Fish and Chips?’ enquired Eddie as he stretched out in his self-allotted sleeping space. ‘Fish and chips are always an essential part of camping.’

‘Fish and Chips! Now who is just being cruel? You can forget all about them and concentrate on getting the rest of the stuff in here. We want to know where everything is before dark, because if Mel’s theory is correct, about the possibility of the odd poacher, we don’t want to be showing any lights round here after dark.’

‘What time does it get dark?’

‘About Half past Eight to Nine o’clock: perhaps sooner. So we need to be sorted out before then and be ready to settle down for the night.’

‘Do you think we should keep a watch?’

‘Well, we are not expecting anything tonight. But if you think it’s necessary, one of us could stay awake until around Midnight or say, One o’clock. That should be enough.’

As no one volunteered it was not mentioned again.

Fred removed the labels from three small tins of soup and, piercing the lids, stood them in the small pan which when filled with water was balanced carefully on the stove. When she was satisfied that the contents of the tins were hot enough they were opened and we were each handed one, along with two sandwiches and a spoon and ordered, ‘to sit down, shut up and eat’.

‘Food cooked in the open air always tastes good, like Fish and Chips out of the paper.’

‘If anyone mentions Fish and Chips again I will scream. Eat what you have and be grateful. If Fish and Chips are so important I will buy you both a large portion when all this is over. But until then, Mel, you eat and Eddie, you pass my coffee.’

‘This coffee tastes odd. Is it that tinned milk?’

‘Probably the glue from the can labels although I thought I had scratched it all off. Apparently not.’

‘What’s that got to do with the taste of the coffee?’ I enquired naively.

‘I used the water from the pan which I used to warm up the soup. I thought you, having been in the Services and lived the rough life, would know all about that sort of thing.’

‘I was and did, for several years but still don’t know what that has to do with this coffee.’

‘Well, when I was in the Navy to save time and water, mainly water when they are at sea and of course the navy being the navy they practice the same methods ashore, they used the water from the cabbage, or from boiling the eggs, to brew the tea. So now here you have your coffee with a bit of glue in it, which is not going to do you any harm.’

‘I see what you mean now. In the RAF it was only the water from the boiled eggs that was used for the tea, or as far as I know it was only the egg water that they used and they told us that the bromide was then added to help get rid of the taste of hen muck which came from off the shells.’

‘Well! Now here conditions are similar. Remember you are in the jungle and surrounded by potentially hostile natives and that bit of glue in your coffee may be all there is between you and eventual capture and starvation. You can’t

taste bromide because I forgot to bring it, but I am prepared to take my chances on that one.'

'In that case, I have decided that I like coffee with glue in it and will drink unlimited amounts if it will make you two lay off each other and shut up,' laughed Eddie. 'By the way, in this outdoor feast, did you say the bromide was in the coffee or the soup?'

'You haven't been listening, have you. I have already explained that yours was in the meat sandwich darling,' smiled Fred. 'I thought it necessary to knobble you as early as possible. His is in everything.'

When the leg pulling finally stopped I took the soiled spoons and pots over to the stream and washed them. The rubbish I put in a neat pile ready for disposal. While I was doing so my mind drifted back over many years and I remembered a big red-faced, red-haired, Scots Survival Instructor. Try as I could, I could not remember his name, but I remembered clearly what he said. 'Never leave rubbish, laddie. It tells everyone you've been there and tells them that they are looking for an untidy bastard. Move it. Bury it. Lose it. Eat it. Shove it in an uncomfortable place but get rid of it.' Its funny, how the little things stick in your mind and stay with you for the rest of your life. I came across another guy, somewhere down the line, who used to say, 'Never put your own interpretation on information you are given, if it is your job to just pass it on, pass it on, word for word', and one of his other favourites was, 'If you have nothing constructive to say then keep your bloody mouth shut', and another I recalled, 'Finally, and above all else, remember the eleventh commandment: Thou must not get caught. Do what the hell you like but don't get caught doing it.'

I felt the gentle pressure of a hand on my shoulder. 'Are you trying to wash those pots completely away?'

'No. I got carried away for the moment and was just reminiscing. Something about this stream and what I was doing, just now, triggered off memories from the past. Nothing important. Just day-dreaming really.'

'Come on, it's almost dark,' she said, picking up the cutlery that I had laid aside. 'It's time to be turning in. You know Eddie is lovely,' she whispered while she was bent down and our faces were close together. 'But I wish right now he was somewhere else and it was just you and me turning in for an early night.'

'There will be other times,' I whispered and standing up, followed her back to the tent.

Eddie was already wrapped up in his blankets when I ducked through the tent flap.

'You're keen to hit the hay tonight,' I said.

'Too true! I'm whacked and intend to make the most of an early night. I can't remember the last time I had the chance to be in bed so early. See you when the sun rises.' And saying that, he pulled the blanket up over his head.

I stretched out on my sleeping bag and folded my hands under my head.

'Are you getting in?' whispered Fred.

'I suppose I should, but I think I will try and stay awake for a while at least, perhaps to midnight or thereabouts. Some sort of half-hearted watch if you like.'

'Well at least get into your sleeping bag because if you fall asleep during your, so called, half-hearted watch, you will be cold.'

She was of course right, so I removed my boots and loosened my waistband. I rolled up my big jumper and made a pillow out of it. I wriggled down into my sleeping bag and zipped up the side. Fred followed suit and stretched out alongside. She was so close but the thickness and restriction of the individual bags made it feel like a million miles.

The blanket covering Eddie's face flopped down, the fingers of one hand appearing by his face. 'I've just remembered something.'

'What is that my friend?' I asked, expecting the worst.

'I wonder if they sent someone into the village, from our firm, to give them a hard time over the damage done to my car; the bastards. Sorry Fred.'

'They can send a winged messenger from there in the morning, for all I care, to assure you if they did, or did not. But for now, get your head down and forget all about it, or you set watch and I will get some sleep.'

'Sorry, Old Chap: good night.' The blanket once more covered his face and all went quiet. In a matter of minutes he was breathing deeply and evenly, totally oblivious to the world around him.

Shortly after, Fred stopped fidgeting, as she too fell asleep. That left me alone to try and keep awake and mount a listening watch. How long that lasted I don't know, for the next thing I knew it was daylight and the seagulls were screaming and making one hell of a din. Why do they have to do that? Is it to tell the world that they are the first up, that they can't sleep any longer and that they are determined that no one else will either?

'Noisy buggers.'

'Who is?' snapped Eddie, sitting bolt upright. 'What's up?'

'Nothing,' I replied wearily. 'I'm talking to the bloody gulls and if you're interested, it's time to get up. So come on the pair of you.'

'Can't you both shut up and let a girl get some beauty sleep? One of you two has snored most of the night.'

'Which proves what?'

'That I can cope with the gulls. After all, they have only just started, while one, if not both of you, has tried to keep me awake all night.'

'Who's a lucky girl?' I said.

'Shut up, you,' was the reply, as she rolled over and pulled the quilt up over her head.

CHAPTER FORTY-TWO

We pottered about having finally and reluctantly, dragged ourselves out of bed and we were going through the motions of working out some sort of plan whereby we could get through the whole day without leaving the cover of the wood. We knew and accepted, that if everything went according to plan, there would be no action until the early hours of the following morning and we had no need to make any final preparations much before that evening.

We decided that it would be safe to move around as long as we did so with caution and avoided the main tracks to minimise accidental encounters with anyone passing along that way. The weather was fine and dry and not as cold as the previous day and therefore perfect and ideal to encourage the casual walker. We therefore, more or less, decided that it would be wisest to confine ourselves to our little campsite and the surrounding woodland.

'I thought I had remembered to pack and bring with me, everything that I would need. But the one thing I did forget was something to read. It's going to be a long day and already, in the short time that I have been sat here, I have almost worn the print off this map,' I moaned.

'I have a small guidebook, somewhere in one of my pockets, that I got from the village Post Office, when I first arrived. If you hang on I will try and dig it out. It's not much, but in your boredom you might pick up something of interest and it will, at least, help to pass the time,' offered Eddie.

'I have a woman's magazine tucked away in my pack. You can read that. It may not be exactly your cup of tea, but if you just want something to help you idle away the time, it might help.'

'How do you two propose to kill the time?' asked Eddie. 'Just, reading? I certainly don't intend to sit here and read at this time in the morning. It's gorgeous out here, so I think I will wander around for an hour or two and I don't have to drift too far away to do that.'

'What about you Fred? Have you any specific plans for this lovely day?' I asked.

'I am just going to lie on my bed and do nothing for now, nothing at all, then perhaps later…' she sighed without finishing. 'It will be absolutely wonderful to be just bone-idle and snooze. So here is my magazine, sit yourself down somewhere quiet and read what the ladies are supposed to like to read.'

So we each passed a couple of hours in our own separate and different ways. One or two of the short stories in Fred's magazine were quite good, whereas other parts were not exactly my scene. Some of the girls portrayed in the adverts were

very attractive but I had no real interest in the tampons, displayed and described on every other page and which they were trying to convince me I needed and persuade me to use. After much careful thought and several re-reads I am still convinced that the letters to the Agony Aunt, are for the greater part, made up and fabricated for the purpose. Or if not, are terribly distorted, to make them larger than life and spicy to read and of course, ultimately, to sell magazines. Especially those that end with – 'name and address withheld' - or – 'name and address supplied' - or – 'different names have been used to protect the victims' - or the worst ones of them all – 'Elsie from Essex; Bessie of Bolton'.

Eddie came drifting back with his hands thrust deep into his pockets and a strange mischievous look on his face.

'These wood are fascinating with hundreds of different plants and trees growing everywhere. I wonder what the countryside was like when most of it was covered in dense woods and forests and bandits and wild animals roamed everywhere?'

'He hasn't been away from civilisation for more than two minutes and already he has caught a touch of the Robin Hoods,' I joked. 'Or does he see himself as Friar Tuck?'

'The Sheriff of Nottingham more than likely, or perhaps it is just the smell of the vegetation that has got to him,' suggested Fred, who had just stuck her head out of the tent flap. Then still laughing, she added, 'Maybe he's been experimenting with the magic mushrooms.'

'Talking of smells and things like that; you see this stream?' he grinned. 'Well I followed it back to the edge of the wood and from there you can see where it flows for part of the way, down the edge of one of the fields.'

'Well?' enquired Fred who was now standing and stretching. 'It has to come from somewhere.'

'Yes, agreed, but only a couple of fields further away, there is a herd of cows taking in vast volumes of grass at one end and happily discharging from the other.'

'Thank you very much Eddie,' said Fred with disgust, as she dropped her arms to her sides and looked directly at him. 'And I thought all the tastes in the water came only from the natural minerals buried in the earth.'

'Or the glue on the soup cans. Ignore him, he's trying to wind you up Fred.'

'No I am not. It's a fact. Go and take a look for yourself. It is just over there and you can see them quite clearly from the fence.'

'Thanks.' replied Fred, throwing a towel at him.

* * *

We passed much of the remainder of the day just chatting about a wide variety of subjects and things of mutual interest. Fred and I learned quite a few things about Eddie and I suppose, in turn, he found out quite a bit about us.

For lunch we ate the remainder of the sandwiches that, by then, were showing distinct signs of going dry and curling at the corners.

'Very nice when you're hungry and not really all that dry when washed down with a hot pot of, cow pat flavoured, tea,' chided Fred.

When Eddie screwed up his face and looked in his pot, Fred just laughed and said, 'don't blame me. You came up with the theory in the first place. You saw the cows and made the deductions, not me.'

'Do you remember? Eddie said, at one point in our conversation. 'The survival courses we did in the Service? You know, where they dumped you off somewhere and you had to build shelters to live in and catch rabbits to eat and daft things like that. There was always one silly sod that insisted in putting it to the full test, while all the rest of us just starved for a couple of days and sat about to conserve energy until it was time to be picked up and taken back. Or the other time when all we were allowed to take with us was a shilling, old money, or it was when I did it and we had to get as far away from base camp as we could, before the Civilian and Military Police were given our Service Numbers and descriptions and told we were deserters and had to be arrested. We got as far as a Chip shop in the nearest town, where we spent our shilling and were picked up outside by the Police while stuffing our faces. Did you do any of that?'

'No we didn't do anything like that,' answered Fred. 'What about you Mel?'

'We did it yes and did a bit better than the local Chippie. We were sent out in pairs and I tagged on to this other bloke. I didn't really know him up until that time. I had of course seen him about but we had never actually met before that. All he said was, "Stick with me pal, I have thought this out. My brother was conscripted and did it all last year. He told me all about it, so I have worked out a plan." I thought fine, for I had no preconceived ideas as to what I was going to do. When it was our allotted time to set off, we walked smartly down the road from the Camp, which was a place called Padgate, a RAF Basic Training Station just outside Warrington, which was then in Lancashire, but I now believe is in Cheshire. Anyhow, there was a Bus Stop just along the road and we got on the first one that came along. "As far as we can get on a shilling each please," requested this bloke I was with.

"You on this escape lark from the camp then?" asked the Bus Conductor. "Did it myself four years ago. If no Inspector gets on, you can stay on and ride for as long as you like."

Eventually we ended up a few miles down the road in Manchester. When we got off the Bus, my newfound travelling companion said, "Now a Taxi to the

Airport." When I reminded him that we had no money, he took off his shoe and removed his sock producing, from inside it, a folded one pound note. "Told you I was ready and had this one sussed out."

When we arrived outside Manchester Airport, I told him that I thought this would be one place they would surely be watching. "Not this entrance, they won't," he said. So we set off to walk about a quarter of a mile round the perimeter fence, where we eventually came to a gate complete with Security Guard. I thought when I saw the uniformed guard that he must have gone completely mad, but no, he walked straight up to the man on the gate. "Hello Uncle Albert, mind if we come in. Don't want to hang about out here; is my Dad at work?"

Within minutes Dad had been located and summoned, by telephone, to the Gatehouse. Over his arm he carried two pairs of matching overalls and, in his hand, two caps. We spent a full week inside Manchester Airport, just wandering round and picking up rubbish inside the airfield.'

'A week and you never got picked up. Where did you sleep? How did you eat?'

'Manchester Airport is a big place and there are vast areas inside the perimeter where no one hardly ever goes and so we stuck mainly to those and if we thought we were being approached or someone got a bit too close, we either wandered off in the opposite direction or nipped smartly round a convenient corner. We ate in a Canteen with a load of other manual workers, which was free, and because our overalls matched the vast majority of those who used the place regularly, no one challenged or even took any notice of us. At night we slept in a storage building on the edge of the Airfield that was never visited at all during the hours of darkness. The key to get in and out of the place came courtesy of "Uncle Albert".'

'What happened in the end?' asked Eddie.

'Well, after much debate we decided that we could make it last indefinitely if we chose, but we thought a week was long enough. So we simply asked "Uncle" on the gate to report us to Airport Security for trying to get in and onto the Airfield. The local Military Police eventually arrived and gave us a ride back to camp. On the way back they assured us that although we had been on the loose for a week no one else, out of our group, had got further than Birmingham and that as a group of escapees we were all useless. A week later, when we were back in camp, two that were still missing sent a card addressed to our group Instructor, from Malta, with a request for extended leave. We all had a good laugh over that. How they got there I never found out, nor did we tell anyone where we had been for a whole week, when it turned out that we had achieved the second longest absence.'

'They were great days and a lot of fun,' mused Eddie. 'But were they really of any value? I still wonder what it would be like to find your-self, alone without contacts, food, or money, or for that matter without any acceptable identification,

in a totally hostile country. Of those who found themselves in that position during the last war and the likes, I wonder how many actually escaped and how many were caught or had finally to just give themselves up the result of sheer frustration and their inability to get anywhere?'

'I don't know, but I bet it was easier in "war days" when there was confusion, underground movements and sympathisers, than what it is in the present day. I still wouldn't rate my changes too highly in some of the countries where there have been recent conflicts.'

'You two would probably end up being caught and shot on the first day,' mocked Fred.

So we laughed and talked, and discussed a wide variety of subjects until Fred, looking at her watch, said, 'Who's for soup and a slice or two of rather dry bread?'

'Is there an alternative?'

'Sorry, darling, most of what was originally on our extensive menu is now off. It's soup or soup. Take your pick.'

So it had to be soup, eaten hot and once again, straight from the can. The tea which followed was a vast improvement, as far as the flavour was concerned, as both Eddie and I had insisted that the water used to heat the soup cans was thrown away and fresh water, cow pats excepted, be taken from the stream and boiled separately for the tea.

Fred returned from the stream, having washed the few utensils we had used and set them aside ready for next time.

'When it gets dark are we going to leave the tent and everything here or are we going to take it all along with us?' asked Eddie as he went about neatly arranged things around the area.

'If we leave everything here then we will have to come back and collect it, or at least two of us will, as there is far too much for one person to carry alone. It worked out just about right when we divided it into three to come here and even taking into account the fact that we have eaten most of the food there is still too much and no way one person can deal with it all on one trip. Never mind attempting it in the dark. Split into two, then perhaps it might not be too much of a problem. Anyhow I am not keen on the idea of even carrying an equal share on a stake out. But I don't follow exactly what you are getting at. Are you actually proposing that we each take a share with us?'

'No, I don't mean it like that. If we stake out, the same as last time, then perhaps two of us could carry everything down and hide it in the woods behind the Car Park and who ever stakes out from there can keep a eye on it. I thought that might either save time later or eliminate the necessity to come back up here altogether.'

'Could you manage half this lot?' I asked Fred.

'If I have to, of course I can manage.'

'Tell you what. Seeing as the suggestion was mine, if you give me a hand, Mel, you and I can carry it all down, find a suitable hiding place for it and leave Fred up here; if she is agreeable to that? That means that I stake out the Car Park this time and you, Fred, the cliff top.'

'I am quite happy to go anywhere. So if you think it would be better to do it that way round, suits me.'

'OK with you, Mel?'

'Yes. Fine by me. So if we are all agreed, we will do it that way. Let's get everything packed before it gets too dark to see.'

* * *

Fred ended up with Eddie's bag, into which she stowed everything she felt she might need. The rest was split into the two rucksacks, to be transported by Eddie and myself to the bottom, where most of it would be deposited somewhere behind the Car Park. One of the last things we did before packing away the stove was make a fresh flask of tea for each of us.

'I don't think it is going to be as cold tonight as the last time we were here, but we still might need these,' said Fred as she carefully screwed on the tops of the flasks and handed them out.

'I have the furthest to go so I will give the first two clicks on my radio when I am in position. Eddie, two pairs when you are ready, and you Fred, three. Everyone got that?'

They both nodded.

'See you both later,' said Fred, giving me a light kiss on the lips and Eddie one on his cheek. 'Careful, both of you, and watch how you go.'

'You look after yourself,' I reminded her and looking round for the last time checked that we had not overlooked anything, remarked, 'It's a bit too late now if we have missed anything. It's too dark to see much. Come on Eddie. We have ample time, if we leave now and can take it nice and easy. A slow, cautious walk, then if we do bump into anyone we will have time, I hope, to take some evasive action and get out of their way.'

The walk down the track went off without incident once our eyes became accustomed to the dark. The most testing time, we decided, would be working our way over the bridge and behind the Pub and then the added risk as we crossed the road to make it to the other side of the Car Park.

We stopped just short of the bridge and at a selected point where we were out of direct line of sight from the back of the Pub.

In a whisper Eddie said, 'It is going to be a bit risky going behind the Pub at this time of the night. There is every chance of some sort of activity around now,

both around the back and the front of the Pub and the Car Park. I know we have not been that way before, but what do you think if, after crossing the bridge, we follow the bank of the stream and go round the outside back wall of the Camping field. That way we can then climb over the wall further up and cross the main road and climb over the other wall to get behind the Car Park. It's further and a more circular route but we will avoid the risk of crossing behind the Pub.'

I saw the logic of his argument so said, 'Let's give it a try. We have plenty of time and if the worst comes to the worst and we hit a snag we will have to double back and go by the original route.'

'OK, but there is no point in us both struggling with these packs, through all that undergrowth, if it only turns out and proves to be, a useless exercise. So you stay here and give me ten minutes. If I haven't come back by then, follow me and I will wait for you to catch me up.'

He set off through the undergrowth and quickly disappeared out of sight, leaving me in total darkness. I waited for what I thought was a good ten minutes. He had not returned, so I hitched up my pack and set out to follow the bank of the stream in what, I thought, would be Eddies tracks. I had no problems at the bridge; everything was quiet. So I slipped across and into the brush on the opposite side. There was no path to follow along the bank of the stream and it was difficult, with so little light, to make out where the grassy bank finished and the stream flowed. The result being that I put my foot wrong on a couple of occasions and by the time I eventually caught up with Eddie, my right boot was full of water and my foot was beginning to feel very cold. When I came up alongside him, I leant against the wall and shook my foot vigorously from side to side to try and improve the circulation and get rid of some of the discomfort.

'What's wrong?' he enquired. 'It's OK, I have had a good scout around, we can talk here. While I was waiting I looked over this wall and there is nothing but the Camping field and it's empty and deserted.'

'Boot full of bloody water!'

'Change your sock, if you have one handy.'

'Not now. God knows where my spare socks are in this lot. Keep going. I will sort it out later.'

So turning, Eddie led on and I followed. We stooped over slightly to keep the tops of our packs below the top of the wall and walked on for a short distance. Eddie suddenly stopped and I nearly stumbled into him.

'Let's check and see if we have gone past the Camping field yet.'

We cautiously stood up and peered over the wall. We were looking into an empty field with the Campsite way over on our left and the dividing wall some thirty yards further back.

'We have come a bit too far unless we want to risk crossing this open field.'

'No. Don't let's take any unnecessary chances. Let's stick along the wall side.'

So turning I lead the way back.

Climbing over the wall, after having dropped our packs off, presented no problems, as it was a dry stonewall, common in this area and it offered plenty of hand and foot holds. I was first over and dropping down the other side, looked about me to make sure we were alone.

'All clear, pass the packs, then over you come.'

Still stooping we followed the boundary wall dividing the two fields until we arrived in the corner formed by the boundary wall and the one that ran parallel with the road.

'So far so good: we have made it to the main road. All we need to do now is get across it and then it should be plain sailing from there.'

'There is a gate just up there,' pointed Eddie.

'Good. That makes life a bit easier.'

The gate proved to be a big help, for not only did it allow us to slip out onto the road without exposing ourselves as silhouettes against the night sky, as would have been the case, if only for a brief moment, had we climbed over the top of the wall, but directly opposite in the other wall of the field on the other side of the road was a similar gate. We opened the first one and then cautiously looking up and down the road, straining our ears for the slightest sound. There was nothing, so we nipped smartly across the road and entered through the gate into the field opposite.

'That's probably the worst bit behind us now,' commented Eddie, as we made our way parallel with the road towards the boundary wall of the Car Park. Once there, we skirted the Car Park and climbed over the final wall and dropped down into the wood beyond it. A few yards further on to our left and we were looking over the wall into the Car Park itself. There were several cars parked there and all clearly visible under the glare of the single floodlight mounted on a telegraph pole and placed specifically so as to light up only the Car Park during the hours of darkness and Pub opening times.

'I don't recognise any of them, do you?' I asked, referring to the cars.

'No. But you let me worry about the Car Park. You still have a long way to go and how's your foot?'

'Still very cold! I think I had better do something about it now, instead of waiting until it goes numb altogether and this is as good a place as any to do it.'

Sitting down, I unlaced my boot and pulled it off. Most of the water had soaked up into my sock and had started to evaporate. Only a few drops ran out from my boot as I turned it upside down.

'Not much to show for all the discomfort and from what felt like gallons, when it first went in.' I grumbled.

Removing my soaking sock I folded it in two and wrung it out. I felt slightly better when quite a lot if water came out of it and fell onto the ground.

Every effort to find a clean sock failed, despite the fact that I felt certain I knew exactly where they were supposed to be and on which side of my pack. Each time I delved into the depths of my rucksack, I came up with something different. In the end I accepted defeat. Short of emptying the whole contents out onto the ground, I was obviously going to achieve nothing and I would have been there all night. So, with no alternative I had to accept the part that I hated most, putting back on to an almost dry foot, a wet, cold sock. But before I did, I squeezed it and wrung it out yet again, then held it tightly screwed up in both hands, hoping that by doing so, I might inject a little warmth into it. The next move was to get it onto a cold foot, before whatever heat I had managed to get into it, escaped into the surrounding night air. It didn't work. My foot was still damp and the process was slow and the sock felt very uncomfortable, to say the least. After much pulling and twisting, I finally got it back on and then pushed a still very cold foot into a wet boot laced it up.

'You will feel better when the damp, still in there, comes up to body temperature.'

'I doubt if it ever bloody will,' I grumbled, stamping my foot. 'Right now the whole lot feels like ice and I can't even remember what it felt like when it was warm.'

'By the time you get down to the bottom, I'm sure the circulation will have improved and you will feel much brighter.'

'I hope you're right,' and lifting my pack away from the wall, I began to repack it, leaving out all the things I planned to take with me and which I believed I might need.

'You won't believe this, but here's a bloody sock now that it is too late,' I said in disgust as I held it up for Eddie to see before stuffing it back.

I checked the items I had set to one side and began to finish packing the remainder when Eddie put his hand on my arm.

'You take just what you need and away you go. I will attend to this lot and stow it all away. I have plenty of time while you move off and get into position. I will then get myself settled down and be ready.'

Checking my pockets and making sure I knew were everything was and I could quickly get at them, I prepared to move out.

'See you later and let's hope everything goes according to plan and we at least achieve something worthwhile tonight.'

'Here's hoping.'

* * *

I headed off along the wall side and through the undergrowth, then made my way along and down the side of the ravine. It seemed to take me longer and to be much further than the last time. Each time I stopped to look around and see if I could pick out any familiar landmarks, there were none that I could recognise. Everything looked so much the same in the dark and yet I knew I was going in the right general direction. However, I continued until I finally reached a point where I could see the track through the trees as it came down the ravine and opened out onto the beach. I stopped and studied the area as far as my range of vision allowed. I knew that last time I had been somewhere over on the other side, but decided that somewhere around where I was at that point would be equally as good providing I could find adequate cover and have the widest possible field of vision.

The overhead tree branches and the surrounding undergrowth, made it very dark where I stood and I felt confident that if I remained very still, someone would have to walk almost straight up to me, before I would be seen. The sky, reflecting on the sea, however, provided sufficient illumination for me to observe the area some distance out in front. As I listened, I knew I would have to pay particular attention to sounds and anything else that might appear over and above that which was already coming from the wind in the trees and the waves, as they crashed onto the shingle. The natural noises could, I realised, of course, work both for and against me. Against, meant that I would have to concentrate hard to pick out the unnatural and unfamiliar sounds, but in my favour was the fact that those already surrounding me would cover any minor noises that I might be obliged to, or accidentally, make.

As I became more familiar with my surroundings I shifted my position slightly; in fact several times, before finally deciding that I was, with my restricted knowledge, in the best place. I settled down and prepared for a long wait. I knew that by this time, Eddie would be set up and not have moved very far, but I wondered about Fred. Would she have moved into her selected location more or less straight away after we left or would she still be waiting in the woods and then moving nearer the time? There was only one way to find out. Checking my radio to ensure it was on the correct setting, I put on the headset and replacing my woolly cap, depressed the transmit button twice. Click. Click.

'Click-click, click-click,' came the reply through the headset. Eddie was in position and ready, as I had expected.

A few seconds later, three pairs of clicks came through loud and clear and confirmed that Fred had heard us both and that she too was there, set up and waiting. Bless her.

That was it for the moment.

I suddenly felt isolated and rather lonely and wished that I could have been on the top of that cliff, cuddled up close to Fred. But that was not to be. For the present things were very different and I had to be satisfied with standing there

and day dreaming and thinking about all the exciting things we had done together so far. In reality it had all taken place over a very short period of time, since we first met and yet I felt we had been together for ages. I stood there feeling rather depressed at the thought that it might all eventually come to an end. There was I, on a cold dark night and with a wet, cold foot, alone and isolated, in a wood, close to a beach, on the Yorkshire coast, not knowing what was about to happen. All very good, sound reasons, I thought, for wanting the job over and yet at the same time feeling depressed at the thought that it might not last much longer and then all the good things about it would eventually come to an end. Get a grip or yourself, I told myself. The last woman that made you feel like that, nicknamed you Mel, then pissed off and left you.

* * *

Time dragged on and due to my, then, state of mind and circumstances, provided me with plenty of time to contemplate my past and what it might have been. My future was now perhaps a bit more complex and the more I thought about it, the more I found it somewhat difficult to get it into any form of perspective. But perhaps I had no future at all and should be happy in the knowledge that if I could accurately predict it, I would probably scare myself to death. So I settled for my daydreams. They were less painful than the reality of the past and it made me feel good when I dreamed of a future with no debts and winning the football pools; which is extremely difficult, if not impossible, when you don't do them. But then perhaps out there somewhere was the unknown, obscure, and very rich aunt who was about to turn up her toes and provide me with the ware with all to solve all my financial problems and fund any and all of my future schemes. The thought of not having to work for a living or take orders from people like the Old Man and other people, who aren't even street wise or who don't have one iota of common sense. Doing just what I wanted and when I wanted and doing all the other things that most people desire for themselves but fail to achieve. All the things, that if they all came true, would no doubt make life rather boring, empty and meaningless. I suppose we all need a bit of aggro, a bit of pressure and something to gripe about, so from that, I decided to settle for a life without debt. Of them all, I definitely decided, that was the most important; a simple life with an active career and free from the worry of debt and the pain that goes with it.

'Click, click. Johnson's car into Car Park.'

I jumped almost three feet into the air. Or it felt like that at the time, as I was brought back, with a severe jolt, to reality and a very cold night. I fumbled, taking a few seconds to sort myself out, before I was able to locate and depressed the button on my radio, the necessary twice, to acknowledge receipt of the

message. I then heard two more clicks in the earpiece, which I assumed were Fred's acknowledgement.

'Johnson into pub.'

Same acknowledgement, my two clicks followed closely by Fred's, then silence. The waiting continued, perhaps for half an hour or more, although at the time it felt much longer than that.

'Fisherman into Pub.'

I acknowledged again and heard Fred as she followed suit. It was then that I remembered we had never found out that Fisherman's name, although we had his picture and could readily recognise him by sight.

More waiting and prolonged silence but at least something might be happening.

I was beginning to feel distinctly chilly although, by then, my foot felt a lot more comfortable and was, I assumed from that, almost dry. For want of something better to do I attempted to find out by wiggling my toes, but came to the conclusion that it was either dry, or now so numb, that I just couldn't feel the dampness. I decided that my overall physical state was such that this was perhaps the time and excuse, to indulge myself and have a hot drink.

I wrapped my hands round the plastic cup from the top of my flask and savoured the heat that was truly appreciated and most welcome. The tea, which I swore had more whiskey in it than water, slipped down, a sip at a time and warmed me through. Time, itself, I felt, must now be getting on, or my mind was distorting from the prolonged waiting to such an extent, that it only appeared to be passing slowly and that it was all due to nothing more than an overall lack of stimulation?

I screwed the cup back on the flask and carefully laid it to one side. I shone my torch on my watch. Well past Midnight. The Pub must surely be emptying out by now, if not already empty. Sadly I had no way of telling and knew that Eddie would not pass on information of that nature, which he would probably consider to be none essential. All that I could do was speculate and wait patiently. In desperation and in an overwhelming desire to break the monotony and speed up, if I could, the passing of time, I took out my pocket knife, selected a piece of dry twig and started to sharpen a point on one end. Why, I don't really know, but it just seemed the right thing to do at the time. It was something that I could do in complete silence and gave me both physical and mental stimulation whilst at the same time did not interfere with my prime reason for being there. I continued to pair off the slices of wood long after I had made a point on it. After a while I examined my handy work. The pointed stick served no practical purpose other than it had given me something to do. I turned it round and started to sharpen the other end.

'Car arrived. Stopped. No movement.'

A further period of silence, during which I continued to slice away at the stick.

'Land Rover arrived. Stopped. No movement.'

Something was beginning to happen as I began to try and picture the scene in the car park at the top of the hill.

I estimated a further fifteen minutes elapsed before there was more.

'Johnson and Fisherman returned to Johnson's van. No further movement.'

One o'clock, two o'clock, half past two. I was slicing away at my second twig, the first one having been reduced to a mass of slivers, which had all ended up spread out on the grass, around my feet and then had been carefully picked up and thrown into the surrounding undergrowth. During all this time, I assumed, the result of no further information from Eddie that Johnson and the Fisherman must have been sitting in Johnson's van. But then, shortly after that and whilst I was bent down picking up the waste from my latest efforts, there came, 'Fisherman on the move.'

It was then, as I brought up my arm and reached to press the transmit switch on my radio, to acknowledge Eddie, that I almost stabbed myself in the mouth with the knife. I snapped it shut and slid it into my pocket at the same time throwing the stick into the undergrowth. It was time to concentrate on the job in hand and abandon my attempts at totem pole carving, at least for the time being.

Two, perhaps three minutes further elapsed.

'Fisherman gone round back of Pub.'

That move was of particular significance to Fred and I knew she was aware of it as soon as I heard her two clicks.

Suddenly I was more alert. Something was definitely beginning to happen. Of that there was no doubt. But at the same time and being honest about it, I did not like the thought of someone heading in Fred's direction when she was out there alone. I tried to assure myself that she was a very competent and capable girl and could well look after herself. As I dwelt on it, that and many other things, as I waited in the dark, I recalled that sometime in the past, I had heard someone, somewhere, expounding a particular theory about men and women working together out in the field. They argued that one male, looking after himself, can give one mans' concentration and effort. Two males, double the amount. In other words: two efforts. But one male and one female, working together, only produce around one and a half efforts. Not because the female gives less than one effort, she might, in actual fact, give more than one, but because the male spends about half his time and overall effort worrying about and trying to look after his companion when she doesn't really need it. The male instinct to look after his mate and protect the female. I could just picture the look of disgust on Fred's face at that hypothesis and I could clearly hear her saying, 'Chauvinistic pigs, it's the men who need looking after. Without women they are a waste of space. Ask any woman worth her salt.' But theory or no theory, I felt it could be partially true, if not by the same

proportions and I just could not help my feelings, at that moment and my feelings at any time for that matter, towards Fred.

'Three others down the track.'

My two clicks followed by Fred's. I took a quick look round. This was my last chance to make any last minute changes. I could see no improvements. I picked up a few of the last remaining slivers of cut twig, tossed them away, and resolved to stay where I was.

Compared with what had, so far, been and definitely felt like long waits between very short bursts of activity, now, in what seemed like no time at all, to have all been set aside as I now heard voices. At first it caught me unawares, not expecting it to materialise so soon, then it surprised me with the speed at which they actually approached and the rise in the volume of their conversation as they did so. But then I realised, that as far as they were concerned, they believed they were alone and there was no one to hear them, so they had no need to take precautions.

'Let's hope the buggers turn up this time,' said a voice that sounded very much as if it might have belonged to Johnson.

'And no bloody balls up, like last time,' said another.

'Are we getting anything out of this fucking trip? I'm short of fucking coin right now,' said the first voice.

'Soddin' hell, you got a big wad for the last one, when no bugger come. How much do you want out of this soddin' job?'

'I could use more than we bloody get, for the chances we takes. I was only thinking… ' As his voice trailed off, as they had, by this time, progressed well past me and were moving all the time further away and out of ear shot.

All three had passed, totally unaware of my presence and although I could no longer hear them, due, not only, to the distance between us, but also above the noise of the waves as they incessantly crashed onto the shingle beach. Also the wind did its share and helped disperse anything that might, at that time, have drifted my way. But despite all that, I could, at least, clearly see them, standing in a close group down on the shingle. Johnson, Scampton, and Raines. All easily recognised.

Two of them had their hands in their pockets and idly shuffled their feet as they stood about doing nothing. Raines was smoking and pushing pebbles about with his toe.

I pushed my left hand deep into the long grass and with a quick flash from my torch, briefly illuminated my watch dial. Ten minutes to three.

'Fisherman on cliff top… Obvious lookout,' came Fred's clear voice. I clicked my acknowledgement and heard Eddie send his.

The three on the beach just stood there and killed time and I, of course, had no option but to wait and watch them. I also had to force myself to relax as I became increasingly tense from standing ridged; scared, I suppose, of being heard

or seen. I forced myself to take deep breaths and told myself they could not hear me from where they stood, so it was safe for me to, at least, breath. Eventually my heart stopped pounding and my breathing came a little easier. All the time, they remained standing in a group and appeared to be just talking among themselves. At one point, Scampton broke away from the others and went towards some larger rocks, and then having relieved himself, returned to the group.

As if at a signal, although I heard or saw nothing from where I stood, they turned and formed some semblance of a line, standing shoulder to shoulder and looking out to sea. They remained in that same position for quite some time, as if watching and waiting for something to happen. I could still not see anything but it became obvious to me that their attention was taken up by something that was happening out at sea.

Again, as if by yet another signal, all three strode further away from me and moved down the shingle beach. At the same time the bow of a rowing boat came into my field of vision. As it came towards the shore line and grounded on the pebbles, Johnson and Scampton, both of whom I could still readily recognise despite the distance between us, strode into the water and taking a firm grip on either side, heaved it forward, on the next rising wave, to make sure it was grounded firmly. As they did so one of the three occupants in the boat, two having rowed it ashore and the third handling the tiller, stepped into the shallow water. After a short exchange, none of which I could hear, shook hands with Raines and then the two of them walked about ten yards away from the main group. The remainder just stood and looked on. After a few moments Raines produced something from inside his topcoat and passed it over to the new arrival. He took it and pushed it deep down inside his own pocket.

I had been so preoccupied with keeping absolutely still and concentrating on the activities down on the beach that I had completely forgotten to update Fred and Eddie. I moved my hand very slowly and depressed the transmit button and whispered as loud as I dared, forgetting completely for the moment, that if I could not hear the group down on the beach, then they would not be able to hear me.

'Boat arrived. Contact made. Three S.O.B's.' I was hoping, from that, that Eddie understood the Coastguard jargon for Souls on Board.

He must have, for I heard the two separate sets of two clicks and no request for clarification.

Raines and the man he had been talking to, returned to the boat and standing one on either side, their legs and feet in the water, looked intently into the bottom of the boat and, by the way their heads bobbed about, I gathered, that a detailed and in-depth, discussion over something was taking place. Eventually everyone must have been satisfied, for the two who had remained stationary and in their places, holding the oars, since they arrived, shipped them and stood up in the boat. They shifted their position then stooping down, lifted a large box, using

the attached rope handles, one at each end and passed it over the side of the boat to Johnson's and his colleague. From the way they needed to hold on to it, using both hands at the same time and with their elbows bent to keep it above the water, and also the clumsy stumbling, as they side-stepped out of the water, made it obvious that it was very heavy for its size. They manhandled it a few yards up the beach before setting it down on the dry shingle. Having done so they returned for a second similar sized package.

This lifting, stumbling and shuffling was repeated for a further five times until they had six boxes in total stacked up on the beach, two on top of the other four. When the last one was in place Raines and his two associates sat on them and slumped forward, arching their shoulders. It was obvious from the way they held themselves, heads forward and down, that a lot of energy and effort had gone into moving them only that short distance. Two of them eventually lit cigarettes and began to smoke. In the meantime the men in the boat pushed it free from the shingle and, setting their oars, rowed seaward and out of my sight.

'Boat left. Six boxes. Three men on beach.' I whispered.

No sooner had I received my acknowledgement, when Fred followed it up with, 'Fisherman signalling.' and I acknowledged her call as, of course, did Eddie.

I continued to watch as the party on the beach remained where they were, the group only splitting up temporarily when Johnson went off to one side to relieve himself. The others just sat and, as far as I could make out, talked.

They remained there for what I can only describe as a very long rest and one that eventually developed into something rather disproportionate to the amount of physical work they had done so far. A quick look at my watch confirmed they had been there, resting and talking, for three quarters of an hour.

I was trying to rationalise why the necessity for such a long break, when it all became crystal clear as they collectively stood up and the bow of the boat slid up onto the beach once again. They had been waiting for a second shipment and not resting for all of that time.

They repeated, more or less, the same procedure as they had with the first shipment. Raines went off to one side with their man and an exchange, of some kind, was made. The cargo in the bottom was examined, discussed, and finally unloaded. There were a further six cases; only this time they were only about half the size of the originals and they were more square than oblong in shape. They were also heavy, for each one required two men to lift it ashore and place it alongside the larger ones. When the task was complete there was hand shaking all round, but after that, the three men in the boat did not loiter and wasted little time before pushing their craft free and rowing away.

'Boat left. Six more boxes landed.'

There was no resting, this time, for the three left ashore. Without hesitation they lifted two of the smaller cases by their rope handles and formed a three-man, two-case, chain. Johnson took the middle place with a handle in each hand.

I pressed transmit. 'Three men, two boxes, leaving beach.' To which, I received acknowledgement from both Eddie and Fred.

As the party of three passed at it's closest point to me, I clearly heard Johnson complaining. 'They took their bloody time with that second lot. You would think we had all bloody night. All right for them bastards, they have finished now and pissed off and we're still here to shift this lot.'

'Shut up and save your breath. We've still a lot to do and you're belly aching don't help.' Then in silence, they passed out of earshot.

'Fisherman leaving cliff top,' said a familiar female voice in my earpiece. 'Follow or stay? Over.'

'Follow,' I quickly replied.

Click-click.

A short time later when I was alone at the bottom of the ravine, with only several boxes on the beach for company, a voice on my radio said, 'Two boxes in Land Rover. Three returning to beach.'

They were certainly not messing about and had made very good time, and in only a very short period after that, they were back on the beach and preparing to lift two more cases. Scampton taking the middle position on this occasion. The only conversation I managed to pick up as they passed close by on the way down, again came mainly from Johnson who was whinging, this time, about the fact that the Fisherman had not caught up with them and was probably, according to Johnson, doing it on purpose to avoid helping.

When they came up from the beach for the second time I relayed the information to Eddie and Fred, then carried on calmly watching and waiting.

'Fisherman in Car Park. No movement,' I heard.

'Two boxes in Land Rover. Four returning to beach.'

Two clicks sent by me and two heard from Fred.

It was obvious that the Fisherman had waited for the second load to come up and was now returning to the beach along with the others.

The four of them passed me on the way down in silence and for their return journey they selected two of the larger cases that they now carried between the four of them, two to a case.

We continued throughout to keep each other informed of all their movements and I learned, from Eddie's concise transmissions, that the larger cases were being stacked, on arrival at the top, in Johnson's van while the smaller ones had gone into the Land Rover. Throughout most of this period Fred remained silent but I knew she was out there somewhere and listening as she clicked her acknowledgement of each and every transmission.

The fourth trip resulted in two more of the large cases being taken up to the top but this time I heard no conversation as they passed close by in either direction. The effort of moving heavy cases had eventually silenced even Johnson.

On their fifth trip they showed distinct signs of fatigue and this was further confirmed by Johnson's statement, as they passed me by on the downward leg, 'I'm bloody knackered!'

'You bloody well will be if this lot is not stashed away from here before daylight. I've said all along, twelve is too many at this time of year. It's light too bloody soon,' someone replied.

They shuffled away onto the beach to return shortly and stagger off up the hill, with the last of the large oblong boxes.

'Four men, two cases coming up,' I whispered.

'Two cases in Johnson's van,' was Eddie's report when they eventually arrived in the Car Park. They were now definitely taking longer between trips as the physical effort obviously took its toll.

There now remained only two of the smaller boxes on the beach.

I had already thought about it, but up to now had not dared to take the chance in case someone, for some reason, had returned to the beach and caught me. But now I decided that this would be my last chance if I wanted to take a close look at those cases. I had timed the previous trips and each one had taken that bit longer due to the onset of weariness. I therefore calculated that I now had time, if I was smart and did not linger, to go down to the beach, take a quick look and get back into hiding before they returned. I would also have the warning from Eddies signal to tell me when they were on the way back.

I broke from my cover and cautiously went down to the beach. The two remaining boxes sat on the shingle. They were solid and made of wood. They were painted a dull dark green, had rope handles attached to each end, and were typical of ammunition boxes that are found with any military unit, anywhere in the world.

There were no markings, or signs to indicate the contents, or their country of origin. The only markings, stencilled on the tops and sides, were characters that looked to me as if they were of an Arabic or Turkish style of writing, but as far as I was concerned they were totally indecipherable. I stood looking down at them, hoping and kidding myself that perhaps, if I staring at them long enough, they might give me a clue as to what they contained, when Eddie's voice came through my earpiece.

'Two boxes in Johnson's van. Four returning.'

I knew I had ample time to get back to my position and conceal myself once again, but still I found myself dashing away from the beach as if my very life depended on it. My heart was beating fast and I was short of breath as I dropped down into my hiding place. I had to force myself to calm down and to breath

slowly and deeply. I was back to normal and, I hoped, in full control long before they returned.

As they passed me on the way back up, for what would be the last time, I transmitted, 'Last two boxes. Four men leaving… Beach clear. Following.'

I then gave them, what I calculated to be ample time to get well ahead. Then, making sure I had left nothing behind, I set off to return to where I had left and last seen Eddie earlier that evening. I deliberately kept clear of the main track just in case they had made an unscheduled stop and I ran into them. I slowly made my way up the hill through the undergrowth.

While negotiating a particular dense patch my radio went. 'Two boxes in Land Rover. Land Rover left. Three standing. No movement.'

I continued on my uphill climb and despite the fact that I honestly believed that I was moving with all the cunning and stealth of a Red Indian stalker, a voice in my earpiece said, 'Thirty yards to your left, Old Boy.'

At thirty, or so, yards distance, Eddie had not only heard me but had clearly seen me. I, despite all my caution, had not seen him and, if he had not said anything, would probably have fallen over him. All credit to Eddie, I thought, on his selection of hiding place.

I came up alongside him and sat down on the ground. He pointed. 'They are sat in Johnson's van at the moment. Scampton has gone off in the Land Rover. I have moved around a bit while you've been away and have been down as far as the wall. From behind it I couldn't see anything but I could hear them. I had to dodge back and forth quite a bit because it was important that I was up here to see what they were doing, but I wanted, if I could, to hear them as well. Also I needed to be back up here and away from them, in order to transmit.'

'Have you any idea where Fred is?'

'Still over on the other side somewhere, I assume. She left the cliff top some time ago.'

'Yes, I know. I heard her,' I said, and turning my head to one side, I depressed the transmit button. 'Foxtrot. Present location, over.'

'Bridge.'

'Safe?'

Two clicks.

'Stay.'

Two further clicks.

'Did you pick up much of their conversation, from the Car Park, when you went down to the bottom there?'

'A fair amount,' replied Eddie as he continued his watch over the Car Park below us. 'Johnson did a lot of moaning about the amount there was to handle. Scampton seemed more concerned over the time available before it got light and the amount they had to do before then. There was some argument when Scampton

left and drove away and told the others to wait. I heard him say quite clearly, "You lot; do not move from here until I get back, understand?" and I assume, that is why they are waiting down there now.'

'Is he in overall charge, do you think?'

'I'm not sure. I get the impression that they each do their own thing, with the exception of Johnson, who appears to do as he is told and mainly functions as a driver-cum-humper, cum-what-have-you, if you know what I mean? I know he seems to be the one all the others tell what to do and he does it, despite the fact that he appears reluctant at the time and moans a lot.'

'Down on the beach Raines was the one who appeared to be the main man and do all the negotiating and it was him who handed over packages on each occasion, which probably contained cash or some other form of payment.'

'On each occasion? Did he pay for each box, one at a time, then?'

'No. They came ashore in two shipments. The six large boxes first, which he negotiated for and then the six smaller cases. He made two payments altogether.'

'Oh, I see. Look! Movement down there,' pointed Eddie.

I looked down towards the Car Park and saw that the Fisherman and Raines were climbing out of Johnson's van and, without a word, that we could hear, got into their respective vehicles and left the Car Park, driving away into what was left of the night. Johnson's van remained stationary where it was.

'I'd give a lot to know why those two have suddenly left and why Johnson is still waiting there.'

'You may get your answer in a minute. There are lights coming down the lane now.'

'Two vehicles left car park. Johnson's van remains. Forth vehicle approaching.'

'Jesus,' I exclaimed as I pulled my earpiece away and reached to turn off my radio. 'Forgot that bastard was still on.'

'Seen them,' was Fred's reply.

In less than half a minute the Land Rover was back. It drove up and stopped parallel with Johnson. The driver then reversed, in a wide arc and stopped when the rear doors were facing each other. Johnson got out of his cab and proceeded to open his rear doors. Then he and Scampton loaded the six large cases from the van into the Land Rover.

'I don't know where he went in that Land Rover, but where ever it was, he has offloaded the other boxes and has now come back for these. Let's move down to the wall and see if we can hear anything.'

We moved very slowly and cautiously and were just in time to hear Johnson moaning, yet again.

'Where the fuck have you been all this time with that bloody stuff? Leaving me here. Them two buggered off, said they were fed up of waiting. Why I couldn't come with you in my van instead of waiting here, I don't know.'

'Because I told you to stay here, that's why. You just do as your bloody told. Stashing the stuff is my worry and the least you know about it the better. You know what you're like when you get pissed up. You loose off at the mouth and that's dangerous, so now, you bugger off home to your dear little wife and slip her a length to keep her gob shut, like a good husband.'

'Sod that. All she's expecting is some dosh and we got bugger all, tonight.'

'You will son. You'll just have to wait and tell her to wait. You know it will be there, it always is. Now piss off. It will be light soon and I still have work to do.'

We heard the van doors close and the engine start and the sound of Johnson driving away. The Land Rover remained silent.

'What's he doing now, do you suppose?' asked Eddie.

'I don't know,' I replied, as at the same time I jabbed my index finger skywards. Eddie nodded, having understood my signal and we both very slowly raised our heads until we could just see over the wall. Scampton was standing with his back to us and had his hands on his hips. He was looking along the lane. Eddie put his lips very close to my ear and whispered, 'Waiting for Johnson to get clear, I expect.' I nodded in agreement.

We ducked back down again and in a whisper I said, 'Did you see the wheels and the state of his boots?'

'Yes. What about them?' he whispered.

I pointed firstly at him and then up at the sky, indicating that he should go up and take another look.

When he ducked back down again, I pointed away from the wall and back in the direction of Eddie's original hiding place, indicating that we should go back there. As we sat down Eddie said, 'Mud. I saw a lot of light coloured mud, all over. He has been somewhere very wet and muddy tonight.'

'And not a thousand miles away, judging by the time he was absent. But where exactly round here, is anyone's guess right now.'

The Land Rover engine started and we craned our necks in order to see and watched him pull out of the Car Park and disappear down the lane. The Car Park was now completely empty and with the exception of the wind, everything was uncannily silent.

I switched on my radio and adjusted the earpiece, pointed at Eddie's so that he could turn down the volume and called, 'Foxtrot. Location, over.'

'Camping field. Where you? Over.'

'Your position on last time out. Over.'

'On my way.'

'Roger. Waiting. Out.'

We gathered all the gear together as we waited for Fred to join us.

She arrived a few minutes later and dropped down beside us.

'Has anyone got anything left to drink? I drank all mine ages ago,' was her opening remark. My own flask was only about half full and the contents not very warm. Eddie's was steaming hot because he had not even opened it. We shared it out.

'I thought I told you to stay put earlier on, young lady?'

'I'm a big girl. Remember? The Fisherman had long since departed and therefore there was nothing else for me to do up there and I was cold, so I made my way in this direction. I bet now you are really glad that I did.'

'Why? How come?'

'This!' she replied producing what looked like a newspaper parcel from inside Eddie's holdall, that she had been using as her pack.

'Not Fish and Chips?' laughed Eddie.

'No, not quite, but I hope, equally as valuable. Mud from the Land Rover wheels. I noticed it when he came back along the lane and I saw it fall off as he turned into the Car Park. I picked it up on the way across. The newspaper comes courtesy of the Pub waste bin. Find out where that mud came from, which you must admit is an unusual colour and we will, at least, know where one of them has been, on at least one occasion, tonight.'

'It's not much to go on really; a lump of light coloured mud. It could have come from anywhere,' said Eddie.

'Yes I know. But it is still better than nothing. I would not have noticed, or bothered about it, had it not been an entirely different colour to anything that I have seen round here.'

'Yes. Your right! It is better than nothing and I'm sorry. I didn't mean it to sound dismissive. What I meant was that we have seen them bring a large quantity of something ashore and drive it away into the night and all we have to show for all our efforts, is a parcel of funny coloured mud.'

'Come on! Let's pull out of here. I'm sure it's all over round here, as far as we are concerned, for tonight. I'm cold and tired and we can talk as much as we like about it, as we walk and the walk will warm us all up a bit. I suggest we skirt round the village and take the Whitby road, until we pick up the path back across the fields to the Caravan Park. It's still early, so we should have no problems passing close to the village,' said Fred as she started to re-apportion our loads.

'Unless Johnson and his lot are still out on the roads or loitering about somewhere,' I suggested.

'Well it's down to you. It's either, take the chance, or go all the way back along the route we came and that's a long way round, after being cramped up in these woods all night.'

Eddie said nothing.

'OK, you win. It's past the village,' I said.

Fred was right. The village, just before dawn, was deserted. We didn't even see a cat and once along the Whitby road, we were able to relax a little. We were able to relax even further, once we had climbed the stile and left the main road. We discussed, as we trudged along, everything that had happened and filled each other in as to what we had each seen.

Eddie elaborated on what he had witnessed from his position overlooking the Car Park and confirmed what we had interpreted from his transmissions. Fred told how the Fisherman had arrived at the top of the Northern track and how she had watched him go to the edge of the cliff and from there, with a lamp, he had signalled to a ship out at sea.

'It was too dark to identify the ship but, against the fluorescence of the sea, the silhouette looked very much like one of those factory ships which move along the coast servicing the fleets of continental fishing boats. I saw signals flashing from it but was unable to interpret them and assumed they were some predetermined code. However, a small boat was launched from it and rowed ashore. The large ship then steamed away to the North but returned later to rendezvous with the rowing boat. I thought at first that that was the end of the operation, but as I watched they lowered a cargo net, down into the small boat, which once again came ashore. This time the large ship steamed off to the South. When it returned it picked up the small boat and then set off due east, out to sea and well away from the coast. I watched it disappear out of sight. After the rowing boat went out for the second time, the Fisherman left his vantage point at the top of the cliff and set off down the ravine track towards the back of the Pub. I allowed him time to get clear and then following the same route, made my way down as far as the bridge. I remained there for a while, then I decided to make my way into the Camping field. I am glad I did because if I hadn't, I would not have seen the mud on the Land Rover and we might have missed the only additional clue to come out of tonight's exercise. I am sorry I passed no information about the Factory Ship or the rowing boat but at the time I was too close to the Fisherman to take the risk and didn't want to pull far enough back to be safe in case I missed something vital that he was doing. Later I picked up your transmissions and knew, from them, that you were ok and had managed without it.'

'At least we know that all the goodies that came ashore tonight went in the Land Rover, which made two trips. What we don't know is if both trips were to the same place. But at least we have some mud which he picked up from somewhere between the Car Park and where he went on the first trip, which is better than

nothing, I suppose,' the last remark being more of an afterthought to myself, than one for the benefit of the others.

'So we need to find the source of the mud,' said Eddie. 'It can't be too far away. We know he picked it up on the first trip and we also know, how long he was away. We should be able to calculate roughly how far he would travel in half the time he was missing and strike an arc on the map to cover a hundred and eighty degrees from the Car Park.'

'Three hundred and sixty degrees! He could have gone in any direction.'

'Oh Fred, think about it. The Car Park is on the coast, so therefore one hundred and eighty degrees of the circle is out at sea and I doubt he went that way even if there is mud of that colour on the sea bed,' declared Eddie.

'Sorry. I'm tired and my brain is not working properly. He was nevertheless away quite a long time.'

'Yes, but he was alone, remember and had to unload. We know that, because he came back empty. He may have had help waiting at the other end, but he still had to take time to unload. If he was working alone he will not have gone far, even if we calculate his travelling time at thirty miles per hour and I guess, that along these lanes, he will have probably gone slower than that. If he had help to unload and therefore spent more time travelling he may have been able to go a bit further and we can take that into account in our calculations, but my guess is that he was working alone. Remember what he said to Johnson in the Car Park, "It's my job to stash the gear", or something similar and my bet, from that, is that when he left the Car Park he was on his own and remained on his own, all the time, until he came back.'

'He could still have gone in any direction once he got out of our sight and reached the end of the lane and that covers one hell of an area. He might have picked that mud up in any old gateway, lay-bye or lane, then what would that tell us?' asked Fred.

'That he went through a particular gateway or down a certain lane or stopped on a particular lay-bye for some reason,' said Eddie.

'Precisely, but not much else,' I said.

'Come on Mel. Drop the doom and despondency. Look on the bright side,' laughed Fred, who suddenly sounded cheerful despite her obvious weariness. 'I should imagine that it is not often any of us gets the chance to stay up all night hidden in a wood. Think of yourself as a happy go lucky woodland nymph or something equally romantic. When you have had something to eat and a good rest you will feel much brighter. Be satisfied with the fact that we are now certain they are up to no good and that for Johnson, this is his second venture that we know of, and if the mud came from any old gateway and we find it, then we have at least a clue as to a route and from that who knows what else.'

'Sorry Fred! I suppose your right. I am tired, the same as we all are, and I supposed I should be grateful for small mercies. I bet our friends are even more tired than we are and it would surprise me if any of them were making any more extra moves tonight after all the humping they did between them.'

After what seemed like endless walking and a constant battle against weariness, brought on by the long hours out in the open, we finally reached the caravanette. We were all shattered and glad to be back.

'Mel, water. Eddie... '

'The loo for me.'

'OK. I will see if the shop is open yet. It's a bit early but you never know and the Ladies loo is in that direction.'

We were all too weary to argue.

I lit the gas and put on a kettle of water to boil. I emptied the flasks and having rinsed them out, generally busied myself around the van waiting for Fred and Eddie to return. When they did, they were in hysterics and almost beside themselves with laughing.

'Guess what? You have been well and truly sussed, my darling,' said Fred, as she climbed in.

'Tell me again,' said Eddie, ignoring me. 'You say you know her?'

'No. Listen. I will start again and explain everything,' and looking at me she continued. 'Mel, you know the other Camp Site we were on, down the road, before we came here and the dragon woman who ran the place with all her inflation problems? Well she is here now, on this site and must be related to the woman who runs this place, because she is bossing her about and the other one is answering her back and calling her "Mother". They must be mother and daughter. When I went into the shop, which by the way is open, with Eddie, she, the dragon lady, looked at me and said, "Oh, hello, how's your mother?" Remember when we left I told her it was because my mother was ill and that was why we were leaving. She then went on, "I knew you were up to no good. Who's this?" and pointing at Eddie said, "Your husband? So that means the other was probably your fancy man. I knew it. You in that van and him in a separate car and you claimed to be on holiday together. Up to no good together, more like it. There ought to be a law against that kind of thing."

'What did you say in reply to all that?' I asked.

Before Fred had time to answer, Eddie interjected, 'She told her I was not the husband but another of her boy friends, as she always had more than one while away from her husband and on holiday.'

'Hell, and how did she react to that?'

'She said nothing really, but muttered something to the daughter about it being a pity they needed the money so badly otherwise she would not cater for the likes of us, as she climbed into her Land Rover and drove away.'

'So that relegates me to boy friend number two, does it?' I laughed.

'Looks like it Old Boy,' said Eddie and we all laughed.

'Poor old soul! But enough of her and her petty jealousies: she has her problems and we have ours. So let's get this gear sorted out and put out of the way. The sooner it's done and stowed away, the sooner we eat and sleep,' said Fred still chuckling to herself.

We sat round the table, relaxed a little in the warmth and almost fell asleep in our seats.

I have never been a real fan of corn flakes but on that occasion, they really tasted good and the bacon sandwiches, that followed, tasted out of this world.

During my semi-conscious state I remember muttering, 'It's probably too soon to contemplate moving back into the village, or should I say, moving back to the Pub Camp Site and yet we seem to be a long way out here.' I wasn't sure if anyone was interested or heard me.

I hung my head and closed my eyes.

'I can hardly move back, after what happened to my car, although I suppose I could, if I had to, in a dire emergency, under the cover of sorting out the damage or something like that.'

'For the moment we have secure accommodation here and we are at least mobile and can get about from here. Before we consider moving we should be carefully thinking out some logical reasons for doing so,' said Fred.

'For the moment I propose we pass on that one,' I said without moving. 'My top priority is to get my head down for a few hours and then perhaps I may be able to think more clearly about it all.'

Someone closed the window that had been opened for fresh air and turned off the cooker, which Fred had lit, to raise the temperature when we first came in. There followed a welcome, peaceful sensation.

I don't know who dropped off first, but if it was not me then I bet, I was a very close second.

CHAPTER FORTY-THREE

I awoke, desperately needing to go to the toilet and quietly let myself out. On my return, the other two were stirring, but showing little enthusiasm towards doing anything else.

'I have brought a newspaper back from the shop,' I said cheerfully as I closed the door behind me and opened a window. I was now fully awake and alert.

'And does that solve any of our immediate problems?' groaned Fred, who then stretched and moaned, 'Gosh, I'm stiff.'

'No, but it's something to read.'

'Didn't you bring any goodies, or any treats back with you?' she demanded, screwing up her face. 'Give me a minute will you to get out from here. Can someone put a kettle on?'

'No I didn't. It's too early for goodies. I brought a paper that's all.'

'I suppose if a girl fancies a bar of chocolate, or something, around here, she has to get up and go and get it for herself!'

'I will go, as a special favour just for you, if you like. Particularly if it will make you feel better,' offered Eddie.

'No, it's OK, thanks, Eddie. It's him that's mean and non-caring and I really need to go to, you know where, so I can call and see what they have to offer, on my way back. You two stay just where you are and read his paper or better still, make a drink for when I get back.'

She stood up and squeezing past Eddie, went to the rear of the van and lifted up one of the seats to get at the storage space below, rummaged inside and enquired, 'What happened to my trainers, my feet need a change from those heavy boots?'

'In the locker under that next seat,' I pointed.

Fred lifted the cushion and seat cover and began to delve into the locker. I picked up the paper and began to read the headlines while Eddie fiddled with one of the radios.

'We really need to get these charged up, if we possibly can. We can still use them from the car battery, using the cigarette lighter socket, but they don't charge up, very well, that way.'

'Present for you,' said Fred.

I lowered my paper to see her clenched fist on the table in front of me.

'What's that?' I asked as she slowly began to open her fingers.

'Mud,' said Eddie, as he leaned across to get a closer look. 'We already have a parcel full of that, somewhere, remember. You carried it all the way back, this morning.'

'True. But look closely at this. Would you say that it is the same colour and the same mud that I found this morning? Even though this is all dried up?'

'It could be, if you go by the colour, but beyond that, it is just dry mud and I am no soil analyst,' shrugged Eddie.

'But didn't we all agree that it was an unusually light coloured soil. Not the common colour we have seen in the fields and surrounding areas, close to here.'

'Yes, I think we are all agreed on that, so what about it?' said Eddie.

'It came from the sole of my trainer. I have just knocked it off and the last time I wore my trainers was the day we went on that walk through the forest. You remember Mel, it was wet and muddy in places under foot and it was where we bumped into that nice guy, who we met again later, when he was playing darts in the Pub.'

'Yes, that's right and later when we were in the Pub, if I remember, he complained to us about Scampton, saying that he was always driving around in the woods and going into places he was not supposed to go. I wonder… '

'Are you thinking the same as me?' said Fred, cutting me off. 'I wonder if he is hiding the stuff in those woods. Actually hiding it somewhere close to where we went. We assumed, or at least I did, that he would be taking it to a house or a storage place and while doing so, had simply gone through that mud on route.'

'So, what you are now suggesting, is that he maybe hiding the stuff in the actual woods. A bit risky doing that, don't you think?' suggested Eddie.

'Not really,' continued Fred. 'It might even make sense if you consider this; it's so dense in parts of that forest, that you could easily get completely lost and there are no paths or tracks, only fire breaks to divide it up so it is a safe enough place and well off the beaten track, to leave almost anything. Also if it was hidden in the forest and someone was to accidentally come across it, then to whom would it belong? Who could it be traced back to? No one? It is not hidden in anyone's house or on anyone's private property where owners can be easily tracked down. The forest maybe just the place and the place we are looking for.'

'So do you think that area, where we came across those woodcutters, might be a good place to start looking? We saw no sign of Scampton on that day, in fact we have never seen Scampton anywhere round there and he only came into the picture when the woodcutter complained about him much later on, and when we had mentioned him first. There is a vast area of forest over there and as you have already mentioned, one that is big enough and dense enough, to get completely lost in.'

'Have you any better suggestions?' demanded Fred. 'At least we have a clue in the mud and nothing much else to go on. Have we?'

'No. I can think of nothing.'

'Let's check it out on the map then first. Let's see if it comes into the radius we talked about earlier,' suggested Eddie.

'You can all wait until I have been to the loo and someone has made me a drink,' said Fred, 'and then, I bet that when you check it, it comes well within the radius.

Eddie and I sat either side of the table and Fred produced the map and then having spread it out, sat in beside Eddie, clutching her pot of coffee. Using pad and pen I set about the calculations while Fred and Eddie discussed the criteria to be included. They decided to do it several ways, using as the basis the only known two basic facts and they were, the time the Land Rover was away and took to return after having disposed of it's first load and where it set out from. In other words: the Car Park and the time factor.

'Divide that out at twenty miles per hour, then twenty five, then thirty. Halve the answers and we have three possible distances that he could have travelled if he did not stop to unload.'

'What have you got?' asked Fred.

'Give me a minute. I'm quick but not that quick,' I complained.

'How long shall we allow for unloading?' Eddie asked Fred, 'a third of the time? Let's knock a third off and see what that gives us.'

'Why not expand on that and see what we get if we knock a quarter and then a half off as well?'

'Why not? Help yourselves, seeing as I am doing all the work. Knock off and add on all you want,' I complained.

'You shut up and just work it out and leave Eddie and I to deal with the technical stuff. You just let us know when you have some answers.'

I double-checked before pushing forward the pad. 'There you are, six distances to two decimal places.'

'I think we can disregard the one at thirty miles per hour and no stoppage time and this one at twenty miles per hour and half the time taken off for unloading,' suggested Eddie to Fred.

'Charming, now he decides, after sitting there and watching me work it all out, that he doesn't want it. You get them all stuck on that map and then we will decide if we want them or not.'

I sat back while Eddie and Fred struggled to take the scale from the margin along the edge of the map and transfer it onto the edge of a piece of paper and then determine the distances they required.

'I wish we had a ruler and a set of dividers, it would be much easier,' complained Fred.

'I had to manage without a calculator, so get on with it. I thought you two were supposed to be the cleaver ones; so be cleaver.'

'OK?' enquired Eddie.

'Yes,' replied Fred.

'If he drove at thirty miles per hour, turned round and did not stop he could have got as far as this,' Indicated Eddie to me. If on the other hand, he went at twenty miles an hour and spent half the time unloading it would be somewhere in this area.'

'And I know what you are grinning at young lady. The forest comes well within them all.'

'It sure does.'

'Right then,' I said stretching. 'What's next?'

'We'll go and have a wander round there. We can go in the car, take the back lanes and miss the village. So shake yourselves Gentlemen, you have work to do.'

Flasks were filled, sandwiches once again quickly thrown together and half a dozen Mars bars, which were purchased later, at the shop on the way out.

Following the back lanes, as Fred had suggested, we went, as near as we could get, to a point where we had come across the forestry workers on the day of our walk.

We parked in the designated place, especially provided by the Forestry Commission, as a Car Park and Picnic Area for visitors. Ours was the only car and as far as we could tell, apart from ourselves, there was no one about.

'I can't hear any familiar noises, can you?' asked Fred.

'Like what?' asked Eddie, 'I can hear the wind, the trees and even the birds, what more are you hoping to hear?'

'The noise of their power saws and things,' she replied. 'You can usually hear them, working away somewhere. But there is nothing today.'

'Let's go straight to that clearing where we came across them the other day. At least it's a starting point,' I suggested, 'and they may still be working somewhere round there.'

'Lead on, seeing as you seem to know where you are going and I will follow,' said Eddie.

We followed a wide gap, created to form a Fire Break through the trees, which were all very tall and straight and covered mostly in pine needles, as opposed to the more common type of leaf and the one with which I am more familiar. Casually looking about me, they all seemed to be of the same type to my untrained eye.

'Do you know what I thought for a long time and thought it because no one had bothered to tell me differently, that they grew all these tall trees just for telegraph poles and it's only recently, and since I noticed, that they now use aluminium ones, that my myth has been shattered. All these hundreds and thousands of giant Christmas trees; I wonder where they all end up? Not in log cabins because we

don't have log cabins in this country and they can't all end up as matches. I wonder how many matches they could produce from this one area alone?'

'Instead of worrying about matches take a good look at this,' said Fred, who had moved over to the edge of the track and was looking down and scrapping the ground with her toe.

'You see here, where these tyre marks have been left. The wheels have sunk in and scuffed the sides. If you pull away the top stuff and all the dead leaves and pine needles, you have the same yellow coloured mud, or near enough the same colour, that I found.'

'So we now have a forest full of light coloured mud. Great, you realise it's a damned big place.'

We carried on walking and eventually reached the spot where we came across the men working, on our previous visit. There was no sign of them on this occasion and judging by the rapid rate of recovery of the surrounding vegetation from man's previous interference, they had not been there for quite some time.

'Look, no prints, no new timber, no signs of disturbance and the fresh grass is all standing tall and growing up through the old sawdust which has now gone dark coloured. I bet they have not been back to this site since we last saw them,' I said as I wander round the immediate area.

'No fresh tyre tracks either,' added Eddie. 'So where to now?'

I looked at Fred. It seemed pretty hopeless, but she obviously was determined not to be beaten, 'We carry on down here,' she pointed; and Eddie and I, having no better suggestions, lamely followed.

* * *

Some half an hour later and with the scenery exactly the same, having not changed one little bit: somewhere behind us, and way off in the distance, a chain saw started up.

'There they are,' said Fred with obvious delight, 'Somewhere over there.'

'But we came past that way not long since and there was no one there.'

'No one that we saw! They could have been further over, that way. Come on,' and turning completely round, she set off at a brisk pace in the opposite direction.

We re-passed the point where we knew they had previously been. Here we turned off and carried on along a new Fire Break. New, that was, only in the sense that we had not been along it before, or I didn't think we had. They all looked so alike to me and for all I knew, at this point in time, we might already be well and truly lost.

'Don't you get us all lost in here, charging about in every direction through these trees. Shouldn't we be leaving a trail of bread crumbs or putting chalk marks on the trees or something?'

'Shut up and follow that noise. They will know the way in and out, even if we don't and who says I'm, lost?'

We came across them in almost identical circumstances to those we had encountered on the previous occasion. They were again just off the beaten track and working away in a small clearing. We once again came up quite close to them before anyone in their group noticed us. The noise of the saw drowning out any noises that we made, as we approached.

'Good afternoon,' greeted the one with the saw, which he had turned off the moment he saw us. 'Nice day.'

'Yes, it's lovely,' replied Fred.

'Well! Hello Miss. Its nice to see you again and you too,' said one of the others nodding his head in my direction. I recognised the voice as belonging to the man we had previously met and later talked to, in the Pub. I didn't at first instantly recognise his face as the bottom half was covered with a coloured piece of cloth, I guessed to prevent dust getting into his mouth. Also his eyes were protected and partially obscured by large Perspex goggles. 'I thought you was leaving here and moving on?' he said.

'We did,' replied Fred. 'But then we were telling our friend here all about it,' Indicating Eddie. 'We told him how lovely it was round here and how we would love to come back. So we decided to do just that and bring him along with us this time.'

'There is nothing much round here to speak of or to get excited about. It's only a load of trees crammed in tight together,' he replied. 'Just trees and more trees and then some more after that.'

'To you perhaps, because you live and work with them every day,' retorted Eddie. 'But to a townie like me, who has never been in a forest before, it is all fascinating.'

'Keeping wandering round, day in, day out,' chipped in one of the other workers, 'and you will soon get fed up.'

'Eventually we might, but for the moment, we love every bit of it.'

'We were hoping to run in to someone we knew and so it is really good to see you again,' I said, looking at the one from the Pub who had lifted his goggles and removed his mouth covering.

'You won't meet many people in here, only the likes of us and what would you want to be meeting people in the middle of a forest for?'

'To ask questions, I suppose.'

'About what? Trees?'

‘Yes, trees and forests. The management of cultivated timber and about the types of trees and why they are planted so densely. How much they cost to produce and what happens to them in the end? Who owns the land and why is it used for forestry and a whole host of other fascinating things I could think of, and all to do with forests?’

‘Then you have definitely come to the wrong place. We work here and just do as we are told. You will have to find someone else to answer all your fancy questions,’ chipped in one of the others.

‘Like that Park Ranger fellow in the, dark green, Land Rover that we have seen driving around?’ I suggested.

‘Hell no,’ he replied. ‘What makes you think you want anything to do with the likes of him?’

‘Well he just seemed the type of chap, judging by his appearance and the Land Rover he drives round in, who would know these things and I thought we could ask him questions about the countryside and other things that we find interesting but know nothing about.’

‘Him? Like I told you before,’ said the chap we vaguely knew. ‘He is nothing to do with us and should not be hereabouts. So if you see him, or have seen him, anywhere in the forest, then he is way out of order.’

‘But he was here the other day and we saw him,’ I lied, ‘and I just thought we might bump into him again, that’s all.’

‘Who’s he talking, about?’ enquired the third man in the group who, up to that point, had just been stood to the side and had said nothing.

‘Bloody Scampton,’ replied our friend.

‘Wouldn’t piss on that bloke if he were on fire. Pardon me, Miss. Bother maker that one and has caused no end of trouble round here in his time. I’m amazed no one has done him permanent injury before now. Every time he comes in here, which he is not supposed to do, I tell him to piss off. Folks is always complaining about him. Thinks he owns the spot and every other spot for that matter, he does. We haven’t seen him down this end for ages but one of our lads, who works in a different gang, says he were messing about over their way a couple of days ago.’

‘Over where?’ I asked before quickly adding. ‘Not that it matters if you say he is no good and can’t help us.’ As the last thing I wanted was not to sound too enthusiastic or to let them know that I desperately needed the information and something had told me to be wary and to tread carefully and to take things casually, for if these guys were hostile towards Scampton, they might be reluctant to say anything which they believed might be to his advantage. I think it worked.

‘My mate didn’t say exactly. Just said he told him to bugger off. Somewhere over t’other end, towards mill it was, where he has been working, so he probably means over that way.’

'Oh well, thanks anyway. But if you say he's bad news then we will give him a miss.'

'You will lose nowt by it mister,' came the reply.

'Great talking to you all and thanks for your time,' I said. Then, addressing the one we already knew, I added, 'We may well be back this way but in the meantime if I see you again in the Pub you must join us for a pint. Remember it's the free ones that don't upset your ulcer.'

He laughed and they all waved, as we set off to retrace our steps.

As we left we heard the chain saw start up behind us.

'Have you got the map handy, Fred?'

'Yes, here it is,' as she offered it in my direction.

I took it and opened it. 'We are looking for a mill and my bet is, that within a forest, the mill they are talking about, will be a sawmill and I guess it will have to have some type of access road, running from the main road, that, if it exists, should be clearly marked on the map.'

It was, as I predicted, clearly marked, and easily spotted. Still looking at the map, I continued, 'We need to go back to the car, which is here, then go along this road here and turn off up there. A couple of miles, I reckon, at the most.'

We found the place with ease and as we came up to the entrance we found that it was clearly marked with a large sign. We drove straight up the approach track and parked close to the actual mill. There were the sounds of machinery working within the building and large piles of neatly stacked, fresh cut, timber all around the surrounding area. The aroma from the recently cut wood was almost overpowering. As I got out of the car a workman, who had been stacking logs close by, greeted me, and asked if he could help.

'I am trying to track down a Park Ranger that I understand comes round here quite often. He drives round in a green Land Rover with a white top. It has a North York Moors name and badge painted on the doors.'

'You won't find anyone like that round here.'

'Oh, I thought I saw him in this area a couple of days ago.'

'You might have done, but if it is the same person I am thinking of and he comes round here when we are working, our boss soon pisses him off. We know, again if it's the same guy we are talking about, that he does come round here at other times because he has been seen and we have been told and you have just said that you have seen him, but he is not supposed to. Your best bet and if it's important that you get hold of him, is to ring the Moors people direct.'

'Thanks very much, we might have to do that, although it is not very important really. But thanks for your help.'

I returned to the car and climbed in. I started the engine, turned the car round, and drove slowly down the lane back towards the main road.

'He is certainly not popular round here. The standard procedure seems to be to tell him to "get lost" every time he shows up and I got no confirmation from that guy back there, that he has been around this area in the last couple of days. So what now?'

'If we can't establish, for certain, that he has been anywhere near here within the last few days, we are wasting our time. All we have is that someone has mentioned him to someone else and that someone was probably not all that interested in him in the first place. Our information is weak and this overall area big, so unless we can find a way of reducing down the search area we have no chance,' said Fred.

'One last chance! I have just thought of something. Turn round and go back,' requested Eddie.

I didn't argue and reversed the car into a convenient opening, turned round, and went back to the sawmill. I parked the car and Eddie got out. He approached the same man that I had spoken to and who was still working in the same place.

'I am sorry to annoy you again but a moment ago, my friend there,' pointing back towards the car, 'asked you about a bloke that might have been here? The fact that he isn't just now doesn't really matter, because we only wanted to ask him a few simple questions about some domestic problems he has been causing.'

'He in trouble, is he? He been bothering again and causing hassle has he?'

'He might have. But a lot depends on whether you can help us or not.'

The quick flash of Eddies' ID card might have helped to influence him or the fact that he had been given an opportunity to get at Scampton might have been the reason. But either way he bit.

'If he's in trouble a lot of people round here will be only too pleased to help you, not least of all, me.'

'Thanks. Now, tell me. Has he been here within the last few days? Two or three or perhaps four at the most?'

'Why?'

'Well he says he hasn't. We say he has and it would be useful for us to know. Because then we have him.'

'Well if he has I haven't seen him but then I'm not here all the time. Some of my mates might have seen him. I'll go and ask if you like.'

'Not just at the moment! The less people who know about our enquiries the better, if you understand. Perhaps later, but for now you might be able to help with another matter.'

'This still got to do with Scampton?'

'Possibly.'

'What do you want then?'

'You see this yellow-coloured mud that's all around here?' Indicated Eddie as he pointed to a particular large visible patch at the side of the track. 'We have not come across it before and it is of particular interest to our enquiries. I wonder if you can tell me if there's a lot of it about in this area? Is it widespread around here or just up this track?'

'Depends on what you mean by widespread.'

'Well, is it found everywhere in Yorkshire, for example? Because so far all we have come across, in the fields round here, is soil from a very dark brown to light red.'

Eddie told us later that, at the time, he had to rack his brains to try and remember the colours of the different soils he had already seen, round and about, in the ploughed fields.

'There seems to be quite a bit of it around here and I was interested to know if it was peculiar only to this area.'

'Peculiar? What do you mean?'

'Only to be found just round here; this light coloured stuff over here.'

'No not really! It's in patches and is all over the place really. There's quite a bit of it on the coast line and on the tops over there.'

'That's strange, because only a few miles North of here it is reddish brown along the cliff tops.'

'I didn't say it ran all the way. I said there's a lot of it on the coastline. Here there's a band that runs right through the middle of the woods here. That's part of it you are looking at just there. Goes well inland, but if you go a couple of miles either side you won't find any that I know of.'

'If I get a map do you think you might be able to show me just where it is?'

'Well, I am no expert with maps or soil and stuff you know.'

'Perhaps not, but I bet you know far more about it than I do and I really would appreciate your help. It's Scampton we're after, so it's important. So let me get the map and you can try.'

As he turned his back and walked the few paces back to the car he raised his eyebrows in a look of despair. He was certainly working hard. I handed him the map through the open window and he spread it out on the bonnet. The forestry worker walked the few paces across and joined him. I got out of the car and joined them both.

'You say it's in a band. Where, along this way?'

'No!' He stabbed roughly with his finger along the line of the coast. 'You come across it in places along here. Don't know of any round here or here. Then there's this lot that runs through here,' as he traced a line through the green shaded area of the forest and roughly over the point where we were standing. 'It goes through here, as far as I know and way back as far as here or I think it does.'

‘As far back as York or Pickering?’

‘Maybe Pickering! I don’t know about York but probably as far back as Pickering. I know it’s as far as here ‘cos my cousin works some land here about.’

‘What about these woods?’

‘Like I said it comes in a line right down here and goes right through to cliff tops.’

‘Is it the full width of the forest?’

‘No, there’s a patch down here where I don’t know of any and there’s a stretch along here where I am fairly sure there is none.’

‘Thank you,’ said Eddie, folding the map and passing it to Fred through the open window. ‘You have been a great help.’

‘No trouble! Any time. But what’s it all got to do with Scampton?’

‘Scampton?’

‘Yes, the Park Ranger you were talking about. I thought this was all about him?’

‘Oh, it is. He claims to have been somewhere else and we are trying to prove differently.’

‘With the coloured soil stuff?’

‘Something like that: that and other things. Anyhow, thanks once again. You have been a great help and I really appreciate it and I would be obliged if you would keep our little chat to yourself. We don’t want to give anything away to Scampton do we?’

He seemed genuinely pleased with himself and was probably satisfied to think, that what he had said, would be to the detriment or demise of Scampton.

As we drove down the lane Eddie sighed with relief and laughed.

‘That was hard work but we came out of it reasonably well. We now know that we have a band of soil starting somewhere this side of Pickering and running right through to the coast and if that fellow is right it is about a mile and a half wide and covers most of this forest area.’

‘And that’s one hell of an area,’ I said.

‘Never mind,’ said Fred, patting Eddie on the shoulder. ‘You did very well to pull it off and it was well worth the try.’

‘Back to base and another rethink,’ I suggested.

‘And something to eat as well, I think,’ added Fred.

‘Sound idea, but we still have to come up with something more concrete to work on. Concrete, do you get it? Mud is not sufficient, we need concrete,’ I said.

‘Ha, Ha,’ mocked Fred.

‘Yes, we do need a slightly different approach,’ said Eddie, still being serious and still deep in thought.

'Cheer up chaps. It's not the end of the world. But while we have our rethink, do you both think we can do it somewhere comfortable and cosy this evening?'

'Suggest somewhere.'

'I don't know, but let's go inland a few miles and find somewhere nice and warm to talk. But above all else let's find somewhere good to eat. Soup and curly sandwiches are fine in their place but lets take advantage of our present circumstances and let someone else do the cooking and washing up,' pleaded Fred.

'I think Eddie and I can go along with that.'

CHAPTER FORTY-FOUR

Fred was fussing round and preparing for an evening out. The return journey from the forest had been rather disappointing, in so much that no one had come up with any good ideas to help surmount our present difficulties.

'Difficulties!' echoed Eddie. 'That's rather an understatement of the facts if ever I heard one. As I see it, we are up against a solid brick wall at the moment. Your earlier remarks about concrete maybe more appropriate than you think. So far all we have done is hide behind some bushes and just watched Scampton and his cronies disappear into thin air, leaving us high and dry.'

'We had little choice. How could we follow them without transport and even with it, we would have been seen? There was no way you could follow any of them without them seeing us once they drove away. We did all we could.'

'Those boxes might be hundreds of miles away by now, hidden away, in some little attic, down an alley, in Manchester or Birmingham, or any other big city for that matter.'

'You could be right, in which case we have no means of knowing anything about it and again, if you are right, then there is nothing we can do about it either, is there?. All we can do is work on what little we have; chip away a bit at a time and hope that while we are attacking it piecemeal, we get lucky. Anyhow, while you mull it over, I am going to ring our boss. I still have to report to him, and although he rarely has anything to offer, by way of encouragement, at least I might feel a bit better bandying a few words with him. It might help to get some of the frustration out of my system.'

'Is that public phone safe? You know what I mean; for passing confidential stuff and the likes?' enquired Eddie.

'It should be or at least reasonably. It has a different number to the one in the office and besides, the office and shop are closed now, and I doubt there will be an extension running anywhere else from a phone box; the office perhaps. Anyhow, anyone listening in isn't going to learn very much, apart from the fact that we are stumped and have no idea what we are going to do next. I will be back in a minute.'

When I returned, Fred had already got back from the toilet and was in the process of drying her hair on a large towel.

'That feels better. A good wash in hot water works wonders and I always feel ten times better with my hair washed.'

I rubbed my chin.

'A shave is the order of the day for me. Where's my shaving gear?'

'You should know that. You are the only one who uses it round here,' answered Fred from within the folds of her towel.

'I will walk across with you, if you don't mind. Then while you shave, I can make a couple of phone calls myself. My people like to know that I am still alive,' said Eddie. 'And then after that I suppose my chin could do with a scrub round if everyone is getting dressed up.'

I washed and shaved and generally attempted to tidy myself up. I noticed, whilst combing it, that my hair badly needed cutting.

I returned to the caravan, to be greeted with a pot of coffee and to find Eddie grinning like a Cheshire cat.

'What's got into him?' I asked. 'Won the Lottery, or something? Anyhow I thought you were coming for a shave?'

'He won't tell me. He said I had to wait until you got back. Well he's here now, so let's have it.'

'I don't believe it, it's amazing, yet I must, because I have just been told and so damned quick, when to work it all out can't be all that easy,' said Eddie.

I looked at him hoping that what he was trying to say made sense to him, for so far he was not making much sense to me and the look on Fred's face told me she was equally puzzled.

'Go on,' I said rather impatiently. 'Explain yourself and in syllables that we can all understand.'

He laughed. 'Sorry. Well. I rang my chief and he told me that your chief; and that must be since you rang, had already been in contact with him and that a plan had been quickly drawn up, and that, as a result, we are to expect visitors tomorrow. That's incredibly quick if you ask me, can your people really do that?'

'Do what?'

'Arrange things so quickly.'

'I suppose they can, if they have to and if they say that is what they have done, then they will have done it or be shortly about to do it.'

'Stop the pair of you. I was under the impression that I was an integral part of this team. So will one of you, please start at the beginning and tell me, in minute detail, exactly what is going on?' demanded Fred. 'Eddie what the hell is it you are on about.'

'Go one Mel, you tell, after all it is your show.'

'I'm sorry. I had every intention of telling you all and I had planned to do so just as soon as we had all stopped flitting about and could sit down and concentrate. If that hadn't worked then I had every intention of telling you this evening, at the latest, while we were out. I did not anticipate Eddie would find out so soon and from a different source. He has however and that alters things a little. So sit down, the pair of you and I will reveal all.'

Fred was now cross and I could sense it.

'I thought we were partners Mel Grundy and working together. Keeping things to yourself is hardly my idea of togetherness or how a partnership works.'

'I said I was sorry. I was not keeping anything to myself. I don't work like that and you know it. If Eddie had not found out and broached the subject, then you would have been quite happy to remain ignorant until I told you later tonight. You may consider it to be important; in fact it is, but it is nothing that requires immediate action on our part and therefore no harm will be done the result of you, not knowing straight away.'

I reached across the table and touched her arm. She pulled it away sharply.

'Forget it, just tell us what you have to say.'

I felt bad, for it had not been my intention that she should take it that way, but she had and there was nothing I could do about it, so I shrugged my shoulders and simply avoided her stare. She would get over it.

I looked at Eddie. 'As you know, I rang the Old Man with a "sit rep" and basically reported everything that has happened so far and also told him, that for the moment, we had drawn a blank from the stake out and the reasons why I thought we had. By way of a change, he was sympathetic and seemed to understand, for once, how we had ended up in our current position. He made me wait, while he thought about everything that I had said. Or I think that is what he made me wait for, as there was a long silence on the other end, which, by the way, cost me an additional fifty pence in the coin slot. Then he made a suggestion, which I must admit, just might work. After outlining his proposal he said he would put the wheels in motion immediately. Then following another short pause, I assumed for more deliberation on his part, he told me to expect a visit first thing in the morning from two people.'

'Who? Just two people, who?' demanded Fred.

'One, an Army Major, probably by the name of Wilkinson, a crony of the Old Man's no doubt and the other, a bloke from Customs and Excise. He didn't have a name for the Customs man because he said he did not know whom they would send. But he assured me that who ever it was that came, he would be fully briefed and be the right person for the assignment.'

'So what are you two still trying to tell me?' snapped Fred. 'That we are being baled out or pulled out? Replaced or something?'

'No: nothing like that. The Old Man is sending the Army to help us out, to give us a hand if you like, but certainly not to bale us out, or replace us in any way, as you put it.'

'What! So to do whatever, he is sending one Army Officer and a Customs man. Tell me; what can they do that we can't? That's all I want to know.'

She was still full of hell and things were not getting any easier. Any moment and steam would come out of her ears. I thought it was time to call a temporary halt if only to buy some breathing space.

'We will have to wait and see. If we are going out tonight, it's time we worked on it, forgot the army and got a move on.'

'Good idea,' said Eddie, who had become very conscious of the tension. 'I could murder a pint. So the sooner we get away from here, the better'

'I think I will join you in that. A pint sounds a damned good idea, just now,' I said.

'Before you two make any deals or arrangements, remember one thing. I am not driving. I am not in the mood to drive. Tonight was my idea and I invited you to join me as my dinner guests and that includes being my chauffeur. Though God knows why I invited you Mel Grundy… partner.'

CHAPTER FORTY-FIVE

Early the next morning, I was about to make my way back to the camper, having had a good wash and shave in the Toilet block, when I was distracted by the noisy arrival of an Army Land Rover. It pulled up in front of the Office Block and a man dressed in the full uniform of a serving Major, alighted from the passenger side.

'Good morning! I have a feeling you maybe looking for me, Major. Major Wilkinson, is it?'

'You have the name correct Old Boy, but a shufti at some form of ID may not come amiss.'

'Of course, Major.'

I rummaged in my back pocket and produced the plastic folder that held my ID card. I opened it and held it up for his scrutiny.

'Thank you Sir,' and drawing himself erect, he saluted with his pace stick. As he dropped his hand, he placed the stick under his arm and went straight to the button on the breast pocket of his tunic. He produced his Army ID, which he promptly pushed forward for my inspection.

'Thank you, Major! Pleased to meet you! If you will follow me please.'

'Is there anywhere my driver can dump that damned thing, or do we leave him here?'

'He can follow us and park alongside my car, in this field alongside here.'

Turning, he raised his voice, and speaking towards the Land Rover, said, 'Driver, follow us. This gentleman will show you where to park.'

There was no reply, only the re-starting of the engine.

We arrived at the Camper where both Eddie and Fred stepped out to meet us.

'Major Wilkinson, these are my colleagues, Miss Huntington and Mr Scott.'

He shook hands with each of them. His only comment being, 'A woman, eh. Sign of the times I suppose. They seem to get everywhere these days.'

Fred smiled and I knew she was ready for him, if he chose to pursue the feminist bit.

Introductions over, we sat round the table. Coffee was served and the map was spread out. Fred then made us all wait while she took coffee out to the driver who was still sitting in the Land Rover.

'Customs man shown up yet?' demanded the Major, looking round as if he half expected that he had and that we had him hidden away somewhere.

'You're drinking him. He's the little bits floating about in the coffee,' muttered Fred, under her breath.

'What's that, Miss?'

'Nothing,' grinned Fred.

'No, he has not. Not yet, Major,' I replied.

'Damn him! We can't sit about all day waiting for the likes of him to turn up just when he thinks fit. We have planning to do. I assume he was told the time to report here?'

'We assume so too,' replied Fred, giving him her best smile. 'But you know you can't rely on some modern time pieces these days so leave it to us to fill in the poor unfortunate and ignorant man when he gets here. I think we will be able to remember all the tiny details and pass them on, when he eventually decides to turn up. What's he coming for anyhow? A day out with the Army?'

If he was aware of what Fred was doing; her dislike of him being very obvious to me, he showed no signs of it and just carried on. 'That's what we want to know. What is he coming for? My brief said he would supply sniffer dogs. Sniffer dogs? Everyone seems to be overly fond of those creatures these days,' snapped the Major, who obviously, for some reason, disapproved.

Fred could not resist the opportunity to have yet another dig.

'Not like the old days, Major, when you used to kill most of the population and blow up half the town to get what you wanted. Now they use sniffer dogs. I suppose it must have something to do with budgets and the cost of ammunition or the fact that someone has discovered, that in certain circumstances, a mongrel dog is far superior to the might of the British Army.'

I gave Fred a gentle dig on the side of her leg to get her to stop. The Major's only reaction was to mutter something to the effect that, 'Everyone has gone soft these days, using dogs to do men's work and they will find out how wrong they are when the crunch comes.'

A polite knock on the side of the van interrupted our conversation, or Fred's mickey-taking, whichever way you looked at it, as the Majors' driver announced, 'There is a Gentleman here from Customs and Excise, Sir.'

'Have you checked his ID, Corporal?'

'Is it my orders to do so, Sir?'

'Of course it is man! Of course it is. We are senior round here.'

'Sorry sir.'

I looked at Eddie, who sat there grinning and then we both looked at Fred whose face was a picture of disgust. She held her lips clamped tightly shut and her cheeks were distended and puffed out, as she desperately tried to control and prevent an outburst of indignation. I laughed and shook my head. One more statement similar to that and he was dead, if Fred's face was anything to go by, as she would just not be able to control herself any longer.

There followed a few moments of forced silence, then, from the Corporal, 'It is in order, Sir.'

'Then send him in.' Turning then to me, he added, as if as a casual afterthought, 'If that is all right with you, Sir.'

Fred still had a look of thunder on her face and I was certain that at any moment she was going to say something, but she didn't.

'Of course,' I said.

A smart young man in his middle twenties climbed into the van.

'Owen Long,' he said to no one in particular.

I made the return introductions and the Customs man further identified himself as being from the Special Investigation Branch of Customs and Excise. He informed us that he had brought two dogs with him, had been briefed to co-operate fully with all the parties concerned and to accept that I was in overall command. The Major raised an eyebrow at that but said nothing. I winked at Fred who slowly and deliberately, exhaled.

'Two dogs! What on earth do you want two dogs for, man?' demanded the Major.

Before he had time to answer Fred cut in, 'Perhaps one is a lady dog to keep the other boy dog, company on cold nights.'

Owen Long looked at her and knew instantly, from the look on her face, that there was no love lost and a certain animosity between those two. He carried on.

'One for drugs and one for explosives, Major.'

'Waste of manpower! Train one to do both jobs. Do that with men, don't need two.'

'I wish we could do that, but each one is a specialist in it's own field.'

'A dog a specialist? Impossible, doesn't have the brainpower. Still think it's a waste. Modern soldiers are trained to do more than one job. My driver doubles as a radio operator and he also makes a good cup of tea. Training and the ability to take orders, that's all it takes.'

'Same with the dogs! Training and orders, very similar really,' said Fred almost casually. 'But these dogs have it even better, for one is trained to get them both as high as a kite on the drugs, while the other is trained to blow them both up while they are in cloud cuckoo land. What a climax to a lovely trip and day out with the Army.'

'I don't think I follow your drift young lady. Who mentioned anything about a trip?'

'I didn't think you would follow, Major. You need to be an intelligent dog to appreciate the trip I am talking about and I bet that in an emergency this Gentleman's dogs also make a good cup of tea.'

He screwed up his eyebrows, grunted and looked at her, slightly bewildered, for a brief moment, before he continued, 'Well, whatever. Get in here, man, and look at this map. These people think there may be some terrorist stuff hidden in these woods.'

We looked across the table at each other. This was the first time there had been any reference to terrorism. What did the Old Man know and in his wisdom had passed on to the Army, but was keeping back from us? Not being present or readily available at that precise moment, we couldn't ask him.

'Forest,' corrected Fred, 'It's a forest, not a wood,' as she gave me a dig under the table. She was not letting up.

'Forest then, if you insist, Miss. However, I have been ordered by my command to find this material, or whatever it is, for you people and this is how I propose to set about it.'

He cleared his throat and sat back. Fred remained silent and looked at him through narrowed eyelids.

'At lunch time today a convoy of twenty army wagons from Catterick Garrison will enter this village here. They will be driven by Learner Drivers and accompanied by their Instructors and their wagons will be marked up accordingly. They will effectively clog up the village and the men will be allowed to wander around the area while supposedly having a lunch break. They will do this having entered the village from this direction. At a point near here each wagon will have dropped off some ten men and NCOs who will assemble here. We will then have two hundred plus men assembled close to the forest area here. Catterick will inform the forestry people that we are exercising in this area. They will be given no reason, security, and all that will be the excuse put forward to keep them quiet. Any locals who become involved or who complain will be told to ring the Forestry Head Office at Northallerton, who in turn have been instructed to say only that an exercise is taking place and that civilians are advised to keep out of the way. Any questions so far?'

'Why the wagons in the village? Why not place them in the forest area?' asked the Customs man.

'To help create the impression, among the local population, that the exercise is not solely concentrated on the forest. It will give them something to focus on and distract their attention away from the concentration in the wooded area.'

'You hope.'

'I know it will and I would be obliged if you would leave military matters, of this nature, to me Miss.'

'How do you propose to deploy two hundred men, Major?' asked Eddie.

'If the area turns out to be, as it indicates here on this map, a cultivated and man-made forest, then I propose to put them shoulder to shoulder and let them walk the entire length searching for whatever you want them to search for. Once

you have clearly defined your objectives, that is and I have passed them on to my NCOs.'

'Yes, it is cultivated, or man-made, forest. It is also very dense in places but should present no problems and your men should, even though they may encounter some difficulty in places, get through.' Here I was assuming that if there were places where the army could not penetrate, it was a sure bet that Scampton, or his associates, would not be able to either.

'My men will get through anywhere, if they have to.'

'Yes, of course! I appreciate that and while they are doing so, what we want them to look for, are any signs of the ground being disturbed recently. Signs of things being buried or hidden in holes, gullies or under piles of timber or brush. Our reasons, which necessitate this search and our prime interest in the forest, stems from the fact that, so far, our only tangible clue that something maybe hidden in there, comes from a light-coloured soil or clay that underlies most of that area. It is unusual in so much that it is a light buff colour and is only to be found in certain areas and the forest is one of them.'

'Just tell me what you want me to look for Old Man; all the underlying reasons, clues or pure speculation and the history behind it, are all your worry. Now if you will excuse me a moment, I will pass details of the route the transports are required to take and the co-ordinates outside the forest area, where I require the men dropping off, to my driver, in order that he can radio them through.'

As soon as he was out of earshot I said to Fred, 'You behave yourself, prat that he is, we need this guy.'

'Do we? You could fool me,' she replied with disgust.

The Major returned and sat down. 'Now you, Sir,' he said, as he twisted in his seat to face Owen Long, the Customs man, 'Where exactly do you fit in? Why do we need you?'

I could literally feel Fred tense up. The Customs man, Long, remained calm and unruffled. He could obviously handle the Major.

'If I let my dogs loose in any area, that I feel may be of interest, they will sniff out certain things, undetectable by humans even if the area has lain undisturbed for many weeks. Certain scents and odours linger a long time and my dogs are trained to seek them out.'

'My wife had a dog once. Silly bloody thing; kept biting my Batman. Disappeared one day. I swear that batman knew something about it, but he denied it of course. Bloody good soldier,' mused the Major from a distant, half dream-like, state of reminiscence. 'Had another Batman once who did a bit for the wife. Had to get rid of that bugger too, sharpish.'

'Do you always work alone?' enquired Fred of the Customs man, totally ignoring the Major.

'Usually. It depends on the size of the operation. I was told that in this particular case, the Army was supplying all the manpower and all that was required from me were the dogs.'

'And so they are! The Army can supply everything,' confirmed the Major, who appeared to be coming back down from his orbit around another planet and where he had relived the time where his Batman did a bit for his wife, while the dog bit him.

'Except the dogs,' Interjected Fred.

'Err! Yes. What eh? Yes. I was saying? Ah, yes. Now, transport.' As he pushed back his shoulders and re-asserted himself. 'I want one of your people with me for comms. You preferable Mr. Grundy. I don't like working through intermediaries; mistakes get made. Have you got transport?' addressing Owen Long.

'Yes, my Dog Van.'

'Oh, and we all thought you walked here or used the dogs to pull you on a sledge,' grinned Fred. I banged her leg under the table. She banged me back.

Her remark did not register with the Major.

'Suggest you use that then. And you two?' looking towards Eddie and Fred.

'We have our own little car, don't we Eddie and we are ever so good at finding our way around the countryside in it, particularly at night.'

'We are not talking about the night here, young lady. We are talking about today and not too far ahead at that.'

'I know, but I thought you might like to be aware of our vast experience and our overall value to your delicate and complex operation. I did not want you to think that we might get in your way. After all this is our job and we would hate to be under your feet the result of that.'

'Right. Let's move out then and get into this village, and set up our operations HQ.'

'Sorry Major, but we can't go into the village. We have supposedly left there, for very good reason and it would not be prudent for us to return at this point in our investigation,' I said.

'What on earth for, man?'

'Let's say we have our reasons, Major,' said Fred very forcefully. 'So let's leave it at that shall we.'

'Damn nuisance that! I was hoping for a convenient and hospitable Pub in the village to work from. So if that is not to be Miss, then my driver will have to find a sheltered spot for the Land Rover and we will have to work from there. Damned bad show that.'

Fred grinned and was obviously delighted and not just at the fact that he had addressed a remark directly to her but that she had successfully thrown a

spanner into his works. I was going to have to keep these two apart, if only for the Major's overall protection and safety.

'There is a Saw Mill close to where we propose to go. We can park on the approach road. It will be sheltered and close to where the action will be. I will direct you and show your driver the way, Major, and you, Mr Long, can follow behind Fred here who will be taking our car.'

'No more questions?' demanded the Major. 'Good, then let's shape up and move out. Don't want the enemy to have slipped off home for lunch before we get there, do we?' he laughed. We all just looked at each other, presuming it to be some private joke with special meaning to those in the know, or to those with a particular fetish for lunch breaks. His humour, or the way he attempted to project it, was certainly not ours.

We assembled outside and prepared to leave. The Corporal stood holding the Land Rover door open for the Major. Owen Long sat in his van with the engine running, waiting to fall in behind Fred. The Major stood, for a moment, with his hand on the Land Rover door, a deep frown on his face, watching Fred as she walked towards the car. I don't know what he was thinking at that precise moment, but I wonder if he realised just how much she disliked him because of his bad attitude towards women. I could only hope, for his sake, that once we got on the job he totally ignored her and got on with his business.

'Are you going to ride in the front with the Major, Sir, or would you prefer to ride in the back?' enquired the Corporal. 'Three in front can be a bit of a squeeze Sir.'

'In the back will be fine,' I replied.

If we proposed going through the village, which I knew we would, then I felt the back of the Land Rover would perhaps provide a better shield and protect me from any curious and prying eyes.

'Which way do we take to the Saw Mill?' shouted Eddie above the engine noises.

'You go round the back way. I will take the Major through the village, so that he can see what is what there and then meet up with you at the mill.'

'See you there,' Eddie shouted back as they pulled out, followed closely by the Customs Van, which I noticed, for the first time, was conveniently painted a plain dull green and unmarked and could have been taken as belonging to almost anything by a casual observer.

'When you are ready Major. To the end of the lane and turn right.'

'Follow those instructions, Corporal.'

'Yes Sir.'

* * *

I positioned myself in the back of the Land Rover and lent forward between the driver and passenger seats from where I had a clear view forward between the two. The back of the Land Rover was typically Army style, spotlessly clean and neat. One side was taken up with a variety of complex radio units and other essential communications equipment. There was a swivel chair secured to the floor for the operator and a variety of lockers filled up the remaining space, no doubt all full of goodness knows what, but knowing the Army, all there for very specific reasons.

'Take the right at this T-junction Corporal. The road then leads straight into the Northern end of the village and you will come to the actual outskirts about five kilometres down the road.'

I chose to use kilometres as opposed to the more familiar miles, as I felt certain the Army would now certainly be metric. What with the EEC and NATO and all that? However which ever they use, the Corporal made no comment and simply drove on.

As we entered the village it looked as if an invasion had taken place and an Army of Occupation had completely taken over. There were ten-ton trucks, in dark green camouflage, strung out along the entire length of the main street of the poor village. There were even odd ones, I noticed as we passed, tucked down the side roads, enveloping the entire area in a dull, drab green. They appeared to be everywhere and first impressions were that there were literally dozens and dozens of them, many more than the twenty the Major had mentioned at the briefing.

'How many trucks are there, Major? There seems to be far more than the twenty you mentioned,' I asked.

'If there are then heads will roll. Count them Corporal.'

'No, don't bother because I am sure you are right. It just looks as if there are more; probably because the truck are so damned big and the streets so narrow and the village only a small place.'

I continued to look around. Some of the trucks seemed to totally overshadow the small cottages and the tiny shops. On top of that there were children milling about everywhere and, at first glance, it looked as if every door, of every building, strung out along the entire length of the main street, was open with at least two people filling each doorframe. Some distance up front the village Constable was remonstrating with an army Sergeant, both were standing in the middle of the road and waving their arms about. The Major had said there would be two occupants to each truck and that no doubt was true, but now, no matter in which direction I looked, there appeared to be soldiers in combat fatigues and green berets everywhere and I began to wondered, as no doubt did a lot of the local population, where they had all come from.

'Pull over close to the Sergeant and that Police Constable,' ordered the Major.

The Land Rover drew up and came to a halt along side them.

'Sergeant.'

'Sir,' snapped the Sergeant and abruptly turning away from the Constable he took one single pace forward and stamped his feet down hard, giving at the same time a very smart and ridged salute.

'Is there a problem here, Sergeant?'

'No Sir! We stopped for a break Sir, as ordered, Sir. The Constable now seems to think we are causing an obstruction, Sir.'

'Then co-operate with him man or order him to co-operate with you and operate a system of single file traffic if that's his problem, Sergeant. Rearrange your trucks if necessary but make sure he understands we are here to stay until I give the order to move out. Is that clear and understood Sergeant?'

'Yes, Sir! But he says he can't operate that system Sir, 'cos he's only one man, Sir.'

'Then give him a hand, detail someone, there's a good chap Sergeant, co-operation with the locals and all that. Use some of your men.'

'Yes, Sir.'

'Carry on Sergeant.'

''Sir,' and with another salute he turned on his heel and marched smartly away.

'Things seem to be working well,' observed the Major. 'Move on, Corporal. Now which way to this Saw Mill?'

'Keep going straight forward, follow this road out of the village; the turn-off you are looking for is on the left and is about half a kilometre further down the road.'

Just short of the turn-off, which was on the left hand side and which led from the main road up to the Saw Mill, we came upon Eddie and the Customs Van parked along the roadside. An Army Captain was deep in conversation with Eddie through the open window.

'Drive round that van; stop by the Captain, Corporal.'

'Sir.'

'What seems to be the problem, Captain?' demanded the Major through his open window as the Land Rover pulled up.

'Sir,' saluted the Captain. 'These people insist they have some sort of right to be here, Sir. I told them that my orders are to stop everyone going anywhere near this wooded area and that they must either turn back or proceed no further than this point, Sir.'

'Good man Captain. Now let them through. They are with us. Then you report to me. Got that?'

'Yes, Sir.'

When we arrived in the open area, in front of the Saw Mill I saw several soldiers, in combat fatigues and camouflaged helmets, standing idly about. When I looked down and saw their shiny boots my heart ached for them and I shuddered to think what state they would be in after they had tramped a few miles through the forest. Also standing around, in the same area, were several of the local workmen who between then looked partly bemused and partly angry.

'What's going on here, Captain?' demanded the Major, as he waved his pace stick in the general direction of the workmen.

'These men are under protective guard, Sir, until after the completion of the exercise. "No civilians allowed in the area" were my orders, Sir.'

'Correct Captain.'

'Oy you! Are you in charge of this bloody lot?' demanded one of the workmen who stepped forward to confront the Major.

'As far as you are concerned yes. Who are you?'

'I am the Mill Manager and I object to the presence of you bloody lot. When I rang our Office, they said it was some kind of Army Exercise and that it would not interfere with us and then this bloody ignorant lot come along and shut us down,' pointing at the Captain and the main group of soldiers. 'On who's bloody authority. I want to know?'

The Major, turning to the Captain, said, 'Captain, withdraw your men, and you sir,' turning back to the Mill Manager, 'Accept my apology and you are now free to return to work. However I must ask you, and your men, not leave the immediate vicinity without my express permission until the exercise is complete. Don't want anyone shot by accident, do we Sir?'

Without any further acknowledgement the Mill Manager turned and addressed his men. 'Come on lads. Let's cut some timber and leave these silly buggers to play soldiers. A lot I know would have shot that snotty bastard in the back in 'forty two.'

'I say old chap.'

'Leave it, Captain,' commanded the Major. 'Where are the main body of your men?'

'Strung out along the roadside, a little to the South of here, Sir.'

'You brought mine detectors along?'

'As ordered, Sir.'

'Good. Now, the plan. Where's our map of this area, Corporal?'

'Here, Sir.'

'It's no damned good there man. Bring it here and spread it out on the bonnet. Gather round, Captain.'

I stood and listened and decided to say nothing; for I felt there was no need to interfere as long as the well-oiled wheels of the Military were running smoothly.

'Captain, I want your men strung out along a broad front bordering this edge of the forest, with detectors, evenly spaced out. On the command, you are to work your way, in line, through the forest until you come out here. Your men are looking for any signs of disturbance or anything unusual that might indicate there has been unusual activity at some time. Concentrate on recently cleared areas and disturbances.'

'What type of disturbances, Sir?'

'Signs of digging! Look for signs of things buried, hidden, covered up: evidence of concealment, or attempted concealment, and things of that nature. Make out you are looking for "Charlie" hidden in the jungle. Look for where he might have hidden his supplies.'

'I get it, Sir. We are to "make out" we are looking for something that does not exist. Jolly good idea if I may say so, Sir.'

'You are not to "make out" anything, Captain,' I snapped. 'Excuse me, Major. Captain, what you are looking for is very real. It exists and I want it. We want you and your men to find it. It is no "jolly" exercise that doesn't matter if you come up with nothing. We want, and fully expect, results.'

'Sorry Sir! You will get them, Sir. If there is anything there to be found, my men will find it.'

'Make sure they know, that they are expected to find something, Captain, because if they don't, then they keep going until they do. Understand?' added the Major.

'Yes, Major. Sir.'

'And Captain allocate two men, with a radio, to accompany that civilian and his dogs. They are to stay with him at all times and ensure he does not get lost. They are to accept all reasonable orders from him and assist in every way. Is that understood?'

'Yes Sir.'

'Then carry on, Captain. Make it snappy, and let me know when you are formed up and ready to move forward into the woods.'

'Sir,' he saluted and turned in his heel and marched off down the lane.

By this time the Saw Mill had restarted and if the volume of sound was anything to go by, was functioning to capacity.

'Corporal.'

'Sir.'

'Set up your listening post here. Inform everyone that we are the field command post and make sure you give, them our position. Everything to pass through us, understand?'

'Yes Sir.'

'Then jump to it man and get yourself a second radio operator and a runner.'

The Corporal disappeared into the rear of the Land Rover to do as ordered; the remaining five of us stood in a semi-circle round the bonnet.

'It shouldn't take them long,' observed the Major.

'Those trees and undergrowth are pretty dense in places,' said Fred who had turned her back on the Major and myself and was talking to Eddie.

'They are good men. They are trained to work and fight in the woods,' and turning to survey his surrounding, perhaps for the first time, the Major added, 'I hate this type of exercise, in a strange and inhospitable place with very little to do but wait about and especially today when there is no field kitchen or anything decent, close at hand, to drink. On these outdoor exercises I prefer my HQ to be in a Pub or a convenient warm billet somewhere. Could have been playing golf today. Good day for it, what. Corporal, have we got anything decent to drink with us?'

The Corporals head popped round the rear doorpost of the Land Rover.

'No Sir! You never said to bring anything Sir.'

'A good Corporal that! He doesn't think, just does as he is told. Would make him up to Sergeant but then I would lose a good Corporal. Hard to find these days: good Corporals. Sergeants are even harder.'

The corporal's head popped round the doorpost once again, 'The Captain on the air, Sir. He is in position and awaiting orders, Sir.'

As if drawn by some unseen force, we all moved to the rear of the vehicle.

'Tell him to carry on, in his own time, and report his progress.'

'Very good, Sir.'

'Sir,' snapped a voice from behind.

As we all turned, we found ourselves confronted by another Corporal and a soldier with a radio pack on his back.

'Sir. We are to report to you, Sir and collect and escort a civilian, Sir.'

'Not "escort". Accompany this civilian Gentleman,' replied the Major, indicating Owen Long. 'Look after him. Accept his orders but do not let him out of your sight. You understand that?'

'Yes, Sir.'

'Then double up and get on with it. The others will be finished before you get started.'

'Wait, I will get my dogs,' said Owen Long as he moved over and opened the rear doors of his parked van.

Throughout the whole time we had been there, there had not been a sound from that van. In fact, had I not been told otherwise, I would not have known there were any dogs in it and I was very surprised, when he opened the rear door of the van and out jumped, firstly, a fat black Labrador, followed closely by a very fast, quick moving and fussy black and white spaniel. Within seconds of hitting the ground the spaniel had sniffed over a very wide area and was preparing to move

off down the lane. The Labrador, on the other hand, sat and with twisted body, used one of its back legs to methodically scratch its ear.

'Here boy!' Long called. Then turning to us, said, 'He's the keenest dog I have ever had. He works and never stops from the moment he gets out of this van. He will be through those woods before this one stops scratching his ear.'

The spaniel returned on command and then immediately shot over to where Fred stood. She bent down and with both hands rubbed his long ears. 'What is your name little fellow and what do you do beside wag your tail and be fussy?'

'He looks for drugs amongst other things. But mainly drugs these days.'

'Other things?'

'Yes, Miss. From the few moments he is with you now, he will remember you for a long time, months in fact and would come to you in a crowd, or seek you out if you were lost, or hidden, from almost anywhere. Won't you old son?'

'The other one?' enquired Fred, looking at the slightly overweight Labrador who was now slowly sniffing the short grass in a bored fashion and occasionally cocking his legs to let any interested party know that he had passed by.

'He's the more sensible one. He doesn't waste energy. He methodically moves through an area and waits until he gets a good sniff and then he's in. If it's there, he will find it, in his own sweet time, despite the fact that it maybe well hidden. If he sits and wags his tail you know something is there, or has been there at some time.'

'What has?'

'Any: or almost any type of explosive. Stick him in a warehouse, for example, and let him roam on his own. Then call him back. If he comes: nothing. But if he refuses to come, when called, then you can be assured there are explosives somewhere in the area. If he sticks his nose against an object and stands sniffing, then that is what you are looking for. He never gets excited, just stubborn.'

'They are both lovely,' said Fred. 'Which one can I have?'

'Some days, when they are both daft side out, you could have them both, but that's not very often and I hope not today. We had better get started if you will excuse me Miss or, like the Major said, they will be finished before we begin. Come on you two. Work to be done,' and at that, both dogs came to heel and fell in behind him as he walked off down the lane accompanied by the two escorting soldiers.

'You know something, Mel?' said Fred, after they had gone. 'I always thought the Military and people like them and Owen Long used Alsatians. I don't know why, perhaps it is because they use them in their Public Display Teams, which we see at shows and on the telly.'

'I agree. I think I expected to see Alsatians. But nothing like, that fussy little Spaniel. It's strange how often you get preconceived ideas and take things, like that, for granted.'

'Anything to report, Corporal?'

'Nothing Sir! The line is getting straggly because of the terrain being thicker and denser in some places more than others. Apart from that, nothing Sir.'

'Tell them to keep it together.'

'Captain say's he is doing that Sir.'

'Good man, that Captain! Every confidence in him! He will find it if anyone can. Not much faith in that mongrel dog chappie. Don't know what he hopes to achieve?'

'I thought "they" would find it, not the Captain,' remarked Fred.

'Who are they, Miss?'

'The soldiers.'

'No Miss! The soldiers are used to find it for the Captain. The Captain finds it for me and then I have found it and having done so, I then hand it over to Mr Grundy, as per my orders. It is, in actual fact me Madam, who finds it. That's how it works with the Army. You use the soldiers only to achieve the objective, that's why they are expendable in times of actual conflict and what they are specifically trained for.'

'Some fine logic,' muttered Fred almost inaudibly under her breath, and as she turned away from him and added, 'Pompous ass.'

'Report Sir! Captain says they have found a patch approximately two meters by one meter, Sir.' He stopped and listened to his earphones and wrote on his message pad. 'Recently dug earth covered with leaves and brush.' He listened intently as more came through. 'Detectors indicate metal, Sir. Captain requests orders, Sir.'

'Tell him to mark it Corporal and post two men there.' Then, turning to me, said, 'don't you agree? I think we should complete the sweep of the whole area first before taking any further action.'

'I agree Major.'

'Right, Corporal! You got that. The Captain is to mark the area and leave two sentries.'

The Corporal transmitted the order and made the appropriate record on his signal pad.

'The Captain acknowledges, Sir.'

Everyone was now smiling, including the Major, at what might be the first bit of good news. 'Good man that,' he muttered, more to himself than to anyone else.

An atmosphere of excitement began to develop, despite the fact that so far, we really knew very little and the reported 'find' could, in the end, result in nothing at all. However the waiting became tense. Everyone stood about in silence and seemed to want to keep his or her thoughts to their selves. Myself included. I winked at Fred and she smiled back. A square of, newly, disturbed

ground. It sounded promising. Had they found what we were looking for? Had we been lucky at the first attempt? What would the Old Man say to this? "Well done, Grundy. So tell me. What is the solution to Edison's disappearance?" Thereafter a million questions, that might follow, shot through my mind along with some possible answers, most of them fabricated by my flights of fancy and completely outrageous and far fetched.

I slowly walked over to Fred and stood in front of her, 'you all right, Fred? You've gone very quiet. But then I suppose we all have this last few minutes.'

'Yes, I'm fine. It was something I was thinking about, just now.'

'I think we have all been thinking quite a bit this last few minutes. But you must have been thinking of something pretty awful because when I looked across, for a second or two, you looked really upset and pale. Want to tell me about it?'

I took her hand and gently drew her away from the Land Rover.

'It's nothing really, just me being silly and allowing my imagination to get the better of me. All I was thinking was, here am I, getting excited over the possibility of finding something out there in the woods, when all the time, it could be Edison and before you say anything, I know what we were sent here for. But it just somehow, for the moment, felt wrong to get all excited about it and especially something, which could be, as tragic as that. On the other hand it could amount to nothing.'

'I know. I have thought about it. The other night I dreamed that we were digging tunnels all over the place and all the time Edison was at home with his wife. She had her boy friend locked in a spare room and I don't know how it came about, but I was obliged to help her so that her Daughter could not get at him. Mixed up in all this was Mother trying to get rid of Father, Daughter trying to knock off Mother and all of them trying to knock off me, because, for some reason, I was preventing everyone from achieving their objective. It was really bizarre and I was actually relieved when I woke and found it was all not true. I often find I dream like that and often have terrible nightmares when I am tense and under pressure. It was even worse the other night because you were not there to cuddle me,' I smiled and winked as I told a little white lie. She responded by giving me a playful tap on the arm. 'But seriously, do you know Fred, there are now about two hundred men out there in those woods and the shear size of this operation is beginning to bother me. I am worried that the whole thing is getting out of all proportion. If this lot find nothing at all, how do we calm it all down and get back into the village and act as if nothing has happened? Does the Old Man really know what he is doing when he set this lot in motion? I'm honestly beginning to have my doubts. It is all getting too big and at any moment could all go dreadfully wrong and then you and I will be left to pick up the pieces and at the same time will probably get the blame. I am beginning to wonder how the hell, from this point on, we are supposed to do our job.'

'Try and forget it,' said Fred, who was now trying to comfort me. 'There is not much we can do at the moment and worrying about it will not help. I have thought about it and it occurred to me, that things might just work out right.'

'How do you arrive at that?'

'Well! Basically the Old Man! Let's take for example his attitude. First of all you can't go by that, and you know that, as well as I do. So you can forget that. Therefore I think, that with attitude and manner to one side, if he were not satisfied then we would not be here. He would have recalled us and replaced us, long ago. He sent the Army. We didn't ask for it. He decided to do it this way, not us. It is all his idea. So if it all goes horribly wrong how can it be down to us? He will have to pick up the pieces, not us.'

'But you know the Service? The Old Man will not take the blame for anything as long as he has the likes of you and me to throw to the lions.'

'That doesn't alter the fact that the Army was his brain child and not ours and what happens if he throws us to the lions, as you put it? He still has the problem, not us. He can't very well sack us for his blatant mistakes and don't forget our report, both our reports, will show that he sent in the Army and that we did not request it. We can make that very clear.'

'Can't he? That's just the sort of thing he can do. But I suppose you could be right and everything will work out. But let's hope Eddie's report follows the same tack and will be there for us to use, as back up, if we need it.'

'You don't think he is doing all this with ulterior motive, do you?'

'I don't know. But you know the crafty old bastard. For reasons known only to himself, he maybe, and is capable of, feeding us rope and sitting back while we hang ourselves.'

'You don't trust him one bit, do you?'

'No I don't. I don't trust any of them, who get where he is, the way he got there. It's like this barmy bugger in charge of this lot. He is typical of the whole damned set up. "No Miss, the Soldier gets it from the Captain, the Captain gets it from me and I catch it from you and that's the way the Army works Miss". Bull shit.'

'Snap out of it! Why this sudden downer?'

'I don't know. I have never had it as bad as this before. I suppose I just don't feel comfortable with all, this crowd around me. I am used to working things out for myself. I prefer it that way. You and I were doing just fine before all this lot. But I will be all right and I will cope.'

'Of course you will. You still have me and it might be fun getting the sack together.'

'Are you sure you have got it right? You understood what I said? I said getting the sack together, as in getting fired, loosing our jobs. Not getting into the sack together.'

She laughed and was about to reply when she got cut off.

'Another report Sir.'

'Pass it.'

'Yes Sir! Captain says they have located a second site.' He stopped and listened. We stood in silence and looked towards him, waiting for any follow up. 'They have marked it, Sir. No sign of recent disturbance Sir. Metal detectors indicate something there, Sir. Orders, Sir.'

'Same as before, Corporal! Mark it and set sentries. Original orders still stand; continue to the end of the search area.'

'Sir.'

'A second possible site! I didn't expect that. Did you?' said Fred.

'No I didn't. I didn't expect anything,' I replied, suddenly feeling the adrenaline beginning to run a little and some of the original enthusiasm return, though goodness knows why? 'Found by detector. Nothing visible. It might be a deposit of iron or something metallic that was dumped there a long time ago. Someone's old cast iron bath or burnt out car? We will have to wait and see.'

'Where's Eddie?'

'He's over there in the car. I think he's asleep.'

Without opening his eyes he replied, 'No he's not. Just resting. I heard everything he said.'

'Units are breaking out at the far end of the wood, Sir. Captain requests short break Sir.'

'Granted Corporal.' Then, turning to us, the Major added. 'That's one sweep complete. Give them a short break then bring them back.'

'Fine, Major. Can we get a progress report from the Dog Team?'

'Corporal, find out what that chap with the dogs is up to.'

'Sir.'

'I thought we might have heard something from them before now,' I observed.

'Sir. Dogs showed some interest at first site and are presently moving on to second site.'

'Acknowledge Corporal.'

'Sir.'

'Two sites, Mr Grundy. I fully expected my men to find one based on the information you supplied. But two! A bit of a bonus, what?'

'Yes. Very good indeed, Major. But hardly on information I supplied. I didn't know there was anything in there to find. However it will be very interesting to see what they reveal.'

Two sites. "What would they indeed reveal?" I thought to myself. I looked at Fred. She smiled but made no comment.

'Sir. Captain ready to commencing return sweep, Sir.'

'Acknowledged, Corporal and tell him to get on with it.'
'Sir.'

* * *

Time always seems to pass slowly when you know something might be happening and all you can do is stand about and wait and basically do nothing about it. Recently we seemed to have experienced more than our fair share of that; mainly from waiting around in the ravine for Johnson and his team, who, on the one occasion, failed to turn up at all and on the second disappeared into the night leaving us high and dry but leading us, more or less, to our present situation. I hoped this was not going to become a habit. Perhaps not and that somehow, this present situation and level of inactivity coupled with the information so far received, would lead to something very positive and it was that which was also, at present, contributing to the feelings of mild excitement.

'Come to think of it, it was damned uncomfortable in those woods the other night,' I said aloud. 'Not the best way to spend an evening and early morning and I am still not sure if my foot has got warm again or not.'

'I don't know what made you raise that subject but I agree and came to that very same conclusion after only the first hour out there,' laughed Fred.

'Sir. The Captain has reached the second area that he marked. Nothing further found; he is continuing on the return leg.'

'Acknowledge Corporal and confirm that he has left sentries.'

'Sir.'

'When the Captain returns, we shall need to implement another set plan. Am I correct in assuming that you propose to excavate these marked areas, Mr Grundy?'

'That's the general idea Major.'

'Good, then leave that to me. Corporal, arrange for transport to be available when the Captain returns and inform whoever it concerns, that digging equipment is required and mobile lighting.' Then turning back to us, he added, 'There is no point in waiting until it gets dark before we call for lighting, get it shipped out at the same time as we move in, even if we don't use it.'

'I hope we are not going to be here long enough to need flood lighting,' whispered Fred to me.

'Neither do I, but you know army efficiency, anticipate every eventuality, overload the job and as long as you have unlimited resources, there can be no problems. Let the Major have masses of lighting equipment dragged all the way through the woods, if that is what he wants.'

'Sir, how many men for digging parties Sir?'

'The Captain must decide that Corporal. He has seen the sites and has the men out there in the field.'

'Yes, Sir.'

That's it Major, I thought. Pass the book. That's always a good sign of Army leadership.

The Corporal busied himself passing all the Major's instructions and the different orders to the relevant sections. He never seemed to stop writing, as he carefully logged all the messages, in the signal log, as they went back and forth.

'Sir, the Captain is back at the first site now and reports nothing further found.'

'Acknowledge, Corporal. Check out the present whereabouts of the Dog Team and make sure transport will be waiting to bring the Captain here on his return.'

'Sir.'

Eddie continued to sit in the car with his eyes closed. Fred and I had shuffled about, but were currently sat on a low, dry stone, wall about four or five yards away from the Land Rover.

'Sir. Captain asks for orders when he returns Sir.'

'Tell him to report to me, here.'

'Sir.'

'Should not be long now,' said the Major.

'Sir. The Captain is clear of the woods and his men are assembling along the roadside. He reports the return sweep complete, no further finds Sir.'

'Tell him to assemble two working parties and two trucks. Stand the remainder down. Tell him to ensure, digging equipment, detection equipment and lighting are all available. Then tell him to report here, in person, to me.'

'Sir.'

CHAPTER FORTY-SIX

We could hear, although we could not see, the Army Trucks as they moved along the road and past the end of the turn off up to the mill. The high pitched whine of the saw in the mill, loud though it was, could not block out the sound of so many powerful truck engines, as they moved along in convoy.

As this almost continuous rumble began to die away the saw from the mill stopped and through the strange, almost uncanny silence, a new sound took over, that of the Captain's boots as they crunched the gravel on the approach road. A distraction that, strangely enough, caused Eddie to open his eyes and twist round his neck in order to see who was coming our way. As the Captain came closer I noticed that what had once been his highly polished boots, were now completely covered in mud and bits of dead and dying vegetation. So too were his gaiters and the bottom edge of his trousers.

He stopped, came to attention and saluted, 'Sir.'

The Major acknowledged with a half-hearted flick of his pace stick.

'Bit rough in there Captain?' asked Fred looking down at his muddied boots.

'A bit thick and sticky in patches, miss and not easy to get through. Also very dark in places and wet.' As he lifted his foot and bent his ankle to examine his boot.

'You will dry out Captain,' snapped the Major. 'Now let's have your report. What have you found and where?'

'We don't know what we have found so far Sir, it needs further investigation to establish that, but so far there are two possibilities, Sir. First one: newly turned over ground, with an attempt to conceal it. My chaps found it almost straight away. Second one: not so simple and difficult to make out at first. Detectors found it. It is a small open area with nothing of substance growing in it. I understand the dogs showed a lot of interest in and around the same area.'

'Damn. That reminds me… Corporal, find out what the dog chap and our two are up to… Carry on Captain.'

'Not a great deal to add Sir: just two possible sites. I now await your further orders Sir.'

'That depends entirely on Mr Grundy. The decision is yours Sir. We all now await your orders.'

'With your cooperation Major, I would like to excavate both these sites, beginning with the first one found. I will go along with the Captain when he returns to the site with the digging party.'

'Correction. We will accompany the Captain when he returns to the site,' said Fred. 'You coming as well Eddie?'

'You bet, if that's alright with you Mel?'

'Yes of course it is.'

'Fine,' said the Major. 'That is entirely up to you. I will remain at my command post, here. You all go with the Captain. I would appreciate being kept informed however, Mr Grundy.'

'My men will see to that Sir,' snapped the Captain as he threw up a smart salute.

'When you are ready Captain, move out and remember, these people are now your responsibility. Look after them.'

I could sense a certain hostility creeping into his manner by the way he said, 'Look after them. They are your responsibility'. It was almost as if he considered us incapable of looking after ourselves; as if we were a gang of juveniles out on a day trip. I hoped this was not going to be the anti-climax, brought about by the attitude of a group of professional soldiers with no genuine battle experience between them. A group, which on this occasion, very much included this Senior Officer, who's only experience amounted to perhaps the pushing around of civilians in Northern Ireland or going on standby for other anticipated conflicts which never materialised, but who now, having started out eager to please and having for the first time in months, managed to get themselves into something with a degree of seriousness and excitement, had ended up, for reasons known only to themselves, feeling rejected and therefore wanting to rebel against having to let go and pass things over to a group of 'civilians'. What had I done to deserve this?

The four of us set off and walked to the end of the lane. The Captain walking a couple of paces ahead leading the way.

'I feel as if I am under escort. The Major certainly doesn't intend to loose overall control or let go just yet. "You go with the Captain. Captain you are responsible for these people. Keep me informed",' moaned Fred.

Maybe I was, after all, not too far adrift in my assessment of the current situation and I was rather pleased that Fred had sensed something similar.

'He's typical Modern Army and so is incapable of accepting that anyone can do anything as efficient, or better, than he can. They brainwash each other into believing this sort of thing. It's called the military machine. In other words, The British Army. Don't let him get you down and for goodness sake, ease up on the sniping at him and being sarcastic, whenever you get the chance.'

'Who me?' she replied, inferring disbelief.

'Yes you. "I thought it was the Soldiers who would find something, and not the Captain",' I mimicked.

'Oh that. He just irritates me beyond belief, with things like that, that's all.'

'He does me. But we need him for the moment, so until he goes, let him play his part the way he sees it and let him think he is in control; if that's the way he wants it.'

'Anything you say, boss.'

'Now you're even having a go at me.'

'No I am not, but I soon will be, if you start behaving like him or don't stop picking on me. When we have finished with him, can I be the one to tell him to go?'

'If it will make you happy.'

'Extremely and you can punish me all you like, for my sarcasm, later, when we're alone.'

I looked at her and grinned, while she lightly puckered her lips and blew me a silent kiss.

'It's not too far into the woods, if we approach it from this point. Ah! There's our radioman waiting for us,' said the Captain from his position up front.

'You say this is the shortest route in, from this corner here?'

'Yes Sir and as you will see, it is a relatively easy march to get from here to the spot, if you head in this direction and take this line. I didn't appreciate that fact until we were on the return leg and I headed this way in order to report to the Major.'

I gave a knowing look at Fred and she responded with a wink. Eddie nodded his head in understanding.

We climbed over the low dry stonewall and entered the light scrub covered area on the edge of the actual forest. Within a short distance, we were out of sight of the road and the boundary wall and were completely surrounded by trees. The level of light diminished, as the daylight became blocked out by the, ever-increasing density of the, overhead foliage. We proceeded along, in single file, with the Captain leading the way. So far he was correct in what he had said; we were going more or less in a straight line. I estimated three quarters of a mile, maybe slightly more, as the roughness of the terrain underfoot and the close proximity of the trees, as they spread away from us in all directions, made it difficult to accurately judge distance, before we came upon a group of soldiers. Some were sitting on fallen tree trunks others were standing about. A few were smoking but all of them were looking bored and waiting for something to happen.

A voice from somewhere within the group shouted, 'Officer present,' and the voice, who turned out to be a Sergeant, stepped forward and saluted. Those who had been sitting jumped up and joined their colleagues in standing to attention.

'Carry on,' ordered the Captain as he returned the Sergeant's salute. 'I hope no one has interfered with this site.'

'No one has been near it Sir. That was your orders Sir. All equipment is on site and a digging party standing by, Sir.'

'Shall we take a closer look. Stand aside you men and let these people through.'

A small group, close by, parted to let us pass and we moved between them to an area just beyond.

'That one at the back is a bird,' said an unknown voice as we passed.

'It's not,' said another strange voice.

'Bloody is. Look at the arse and the thighs. Seen her tits, I did, when she went past. Would shag it afore shag you.'

I turned and glanced back as we carried on walking. Fred was blushing and in a very low whisper, she said, 'They're all lovely, aren't they and they all look so young?'

'Here we are Sir. As you can see clearly from those markers, it stretches from here to here and across from there, back to here. We had to disturb it slightly to determine exactly how far it extended, but I don't think we damaged anything. If we did, then I am sorry.'

'No problem, Captain! I would appreciate if now, you would have the top soil removed and the whole area dug up.'

'Certainly Sir! Sergeant, get a party over here and dig up this whole area. Jump to it man!'

A group of six, under the direction of the Sergeant, began to dig. There was insufficient room for more to dig in comfort at the same time, so the remainder gathered round to watch.

'Where do you want this muck shoving Sir?'

'Over there I think Sergeant,' pointing as he said so, to a reasonably clear patch to the side.

'Within throwing distance will be fine,' I said. 'If this has been a purpose dug hole then that is probably where the earth was piled originally.'

'You heard what the Gentleman said, throw it, not carry it. You there... Yes you, throw it man!'

Not a great deal of soil had ended up on the pile and only a few minutes had elapsed since the start of the digging, when one of the squaddies who was busy labouring away, shouted, ''Ere Sergeant. It's solid under here. Me shovel has hit something and won't go in any deeper.'

'Then scrape the soil off, you dimwit and see what you've got,' snapped the Sergeant.

'There's something solid under here Captain,' said the Sergeant, as if the Captain had not heard what the man digging had said, 'We will scrape off a bit more muck and then we will be able to see what we've got Sir.'

'Thank you Sergeant: carry on.'

As the earth was scraped up and removed, it became clear that less than a foot below the surface, something had been buried there. As the men scraped away; sheet polythene began to show through the loose earth.

'Something wrapped up down here,' suggested one of the squaddies.

'You'll be wrapped up if you don't shut it and keep digging,' snapped the Sergeant.

A voice from within the group piped up, 'Yo-ho-ho and a bottle or rum. We've found Black Beard's bloody treasure.'

'Ay, maybe you have and you know what happened to Black Beard's bloody men after they got finished with his treasure, don't you?' demanded the Sergeant.

'No Sarge.'

'He shot all of the bastards and buried them and that's what will happen to you if you don't stop pissing about. Sorry Miss, forgot you was there for a minute. Having trouble with this bunch of pirates at the moment, I am Miss.'

'Leave them alone Sergeant, they mean no harm. They are only having a bit of harmless fun.'

'Harmless? Miss. All Black Beard's men went to charm school compared to this idle lot.'

'Enough Sergeant.'

'Sir.'

Through the remaining surface soil there were now six distinct squares of polythene clearly visible.

'They look very much like those six boxes,' suggested Eddie.

'You recognise them Sir?' enquired the Captain.

'Not exactly, but we believe we might have seen similar sized ones recently. Do you think we could have them lifted and brought out to where we can get a closer look at them?' I asked.

'Certainly Sir! Sergeant, pull them out and put them over here.'

They dug down two sides of one until they were able to lever it free.

'Bloody hell, it's heavy for old Doubloons, Sarge.'

'Over there… and quietly.'

Six large packages were eventually removed. Each one wrapped in polythene sheeting and sealed with brown sealing tape. Each was similar, in overall size, to the smaller ones we had witnessed being taken off the beach only a short time ago.

'Not been there long Sir, judging by the condition of the wrapping. Polythene tends to go dark and discoloured with age and this is quite light and new,' observed the Captain.

'About two days, unless we are mistaken,' said Fred.

'Then you do know something about them, Miss?'

'Yes, I think we might.'

'There's more down here,' remarked one of the soldiers who was still digging and prodding about with his spade.

'Look here Mel,' said Eddie, as he pointed and peered down into the hole by the soldier's feet. 'There is another layer of polythene down there and it looks very much to me as if there could be some more crates still down here. What's the betting there will be three of them with a further three below that.' Then turning to look up at the Captain he continued, 'I think that when you pull these out, you will find there are three more identical ones underneath, Captain.'

'Get to it Sergeant and see if we can prove the Gentleman correct.'

* * *

Eddie had been right. The hole was now empty and an exploratory pilot hole, dug to a greater depth, found, with the exception of solid earth, nothing further. We were more than satisfied that we had probably recovered the total haul from two nights ago. I felt good and the look on Eddie and Fred's faces told me that they too felt just as delighted.

'An excellent job of work! Thank you Captain.'

'What about the second site, Sir?'

'Yes Captain! The second site, if you please. I would now very much like to take a look at that.'

'Very good Sir! If you will give me a moment to arrange things here, we can move on. Sergeant, take these packages and stow them under guard, in one of the trucks and then make sure there is nothing further here. No one is to go near them or attempt to interfere with them. If that is acceptable to you, Sir, and you do want them removed from here?'

I nodded, 'Certainly Captain and I can't emphasise too much that no one must attempt to interfere with them.' I was thinking very much of the Major as I made that point.

He continued, 'Sergeant, stand down the men who have been working here. Return to the second site with a fresh party. Corporal, you up date the Major on developments here, so far. Give him Mr Grundy's compliments and tell him no one is to interfere with those packages, understand? Now Sir,' and turning to face me, he continued, 'The second site is some distance away from here but if you look at my map, Sir, you will see that yet again it is not too far from the opposite corner of the forest, just here. About the same distance in, a good half to three quarters of a mile, as this site is from the point here.'

As I glanced at his map, I saw where he had marked the two sites and noted that he was correct. From the opposite corner and edge of the woodland, it was about the same distance in, that we had travelled to get to this particular site,

from the road. I was prepared to bet that if we followed the route in from the other corner, it would prove to be reasonably straight and not too difficult to access.

'If I may suggest! Sir. If we move across in this direction, we will come to a Fire Break and we can travel along it. The going is much easier than pushing through the dense woodland. It is also easier for us moving all our equipment. When we reach a point about here… We take a right turn and follow another break. This gets us to a point about here,' Indicating, while he spoke, with his finger on the map. 'It's then only a short haul to where we need to be. Your dog man should be there to meet us, or so I have been informed.'

'Thank you, Captain! What ever you suggest. Please lead on and we will follow.'

'Very good, Sir! Come along Sergeant. Hurry things up there. These good people have important things to do,'

'Ready to move out now Sir.'

'Very good Sergeant, lead on.'

'Sir.'

'By the way Mr Grundy, do you want my men to re-fill in this hole here?'

'No thank you, Captain! We may need to send some more people in, to examine this site in more detail, later.'

'Very good Sir.'

We set off in single file, threading our way towards the Fire Break. We were strung out in a long straggly line and covered quite a distance from the first to the last man, there being a lot more than I realised, at first, in the party. It reminded me of the old party game "The Conga" where people all face in the same direction and dance from side to side and weave in and out of objects; the idea being to do so without breaking the line.

I followed directly behind Fred and although, in general, we didn't say much as we trudged along, I made several attempts to break the monotony by making casual, irrelevant observations.

'I wouldn't like to live in a jungle. Just imagine, nothing but trees and this lot to paddle through every day to fetch water.' Then a few yards further on, I added, 'I hope we reach base camp before nightfall. I have heard the natives are not too friendly in this region. I understand from Carruthers, up front, that they are armed with deadly blowpipes and can knock virgins off at over a hundred yards.'

Fred either laughed or told me to shut up. At one point, she turned and gave me a friendly push, when I remarked about getting bored watching her bum wobble from side to side but, added that, at the same time, I was quite pleased that all the exercise was strengthening her thighs and that might be useful.

The forest was, according to the map, only a couple of miles wide, at its widest point, so to claim that we tramped for hundreds, would be an outrageous exaggeration, but it still felt like that. We seemed to go on forever through

unchanging scenery and towards the end mostly in silence. Occasionally, Fred would look back and I either winked at her, or blew her a kiss. On one occasion I actually got close enough to nip her bottom. She sideswiped at me with her hand swinging behind her and knocked mine away.

* * *

'Looks as if we might be here, at long last.'

'Are we? Good.'

'Well everyone up front appears to have stopped and they are gathering in a group. Look, here comes my favourite dog. Come here boy, and let me fuss you. Who's a good boy then? What have you found for us, so that big fat, horrible man, sat in his great big warm London office, will think we have done a wonderful job?'

'The actual site is just through here Sir, Miss. Make way there and let these people through,' commanded the Captain's voice from somewhere up ahead of us.

We threaded our way through, passing the soldiers, who each carried a variety of gear, in preparation for the next dig, until we came out in front of the group.

'We picked up something in this region with our detectors, Sir, but as you can see for yourself, there is very little to be actually seen, so all we did was mark it. We did not investigate any further at the time. If you wish Sir, we will sweep the area again and peg it out in greater detail.'

'If you would Captain.'

The area we had arrived at was not unlike several others, we had passed on the way to reach this particular spot. A naturally formed grassy area where the trees had not been planted close together, or if they had, then perhaps one or two of them had died off as saplings. In which case, if they had, then their remains had long since rotted away to leave an open space within the surrounding dense woodland.

'Right Sergeant, get your men over here and let's have this area accurately pegged out.'

Two men, each equipped with Electronic Sound Detection gear, or as we humble civilians call them, Mine Detectors, moved forward and commenced a systematic sweep of the area, moving the base plates of their detectors gently from side to side as they went. Occasionally one would stop and go over an area a second time, or he would stop and bend down to push a short wooden peg into the soft earth. Before long, the pegs began to form a pattern, and the shape of a rectangle began to emerge, then a second rectangle close by. One was twice the size of the other but both were considerably smaller than the area we had already unearthed at the other end of the forest.

'Nothing more here, Sarge, only these two,' remarked one of the searchers as he pulled his earphones clear from his head.

'Spread out, away from here and sweep right up to that tree line over there.'

The soldier nodded and replaced his head set and then touching his colleague, who had heard nothing of the conversation, on the arm, indicated with his forefinger, making first a circular movement and then a pushing sign, with his flat hand, held out and up, in front of him. He gave the impression of stirring something up and then pushing back an invisible barrier. His mate understood perfectly and moved away towards the trees, sweeping all the time, from side to side, as he went.

'Shall we begin to dig here Sir, while they continue the sweep?'

'Yes please, Captain.'

'Sergeant, get some men in here and dig out these marked areas.'

The ground on this occasion was much harder and more compacted than the previous site and required considerable pressure from some heavy army boots, to force the spades to cut down into the earth. On the other hand, there were some similarities. At approximately the same depth, below the surface, resistance was met. The earth was carefully removed and the larger plot of the two, proved to have two cases buried in it. The other had just one. Each package, as it was pulled free, proved to be of a similar size, to the larger ones, from the first dig. Probing further satisfied us there was nothing buried beneath them. The outer wrappings of these cases were much older, brittle and badly discoloured. Some of the sealing tape had started to split and peel off. They showed every sign of having been there for some considerable time.

When they were finally pulled free and set to one side on solid ground, we were able to confirm that they were, in actual fact, of the same size as the larger ones brought ashore by Johnson and his team two nights ago.

We deduced from their overall condition that they had been there some considerable time and that the one, buried singly, had been there much longer than the other two, which, in turn, had been buried side by side.

'Sergeant. Your men found anything else over there?'

The sergeant stepped forward and touched one of the searchers on the shoulder. When he attracted the man's attention he held his hand out, palm down and moved it in a circular motion, then using his other hand, jabbed his forefinger towards his ear. The reply was a swing from side to side, of the listener's head, indicating 'No'. The sergeant passed his index finger across his throat in a cutting motion and both men switched off, disconnected the sweepers from their power packs, and removed the headsets. Everything was then carefully dismantled and laid aside.

'Nothing else that we can pick up around here, Sarge,' said one.

‘Sir. If there is anything else round here, then it is not metal and my men can’t pick it up with that equipment,’ confirmed the Captain.

‘Thank you, Captain and you too Sergeant, and thanks to you two chaps. A good job.’

I stood for a moment and stared into the nearest hole. I then looked across at the polythene-wrapped cases. Three found on this site and twelve from the first site and all detected by army Mine Detector, which through ultrasonic sound had responded to their metal content.

‘I can guess what you’re thinking, Mel. For us to find these cases, as we have, means that each one must contain a fair proportion of metal and that Metal Detectors don’t react to other things. For example they would not pick up drugs, would they?’

‘You’re quite right, Eddie. It has crossed my mind, but until we open these boxes we cannot be sure what we have. Drugs could be sealed in metal containers before being boxed up for shipment. The only reason I’m thinking about drugs is from our experiences with Johnson and the Builder, and their distribution trip that we took all the trouble to follow them on. Maybe this is an entirely different operation and has nothing to do with their drugs.’

‘There are no drugs here, Mr Grundy,’ cut in Owen Long. ‘If there were, the chances are very high that my dog would have found them and even more so now, when the ground has been disturbed. If any drugs had been anywhere near those cases he would have gone mad. But look at him, not interested in the slightest and the same with the other dog. If there were any explosives in any of these cases he would have flipped. He reacted rather strongly at the other site the one over there, and my bet is that there will probably be something of that nature there. But look at him right now. He is more interested in rabbit holes than anything else.’

‘He looks to me, more as if he is trying to bury a bone, or dig one up, than find a rabbit. My mutt, back home, digs furiously, just like that, when he thinks he has found a buried bone, especially if he thinks it might belong to another dog,’ remarked one of the soldiers standing close by.

‘If it’s your flea bag, or anything to do with you, then it will be a bloody nutter,’ tormented one of the other soldiers.

Owen Long looked across at his dog. ‘That is a bit unusual for him, I must admit. He doesn’t normally dig with such enthusiasm. If he finds something, or thinks he has found something, then he tends to sit and bark and whine.’ Walking over to the dog he continued, ‘you developing a new technique all of your-own, boy? You have never dug like that before. What’s the problem? What have you found that is getting you all excited? Come out of the way and let’s have a look.’

The dog flatly refused to give up on his efforts following the verbal command and when Long reached out to pull him back by his collar, he turned, growled and snapped and made frenzied attempts to get back to his digging. Long

looked surprised and had to exert considerable effort to pull the dog away. When back a couple of yards, he settled somewhat but still had to be held. Fred tried to pat him on his head and he snapped.

'That's strange. Do you mind if we dig up the ground round here, if only to satisfy me and my dog?'

'Sergeant. This Gentleman requires some digging. Get two men on to it, straight away.'

Two were singled out and set to work and while they dug Owen Long came to stand beside us. He still held the dog tightly by his collar. The dog for his part was agitated and would not settle.

'You keep back out of the way, dog. You be good and let those two men do the digging.' Then, looking at us, he continued, 'I was confident there are no drugs or other explosives round here, but the way this dog reacted earlier today, at the other site, I think it is a fair bet to guess there are, or have been, explosives or something there.'

'Sergeant. There's plastic stuff buried here but it's like a soft parcel,' said one of the men delegated to dig.

'If it's not solid then go careful and take it easy. Don't damage it.'

Without warning they stopped and stepped back, as if to rest from their efforts. One lent on his shovel and just looked, while the other dropped his shovel and began to light a cigarette.

'Who told you to stop digging there. Put that cigarette out man,' barked the Sergeant.

'Better take a look at this, Sarge.'

Everyone had now stopped what they were doing and all attention turned to the diggers and the hole they had dug, and stepped back from. My stomach tightened as I hoped, against hope, that it was not what I immediately thought it might be.

Five minutes later all my initial fears were confirmed.

'I think you had better take a look at this, Sir,' said the Captain. 'I don't think we need to open the wrapping to see what it is. We can guess from the shape and size of the bundle, that what we have here is, very probably, a corpse. But I don't suppose a guess is good enough. Is it Sir? If we do have a corpse then the situation has become very serious, so I further suggest we had better split open the wrapping for definite confirmation.'

'I agree, Captain.'

'Sergeant. Split that end open. Go easy man. We only need confirmation of the contents.'

The sergeant knelt down and bent over the bundle, he then stood up and moved to one side. We could all see the toe of a black gumboot sticking out through the hole he had slit in the plastic.

'Doesn't smell too bloody good, either,' muttered the Sergeant.

Everyone had gone very quiet but now started to edge forward gathering closer round the bundle.

'Hold my dog for me, please Miss and don't let him come near. I'm going to have a look.'

I wondered afterwards if perhaps, he did that on purpose to give Fred a reason, or excuse, to stay back, or was he perhaps so strongly drawn to it himself, that he had to get someone to hold his dog and Fred just happened to be the nearest. He never offered any reasons for his actions, either then, or later, so I will never know, but I still feel very grateful to him for when I turned back, to look at Fred, she had gone very pale and could only whisper, 'Edison?'

'More than likely,' was all I managed to say in reply.

'Right,' said the Captain, who seemed to pull himself together before the rest of the onlookers. 'Some of you have seen dead body's before. Those who haven't take a good look. Then if we are all through here now Mr Grundy, we can all move out.'

'What do you think?' I said to Owen Long as he moved back alongside Fred, who still had hold of his dog. 'Do you think there might be something else?'

'I will let the dog have one last go, but I don't think so,' and reaching towards Fred, he took hold of the dog by its collar and snapped on a short lead.

'You can let go now, Miss, and thank you very much. He can pull a bit when he's excited, can't he?'

'He certainly can but he's still lovely.'

When Fred released her grip the dog made straight for the corpse, sniffed it briefly, then just moved away and walked rapidly too and fro covering the surrounding area with its sensitive nose almost touching the ground. As it passed each individual soldier it stopped briefly to give him a quick sniff before moving on to cover fresh ground. Eventually its initial enthusiasm waned and its intense sniffing became the normal canine interest in its surroundings. It went up to individuals to be fussed and played with. Stopping for the occasional scratch and to cock a leg against a bush or tree trunk.

'There is nothing else around here,' declared Long. 'You can all pack up and go now as far as I am concerned. Come here boy. Good dog.'

'Sergeant. You clear up here and then get these men back to the road. Corporal, a sit-rep to the Major, and have a body bag sent up here at the double. We are returning to the command post Sergeant and don't you forget everything is to remain under close guard. Report when you are through and fallen in by the trucks.'

'Sir.'

* * *

As we trudged back towards the road and the Major, I suddenly felt very weary and totally deflated. It felt as if we had been in those woods for a lifetime. In fact it was still daylight and when we finally emerged at the end of the Fire Break and came out on to the road the evening light was still quite bright. The fact that we had not eaten since before lunch did nothing to help my mood.

'It's not as late as I thought it would be,' said Fred. 'I feel all in.'

'I will have you escorted back to the Major, Sir. I intend to stay here with the trucks until things are sorted out.'

'Not necessary! Thank you Captain. I think we can find our own way back quite safely,' I said.

'Yes of course, Sir. Perhaps you might do me a favour and pass on to the Major all the small detail as to what has happened so far. It will save me considerable time later. I am sure that by then I will be through here and, if the Major wishes, ready to join you.'

'I will do that for you, with pleasure Captain.'

'Thank you Sir.'

'You sound to be as down as we are,' observed Fred.

'I am Miss and it's not that I don't want to have the trouble of reporting to the Major, it's just that I would like to get my men away and fed as soon as possible.'

'If there is nothing further, I too will also be getting along,' said Owen Long. 'We have a fair distance to go and the dogs need feeding and taking for a walk before they are bedded down.'

'A walk!' exclaimed Fred. 'After all of today's activity?'

'Yes, Miss. Work is one thing for these two, but we always end the day with a long walk. There are some fields close to where we live and they are allowed to roam free and do their own thing. Also, by way of a reward, they always come into the house to be fed, by my wife, during the evening when we are not working away. It has been a pleasure to meet you all and perhaps we might meet up again sometime in the future. I will submit my report straight away which will then be ready and available to you, should you need it.'

'Thank you for everything: that you've done. It has been a pleasure working with you and those dogs of yours have been magic and I do hope we meet again,' I said.

'Let me stroke them both, just once more, before you close that door,' said Fred. 'Who's a lovely, clever dog. Yes, and you are too. Both good dogs. Be good. Bye-bye.'

CHAPTER FORTY-SEVEN

When the three of us arrived back at the Major's command post, in front of the Sawmill, he had, for the first time, a smile on his face.

'Damn good man, that. Knew he would do the job. One of the best Captain's I've got. Give that man a job and leave it to him. Damned reliable.'

'Well at least the Major is happy. Just look at the way he is strutting about, you would think he had found a formula for world peace,' said Fred, aside to Eddie and with more than a touch of sarcasm.

'Watch it, you,' I cautioned and she laughed.

'While you were out there observing my men at work, I arranged with my HQ to have the body removed to a suitable location and the other stuff stored away safely. At the moment I am awaiting their confirmation. Can't understand the delay in receiving the all clear to get on with it. Not like my people, but they won't, apparently, give a decision until they have had a word with your people. Can't understand why myself.'

'Thank you Major but for the moment what I need is a telephone.'

'No problem Old Man, there's a mobile in my Land Rover. Corporal, pass the telephone to Mr Grundy. Help yourself Sir. The sooner we get this sorted out the sooner I can get on.'

The Corporal handed me a military type mobile telephone. I lent against the low wall and after checking the operating instructions, pressed the buttons, and held the instrument up to my ear. It began to ring but no one answered it straight away. As I waited, I casually strolled down the lane. The idea being to take myself out of ear shot of the main group. It was the Major and his Corporal that I particularly wanted to be furthest away from. What the Major didn't know, he would not be able to try and take credit for.

Had the search revealed nothing, he would probably have rode off, in his battlewagon and reported a very successful exercise. But as things had turned out, I felt sure he now saw a god sent opportunity to grab all the credit. In fact, if I was not careful, I felt he would do his utmost to take over completely from this point. I think he saw himself as the 'cavalry in khaki to the rescue".

The phone was finally answered. 'Hello Sir! Grundy! Before I proceed let me tell you this is a mobile phone Sir and therefore not secure. The only reason I am using it, is because we are out in the open countryside and there is no land line close at hand.' I didn't mention, for obvious reasons, that it was an Army Mobile Phone and was probably, at that very moment, being monitored in the Majors' Land Rover.

'I know where you are Grundy. My phone has been red hot for the last hour. The Army are proposing to launch a full-scale operation. They claim they are now in full control due to the nature of your findings and will be in full command from now on. They say they have a Major in the field who is already in direct command and who will take full control.'

'I know Sir. He is standing not a million miles from me right now and I wouldn't let him loose on a game of War Games with tin soldiers.' Monitor that major, I thought. Teach you to listen in.

'Listen Grundy, get this straight; you use him, if you need him, but we are still in charge. I have been on to Whitehall to sort out the Army and their priorities and no doubt, given time, it will finally filter down to your Major. The Army were requested to supply nothing more than equipment and manpower. If they have transport and you need it, use it. The other thing Grundy, if what I understand the Army claim to have discovered is correct and don't elaborate on it, to me, over that mobile phone, get in touch with me on a more secure land line as soon as you can. The reports, I have received so far, from the Army have told me enough for me to know that you have made good progress. Don't delay. Come back to me with your report. In the meantime, is there anything you immediately require that I can attend to?'

'Not that I propose to ask you for over this phone, Sir, I will come back to you - land line.'

'Make it quick and in the meantime don't forget to keep that Major where he belongs; at arms length.'

'I will Sir, bye Sir,' and I switched off the phone.

I went back to the group and handing the telephone over to the Corporal, thanked him.

'Right Mr Grundy, now that you are through with the phone and your personal problems; what I now propose to do… '

'HQ Sir,' called the Corporal.

'Excuse me. This is probably what I have been waiting for. Hand me the set Corporal.'

We stood in silence and waited. The Major listened and muttered a few odd words. Finally he handed the radio set back to the Corporal and stretching himself to his full height said, 'Well that's it then: orders from HQ. I am to withdraw after you, Mr Grundy, officially release me. Seems that after all I am to take orders from a civilian, whether I like it or not and believe me Mr Grundy, I do not like it one bit, and I am prepared to say so. I am going to leave you the Captain so that you can give him as many orders as you please. Corporal, tell the Captain to report to me and prepare to move out.'

'Yes Sir.'

A few moments elapsed, during which everyone just stood around feeling somewhat embarrassed at the Major's outburst. No one said anything.

During this time the Sawmill engine ran down and stopped for, what was, the end of the shift and that added to the uncomfortable silence. The men from the Mill filed past and climbed into an old minibus that was parked alongside one of the outbuildings. Two of them actually managed to mutter a polite good night, as they passed. The bus started up and made its way down the lane to finally disappear out of sight. The atmosphere became more tense as the Major snorted and snapped at the poor Corporal who simply carried on as if nothing out of the ordinary had happened.

'Mel, can I have a word with you in private, if you don't mind. Excuse us, Eddie please.'

Fred started to walk away from the main group, and I followed. Once out of earshot, she stopped and turned. 'Has he spit his dummy out?' she asked, referring to the Major.

'I think he has, because when I telephone the Old Man just now, he said he knew all about our progress. He said the Army had kept him fully briefed and he knew, or had a pretty good idea, what had been found. He also told me that the Army had informed him that they had a good man on the scene who, due to the nature of the finds, would now take over and sort everything out. He didn't exactly say he would, but I assume he has put a block on that straight away and the Army has been told to back off. That is what, I presume, has happened just now. The Major has been told that the Army is not in charge and he has to take his orders from us, but before do that, the pompous bastard is going to pull out and leave the Captain in charge here.'

'That's alright by me, because I think the Captain is a much nicer man.'

'I thought the Major was OK at first; a typical Major perhaps, all bristle and pompous efficiency, but he changed somewhat when he saw the opportunity to go glory hunting.'

'What's our next move? Wait for the Major to clear out I suppose?'

'I think so. Don't you?'

Further discussion was interrupted by one of the Army trucks, which came up the lane and stopped just short of us. The door opened and the Captain jumped down. He saluted.

'I am to report to the Major, Sir. Is he still in the area?'

'Yes he's still in the same place, as far as I know. Possibly in the back of his Land Rover.'

'Thank you Sir! Driver, you wait here. Excuse me Sir.'

As he strode away we followed him back and joined Eddie who was then half seated and leaning on the low wall.

'Captain,' we heard the Major snap.

'Sir.'

'I am withdrawing. You are to remain here until Mr Grundy dismisses you. You are to take orders from him, is that understood?'

'Yes, Sir.'

'Where are the men?'

'All stood down Sir and returning to barracks, with the exception of four men, a driver and one truck on which are loaded the items we found in the forest, Sir.'

'Good. Carry on. Come along Corporal, time for us to move out.'

'Are you leaving Major?' enquired Fred.

'Yes Miss, immediately.'

'On whose orders Major?'

'My people Miss.'

'Not us Major?'

'No Miss.'

'Well then; as we are finished with you, you are still free to go and thank you Major for your small, though valuable, contribution to our overall success.'

He went red in the face and gave, to no one in particular, a half salute with his pace stick. Then, without uttering another word, climbed into the Land Rover. It immediately started up, did a three point turn and headed off down the lane. At some point, we heard it stop and way above the engine noise, we heard the Major holler, 'Get that truck out of the damned way and let me pass, man.'

'He can bristle a bit at times,' observed the Captain, 'and he is certainly annoyed at the moment. I wonder what's eating him?' and without waiting for an answer continued, 'Right Sir, I am at your disposal. Have you any immediate orders Sir?'

'Eddie; I feel really good now,' said Fred with a malicious grin.

'My first priority Captain, is to get away from here and find a telephone. The Mill is probably secure for the night now, so there will be no access to theirs.'

'If our radio telephone is not suitable, may I suggest the village along the road Sir?'

'No Captain! I want to avoid going into the village for very good reasons.'

'Back to the camp site is probably the best bet,' suggested Fred. 'It will be quiet and the management, or whatever they are, will have gone home by this time, so no one should object to the Army truck. If Eddie travels with the Captain and shows him the way, we can take the back roads and should have no problems.'

'OK with you Eddie?' I asked.

'Fine by me Mel: see you back at camp. If you are ready Captain?'

The Captain beckoned for the truck that promptly came up to the end of the lane and turned round in the open space in front of the Mill. As it pulled away Fred and I, in my car, fell in behind it.

* * *

The journey back along the back lanes, despite the twists and turns, allowed us to average a steady thirty miles an hour. I was beginning to feel weary as I relaxed a little and Fred drove.

'You tired?' laughed Fred. 'I don't know about tired. I am more hungry than tired right now. Am I expected to feed all this lot, when we get back?' pointing at the truck up ahead.

'I doubt it. The Army usually looks after itself.'

'I hope so. Feeding three is about my limit with the faculties we have. What are you planning for, when we get back?'

'The first thing I want to do is have a long talk with the Old Man. We now have a body in that truck up ahead and that is very serious. We don't know for sure who it is. We are only speculating that it is Edison and as I say, until we confirm that, one way or the other, it could be anyone. Nor do we know what is in them polythene wrapped parcels, or should I say cases, or crates, or what ever you want to call them. Whatever they are, I am fairly certain that the batch of twelve which came out of the first dig, are the same wooden crates we saw come ashore the other night. We need to find somewhere secure to examine them and that's just one of the reasons I need to talk to his nibs. I need him to make some contacts and arrangements for us.'

'What do you think we have really found Mel? It looks very much, to me, as if the body in the bag will be that of Edison. I am no pathologist but I would guess, looking at the state of the wrapping, that it has been buried for the right length of time and perhaps buried at the same time as those small boxes found near by, or perhaps even as a separate issue, but never the less somewhere about the same time. The black Gum Boot is typical Coastguard issue but then black Gum Boots are very common and readily available almost anywhere. No doubt science and the right people will solve that one, along with everything else, but I am sure they are all connected. Edison must have stumbled onto something and, for some reason, paid a very high price. Scampton and Johnson and their lot, are, for my money, all in this up to their eyelids.'

'They may well be and as you say, probably are, but proving it, is going to be difficult.'

'At the moment I agree, but that's a separate issue which we will get round to and deal with, shortly. What do you think is in all those boxes, cases?'

'I don't honestly know, but once again, it could be anything. For the moment I am tempted to rule out drugs, as they are not the type of thing, that responds well, to being buried. Warm, dry storage is more for them. But we will know just as soon as we get a chance to open them and take a peak inside.'

'They definitely look like ammunition cases despite the fact that they are wrapped up and you can't see any markings or handles on the ends. They are the right size and shape. You saw some of them on the beach, which confirms that and I think that is just what they are.'

'Ammunition or guns and the like?'

'Yes. Something like, that, probably both. There might be other things, but my bet is that we have uncovered an arms cash of some kind. I also think it is a separate operation from the drug smuggling that Johnson and the Builder are in to. It is going to be very interesting finding out.'

'And how do you propose we go about doing that?'

'Ring the Old Man. Find a place to open the cases. Establish the identity of the body and take it from there; which is plenty to go at and not bad for starters.'

'Did you feel good, back there, when you dismissed the Major?'

'Yes, it made my day. The pompous ass. He had a down on women and made me feel uncomfortable from the very beginning.'

'I'm glad I'm on your side,' I laughed.

'You make sure it stays that way,' She said as she turned the car into the campsite.

CHAPTER FORTY-EIGHT

The Army were, as I expected, self-sufficient when it came to provisions and feeding themselves. They sat about on the grass or leaned against the wall and ate their issue packed rations. The Captain accepted Fred's invitation to join us in the Camper. He appreciated the shot of whiskey and the opportunity to relax a little out of sight of his men.

While Fred delved in the cupboards and scraped together what she could from our provisions, I excused myself and left Eddie and the Captain chatting over their drink, while I went to the public phone and rang the Old Man. I quickly related to him all the events of the day and was pleasantly surprised at how much he already knew. Apparently he had been linked into Whitehall and had received all the Army Intelligence Reports, as they came in. When I finished my report he said, 'You say, you are now back at your base camp with an army truck and how many men?'

'A Captain and five men, Sir.'

'So the Major has left, has he?'

'Yes sir, he left his Field HQ in the forest to return to his barracks, just before we left to return here.'

'Good. From his reports and the way in which he was interpreting everything as it developed, I felt it was necessary to get him out of the way. His attitude was completely wrong, but you know these army types, bored out of their minds for most of the time, so that if you give them an inch, they take a mile.'

I remember thinking, 'I do indeed Sir, you were one of those types and as far as I am concerned, still are', but I said nothing, diplomacy being the mother of survival or whatever the stupid expression is.

He continued, 'From the way his reports were coming into Army HQ, it was obvious that he felt, he was the only person capable of handling the situation, so I, in turn, felt it was expedient to relieve him before he stepped too far out of line. What about this Captain he left behind? Are you satisfied with that arrangement?'

'He's fine Sir. A first class chap and I don't envisage any problems, at the moment, in that direction.'

'If there are, then you come straight back to me, understand?'

'Yes Sir, I will.'

'Excellent. Now listen, Grundy, this is what I have arranged. You are to leave, as soon as possible, and proceed to Thornley. There is an Army Depot there, which has not been used since the Guards pulled out some time in the Fifties, but it has been retained by them and is currently used to house a Territorial Army unit.

The chap, who is responsible for the daily maintenance of the place, is currently being told to meet you there and when you arrive, to provide secure storage for those crates and anything else you may wish to leave. You will then take the body to the local hospital. There, at the mortuary, the Police will meet you and it. The Police have been fully briefed and will make all the necessary arrangements to bring all interested parties together. They know all they need to know regarding our involvement and the necessity for a security clampdown. There will be no statements to the press or media from either them or the Army. As far as everyone is concerned this is still an ongoing investigation that may have far-reaching implications. I don't need to remind you of that of course, but thought you ought to be reminded of the need for utmost discretion, at this time, now that so many people are involved and will continue to be drawn in. Security is always threatened once the lower ranks of either the Army or the Police become involved. So watch your step, Grundy, and use the Captain only as much as you think fit, but don't involve the Army in the field, any more than you need to. This really has nothing to do with them and I want it to stay that way, at least until final reports are prepared. If then it is deemed necessary to involve the Army, it will be done at the correct level and only the right people will be informed. The same applies to the Police and all other interested agencies. So remember, Grundy, this can no longer be exclusively our show. We may be responsible for the investigation but the clearing up involves a lot of other departments and agencies.

'Yes Sir.'

'Keep me informed,' he demanded and then, true to his usual form, he hung up.

I returned to the van and rejoined the others. We then all sat down and had a very welcome bite to eat. No matter what the circumstances, Fred always managed to come up trumps, when it came to producing food out of thin air. The soldiers continued to lounge around outside, taking full advantage of the extended break.

'It's not much I'm afraid,' apologised Fred, as she placed a bowl of soup in front of me and beside it, a plate of assorted sandwiches. 'It is all we have in, at the moment, so it will have to do.'

'This will do me fine. I am getting quite used to a diet of assorted sandwiches and who cares anyway as long as it fills me. After today and all that time out in the open air, anything would be welcome.'

Our meal and the general conversation that accompanied it, was interrupted by a light tap on the side of the van and a voice from outside, which said, 'Excuse me, Sir. There is a radio message coming through for the Captain.'

'Please excuse me,' said the Captain as he stepped out of the camper and, escorted by the soldier, went towards his own truck.

When he returned, he politely knocked on the van side and climbing back in, announcing, 'That was my people. I understand that you, Mr Grundy, will provide the briefing for our next moves and that I am to stay here, and remain under your command, and to co-operate fully with you, until dismissed or relieved.'

'Good. Well there is no time like the present. So Fred, can you break off from over there, just for a moment and come and sit down. Then if you will excuse me, if I talk while we all finish our meal, I will give you all the general outline of our proposals and next moves.'

I waited until Fred handed out hot drinks and sat down, before I continued.

'We are leaving here, as soon as we are ready and going into Thornley, which is a few miles West of here. Apparently there is a barracks there, that will be made available to us and is there for our immediate use.'

'I know it well, Sir,' said the Captain. 'It's now used for weekend soldiers, the TA. I've been there a couple of times, when I drew the short straw, to give lectures to those weekend wonders.'

'Good. That will save us time driving round looking for the place. From there we go to the Hospital Morgue where there will be a tie-up with the Police who, I understand, will then take us, from there, to the local nick and a conference.'

'We are to go now? Straight away,' asked Fred, looking across at all the accumulated dirty crockery, discarded food wrappers and empty soup cans.

'As soon as we can, is what the Old Man said and I assume from that, he means now.'

'If you will excuse me, I will go round up my men and be ready to move out as soon as you give the order, Sir. Miss, thank you very much for the simple, but excellent, meal.'

'Such as it was, Captain.'

'It was fine and very welcome, and so was your hospitality Miss.'

'Thank you Captain,' smiled Fred before turning to me, 'Are we taking the Camper?' she enquired.

'No. We three will go in my car and if the Captain knows where the barracks are, then all we need to do is follow him. So are we anywhere near ready?'

'Only, if we are going to go and leave this lot. Someone collect the empty cans and the rubbish and get rid of them while I just nip across to you-know-where, it will only take a minute.'

'Off you go then. We will see to this lot and pick you up on the way out.'

We made sure everything was secure, then, falling in behind the army truck, stopped to pick up Fred outside the Toilet Block. We then set out, turning left at the end of the lane and heading inland towards the market town of Thornley.

Somewhere along the route we were approached and caught up by a Police Patrol car that just appeared from nowhere. It ran alongside us and the Policeman,

on the near side, wound down his window and indicated with his hand for me to do the same.

When I opened my window, he shouted, 'If you will follow us, Sir, you are expected and we will show you the way.'

I acknowledged with a wave and wound the window back up. I could see no point in trying to tell him we already knew the way and only had to follow the tuck up front.

The Patrol Car pulled forward until he was parallel with the truck. I assumed he was passing the same message to the driver, but appeared to be having some difficulty. Twice he stuck his head out of the side window and waved, quite furiously, with one arm. Eventually the driver must have understood, as he too stuck his head out of the cab window and glanced down at the patrol car, before returning his attention forward to the road head. Seconds later the Police Car pulled further forward and drew in, in front of the truck. I assumed we were all now following him.

From that moment on our overall speed dropped and held at a steady forty miles per hour until we reached the outskirts of the town, where it immediately dropped to thirty and remained at that until we slowed down even further, to drive slowly through the open gates of a compound, surrounded by a high wire boundary fence.

The barracks were not large, as Military Barracks go, but had the typical military atmosphere about them: everything exceptionally neat and tidy and spotlessly clean: all the paintwork in pristine condition and white lines crisscrossing everywhere. Dozens of signs, of an infinite variety of sizes and colours, gave directions to every last nook and cranny.

The Army always excels itself when it comes to this type of thing. They design and label everything, in order to reduce the need to think almost down to nil, for anyone who is confined to, or lives and moves within, their perimeters.

It reminded me, very much, of my own first experiences of Army Barracks, many years ago. I remembered the mass of signs that were everywhere you cared to look. They were designed to save time, but by the time you had read and studied them, you had lost the time they were designed to save and you were inevitably late. I particularly remembered entering a Toilet Block, having been taken short while studying the profusion of signs outside and half expected to find the cubicles clearly numbered with a large sign saying 'Relieve yourself in strict numerical order'. I was most disappointed to find that, in the case of personal requirements, one was actually given a small amount of choice. My sense of humour being what it is, I quickly saw the funny side and wondered what would have happened, if that had actually not been so and there had been specific instructions as to how the toilets should be used. I could imagine some bone-headed Sergeant, standing in the middle of the latrine and screaming, 'What are you doing in trap number

four, laddie, when number three is empty?' and a pathetic reply coming from deep inside, 'But it was occupied when I came in, Sarge', and then the thunderous response, 'Don't give me that, son. Up with your trousers and move along a trap. Next time you will not be told, you will be on a charge'. Or again, if there had been numbers on the doors, then the Orderly Officer, on his routine inspection, could have put into his report "Trap numbered so-and-so is below standard and trap number three was occupied when trap two was empty". Think of the time saved; instead of having to count from left to right and being obliged to put in his report, the lengthy statement; "The forth from the right, when stood facing, is below standard in Toilets, North, North East of Main Gate, Soldiers, For the Use Of", he could just write down a number.

However, which ever way you look at it, according to army logic, counting takes time and above all else, brain power, and so they revel in their attempts to save both whenever, and wherever, the opportunity presents itself.

The Captain jumped down from the truck and walked the short distance back towards the large wire mesh covered gates, which, at the time, were being closed behind us, by a middle-aged man in civilian clothes. He stopped as the Captain approached. They exchanged words, after which, the Captain returned and approached our car.

'That fellow's a T.A. Captain. Claims he hadn't time to don his uniform but as soon as he has locked the main gate, he will join us and show us where to go.

We waited a few moments.

'Down that way, second left, you will find the Drill Hall, Captain. Just follow the signs. You can't miss it. The lights are already on,' said the Captain in civilian clothes. 'You can either drive your car round, Sir, or park it in the visitors' reserved space. Over there, Sir, under that sign,' and he pointed to a large board, mounted on a wall, which said "Visitors to the Main Office. Park Here. Cars only. Trucks, Light vans, and other personnel carriers, second left. Follow signs".

'Better leave it here,' sniggered Fred. 'We don't want to get lost driving unescorted round a Military Base or park in a place for "other personnel carriers". Do we? Which reminds me, where has the Police Car gone?'

'I never noticed. But come to think of it, I didn't see it drive in here with us. I suppose he was sent as escort only and has now gone off and resumed his normal duties or something.'

The truck moved slowly forward and away then turned left, and went out of sight. The civilian Captain walked after it. I parked the car, then the three of us, walked the short distance along the road.

As we turned the corner we saw the truck parked outside a large Drill Hall, where light spilled out from the open doors. The canvas back of the truck was up and the tailboard down. The Captain and his men were stood in a group, waiting.

'We can unload these cases into here where they will be perfectly safe and secure, Sir. My men are available and will attend to it straight away.'

'Thank you Captain: if you would.'

'Unload this lot and lay them out neatly down the centre. Leave space between to move around.'

The soldiers offloaded and carried in the crates, one at a time and laid them out as instructed. When the first one was in place and the men who had carried it in had gone back outside, Fred touched my sleeve and suggested, 'Don't you think we ought to take a peek into one of these now. It would, after all, be nice to know what we have discovered and be able to talk intelligently and knowledgeably about the contents, instead of referring all the time, to those boxes or parcels wrapped in plastic.'

'Just what I was thinking! Captain, have you something we can use to open these cases?'

'One moment Sir… You there… Get some tools to open these cases. At the double!'

While we waited for the tools to be brought in, I took a small pocket knife, which I carry on my key ring, and bending over the first crate, began to cut and peel away, the plastic sheeting; to reveal one of the cases. It was very similar in colour. At least it looked that way in the artificial light, to those I had seen brought ashore the other night. The lid appeared to be securely fastened down with screws.

'Crow bar here Sir,' said one of the soldiers, offering me an eighteen inch long bar.

'I think we need a screwdriver first.'

'Coming up Sir. Allow me Sir,' and kneeling over the crate, he began to remove the screws one at a time.

The task was time consuming as the lid was well secured down. As the soldier continued to remove the screws, the drill hall floor progressively became covered, as each additional case was brought in and put in its place.

Eventually, the Captain came in and said, 'that is it Sir. They are all in place and accounted for. Only the body remains in the truck.'

'Thank you Captain! We are going to have a look in this one, then perhaps one of those smaller ones, before we move on.'

'Very good Sir! You over there come and give a hand. Open that.'

Eventually when all the screws were removed, the lid was prised off using the crowbar. Inside the case, the first thing to be revealed, under the lid, was an outer wrapping of greaseproof paper, which when folded back, unveiled four, heavily greased, automatic rifles. On closer inspection, we found that packed between them, were several handguns, greased, and wrapped separately.

'If each case contains the same, then we have quite an arsenal,' declared Eddie. 'I wonder if the smaller cases are more hand guns, or ammunition?'

'We will soon find out. How's the work progressing on that one Captain?'

One soldier had removed the outer wrapping of the nearest small crate and two others had set about removing the screws.

When the lid and top layer of inner wrapping had been removed we were able to inspect the contents. It was not ammunition, as we first suspected, but a large package of explosive materials.

'Semtex at a guess,' volunteered the Captain, 'or something equally evil, but definitely explosives.'

Everyone stood round and looked at the open boxes and their contents. Before us lay Automatic rifles, handguns and explosives. What were those people up to?

'So the dog handler was right; he said one of his dogs had reacted to explosives,' said Fred. 'And just look at this lot.'

'Now that we have satisfied our curiosity, I suppose we should be making our way to the Hospital. There are probably people waiting there for us. Can you leave some men to keep and eye on these, Captain?'

'Yes Sir.' Then turning. 'Driver and you, into the truck,' pointing at one of the soldiers, 'the rest of you stay here. You are in charge,' pointing to a Lance Corporal within the group, which were to stay behind. 'You let no one in here unless you recognise them as being one of our group. No one! Understand?'

'Yes, Sir.' Before adding, 'Shall we be opening these other ammo boxes, Sir?'

'No. You touch nothing.'

'I will go and open the gates ready to let you out,' said the resident Captain.

As he moved towards the door I said, 'Captain, may I remind you that you have seen nothing in here tonight.'

'Very good Sir,' he replied as he disappeared out into the dark. We followed close behind and walked back to where we had left the car. The truck caught us up and stood, engine running, waiting to be let out. It was then that I noticed the Police Car parked on the roadside, opposite and a little further along. As we drew parallel with the car, Eddie wound down his window, as did the Police Officer in their passenger seat. He enquired of us, 'Where to now, Sir?'

'The Hospital morgue please.'

'Just follow us, Sir. It's just along the road.'

In a matter of minutes we arrived at the Hospital and following the police car, entered a gate that was signposted, 'Emergency Vehicles Only'. We wound our way round several buildings and finally stopped round the corner of one, which was well away from the main part of the hospital. There was a plain metal door, set in a windowless wall, with a small emergency light above it. One of the Police

Officers came over to our car and said, ‘Here we are, Sir. I will go and see if there is anyone about. If you would care to wait here Sir.’

He disappeared through the door and reappeared several minutes later accompanied by two other men, both wearing green coloured, hospital, protective clothing. Between them they pushed a stainless steel trolley.

‘In the back of the wagon, is it Sir?’ asked the Policeman as the hospital staff went towards the rear of the truck. We followed and watched as, assisted by the soldiers, the body bag was unceremoniously pulled out of the truck and dumped on the trolley.

‘Shall we wait here Sir?’ enquired the Captain.

‘Yes please. We will try not to be too long.’

One of the men pushing the trolley, said, ‘Which of you Gentleman is Mr Grundy?’

‘I am.’

‘My name is Bruce, Sir. I am the Coroner’s Police Sergeant. This is the Mortuary Attendant. Are these two with you Sir?’ Indicating Fred and Eddie.

‘Yes they are, we work together.’

‘Will the young lady be alright Sir?’

‘Why not? My mother used to tell me that it was the living that did you harm and not the dead. You lead on Sergeant and ignore me.’

‘Yes Miss.’

Mortuaries must be the most cold and impersonal places in the world. In this one, as indeed I have found to be the case in all the others, which I have had cause to visit over the years, was no exception when it came to the smell of disinfectant. It was overbearing and got into the nose and mouth until you felt you might actually choke on it. The light, from a bank of overhead neon lights, was extremely bright and a cold, greenie white colour. There were no windows and the furniture, if dissecting tables and glass fronted instrument cabinets, all made of dull stainless steel, can be called furniture, was cold and uninviting. There was, as there always seems to be, a constant sound of trickling water and the floor was wet as if they had only just finished with the last visitor. The bank, in this case, of six, large steel cabinets, set in the wall, for the cold storage of the deceased, always catches the attention and seems to dominate over all the other fixtures and fitting, with perhaps the exception of the centrally placed dissecting table. Everyone who enters cannot avoid seeing the draw fronts and are always drawn closer by the white cards slotted into the holders in the centre of each, which indicate the occupancy levels at any particular time.

‘This smell! It’s dreadful. You can almost taste it,’ muttered Fred, who, with the rest of us, watched as the body bag was transferred from the trolley onto the stainless steel slab.

The trolley was then pushed aside and placed against a convenient blank piece of wall.

Having put on a pair of surgical gloves the Sergeant began to unzip the bag and as he did so, he enquired, 'Have any of you, any idea who this is?'

'We have our suspicions, but are definitely not sure.'

'I see what you mean,' he exclaimed as he saw the well-wrapped body with its outer envelope of discoloured polythene and parcel tape. 'Not easy to identify trussed up like this, is it?'

With the help of the attendant, he pulled the body bag from under the corpse. Before laying the bag aside, he examined the interior, finally turning it completely inside out. His next move was to select a large pair of cranked scissors and with remarkable dexterity and speed, cut the polythene wrapping the full length of the corpse. Using both hands, he tugged at the wrapping in order to pull it apart and reveal its contents. Laid there and very dead, was the body of a male, clothed in a black anorak, complete with a Coastguard badge on the breast pocket, blue overalls and black gum boots.

'Exactly as Pat Edison described her husband when we asked, if she had any idea, what he was wearing,' muttered Fred.

'Do you know this man Miss?' enquired the Sergeant.

'No I have never met him, but the clothing is as it was described to us.'

'Oh I see Miss. Pity.'

'Why is that Sergeant?' I asked.

'I thought I might get a positive identification from you now. It would have saved me a lot of time, that's all.'

As he spoke, the door opened and in walked a man wearing a loose white coat. The stethoscope, round his neck, didn't make it difficult to guess who he might be.

'What have you here Sergeant?'

'One to certify as no longer being with us, Doctor.'

'Pass me the board. Now let me see. Time. Male. Look, let me just sign it, he is without doubt deceased, our man here can fill in the relevant details later. I need to get back to casualty. We are busy at the moment. Goodnight everyone,' and with that, he handed the clip board to the attendant and left.

'Seems strange, when you look at the state of this corpse, that only a Doctor can declare it dead.'

'It's maybe as well,' said Fred. 'Because I have seen some people, in hospital, who look as bad as that, yet were still alive.'

'As bad as this?' smiled the Sergeant.

'Well, you know what I mean?' replied Fred. 'You can't be too careful.'

The Sergeant did not answer but began to unzipped and go through, each of the anorak pockets, in turn. The contents, which were not much, were carefully

laid on a convenient flat surface, no doubt to be looked at closer, later on. When satisfied there was nothing further in the outer pockets, he unzipped and opened the anorak. He continued to search the inner pocket revealing more pieces of folded paper. He then turned his attention to the breast pocket of the overalls. From the first one, he produced a navy blue plastic wallet with a gold Coastguard emblem embossed on the front.

'Ah, now this looks encouraging,' he said as he opened the wallet and turning it round to get it the correct way up, examined the contents.

'I think we might have what we are looking for here. According to this we have one Philip Edison of Her Majesty's Coastguard, or so this warrant states. Sadly, as there is no photograph, I shall have to get a formal identification of the body from the family or next of kin. But for the moment this will do.'

He continued his search for pockets and when located, extracted all their contents. When satisfied there were no more to go through, he produced, from a drawer, a large self sealing clear plastic envelope and inserted all the contents of the pockets into it. He wrote the necessary identification on the white label that was moulded onto one corner. He removed his gloves and dropped them into a bin. Addressing the attendant he said, 'I will leave this with you for now. No doubt I shall be back shortly and the pathologist will want to take a close look.' Then turning to us he continued, 'and if you good people are ready, I am to escort you to the Police Station as soon as we have finished here. By the way you maybe interested to know that there is no suicide note, or anything of that nature, on the body. Only personal effects which, by the way, you are free to examine now before we leave, if you wish.'

'Not at the moment, thank you. Providing we can come back to them later if we want.'

'Yes of course. They will be going along to the Police Station now with me.'

As we left, the bright lights were blocked out when the door closed behind us. The cold and what felt like very fresh air was a welcome relief.

'It got more than a bit overpowering in there,' said Eddie, who spoke for the first time since the Sergeant started to cut open the wrapping. 'At one point I thought I was going to choke and the smell when he opened that plastic, no wonder they need that lousy disinfectant. That copper never batted an eyelid, or that Doctor when he lent over it with his stethoscope, while the other fellow with them, just stood and watched. He hardly blinked.'

'I suppose you can get used to and become immune to anything, given sufficient time and experience,' said Fred. 'But I am glad it's not a regular experience for me and I agree with you about the smell. It was dreadful.'

'What's that Miss? The pong get to you a bit?' said the Police Sergeant, who had just walked up to us. 'It does. You will soon get rid of it. If you are ready

Sir, you can follow me and I will lead the way to the Police Station. What about these Army people Sir?'

'I will send them back to the barracks and they can make themselves comfortable there, for the time being.'

'I'll tell the Captain.'

'Thanks Eddie.'

As Eddie disappeared round the back of the truck, Fred whispered, 'Poor old Eddie, he was glad to get out of there. Mind you, so was I. But did you notice, he was starting to go a bit pale?'

'He'll be all right. Probably a first time or something and he is just not used to it. Who knows? I've had quite a few over the years but still don't find it a pleasant experience. If it wasn't part of the job, sometimes, I could well do without it.'

The Captain and his men left and disappeared into the night, I presumed, to return to the barracks, although, I did overhear him say, something to the effect, that they should go and look for something to eat. We had no such luck. We followed the Police Car through the streets and eventually parked in a compound for police vehicles, behind a large, impressive, Police Station. We were taken in through a back door and up to a third floor, via a lift.

CHAPTER FORTY-NINE

The Police Station was typical of any modern central, crime-fighting unit, which forms part of the skyline of any large town or city. It was housed in a fairly modern building and was spread over several floors. It was a mass of concrete and glass and was located bang in the centre of the town. Internally, it was divided into miles of corridors and glass-partitioned offices. Office furniture was everywhere, with an abundance of filing cabinets piled high, on top, with boxes and folders. There were desks of all sizes and each one seemed to be cluttered with typewriters, computer terminals, and telephones. There were notice boards and posters on every wall, and spread throughout and covering all remaining flat surfaces, were masses of loose paperwork. We passed by coffee machines, tucked into corners, stairwells, and lift shafts. Everything was either painted cream or grey with the odd splash of pale blue thrown in. The whole atmosphere was one of hustle and bustle, with uniformed officers hustling back and forth, as they went about their business. We must have passed at least half a dozen in the short distance we walked along the corridor from the lift. I noticed several females among the predominantly male occupants and although I have never been particularly attracted to females in police uniform, woman in black stockings, never the less, do something for me.

'She's ugly. Even I can see that.'

'I know she is, but look at the legs.'

'What about them?'

'The black stockings.'

'Are you into black stocking now?'

'Always have been. Black or dark blue: they do something for a girl and I find them magic.'

'What about green or red?'

'No, sorry: not for me. Green makes them look like Brussels sprouts and red reminds me of pantomime dames. No it has to be black or blue; although a good looking girl in nothing but red stockings and suspender belt might make we change my mind.'

The Sergeant held back a door to allow is to pass through. As we did so, he followed us in and announced to those already seated at, or standing round, a large table, 'The Coastguard people Sir.'

A Police Officer, wearing the uniform of a Chief Superintendent, rose from a seat at one end of the table and approached us, hand outstretched.

'Thank you for coming: particularly at this late hour. If you will join us, I will try not to keep you too long. If you will just take a seat, I will be as brief

as possible, because we all have a lot to do and I feel it is essential that we move quickly.'

We spread out and sat down on the vacant seats that he indicated. As we did so I glanced at the people already present. One I instantly recognised as the Drug Squad guy, Len somebody or other, who had turned up at the Dog and Gun posing as a fertilizer salesman and who we had asked to go. Sergeant Bruce from the hospital and who had been our escort to the Police Station and the third, a complete stranger. With the three of us, and the Inspector, that brought the total present to seven.

'Right Ladies,' while smiling at Fred. 'and Gentleman. My name is Adams and I am here to chair this briefing, in order to establish what immediate action shall be taken, to draw this investigation to a satisfactory conclusion. The Gentleman here, on my right, is Mr Ron Williams. He is Customs and Excise, covering Drugs and Arms importation. The Gentleman next to him is Mr Len Jones of the Police Undercover Drug Squad. At the far end of the table is Sergeant Bruce, who you have already met and who is the Coroner's Sergeant, but who I have asked, on this occasion for expediency, to act, in addition to his own brief, as minute and record taker and be my general assistant. You are Miss?'

'Winifred Huntington, Coastguard Special Investigations.'

'Thank you Miss and you Sir?'

'Eddie Scott, Metropolitan Anti-Terrorist Squad, Sir.'

'That leaves you Sir and you are, I take it, Mr Grundy, also of the Coastguard Service and working on this case with the charming lady here.'

'Correct.'

'Tonight, or should I say in the early hours of this morning, arrests have to be made. They must all take place at about the same time and before the people concerned fully realise what is happening to them. But most important, before they have time to rouse themselves sufficiently to warn or inform others. We must, at all costs, prevent them from tipping each other off, which they would do, if they had any warning or were randomly arrested over a period of time. So you understand why we must be as brief as possible and then get these people into custody as soon as we can. The charges will be, smuggling and suspicion of murder with possible terrorist implications. Now, who do we specifically target in this operation Mr Grundy; at least to start with? Are you ready to get this down Sergeant.'

The Sergeant looked up but said nothing.

'I think you will agree Fred and you too Eddie, we certainly need to detain Raines, Johnson, Scampton, the Fisherman and the Builder. They are the ones we are sure of. There are probably others implicated, but those five are the big fish in our operation, so to speak, as far as we know.'

'Does this Builder and Fisherman have names, Sir,' enquired the Sergeant who was painstakingly recording everything that was said.

'No. But we do have an address for the Builder and your man in the village will know his name. The Fisherman we know even less about. All we have is a photograph, but we believe he lives in Whitby.'

'If you have a picture then, that will be very useful. Will you pass it to the Sergeant and he will arrange to have it circulated in the Whitby and surrounding area.'

'We don't have it with us.'

'That is unfortunate. Where is it? We shall need it as soon as possible.'

'It's in our Caravanette which is parked on a Camp Site and which we have been using as our most recent base.'

'Write the description of the van, the Registration Number and the address of the Camp Site, on a piece of paper and pass it along, with the keys, to the Sergeant. Sergeant have it picked up and brought here straight away.'

'Here are the keys Sergeant,' said Fred, as she slid them along the table towards him, 'and if you will pass me a piece of paper, I will write everything down, that you will need to know.'

I was relieved when Fred volunteered to give the information because I could not have remembered the Registration Number to save my life.

'At the same time Sergeant, arrange for warrants to be issued and brief the duty Inspector. All on my authority, tell him.'

'Very good Sir,' and raising from his seat, the Sergeant collected his papers, including the one slid across by Fred and left the room.

'That's the most essential and important part for the moment, but before we break up for tonight, will you fill me in with a few details in order to bring me fully into the picture. But perhaps before you do, let me tell you what I already know. As far as I gather you originally came to investigate the disappearance of one of your people, a Coastguard. While you were here you discovered that drugs were being smuggled in, and distributed.'

'Something like, that.'

'Where do the arms, if that's what they are, come into all this?'

'Yes, they are indeed, arms and explosives. In our last report we could only, truthfully, state that we had found several large cases that, we believed, might contain arms and ammunition. Since then we have opened two of the crates. One had automatic rifles and handguns in it. The other had explosives. We have no idea what the others contain, but can guess that the contents will probably be very similar.'

'And these crates are now secure in the barracks, here in town and being guarded by the Army. How did you get on to them? The arms and ammunition, I mean.'

'By natural progression really, while we were investigating the disappearance. One thing led to another and we followed it through. We believed it was somehow tied in with our investigations.'

'Your people Mr Scott, will be wanting to arrange the removal of these cases, no doubt?'

'Yes as soon as possible, I should imagine,' replied Eddie. 'If there had not been this nasty business involving a body mixed up in it all, my people would probably have preferred, for the arms, once discovered, to have been reburied and left at their original location to allow the net to widen. In other words, we would have tried to sit on them and wait to see who came to collect them and if possible find out where they were destined to end up. As far as we are concerned the people who are about to be arrested could have been picked up at any time. They are small fry and only part of a complex chain, but now murder has come into the picture the whole scene has changed and I realise they must now be nailed and taken out of circulation.'

'I realise, the same as you, the seriousness of the situation, but why then did your people not pursue that line? Why did they not simply request the removal of the body, create some sort of suitable cover up, and leave the arms on site? A cover up, on the discovery of a body, would be of a less serious nature, from the national security point of view, if it, in the long run, lead to the discovery of where arms and explosives were possibly being distributed or accumulated in storage areas across the country.'

'My people decided not to interfere because of the level of activity surrounding the discovery. The massive army exercise and all that, is bound to leak out and get back to the people concerned, despite any precautions we took. The workers at the Saw Mill, alone, would soon let it be known that there had been unusual activity in the forest and our past experiences have taught us that when we have come across similar cashes of arms, under similar circumstances and intentionally made no arrests, we found the arms were simply abandoned. The supplies must be so plentiful, that if there is any suspicion surrounding any one cache, it can be abandon and just left to rot. On other occasions, again in the past, when we have made actual arrests and interrogated those involved, we found that the stuff was not always for immediate use and that it was meant to remain in situ until a specific use for it arose. Therefore, in that case, we may have had to sit on it for years and leave those, so far involved, to get on with their dishonest lives. On this occasion, taking all the known factors into account, we feel it's better this way. At least we have taken a lot of potentially dangerous material out of circulation, broken up this line of supply, and with it taken out some very dangerous and misguided people. All in all, my people are very happy so far and go along with everything that has happened. We of course will continue to try, along with the other agencies, to establish where it originated from and how it got here

and maybe with a bit of luck, where it was meant to go, if and when it was moved on. Also we will keep a eye on the site and surrounding district to make sure no other idiots decide to step in and re-establish a point of entry.'

'Yes it would be very nice to bring to boot the people who do the ordering and the supplying and find out where that delivery ship came from,' added Fred.

'We have a pretty good idea on that Miss,' Interjected Ron Williams. 'We believe the Poles have a lot to do with it at the moment. Suppliers change and vary according to international pressures and political issues and as they do so, they also change the supply routes and the carriers. At the moment the Poles are fairly active, not as direct suppliers, but as carriers, they are the transport men and some unscrupulous Dutchmen know a lot more about the drug side of things than they would like us to know. Some of our own people are not exactly squeaky clean when it comes to popping over to the continent and making a bob or two on illegal drugs. But, it's a bit late now to go into all the details tonight and I have a few things I need to attend to, so if you will excuse me, I will bid you all good night. What time tomorrow Mr Adams?'

'We should have things pretty much tied up and have something to show for our efforts by lunch time, so shall we say Two in the afternoon and thank you Mr Williams and good night.'

'I think I will call it a day as well,' added Len Jones. 'If you don't need me further Inspector. Good night all,' and he got up and left.

'It has been a long night,' said the Superintendent. 'By the way, when you go down to the Front Office and Reception, you will find arrangements have been made for your accommodation. I took the liberty and trust you will find it OK.'

'I am sure we will and thank you,' I said.

'Been a long night has it Mr Adams?'

'It has Miss.'

'It's been a long day for us and tonight has only been a very small part of it. I am glad that you propose we meet at Two tomorrow afternoon, because if you had suggested any earlier, you would have had to manage without me.'

'Well, in that case, the sooner we get you out of here, the better then. Follow me and I will show you to the lift. When you come in tomorrow, just ask at the front desk for me, they will have been told to expect you. In the meantime if we should need you for anything, we know where you are.'

'I hope it doesn't come to that, not tonight,' said Fred.

'We will have to do our best to make sure it doesn't; won't we Miss?' smiled the Superintendent.

We left the Superintendent at the lift and found our way to the front desk. From there a car was laid on, which took us to a medium sized hotel, somewhere in the town. By unanimous decision we sat in the lounge, which was deserted due to the late hour, to wind down before we went to bed. We downed a large quantity

of whiskey which the night porter continued to produced from somewhere behind the scenes.

'Do you realise what time it is and have you seen the state of us? Little wonder the porter keeps giving us a strange look and do you know this drink is going straight to my head. We have had hardly anything to eat for ages and that is not good for me. Does anyone want anything to eat now, because if you do, I will ask that nice porter man to get us something and I am sure he will, because he is a nice man, and I am a nice lady… and don't I go on… and on, when I am drunk.'

Eddie and I laughed as Fred let her chin drop onto her chest and let go a big sigh.

'Come on girl, give me that glass, it's time a nice lady, like you, was up those stairs and in bed. You have had far more than your share of drink for tonight.'

The rooms allocated to us were all on the same corridor and situated side by side. While Eddie looked bleary eyed and tried to focus on the key fob in his hand, to determine the number of his room, Fred lent against the wall and muttered, 'Hurry up someone, before I fall asleep and fall down.'

Eddie, after a great deal of fumbling, found the door lock and let him-self into the first room and once the door was fully open, he turned and looked towards Fred who was barely standing. It was difficult to tell, through the drunken smile and the swaying, if he was indeed focusing or just facing in that direction. 'Good night you two, see you in the morning,' and he swung the door closed, not really caring if it shut properly or not.

'No you won't. Tomorrow afternoon,' drawled Fred. 'Where's my bed?'

I looked at the key in my hand. It had a number on it somewhere, but it would not stay still long enough for me to read it. 'Give me your key and I will open your door.'

'But that one was open.'

'I know but that one is Eddie's.'

'Tell him to come out here and find another. I want to go to bed.'

'Then give me your key.'

She pushed her hand into one of her pockets and tried to extract the key. The more she tugged the worse she made it. The lining of the pocket turned inside out and loose change fell all over the floor. As I bent down and attempted to retrieve it, she muttered, 'Leave that for the nice man who served the drinks. You just open this door and let me get to bed.'

I managed, eventually, to get her to release her hold on the key and let me have it. I opened the door, not at the first attempt, but I opened it in the end and taking a firm grip on her arm, or that's what I thought it was, guided her into the room, and closed the door behind me.

'Are you going to be alright now?'

'Of course I am. All I have had is a little drink, or two, or three, and now all I intend to do is crash out on this bed and sleep. You go to bed darling and I will see you sometime somewhere. Don't leave me, I'm pissed and won't love you anymore if you leave me.'

She stood in the middle of the room and swayed violently from side to side, as she clumsily removed her anorak. Once free of it, she let it fall to the floor. Then, still wobbling in a very unsteady manner made a clumsy attempt to remove her jumper. The more she pulled, the nearer she got to overbalancing and falling down.

'Let me give you a hand with that,' at which she immediately hoisted both her arms high up into the air and muttered, 'I surrender, you can have anything you want. They tell me it's much less painful than rape.'

'Thanks,' was all I could think of by way of reply.

I took hold of her jumper by the waistband and raised it up over her upper body. There was only one way to get it off in those circumstances and that was to pull at it, and allow it to turn inside out, and slide off her arms.

'Put it there,' she said pointing up into the air. 'That's where it belongs and it will be quite safe there… just there…' as her body shuddered and her knees buckled that little bit more.

I ignored her and turning the jumper back on it-self, so that it was once more the right way round, placed it on a chair. As I turned back and checked my own balance, which was not all that good, it was to see Fred, about to fall on her backside on the floor. She had managed to drop her jeans and had them, in a jumbled mess, around her ankles. She had one leg partially pulled out and her panties were stretched tight and at an angle just above her knees, as she hit the floor.

I stood and watched, trying desperately to keep my brain in gear, as I too was slightly worse for ware, or was it for drink.

'Oh sod it. I will sleep just here,' and rolling slowly onto her side and still all entangled in her jeans and knickers, she closed her eyes and immediately began to breath slowly and deeply.

'Hold on Fred. Let's get you out of these and into this bed.'

I knelt down and shook my head, to try and clear the fuzzy feeling. Then I pulled and worked on the jeans, until they too, turned inside out and came off. I straightened them and placed them over the chair with the jumper. At first I tried to pull her panties up but it didn't work. 'Off is my speciality girl.' I muttered as they too joined the rest. I was knackered.

Turning down the covers of the bed, I bent down to pick up, the now sleeping, Fred. For someone so slim and light, she was remarkably heavy. Ask anyone, except the exceptionally strong and they will all tell you that when you try and lift a grown person from floor level, they are very heavy and the fact that they are all loose and limp doesn't help very much either. Nor does the fact that,

on this occasion, the person attempting the lift was also very much worse the wear for drink. After much pulling and tugging I finally managed to lay her across the bed. Throughout the entire manoeuvre, all she managed to do was moan a little and throw her arms about. I lifted her legs and whilst still hold of them, used them to twist her body round, so that eventually, I was able to push her feet under the covers. Before pulling the bed covers up and covering her completely, I stopped for a moment and through bleary eyes, took one final look at her gorgeous sleeping body. It looked so tantalizing in the pale blue bra and nothing else except the tiny white socks that still covered her feet. I was drunk, I was tired, and she was asleep. The socks stayed where they were. God she looked good. I shook myself.

I staggered across the room and turned off the light and closed the door behind me. Fred was away with the fairies and was totally oblivious to everything going on around her. I found my key in a pocket, where I remembered carefully putting it earlier, for safekeeping. After much swaying I opened the door and let myself into the room next door. My room, as I hoped it was, through bleary eyes, appeared to be identical, in almost every detail, to the one next door. Or that is what I thought, as I looked at the bedspread and was convinced that it was of the same pattern and shade of pink as the one I had pulled over Fred.

I stood for a moment and hoped to relax and wind down a little from the strenuous efforts of getting Fred into bed and it was then that I became fully aware of the total effect the alcohol was having on me. I suddenly felt very light headed and weak. I remember thinking the sooner I climbed into bed the better before I finally fell down. I managed to strip off and deposit my clothes, not very neatly, in a pile on the chair. Totally exhausted I managed to climb into bed and within seconds of doing so, drifted off. My last conscious thoughts were of the Police and if they had located our Camper and found the photographs where Fred said they were. I also remember not caring very much, as the night shift at the Police Station had a full eight hours to do it all in and would, in addition, get paid for any overtime. Fred and I worked as and when required and we had had a long day and the pay still remained the same.

I had no idea how long I slept, because I had no idea what time it was when I went to bed. I only know that when I was disturbed and woke, it must have been very early in the morning as daylight was just beginning to filter through the curtains. Curtains I did not remember pulling.

Someone shook me again. I tried to clear my head. 'Move up and make room for me. My bed is too small and there's no man in it. How can a girl expect to get a cuddle like that? Quick, move up, I am freezing to death standing here.'

I pushed back, towards the edge of the bed and away from the warm centre and soon felt a distinctly cool body, pressed up tight against mine.

'That's better,' she shivered. 'Now for some real warmth,' as both hands slowly closed over my meat and two veg. Her fingers were icy cold and I shuddered from head to foot. It was lovely.

'After the pain will come the pleasure,' she teased. 'Come on be a big boy, just for Fred.'

'How did you get in here and go easy, your hands are like ice.'

'Do you care? If you must know, your door was open, so I walked straight in.'

'I didn't think I was that drunk.'

'How do you mean?'

'To leave the door unlocked and what would you have done if I had remembered to lock it?'

'Standing out there in just my bra and socks and feeling as I do now, I would have bashed it down. Don't just lay there looking all smug, kiss me, cuddle me.'

She then gently eased herself on top and slowly flexed her thighs so that her stomach gently slid up and down along mine. 'Hold me tight, this bed is very narrow and might not stand too much activity.'

I put my chin on to my chest and gave myself a perfect view of her cleavage and hanging breasts, cupped in delicate blue.

'Take it off, if it will improve things for you,' she grinned as if reading my mind. 'It might as well join all the rest that are goodness knows where. Here let me. You always fumble too much.'

After some manoeuvring of shoulders and arms the bra drifted down to the floor and I felt her cool breasts press down on to my chest. She then split her legs to either side of mine and drew up her knees.

'Stick a pillow under your bum darling. I have waited so long for this and right now, I am in the perfect mood to ride the Grand National, fences and all.'

CHAPTER FIFTY

We arrived back at the Hotel about mid-day and went straight into the dining room, to find Eddie already there and eating.

We had earlier dragged ourselves out, having decided to stroll around the town and discuss our current situation and evaluate, if we could, our progress and what, if anything, we planned to do next. Several things came up for serious consideration but all seemed to get lost or loose there initial impact whenever Fred broke off to admire a particular dress or some other item of clothing in a shop windows or if she decided it was time for another coffee and dragged me into yet another snack bar or tea room.

Despite this distinct lack of progress as far as forward planning was concerned, I did manage, at one point, to drag her into a public telephone box and made her promise to concentrate and be quiet, long enough for me to ring and speak to the Old Man. He, to my utter amazement, unintentionally, perked me up no end, by stating that he was satisfied with the progress to date. He told me that he was currently receiving a feed back of information from numerous sources, which I guessed he would be. He knew for example; which was more than we did, that arrests had been made and that it had not all gone smoothly and assured me there was no cause for alarm and that we would get all the details when we attended the afternoon meeting. Something else he knew all about.

His only criticism and of course he had to have at least one, even though he had started out by saying that as far as he was concerned everything was going well, was that he thought we might have submitted our report to him, much earlier in the day, when Fred, who, up to that point, had been stood quietly beside me, content only to listen in, intervened saying, 'Tell him we were up late last night working on this damned case.'

He exploded!

'Have you got that woman in the phone box with you again Grundy?'

I could not resist and found myself replying, 'Yes Sir, I have and you really should try it sometime. It does wonders for the ego.'

'Ego,' he hollered. 'You are not employed by this department to boost your ego. I shall certainly have to review procedures and working practices for our operatives out in the field. This behaviour just will not do,' and with his usual courtesy, he hung up.

'I wonder what his poor wife is really like?' giggled Fred as we left the confines of the phone box. 'Long suffering I'll bet, poor dear, who ever she is.'

'She might be worse than him and that maybe why, he is like he is to us.'

'Maybe. Who knows?'

* * *

As we approached Eddie, he rose politely from his seat and invited us to join him.

'Sorry, I started without you. But I had no idea where you were, or what you had planned and I was damned hungry, as I slept in this morning and missed breakfast completely.'

'That's OK. We had a few loose ends to tie up and you were not about at the time to tell, so we went out. We didn't have all that much to do really, but what we had, the mood this one was in, kicked all that into touch. So we have spent most of our time in either coffee bars or window-shopping. Haven't we?' I said nudging Fred, who just grinned and sat down.

'I saw a lovely two-piece suit and a gorgeous skirt in another shop but he wouldn't even let me look properly. All he wanted to do was talk shop. He even begrudged me a coffee. At least we found out where the Police station is relative to this place and he insisted we came back here in his car so it wasn't exactly a wasted morning.'

'Fibber. It was and you know it.'

'I was up quite early,' said Eddie. 'Considering the state we were all in last night, but it was too much, so I got back into bed and then over slept. When I finally got up I was annoyed with myself, as there was a fair amount that I wanted to attend to. I needed to tie up, the same as you, a few loose ends. But I also needed a substantial amount of information for this afternoon's meeting. So, since I managed to drag myself out, I have been rushing around like the proverbial blue arsed fly. I then decided that enough was enough and I needed food, so I came in here. Before you came in I was wondering what progress the Police have made?'

'According to our Chief, there have been some arrests, but that is all he told us. No doubt we will find out all about it, this afternoon.'

'If I remember rightly, the Police had plans to collect and bring your Camper here. If that proves to be the case, then I will collect my things out of it and set up my base here, in this Hotel and work from here from now on.'

'We will miss you, won't we Mel?' as she stroked the inside of my thigh, under the table.

'Yes we will.' I replied as I put my hand over hers and attempted to draw it higher up. She countered by pulling it sharply away. 'It has been good working with you so far, and I really mean that, despite the fact that recently we were all rather cramped for space.'

Eddie looked at me with an odd expression. He must have had no idea that my last statement was only a follow up and a cover for Fred's earlier remark, "We

will miss you" and meant nothing more sinister or profound and that we had no immediate plans to part-company.

'Why. Are you leaving? Going away from here? Going to live back in the Camper?' he asked in amazement. 'I thought you would have stayed on, in the relative comfort of this place, for the time being at least?'

'As far as I know, that is what we propose to do. We haven't really discussed it; we have been more interested in frocks. But I can see no reason to leave just yet. What I meant, when I said, we will miss you,' and then racking my brains to think of a plausible explanation for Fred's initial statement and my stupid follow up, 'Is that now we have left the confines of the Camper and we are spread out in here, I shall miss the closeness of it and your company. You know, as well as I do, that sometimes, when operatives from different departments cross paths, it does not always work out as it should. I have been guilty of causing problems in that direction myself, many times in the past and not always through choice. It has often been the results of instructions from outside or above and these have led to problems with close working relationships. How often have I heard, "Don't tell them this or that. Find out what they know and tell them nothing," but in this recent case and between you and us, so to speak, everything has worked out fine and as I have already said, it has been great working with you. But, just listen at me. It is not over yet. There are quite a few loose ends still to tie up and the job is far from finished. No doubt we will all still be seeing a lot of each other over the next few days, at least.'

'When this is all over we will have to see if we can arrange a farewell drink or something before we finally part,' said Eddie as I sighed, a sigh of relief.

'I am one hundreds percent in favour of that,' enthused Fred. 'Any excuse for a party.'

'After last night?' I asked.

'Yes, even after last night. So I was a little tight. You were not exactly sober yourselves, or so I vaguely remember, before I slipped off into oblivion and so, you Mel Grundy, you have no room to talk. You should have seen yourself trying to help a poor girl into her room. It was most embarrassing and not only for me, but also for all the other guests. Anyhow I was tired, not drunk, that's all.'

'And cold later on.'

She tapped me on the shin with her foot. 'I don't remember you objecting.'

If Eddie gathered anything from that last remark, he said nothing. Perhaps he was still tired or wrapped up too much in his own thoughts.

We ordered and ate, while Eddie, who had excused himself and left the table, sat in the lounge reading documents and making notes.

As we finished Fred said, 'Excuse me a moment Mel, I won't be long, back in a second.'

She return shortly after. 'I have just rung the Police Station and they have our Camper in their compound, so I have rung for a Taxi to take me round there. I need a change of clothing if nothing else. One of the hooks on my bra somehow got damaged, probably when horse riding in the early hours of this morning. But anyhow, what ever happened, it doesn't feel comfortable and I need to do something about it. Are you coming with me or can I get anything for you while I am there?'

'I think I will come with you. A change of underwear sounds a good idea and a shave would certainly not go amiss,' as I ran my hand over the stubble on my chin, 'but why the Taxi? There's the car round the back.'

'Because, I anticipated that we would be staying there when we got there? Thereafter, the Police seem to have this idea that they should chauffeur us around. So why not let them?

The Taxi arrived. As we passed Eddie on the way out, I said, 'See you along at the nick at two.'

'See you there,' he replied and returned to reading, whatever it was, that was holding his attention.

* * *

I felt a lot brighter for the change of clothing and the opportunity to clean myself up. The Police had been most obliging and allowed us to use their washrooms, where hot water was plentiful and so I was able to get a good shave if nothing else. We were also just in time to get our things together, lock the Camper and go straight in for the meeting.

The young Constable at reception released the security door to let us through and as he did so, he said, 'the same room, on the Third Floor, that you used yesterday. Would you like someone to take you up?'

'No thanks,' smiled Fred. 'If we get lost we can always ask a Policeman.' At which he laughed and replied, 'That could be very dodgy in here Miss'.

As we entered the Conference Room, some were already assembled, having arrived before us. Looking round I nodded a greeting to those who glanced across in our direction. Fred chatted to Eddie who must have arrived while we were busy changing.

The Superintendent entered the room, neatly turned out in his full uniform and with his hat, pace stick and leather gloves in one hand and a large folder in the other. Placing them all on the table, he addressed everyone present.

'If you would all take a seat please, we need to make a start. Is everyone present that should be?'

There was no reply. Which did not surprise me, for I have often thought that that particular statement must surely be, not only one of the commonest used in circumstances similar to these, but must also be one of the most misleading.

How can those present answer if they don't know who should be there and how can those, who should be there, answer when they are not? However the absence of any sort of response did not deter him, as he drew out a chair and seated himself at the head of the table. Everyone else spaced themselves out around the adjacent sides. By coincidence, I happened to be standing by the same chair I had occupied on the previous evening. Fred pulled out the one beside it and sat down next to me. There were two new faces from the night before.

'Right Ladies and Gentlemen: if I can have your attention. With the exception of Inspector Bob Molescroft here, who is Duty Inspector, and WPC Kath Smith, who joins us as a Stenographer, we are all known to each other. For the record and for the benefit of Kath, I will call out your names individually. Starting on my left, we have Mr Grundy, Coastguard, Miss Huntington also Coastguard, then Mr Scott, Anti-Terrorist Squad.'

As he progressed round the table he ignored the WPC who was seated at the opposite end and facing him and proceeded to the Police Sergeant, sat beside her, and continued, 'Sergeant Bruce, the Coroner's Sergeant, Mr Jones, Drug Squad, Mr Williams, Customs and Excise Special Investigations and finally Inspector Molescroft, Duty Inspector.'

He then paused for a moment while he opened his file and arranged his papers into individual piles, swapping them about until he had them in the way he obviously wanted them. At the same time, some of the others present did the same. The WPC passed round blank notepaper and pens. He waited until everyone had settled and had, more or less, stopped fidgeting.

'Warrants were issued and in the early hours of this morning, several significant arrests were made. We now have a number of people in custody. No one has yet been formally charged, but arrangements have been made under the Prevention of Terrorism Act to detain each one for questioning. Perhaps as Duty Inspector, you will give us more details Mr Molescroft?'

'Shall I take notes for us?' whispered Fred as she reached for a pad and pen.

'If there's anything significant, that you think we need to remember, you can make a note of it,' I whispered back.

The Inspector cleared his throat and, shuffling his papers, selected one and placing it in front of him, used it as his prompt.

'At dawn today, in simultaneous raids, several houses were visited and the following arrests made: one Albert Thornton, Builder; one Alfred Scampton, Park Ranger; one Michael Johnson, described as a Jobber; one Ronald Raines, Labourer; one Pauline Johnson, housewife; and a further warrant, which was not served, was issued for the arrest of one Philip Whiting. That is all so far, Sir.'

Fred pushed the scrap pad towards me. I took it and looked at it. Written, in very neat handwriting, it said, 'That's a posh name for a scrubber!'

I reached across and took the pen out of her hand. I wrote on the pad, 'What is?' and slid both pen and pad back.

Fred tore off the top sheet and wrote on the next page, pushing the pad back to me. I looked at it and smiled. She had written, 'Pauline. Johnson's wife.'

We discovered later that her name was truly Pauline, but she preferred to call herself Lena.

I raised my finger to attract the Superintendent's attention.

'Thank you, Inspector,' he said. Then looking at me. 'You have a question, Sir?'

'Yes. Why the arrest of Mrs Johnson?'

Everyone turned to look at the Inspector who consulted his sheet of paper before replying, 'Apparently when attempting to apprehend Mr Johnson, she intervened and as a result was arrested and will probably be charged with obstruction and threatening behaviour. It says in the arrest report here, that she produced a firearm, namely a Shotgun and threatened to use it. There is no mention of whether it was actually discharged.'

'Philip Whiting! Is he the Fisherman?'

'Yes, Sir! Identified from the photographs. Philip Whiting, Fisherman of Whitby and well known to the Police for various other minor misdemeanours in the past.'

'Why was the warrant on him not served?'

'Simply because the Police at Whitby were unable to track him down. He was absent when his home was raided and at present his whereabouts are unknown. But we will get him. I have no doubt about that. Just a matter of time.'

Sergeant Bruce was the next to speak. 'If you will excuse me Sir, I have an appointment with Mrs Edison, who has been asked to attend and make formal identification of the deceased. After I have finished with her, I will make arrangements for her to be formally interviewed in connection with this whole business.'

'You carry on Sergeant and thank you for attending this meeting. I will send for you if we need you further.'

The Sergeant stood up and after gathering his papers, gave a polite nod to the whole assembly, and left.

'Mr Grundy! I have made arrangements for you and Miss Huntington to make full and detailed statements and to provide us with all the relevant details, that we need, to further our enquiries. If you would care to remain here for a few more minutes, I will make arrangements for someone to collect you and take you to an Interview Room, where we have better facilities.'

The Superintendent then excused him-self, and left, closely followed by all the others, leaving Fred and I alone.

'Five minutes at the most: that's all it's taken. Some meeting,' I said.

‘A bit of an anti-climax after all this time.’

‘I suppose it is, now that you mention it,’ I replied. ‘We seem to have been at the sharp end for so long and so closely involved and spent so much time in the thick of it, that now it has all been suddenly taken out of our hands, it leaves a kind of empty feeling. The Inspector’s last remark, “We will make arrangements for you to make full statements,” leaves me feeling that, as from now, we have been reduced to just another Police Witness, helping in their enquiries.’

‘I couldn’t agree more. But I hope not. I sincerely hope it hasn’t really come down to that. But I admit it makes you want to say “Well, is that it then? Can we all go home now?” I know that you and I, do not have the necessary skills, to interrogate the likes of Johnson and his team but it might have been more satisfactory if we could, somehow, have been more closely involved towards the end. To be invited just to sit in would have satisfied me.’

The door opened and a young Constable stuck his head into the room, ‘If you would come this way, please. I will take you to a vacant Interview Room.’

We looked at each other, shrugged, and dutifully followed him. He said nothing more until he reached a room and then, holding the door open, said to Fred, ‘If you will make yourself comfortable in here Miss, there will be someone along in a moment to see you. Sir, if you will come this way.’

He opened a door a few yards along the corridor and I entered the room. He immediately closed the door behind me and left me standing, alone, in the middle of a very uninviting place. It was a small square room. There were no windows and the only illumination came from a single strip light suspended from the ceiling. The walls and woodwork were clean and painted a uniform cream colour. The floor was tiled and a mottled grey. How one was supposed to make oneself comfortable was beyond me, for to start with, the only furniture was a tubular metal table with a grey Formica top and three chairs, also tubular with moulded polished wooden seats and backs. I pulled one of them out and sat down, resting my elbows on the table. It was very quiet, the only sounds being a barely audible noise, caused by people passing along the corridor outside the door and the general hubbub of the Police Station. No way was it possible to make out anything specific. I began to think how inhospitable and uninviting this small room really was. I wondered if Fred was at that moment, in similar circumstances and how she was feeling about it. I was glad I was not claustrophobic. I even found myself wondering if the door would actually open if I tried it, or if, to add to the whole atmosphere of depravation, it would be locked.

To complete the decor, there was small spy-hole in the solid flush door. I had just made up my mind to try the door and was on the point of getting up from my seat, when it opened and in walked Inspector Molescroft, closely followed by another man in civilian clothing.

'Sorry to have kept you waiting, Mr Grundy, but we are trying to cover so much ground, in so short a time, that we are having to pull in extra manpower from all over the place. We have such a limited time allowed to us these days, in which we can detain people without charge, that if we don't move quickly we lose the advantage.'

'So I am being held, am I? I suppose that accounts for these luxurious surroundings?'

'Indeed you are not being held, Sir. But you will appreciate that you have vital information that we need straight away, if we are to nail those that we already have in detention. What you have to tell us, we need now, to use against them. That is why it is essential that we talk to you straight away.'

'So why was it necessary to split us. My partner, Miss Huntington, and I work together and have done so throughout and will only tell you the same things.'

'I am sure you will, Sir, but if you will forgive me, it is our method. We always interview separately. We find it works much better that way. As for the accommodation, it is all we have available, at the moment and at least in here we can talk openly and confidentially without being overheard.'

'I bet we can and I wonder, how many times you have said that to some poor defenceless suspect in this room Inspector?'

He chose to totally ignore my remark, which annoyed me, and, indicating towards his colleague, he said, 'This is Sergeant Burrows of C.I.D.'

The Sergeant extended his hand and, as I reluctantly shook it, he said, 'Good afternoon, Sir. I'm pleased to meet you and as the Inspector has explained, Sir, we are pushed for time, so if you would be good enough to draw up your chair we can make a start. My responsibilities are to co-ordinate this investigation and ensure that all relevant information gets passed to all other Investigating Officers. We are not asking you, at this stage of our enquiries, for signed statements, although it will probably come to that later, when we need them for evidence. What I need, for the moment, is factual and detailed information on your investigation to date.'

"I bet you bloody do and as far as signed statements are concerned, you can stuff that," I thought to myself.

I did not like this man or his attitude and I got the distinct feeling that he did not consider me to be any different to those they already had under arrest and probably residing, at this very moment, somewhere else in the building, probably in a similar room or a detention cell.

'I am not sure that I am at liberty to divulge everything to you Sergeant. I have not had appropriate clearance from my people.'

This of course was not true, as the Old Man had categorically instructed me to co-operate fully with the Police. But I thought, "What the hell!" A big change in attitude, by them, was required here, if they hoped to get my full co-operation.

'That's not our understanding Mr Grundy. We were led to believe that you would co-operate fully with us.'

'Your co-operation, with us, is vital to this investigation,' pleaded Molescroft. 'So please, Sir, I have Officers waiting for information which only you and Miss Huntington can provide. So if the Sergeant can please get started.'

'Yes, but before we do, there are one or two things to sort out, which I am not at all happy about Inspector. If you want co-operation you will find somewhere better than this room and you will talk to us together and a cup of coffee, into the bargain, wouldn't go amiss.'

Molescroft looked at Burrows. 'Can I have a word outside? If you will excuse us a moment Sir.'

They left and as the door closed behind them I stood up and moved over towards it. I put my ear against it. The conversation, due to their close proximity to the other side of the door, could just be made out. The Inspector was saying, 'Go get someone to make their office available. Organise some coffee and collect the woman and lets start treating these people as if they are on the same side.'

The Inspector returned and as he closed the door behind him, was about to say something. But before he could, I could not resist smiling at him and saying. 'That's better Inspector. I too thought we were all supposed to be on the same side, or do Policemen only have one side, their own?'

'You must try and understand, Sir. We tend to be fixed in our ways and are so used to being on our own and on the one side that I must admit, we often forget that it is not necessary to be suspicious of everyone. No offence, you understand and I promise I will sort it all out to everyone's satisfaction.'

The young Constable, who originally showed me into the Interview Room, opened the door and announced. 'The Sergeant has found an office, Sir, number eighteen. So if you care to go up. I will bring the Lady along.'

We travelled, by lift, up two floors and came out into another corridor. The Inspector opened a nearby office door.

'If you will step in here, Sir, we should be more comfortable. The Lady will be along any moment and, with a bit of luck, we will all be getting some coffee.'

The office was large and roomy with one wall almost entirely constructed of glass that gave a panoramic view, over the rooftops, of the surrounding area. There was a large desk with a swivel chair that backed onto the window. Several other chairs were set out in front of it and along the back wall was a two-seater settee. I noticed, what I thought to be, when compared with all the other rooms and offices that went to make up this building, the above average quality of all the furnishings in this office and in particularly the thick wall-to-wall fitted carpet and the attractive pictures on the wall. Another Constable, having politely knocked on the door, entered and placed a tray containing several cups and saucers and

two large stainless steel thermos flasks, on the corner of the desk. He left without saying a word. The door had hardly closed before it opened again and in walked Fred. Someone closed the door behind her. Without a word she sat down on the settee and crossed her legs. The look on her face told everyone and in particular me, that she was far from happy.

'So what are waiting for now?' she snapped.

'The return of the Sergeant,' replied Molescroft, somewhat taken aback by her abruptness; a side of Fred he had obviously not seen before. 'He should be along at any moment.'

'Well, if he doesn't hurry up I am going. If you people think you can dump me in a small empty room and just leave me, you have another think coming.'

'I am sorry, Miss. I understood someone would come to see you straight away and put some questions to you. I have been trying to explain to Mr Grundy that we are short of space and very limited for time. I had no idea you had been left alone and once again, all I can say is, I am very sorry.'

'Well I was and you are not half as sorry as I am.'

There was a bustle of activity, the noise of which made us all turn towards the door.

'Sorry to keep you all waiting,' quipped Burrows as he sprang through the door, with a smile on his face that was so false it was laughable.

'Who is he?' demanded Fred. 'Another of the establishment's heavy mob, someone from "Z Cars" or "The Bill" or just another look-alike?'

'No Miss, please,' the smile, disappearing from off his face.

The Inspector looked uncomfortable to say the least. He was beginning to realise that they had got off to a very bad start and should have brought us to somewhere similar to this office, in the first instance or at the very least, talked to us in somewhere like the Conference Room.

'Let's all have a cup of coffee and then see if we can settle down for a friendly chat. Things should be much better in here. At least we have the use of a tape recorder, which will save us all waiting for me to slowly write it all down.'

'Assuming you can,' threw in Fred.

Now thoroughly demoralised, all he could reply to her remark was, 'Yes. Assuming I can Miss.'

A hint of a smile began to appear on Fred's face as she softened and soon became her usual self. I could see she was now satisfied that she had made her protest felt.

* * *

Coffee cups empty and put to one side, we sat down for what turned out to be a long interview, consisting mainly of hundreds of different questions. The

Sergeant may not have been very strong on the public relations side of things, but he was very skilled at asking the right questions and extracting accurate and detailed information. He went laboriously over several small points until he was satisfied he had a clear picture in his mind as to exactly what we had described, said or heard.

A "persistent prat" was the title Fred was to give him later.

It was late in the evening when the Police car dropped us back at the Hotel. We had spoken very little to each other since we left the Police Station but once back in her room Fred let forth a tirade of pent up anger and frustration.

'They tried to treat us no better than criminals, putting me in a small room and leaving me. What was I supposed to do there, sweat it out? Contemplate on my guilt and wrong doings? I was embarrassed, hurt, and humiliated. What did they hope to gain by splitting us up? Catch us out as liars? Find flaws in our statements, to use against us, or something? Try and destroy our credibility? I have had a belly-full of Police Stations to last me a lifetime. "We will give you a ring and send a car for you if we need you." Cheeky sod. He didn't look too happy when I said, "Not tonight you won't, you've had all you're getting out of me for today". The whole episode was mind-boggling and I can just imagine that Sergeant in a courtroom, right now, reading out his written evidence: "I was proceeding in the course of my duty and on several occasions, five in total My Lord, I had cause to remind the Lady of the necessity for accuracy in her testimony, as she was totally ignoring the fact that she was supplying vital information, crucial to my enquiry and without which I would still be a useless numb copper. Without her co-operation, encouraged I must add, My Lord, by leaving her alone for long periods in an empty room, I would not have achieved anything or got anywhere and would still be as thick as pig muck. A problem I have had for most of my life, My Lord."

'He certainly got under your skin.'

'Not only him, the whole damned lot of them before they had finished and the way they went about it. Once we were out of that Conference Room their whole attitude changed and I knew they had rattled you also because I could see it plainly on your face.'

She walked across the room, stood in front of me, and gently wrapped her arms round my shoulders, placing her cheek against mine, she sighed. 'I've had enough for today. Shower and bed and I don't care if it is only a three quarter bed or the shower isn't big enough for us both to squeeze in. We will work something out.'

'You wouldn't rather go for a walk to blow off all the cobwebs and cool down, or go somewhere for a drink, or something like that?'

'No. We might bump into Eddie and much as I like him I couldn't face even talking to Eddie tonight. We would end up talking shop and that would be just too much. I have made up my mind. I am going to shower and crawl into bed and

screw my favourite man. If you would care to join me you will be most welcome,' and releasing her arms from round my shoulders she stepped back and pulled her jumper up over her head. All ideas of going out for a walk were immediately cancelled and the idea of a shower became very attractive.

We may have got into bed early that night, but we certainly did not get to sleep until quite late.

CHAPTER FIFTY-ONE

The telephone at the side of the bed shattered my dreams. I reached out and lifted it off its cradle. Fred stirred, groaned, and turned over.

'Yes,' I said.

I listened to the voice on the other end, trying desperately to absorb what it was saying, when he finished, I hung up.

'Come on lazy bones, time to get up.'

'Who was that at this unearthly hour of the morning?'

'Take a look at the time. It is not that unearthly. Anyhow we have to get up. That was some of your favourite people from the nick. We are invited to attend and a car is being sent round to collect us.'

Everyone was already assembled in the Conference Room when we arrived and it was obvious by the lack of conversation that they were waiting for us. All the same faces, from the day before, were there and all seated in more or less the same places they had previously occupied. There was however, one exception. Seated between Williams the Customs man and Jones the Drug Squad Officer, was a thickset man in plain clothes. He was a complete stranger and someone I had not seen before. In front of him, on the table, was a substantial file.

Chief Superintendent Adams, from his seat at the head of the table, opened the proceedings, 'Good morning Ladies and Gentlemen. Before we get underway with today's business, I would like to introduce Inspector Cameron of the Royal Ulster Constabulary.'

The newcomer politely nodded but said nothing. The Chief Inspector continued, 'He has a special interest in this case, as part of an on-going investigations and will, in due course, make a valuable contribution to our enquiries. In the meantime, to start the business for today... The man Whiting, who we only previously knew as the Fisherman, was readily recognised from the photographs supplied by the Coastguard, and was arrested during the early hours of this morning while attempting to board a deep sea fishing vessel in Whitby harbour. He was brought here and is currently in detention and is being interviewed at this moment. I hope shortly to have a transcript of the interview, but while we are waiting for that, let us deal with the prisoner, or should I say detainee, Johnson. I have chosen to deal with him first, because of all those interviewed, he proved to be, as we say in Police jargon, the most cooperative. Of them all and that includes his wife he was the weakest. According to the Interviewing Officer's report,' and he hesitated as he shuffled through the papers in front of him, before selecting one and then reading from it, "The level of Johnson's intelligence is not very high.

He was easily confused and this was used to confuse him and to our advantage." The officer goes on to explain that Johnson, when told the others were pleading innocence and had all placed the blame on him, quickly implicated all of them, in his attempt to shift the accusations away from himself. At that point we knew little about their activities but, with bluff, we managed to convince him that we knew everything. When it came to those areas where our information was a bit sketchy, the officers skirted round it, or fabricated something, which they hoped, sounded convincing and it obviously worked. However, the threat to blame everything on him and hints as to the severe penalties he might get the result of that, did the trick. He fell for the age-old ploy of - "tell us everything you know and we will go easy on you". He obviously isn't bright enough to realise that it has nothing to do with us and that in the end it is all down to the Courts to decide the sentence and punishments. Also according to this report he was very shaken when it was hinted that the Home Secretary was being lobbied by the Chief Constables Association to consider reintroducing the death penalty for terrorists, drugs and arms dealers. Not strictly true of course, although it may well have been discussed at some point and might have been mentioned publicly at some time.'

He hesitated and checked his notes before continuing, 'Most things relating to crime or law and order, come up from time to time for an airing and I am sure the suggestion of hanging arms dealers, will have had its turn. On these issues we allow ourselves a little licence if it achieves our aims and rids, like now, society of some of its rubbish. To add to his agony, he was told that arms dealing might be considered by some Courts to be treason and that the death penalty was still in force for that. We all know of course, that the death penalty still does exist for treason. We also know it has not been used since the late Forties for that crime, but no one cared to elaborate on that to Johnson. Nevertheless it appeared to rattle him sufficiently to work to our advantage. Johnson, although up to his neck in this operation, is only a minion in the whole set up. His part in it is virtually nothing, but, never the less, he knows enough about it to be of value for our purposes. He is a local man who was easily recruited for cash and was, because of the substantial amounts of money involved, reasonably reliable to keep his mouth shut. In other words, he did as he was told as long as he was well paid. He was more muscle than brain and there mainly to be used in that capacity, as and when required. The builder Thornton used him to help bring in drugs and alcohol and to distribute them. The others used him for the heavy work in the arms dealings. He swears he knows nothing about the arms. He claims he was paid to carry boxes from the beach to the Car Park. He says he did not know what the cases contained or where they went after they left the Car Park. We of course, said he did and that we could prove it and from that, we said we were going to charge him with organising all the deals, being responsible for transport and distribution and that all the others were employed and paid by him. We know of course that none of it is

true, but it worked to loosen him up. When confronted with the evidence of drugs and alcohol found in his home, which incidentally amounted to very little, he was only then too willing to implicate Thornton the builder and his wife. According to this transcript, Johnson knew considerably more about the drug deals, than he did about the arms. He claims that Thornton purchased, legally, through his wife's business, large quantities of quality clothing, mainly Denim Jeans. These were exchanged via foreign vessels, for drugs and alcohol. He insists he knows nothing of the arrangements for deliveries, but went down to the beach to collect and pay for goods when the Builder told him to. He said the Builder gave him the money and told him when exactly to go. He then went, later, with the builder Thornton, to distribute them. Thornton was the banker. Johnson received cash payments for his contribution and was allowed to sell a proportion of the alcohol for his own personal gain and as a form of bonus. He also retained small quantities of the soft drug, cannabis resin, known as slate, for his own use. He unwittingly implicated his own wife when he admitted she sold small quantities to friends and acquaintances. When asked why clothing was used in the dealings, he stated that he really did not know, but remembered that at one time, Thornton, had remarked that anything with a Marks and Spencer label on it was more valuable than cash. He apparently doesn't understand the logic in that and claimed that he only did as he was told.'

'More valuable than hard currency; almost impossible to trace and very easy to get rid of in Central and Northern Europe, where a pair of Jeans costs more than a month's wages,' Interrupted Ron Williams, the Customs man. 'When currency is involved, it has to be exchanged or dealt further and in the process and particularly in the hands of illegal dealers, can and naturally does lose some of its value. On the other hand, where something is very desirable, fashionable and in very short supply, as in the case of Denim Jeans and the likes, means that in the Communist States, at the moment, inflated prices can be and are charged and so profits are good and very high. Making the dealings, generally, worthwhile and the overall trading more lucrative than it would be in the case of straightforward cash transactions. There is also much less chance that someone, perhaps in authority, concerning themselves over the origin of a pair of Jeans or Marks and Spencer underwear, than they would over Bank of England Bank Notes which could, without doubt, attract a lot of unwarranted attention. Although I must admit, that it is a well know fact, that hard currency of any denomination, or country of origin, is always welcome in the, so called, Eastern Block and always has been.'

The Superintendent waited politely until he had finished then continued, 'We accused him of discharging a Shotgun at Mr Scott's car and claimed we could prove that the gun, taken from his wife, was the same one that he used, to shoot at the car. Of course we can't do that as we only have, as evidence, mutilated and spent lead pellets taken from the car. They don't have any traceable identification marks on them that could link them with any particular firearm. Even taking the

pellets from the car and trying to link them to an un-discharged cartridge in his possession, would be extremely difficult and perhaps impossible. When we said that all we had to do was prove it had been discharged recently, he made a very bad mistake. He said we couldn't prove anything by that, as it had been fired several times since he shot at the car, so our claims didn't prove anything. When the officer, in charge of the interview, pointed out that proof was no longer necessary, as his own statement was now sufficient, he became confused and claimed that he had shot at the car, but did so for no reason and couldn't understand what all the fuss was about. He said he was drunk at the time and that he, and a lot more like him, was fed up with strangers around the place. He blamed their presence for deterring the local Landlords from buying his booze. So, according to him, he just shot at the car to scare off the owner and warn off everyone else. We have since made arrangements for the car to be collected from the village and impounded as evidence. Sorry about that Mr Scott. It will, of course, be released back to you in due course, but, for the moment, back to Johnson.'

'That's very kind of you,' muttered Eddie, without looking up.

'Whenever we mentioned anything in connection with his wife, Johnson did his utmost to protect her, claiming that she was totally innocent of everything, and that she only sold cannabis to supplement their income when his was low. She had only produced the shotgun to protect him and their children. The officer states that he made no comment when he was asked, if he could produce a licence and gun certificate for the firearm. So far so good and according to this, that appears to be as far as we have gone with Johnson. I propose to deal, in detail, next with Mrs Johnson, but for the moment we must leave Johnson himself, as his interviews have been suspended for a short time, to allow him to sweat a little and while he does that, we will use what we have gleaned from him, on the others.'

'And what about Mrs Johnson, Mr Adams?' enquired Fred. 'What of the charming Pauline?' and leaning towards me, added, in a lowered voice, 'I still think Lena suits her better and I wonder if she has had a wash or combed her hair since we last saw her?'

'Yes. Mrs Johnson!' As he rummaged through his papers and re-arranged them. 'According to the Arresting Officers report, which I have before me, Mrs Johnson's attempted to interfere with Johnson's arrest by producing a Shotgun and threatening to use it. She did in fact discharge one cartridge into the air that resulted in her overbalancing and falling, due to her not being totally familiar with the firearm. While recovering, she was overpowered and the gun taken away from her. According to the report, she said at the time, that she would kill Johnson before she would let them take him away. She was, she said, going to kill everyone present, then her children and finally herself. When the firearm was examined by a Police officer, it was found to have been loaded with only one single cartridge. She had no additional ones about her person and none were found in the house. Later in

her statement, made in custody, she claimed she did it because she was frightened that they would find drugs in the house and Johnson would be in trouble. When questioned about her husband's relationship with Thornton the builder, she claimed he did casual work for him and went fishing with him most Sundays because he paid Johnson cash to show him how to fish. That is an obvious lie, but was probably based on the story told to her, by the husband. She told us that the Builder's wife, who she affectionately referred to throughout as, "A stuck up cow" - was probably responsible for informing the Police and getting them all arrested. She had some strange notion that the Builder's wife is jealous of her, didn't like her children because she didn't have any of her own and resented her husband going fishing with Johnson. She further claimed that Mrs Thornton resented the fact that Johnson supplied her husband with an ample supply of cheap alcohol. We of course realise it was probable the other way round and it was the Builder who did the supplying and Mrs Johnson who was jealous. However, that is speculation on our part and we must stick to the facts. Finally, when questioned about Philip Edison, she claimed she did not know him. We of course are keeping an open mind on that.'

'You are right about the jealousy. If you saw both women together you would soon realise that Mrs Thornton is in a different league and has very little to be jealous of in Mrs Johnson. What do you think Mel? Don't you agree? You have seen them both,' said Fred.

'They are definitely as different as chalk and cheese and Mrs Thornton is without doubt in a superior league,' I replied.

'If anyone were to be jealous it would definitely be Lena Johnson of Mrs Thornton, or "Fancy Pants" as we have often heard her called,' added Fred.

The Superintendent re-arranged his papers once more before continuing. 'We are still interviewing the village Police Officer and the two Pub Landlords. We propose to take statements from them all.'

He flicked through more papers, spread out in front of him, and stated, 'That appears to be the position regarding them. As for the others, we are currently finding Whiting a hard nut to crack and interviews so far with Mrs Raines, indicates we may have a struggle there.'

'Mrs Raines?'

'Yes, she is deeply implicated and has therefore been brought in with the rest, as you will learn in due course from Mr Cameron, when he gives his report. Before that there are one or two minor points which Inspector Molescroft here, will now clear up for us.'

'Thank you, Sir! As you may, or may not know, Mrs Edison formally identified the body as being that of her husband Philip Edison. She is currently being interviewed and I expect a report shortly. In your statements, Miss Huntington and you, Mr Grundy, you both made reference to the fact that a body had been washed up on the beach and the fact widely publicised and at the time you believed it might

have been Edison and the publicity from it did little to help your investigation. The identification of this person still remains a mystery and probably always will be, along with many others who, over the years, have been lost overboard from foreign vessels and ended up on our shores. Some foreign countries have, to say the least, some peculiar ways of dealing with people lost at sea. They often don't bother to inform us if someone goes missing from a vessel that happens to be sailing close to our shores. What they do about it back at home, we have no means of knowing. We have had, in the past, some intelligence, passed to us by other agencies, that indicates that they are quite capable of disposing of the odd "nuisance body" over the side of a ship if it suits their political or criminal purposes. We are therefore always suspicious when a body washes up totally devoid of any form of identification. We can only hope that someone, in the foreseeable future, might make enquiries about a missing person and give us some clues to help solve the mystery. In the meantime all we can do is dispose of the body, as prescribed by law in these circumstances and leave the file open. Finally, and to conclude my report for today, a question you put to us earlier Miss Huntington, regarding mud removed from your Trainer Shoe and from the tyres of Scampton's Land Rover. The samples matched each other and also matched a further sample taken from the lane, which led up to the Sawmill, in the forest. Useful circumstantial evidence to use against Scampton.'

'Does that conclude your report for this meeting Inspector?'

'For the moment, yes sir.'

'Thank you Mr Molescroft! Perhaps now, you will give us the Customs and Excise report Mr Williams.'

'Thank you Chief Superintendent! Good morning Ladies and Gentlemen. I don't have to remind you good people, gathered here round this table, that Customs and Excise are very active in all forms of illegal activity. Nor do I want to sound as if I am lecturing you all, when I remind you that, originally our concern was to prevent the Revenue from being cheated out of its dues, as a result of any illegal trading, falsification of accounts or documentation, in particular the import and export of goods on which a Government duty was levied. However, over the years, our brief has expanded by Government decree until now, there are not many areas left, in which we don't have some form of interest. As a result we collect and collate a vast amount of information and intelligence that we either use ourselves, or make available to other interested parties. Amongst many other things, we were getting strong hints that there might be some form of illegal activity in this area. In fact we were almost certain there was something, when one of our patrol vessels had cause, for another reasons, to board a small vessel off the Norfolk coast. During a search they found charts, in the wheelhouse, that clearly showed markings, bearings and tidal information applicable to this area. At that time that vessel was clean, as we say, when we can't find anything on which to detain it and

so it was allowed to proceed on passage. Nevertheless, the chart information was recorded and we decided to investigate further and one of our men was sent to take a closer look. When he arrived he found the Coastguard people already there and decisions taken at a higher level, decided that, in the best interests of all concerned, he should be temporarily withdrawn. I see you mention that fact in your statement, so you obviously met him.

'And kicked him out,' wrote Fred on her pad before sliding it sideways, to me. I tore the sheet off and put it in my pocket.

'We have known and no doubt you all know, that for quite some time, vast quantities of illegal drugs, of every description, and illegal spirits, along with many other things; electronic equipment, pornography and the likes, have all been finding their way into this country. Of the drugs in particular and this area of Northern England, it has been mainly cannabis resin, which before it arrived here, started out from a number of locations spread throughout the world. The spirits, which recently, have been mainly Polish, Russian and Bulgarian Vodka, have continued to creep in, in ever increasing amounts and could have started out from almost anywhere. They will continue to be part of a lucrative illegal trade as long as we, in this country, impose high levels of duty on them. We also know it comes in, in relatively small quantities, in terms of bulk and volume, but it is the frequency, of the individual trips, that builds up the total amount and results in the overall embarrassing quantities being distributed across the countryside. I don't have to remind you of all the hundreds and thousands of sailings, of small vessels, of all types and sizes, that there are, at any one time, in and out of British ports and along our coastline and taking place all year round. Some of these are very small, sail rigged pleasure boats or yachts and some are powerful launches and cabin cruisers. It is virtually impossible for anyone to observe them either physically or electronically, let alone log them all. So we, with our limited resources, have to target specific areas at certain predetermined times and concentrate on those. In the meantime everyone else, employed on illicit dealings, is free to get on with it. The North Sea is no exception and sees well above its fair share of illegal trips. The continent is very close and the winds, tides, and weather are ideal for anyone who chooses to get up to no good. Anyone who has experienced a good North Sea fog or sea-fret will tell you that conditions round here can, for most part of the year, be ideal. There are dozens or even perhaps hundreds, of small commercial harbours, suitable inlets, and uninhabited coves all along the East coast, which will provide safe landing grounds for almost anything. These areas are particularly useful and vulnerable to exploitation, during the hours of darkness, but even that is not necessary. Who takes any notice if one of their own, locally known, pleasure boats sets sail and returns from a pleasant days sailing, that same evening, or even returns the following morning - no one. Who knows what changed hands over the horizon? We know that, beside ourselves, the local Coastguard and the Port

Authorities do their utmost, but each one has its own priorities that absorb most of its time and resources. We therefore have to rely on luck, random spot checks and collected intelligence. Fortunately, all of which have improved tremendously in recent years. In recent times we have also had problems with the smuggling of illegal immigrants. Knowing what little attention we have been able to give to this and other areas, I shudder to think how many illegal immigrants there are, in this country at the moment that passed through any one of a hundred possible safe entry points along this coast alone. I believe that if we were to grant them all amnesty, many clothing firms and many of the thousands of sweatshops there are in the inner cities, would probably collapse through a lack of cheap labour. They need only to arrive in ones and twos at a time, but then multiply that by the number of small boats that can, and do, sail into isolated spots at night and the potential is frightening. If fifty per cent get caught, it may look good for immigration and government statistics, but then what happens? They are sent back only to save up and try again, probably with success, next time. I received an intelligence report, submitted by one of our chaps working along this coast, who reported that while relaxing in a Seafront Pub, he actually overheard a guy bragging to colleagues, that if he was short of cash and the fishing was bad he "fuelled up, bought a few bottles of Newcastle Brown ale and nipped across the water and brought back a couple of 'wogs'. Quick five hundred quid," he boasted. When asked what happens if he is intercepted on passage out, he stated that he would say he was on a pleasure trip and that is perfectly legal. If intercepted on the way back he would say that they had hired him for the day and to cover that he always had fishing rods and lines out, which were, in actual fact, part of his legitimate business. He would then promptly turn back, to avoid suspicion and dump them off at the nearest continental port. His final brag was "what could they charge me with? I'd not landed them." But he also stated; and I think this is quite significant, that on one occasion, when apprehended, on this side, with a Dutchman on board, he had, as a result, spent a few days in jail, been fined and the Dutchman sent back. All worthwhile; if only for the amount of cash he had retained or could make up later, he claimed. So you see, we have almost insurmountable problems with the very limited resources at our disposal and the vast arena we have to cover. We are therefore, very grateful when people, like yourselves, who are usually involved in investigating something else, stumble on, or painstakingly work something out and pass the results onto us. Customs and Excise are always very grateful for any assistance they can get, which is more than can be said for the thanks they received from the general public, who choose to ignore their role in preventing the spread of drugs and the likes and only see them as evil Tax Collectors. Do you know and forgive me for digressing for a moment, but Customs and Excise now play and fulfil the part of being Britain's National Sport? It used to be Cricket, but not anymore. Britain's National Sport is now, without doubt, Tax Evasion. We are one team, who stand-alone and all the

rest are on the opposing side, and the idea of the game is to avoid, by any means, the payment of tax, but enough of us and our prejudices and petty problems. Let us once again be serious and deal, at this point, with the arms and ammunition and with that, of course, I include the explosives.'

'Before you do Mr Williams, where do you believe most of the drugs, which end up on the East coast, come from?' enquired Adams. 'You did say, they can come from a variety of sources, but where do you think the majority comes from at present, or is that rather a silly question?'

'Not at all and as I said, they come from all over the world and pass along very long and devious routes, often covering thousands of miles and changing hands many times before ending up here. The last leg of their journey often takes the shortest route and by that I mean via the cross Channel ports. That is why we target those areas and give them as much saturation as we possibly can. That unfortunately leaves other areas a little thin and the drug boys are quick to catch onto this. Therefore of recent times, Holland has become a favourite and from that the East Coast. I am not blaming the Dutch, for I know the Dutch Government is doing all it can to curtail these activities, despite its own liberal attitude towards soft drugs. But they have the same problems as us, as unfortunately, there are good and bad on both sides of the water, and ours, and their problem is catching them. We do have our successes and I have to admit that when caught the Courts deal quite harshly with them. Unfortunately however, when that happens, someone else usually takes over and plugs the gap and the evil trade goes on. As I said, routes vary, as pressure is applied and are often changed very quickly when special attention, or the spot light, so to speak, is turned on them. At the moment we're concerned over the amount the Spanish are allowing to get into their country from North Africa. Africa being the vast, unsophisticated country that it is, is an easy target for world suppliers. It is than a relatively short haul into Spain and from there the rest of Europe. So to answer your question, at the moment, Holland, Spain, Belgium, France, but not necessarily in that order and not necessarily limited to only those countries, are quite active. Remember this is big business, so those involved are very cleaver and can switch their activities at almost a moments notice, so all we can hope to do, is occasionally get one step ahead of them and cramp their style.'

'Do the arms, ammunition and explosives come from the same sources then?' asked Adams.

'Some may well do, for we do know that arms and ammunition are available, in unacceptable quantities, from a wide variety or sources. Vast quantities of arms and explosives are being moved around the world all the time, both legally and illegally and while they do, large quantities are apt to slip out of the system and disappear, so to speak. Corrupt Governments and their employees, agents and even relations, and sadly there are quite a few of those, see to that. How do you think Libya's Gadaffi or Iraq's Saddam Hussein get all theirs when the bigger nations

put arms embargoes on them? Then there's Angola, Somalia, Palestine, or should I say the Lebanon, Kazakhstan, and Afghanistan to mention only a few? There are also people very close to home. Remember the Big Guns to Iraq and the American Contra arms deals; there are people willing to buy and sell every kind of weapon with which to wage war or terrorism. Our chaps in the Falkland's conflict were trying to stop missiles hitting them that had "Made in France" stamped all over them and we and them are both in the Common Market.

We are fortunate in some respects and the situation is not as bad as it might be, because of the unique position we occupy as an island, but as time passes even that does not protect us completely and increasing amounts find their way onto our shores. Wait until the Common Market becomes a full European Union, the floodgates will really open then. Even the present liberal attitudes towards boarders aren't helping very much, so what it will become later, I shudder to think. But for the moment, along this East coast, all our intelligence tells us that the majority of hardware is coming from Poland and associated territories. Polish factory ships are a common site in the North Sea and are accepted as long as they pursue their legitimate business, which unfortunately for us is not always the case and provides them, through their methods of working, with opportunities to get up to all sorts of double dealing. Each large vessel employs, as part of the set up, several smaller ones, usually around six, who's individual function is to dredge the sea clean of all and every type, of fish that they come across, without thoughts of conservation or the future. These factory ships and there are one hell of a lot of them, from other continental countries as well as Poland, have insatiable appetites and devour millions of tons of fish per year to keep their on-board canning plants operating twenty four hours a day. But despite this, most of the countries of origin, for these vessels and this includes Poland, are economically very poor and the Skippers of these State-owned floating factories are not exactly overpaid, nor are their crews. So it doesn't take much imagination to realise what happens if someone puts a lucrative proposition to them whereby they could earn a lot of extra cash on the side.'

'So how do they work it?'

'Basically the factory ship, or Mother Ship, steams back and forth through the North sea collecting fish from the support fishing vessels which accompany her and by the way, as a point of interest, our own fishing boats have been known to sell their catches to these floating factories. That is usually if their catch is likely to attract attention at home, because of Ministerial legislation imposed on size, or restricted type. So why then, according to the rules, dump it at sea, when there is readily available floating market that pays cash and asks no questions. But to get back to how they operate. At predetermined times, set up through simple contacts, the factory ship arrives at a predetermined point and anchors. Nothing illegal in that, particularly if it is just outside territorial waters and in our case, that is

only twelve miles. Some of them are very cheeky and come in closer, claiming breakdown or power failure and then blame the wind and tide for causing them to drift in towards the coast. These however are few and far between because once in our territorial waters, they tend to draw attention to themselves. You see, that when they claim breakdown, having been challenged and the reasons for their present location requested, over the airwaves, they attract numerous offers of help. The locals can be very quick to seize the opportunity to earn a little from a big boat in trouble. However, that is digressing, but still gives you part of the overall picture of how things work out. As I said, the factory ship anchors at a predetermined place and at an agreed time. No one takes any particular notice of it and in fact and quite often it might not be the only vessel doing so at the time. The Master continues his business of unloading his feeder trawlers, taking their catches on board and processing, canning or freezing them, below decks. Under cover of darkness, again at a predetermined time, one of the support trawlers quietly slips away from the main group and slowly eases her way, the few miles, towards the shore. Once close in, she stops and if challenged, will in her turn, claim breakdown and drifting tides, or faulty navigation equipment. If not and all is quiet, a small boat will be lowered, over the side, and the illicit cargo rowed ashore to be picked up by the likes of the group we now have in custody.'

'How do they get away with it so easily?'

'Because no one, of consequence, sees them, that's why. During the night there are very few people about, anywhere along the coastline, to see anything and if there are, and they do see something, then due to their lack of knowledge, or ignorance, they simply ignore it. They see a vessel close in, so what? We see dozens of our own vessels during any single day of the week and everyone knows that they also go about their business at night. They are a very common sight and all vessels look alike to a landlubber. As for our own seamen, it might be different. They might recognise the vessel, but why do anything about it, after all, don't they too, go all over the North sea and sometimes, through no fault of their own, get close to foreign shores and do things which might be considered a bit naughty, so what is wrong with the situation in reverse? If a vessel is just sat there, bobbing about and making no attempt to fish in our territorial waters, then to our fishermen, he is doing no harm. Nine times out of ten, one of our own vessels, out at sea and passing close bye, would probably call the stranger, on the radio and ask him if all is well. When assured it was, they would pass on their way. Fishermen, in particular, live in a different world once they get out to sea. To them, at sea, survival is paramount and towards that they will give help when requested and expect it back when it is needed. But apart from that they tend to just get on with the hazardous and precarious business of earning a living, mind their own business while doing so, and leave everyone else to get on with theirs. Life, at sea, can be tough enough without interfering or concerning ones self with other

people. Spare a thought for these guys, will you, the next time you are eating Fish and Chips. The fish did not come to you easily. Or think, the next time you eat a tinned Norwegian pilchard, it may have been caught by a British boat, sold to an Eastern Block factory ship, canned by them and then sold on, to the Norwegians, for export to this country. So you can see, the foreign trawler has little to fear from other shipping. He also has and it is improving all the time, sophisticated electronic equipment on board, which will tell him, long before it comes into sight, if any other vessel is approaching. If he's then in any doubt, he has ample time to break off the illegal operation, stop his engines and hoist the necessary signal flags - "Stay Clear. Manoeuvring with Difficulty" - intimating also power failure and thereby giving to him-self an excuse for not answering any radio calls when hailed. Or he may even simply put the vessel into drive and calmly steam away. Don't forget, he does not have far to travel before he no longer attracts attention as he will be once again outside our territorial waters and therefore our jurisdiction.'

'But I thought the Navy had patrol boats to specifically check on things like that?'

'They do. They are known as - Fishery Protection - vessels. The Navy provides and man them, but they are primarily to look after the interests of the Ministry of Agriculture and Fisheries and not exclusively for Customs use. Their main task is to protect anything associated with our national interests and as I say, in particular fishing. Also, with only two or three operating at any one time, round the whole of the United Kingdom, what real chance have they? They do a marvellous job and they do provide intelligence to anyone who maybe able to use it and whilst they are considered to be the Policemen of the sea, they are like most other agencies, limited in what they can do with their resources, so tend to concentrate on chasing the "big fish." Granted they supplement their main capability with small shore based craft; there's one such vessel based in Whitby. But the sea is so vast and so busy and they too, are stretched so thinly, that they are virtually fighting a loosing battle. But having said that, if they weren't there, or we were not there, and not forgetting the Coastguard, then this country would have a massive drugs and arms problem. But then that, sadly, in itself, becomes a debateable point, for there are those who would argue that we already have a massive problem and that if it hasn't already reached a point of no return, then it can't be far off. I would like to think otherwise.'

'Is drug dealing, on the scale that Johnson does, or should I say, Johnson did, profitable?' asked Fred.

'Very. The demand is so great that the street value is very high and therefore even small quantities are very valuable and realise vast sums and profits. Intelligence tends to tell us that each time a quantity of drugs changes hands it can double and often treble in value up to the point where it reaches the user. So, take the one small operation we have just uncovered. If drugs to the value of only a

thousand pounds, purchase price, are landed, they are worth two or three thousand by the time Johnson's team have stored them away. In other words, that is what they can expect to get for them when they sell them on and this is on only one delivery. Multiply that by the frequency of deliveries and you have a very lucrative income for the likes of Johnson and his cronies.'

'You said, take drugs worth only a thousand pounds. What do you mean - only?'

'I used that figure only to illustrate my point. The actual amounts involved are probably considerably more. You see, relative to their size and bulk, drugs are very valuable. So you will be able to work it out for yourself, the kind of profits involved relative to the volume handled. Take cannabis. Cannabis, of a relatively good quality and worth a thousand pounds import purchase price, could easily be carried away in a Tesco plastic bag. To illustrate further, not long ago, a large red fire extinguisher was removed from a Fishing Trawler, in the Yarmouth area. It contained, good quality, hard drugs and had a street value, in other words, the top price the user pays, of half a million pounds. A yacht and just think how big the average family owned yacht is, sank off the North East coast and was known to have a cargo of cannabis resin on board, one of the cheapest and commonest drugs, to the street value of five and a half million pounds. Need I say more?'

'I shudder to think what the really big boys make,' added Fred.

'Let's put it this way, Miss. I don't think gambling, numbers rackets, prostitution, or bootlegging, or any of the other old Mafia favourites, are any longer in the top ten of illegal businesses.'

'At that rate and dealing in those amounts, I am sure they are not.'

'A tremendous amount of profit is being made out of the drug scene, not to mention the harm and decimation that goes with it and there are whispers that the amount of money involved world wide, is starting to have an effect on the world's economy. A frightening thought and yet it can happen if the amount of money involved, becomes big enough and a very large proportion of the population becomes drug orientated. Which, let's face it, is rapidly heading that way on almost a daily basis. In some areas of the world drugs are the only commodity that count for anything and the underworld backing it is frightening. But all the time we, in this country, are getting better and slicker, or we like to think we are and as a result, more and more of the bigger boys are getting caught. Let's hope for all our sakes that if things don't get any better in the short term, at least they don't get worse. If only the world's governments would come together and formulate a plan, to wipe out the whole scourge. But they won't because politics and corruption have become inexplicably involved and run right through the middle of it all and whenever this subject comes up for discussion, I always think of the Americans, so called world leaders and policy makers, who cultivated and manufactured cocaine, to feed their own troops in Vietnam. The Vietcong quickly latched on to this and flooded the

market. The Americans lost the war. Try convincing idiots like that, that there is a problem. Sorry we are getting way off the main subject again, but until we get to the bottom of the philosophy behind it all, we have no chance of finding a permanent solution. But to come back nearer to home and our present priorities, all we can do is keep nibbling steadily away at it, in the hope that one-day we might win. As long as we can keep on removing the Johnson's of this world, we must be achieving something. I know there is the argument, often put forward by those in despair, that each time you take one out, there are two ready to step in and take his place. I know this is true and that is why we must keep on after them until they are eventually starved out by the elimination of the big boys, the growers or producers and the manufacturers.'

'Do you see that happening?'

'Definitely not in the short term no. Not as long as Governments and Dictators, are directly or indirectly involved. Not as long as the youngsters have the money, or can get the money, by stealing or what have you, to buy and create a demand for the stuff. As long as that state of affair exists, then so will demand and that demand will remain until the fashion dies out.'

'Do you see that happening?' asked Fred.

'No, I am sorry to say; that is something that I again just can't see happening in the foreseeable future. Drug taking may eventually go out of fashion and the users may finally destroy the industry, but not as long as there is the imbalance within the world's economy. As long as you have poverty, haves and have-nots, then such people as farmers, in under-developed countries, will grow literally any cash crop that sells for high prices. Corrupt and bankrupt Government, forced into that position, by affluent Western Governments are happy to turn a blind eye to what is going on, or to even join in to share the spoils. It keeps their population quiet, particularly if they encourage the abuse amongst their own people. It keeps them all happy and inactive. It stops revolutions and backs corrupt administrations. It buys guns and who better than the high moralistic West, to supply them and the whole rotten world is happy to sit back and let it all happen, because a very large proportion of it is, no doubt, as high as a bloody kite. I bet the chinks are laughing like drains as they sit back and with their infinite patience, wait for us all to eventually, economically, if not physically, destroy ourselves and then, when we, particularly in the West, are all a nation of junkies, sweep us to one side or if it comes to a push, wipe us out.'

'Have you Mr Williams, by any chance, got any strong political views that make you feel as you do and express yourself in this manner and so strongly,' asked Adams.

'Hell no and forgive me if that is the impression I have given. I leave that very much to other people. If anything I am the opposite and have no interest in politics or anything remotely connected with them. If I can be accused of being

anything, then it will be that I am a Customs and Excise man, who does my job to the best of my ability and who cares very much for my fellow man and does not feel too happy at the way thing appear to be going at the moment. No I have no political persuasions nor do I support any radical movements, if you are thinking along the lines of the anti-establishment schools of thought and the likes. My job brings me into close contact with this sort of thing and I think about it a lot and just don't like what I am seeing at the moment. That's all.'

'Some may not see it quite like that.'

'Then that is their worry because that is how it is, and can I ask you, Inspector, why are you so interested in my possible political persuasion?'

'Because; you feel so strongly about it and that's all. But let us not forget why we are here and it is not to investigate you. Is it?

Fred and I exchanged glances. The others all sat in silence.

Fred took it upon herself to release the tension. 'I know we are drifting away from the main point, but I find all this fascinating and I love to hear other people express different points of view. Before we move on can I go back, for a moment, to one of the points you raised? You said as long as it is in fashion, the youngsters will buy it. What do you mean by fashion? Surely drugs are not fashionable?'

Williams, unperturbed and unruffled answered, 'Yes they are Miss and it is not only the youngsters, sadly, who are keeping them in fashion and I believe, at the moment, that our only hope is for these drugs to go out of fashion. Kids and youth and for that matter a large proportion of our population in general, are fickle, always have been, always will be and each generation has its fazes, fads and fashions. I know some people want to view drugs as an entirely whole new ball game, something new and permanent. But I hope it isn't and that it will go the same way as - Ban the Bomb – Beetle-mania - Elvis - Flower Power and Burn your Bra. I might even include the Mini-skirt although that was one fashion I truly appreciate and don't consider corrupting. But it is never the less a fashion which goes the rounds. Even Hoolla-Hoops and Rubik Cubes came and went and who would have thought we would see the collapse of Communism or the demise the Great British Pub, but we have and so I remain the eternal optimist and hope that, eventually society will wake up before it destroys itself and drugs will slip quietly into history and take their place along side the ancient sport of throwing Christians to the Lions or more recently, the burning of Jews in large numbers. Whenever I feel depressed about the whole thing I tend to look back and remember our own government, who were adamant, quite a few years ago now, that the AIDs virus would wipe out the whole population and do so, in a very short period of time and a decade along, granted it is still with us, but has not done any irreparable damage and will soon find its place in history along with all the other diseases that were to wipe us out when they came along, the plague, polio, diphtheria,

syphilis, tuberculosis and dozens of others that have all come and gone and for which permanent cures have been found.'

'Thank you so much! I could discuss this and talk to you about it for hours. But sadly this is not the time or the place, so once again, thank you.'

'My pleasure Miss. But please don't think I have the answers to anything or that, as Mr Adams thinks, I am a Chinese Communist or something like that. To repeat myself, I am only a humble Customs Man, doing my job, to the best of my ability. Where the real answers lie, is anybodies guess and beyond me.'

'Aren't we all,' echoed Adams causing everyone to look in his direction through lack of understanding.

'Aren't we all, what?' asked Fred.

'Doing our best, Miss.'

'Yes, I do believe that, in general, we are. Although earlier I began to have some doubts when dealing with your men. I am sure someone had forgotten to tell them, that there are other people, beside themselves, involved in this business and all on the same side and doing their best.'

Adams said nothing, while the Customs Man continued, 'I think I have said enough about drugs for the moment and hope you will all forgive me for waffling on a bit and expressing some of my strong views. But now let me see if I can summarise the arms issue, from the Customs point of view. As long as there is a demand, the result of conflicts, such as we currently have in Northern Ireland, to use a ready made market and an illustration from close to home, then there will always be, as is the case with drugs, a willing supplier. People like Gadaffi are not only willing suppliers, but are quite open about it and laugh in the face of opposition. But sadly no Government, in the world, has clean hands as far as arms and arms dealing is concerned and that is not one of my pet theories Inspector.'

I could see now that the Inspectors' earlier remarks had not entirely gone un-noticed by Williams. To hear the pair of them in debate might have been quite interesting. Sadly this was not the time or the place.

Williams continued, 'In the United States alone, the manufacture and supply of arms is a stable part of their economy. Without war, any one's war, they cannot survive. Why do you think they start so many, or become directly or indirectly involved in other peoples? Look for a conflict anywhere in the world and the yanks won't be too far away. The French and Belgians will sell to anyone and we, in this country, have above our fair share of dodgy dealers. So there is, as you can see, a similarity between drugs and arms. As long as there is a demand, someone will be willing to supply. It is as simple as that. Fortunately in this country, despite the small demand created by the criminal fraternity, we do not have a big arms problem of our own, as yet; and I say as yet, because the drug dealers are slowly increasing the demand as their belief in the need to protect themselves increases. Therefore the vast majority of arms and explosives that do come into this country

are brought in by outside organisations, who's propose to ship them out later, or use them to create terror here. Who knows what they have planned for them. We do our best, along side all the other agencies, to find out and that basically is all I have to say about arms.'

'Thank you! I am sure we are now much clearer in our minds as to how these things come about and how simple it is to satisfy demand. I also find your opinions very stimulating, to say the least and do hope you are wrong on several points. However, I have one last question, if I may?'

'Go ahead and please ask Mr Adams.'

'Why bring arms here when they are destined for Ireland, which we assume most of them are, or for that matter, when they could be destined for any other country. But in the case of Ireland, why not directly there?'

'In the first place: because it is easier to bring them here. There are greater opportunities to get them in. We are world renowned for our laid back attitude towards Northern Ireland and perhaps, as a result, are seen as an easy option by those in the business. Perhaps we don't direct as much effort and resources towards routing them out as we might. Remember there is a vast intelligence network operating in Ireland and the fact that the place is crawling with trained British troops on the ground and all that implies naturally makes here the easier option. It is therefore much more attractive and perhaps that much safer to land them in quantity here, where security is much more lax and then break them down and transport them across piecemeal, to Ireland. Guns break down into small pieces and bullets down to single rounds. But we do not believe that many of the arms imported here are destined for use in Ireland. Some maybe of course, but we feel it is more the case where the Irish Terrorist Organisations import them here for use here. We may of course be way off beam and large quantities may pass through this way on their way across to Ireland. Perhaps even using similar methods to the one we are currently investigating here, now. Despite the heavy resources of the Intelligence Services and the vast number of troops deployed over there it maybe considered by those making the policy that policing, if that is the right word, between the mainland and Ireland to be somewhat of a low priority. Also you have the almost impossible task of trying to cover everything. We are not at war in Northern Ireland and our troops are there as a piece keeping force and as such, must allow the population, as a whole, to go about it's business unmolested. With the thousands of commuters who pass between England and Ireland in a single day, not to mention those who pass through the boarders, which literally stretch for hundreds of miles, between Southern and Northern Ireland, it is little wonder that things, when broken down into small units, get through relatively easy. We know they have tried to do it in bulk, both directly to Northern Ireland and to the South for subsequent transportation North and the reason we know this, is because we have caught them. But how many of these smaller operations do we find? Not many

and we have no means of knowing how many exist and have operated unmolested for years. Will we ever know how long Johnson's team have been in business? They maybe new to it or on the other hand they maybe old hands and have, over a long period, been responsible for handling vast quantities. However, there is, as I have already mentioned, the other aspect to be taken into account. Not all these illegal arms and in particularly explosives, are destined for Northern Ireland. Where do you think the Birmingham Six, the Watford Pub Bombers, or the central London Bombers got their explosives? Or those used to blow up the Army Coach on the motorway, the Band Stand and Mounted Guards in London or the Marine Band Barracks, killing all those youngsters. I could go on and on, but the point I am trying to make, is that they all needed supplies of raw materials and without them they would have achieved nothing. What has brought about the upsurge in armed robbery, or for that matter, the ever-increasing number of murders or violent deaths, where firearms have been used and there are no obvious links to organised crime? From terrorist cells, set up and operating in this country. The IRA also needs cash and what better way to raise it, than through armed robberies or the actually selling of arms to the mainland underworld. I am sure that if you were to ask Mr Scott, he could enlighten us even more on this subject.'

'I am sure he will do just that, if he thinks it necessary, when he presents his report, in due course. But in the meantime has anyone any further questions for Mr Williams?' enquired Adams.

'Not a question, but more by way of an apology, if I may,' I said. 'I am sorry we had to request the withdrawal of your man when he originally turned up. As you will appreciate, it is only a small village and I was concerned that we were overloading the place with strangers and perhaps, as a result, drawing undue attention to ourselves and putting the outcome of our own investigation in jeopardy.'

'No hard feelings what-so-ever,' Interjected Len Jones. 'It was your patch and you were making the decisions. It presented no problems, as the outcome has proved and I was able to carry on with other work. You confirmed our suspicions, when you established that drugs were being moved inland, although we did not know and are therefore very grateful for the information, that they were being distributed further inland under the cover of innocent bogus fishing trips. However all this has helped to establish that most of the stuff; that started out from around here, ended up in the Leeds area, for re-distribution even further afield. We were also able to establish and tie in the fact, that some of it actually found its way back to a ready market on this coast. Special trips being organised, mainly by youths on fast motor cycles, to buy and collect the stuff in Leeds and bring it back this way for distribution in even smaller quantities. This time it being the end of the line, as we originally believed, suspected and partially knew but have now been able to confirm. You maybe interested to know that we learnt that fishing, once

again, plays a big part in the final distribution along the coast, only this time it is the shore based, Beach Casting Fishermen. The hobbyist or spare time fishermen, who leans over the sea front railings. Many of them stand there all night long. They stamp their feet against the cold and chat away to each other, often within sight and hailing distance of a genuine and innocent all night Fisherman. The genuine and not so genuine come and go at random and change their positions all the time. The result is that there are always people moving back and forth along the sea front. Perfect for those in "the know." When you are wise to the set up, you can spot them easily. First of all, the potential buyer, he will have a rod out over the railings and his line will stretch out into the darkness. He maybe smoking or stamping his feet to keep warm, he may or may not, according to his enthusiasm and willingness to take risks, have all the gear set out. The thing he does not do, is attend very closely to his rod; he is not really interested in it. Other potential buyers or even genuine Fishermen will pass him by or come up to him and chat. Eventually, an innocent looking car and only one of many that will pass that way during the night, will come and park some distance away. This time the "fisherman" is that bit different; the driver gets out and sets up his rod. He strolls over to the nearest group and in a hail fellow well met, let's all be fishermen pals together attitude, calls out "Caught anything lads. I have some good bait over in the car if you want it." Or some such similar greeting. However, contact has been made with those in the know, to anyone else, they hear a perfectly innocent remark. In the meantime those interested go to the car, where there will inevitably be someone else sat in it or there may be even more of them; another give away for us who know what they are up to, but for them, they are a necessary precaution and security, as there is a very valuable cargo in the boot which needs protecting from fellow villains. Within minutes of the visit for "bait", the first group will have packed up all their gear, taken their purchases and gone, and no one will have taken any notice. The car owner may stay where he is and wait to be approached by other potential buyers, or he too may remove his rod and move a short distance along. How do I know all this? Because I have stood along those railings for hours, with a rod and line and watched them come and go and logged their activities. On one occasion, after only the first couple if nights, I was approached and asked if I had caught anything. When I said no, it was suggested that perhaps I was looking for some special bait and that if I was, there was plenty available, but it would cost me. I purchased a small quantity of cannabis resin about the size of an aspirin tablet and paid five pounds for it. That was kept as evidence along with the tape from the mini-recorder in my oilskin pocket. Later I recorded details of the car; a description of him and his silent passenger, along with the registration number. They were put under surveillance, not with a view to arrests, but to try and establish their sources of supply and the extent of the operation locally. I must remember to enquire if any of them were ever taken out of circulation, or if they were left there and are

perhaps still there, and if they did lead us on to other things. Often the local Police will inadvertently, without realising it, spoil it for us. They have their local Drug Officers and they patrol around, and pick up these people. Perhaps, in the first instance, for something entirely different, perhaps a minor traffic offence, or in connection with burglary or shoplifting or even just to harass them in the hope of finding small quantities of cannabis in the car and then, bang, they have a sure fire nick. You see, a fair number of these small dealers, but not all, are local bad boys and in a small community, are usually know to the local law enforcement troops. From there, the local Court and local press have a ball and we have lost a valuable stake out. We don't blame them, they have their jobs to do and pick up a few dribs and drabs. At least they go someway towards assuring the "do goody" section of the local population that the drug problems, in their area, are firmly under control. I smile when I think about it. If only they knew. On one of our numerous undercover jobs, when we were blitzing one particular area, we came across a young woman, who commuted regularly, to York by train, to entertain, in the streets, as a busker. She returned to the coast and don't forget, this was on several days a week, with cannabis in blocks the size of a half pound block of butter, casually laid in her instrument case. Because we found out about it, thanks to colleagues in York and because of the quantities involved, she is no longer in circulation. Or the two youths who invested in a Mobile shop and toured around the large housing estates? We may never have found out about them had it not been for a rival gang who decided to rob them of their cash and stock and in the process wrecked the van and severely hurt the occupants and an innocent bystander. But I use these and could quote many more, to illustrate to you, how easy it is to get the stuff in the first place and how then it is simple to distribute, with a little bit of original thought, and how widespread the problem really is. Look at the operation, that I read about in your report, Mr Grundy, involving Johnson and his Builder friend. Every Sunday they take a trip inland and all so innocent. I shudder to think how much those two alone, have distributed over the time they have been at it. Something I sincerely hope we might find out. But even if we don't, having taken them out, must have made one hell of a hole in the supply network, to that area at least and if only in the short term. Not only do I admire these people for their ingenuity, when I know I really shouldn't, but I am always tempted, having come across something like this, that combines simplicity and cunning, to stake out the same place on the off chance the operation will be restarted and we can nip it again while it's still in the bud. But, from experience, I know they won't do that. The supply line has been severed and they are not daft. They will either abandon the site altogether or leave it dormant for quite some time. Anyhow, that's all I have to say and I apologise for taking up so much of your time.'

'Not at all and thank you very much Mr Jones. I think before we ask Mr Scott for his report this might not be a good time to take a short break.'

* * *

'To continue Ladies and Gentlemen; Mr Scott, if you please.'

Eddie shuffled in his seat and drawing one of his papers towards himself, glanced at it briefly, then began, 'Most of my time, on this operation, has been spent with the Coastguard and there are one or two items that concern my Department and which you may find of interest to this enquiry. Being the Anti-Terrorist unit of Special Branch, we are not too concerned with the import and distribution of drugs. We like to leave that to other agencies although we would never ignore it and, as in this case, we were only too pleased to help and would go for it, with greater enthusiasm, if we believed the drugs were being used, in any way, to fund arms dealings or terrorist activity. However it is now my belief that in this case, they are not and should be treated as two separate issues. Never the less, we will not ignore the drugs and will pass on everything we have discovered and will continue to pass on, anything we come across in the future, to all the relevant and interested parties. Our main concern therefore, in this investigation, is arms. My brief, as a result, was not to specifically concerned myself with where the stuff originally came from, although, at the expense of repeating myself, if I found out anything relevant about that, I would naturally pass the information on. I was to concern myself with, among many other things, where it was going. In other words, where is the final destination? Who will be using the stuff and for what? We are confident that, in this case, they are, or should I more accurately say, were, destined for terrorist activities and with a very strong possibility of doing so, in this country. We desperately would like to know where and who, is the individual who will eventually put the bullet in the gun, or set the fuse on the explosives; which Cell he or she belongs to and who is their area controller or "Cell Commander" and what, if we get really lucky, are their proposed targets. Although that is probably asking a little too much and the hope of eliminating the whole Cell is probably a bit too ambitious also. But that is, ideally, what we would dearly like to achieve. Ignoring, of course, the fact that we would really like to eliminate the whole damned lot of them, in their entirety, if we could. Sadly as things are at the moment that is very much pie in the sky and will remain so for the foreseeable future. To achieve that, in my opinion, requires Government intervention at a very high level and I don't see any signs of that happening at the moment.'

'I am not sure about the others,' said Adams. 'But for myself and for the benefit of the records, I would appreciate a little of the background to all this. I feel that a clearer understanding of how all this came about in the first place would help tremendously; as it is also my opinion that to clarify it and be more concise, will greatly assist in the preparation and understanding of our final report.'

Eddie looked up and he and Adams scanned the faces round the table. As no one showed any obvious signs of decent, Eddie continued.

'In the early days, as I believe has already been mentioned round this table, most arms were being illegally imported directly into Ireland and in particular, Southern Ireland. That initially suited and satisfied the demands of the terrorist organisations operating their campaigns in the North. But when they decided to expand their sphere of activity and terror onto mainland Britain, they ran into several problems. Firstly the network of intelligence developing and operating in Northern Ireland, made it difficult, for known activists, to move around freely and don't forget that in the early days the real activists were few, many of them were not exactly discrete, through lack of proper training, and were well known to the Security Forces. Something, I now admit that they have since worked hard on to rectify. Secondly security at Irish Ports and Airfields had been stepped up to such an extent that, if it was not exactly impossible to smuggle arms and explosives in and out of the country, the risk of doing so was so high and the chances of success so very small. After many unsuccessful attempts, when their efforts were thwarted and they lost a lot of their best men, and the Maze prison began to fill up, they decided that it might be easier if they imported directly into this country. So an organisation, which had been established over here on the mainland, for some such eventuality, but which had laid dormant and inactive for a long time and probably never used since it's inception, was opened up and developed to actively operate here. From this were set up, what were to become known as, - Cells or Dormant Units, staffed by Sleepers. Active or activated, when necessary, and self-sufficient units, fragmented to such an extent that each unit had little or no knowledge of their immediate neighbours or the overall size or structure and in particular the command structure, of the set-up as a whole. This was purposely done and incorporated into the structure and organisation to protect their internal security network; for if one of the Cells were to be uncovered and taken out, it could then not jeopardize the security or compromise any of the others. Organisers were originally sent over, which presented no problems, as they travelled on the Ferries as transport drivers, construction workers or even holidaymakers and job seekers. They could pass freely, passing almost as anything and had little to fear, as they carried nothing incriminating on their persons and simply mingled with the thousands who commute, back and forth, across the Irish Sea on a daily basis. Other "Cell" staff, and later workers, or Soldiers, as they prefer to call themselves, were recruited from the Irish community already living and working on Mainland Britain, having perhaps crossed over originally for that very purpose or if not, having later been recruited into it. Even sympathisers of non-Irish origin were and still are, to some extent, used. A Cell Organiser would be a lone individual, not even being aware, again for security reasons, of even his immediate colleagues and sympathisers working at the same level and perhaps doing so in the same

district. The idea is that he and there is a strong possibility that it might even be a she, is totally responsible to the main Organisation, controlled from Headquarters somewhere in Ireland, for the organisation, the setting up and taking charge and responsibility for the illegally imported arms, explosives and all the other trappings of terrorism designated for that particular cell and finding a safe place to store them, until they were required, when he would then be instructed further, through the command structure above. Up to that point he or she would know nothing of further or future plans and was therefore, in that respect, a limited security risk. He was, for want of a better title, a store man or custodian and would often use for his purposes an innocent terraced house or a respectable bungalow in a modern suburb and there they would have, carefully hidden, within their cellars or attic, vast amounts of illicit materials, all tucked safely away and stored, often for long periods, until required for a specific operation. Back rooms in these places could be and often are, used as make shift bomb factories or assembly points for home made mortars and booby traps and what have you. Somewhere, further behind the scenes, there is a Commander or several Unit Commanders who will receive and take their orders, directly from their superiors, in Northern Ireland and pass them on, or carry them out, as and when required. The methods used to do this, again for security reasons, do not involve any direct contact between individuals and can vary tremendously, ranging from simple messages inserted in the personal columns of newspapers to pre-arranged code words over the telephone or through the mail. I am sure you are all very familiar with the range, of non contact methods, for passing information and don't need me to elaborate on them here and you must also take into account the fact that there are so many individuals of Irish decent, resident and travelling round this country, that even two or more talking together in a Pub or other public place arouses no suspicion. So you see the passing of even the most confidential of information is no real problem.'

He hesitated as once again he consulted his notes.

He then continued, 'another section of their now, worldwide network is responsible for the ordering and the delivery, to the points of entry, of the necessary hardware. Most of these deliveries are paid for in advance with the exception of the final leg, which is often paid for, in cash, at the time of delivery to a middleman who has the incentive, by not being paid until then, to ensure the actual delivery is made. Again this deliveryman, or last leg runner, will be only a small guy, who if taken out knows little that can jeopardize or compromise the whole. He is what he is, "a cash on Delivery man", who knows nothing of what happens before he becomes involved and couldn't care less, as long as he gets his money, what happens afterwards. But let us now consider the bulk of the money and why most of it changes hands overseas. There are obvious reasons for that, the main one being that it is easier to move large sums of money around on the continent, where most of it is raised in the first place, or at least held there until required, than it,

fortunately, is in this country. Although, sometimes, I even have my doubts about that and prefer to assume that the cash changes hands on the Continent because that is where they draw much of the support for their cause. There and the USA of course, but mainly the continent when it comes to making the deals. There and in the Middle east or even further afield, I really don't know. I do know that it keeps it as far away from our security people, as possible and suits them as a result. The larger the proportion, of all high level dealings, that can be kept out of Ireland or off mainland Britain, the better, as far as they are concerned. So the initial deals and purchases can be made almost anywhere in the world and the cash transferred with the minimum fuss and risk. The arms then begin their devious travels and finally end up here and despite everything that has been said about lax security and laid back attitudes towards Northern Ireland, everyone involved, in this country, takes a very dim view of terrorism and will go to great lengths to counter it. That, unfortunately for them, makes the final leg, in the movement of any arms, the most dangerous and if anything their weakest link in the whole chain of events. That is just one of the reasons why they are prepared to, or have to, use detached links and pay extremely well, in cash, for final deliveries. They do it also, to make sure that the Poles and other vessel owners, crossing the North Sea, or wherever else they decide to cross, have either a suitable incentive to do so or too much at stake, once involved, to back off. Also it would not surprise me to find out that once these final delivery people do become involved, they find themselves under some sort of heavy pressure, through threat or blackmail, to deliver, from the original dealers. After all, the world's illegal arms dealers are a very powerful and ruthless lot and the individuals involved are definitely dispensable if they slip up, fail to perform as expected, or make any mistakes. Who knows if that body that washed up down the coast, might have been involved in something like this and dumped as a punishment, or incentive, for others to fall into line. I don't know, but there is always something highly suspicious about a body that shows up with no identification on it what so ever. An accident in those cases is very hard to imagine.'

At that point Eddie broke off once again and rearranged his papers, selecting one before he continued.

'Where was I? Oh yes. Explaining incentives and cash. Large sums of money are always a temptation and I should imagine even more so, to the low life involved at the bottom end of terrorism, so perhaps that is a further reason why very large sums are kept out of their reach. What changed hands on the beach the other night was probably, by our standards, a very large sum, but was meant only as payment for final delivery. If anything else had been paid, in addition or in advance, to these transport people, we have no means of knowing and the money handed over on the beach, though considered a substantial amount in our judgement, was probably only made available for that particular purpose and came via some safe route, shortly before the scheduled delivery.'

He looked again at the paper in his hand, appeared to change his mind, so placed it to one side, and selected another.

'When the perpetrators of terrorism decide to mount a campaign on the mainland, those who are to do the dirty work, or who are specialists in some way, again travel relatively safely across the Irish Sea. We also know that many of them had and have been, in mainland Britain for years, just keeping a low profile and behaving normally, and waiting patiently to be called upon to serve "the cause". Again part of the elaborate security system, for if the Cell is taken out then the specialist is not lost and vice versa, but to bring us more up to date, and the reasons for our being here today. What the Coastguard people have found, as a result of their investigation into another matter, was a point of entry, into this country, for arms and ammunition, and judging by the amount of hardware involved, I would say a fairly important one. However, what requires our careful consideration here is, the significance, or importance of this dump and why there.

'My guess is a staging post or half way house,' suggested Fred. 'The site is too far away from anything significant to be of any great value.'

'Not necessarily Fred, distance, on the mainland is no real problem and the more isolated the spot the better for those significant quantities. But I believe they were there because of the ideal location for an entry point if nothing else. I further believe that eventually the bulk would have been split up into various smaller quantities and used to re-supply and replenish existing Cells or used to set up new ones. As I think I mentioned earlier, or if I didn't then I will now, that is one of the main reasons why our people would have preferred to have left the stuff on site, but realise because of the seriousness and demise of Philip Edison and the circumstances under which they were recovered, that that was not possible. In order that you have a clearer picture of our logic and the way we apply it on these occasions, let me explain.' At which point he stopped and looked at Adams.

'Please do.'

'OK. Arms and explosives start somewhere and end up being used somewhere, as that is the purpose of the plan and sadly they do so, in the hands of someone, who we would all rather manage without and I know we could all certainly well do without the death and destruction, not to mention the heartache they cause, and please forgive me for stating there, what must be to all of you, the obvious. But it is never the less a cold hard fact and something which bothers me personally and effects me tremendously. I know also that it is ironic, but the only people, who might get anything out of any of it, are the Insurance people and God help us if that is the only way we can fund an important section of this countries economy. The Anti-Terrorist Squad, along with other worldwide anti-terrorist organisations concerns itself, very much, with the discovery and illumination of the origins and movement of all illegal hardware, their points of import and export and preventing, where ever possible, their arrival and use at their ultimate destinations.

My people, naturally, have more than a special interest, at the moment, in the movement and potential uses, of anything, within the whole of the United Kingdom and that, of course, includes Northern Ireland. Sometimes, as we go about our business, we often discover things that don't really directly concern us, but, as I have said, when we do, we pass it on. For example this current find shows us that at sometime during their travels, this particular batch of arms passed through Libya and both the arms and explosives are of French and American manufacture. We shall make that widely known to all legally interested parties, but I hasten to add, for your benefit, that that does not follow that they were sold by the French or the Americans directly to the Libyans. They may well have acquired them from other friendly Arabic states who in turn may have bought them from yet another country, who might even, in their turn, have obtained them initially, legally, or bought them from a reputable international dealer. If there is anything remotely reputable about an arms dealer, or their agents, or the Governments that back them and there are plenty of those about. Think about the recent grant to Malaysia to build a huge dam. This is to be done in exchange for their purchasing vast quantities of arms that they probably didn't want or need, from us. Now I am not blaming the Malaysian Government. They desperately need a dam, or the money to build one and because they don't have it, they become the victims of Western political intrigue. We send them experts and engineers and lend them the ware-with-all and then say - don't pay us back - because we are confident they can't. We have done our homework beforehand and know they can't. So then we just say - if you don't have the ready cash, sign this agreement to buy arms and technical aid from us at twice or treble the value and pay for them in instalments, and we know that with a bit of luck they will struggle, because we will see that they do, with more double-dealing and intrigue. That way we ensure they won't be able to pay us back and therefore will become victims of our jiggery-pokery, or come under our Cultural Influence as the politicians prefer to call it, in their part of the world. Now these people don't want these arms, nor can they afford them. So why not dump them out on the open world market. Why not get the best price they can to help pay off some of the debt and make a bit for themselves in the process; some of the big boys in some of these countries being prone to that and it is all made that much easier, for the bad boys who want to buy, when not too many questions are being asked during the actual transactions. Or where no one dare ask any, because everyone, along the line, is a party to it all and probably stands to make a bit out of it. Just one more, of thousands of similar deals, that are made worldwide every day of the year. It is called Politics and Development and Economic Aid, where considered to be acceptable, though God knows by who's standards and Corruption where it is not acceptable, but practised by those who stand to make a lot of money out of it and where, along the line, no embarrassing questions are ever asked. Every now and again the driver of a wagon, delivering big guns to Iraq, is arrested and

thrown to the "do-gooders" to satisfy, or appease, the few who claim to represent the national conscience.'

'So the British Government is in it also? Is that what you are suggesting?' enquired Adams.

'Who knows? I am not suggesting anything. But they know an awful lot about those "Big Guns" and the poor bugger arrested for carrying them and the Malaysian Dam. However, to come back to our minor consignment, of more recent times. As we have already noted, it probably arrived here after travelling along a complex and devious route and with many people making a great deal of money out of it along the way. From intelligence available to us, we know that Libya, in the case of the Irish cause, has a lot to answer for and is one of the many countries that openly supply and supports terrorist causes. Ask Israel or perhaps Yassa Arafatt where most of their stuff comes from. There are many countries and many causes, with no conscience. The Poles, as we have already mentioned, are, with or without their government's knowledge and blessing, the present favourites for distribution and final delivery to this country. So at the end of the day, what I am saying is, that these arms probably arrived, if not via the country of Poland itself, but by Polish owned, or operated, transport and first and foremost, what we have discovered, and probably severed in our operation, is part of the transport system in a long chain, to either set up a cell, as I mentioned, or to feed existing ones. Which brings me yet again to another point and one which I again have previously mentioned and more than once now, I think, of why we would have preferred to have left things hidden, where they were, in the woods and left the site untouched and exactly as it was. Granted what we have done is break up a very important supply route and taken out of circulation a large amount of undesirable material and those responsible for doing that are to be congratulated. But what we would really have liked was to find out more about their future destination and the set up surrounding them. The woods, I do believe, and forgive me if I am repeating myself yet again, was not their final resting place, and base that assumption on the amount involved and past experience. We would have liked to have, exploited the situation to find out who is behind this particular Cell as it must be a part of, or an offshoot of, an existing and perhaps very large one. We would dearly like to know why it was set up. What was its purpose and where does it fit into the overall network and plan? To have known or found out a final destination for the goods would have been of immense value. Even to have actually discovered if the site was purely a temporary holding point, or if it was meant to be for long-term storage, would have helped enormously. If temporary, we might have had the opportunity to discover the next link in this particular chain. If found to be permanent that would tell us that it was meant to supply some future planned act of terrorism locally. The North may strike you as an unusual place for terrorist acts, but don't forget, many of the large Political Party Conferences take place in coastal resorts and Scarborough, for example, is

only a few miles down the road. To be able to discover when and where, would have been the ultimate. You see we do have, even though rather lean and sketchy, some semblance of a layout of most of their known, so called “safe houses” or “safe havens” if you prefer to call them that, that we have chosen not to interfere with based on the assumption that they may lead us to bigger things before we take them out. But up to now, we had nothing round that area.’

‘Won’t we be able to find out some of that from Johnson or Scampton and company?’ suggested Fred.

‘I doubt that very much Fred, because they are all such small fry and will know very little. There will be no one at Unit or Cell Commander level with them, they purposely don’t get that closely involved and so therefore, as in this case, do not get caught that easily. People like Johnson are locally employed labour and know nothing of value. One or more of the others may know a little bit more and maybe we might get lucky and get a few clues from them, but the chances that they know something of real value are virtually nil. There is probably not one of them who is an actual member of the “cell”, but never the less one of them will still have to be a contact. But remember we are dealing with a very clever and sophisticated terrorist organisation. Don’t ever try and tell me that the Irish are as thick as their humour tends to suggest. They will ensure that the likes of our group, know nothing more than the limited knowledge they need to function. It has all been carefully planned so that if someone gets caught, as now, they pose no threat to the overall set up.’

‘But there must be something: how do they plan or pass information? How did they get, if what you have told us is correct, a large sum of money down onto the beach? Where did it come from? Not drawn out of the local Post Office. They must communicate and pass things?’ observed Fred.

‘Yes, they obviously do. But it is done by the anonymous voice on a telephone, the unsigned note in the plain envelope, the dead letter box, widely used by most intelligence agencies. There are so many ways available to them and which they can, and do, use.’

‘Excuse me! The what?’ asked WPC Smith. ‘I missed that last bit. The dead what?’

‘The dead letterbox! Where a simple message or parcel, perhaps containing a large sum of money, is left at a safe place to be picked up later by a second person. The left luggage locker in a railway station, for example, though I must point out not a very sophisticated one due to the ease at which it can be observed and opened. But it is typical and the one most favoured by the film industry when they need to show the ingenuity and deviousness of their fictional spies and I use it now, as it serves here, to illustrate the basic technique and I would add that it is still used. The method of using the dead letter box is so that the individuals involved never meet, never see each other, or are never seen to meet by a snooping third

party, thus preventing the establishment of a chain of contacts either from within, or from outside, the organisation. So I hope you can see my point, when I said we would dearly have liked to have, left those cases buried in the woods. That way we had something to stake out. If those in custody can tell us nothing, which I doubt they will, we would have had at least another chance of a lead, even though I must admit, only a very slim one because the arrests alone, will probably have sent out enough warning signals, to those along the line, to abandon the site altogether and clear out of the district completely leaving everything behind. The lost and forfeited hardware can, and no doubt will, be replaced later. However, slim chance or not, it is not to be, and we are not to get another crack at it, in this case, and so that, for the moment, is all I have to report. Has anyone any further questions? If so, please fire away and I will do my best to answer them.'

'How could you stake out boxes buried in the woods? You couldn't hide a man up a tree for a long period of time?'

'Easier than you think, Fred and one method that readily springs to mind is this. Consider for a moment all that grease that was about in those cases. It is, using that grease, a simple matter to hide a bug in them and after that monitor their movements. The removal of a single round of ammunition, or a detonator for example, taken out and then put back, after the necessary electronics have been inserted inside it, presents no problem for our wiz kids and cleaver tricks people. But an even simpler and perhaps much more effective method, would be to actually stake out the place and that is not as difficult as you may think. When I came and met you, what was my cover? When you first met me, what did everyone think I was doing in the area?'

'Selling Farm Insurance.'

'Exactly. So along come two or three additional Forest Workers transferred from down South to study forestry techniques on the Duchy of Lancaster estate. No problem to arrange it and to do so, in such a way that they are free to move around and stay as long as necessary. Within a matter of weeks they would be part of the scenery and ignored by everyone. Perfect cover.'

'Thank you very much Mr Scott. If nothing else, your explanations have allowed us all to understand a lot more about the terrorist network and how it operates in this country. By the time we are through here our Miss Smith, down there, will have become quite an expert on terrorism. I don't need to remind you, Kath, that everything you hear in the room, is in the strictest of confidence and that you were selected for this job as part of your training and future career prospects.'

'Yes Sir.'

'My pleasure, Sir,' said Eddie, 'and I am sorry if I sounded rather disgruntled or dissatisfied about certain things or if I waffled on too much and bored you all to death. But in our line of business we always seem to need more than we get, when

really I suppose, I should be satisfied and more than grateful for what we have, and hopefully we have, as a result, plugged up yet another point of entry and severely damaged their network in this area.'

'In your line of work, I don't suppose it is a bad philosophy never to be satisfied,' observed Adams.

'Philosophy or not,' laughed Eddie. 'We never are and my Chief must be one of the worst.'

'We know the feeling, don't we?' smiled Fred, looking at me.

I nodded.

'Time for coffee Ladies and Gentlemen,' declared Adams.

* * *

'Have you any comments Mr Jones? Because if you have, we would like to hear them before I invite Mr Cameron to address the meeting,' said Adams as we reconvened.

Len Jones cleared his throat. 'Our success in this matter is similar to that of the Anti-terrorist Squad. We of the National Drug Squad, as you all know, laboriously nibble away at what is becoming an, ever increasing, problem. I don't intend to lecture you on the vastness of the problem, or on the availability of drugs of every style and type, as I am sure you are all, already, very familiar with that and that you are also aware that there is a colossal black economy growing up, and thriving, around the whole drug scene. Our job is to fight and stop it, or at the very least, damage it, if we can and I personally believe, that despite all our efforts, we will never be totally successful in our attempts to completely eradicate it. It has now gone too far for that and the fight against it is grossly under funded. Nor do I believe it is a fashionable trend and will die out, as has been suggested round this table, but nevertheless there is a similarity between the drugs scene and the gun running. Thanks to the Coastguard, this operation has broken one of many links in the drug-running network and although very small in comparison with some of the more recent larger seizures, if allowed to continue, even this small operation, would handle a fairly substantial amount over the years. We are hoping, from this bust, for a knock-on effect. We are banking on the fact that drug smuggling is less sophisticated and more lax, than the arms dealing and that those people presently downstairs may be persuaded to part with useful information that we can use to further our aims. I nearly said, further our investigations, but then remembered that words like investigations and other very long words, like sophisticated, come from watching too much television. But joking apart and ignoring the fact that on television they are always hellish successful and nail everyone. Ours is very similar to many other very real agencies where it is nothing more than a continuing uphill struggle and where the success rate is not quite so impressive or guaranteed. The

demand for illegal drugs, of every type, is currently so high and is expanding so rapidly that the sad, world-wide network of suppliers, behind it, is also expanding at an alarming rate and we currently seem to be so ineffectual in stopping it. If only we could reverse this trend then we might begin to see some light at the end of the tunnel. But at the moment it is all blackness. So all we can do is stick with it and be grateful for anything we get. One day we may win. Who knows? Perhaps cows may fly and mad cow disease become the "in thing", if the whole population has not already overdosed by then.'

'And I thought I was the defeatist,' laughed Eddie. 'To listen to you, you make my job sound easy. Do you really believe all that about never winning?'

'I don't know what I really believe. I seem to blow from hot to cold these days. Maybe at some time in the future a whole new generation will see the stupidity of it all and turn their backs on it and the fashion theory may then, after all, prove to be correct. But that's an argument I don't want to pursue right now. At the moment it is only a dream of mine, that one day we will all live in a drug free world. But to sum up today: in this particular operation I feel that my department has gained considerably more than we have contributed and for that we are grateful. Thank you all and in particular, the Coastguard.'

'Thank you, Mr Jones; perhaps next time it will be your turn to contribute the larger proportion. But to round off today's meeting I would like you all to hear what Mr Cameron, here has to tell us.'

'Thank you Superintendent! Good afternoon all. When reports began to filter in, to our department, and were being collated, filed and then circulated to interested parties, my attention was drawn to the fact that during a Coastguard investigation on another matter, over here on the mainland, illegal arms had come to light. This is an area where I, currently, have a special interest and so, while studying these reports, I came across a name that cross-referenced to certain individuals who feature in one of our top, special security, lists. We have had an interest in the man Raines, and his wife, ever since there was an episode, in the town where they lived in Northern Ireland and after which, they moved out, leaving rather suddenly. These people first surfaced and came to our attention some years ago when terrorism, in the province, was at one of its peaks. During that period there were many splinter groups and other minor groups of idiots and indeed, sadly, there still are, who formed their own individual organisations and hid behind the ideology and universal claim, of "freedom fighter" and supporter of "the cause". When in reality, all they were interested in, was private vendettas or extortion, through general thuggery, for personal gain. Arms were always readily available to them and, to understate the case, were not always in the hands of individuals who could be controlled and certainly not by those, supposedly, in charge of the overall "cause". Hence there was wholesale slaughter and very often, motiveless murder. Raines' wife, Bridgett, was one such victim. She had a brother,

who declared himself for "the cause of freedom" and managed to get himself involved with one of the so-called Paramilitary groups. They did a lot of drinking and bragging, and hanging around in the back rooms of bars. They covered their faces, wore silly hats, and marched up and down. They painted slogans on walls and waved banners and threw stones at anything, and everything Military, or what they believed might possibly be connected to the military, or the Police. Often they were not concern about any connection to anything and simply revelled in the childish delight of throwing stones. On one occasion we received a report of stones actually being thrown at a funeral party for no apparent reason and, I think, we have all seen television pictures of shootings and bombing, taking place where one side or the other, has felt it justified to interfere with these solemn proceedings; however to come back to Bridgett Raines' brother. During this time his group were drawing attention to them-selves, and were becoming well know to the local RUC. One day it all went horribly wrong and Mrs Raines found herself at her brother's funeral. He had been gunned down, after an all-day drinking session, in the street by some of the local thugs. The detail of how this came about is very sketchy as both sides were, and still are, notorious for seeing nothing, hearing nothing and, if they think they can get away with it, claiming they were not even there. Up to that point, while her brother was consuming vast amount of Liffey water and playing the part of the brain-dead freedom fighter, she remained at home, and alongside her parents, tried to live a normal, trouble-free life. It was during this period that she met up with a young man, who impressed everyone with his bright personality, his obvious intelligence, and his aptitude for hard work. He was English by birth and for reasons, know only to himself, had chosen to go to Northern Ireland, perhaps, everyone thought, just for the adventure or for the opportunity to live and work in a different part of the United Kingdom. However, he was working locally, on a building site, as a labourer, when he met Bridgett and from there one thing led to another. Eventually they were married, much to everyone's delight and in particular her mother, who saw in her new son-in-law, everything that her own son lacked. They had been married about six months when the brother was killed. The family took it very hard and her father, who up to that time, had been a peaceful man, took to drink and cursing all and sundry and blaming every stranger, he met, for his son's death. He was, as a result of his irrational behaviour, arrested on several occasions and charged mainly with public order offences and, on one occasion, criminal damage. While all this was going on, and the whole family was in turmoil, someone must have approached Bridgett and convinced her, that her brother had been singled out for a revenge killing. No one, of course, will ever know if this was true, but we do know that Bridgett suddenly became very active out on the streets and at political rallies, and eventually drew herself to the attention of the authorities. She was now on file and known to be an active political dissident and potential terrorist. Then one day, without any warning, she and her husband left

the province and came across to the mainland and set up home, here, in North Yorkshire. They made no attempt to go back to where he originated from, but came straight here and set up home. He got regular work and lived a quiet, trouble-free life up until this episode. We believed, at first, that she had decided to turn her back on everything and leave Ireland to get away from all the trouble. After all, her brother was dead and all she was getting was hassle from the authorities. Her mother never really recovered from the shock and, on top of that, her father was spending more and more of his time in custody, than he was spending drunk in public bars. Like I said, we thought that perhaps she had had enough and with the agreement of her husband, had come across here to make a clean break. When we were informed of their arrest and the circumstances surrounding it came through to me, I flew straight over. I came to find out why they had been arrested and to see if there was more that I could learn, or if there was anything I ought to know that I don't already know. So until I receive further ongoing reports, that is all for the moment.'

'Thank you Mr Cameron! From what we have just heard, we can now begin to see the seriousness of the situation and the importance of your discovery,' said Adams as he nodded towards Fred. 'We may well, through you two, have some very important links that, let's hope, will lead to bigger things. But for now, thank you all very much. I think this is probably a good time to make a break, so if you will all make yourselves available for two-fifteen this afternoon, we will reconvene then. That will give me some time to update myself and check on the progress made, with this morning's interviews,' and standing up, he collected his papers, nodded to everyone and left the room.

The others stood up stiffly and gathering their papers together, slowly filed out. Only the Irishman remained and as I stood aside to let him pass he said, 'I wish I had a pretty girl to work with. You're a very lucky man.'

'Yes he is, isn't he?' laughed Fred, 'but he doesn't appreciate it,' as she squeezed my hand. Then she said to me. 'Where are you taking me for lunch you lucky man?' and then, stepping back a single pace, gave me a mock salute, and added, 'Where ever it is, you must make it snappy. You heard what the big man said; must be back for two-fifteen, on the dot and all that.'

* * *

'My shout,' called out a voice from behind, as we stepped out of the front entrance and into the noonday sunshine. We both turned to see Eddie making a dash to catch us up. 'This may be my last chance, so you must let me stand lunch.'

'Your last chance?'

'Yes Old Boy. I am on my way back to the buildings, as they say, at the end of this session. I have a lot of other work to do and masses of reports to prepare and

as usual, am always behind and under pressure to produce. After this afternoon I will have to rely on reports, submitted to me, from here.'

I knew then, that I was really going to miss him. We hadn't known each other that long and yet I felt I could have know him all my life and that, given the chance, we could have become really good friends. Fred also sounded rather saddened and deflated when she said later, whilst Eddie happened to be out of ear shot, 'I do hope we bump into him again, sometime, in the future. He is such a nice guy and I will miss him.'

'Me too,' I replied.

After that, lunch seemed strangely subdued with little fun in it and all the time it felt as if there was something uncomfortable and terribly final, about it all. Fred had so little to say that I was rather glad when time ran out and it was time to return for the afternoon session.

CHAPTER FIFTY-TWO

We filed back into the conference room, for what felt like the umpteenth time. Lunch, to say the least, had been a little strained and more like the last supper, as Fred had put it to me on the way back. I checked, with my watch, to make sure we had not miscalculated and arrived too early, for the last thing I wanted to do was sit around in that large, over warm, Conference Room, feeling uncomfortable and trying to make small talk to Eddie as we waited. My watch told me that we were, in actual fact, a full three minutes late and yet the number of people already assembled seemed somewhat depleted. The thought passed through my mind that perhaps there had seen some delay, or unforeseen development that we were not aware of. I was about to remark about it to Fred, when in walked the WPC, and smiling all round, took her place at the far end. She dropped her note pad down on the table in front of her.

'The Superintendent sends his apology, he will be delayed for a few minutes,' she said to the few already seated.

'Something must have happened,' suggested Fred, and I was about to agree with her when a rather flustered Chief Superintendent barged in.

'Sorry about this: the Raines woman has tried to do herself some harm. That's all we need - a suicide in custody and during the bloody morning. There will be a Bridewell Sergeant and maybe an Inspector and several Constables looking for other jobs by the end of today, if someone does not come up, in the meantime, with some pretty good answers. We expect less supervision during the night but during the morning,' he repeated. 'I thought things were going a little too smoothly.'

'Is she all right?' asked Fred.

'Yes, we found her just in time, thank God. The doctor is checking now to make sure. We had better get on with our business before I go over the top and sack everyone who has been within a mile of that cell in the last twenty four hours.'

He bounced the edge of his papers on the desk top and let out a long sigh, then, laying the sheaf of papers flat, looked up and said, 'I think everyone is here. The Inspector is attending to last minute reports and I have released the Sergeant to try and help sort out the mess downstairs. We don't need him here anymore and he has other things, as well as the fiasco below, to attend to, and, I am told, that you are leaving us at the end of today Mr Scott, is that correct?'

'Yes, I have another assignment that I must attend to, but I will make arrangements to have reports, from here, passed directly onto me and I will arrange it so that you will have access to me should you need anything further from me.'

'Good, I am sure you are perfectly capable of sorting out your own affairs, so let's get on.'

'Gosh, he does sound cross,' whispered Fred.

There was a shuffling of papers, while the WPC offered scrap pads, before settling down to take notes. I had noticed that when she came in, she had, for this afternoons' session, removed her uniform jacket and that she was sitting in shirtsleeve order. I was obviously not the only one who had noticed and been affected by, the heat in the conference room. While all the others were absorbed in sorting out, or referring to their paper work, I sat back in my chair and looked at what, I now realised, was a very charming, and neatly formed, young lady, in uniform. I tried not to be obvious, although I must admit that once or twice, while I glanced in her direction, she caught my eye, smiled, and flexed her shoulders. I am sure she was not doing it purely for my benefit, but as a direct response to the fact that she knew someone was looking at her. The body was good and she was well worth looking at.

The first thing I noticed, after the pretty face and short and immaculate hair-do, was the faint outline of the white bra through the crisp white uniform shirt. I don't know enough about bras to know if it was a "lift and separate", "cross my heart", or an "eighteen hour wonder bra". I know the terms used for them of course, from the television advertising, but not being a user, I am not familiar with the different types. All I knew was, the fact that, the bra in question was doing a wonderful job of work, as it supported and displayed to their full potential, two ample breasts.

What could be seen, from where I sat, of her black stocking clad legs, protruding below the hem of her skirt and which I had already had the chance to notice, on previous occasions, when she walked back and forth, or in and out of the room, were a pleasure to behold. Or were they tights, I wondered? Again there was no way of knowing, short of asking a direct question or a direct assault on her person. But at least she had knickers on. I knew that, as I had seen the outline of them, through her skirt when she bent over to pass out the scrap pads. The legs? Yes, very nice indeed, despite the flat shoes. How often, I mused, have I noticed in the past, how WPCs' appear to have short, slightly thickened legs on the portion that shows below the hem of their skirts, perhaps because of the flat heeled shoes that they are required to wear? I don't really know, but would advise all other males, and females, if they happen to be that way inclined, to take a look for themselves, and see if they agree with my observations. Also to check and determine if I am right when I claim that a large proportion of them also tend to be slightly bow legged. Sorry Police Ladies, but I consider myself an expert and that is how I see you and you may wrap those, ever so slightly bowed legs, round me, any time you choose. I can't say fairer that, now can I? Although wait a minute, maybe they are not bow legged at all, but some only appear to be that way, the result of their owners

overall fitness and training, or is it perhaps, something to do with where they keep their truncheons. I could not see any sign of one, hidden away, on our WPC Smith. Perhaps that is why she had very nice legs. But I could see her handcuffs. They were attached to her waistband alongside the power pack for her radio.

As she prepared to take notes, she stretched and reached for something on the table out in front of her and I swear, that for a brief second only, I saw the outline of a nipple. It was not cold in the room, as she had confirmed by the removal of her uniform jacket, so perhaps after all, she was glad to see me. I have never had a date with a policewoman, so I decided to make a mental note of the fact and store it away as something, which perhaps, could be rectified in the future. That is, if they don't all take my observations too personally and smack me in the eye before I have time to ask.

'When you are ready, Mr Grundy.'

'Oh, sorry Mr Adams; I was just thinking about something else and not concentrating. You were saying?'

I glanced back towards the far end of the table and the girl and she was looking straight at me, with a broad smile spread across her lovely face. Hell, I thought, I hope she is not psychic. No, probably not. Just having a quiet, secret laugh at my expense.

'We have interviewed the village Police Officer, who as a result of the statements he has made and the records he has not kept,' and he emphasised the word Not, 'has given us grave cause for concern. No doubt his evidence, or distinct lack of it, will be the subject of a serious internal enquiry, leading to a possible disciplinary action. His overall attitude towards policing, leaves a great deal to be desired and the opinion of the interviewing officer is that, to put it mildly, this Constable, has of recent times, opted for the easy life. He was aware that illicit alcohol was circulating freely and chose to do nothing about it. He thought there might be drugs about, but did not report, or pursue it, and when questioned about the part he played in the search for Edison, he can not account for why he chose for himself, an area to search, at the furthest point away from the village and the main search area. We shall need to also, investigate further, his claim that he was diverted, during that search, to attend to an incident in the village, which he says he discussed with you Mr Grundy. He stated that it concerned two locals and required no Police action. He made or kept no record of it. We are suspicious that this incident occurred and involved one of the transport vehicles being used for illicit purposes and that the Constable may have been aware of this fact and tried, for some reason, to cover it up by ignoring it. If nothing else he maybe one of two things, either part of the illegal trading, or simply aware of it, but chose not to become involved. Either way he has been suspended from duty until we can get to the bottom of it. We have further evidence to support our suspicions, from the statements made by the two Pub Landlords, which I propose to deal with next.'

Papers were put into their respective folders and others were extracted and spread out.

'Many of the local villagers have been reluctant to give statements, or discuss anything when interviewed or invited to comment. They are, as one might expect, a tight-lipped lot and typical of rural village inhabitants. They have virtually turned in on themselves and closed ranks, having collectively, subconsciously decided that their silence is their best protection against possible involvement or intrusion. There were, nevertheless, several derogatory comments passed regarding local policing. If what they have suggested is correct, then our Police Officer has developed, over a long period of time, a very nasty habit of claiming to have been either on his day off, or somewhere out of the district, whenever he was needed. One very bitter villager made a snide comment, which was recorded and I have here, relating to a past incident, where Johnson had become very drunk and caused considerable damage to other peoples property and the Constable would do nothing about it, because it was his "day off", and he was actually with Johnson and others at the time and was also falling down drunk with all the rest. We definitely need to look into this Officer and his working methods much further.

'Strange, because when we talked to him he seemed pleasant enough. But now come to think of it, he didn't tell us very much and was ready to refer us, all the time, back to his superiors,' said Fred. 'Funny how you don't realise it at the time, but now, in light of all this and with hind sight, it becomes obvious.'

Adams looked away from Fred, without making any comment and glanced back down at his papers. 'Now the Landlord of the Dog and Gun, one Harold Spinks, when told that Johnson had admitted supplying him with illicit Vodka and other spirits, admitted to taking it. So when it was suggested that we might overlook the matter, in exchange for the supply of additional information, we were able to extract some minor points that might help to tie in a few loose ends. For example, he confirmed that it was Whiting, who followed Mr Scott from the Pub Car Park, on that occasion when you had to abort your visit to the camp site and found it necessary to go on a wild goose chase, in order to eventually loose him. During a conversation between Spinks and Whiting, Spinks remarked that he had overheard you making a phone call, from the Public Phone, in the Pub, where directions and a map reference had been part of the conversation. He did not know exactly what they were because he said you only referred to them but did not quote any numbers or anything. He says this information seemed to infuriate Whiting, as he seemed to have a desperate need to know what they were and actually tried to blame Spinks for not getting them. However, not long after you left Mr Scott, he claimed that Whiting said, and I quote "I will find out where that bugger is going," and he left the Pub. What happened after that, he says he has no idea.'

'Silly sod chased me for miles,' muttered Eddie, 'and at the time threw us into a bit of a panic.'

'Further to that, he, Spinks that is, told us that on one occasion, when Philip Edison visited the Pub, Edison apparently, according to Spinks was a regular there, had a violent row with Raines during which he accused him, Raines that is, of having, or trying to have an affair with his wife Pat. Raines categorically denied it, but Edison would not let it drop, although according to the Landlord, when challenged by Raines to prove it and bring along the wife to confront him, could not, or would not, do so. There must have been quite a strain on their relationship after that and it must have affected their working in the Coastguard Service. When questioned further about his knowledge of Mrs Edison and her suspected extra-marital activities, he said he had never seen Mrs Edison in the company of Raines, or ever heard Raines make any remarks about Pat Edison. He said it was fairly common knowledge in the village, that she and Scampton were up to something, to use his expression, and that Scampton was not the first, and would not be the last according to public opinion. Apparently she is considered to be a very amorous lady and shares out her affections to cover as wide an area as possible. She is not very popular in the village, as a result of this, particularly with the female inhabitants, because of her flirting and the way she has honed in on any man who happened to come her way, and who she fancied. Again according to the Landlord, Spinks, one regular customer in the Pub and a near neighbour of the Edison's, often loudly proclaimed that Pat Edison had had more odd-job men in her bungalow, than the rest of the village had had hot dinners. Whether that is true or just a bit of bitchiness on the part of the neighbour, we will never know, but the more people we interviewed, the more it became clearer that Pat Edison liked men and the more she could get very close to, the better she liked it. In another statement, one lady, Mrs Wilmot, even went so far as to suggest she should have had a revolving door built into her house and that on wash days, one never saw knickers hung out to dry as she didn't have time to wear any. I don't know what exactly a nymphomaniac is, but if my preconceived ideas are anything to go by, I should say that if Pat Edison is not one, then she must come very close to being one. We can now see why the men liked her and the women did not. We have as yet, or course, to establish exactly what part, if any, she played in Edison's death. It is always complex when there is the eternal triangle, or any combination of husband, wife, boyfriend, lover, or what have you. Who knows what is planned, hinted at, or threatened during those intimate moments when two illicit lovers come together. We must remember that at the end of the day, she maybe totally innocent and be nothing more than the victim of malicious gossip. Small, insular village communities thrive on this sort of thing. It adds spice to what would otherwise be a boring, humdrum existence for them all.'

He broke off and re-arranged his papers once again. He had quite a considerable sheaf spread out in front of him by now.

'Kath, do you have anything down there concerning the village Landlords?'

'No Sir, I have no statements or anything like that with me.'

'Damn. I must have left them behind in the confusion over that bloody woman trying to top herself.'

'Can I go get them Sir?'

'No. Stay there. I know exactly where they will be. If you will all excuse me I won't be a moment.'

He got up and left. I smiled at the WPC who ignored me.

* * *

After only a few moments silence during which time those who remained either looked into space or occupied themselves shuffling papers Fred turned to me and in a lowered voice said, 'Talk about give a girl a bad name and it sticks.'

'Do you think that is all it is?' I whispered back.

'Why? Do you think there is more to it? Do you think she might be a murderer or be a party to murder?'

'I have no idea. Perhaps the Police know a lot more about her and her murky past, than they have so far told us today, but as far as first impressions go, Pat Edison didn't strike me as being a murderer or a man-eater or a nympho, or whatever they are called. Mind you, do murderers ever strike anyone as being murderers? I don't think they do, but Pat Edison? Attractive, yes: sexy, yes and not the type I would readily kick out of bed, but a murderer or a party to murder? I doubt it, for I now honestly believe, from what we have heard so far, Edison's death probably ties in with the smuggling and not his wife's love life.'

'That's exactly my point. She also struck me as an ordinary person and just because she is attractive and may like men, it doesn't follow she goes about sharing it out in all directions. I sometimes wonder about these, so called, Policemen and the warped way they see things. They certainly don't know much about women. They love tittle-tattle and are quick to destroy any ones character, if it fits in with their preconceived ideas, based, it strikes me, on nothing. Here they are now, wiping the floor with this poor woman and no doubt will try and fit a whole theory round it. While in one breath, Adams is labelling Pat Edison a nymphomaniac, in the next he admits he doesn't know what one is? They are obsessed by motive and will try and hang one on anyone who happens to be handy, when, at the same time, some of their own kinds are a bit dubious in the first place. You don't have to look any further than their-own village bobby in this case for that. What sort of logic is that? They continuously bleat about sticking to the facts, when if they did, instead of wrapping everything up and embellishing it, in village gossip, they would have little or nothing at all.'

‘Are you defending Pat Edison then?’

‘No I am not. I’m not defending anyone, for as you well know, I can’t do that; now can I? All I am saying is that if Pat Edison is guilty of either her husband’s death, or is any way involved in arms or drug dealing or an accessory after any of the facts, then let’s prove it and not assume so much.’

‘Leave it for now, Fred. I full understand what you are getting at and see your point, but let’s just wait and see what develops. There is a lot more to come and remember the Police do have to make out a solid and sound case for a prosecution to stick, and at the end of the day it is down to the Courts to decide and apportion the degrees of guilt or innocence. Remember the likes of you and me only dig up the muck, someone else sifts, strains, dissects and finally slings it, hopefully, in the right direction.’

* * *

Adams returned and so I swivelled in my seat to face him, shifting as I did so, my gaze away from WPC Smith.

‘Right, Ladies and Gentlemen, sorry about that, but I seem to have accumulated so many pieces of paper and for some reason seem to have got them all out of order and spread out all over the place. But I think I now have some semblance of organisation, so let us get on and deal now, with the second Landlord.’

He still shuffled his papers. Fred squeezed my leg and then gentle traced a line with her finger towards my crotch. I smiled at the WPC.

‘The second Landlord, James Lacey of the Grapes Public House has also admitted to purchasing alcohol, mainly in the form of foreign branded spirits. He was also aware that Johnson could not have obtained his supplies legally by virtue of the obscurity of the brands and the low prices he charged. He admitted there was often a lot of activity in the vicinity of his establishment, although it is off the beaten track and some distance away from the nearest dwellings and the outskirts of the village. He claimed that as far as he knew all the activity, which he admitted often went on throughout the whole night, was organised by the locals who went out on fishing trips. He allowed them to store a small boat, for that very purpose, at the back of his Pub and was quite pleased to receive a regular supply of fresh fish, by way of some form of recompense or rent. When smuggling was first suggested he dismissed the whole idea as ridiculous and said that everyone knew that smuggling died out with the decline of the cloth trade across the North York Moors, over a hundred years ago. He claims there are historical records that show that, in those days, his establishment was very popular with both those engaged in the illicit trading and those of the Government, who were trying to discourage and stop it. Today the stories are retold and elaborated upon, purely as a means of

attracting tourism. Since the introduction of the drink and drive laws he says he has to employ any means, that he can, to attract customers and if one of them is to tell tales, tongue in cheek, about smugglers and ghostly Customs men on horseback, who all haunt the place and disturb the piece after dark, then he is guilty of telling tall stories. He strenuously denied any suggestion of modern-day smugglers and said we have been listening to Yankee visitors repeating sagas. He reluctantly confessed that he allowed late night drinking, again blaming drink and drive and a rapid decline in the tourist trade, for the necessity to do so. That, he said, and the frequency with which the local lads went fishing, may have contributed to the fact that people got the impression there was something unusual going on in the area. He assured us there was not and cautioned us not to take any notice of the Landlord of the Dog and Gun, who's trade had also declined and who was blaming anyone and everyone for it, and had been jealous of the Grapes and its success, since he moved into the village. It was also hinted at, and I assume by way of some form of retaliation or an attempt to take some of the pressure away from himself, that we take a closer look at the optics behind the bar of the Dog and Gun and ask him why Johnson frequents the place as often as he does, when Spinks claims he is not welcome. When we pressed him on the subject of locals or regulars who use his Pub and drew his attention to those particular individuals we are interested in, we believe, he cleverly skirted round the issue and that in the end we only got a small proportion of the whole truth. He denied nothing and openly admitted to having them all in his establishment, but emphasised only from time to time and as nothing more than strictly paying customers. What they did outside or if they were ever part of the fishing trips, he claimed he had no knowledge, but said they could be, on the grounds that, occasionally, the odd one had given him fresh fish. Even Johnson, as far as he was concerned, was nothing more than a customer, even though perhaps more of a regular one than the others and that he could sometimes be a nuisance. He claims also, that Johnson's offers of alcohol were no more than any other customer might offer from time to time. After all, he claims, Pubs are notorious for wheeling and dealing. He claims that everyone, including himself, knows that Johnson is nothing more than a local bum and as far as he is concerned, probably gets his alcohol in dribs and drabs from foreign vessels who visit and come into Whitby harbour. He also grumbled that he has had trouble, on more than one occasion, with Johnson during after-hours drinking. He claims that on at least two occasions, that he could readily recall, Johnson, during the extended drinking period, had consumed more than was good for him and as a result became very aggressive. It was during these periods that Johnson attempted to press him into buying more illegal spirits than he wanted. He claims that according to Johnson's besotted, irrational thinking, all Landlords have more cash than sense and should therefore purchase anything and everything, that was available, particularly when Johnson had it for sale and was short of ready cash. It was usually the refusal to

do so that would provoke Johnson's aggressiveness. Beyond that, he would say, or admit to, nothing. We may have to go back to him, but the for the moment we have released him, as we have also the Landlord, Spinks.'

At that point we were interrupted by the arrival of coffee. The short walk round the table and across to the little side table, where the cups and saucers had been laid out, provided a much-needed stretch for my legs.

* * *

When we resumed the Superintendent continued.

'We will now deal with Mr and Mrs Thornton. Let us take Mrs Thornton first. She used her retail business, in the main street of the village, to purchase legally, selected items of clothing for which she claims her husband paid her cash. She claims that there was nothing unusual in the dealings, as she is a legitimate trader and as such, can purchase an infinite variety of clothing from a wide variety of sources at both trade and wholesale prices and, while doing so, is able to negotiate special deals for quantity and regular purchases. This she has done in order to supply her husband who, in turn, sold the goods, at a profit, through Sunday Markets held in and around the area. It is interesting to note that she could give no satisfactory explanation as to why her husband felt it necessary to operate a Sunday Market business when he was already very successful as a local builder. She suggested that perhaps it was to help Johnson? But could, or would not, elaborate further. She made it very clear that she had no liking for Johnson and found it very strange that her husband associated with him. She said that she had, in the past, raised the subject with her husband only to be told that Johnson, despite being employed on a casual basis, as a labourer, had his further uses and one of them was his knowledge of fishing and market trading and that the two were basically a hobby. According to his explanation, to her, the markets providing a useful extra income and financed the fishing, thus turning the whole thing into a profitable sideline. She also said that her husband claimed that Sunday was his day off and how he spent it or with whom he spent it with, was of no concern to anyone. She admitted it was a strange way to spend Sunday and could not understand the need for the Market Trading, but had no real objections, as it allowed her the whole day to pursue her own interests.'

'And we know what they were,' I whispered.

'Yes and just think, she must have been at it all day Sunday. No wonder she had no objections to her husband being away,' replied Fred.

'What was that, Miss Huntington?'

'Nothing. I was just checking a minor point with Mr Grundy.'

'Why, is there something you disagree with, or you wish to add to what I have just said?' enquired the Chief Superintendent.

'No, not at this point Mr Adams, but if anything comes to mind, you will be the first to know.' replied Fred rather sarcastically I thought.

He looked away from Fred and selected yet another piece of paper from the masses of typed sheets in front of him.

'For some reason the interview with Mrs Thornton was interrupted at that point and had to be taken up by a second officer. In order to maintain continuity the new officer found it necessary to go over some of the ground already covered by his colleague. However this is basically what he has to report: he states that he is not sure how much she really knows, but for the moment, she is leading us, rightly or wrongly, to believe she knows very little. When questioned about her wealth and life style, she defended that by claiming her husband was a very successful builder. When asked why, if he was a successful builder, did he need to work the Sunday Markets, she said it was to pay for the fishing and help out Johnson who was only an odd jobber and had several children to support. Also, she said, that over the years all her husbands hobbies have tended to be those where a profit could be made. He is, she said, that sort of man, hence his success as a builder. When asked if her husbands' hobby, of fishing, was an expensive pastime she replied that it must be, but added that she really did not know. When it was suggested that her husband could have given Johnson full-time employment as opposed to providing him with spare time income, she replied that he had tried to and that Johnson had refused and preferred his present life style; yet another reason why she could not understand her husband's relationship with Johnson. When it was put to her that they may have been into something more sinister and perhaps illegal, and that was the true reason for their relationship, she broke down and made a remark to the effect that, to her knowledge, most builders, to be successful, are not exactly honest and a lot of things go off on building sites that might be suspicious. When the subject was pursued she flatly refused to say anything further, as she said she knew nothing about building and dishonesty and stated that we would have to ask her husband. When her husband's success was further equated with the necessity for her to run a retail shop she claimed that she was an active person and could not, or would not, be confined to a large, mainly empty house all day long. She claimed the shop gave her something with which to occupy herself and provided some degree of independence. When questioned about her friends she claimed she had no particular friends but knew and associated with quite a number of people, that she came into contact with, through the shop.

She states that Pat Edison is not a friend, although she comes quite close to being one, being a very reliable, casual employee. She has met, on numerous occasions, Philip Edison but states that she really did not know him.

Pat Edison's main value, she claims, was as a trustworthy person who could be left, unsupervised, to take care of the shop while she, Mrs Thornton, "took her breaks and attended to her personal needs", as she put it. She says she knows

nothing of any relationship between the Park Ranger Scampton, and Mrs Edison, but says she was aware, having been told, that he had visited the shop on several occasions to see Pat Edison when she, Mrs Thornton, was absent. She recalls, something to the effect, that Scampton did some work on the Edison's garden, as an ongoing thing, and that he had called in the shop to discuss the matter. At the time she thought there was nothing unusual in that. She also denies any knowledge of any relationship between Scampton and Edison's daughter. Exactly how much she really knows is difficult to establish, but for the moment we are treating her as only a minor link in the overall chain of events and not exactly an integral part of her husband's illegal activity, but only as a useful supplier. In other words, she happened to be there, so he used her. It will require further investigations to establish if the business was set up for her benefit in the first place, or taken over specifically as a means of obtaining goods for illegal trading, with her and the legitimate side of the business, being merely a front. She cannot be wholly innocent because of the amount of clothing involved and the large amounts of cash that must have passed through her the result of it. That alone must have told her something was not quite right, despite the fact that she may honestly believe she was supplying a Sunday Market. But for the moment we are not pursuing that line, but no doubt will have to later, as part of the overall and final, full investigation. Customs, from the VAT point of view, and the Inland Revenue, might both be interested to know how she accounted for all the goods purchased, as our guess is that everything was transacted in cash with the invoices simply disappearing. The stuff cannot have been put through the business, because to do so would have shown no profit and perhaps even an overall loss. That in its-self, would have attracted a lot of interest at the end of the financial trading year when accounts have to be submitted to the revenue. We will, in due course, of course, bring in the revenue people and maybe they will, at the same time as they make their investigations, uncover something of value to us.'

'So you don't think Fancy Pants has a great deal to do with it?' suggested Fred. 'Apart from supplying her husband with goods for resale or barter.'

'Fancy Pants, Miss?'

'Yes, a nickname we heard, in the village, that was applied to Mrs Thornton and one which we used regularly before we knew her real name.'

'Oh, she is a part of it. Of that there is no doubt. But let's put it this way; at this point in time we believe she was conveniently there and was exploited by her husband, rather than being one of the principal players in the actual drama. Which, talking of principal players, brings us to her husband, Albert Thornton. Let's see what we have managed to put together on him.'

While he rearranged his papers and folders yet again I stretched and winked at the WPC who happened to be looking my way. She smiled and lowered

her eyes back down to her pad. A sharp pain in my shin made me turn and look directly at Fred.

'Have you got some dirt in your eye or are you developing a nervous twitch in the presence of another woman?' she hissed.

'You're jealous.'

'I am not. Just leave the girl alone.'

'I'm not doing anything, and if you....'and at that point I was cut off in mid sentence.

'Thornton,' said Adams, who then went quiet again for a moment while he studied the sheet he had finally selected.

I again looked at the WPC but she had her head down.

'Looking at the summery here, the main conclusions so far, are that he has been very stubborn and very uncooperative. However, we have managed to extract one or two items of interest from our enquiries and these are as follows. When he realised we knew all about the bulk purchases of clothing and could readily prove they had been made, he admitted to buying them, but stated that they were only a few in number and were mainly to help and supply Johnson. He said he also went with Johnson to the Sunday Markets to sell "odds and sods" as he enjoyed the day out and the atmosphere of the market. But says he made no money from it, or in any other way profited by it. He claims he didn't need to, as he is very successful in the building trade. His reasons for the fishing trips with Johnson can, according to him, be easily explained; he was interested in fishing and so was Johnson, and Johnson was the more knowledgeable, so what better way to spend Sundays than fishing with someone who knows what they are doing. He claims that everyone needed to relax and his method was to either wander round the Sunday Markets, while Johnson did the trading, or sit on a river bank, fishing. He claims that despite what his wife thinks of Johnson, or his background, he will still pick and choose his own company and if his wife does not like it, then she does not have to be a part of it. He claims that Johnson is better company than the "ponces" his wife would like to call their joint friends. When we said we had removed evidence, from his home, to implicate him in possible drug dealing offences, he replied, "Bollocks". He claims that the boxes, that we allege are involved, are some of those which he has occasionally stores in his garage for Johnson and that they only contained goods for sale on the markets.'

'Well that is true to a certain extent,' exclaimed Fred. 'They certainly contained goods for sale on the market, but not our understanding of a conventional Sunday Market. Not on a Pub Car Park, or in a Farmer's field where everything is open and in full view of the general public and Trading Standards Officers. But if you take the goods to mean, drugs and the market to be, two men sat on a lake side, then he could be right.'

'He probably realises that we are well and truly onto him and that he is not going to get away with it, so being the type of character that he is, he can see no reason to cooperate. It just means that it takes us a little longer to work out where exactly he fits in, but we will get there in the end. Now let's see what else we have gathered on him.'

After a short pause, he continued.

'When we said that we had evidence of him going to Kinder Hall on one of his alleged fishing trips and had witnessed him drug dealing he replied, "Bullshit" and claimed he was either away that weekend on business or at a market with Johnson but then went on to say that he couldn't remember which and we would have to "Bloody prove it". He also became abusive and aggressive when asked if he could explain why the type of plastic sheeting used to wrap up the ammunition boxes and Edison's body, was identical to that used in connection with his business. We told him we had recovered several identical rolls from a building site he is currently developing and that a partial roll had been removed from his garage. His first line of defence was to claim that he had no idea what we were talking about and that if we thought, that for one moment, we were going to implicate him in anything remotely connected to anything like that, then we could all go to hell. Secondly the sheeting in question was of a common type, widely used throughout the building trade. It was produced in vast quantities and that he himself had purchased large amounts over the years. When asked how he knew that the plastic used to wrap up Edison's body was of a readily available type, he was clever enough to say he didn't know anything about that, but assumed we were referring only to the sheeting removed from his site and garage. That, he said was very common and the only sheeting he knew anything about. He then began to loose some of his arrogance and settled down, to vainly attempt, or so we at first thought, to clear him-self, by making several random statements. At first he claimed he was not the only one in the area to use that particular plastic, and that it was common and used extensively by farmers and builders alike. That, we said, we could accept and would he give us the names of people he knew who used it extensively and who might have provided the sheeting we were interested in, to which he replied, "Piss off, you go find out. That is your job not mine. But remember it was not me". We then assured him we had been unable to find anyone and must therefore assume he must be the only one. He then said he could think of two others beside himself. When asked if he could verify that fact and tell us who they were and also assure us that it was indeed the same plastic, he could only claim that in the past the people he was thinking about, had borrowed from him, and as far as he could remember had returned a similar type. All a bit vague before he then compounded his problems further, by claiming that a large quantity had been stolen from one of his sites and never reported, or recovered. He could not explain why someone would just steal heavy, bulky rolls of plastic sheeting

from a building site, when there would be other far less bulky and more valuable materials to be had. He tried to claim he had sold a roll, one night, to a stranger in a Pub. He made no comment when it was suggested that it must have been very handy and indeed very convenient, to have a roll with him when he went into a Pub, or was it that, he was simply in the habit of carrying a roll around with him and perhaps also a selection of other useful building materials, in the back of his car, on the off chance he ran into a stranger in a Pub, who just happened to have an urgent need for a roll of plastic sheeting one hundred meters long and two meters wide. He said that was possible and claimed that over a long period, he had given a considerable amount away. Lengths varying from a couple of meters up to a part roll, or even a full roll. He said he had certainly given Johnson several pieces, in the past, for his own personal use. At one time he had given several large pieces to the local garage owner and we were free to check if we wished. He agreed the material could be considered, by some, to be expensive, but claimed that when the mood took him he was a very generous man and was quite happy to give away a full roll, even to a comparative stranger. He once again became aggressive when it was suggested to him that, on investigation into his accounts, it had better show that he could afford it and that the Inland Revenue and VAT people would no doubt be very interested to learn why he bought very expensive materials with a view to simply giving them away in Pubs, or allowing them to be stolen and their loss not reported. In conclusion, we believe he is running scared. We believe that at present, he feels we might be attempting to pin more onto him than he is guilty of. We know that Johnson is implicated in both the arms and the drug dealing; he has more or less admitted as much. We know that Thornton is definitely involved in the drugs, but we have yet to prove it conclusively that he is involved in the arms. In the supply of the plastic sheeting, his part may be similar to that of his wife, in her supply of clothing. She has supplied clothing and may not have known the real reason. Thornton may have supplied the plastic sheeting in similar circumstances. We will no doubt find out eventually. Perhaps Johnson will be good enough to provide some answers and we should have more on him shortly. In the meantime WPC Smith, would you go and see if there are any further reports available for us. Try Inspector Molescroft's office first.'

* * *

As we waited for the WPC to return, everyone took advantage and relaxed and chatted between them-selves and discuss progress and developments thus far.

'Don't these people make it all sound so simple. We all sit round this table and they refer to papers and read from reports and all the time a girl, who can't keep her eyes off you, takes notes. They make it all so straightforward,' grumbled Fred.

'All jealousy on your part, particularly the girl.'

'How many more times do I have to tell you. No it is not. Jealous of her: me? She has nothing that I don't have.'

'Big boobs,' I suggested in a whisper.

'So what? I seem to remember, not too long ago, some comments about anything after the first mouthful being surplus and that only so much can he held in one hand, or have we changed our minds since the big-titted wonder, at the end of the table, turned up? Better make up your mind lover-boy, otherwise you can look forward to some long lonely nights in the future.'

I laid my hand over hers and squeezed, she snatched it away.

'You won't get round me that easily.'

'Who's trying?'

'You are.'

'I'm not.'

'Yes you are.'

Thank God for the expression, "Saved by the bell". For that is what I needed and thankfully got, when Eddie, bless him, turned to Fred and touching her gently on the arm said, 'Fred, don't you feel this is all a bit of an anti-climax. I have sat here patiently listening to everything that has been said and all the time these Police types make it all sound so straightforward. Everything starts or ends with - "give us time and we will get to the bottom of this". "We will have to go back to that". "We will have to investigate further". "Give us time for this, give us time for that". Everything sounds like - "We've got the buggers, now we sweat them, then we nail them". Don't you agree?'

'Yes I do and that's just the point I was trying to make to Mel, before he got side tracked by the Policewoman at the end of the table.'

'Yes she is rather nice.'

'Don't you start. You're as bad as him. In fact the pair of you are hopeless.'

'Sorry I didn't mean anything by that.'

'I know you didn't, but he did,' she said as she leaned sideways and in his direction, and very pointedly gave him a big kiss on his cheek. She then promptly turned in her seat, looked me straight in the eyes, gave an exaggerated wink, stuck out the tip of her tongue and turned back to face Eddie.

'You were saying Eddie about anti-climax and simplicity.'

'Yes!' exclaimed Eddie somewhat taken aback by the show of affection that had just landed his way. 'Don't they make it all sound so simple? Sat at this table, if you didn't know differently, you would think that all they do is politely ask questions and from those simple, straight forward requests get all the answers they want, write it all down and submit it in reports.'

'They do make it appear to be a bit like that, I must admit, but I bet in reality, that right now, there are several people downstairs, locked away in individual cells, who are sweating and frightened to death following all the promises and threats that have been made to them. I bet each one of them has been brow beaten and accused, in their turn, of just about everything, all neatly backed up with threats and unseen evidence, and then promised all sorts of reprieves and leniency, if they help implicate others. "We can always be lenient with you if you help us" or "We are on your side really and understand, and only want to help you get things straightened out so that you can go home". Lying beggars. Thinking about it, I don't know if I really like Policemen and in particular, after what they put me through when they took me, and left me, in that room, all alone and for all that time. The more I think about it, the more intimidating I feel the experience really was. It was not necessary, so why did they do it? There is no doubt in my mind, that after that episode, they lost a lot of "Brownie Points" in my book,' complained Fred.

'It's in cases like this, that I can't help feeling sorry for the semi-guilty or those partially involved. The implicated innocents,' I said, joining their conversation.

Fred half turned and leant back, so she could observe both Eddie and me at the same time.

'What exactly do you mean by the "implicated innocents"? That sounds to me very much like a conflict in terminology.'

'Yes, come on Old Boy. What do you mean?' demanded Eddie.

'I was thinking along the lines of such people as Pat Edison or her daughter. Fancy Pants, Johnson's wife, even Raines' wife.'

'Johnson's wife: Raines's wife? What are you getting at Mel, Old Boy? Explain yourself.'

'Yes, please do,' added Fred.

'Well firstly, take Pat Edison's daughter, innocent or guilty? I don't know. But, if innocent, dragged into all this mess just because her father gets killed and she happens to be having an affair with a Park Ranger. That isn't exactly a crime, unless you want to become "all" moral about it. But look at her now. Up to her eyelids, whether she likes it or not. Then there is Pat Edison herself. More closely involved, I admit, but only because she is the victim's wife. But in addition to that, if all she is guilty of is an affair with Scampton, then look at the mess she is in right now. Fancy Pants? OK, we all agree she is rather a rum character. She loves the men and they love her. She doesn't appear to have the best of relationships with her husband and she used Pat Edison to look after her shop, so that she could slope off and have a bit of extra nookie on the side. Neither did she like an empty bed when her husband was away. Not exactly a crime. Even allowing her husband to use her business to purchase clothing and being a bit suspicious of his motives, is not exactly a major crime in my book. If their relationship was somewhat strained, as

it would appear it was, then why should she concern herself too much about what her husband got up to. The more he was up to, the more freedom she enjoyed.'

'Yes, but if we accept your argument, that they maybe innocent victims, I still don't follow where Raines' wife, Bridgett, fits in?'

'Think about it.'

'I am, and that's why I don't follow.'

'Bridgett, what ever her maiden name was, Raines as she is now, is one of the millions of young girls growing up in an ordinary, law abiding, loving family, only, in her case, she had the misfortune to be born in Ireland. Living there during rather difficult times and because of circumstances completely out of her control and the actions, attitudes and beliefs of others, over which she has no influence or control, she ends up where she is today.'

'Totally innocent?'

'No, I did not say that. Her innocence or guilt will be decided, fortunately for me, not by me but by others. I just sympathise with her position. I can not and will not, accept such arguments, as there being freedom of choice, or knowing what she was getting into, before she became involved or that she could easily have turned her back on things when ever she chose. She, like many others, is the victim of circumstance and the degree of guilt or innocence, attached to it, is very debatable.'

'You could extend that argument onto all the others, even onto whoever it was, that killed Edison?'

'I suppose you could if you wanted, but the point I am getting at and trying to make, is the fact that if not guilty, what a mess these innocent victims of circumstances are in right now. How can anyone of them, even hope to return to a normal life after this lot. Not one of them will be able to carry on as if nothing has happened and that is what I feel so sorry about.'

'What about people like Johnson?' Eddie asked.

'What about him? He maybe the victim of God knows what. It is easy to look at his overall appearance, note his attitude, log his behaviour and then call him a scum bag, or low life, or to be more polite a drop out, undesirable or misfit. He hasn't always been any of these. The day he was born he did not draw his first breath and proclaim to the whole world, "Hello, please note I am a future scum bag and I propose to piss on the whole of society from a great height". No. He is yet another perfect example of a victim or circumstance, starting way back with the environment into which he had the misfortune to be born and the adults surrounding him and who initially, moulded his character.'

'I am not sure I wholly agree with you there, Mel,' said Fred. 'What about all those from the, so-called, decent backgrounds and of good upbringing's, that go wrong, as may well have been the case, in your own illustration, with Bridgett

Raines? Or what about the hundreds of thousand from rather deprived backgrounds who don't go wrong at all and often make it right to the top?'

'Well apart from the fact that you will never have all the minute details and full knowledge of their individual backgrounds and can therefore not say with any degree of certainty, that they had a perfect upbringing, or what influence that background has had upon them up to now, or will have in their future. But also and despite all that, I still believe that they can all still become the victims of circumstance. Let's stick with Johnson. Let's suppose his background was everything it was supposed to be, which I doubt, and later things went wrong. He, in his way, then becomes and still is, a victim of his circumstances. The current state of the economy, the availability or should I say, the non-availability of honest work. All goes against him. Then along comes, what to him and others like him, are rich pickings, in return for very little effort. Maybe in the first instance purely by chance but feeling cheated and abandoned by society he goes for it and all that sort of thing.'

'Does it really work like that? Can you simply throw the blame back onto the system, when it is almost impossible to identify what that system is?'

'I believe, that to a large extent, it does work like that, but I am the first to admit that if I fully understood it, or had all the answers, then I would be only too willing to solve all of societies present day problems and would not be sat here at this point in time, idly chatting to mere mortals such as yourselves. Come to think of it, if I were that cleaver I could perhaps change my name to JC2.'

'I am still not sure I follow what you are driving at and where all your alleged understanding and sympathy comes in, but I do see some logic in your argument,' said Fred.

'Thank you dear Lady! So you do still love me then? If only a little bit.'

'Shut up!' she hissed, elbowing me in the ribs

The door opened and the WPC entered.

'An update on the interview with Johnson Sir and Mrs Edison's statement.'

'Thank you Kath; we can progress a little further now at least. Give me a moment to digest what we have here and then I will be with you.'

* * *

'Why do you think people get involved in drugs and arms dealing and dubious things like that?' asked Fred, breaking the silence and returning to our original discussion.

'I would hazard a guess and take the chance on you disagreeing with me, and say that the vast majority get into it by chance or accident. They happen to be there at the right time and their circumstances are all conducive to it. Which is

part of my original theory, which we discussed earlier, if you're asking me. They may be drug users who have drifted down the long lonely path of addiction and see dealing as a way to finance their habit. They buy and split it, selling half on for what they paid for the original whole and use the remaining half, which in effect they have got free, for themselves. To the others, whose unfortunate circumstances happened to be just right at the time, it is a, so-called, business, where personal use and abuse of the drugs themselves has nothing to do with it. To them, both drugs and perhaps here you might include arms and ammunition, are a commodity. There is a demand for them and the profits are high the result of that demand, and that in itself is one hell of a motivation and incentive for the risk-taker who, to achieve his aims, requires little physical effort and very little business acumen. In Johnson's case, I just believe, he was conveniently there to be used and exploited by all the others who took full advantage of him. He was prime and ready for the picking. He is not a drug or arms dealer in the true and strict sense of the word. He is a wheeler-dealer, an opportunist and will do anything, legal or otherwise, if the rewards are high enough. All that concerns him and the likes of him, and their level of mentality, is survival and the making of a fast buck in the process. Also the fact that he is not a businessman does not stop him believing that he is, neither does it bother him that what he is doing is illegal, in fact everything he does he believes all contribute to the fact that he is a very successful businessman and prides himself in that achievement. But forget the merchandise for a moment. Here we have Johnson, who contracts for high returns, to transport batches of goods from A to B. He keeps no detailed records, submits no tax returns and either receives in cash, or pays out in cash, for all his transactions and therefore there aren't even any Banking records to show he has done anything. Life is relatively simple, the work straightforward, and the returns very high. The perfect set up for the likes of Johnson.'

'Until he gets caught.'

'Until he gets caught; but even then that won't bother the Johnson's, or the Fisherman of this world and their type. They are versatile and very adaptable and dodge and duck anything life throws at them, remember they are, above all else, survivors and if part of that survival means settling down, and adjusting to, the odd stretch in jail, then so be it. It presents no problem. The state can then take over and look after their dependants for a while, if they are not already doing that. Remember they are businessmen in the dodgy world and know all the wrinkles and what's available to them through the system. It would not surprise me in the least, if to them the DHSS meant Department of Handouts to the Slick and Sudo-sick.'

'Right Ladies and Gentleman,' said Adams as he looked up and surveyed the room. 'Of the items of information I have just received, the most relevant appears to be a series of statements made by Mrs Edison, so I will deal with those first. Mrs Edison claims she now has nothing to loose, her husband is dead and Scampton has betrayed her, so she has made, what she claims is, a full and frank

confession. She knew that her husband had had a row with Raines. He told her so, several days after he had accused her of having an affair with him. Not only did her husband tell her he had confronted Raines in public, but she had also heard things for herself, in the form of gossip, in the village. She denies any actual involvement with Raines. She claims she knows him through her husbands' work, but says she does not particularly like him. She does, however, admit to a fairly long-standing affair with Scampton that went wrong. She is quite certain that her husband knew nothing of this affair, but wondered if vicious and distorted gossip, round the village, caused her husband to draw the wrong conclusions and as a result, confronted Raines by mistake. She knew that her husband had known Scampton for quite some time from his frequent visits to the Pub. The pair of them apparently socialised quite freely during Edison's regular visits for an evening drink, when he was out exercising the dog and her affair with Scampton started when Edison arranged to buy some fencing from him and where he also agreed to erect it, and to do some gardening in his spare time. He claimed that as a Park Ranger, he could arrange his workload so that he took his time off to suit himself and conveniently did so during the day, when Edison was away at work. He arrived at the house on the appointed day and started digging holes for the fence posts. During this period Mrs Edison made and supplied him with tea. On a couple of occasions, when Scampton was working in the garden, the daughter visited and they all chatted over tea and biscuits in the kitchen. The work in the garden continued at a leisurely pace and the two of them became friendly and talked a lot to each other and about each other. She found out that he lived alone in his little cottage, had few friends, and apart from his work and his own small garden plot, had little other interests, or so he claimed. She told him she was bored. With only herself and Edison living in the bungalow, she was always on top of the housework and the only interest she had, was her spare time job in the village. Eventually he invited her to go to the cottage on the pretext of looking at the layout of his garden and to get some ideas for the layout for her own. She admits that she should not have gone, but she did. It was there that she saw more than his garden and decided she liked what she saw, and wanted more. From then on they had sex regularly at her house, while he was working there and when ever they thought they dare, they went to his cottage where they were less inhibited, there being less chance of being caught out. When the work in the garden was complete, he still visited her on some small pretext or other. Everything went smoothly and she enjoyed the intrigue and excitement. The nicest part was that it was purely physical sex with no emotional hang-ups. That was until one day when she returned from the village to find both Scampton's Land Rover and her daughter's car in the drive. She wasn't unduly perturbed about that because she knew Scampton would have the perfect excuse for being there. It wasn't until she let herself into the house and heard giggling from the direction of a bedroom, that she suspected something. On opening the door, she discovered

Scampton and her daughter on the bed and from the position of their bodies and the amount of bare flesh on view it was obvious they were not discussing landscape gardening, or the layout of flowerbeds. Naturally there followed one hell of a row, during which it emerged that the daughter had been visiting Scampton's cottage, on a fairly regular basis. How it started in the first place, she has no idea, but remembers the daughter boasting that Scampton had said that she was the "Randiest Bunny" in the woods, a place where Pat Edison had always refused to go. Not only had she now lost her lover, but also for the sake of her marriage she had to keep it all very quiet and bottled up inside. On several occasions, she was on the point of confiding in Mrs Thornton, whom she knew would understand and, because of her own behaviour, would probably respect the confidence, but for some reason each time, she changed her mind. She managed to keep her feelings under control until that day in the village, where you,' Indicating Fred and myself, 'saw her physically attacking Scampton. Apparently, that was the first time she had seen either him or her daughter, since a row developed between her-self and the daughter following your initial visit to her house when apparently the daughter had arrived just prior to you. She claims that if Scampton is in trouble, then she hopes it is sufficiently serious for him to end up in jail. When questioned about her husband she claims she knew little of his work, as he rarely discussed it, but knew he worked fixed hours during the week, but was on call to respond to emergencies twenty-four hours a day. He was apparently, a very methodical man and planned to the last detail most of what he did, and did so, if he possibly could, well in advance. Once he left home for the days shift, he very rarely returned and if he did, perhaps to change his clothing, following an incident, he would ring and give warning beforehand. It was, as the result if this habit, that she was able to pursue her liaison with Scampton. Often she would spend the bulk of the day with him at his cottage and her husband would not even be aware that she had been away from the house. She is now very angry with Scampton for betraying her and going off with her daughter. Anyone else she says she could have accepted, but not her daughter, whose marriage was now, as a result, in ruins. She will not accept that Scampton might have killed her husband or been in some way, involved in his demise. We believe she makes this assumption based on her recent close relationship with him and has not taken any other factors into consideration, as she claims he knew she would not leave her husband and they never discussed anything along those lines. He was very happy with his lifestyle and she with hers. The rest was a bonus, a diversion, they both liked sex, and she claims that's all there was to it. She further claims that if he wanted, or was getting, more out of their relationship than pure sex, then he would not have been attracted to the daughter. She obviously has, despite her anger, a soft spot for Scampton and sees him only in the light of their relationship. So at this point we propose to keep an open mind as to her further implications, but don't feel the need to press her any further at the moment.'

‘So what happens to her now?’ asked Fred.

‘Nothing. She was invited to come in and make a statement and nothing else. She is now free to go. She will of course be required, at some time in the future, to appear as a witness and we may have to speak to her again, but in the meantime she is free.’

‘Just like that. Kicked out to get on with her life. Some life. Husband dead, almost certainly murdered, boyfriend destined for jail and daughter’s marriage in ruins. The poor woman and to put it into your words Mel, definitely a victim of circumstance and with the exception of her little affair, non of it of her own making.’

Adams looked at her but made no comment. He shook his head as if to clear his mind then, continued. ‘To conclude, we have more information and have made some further progress with Johnson. When we have gone through this, we will break for today and reassemble again tomorrow morning,’ he then glanced at the selected piece of paper in his hand before continuing. ‘When we put it to Johnson that he knew all about Edison’s death, he replied that of course he knew all about it, he was dead. When we asked how he knew, he replied that Edison had disappeared and that everyone in the village knew and said he was dead and that’s how he knew. When asked how the people in the village knew he was dead, he replied, “Because they said so”. When asked if he did it, he replied, “No. Don’t talk crap.” When asked if he was there at the time it happened, he again replied, “No. Don’t be fucking daft.” We told him that they, without disclosing exactly who “they” were, said he had done it and he was only denying it to try and cover himself. He said they were all talking, “a load of crap and were full of shit,” and that they knew who had done it, and it was not him. If he had done it, “Then them in the village would not have had to tell him, would they, as they would have known he already knew, wouldn’t they?” Some logic, you must admit. When pressed, he became somewhat confused and was, as a result, easily tripped up and talked himself in and out of all sorts of corners. To the question, if he had not done it, but knew it had been done or had been told it had been done then he must know who did it, he said, “No. Do I fuck.” So, we then suggested that if that were the case, then it must be him who had done it. He then compounded his problems by stating that he could not have done it, when in the first place, he didn’t know who had done it and that he, himself, was not there at the time when who ever had done it had done it. Takes some working out. But then we said that he was there, not when Edison was actually killed, but when they were all talking about it and that if they were talking about it, he not only knew who did it, but also who did not do it. Would he then tell us, if he was innocent, who else was also equally innocent and therefore did not do it, and that we should not accuse them of doing it, as to do so would be wrong and grossly unfair. Although totally confused at this stage and under immense pressure, he still gave nothing and referred to the group

as "they" or "them" and would not give any names, descriptions, or any further information. He said that if he told us who they were, they would "have him" later, when we let him go. We said he would be quite safe, because if he told us who they were, then they would not be let go, by us, to get him. But if he did not tell us, we would blame him and he would be locked away for a long time and be blamed for it all, and be quite safe from everyone, but only until later, when we finally let him out and where they would still be waiting, on the outside, to "get him". According to this report, he was even further confused by all that and I must admit I am not surprised, as I had to read through it more than once to make sure I was following the gist of it. However, after contemplating in silence for some time, he came up with a final statement, in which he claimed categorically that he did not do it and that was that, and he was not prepared to discuss the matter any further. The interviewing officer made a note that extracting information from Johnson is a relatively simple matter and the fact that no further progress is being made through him in certain directions, is simply because Johnson had nothing to do with it. Was not there or in any way directly or indirectly involved, even to the extent of overhearing others or gleaning information from hearsay. What he does know will all be extracted in time. There is, however, a separate report here, on the interview, concerning Johnson's involvement in the drug and alcohol dealings. When told how he and the Builder collected, transported, and distributed drugs on their alleged Sunday fishing trips, he replied, "Who told you?" When, we said no one had told us, and that we had followed them both and had seen it all, for ourselves, he replied to the effect that if we knew all that, why were we asking him. When asked what happens to the drugs after he sold them, he claims he does not know and that they sold only to people who approached them and whom they had become familiar with. He knows no names and only sells to recognised buyers, no strangers, as it is strangers, the Builder told him, that would get them caught, and it must have been a stranger who had "shopped" them now. We said, "Yes it was", and left it at that. When we referred to his alcohol dealing, he said the two Landlords were lying bastards and had only said what they had, because they were jealous of the fact that he always had plenty of money to spend and sometimes got the odd bottle of booze given from a foreign skipper when he did odd jobs for them on their boats. He admitted that on occasions he had sold the odd bottle, but claimed he did that solely for cash with which to treat his wife and kids, or to buy more beer, as he preferred beer to spirits. When we said we had evidence of him selling, or attempting to sell, in large quantities to the Landlord of the Dog and Gun, his reply was, "That's a load of bollocks that you have got from that lying bastard who doesn't like me and who is always trying to drop me in the shit."

'There was also that rubbish bag full of empties beside the waste bin on the campsite, belonging to the Grapes. You and I saw them Mel. Remember we

sent one of the labels off in an attempt to find out where they came from. I hope we remembered to put that in our report.'

Adams looked at Fred before instructing the WPC. 'Make a note and check on that Kath. Then if it was omitted, you can get the details from this young lady, but to return, for the moment, to this. There are a couple more sheet here to complete the current run down on Johnson and I see that this is for a separate interview and refers once again to the arms dealing. Here Johnson claims his only implication in the arms dealing, which by the way, he denies has anything to do with actual arms and says that it is us, that claim they are arms, only to make it look bad for him. He says he was told that the wooden boxes contained engine parts, that were purchased cheaply and were for resale, and that he had nothing to do with any of that side of the dealing. He never saw inside any of the cases. His job, or the other job, as he prefers to call it, to separate it from the drug dealing, was to carry what ever was landed on the beach, up to the Car Park and load it onto a vehicle for one of the others to take away. He will not even give a description of the others, trying to make out, as if he expected us to believe him, that it was too dark to see, nor can he, as he again claims due to the lack of light, even identify the type of vehicle used. He says that if he does tell anything, they will definitely "have him no matter how long it takes." We said that we did not believe him, to which he replied, that we could please ourselves, because all he knew was that he has been told and reminded, on numerous occasions, that if he ever breathed a word to anyone, he would be found floating. He was told, at one time, that this method of landing goods was used only to save paying harbour dues that, if they did, only added to the cost and made the deals too expensive and not worthwhile. He was also told that he received enough money, for his share in the work, not to know or see anything. When suggested that his colleagues were Scampton, Raines, and Whiting, his reply was, "If you know so bloody much, why ask me? Ask them," and despite all our efforts, or should I say, the efforts of that particular interviewing officer, we could not get him to admit or deny the fact. Come to think of it, that's somewhat contrary to what that other officer claimed about Johnson in the previous report. Kath, make a special note of that to remind me. A change in DC might prove useful here. But back to what we have for the moment. Johnson did however deny; inconsistent character that he is: isn't he? That the builder Thornton, had anything to do with the arms, or as he insists they still are, the car parts, but while telling us this, nicely implicated Thornton in the drug dealing. When asked how he knows when something is scheduled to arrive and when it was time for him to go down to the beach and collect it, he claims he is simply told by one of the others. He said the Builder told him about the drugs and one of the others about the car parts. When pressed on the point that if he knew it was the Builder who told him about the drugs why did he not know who told him about the car parts, he still stuck to the unbelievable story that it was always too dark to see who it was that

approached him. Incredible man, isn't he? He does not know where or how the Builder gets his information and we have yet to establish if there is any possible link between the two activities. This unseen person, who creeps about in the dark and is never seen, may turn out to be one and the same or it may well prove to be two separate and distinct set-ups with the only common link being Johnson, who just happens to work for both teams. He may well be an active part of Thornton's set-up and only be a paid labourer, or hired hand, in the arms smuggling. We, at this point are not at all certain about that, particularly when the photographic evidence from the meeting in the Whitby Pub is taken into consideration. In his statement he claims he only carried boxes from the beach to the Car Park when told to do so. He will not implicate Scampton, Raines, or Whiting and says he has never heard of any of them and yet Scampton is almost a local, living on the outskirts of the village and drinking in the local Pubs and Raines is a Coastguard and spends much of his time locally. When we eventually showed him the photographs taken in the Pub at Whitby, he simply said, "Yes I go there and that is me. It is always busy and I sit and chat with anyone who wants to talk." He refused to say how often he went, or why, except saying that he only went for a drink and to look for casual work on the boats that he claims is how he makes his living. He would not say if he spoke often to any of the others in the photograph, as he claims they might not like it if he did. On the one hand, he tells us that he doesn't know them, but on the other, knows they would not like it if he said something about them to us. He denies most things initially, but then quickly admits to them when tripped or confronted with the smallest piece of evidence. We will continue to work on him for we are confident that he will eventually provide us with a substantial amount of information that we can use against the others and that, would you believe, Ladies and Gentlemen, just about sums it up for today.'

Eddie was the first to stand up.

'Well! Thank you all. It has been a pleasure working with you and I hope our paths may cross again sometime in the future.'

'Goodbye Mr Scott! It has been my pleasure meeting you and may I take this opportunity to thank you personally for your valued contribution. I shall, of course, be submitting a full report of all our findings to your department, and expressing our thanks at the same time. Once again, thank you and have a safe journey.'

'Thank you Superintendent.'

As we all filed out, Eddie came up behind us in the corridor and said, 'I intend to get away as soon as I possibly can, but certainly not before we have had a farewell drink, preferably back at the Hotel. I have arranged to pick up a hire car from there and I also need to settle my account and tie up any loose ends.'

* * *

There was little conversation on the way back to the Hotel in the Police car that had been put at our disposal. To start with, there would never really be very much said under these circumstances, as we all knew that it is never wise to talk about things in front of others which did not concern them and who were not directly involved; in this case the driver. Secondly, for some reason, we simply did not have anything in particular to say. Possibly due to the way we felt about Eddie's impending departure.

As we climbed out of the car, which had drawn up in front of the Hotel, Fred's first words were, 'I need a loo.'

'Right then, see you in the bar in a few minutes. I have my things to bring down, so I will meet in there. If that's okay by everyone,' said Eddie.

I popped into the Gents, showed Percy the porcelain, swilled my face, and combed my hair. When I went into the bar Fred was already there and was asking the barman to wait a few moments when she would then give him an order. Eddie came in and placed his bags on the floor, just inside the entrance, and walked towards us.

'Well, it seems such a long time, doesn't it? When in actual fact it has only been a few weeks and then with a gap of a week in between when you two went off for a break. I suppose all good things must come to an end and in this case I regret that very much, but on the other hand, I am more than satisfied with the results so far which seem to have made it all worthwhile. What's it to be, Whiskey and a Gin?'

'No. Vodka and Lime for me, please, Eddie.'

'And a Whiskey and Water for me please.'

'Right. So that's a single whiskey for me. I'm driving and a double Whiskey and Water for this guy and a double Vodka and Lime for the Lady please,' he said to the barman.

'Hey, hang on. It's a bit early for doubles,' said Fred. 'I hope you have no evil plans to slope off from here and leave us behind drunk.'

'Who cares? It's my last chance to thank you folks and wish you all the very best.'

'Cheers then.'

'Cheers.'

'What's next then? Have you anything exciting lined up to look forward to? Anything to keep you on your toes?'

It was rather a silly question and I knew it, because I didn't expect, for one moment, a direct answer and if he had given me one, I would have automatically expected it to be a lie or at the most a half-truth. Personal questions of that nature are not part of our business and we would only ask them, if they were relevant to something that was ongoing in an investigation and then only if it concerned us all.

In any other circumstances, direct questions between different agencies are taboo and something that is just not done. It is only at the levels where Cruickshank and his equals operate, that there are interdepartmental exchanges of information and sometimes even then, that can be guarded or limited in it's content and even considered, on many occasions, with distrust and suspicion.

'I have no idea what they will give me next and I still have plenty of my own loose ends to tie up, which will keep me out of mischief for quite some time.'

The perfect answer, I thought. I couldn't have put it any better, or more vaguely, myself.

'No doubt someone in our department will be lining up something for us for when we get back,' I said, working along similar lines.

'I know what your first job will be,' said Fred, which made me look at her with some surprise. I didn't expect a direct statement or even a hint about our future to come from Fred.

'And what might that be?' I said, laughing.

'Designing a telephone box big enough to hold only one person no matter what the circumstances,' she giggled, 'or submitting a full report to the Old Man justifying the need to have two persons in one phone box at the same time and enjoying it. With emphasis on the enjoyment.'

'What's all that about?' asked Eddie. 'It sounds to me, from that and the bits you have already said about him in the past, that your Chief really is a bit of an odd-bod.'

'Not really! Well yes he is. He has some very strange ideas and his sense of humour, we think, is nil. We blame his wife but it can't all be her and I suppose in a strange way, he does have some sort of humour, or thinks he has, particularly when it emanates from him and he is the one trying to be funny. But at the moment he has developed this thing about phone boxes and just can't see the funny side of it and yet if it were him telling it as a tale, then it would be considered hilarious.'

'Hilarious! Tell me one thing he has said that is remotely funny or for that matter one thing that he has ever said that he thinks is funny. I have never heard him,' I said.

'Have you never been there when he tells his favourite story of the time when he was at GCCS Bletchley, either working there or running a department or something and everyone said, according to him, that GCCS stood for Golf Club and Chess Set. You must have and then seen him fall about, when he tells it, which he does with monotonous regularity. He also tells others, along a similar vein, but that is definitely his favourite and is bound to come out at sometime around Christmas.'

'Now you can see what I mean when I say he is not exactly our scene when it comes to humour,' I laughed.

'I definitely do. But tell me, just as a matter of curiosity what is all this about him and the phone box? Unless you are talking about the newer, open fronted, types there is hardly room to do anything in a phone box?'

'Oh yes there is. It's easy. First of all I get Fred…'

'Shut up you! If you don't want to end up in big trouble.'

'Sorry folks, forget all about it,' said Eddie. 'The last thing I want to do is cause a riot.'

'You won't. But he might if he pursues that line,' replied Fred, laughing.

'But joking apart and trying to be a little more serious for a moment, if I can,' said Eddie. 'What I shall really be looking forward to is…'

'Oh yes! Is what? Come on out with it. What might that be?' enquired Fred, who was still laughing and had cut him off before he had time to finish his sentence.

'No, I am being serious and thought you might have already guessed. Finding out who killed Edison of course. But I suppose I will have to be patient and wait for the final reports and the results of all the Police findings. What do you think the outcome might be, Mel?'

'Thinking about it so far, it could have been anyone of them. But let's see; who have we got in the first place that could have done it, or had good reason to do it, or for that matter, had cause to do it? Almost anyone I suppose. What do you think, Fred?'

'Well, like you say. Who do we have? We have Johnson and Scampton, Thornton and Raines, and also Whiting; there's plenty to go on for a start and all are possibilities and suspects,' said Fred.

'Don't forget Pat Edison or even Johnson's wife,' suggested Eddie. 'Or Thornton's wife or even his own son-in-law if he believed that Edison had anything to do with Jenny's affair.'

'Johnson's wife or his son-in-law?' repeated Fred, somewhat surprised.

'Yes, why not? Take Johnson's wife. She is a mad little bitch who loves money and possibly also loves her man and who knows, she may have found out Edison was on to something which she believed was a threat to either one of them or for that matter, to both of them. Johnson himself may have told her something and she with her tiny brain cells may have decided to do something stupid.'

'Like knock Edison off? How on earth could she get to him without him being suspicious? I can't see him being the type who would go anywhere near the likes of her, unless he had to in a professional capacity, let alone be influenced by her feminine charms and advances and then let her get close enough to clobber him,' said Fred.

'I don't know. Who would have thought that Pat Edison would have gone with Scampton and what about Pat Edison herself? She may have harboured some notions that, with her husband out of the way, everything would be fine

between herself and Scampton. She had a motive and although she claims she knows nothing of her husband's work, may, in truth, have known all about it and knew why and where, he was going on the night he disappeared. Perhaps her and Scampton followed him on that "fateful" night, as they like to describe it in the media and Law Courts.'

'But was Scampton all that interested in Pat Edison? Don't forget he appears to have dumped her and gone after the daughter.'

'Maybe he did. Maybe he felt quite safe in doing so, particularly when he had a hold over Pat Edison, in so much, as he was her accomplice in her husband's death. Pat might have wanted her husband dead to lay the way clear for her to be with Scampton. Scampton on the other hand may have had entirely different motives. He might have wanted Edison out of the way because Pat had, unknowingly, given him information as to what her husband was up to in his work, without realising how this directly affected Scampton and his illegal activities. I doubt if Pat Edison had any idea he was up to his eyes in smuggling. So at the end of the day both Pat Edison and Scampton may have wanted him out of the way, but for entirely different reasons. There's even the remote chance that Edison knew about his daughter's affair with Scampton and went after him one night to confront him and ended up dead for his trouble.'

'What about the others? Anyone of them could have done it also, and had a very good motive for doing so and you, yourself, mentioned even the son-in-law just now.'

'True. I agree. They certainly could. But let's take the son-in-law. Highly unlikely I know, but what if he believed that his father-in-law was in some way involved in Jenny's romance, either condoned it, or covered it up, or even caused it, or in some way allowed it to happen in the first place, who knows? Then take Thornton for another example. His wife has a shop and Pat Edison works for her in a spare time capacity. We have no way of knowing what they discussed when they were alone in that shop. They may well have confided all their little secrets to each other. Thornton's wife, Fancy Pants, may have complained bitterly about her husband always being away in connection with his work and then associating with Johnson in his spare time or told her how, in truth, she was happy about it all as it allowed her plenty of freedom to pursue her own affairs and indiscretions. Pat Edison may have been aware of her husband's activity and mentioned this to Fancy Pants who, if she was truly aware of her husband and Johnson's dealings, had passed the information on to them, or at least her husband, who, as a result, had panicked and knocked Edison off.'

'There was one thing in the Police reports which makes that highly unlikely,' said Fred.

'And what was that?'

'Johnson, assuming, of course, that he is basically telling a fair amount of the truth, or we can for the moment accept that he is, said he did not do it, but was there when the others, plural, talked about it and knew from that who did it. The others, he specifically said. Now remember, that as far as we are aware, there have been two different types of smuggling taking place. One, drugs for cash and clothing, the other - arms and explosives for cash. Johnson is common to both and for the benefit of my argument, we have to accept that, and I think we can. Therefore we also have to accept that, as far as we are aware and Johnson claims, the drugs were only a Johnson and Thornton operation. So there could hardly be "others" for him to refer to there and it is fairly certain and confirmed again by Johnson's statements that there were only the two of them involved. That being the case then Thornton had nothing to do with the Johnson, Scampton, Raines and Whiting group and could therefore not be one of the "others" mentioned by Johnson who in actual fact, by that inference, almost gives him an alibi. I know it doesn't rule him out altogether and relies a lot on Johnson's statement and also I accept he also had a motive, but Johnson refers specifically to "others" when he talked about it? So I would be tempted to eliminate Thornton as I would any of the "others" if they were meant to include Pat Edison, Fancy Pants, the daughter, and most definitely the son-in-law. So you have left, after that, the four in the arms deals.'

'Unless there was of course, more than the two of them in the drug dealing; someone we, as yet, don't know about.'

'Could be and I realise that of course.'

'Raines and Whiting we don't know much about as yet, but what we do know is that again, each had a very good motive. For example Edison had accused Raines of having an affair with his wife, which we believe was a mistake on his part and it was Scampton he got Raines confused with. We also know that Raines had Coastguard connections with Edison and through that could have found out that Edison knew something that threatened their security. After all we are dealing with arms and the possible Irish connection here and we now know that Raines has strong connections in that direction. Whiting is the one we know the least about. We don't know, as yet, if he knew Edison or if the others passed him information, which I can see no possible reason why they should not, about him. He, Whiting that is, was very much part of the set up and his security would be threatened just as much as anyone else. So there is every reason to keep him well informed as to what was happening or to pass on to him any bits of relative information. We are only suspicious of him, or should I say, we are only more suspicious of him, or I am, if you like, than the rest, because we saw him go along and alone up the ravine path to the cliff top where Edison was known to have been. So then if that was his allocated and specific task on each occasion in the operation, always assuming there has been more than one occasion, and it was him who always went up there,

then it was very probable that it was him who came across Edison and, I assume, rightly or wrongly, attacked him. If on the other hand they had prior knowledge of Edison's intentions or they suspected he was even remotely on to something, then anyone of them, or maybe two of them, or for that matter, all of them, could have followed him, or lain in wait and attacked him that particular night.'

'There may be others outside the group that we know absolutely nothing about and, I suppose on that basis, we could go on speculating for ever. Really it is now all down to the Police and your boys Eddie, to clear up the mass of details.'

'Not so much our boys: as the Police from now on. Granted the operation comes indirectly under the umbrella of our programme of anti-terrorist activity, but dealing with exposed pockets, such as this now is, falls very much into the lap of the Police working under their Special Branch. We, of course, will keep an eye on things and see if it effects other things on a broader front, but that is not my direct responsibility and that is, the main reason, why I have now been recalled. But that won't stop me following the progress on this case, if only for my own satisfaction. Will you two still be around for the final outcome? In at the kill as they say?'

'I don't know, but I hope so. Having got this far it would be nice to see it through to the end. But like your-self, it is really now out of our hands. I suppose, in a strange way, we have done all we were sent to do and the rest is now down to "the powers that be". Our Chief, no doubt, will decide what happens next, but if your set-up is anything like ours, where it blows from hot to cold, on almost a daily basis, you never know exactly where you stand at any one time. We could be left here to the end and beyond, or we could be pulled out and recalled at a moments notice. No doubt we maybe a lot wiser the next time we phone in our progress report. In the meantime, another drink anyone?'

'Not for me thanks, you understand,' said Eddie as he dangled his car keys up in front of my face. Fred shook her head indicating no and remained silent.

As we stood there, for those last few minutes, making polite conversation, we were obviously all affected by the fact that we were about to break up.

Eddie's departure, I felt, I could cope with and would quickly adjust to, but eventually parting from Fred was something I dare not contemplate as I knew that would be a different ball game altogether. I think I was somewhat relieved when Eddie broke my depressing line of thought, by saying, 'Well, folks, I have a long way to go and it's getting on,' and putting his empty glass down on the bar, stuck out his hand and said, 'Cheerio old chap, been lovely to meet you and it has been good working with you. Look after this girl, she is something special.'

We shook hands, during which time I felt a genuine affection for him and when we broke free he offered his hand to Fred.

'What can I say when I have to leave the prettiest girl I have ever had the pleasure of working with? And I shall remember you, your looks, and your bacon butties for a very long time. Not to mention the tea made with glue water.'

'Say nothing now. Just remember the nice bits,' she said, and taking his hand in hers she placed her other hand on the back of his neck and drawing his head forward, kissed him. Then, still with her hand around his neck she said, 'If I could escape from the charms of this horrible man I might be tempted to ask if I could come with you.'

'Well, that's that nicest thing anyone has said to me in a long time. Your offer is really appreciated although I don't know what my wife would make of it. Bless you and see you both sometime. Take care.'

'And you. Look after yourself,'

We both stood and waved and before we actually realised it, he was gone.

With the back of her index finger Fred wiped away a little tear that was just about to fall down her cheek and dashing towards the door stammered, 'I need to wash and change before dinner.'

I ordered another drink and when it arrived, I sat alone for a few minutes, perched on a bar stool, and thought about everything that had happened to us all, during this last few weeks. Events that had, not only had an effect on my life, but which would change the lives of a lot of other people, sending many of them in directions they could never have possibly imagined before we arrived on the scene.

As I contemplated the various issues and our experiences to date, one of the minor events among the thousands of others, which ran in a continuous jumble through my mind, was that I too, without doubt, along with Fred, would miss Eddie. There was something endearing about him.

'Simply a lovely man,' was the way Fred put it later.

CHAPTER FIFTY-THREE

Eddie had gone and we were beginning to adjust and slowly get used to his absence. We had, among many other things and as part of our routine chores, made our report to the Old Man from the phone box down the road. He was pleased with our progress and appeared to be remarkably well informed, from which I could only assumed, he must have been receiving reports, more or less immediately they became available and it would not have surprise me, to have learnt that in some instances, that was even before us.

We spent the remainder of that evening crossing between the bar and the television lounge or should I say, Fred did most of the paddling back and forth as she was the one who always seemed to be the first to require a refill and insisted she went for them.

We were fortunate and had the TV and the lounge, set aside for it, to ourselves. It had been a long time since I had had the opportunity to sit in comfort and watch television, uninterrupted, for any length of time. I took full advantage and, as is my regular habit, nodded off through the middle of most of the programmes. Something I have always been very good at when not disturbed. Fred found it highly amusing and admonished me for daring to go to sleep in her company and then reminded me, and taunted me, over all the interesting things, she claimed, I had missed. I really didn't care for I felt better for the sleep and after all, who really cares who won tonight's star prize or what Bogdan Sodoffubitch has been up to in some obscure central European state or what is the latest act of crass stupidity that has been perpetrated by a Raghead Arab leader. Let them all blow themselves to bits for whatever political or religious beliefs they may choose to support and use to justify the stupidity of it all. I enjoyed my snooze and that was all that mattered to me.

* * *

The following morning found us once again gathered in the conference room of the Police Station and with the exception of the recently departed Eddie, everyone was there who had been there, on the previous afternoon.

'Good morning once again,' greeted Chief Superintendent Adams. 'We can start this mornings' proceedings by looking at what Mrs Raines has had to say for herself. She has recovered from her suicide attempt but after the scare she gave us, is still being very closely watched. According to the Doctor she is still very deeply depressed and shocked by her present predicament. Her bra has been taken away

from her, as this, apparently, is what she tried to use in her attempt to hang herself. Fortunately, it proved to be unsuitable and sadly let her down, but to get back to her statement. When confronted with the information about her-self, supplied to us by the RUC, and our own collated knowledge of her background, the relief she showed, according to the interviewing officer, was immense. He states that it was as if she had been waiting for a very long time to get out of, what she herself described as, a bloody nightmare, following her brother's death. She tells us that when her brother died, the shock numbed her and then left her filled with hatred and an almost uncontrollable anger, not only at the unknown perpetrators of his murder, but at the whole ugly business in Northern Ireland. She began, from that point in time, to hate everyone and blamed, what she believed was, their general apathy towards everything and their total unconcern at what was going on around them, as being responsible for what was happening to them all. The bombings, the sectarian murders, the church interference, which she calls "the holier than thou brigade" and the self elected leaders and politicians, who she claims, talked out of, and I quote, "their arses as their heads are so full of shit". She desperately wanted revenge for what had happened and was so blinded by the need for retribution that she didn't even stop to think how she could possibly bring it about. She claims that, had she stopped to think, she now realises that there was nothing she alone could effectively have done and so she would probably have done nothing, thus preventing herself from ending up in her present predicament. But she didn't stop to think. She took to the streets and attended radical and paramilitary meetings, often getting very drunk and making a wide range of ridiculous threats and promises. She doesn't know and can't understand how her husband stuck with her during this period. But he did and it didn't take long before she attracted the attention of those who were only too willing to draw her in and use the likes of her, to further their own ends. They took her under their wing and fuelled her anger and filled her head with all sorts of ideological rubbish about unity, self rule and independence and of course, "the cause". She is still not sure if she fully understood what most of it was all about. But those a little higher up in the organisation, probably realised that behind her anger there was some intelligence and this they could exploit and so therefore decided to do so and to use her. They eventually persuaded her that she could better serve the cause and thus avenge her brother's death, by becoming a part of their underground organisation. Hard men, they told her; those thugs and the likes out on the street, were ten a penny. Brains and organising ability was thin on the ground. She says she easily fell for this and soon realised that this suited her much better, as her initial irrational desire to kill everyone who she thought might have been remotely involved in her brother's murder, was not only stupid, but was impossible. She still wanted revenge and was determined to get it, but if it meant going onto the street and committing acts of violence, she now realised she would far rather someone else did that on her behalf. She

says she is not a killer, never has been and could never become one, despite her tragic, and what she still believes is, her unjust loss. However, the people who recruited her must have found her sufficiently responsive to their particular views and the principals of “the cause”, as they all saw them, for they finally integrated her into their undercover network. Something, she says, she willingly accepted initially. She was well and truly indoctrinated and was persuaded that she would best serve the cause from a distance: from behind the scenes, as they put it. She was given basic instruction on how her part in the set-up operated. She was told where to go and what to do when she got there. At the same time she was provided with adequate funds to cover all her expenses and more besides. She says the organisation was always very generous when it came to the funding. But at the same time adequately covered and protected their investment, with their own ideas of security, as she was to find out later. After having been told where she was to go, she was also told how she would be contacted. Until that contact was made she was to make no moves, or do anything, without having firstly been directed by them and certainly nothing, like making contact with her family, for example, which might have compromised her whereabouts and position. Part of her training, immediately following her recruitment and before her placement, was in the art of undercover contact procedures. She was also told her husband was to accompany her and to persuade him to do so, and eliminate any doubts he may have had about not going, they suggested it might not be safe for him to remain behind. He therefore was only too willing to go, as, in the first place, he had no desire to be parted from his wife, and in the second, they were, the organisation that is, after all providing a good incentive, through generous funding and subtle threats. She thinks they both now realised, but never discussed it, that the threats to her husband’s safety may not have been strictly true but were made only as a means of persuading them both to come over here onto the mainland and to work together as a team, or at the very least, to appear as a respectable, inoffensive couple.’

‘I think she may have been in for a bit of a shock if ever she had tried to put it to the test,’ Interjected Cameron from the opposite side of the table.

‘Possibly,’ added Adams as he continued. ‘So when the time came, they came across to the mainland and set up home in the designated area. As instructed, they opened a Giro Bank account and sent details of the account to a Post Office box in Belfast. Shortly after, and thereafter on a regular basis, sums of money appeared in the account which more than adequately covered their living expenses. Her husband found work and they settled down and, as far as she could tell, they seemed to fit in well with the local population. Nothing happened for months and her anger began to subside and almost disappear, as she began to adjust to her new surroundings and the different lifestyle. Even the regular monthly cash deposits, paid into the bank account, failed to fuel her enthusiasm and reminded her less, with the passing of time, of the reason why she was where she was. Then one

day, completely out of the blue and totally unexpected, it all came flooding back. She was in their local Pub having a quiet drink and mixing with the locals, when a complete stranger, seizing on an odd moment when she was alone, approached her and addresses her directly by name and mentioned the contact code word she had been given all those many months before. He arranged to meet her and at that meeting, told her what was required of her. He briefed her and during that briefing she was given sufficient information to identify a particular Customs and Excise officer. This information included a photograph, his name, address, type, and colour of the car he drove and its registration number. Her task was to befriend him and extract information concerning certain activities in the local and surrounding area, all of which was to be carefully listed and logged in detail. She remembers asking at the time, rather naively, how she should go about befriending this man, only to be told that girls with a big smile and no knickers, usually had no trouble. Should he prove to have other sexual preferences then the job should be transferred over to her husband. Initially she was appalled, being a religious girl and flatly refused, as the method suggested was not to her liking or the "way she had been brought up". It was then that the contact referred to the guarantees that the organisation held, which he assured her, were there only to be used as a last resort, but would be used if necessary, to ensure her loyalty and obedience. She says that at first she failed to fully understand what that implied, so it was spelled out to her in no uncertain terms. She was, she was reminded, part of the organisation and all that meant, and would do exactly as she was told, and do it without question. As if to reinforce this and leave her in no doubt, she was further reminded that her father was currently in prison for some minor offence and that prisoners died by accident, while in custody, with monotonous regularity. Particularly when and where, there are gathered a large population of biased and bigoted political prisoners and others supportive of the cause, who would all willingly oblige if it would help to persuade a "colleague" to co-operate and do exactly as they were told. Also, she was told, the planting of explosives was a simple and almost routine exercise. Therefore to blow up the family home; her mother and any other occupants presented no problems. It could all be arranged by a simple telephone call if all she required was a demonstration of the organisations efficiency and persuasive abilities, when it came to reminding members of their sworn loyalty. All the old nightmares then returned and she realised that she was still trapped despite the many months of inactivity and the mellowing of her anger. She also knew there was no way out. She had no choice but to go along with their wishes. She claims that later, when she got over the initial shock, she had discussed it, in great detail, with her husband, to see if there was any possible ways out. But they came to the conclusion that there was not, except for the unacceptable exception of suicide, and that being out of the question, as she was not only a coward in that direction and a good catholic and she also feared they might blow up her family out of revenge if they killed themselves,

they accepted they were well and truly trapped. No matter how long they discussed it or however many times the subject was raised, there was still nowhere for them to go and they feared that the organisation, which they knew is vast and complex, would be certain to catch up with them sooner or later, even if they took the chance and simply ran. That and the threat to harm her parents was all a bit too much, for there was no way she could permit or cause harm to befall them. According to this report, she then broke down and was extremely distressed and was unable to continue for quite some time. Strange when not too long ago all she wanted was to kill everyone in sight in revenge for her brother.'

'But attitudes do change with time,' sighed Fred.

'They do indeed Miss and in particular with changed circumstance, and with changes in pressures, particularly from outside sources, but to continue. When she resumed she said, the man who paid her the visit and set all this up, disappeared and was never seen again. All she remembers of him, is that he had a strong provincial Northern Irish accent and even if she could describe him, or recognise his picture, she would not, as she now fears even more for her parents safety, following the recent events and her arrest.'

The Inspector broke off while he selected another report sheet from his pile. Satisfied it followed on, he continued, 'It didn't take her long to strike up an acquaintance with the Customs man, who she did not find all that disagreeable and shortly after that, they were having sex regularly in the back of his official, little dark green, Customs van. He was a member of the uniform branch and as such, travelled extensively back and forth along the coast. She experienced no problems meeting up with him and did so within a matter of days once she realised she had no choice in the matter. She then gave him the chat line about being married with a husband away at sea, which, she told him, left her bored and lonely. She told him she loved men in uniform and that was one of the main reasons why she was initially attracted to her husband and eventually married him. To this she added that she was fascinated to sit in his van and listen to his radio, stating that her husband had one like it, which she loved to listen to, but dare not switch on when he was away. She made out that she loved to watch him working and thought that what he did was fascinating and exciting. It all reminded her of her husband, she claimed, and because she missed him wanted the Customs man to make it all up to her. She had no idea if he accepted her story but he was more than willing to make up for the alleged lack of physical contact. This led to her spending more and more time with him and only breaking off for the odd day or so when she claimed her husband was home on a short leave. After each break she would ring him and they would resume their liaison. All the time she continued to collect information and often whist doing so, to maximise her gain would pretending ignorance and ask questions or request detailed explanations. She now thinks it all sounds rather corny, to use her expression, but it worked at the time, and he seemed

very happy with what he was getting in exchange for answering all her questions. She did not concern herself with the value of the information; that she had been told was someone else's worry. All she did was repeat everything she heard, from whatever source she gathered it, to her husband, who recorded it, as instructed, on the inside of a greetings card of the type that folds into four. He then posted it off in rotation to one of five private addresses, that they had been given for different places, in and around the Midlands. She is prepared to tell us that there were five different addresses, but won't tell us what they are, or even give us a clue as to their whereabouts. She claims she never knew them but we believe she did, but is still very scared of the consequences of divulging any information of that nature which she believes maybe traced back to them. We realise, of course that these threats are only too real and that this, along with other things, are all part of the dreadful mess she finds herself in. But then she got herself into it, not us. We will have to do a lot more work on this one and with a bit of luck perhaps find out a bit more. A thorough search of their home, which is currently in hand, may well prove of value in that direction. Pity Mr Scott has left. He would probably have found that snippet, concerning the five addresses, very interesting. No doubt his department will want to look into that one also, if they don't already know all about it, of course. It is amazing how well informed they always seem to be. You, on the other hand, Mr Williams should have no problem in singling out and identifying the uniformed Customs officer.'

'No problems whatsoever,' answered Ron Williams, from the opposite side of the table. 'He is as good as nailed already.'

'It was from information obtained from this Customs Officer, that resulted in the first drop, that you Mr Grundy and your partner there, so painstakingly staked out, only to find it had been called off. Apparently one evening, when they were sitting in his van, his radio was particularly quiet and he was complaining that he was bored with his work, but not of what they were doing at that particular moment, and that the only bit of excitement that had occurred all that day was information from his superior, to the effect that one of their Senior Investigators was travelling up from the South and would be in the village on some special assignment. In the meantime all other Customs Officers were instructed to stay away so he did not know if he would be able to meet up with her as she had no transport to come to him. She was alarmed by this, pressed him for as much detail as she could safely extract and then, naturally, passed this information straight on to her husband, who immediately logged it and posted it off. She remembers he also rang someone else and passed on the same piece of information. This is the first reference we have to passing information to anyone other than via the post to the designated address. When pursued and pressed she now says she can't remember who exactly it was that was rung, but believes, following our prompting, that it might have been Whiting. She then tried to change her mind yet again and say she thought the phone

call had nothing to do with the information regarding the Customs people and was probably a normal private call that her husband just made, as he often did, to one of their friends. We think she probably does remember clearly and knows very well who it was. But simply chooses to claim loss of memory and withhold information each time she reminds herself of the very real threats from the organisation behind her and panics at the thoughts of what their future reactions are now going to be. I can't say I blame her for they are well known for the ruthless bunch that they are. However, later she then remembers, when the desire to get it all off her chest is at it's strongest and the threat of the organisation has been pushed temporarily into the background, that someone was told and she knows that as a result, a radio message was sent and the planned drop aborted. She also found out on which day the visiting Customs Investigator was due to leave and from that information the drop was rearranged and we can safely assume that it was the one you witnessed along with Mr Scott.'

'So she managed to get to the Customs man despite transport problems and from that knows all about the arms drop then?' enquired Fred.

'What some girls will do for nookie,' I whispered only to get a kick on the shin by way of an answer.

'Indeed we believe she does Miss and despite her reluctance to give names and remember, on occasions, selected detail, she has told us a great deal. I think at this point we should all remember that Mrs Raines is under a great deal of stress and is suffering from confusion and the effects of conflicting emotions, even to the point of attempting suicide, as we well know, the results of her current and passed ordeals. In one respect, her being caught and arrested has no doubt been a great relief to her, and I believe accounts for the present upsurges in cooperation where she wants to get the whole thing out of the way and behind her as quickly as possible. But their remains with all the confusion and conflict, and the problems associated with it, the safety of her parents. In that respect the organisation still holds the upper hand and she knows it and that is where most of the conflict comes in. Each time she finds herself cooperating with us, she is then pulled in the opposite direction, by thoughts of what might now happen to her family, and this causes her to suddenly pull up and stop. But as long as we recognise this, take it fully into account, and adjust accordingly, we will make progress. At the moment we are taking it very easy and coaxing her along slowly, and letting her set the pace. Believe me, we are very grateful for everything we are slowly extracting from her and what she is reluctantly releasing. What she chooses to leave out at the moment, we will go back to and deal with later when, we believe, the time is right.'

'Can her parents not be got safely out of Ireland?' enquired Fred. Then as an after though, quickly added, 'Sorry I should not have asked that. Of course they could. It would be no problem for Eddie Scott's department, but then none of them are on our side, are they? So why should we. After all, she didn't give herself

up, did she? We caught her? I was thinking more as one woman for another and, for the moment, I failed to realise who and what, she represents, even though at the moment she does appear to be repentant and very vulnerable. Sorry, you were saying Superintendent?'

He smiled and continued, 'She initially started out by saying that she was not sure if there had been previous drops, but thought there might have been. But she knew exactly what was going on concerning the drop you and your team, witnessed Mr Grundy. So she probably knows all about previous arrangements if there were any. But then, apparently for some unknown reason, she chose to become vague again on that point. This time, we believe, because we chose to change the subject slightly and question her about her husband and the part he played in the drop. To this, she tried to claim, that she was not sure if her husband was directly involved in anything, let alone our references to this current shipment of arms. Yet prior to that, we reminded her, she had said that her husband had informed a second or third party of something and, as a result, a drop had been delayed and that also he was the one, she said, that sent off the information, she gathered, through the post. She then claimed she had misled us on that point and that in actual fact she recorded and posted off this information herself. However, from all that, this is what we gather, partly from what she has previously told us and which fits in, and partly from what we have summarized, put to her and she has not denied. When the drop was finally made, she was given a hand drawn map, complete with grid references, showing exactly where the stuff was hidden. The only other information shown on this map, or sketch, was a time and a date. She will, however, not tell us who gave her the map, or how it came into her possession, or if her husband knew of its existence, or if he was in any way implicated in its manufacture. All she will say is that she put it into a Birthday Invitation Card, as instructed, and posted it to a Post Office box in Birmingham. That is something else for the anti-terrorist boys to pick up on. Now, from that and picking up on the map, according to your report Mr Grundy, you saw only Scampton take the stuff away from a Car Park, which was being used as a staging post, following it's movement up from the beach and you are confident that he alone could not handle the cases, at the final point of offloading and delivery.'

'He might have done, at a push, if he had sufficient time. But they were heavy and we calculated that he didn't, according to the time factor involved, and so therefore it is very difficult to accept that he could have completed the operation without some help.'

'Thank you! So we must assume that having had and needing, assistance to load his vehicle in the Car Park, he must also have had to have additional assistance from at least one other person, perhaps more, to off load the stuff at the other end. Also at some point along the way, the cases were carefully wrapped and sealed in polythene before being buried. That also takes time. We can also assume

that at sometime around then, or shortly after, the map would be marked up ready to pass to Mrs Raines. Who actually gave it to her, we don't know and so far cannot find out, as she categorically refuses to say. We, of course believe there is a strong possibility that it was Scampton but we suggested, if it was not her husband, was it: Scampton, Johnson, or Whiting and at the same time showed her the photographs taken in Whitby, which of course, included her husband. She said her husband may know the others but she did not and none of those in the pictures passed her anything. When we said they were all implicated and that if it was not her husband who had produced the map then it must have been one of the others. She said we could claim all we wanted, but she was saying nothing, which might harm her husband further or indirectly her family. She then tried to retract all her previous statements saying she had fabricated them all to confuse us and throw us off the real issue, which was, that her husband knew nothing, including any knowledge of the men in the pictures, and that she recorded all the information herself, that she alone gathered and posted it all off herself. Her husband, she said, was ignorant of any of it, including the reasons they had come across to England from Ireland. She then actually tried to compound the issue by claiming that she told her husband nothing, and that he knew nothing of her brother's killing and that by knowing nothing could not be implicated or blamed for anything. The interviewing officers decided a break was necessary at that point. When the interview resumed she appeared more composed, but would not be drawn on anything previously discussed. She said she had told only a pack of lies and she had made it all up to keep us happy and that as far as she was concerned, we could dump the whole lot in the waste bin, for that was all it was worth. She would no longer agree to anything and said we could go to hell if we expected her to sign anything and we could all go and play with the wee folk, which is where we all belonged. Obviously a bad bout of fear of reprisal had set in at this stage.'

'Was that the end of it then? I assume it must have been. If things had really begun to deteriorate so badly at that point?' enquired Fred.

'More or less Miss, or it was for the time being. But we went back to her, as indeed we will continue to do so until we are satisfied she can tell us no more. A little later we did manage to get some additional information out of her that may well prove useful. She reluctantly told us, that her husband had joined the Coastguard Service as an auxiliary, whilst living in Northern Ireland and that there had been the opportunity to transfer to North Yorkshire when they came to live over here, so he took it. She claims he was involved with the Service before she met him and that he was in it for all the right reasons. She denies any tie-up between his Coastguard activities and the reasons they are currently in custody. No doubt you, Mr Grundy will quickly ascertain the truth on that particular point.'

'At the first opportunity,' I replied, but did not add that we had requested and had already received, and had in our possession, a run down on Raines, which

told us all we wanted to know about him at the time, but nothing about his current illegal activities. I wondered if the Old Man would still be happy when he discovered the whole truth about Raines, particularly when his proud boast has always been, that he knows everything there is to know, about everyone in the Service.

'On the question of Philip Edison, Mrs Raines claims she knows he went missing but did not know him personally, or has she ever met him and she refuses to say anything that would suggest an unhappy relationship between her husband and him, or a tie-up, which may have provided Edison with information which allowed him to find out what was going on in the area, and as a result of that knowledge, act upon it, and ultimately meet his death. She said it was highly unlikely there would be anything between them, as her husband detested Edison and had been accused by him, of having an affair with his wife Pat. Her husband, she claims, refused to work with Edison from then on, and would only set Coastguard Watch when the other full time officer was on duty. Our Interviewing Officer, and here's a turn up for the books, had a cup of coffee thrown over him, when he suggested, first of all, that he could not accept the first suggestion that there was not an unhappy relationship, as she put it, between her husband and Edison when later and almost in the same breath, she said he would have nothing to do with him as he had been accused of having an affair with the wife, Pat. Secondly, when he suggested that her husband may well have been implicated with both Edison and his wife, as she, Mrs Raines, had, by her own admission, spent a great deal of time with the Customs officer and while doing so, was generous with her sexual favours and had perhaps neglected her husband so that he might have gone elsewhere. Perhaps to Mrs Edison. Finally, and this is the point where the coffee was actually thrown, it was suggested that her husband may have approached Edison from the point of view of exposing the group. Perhaps because he was scared, perhaps because of her behaviour with the Customs man, or perhaps for other, unknown, personal reasons. She apparently screamed that her husband was not a "snitch" or would he betray her, nor was he a traitor to "the cause". It appears that at that point the interview had to be terminated so that the officer could go and get himself cleaned up and she could be confined to her cell to settle down. At least the statements she has made so far, even though she may now be trying to withdraw them or distort them, are of immense value, whether she intended that in the first place or not, and I think that by filling in the blank spaces ourselves, we are now beginning to get a very clear picture of events and happenings that have revolved around Mr and Mrs Raines and some of their close associates.'

'Poor girl and all because she was in the wrong place at the wrong time,' sighed Fred.

'Yes indeed Miss. I think it is called, Sods Law,' suggested Len Jones from the opposite side of the table.

'It's sods' something,' retorted Fred.

'What do we have on Raines himself?' I tentatively enquired, looking at Adams.

'One moment, for I am sure I have something here, somewhere, deep down within this lot, on Raines.'

The Superintendent was beginning to show definite signs of enthusiasm and personal satisfaction as he sorted through his papers. It was obvious, that to him, everything was going exceedingly well.

'Ah, here it is. Ronald Raines. As we know from his wife's statements and from our own cross checking, he went to Ireland initially to find work. He had no previous criminal record and his employment records show that he had been out of work for some considerable time, before he left for Ireland. There is no record of why he selected Ireland and in particular Northern Ireland, but that is where he chose to go and where he went. There he met and eventually married his wife and everything went relatively smoothly until the day his brother-in-law was shot and killed. He claims that it was because of that and the traumatic effect that it had on his wife, that they decided to come back to mainland Britain and for no other reason. He had joined the Coastguard Service whilst in Northern Ireland and transferred from there to North Yorkshire, another reason he claims, why they chose to live near to the coast. He openly admits he did not like Edison and had a serious row with him, but states that that is no reason to kill him or anyone else for that matter. He says that if he went round killing everyone he didn't like, then the place would be littered with dead bodies, starting with all of us in here and the likes of us outside. He laughed and ridiculed any suggestions that his wife was involved with a Customs Officer and the further suggestions of a close tie-up with terrorism and smuggling. He dismissed it all as the biggest heap of "bullshit" he had heard in a long, long time. Our obsession, as he puts it, with Northern Ireland, can only mean that we have all been "shagged by Leprechauns," and that we are all away with the "fairies," to quote his own words. The photographs are all "crap" and only show him having a drink with a few casual acquaintances and strangers and nothing more. When asked to look at the pictures again he claimed he remembered that night well and that the Pub was busy and there was only one spare seat, so he took it, and that he had never seen anyone else in the pictures before that night or since. When it was pointed out to him that the pictures showed him in conversation with the others, he replied to the effect that it would only be "numb buggers," like us, who would sit in a Pub and not speak to a stranger who spoke to them first. He said that if a guy asks you the time or a football score and you know it, you tell him. The photographs prove nothing according to him. When told he had been observed on the beach and in the Car Park and that they had not been alone, as they thought, on that night, he replied that he could now smell the "bullshit" and see it running out of our ears. He is considered, by the Investigating Officers, at the moment at least, to be still very hostile and uncooperative, and he is treating everything as

being pure speculation on our part and all a huge joke. He says we are fabricating it all for our own entertainment and deeply resents and reacts very violently to all our suggestions that his wife neglected him in favour of the Customs Officer. At one point, during one of his outbursts at what he claims are “bloody lies thought up by idiots” and following a request for a drink, he asked the WPC who delivered it, if she were Alice in Wonderland and where did she fit into this Mad Hatter’s Tea Party. He also asked her if all the inmates of this lunatic asylum, were dressed in blue and if she could tell him what time the bell went for playtime, and would she go for a feel round the back of the bike sheds with him. He won’t be laughing for much longer. Wait until we threaten him with Edison’s murder.’

‘Do you think you are actually getting any closer to discovering who killed Philip Edison?’

‘Of course we are. We feel we are getting closer all the time and the net is being slowly drawn in tighter. But if you were to ask me the exact position at this precise moment and who I actually believe to be guilty, I would have to tell you that we still have an open mind and are continuing with our enquires, as the official jargon goes. But you don’t want official jargon or a press release type statement, do you? So I must simply say, No, we don’t know who killed Philip Edison. Yet.’

‘I see. Thank you.’

‘We have in custody at the moment, four prime suspects and yet we cannot be sure it was anyone of them, or if it was more than one of them, or if, for that matter, it was a complete outsider and someone, not as yet, even entering into the equation. We have already noted the fact that Scampton was observed leaving the Car Park alone in his Land Rover and we do not believe he could have carried out what, we think, he might have done in the time available, unaided. So if we assume he had help, which at this point I feel we must do, that introduces an additional person, or persons, unknown and we don’t know exactly where they fit in to the overall picture. All we can do is press on with the interviews and cross-questioning. Falsely accuse and suggest that others have made statements and given us facts that they haven’t, until finally, piece by piece, we draw out the truth. It will all come out with patience and I feel confident and so do my officers, that we are currently holding the guilty party and either they will give themselves away or one of their associates will, inadvertently, do it for them and give us the clues we are looking for, and we will then have our guilty party.’

The door opened and a Police Constable entered carrying more report sheets. Without a word he placed them in front of his Chief, who nodded his acknowledgement. Then as quietly as he entered, he withdrew closing the door behind him. The Superintendent scrutinised the latest arrivals, which added even more to the now quite substantial pile of paper work in front of him.

‘A further report on the man Scampton… He has apparently admitted to his association with Pat Edison and her daughter Jenny, but maintains and

categorically denies, that he had anything to with Edison's death. He said he was a good friend of Edison and used to do numerous odd jobs for him around the garden and his bungalow. When we told him we had recovered plastic sheeting and a quantity of cannabis resin from his cottage at Woodend, he replied and I quote, "So what. I use a fair amount of sheeting in my work and there is a load of it in our central stores. It is used and taken, by lots of other people beside me. Ask them, which of them wrapped up Edison's body in the same sort of plastic. There's enough of it about." As for the cannabis, he said we could not have found very much, because he did not keep it in any quantity. "Just a bit for my own use and the girl friend and if you are going to nail me for that, then you had better pull in and charge, over half the village, there is that much of the stuff about." When asked if he could suggest where someone might go to obtain supplies of cannabis, he laughed and said, "Get wise. Try any Pub for a start." He was unimpressed when we raised the point of the mud on his Land Rover tyres, again claiming that he drives everywhere in the course of his occupation, and for all we knew, he was going about his lawful business when he picked it up. He is, according to him, completely innocent of everything we suggest, and it is others, unknown to him, who did everything we are accusing him of. He said he could not help and we should "wise up" when we asked who those others might be, as he repeated yet again that he works alone and therefore can't possibly know what other people do as they go about their business. He denies that he had an accomplice, or possibly two, with him at anytime in the forest and says that not only were we not listening when he said he works alone, but if he does go in the forest, which is not that often, it is only to legally buy fence posts or dig compost for his gardening jobs and he always does that alone. When we told him we had statements from the Supervisory Staff and Forestry workers that he was regularly in the forest, or always in, as one worker put it and had, on numerous occasions, been told to keep out. He said that was rubbish and perhaps someone may have said something along those lines, on the odd occasion, but that was based on jealousy, as they knew that the materials he took were earning him a bit on the side, which they seemed to think they should have earned, as they nearly all had spare time gardening jobs, as forestry work is poorly paid. When we suggested that he might also have been alone when he dug graves or holes in which to later bury boxes, he just laughed and said, "You have got a vivid imagination and you won't catch me out on that one. Ask them other cleaver buggers. If they were always seeing me in the forest, how come they didn't see me dig these, so called, holes you are talking about. Because I didn't dig any bloody holes, except them to take compost out of, and that's only shallow and on the surface, that's why".

At that point the Superintendent stopped talking and fell silent, concentrating his attention on the pieces of paper in front of him. He continued to read while we all waited and looked in his direction.

'I think I should read the remainder of this statement exactly as it is written, as opposed to extracting the relevant information. You will appreciate why as I go along. It goes like this, "Why, if I am not going to catch you out on that one is there something else to catch you out on?"

"Of course their bloody well isn't and you damn well know it."

"No I don't. You tell me."

"Tell you what?"

"Is there anything to catch? For example if I went into a Pub, as you suggest, would I catch Johnson selling cannabis?"

"Piss off! You are not going to get me to pull in Johnson as easy as that."

"Then you perhaps?"

"You must be sodding joking. I admit I use it, but I don't deal it. Grow up."

"Then who does?"

"You find out. You're the clever ones round here. Try talking to your own Copper."

"Can we ignore the Copper for the moment and talk about Pat Edison?"

"Can I stop you? But why Pat Edison?"

"No. Because she says you had an affair with her."

"So what. If you ask round the village you will find out she was not the only one I had an affair, as you call it, with. I have already told you about her and her daughter, a younger, fitter version of the mother and she loved it, she did. Out in the open was her favourite place. Liked the soft grass against her arse, she did. Jealous are we Inspector."

"Yes, but only to the fact that you have already told us that. I though for one split second you might be telling me something new, and the answer is, No, to my being bloody jealous of you over anything really. In fact at this point in time I feel very sorry for you. But back to my point, what about the mother, Pat? Let's talk about her for a minute. You were quite involved with her at one time and she says, very seriously. So much so that her husband was becoming a real threat to you both and was constantly in your way and you felt a strong need to do something about it."

"Piss off. Your imagination is running riot and you won't catch me on that one either. How do I know what she says or what rubbish she's told you? He was no problem to me, that's all I know."

"Catch you out on that one Mr Scampton, which one? I seem to be getting a very strong feeling there is definitely something you desperately want me to catch you out on. Are you sure you wouldn't rather tell me about it. But forget that for the moment. Let us go back to Edison. If he was not a problem to you then who was he a problem to? Is there more than one person you are afraid of being caught out with. Or is there more than one thing I might catch you out on? Perhaps

in reality there are several. Tell me Mr Scampton catch you out on which or what? You are now getting me confused so let me ask you again and this time can you be more specific? Is there something there to catch you out on?"

"You tell me pal. You're the one who is admitting to being confused now, which is not surprising, your all wind and piss to start with. So you bloody tell me, cleaver bugger."

"Go on then. Yes I will. Let us talk about Philip Edison. The late Philip Edison. Tell me Mr Scampton, who mentioned Edison's body being wrapped in polythene before you did? I didn't and my colleague, sat quietly here, has not said a single word throughout this interview. So what do you know about it. Before you say anything, would you like us to go back through the transcript, play back the recordings of this and previous interviews, to remind you and jog your memory, or would you care to tell us now, how you knew Edison's body was wrapped in polythene or more precisely how it came to be wrapped in polythene sheeting of the type commonly used by you? Why was he buried in the forest where you admit you go regularly to dig compost and why you killed him?"

"I didn't bloody kill him."

"Well who did then? Your the one who seems to know all about him being wrapped in polythene sheeting."

"I don't bloody know, but it was not me. You said he was wrapped in my polythene, not me. I said fuck all about it. You said it or some other bugger said it, not me."

"No I did not. Are you sure you don't want me to play the tapes back to you? I will with the greatest of pleasure Mr Scampton if it will help to jog your memory and set the record straight. But if it was not you then tell me who it was, or I will have to assume, because you can't give me any alternatives, that it was all down to you, and pile all the evidence I have onto you. To be accused of his murder is a nasty business if all you did was wrap him up and bury him, out of the way, safe in the woods, and all the time it was someone else who actually knocked him off and is likely, because you choose to clam up, to get away with it."

"You can't do that. You have no bloody evidence of anything. You're filling me full of shit and are trying to stitch me up."

"Haven't I done that already? Or to be more accurate, haven't you already done that to yourself. If you don't think so then you wait and see. Let me ask you again, so that I get it clear in my own mind. Why did you do it?"

"I bloody didn't and you know I didn't, and you can't prove I did."

"Why are you so sure."

"Because it was not me and so must have been one of the others."

"That's interesting. Are you sure it was one of the others? Which others? Who then?"

"Piss off. I'm saying nothing. I know nothing about it and you take it from me, I didn't do it and as far as I am concerned, that's all you need to know."

"You say you know nothing about it and yet you say you know you didn't do it. Come on Mr Scampton. Make up your mind. You can do better than that. First of all tell me what you do know, then you can tell me, slowly and in your own time, all about what you don't know."

"Fuck off. I want some coffee and a fag?"

"No chance. You get neither and sit down. Sit down. I said sit down. You get nothing until you have told me all I want to know about Edison, the polythene, and why you killed him. Then you can have as much coffee as you like and if you can really convince me that you did not do it, I might even consider letting you have a cigarette and sending you home."

"Piss off. I am saying no more and you can fucking dream on."

"That's fine by me. We've got all we need. Johnson said all along that it was you and as far as I am concerned you have just confirmed it, with your knowledge of the polythene and the fact that you say it was someone else, but can't, or won't, give us a name because you haven't got a bloody name, because there isn't a bloody name, other than yours. It's all down to you, and that, as far as I am concerned, just about wraps it up Mr Scampton. You're facing life imprisonment and just for wanting to get your end away with Pat Edison or was it her daughter? I hope you think it was worth it. Perhaps you should have settled for just the daughter and a bit out in the open air."

"Johnson's a lying bastard and you know it. He only said that to save his own skin."

"Why does he need to? Are you now saying he did it?"

"No he's too bloody thick. All he's fit for is graft and a bit of simple dealing. You send him to dig, not kill, he'd only balls up something like that."

"What sort of simple dealing? Booze do you mean?"

"That and others."

"Others? Like what?"

"The bloody cannabis if you must know. It's him and his bloody wife that spreads it round the village and if he is going to shit on me, then he better look out because I can shit on him from a much greater height."

"That's not very nice Mr Scampton, shopping your partner in crime."

"He's not my partner and it's him who's tried to drop me. Not me him."

"Did he?"

"You said he did."

"Did I Mr Scampton? I don't recall."

"Bastard."

"Now, now Mr Scampton. So it was either you, Raines, Johnson, or Whiting that did it and you say it was not you and it was not Johnson because he

is too thick. So it was Raines or Whiting, or both. Whiting says he was not there that night and Raines has come up with an alibi. So what am I to deduce from that? That it must be you. See, we are once again, back with you. It's you that is in the frame all the time. I can't get away from you, can I? Can't be anyone else. Notice how all the time, no matter how we try, it comes right back on you."

"They are both lying bastards. They're all lying, bastards. They were both there and they know they were."

"You sure about that, Mr Scampton? I think you had better have that cup of coffee now, before you go on to tell me a lot more I already know and I tell you, in exchange, that I have not been exactly honest with you and some of the things I may have said may not have been exactly Kosher."

"What do you bloody mean? Not bloody honest, not fucking Kosher. You bastards are never Kosher when it comes to telling the truth because you don't know it when you fucking hear it."

"That may well be so Mr Scampton, but I do know, that on this occasion, I have not exactly told you the truth. You see Johnson says that on the night Edison died, he and Whiting were on the beach, Raines was in the Car Park, and you went up to the cliff top. Later you came down and said that Edison, the Coastguard, was up there when you got there and waiting, and that you had 'done for him'. You were in a panic, he said, and wanted them to give you a hand to get rid of him. Whiting agrees with that and has given us a sworn statement to that effect."

"Bring the lying bastard in here and I will soon show you who is telling the truth. It was him who said that, not me. He went up the fucking cliff that night. It was him."

"Is that so? And if that's correct then who gave him a hand to bring Edison down?"

"I don't know."

"Put that cigarette down. I didn't say anything about a cigarette. I only mentioned coffee. Hysterical blindness was it that night? Brain shut down did it? There, but saw nothing? Or another bout of amnesia conveniently brought on for now and for my benefit? Come on Scampton, you can do better than that. It was you, unless he flew down by himself, wrapped himself in polythene and walked into the woods and laid down for burial? Perhaps he even covered himself up and forgot to say where."

"Can I have that coffee now?"

"Constable would you get Mr Scampton a cup of coffee and give him a light for his cigarette while he and I go back to the beginning and eliminate some of the porky-pies he has been telling me."

"The what's?"

"The porky-pies. The lies Mr Scampton! You are now going to tell us how and why, you killed Philip Edison and how you wrapped up and disposed of his body."

"I keep telling you. It was not me: you need to be talking to that arse-hole, Whiting."

"So we do Mr Scampton, so we do. Now let's see. Was he heavy to carry when he was dead? Did you put him over your shoulder to carry him down or did you share the load with Whiting? Perhaps you took Johnson along with you to give you a hand. After all, he is the strong one. The one used for all the heavy work, you have said as much yourself. Where shall we start? At the beginning might not be a good idea? What do you think?"

He stopped reading and everyone sat in silence and looked at him, waiting for him to continue

'And that, Ladies and Gentlemen, is the update on Scampton. It would appear that he has fingered Whiting. It will be interesting to learn what progress is currently being made. He is now obviously cornered and scared and realises we know far more than he gives us credit for. Unfortunately progress with Whiting has not been so good. So far he is neither ruffled nor scared, according to the reports. He, so far, denies everything, is self-confident and gives one standard answer to all the questions put to him, - "piss off". He even gave the same reply when we accused him of following Mr Scott on the evening when Mr Scott set out to visit the Coastguards, on the campsite. He has not given an inch so far, not even on very minor issues. But it's all a matter of time and we have as much of that, as it takes. We have plenty to go on now and will, without any doubt, make a substantial break through soon. I feel confident that I could well be drafting my report on him, later this afternoon and have it ready and available for you by tomorrow.'

That concluded the business for the day, or so we realised, when the Chief Superintendent bade us Good Afternoon and got up and left.

Everyone else followed him out, including Fred and I and we found ourselves free to enjoy the rest, or what little was left, of the day in whatever way took our fancy.

CHAPTER FIFTY-FOUR

The weather, that late afternoon and early into the evening, was fine and sunny so we took full advantage and wandered round the town.

We were rather disappointed that we only had the end of the day left to us for leisure and could therefore not fit in a trip to visit, either the privately owned and well known, scenic railway, which we had been told, runs between the nearby market town of Pickering and Grosmont, or the ancient castle and a very popular local museum in the town of Pickering itself.

'There's a lot to be seen and plenty to do round here. For anyone who likes the rural type holiday there's more than enough to keep yourself fully occupied,' observed Fred. 'I wouldn't mind spending some of my leave in, and around, this particular area. It would make a pleasant change from the crowded beaches of Spain or some other overcrowded, over priced and over commercialised continental touristy place.'

Later, we decided to take the car and motor the few miles inland to the pretty little market town of Kirkbymoorside. There we visited all the Pubs and Hotels, which are quite numerous and all of which go to form a large part of the buildings that surround the central Market Square, a rather unique feature of that lovely little town. Fred once again played the hero and drank very little, so that she was legally fit and capable to drive back. She enjoyed the food in the Hotel, selected after much deliberation, having been spoilt, in the first place, for choice. At the end of a long day, having, before we finally left, sampled all the other hostelries and sinking above my fair share of the local brews, we made it back to our Hotel, arriving there just before midnight.

* * *

The following morning the Police car arrived spot on time, and once again we found ourselves in, what were now becoming, very familiar surroundings.

People, if that is the correct title for the inhabitants and occupants of a Police Station? But now, come to think of it, what do you call the inhabitants, or is it the occupants, of a Police Station? Are they blessed with, or allocated, a special name or title? For example are they, 'A group of Up Holders of the Law,' or 'a Gaggle of Constables,' or 'a group of Uniformed Bluebottles,' or are they simply a group of 'Nick-nicks'? I don't really know. However, those in this Station were beginning to become familiar with us and with our comings and goings. They began to recognise us as individuals and I was quite surprised at the number who

nodded, or spoke to us, as we passed along the corridors and went up and down in the lifts. From some of the cheery and topical comments that were made between them and which we overheard, it was obvious they all knew why we were there, and what we were involved in.

The Superintendent looked particularly pleased with himself as he sat down and placed a large pile of bound reports on the table in front of him. As usual all those who were supposed to be there were there and already seated and waiting

'I dictated my interim report and a summary of events and had it typed and bound up by the night shift and I have it here now, and ready for distribution. I would however point out that, this is only an interim report and as you will see has been literally thrown together and consists mainly of photocopies of documents and hand written reports and statements. It should however be sufficient for all our purposes until the final one, which will not be available until we have secured convictions and finally neatly wrapped everything up. There are still several loose ends to tie up, but these will all be taken care of by routine Police work. We feel confident that we will be able to charge Whiting with the murder of Edison and Scampton, at least, as an accessory. The others will all be implicated and charged with other, and in some cases, slightly lesser offences. But murder and the smuggling of arms, and not forgetting, of course, drugs, and anything closely associated with them, are all pretty high up on the scale of serious offences, so there are a number of people who are looking at some lengthy custodial sentences. Anyhow, you will become familiar with the details and the proposed charges when you read my report. There is a copy for each one of you, so if you will allow me, I would like to thank each and every one of you, for your contributions and tremendous input, and I further take this opportunity to tell you that I am delighted with the outcome. My final report, when complete, will be submitted directly to my Chief Constable and Special Branch who will then authorise and control the distribution to all interested parties. In the meantime should any of you require clarification on any minor points, please do not hesitate to contact me directly. You all know where I am. But not this afternoon, please. I am due a well earned break and propose to take it trying to knock a little white ball down, what always feels to me like, an ever decreasing small hole.'

'Then why bother to even try in the first place? How boring can one get?' whispered Fred, so quietly that only I heard her. I smiled but did not voice any agreement.

As everyone stood and made their way to the head of the table, they were each handed a copy of the report and were, at the same time, warmly shook by the hand and individually thanked, once again, for their efforts, by the Chief Superintendent.

When Fred approached; she being slightly ahead and in front of me, he handed her a copy of the report and said, as he held her hand, 'I shall miss you, young lady. I have got quite used to your company and your witticism over this last few days. Thank you very much for all you have done and tell me, before you go, did you think that when you first set out, it would all end up like this?'

'I don't really know what I expected. I think that at the outset, I thought, we would probably find that one of our people had perhaps had enough and decided to turn his back on everything and just disappear, perhaps with another woman. It has, after all, happened before. On the other hand, if there had to be a corpse, then I felt we would probably find a simple cause of death. Natural causes whilst on duty or something like that, or a simple, but rather unfortunate, accident, something basically along those lines. I honestly didn't know what we would find.'

'What about you Sir? What were your feelings?' addressing the remark to me.

'My feelings were very much the same as Miss Huntington. We were working together, as a team, on this job and therefore discussed all the possibilities on our way down here, or up here, as I find you Yorkshire people prefer to say. But, as you must realise, you can have no real idea of what to expect beforehand and somehow you always anticipate, or hope, that it will be a simple and straightforward issue. Unfortunately it rarely is and this case was no exception.'

'You have both done an excellent job and it is much appreciated. I will certainly see the right people are informed.'

'Thank you,' said Fred. 'But when you do, will you please avoid any mention of phone boxes.'

'Phone boxes Miss?'

'Sorry, you must forgive me. I should not have mentioned that at all. It is a private, interdepartmental joke and should be confined to the Service. To understand it you need to know our Chief and the special thing he has about the work we do and phone boxes.'

'Even though I don't understand and can't even begin to imagine what you are saying, you have my word. There will be no mention of phone boxes, and you Sir, once again thank you and take great care of this young lady.'

I looked at Fred and smiling, said, 'Why does everyone tell me to look after you?'

'Probably because we are all insanely jealous of you Old Man,' said Adams.

'Or perhaps it is because I don't have monstrous boobs and black stockings,' grinned Fred.

'So, even you noticed our Miss Smith, did you, Miss Huntington?'

'Not half as much as he did,' nodding her head sideways at me.

'A sign of very poor taste if you ask me Miss.'

'You're as smooth as this guy,' laughed Fred.

'Yes Miss and you will please note that it always takes a pretty girl to bring out the best in all of us.'

'Super-smoothie. Come on, Grundy, take me away from here before I begin falling for all this smooth talk and super slush.'

A final handshake, some last pleasantries and we were outside Thornly Police Station.

* * *

There was no Police Car waiting on this occasion and when I remarked on the fact, Fred replied, 'Of no further value, are we? So no more transport. I suppose we will have to walk back to the Hotel. We should have left the camper at the Police Station, but no. Who said, take it back to the Hotel and leave it there with the car? Not me, as I recall. But, not to worry, at least we can stop off at one of those nice little cafes, that you have dragged me past, these last few days and indulge ourselves. Unless you insist on going straight back, in which case you had better find a Taxi.'

We walked until we found the cafe that had particularly appealed to Fred and went in. But not before having stopped, on several occasions, each and every time we came upon a dress or fashion shop.

As I finished my coffee I said, 'What say we now make our way back to the hotel and read through this thing?' pointing at the report on the table beside me. 'Judging by the thickness, we won't get through it in five minutes, even if we speed read and skip every other line. There must be dozens of transcripts and God know what else in there.'

Rolling her shoulders, then pushing them both back to force her shoulder blades together, Fred said, 'Just give me a sec while I pop in the loo and sort myself out. Something is cutting into my shoulder and I can't get it to come right. I'll be right back.'

'Don't you be doing a Raines on me in there.'

'A what! Doing a Raines? What do you mean by that?'

'You know what I mean. Don't you be trying to commit suicide with all those tangled and twisted straps, in there.'

She just laughed and disappeared into the Ladies.

Once outside, I said, 'Feeling better now?'

'Yes thank you! Them damned straps, if they are not flat can really cut in and hurt.'

'Funny thing them bra's, aren't they?'

'No, they're not and how would you know anyway?'

'I know a lot about bra's.'

'Pull the other one. You only know about them from taking them off, I'll bet. Unless, of course, you have a dark secret that you have not yet told me about and you are a secret cross dresser? Grundy in frilly knickers, the mind boggles and so would the front of the knickers. Kinky,' she laughed.

'I do know a lot about ladies uplifting equipment. For example I know that they are strong enough to hold up some rather large and important bits on some very buxom ladies but are not strong enough to support the full weight of the wearer.'

'What on earth are you on about?'

'Mrs Raines! Her bra was strong enough to support her important bits but not strong enough to support all of her body when she tied it round her neck.'

'Want to bet. If you take the shoulder straps and attach them to the open bra in a way that would make it pull tight round your neck, then you can take my word for it, it would be strong enough to hang you. Why do you think Adams got as wound up as he did? If they had not found her when they did, she would have been a goner and he would have been in a terrible mess. You stick to cross dressing or whatever turns you on and leave the suspension of boobs to those who have them and know all about them. If you really want to experiment with lifting equipment, or you want to try and shock me, try parading around in a selection of posing pouches. The see through variety preferred.'

* * *

On our return to the Hotel we settled down, by agreement, in the relative peace of our own rooms and began to read the report.

It took me over two hours.

Most of the contents I was naturally familiar with, having all been fairly well covered at the briefings. I was, of course, very familiar with our own testimony and the statements we made and so skipped quickly through them. Some sections, however, required reading more than once because of the sheer complexity of the legal and police jargon inexplicably woven throughout them. Some of the incoherent statements made by the detainees and witnesses took some understanding and digesting. Once or twice I found I was just not taking any of it in and therefore was obliged to back-track and cover a particular section for a second, or even a third time.

When I finally finished I laid the whole thing on the table beside me, yawned and rubbed my eyes, then wondered how Fred was getting on.

One of the main reasons, that had prompted us to decide to go to our individual rooms and study the report separately, was to reduce distraction and the temptation to discuss the contents as we went through it. I had elected to read mine while laying full length on the bed. So having finished I swung my legs

over the side and, picking up the report, was about to leave the room when there was a knock on the door. My first reaction was to think that it might be Fred but then I realised, that even if she chose to knock first, she would not then hesitate before coming in. I walked across the room and opened the door. Standing there, with a charming smile on her face, was the young lady who normally served table downstairs.

'Sorry to trouble you Sir, but there is a telephone call for you down at the Reception Desk. A Mr Adams and he says it is rather important that he speak to you Sir.'

'Thank you! Lead on and show me the way.'

I followed her downstairs and across the hall to the reception desk, where she pointed to the telephone, which was off the cradle and laid on the polished surface. I picked it up, put it to my ear, and nodded my thanks to the girl, as she turned and disappeared through an open door.

'Hello, Grundy here.'

'Ah, Mr Grundy, Adams! I have just received a snippet that I believed is good news and thought you might appreciate hearing it. During the recent proceedings my backroom boys have been doing a lot of cross referencing and double checking, and sifting through our records, and those of other people and have come up with something which may prove very useful to our enquiries. In the very early hours of the morning following your stake out, in the village, the North Yorks traffic boys pulled up a van which was being driven erratically on the Malton Bye-pass, of the A64. The occupants were both Irish and drunk and the driver in particular, well over the legal limit, so they were taken in and the driver charged. They claimed that they had been to a party but could not remember where. A friend they had recently met at the seaside, they claimed. Do you believe that? Anyhow, the vehicle was taken into the compound where it was routinely examined for mechanical faults. Several minor things surfaced, like the odd light failing to work, wipers inadequate and the likes, but along with the overall report it was recorded that the van was heavily splashed, on the lower parts and up onto the windows, with light coloured mud and was still damp in places on the underside despite the fact that the road conditions were dry when, and where, they were pulled in. It was that which attracted our attention and so our boys followed it up. I have just got the report; the mud is identical to that found on Scampton's Land Rover, the same as that in the lane up to the Sawmill and on your partners trainers. We may well now have Scampton's accomplices from the night in question and I have asked for a fax to be immediately sent through to Mr Scott, for we may well also have the outside contacts to the Cell, he was most interested in.'

'That's brilliant. Three cheers for the Irish and their inability to stay off the bottle or should I say well done your people for spotting it?'

'Probably a bit of both but I thought you would be pleased to know. So now if you will excuse me I have a pressing engagement and will have to leave you. My kind regards to your partner. Goodbye.'

'Goodbye Mr Adams and thank you.'

I stood for a moment smiling before replacing the hand set and rushing upstairs.

I walked straight into Fred's room, without knocking, to find her still engrossed in the report. I had to forcedly restrain myself and found it difficult to contain my excitement following the news I had just received. But I had to, as I realised Fred was still reading and concentrating as she studied the report. I noticed that she too had chosen to stretch out on the bed.

'I've nearly finished. Come in and keep quiet. Isn't some of this hard going? Give me just a couple more minutes will you.'

I said nothing, despite the fact that I desperately wanted to, but in order not to disturb her, I stood looking out of the room window watching the world go by. I was watching a particularly smart young lady, who was on the point of disappearing out of sight, when Fred said, 'Finished. So now come and stretch out alongside me while we discuss it. At least we can have a cuddle, which is much better than just laying here and looking across towards that window in order to be able to see you.'

I turned to face her and blurted out, 'I have just had a phone call from Adams.'

'When?'

'Just now, before I came in and guess what?'

'What? But stop! Wait a minute. Before you even start to tell me, come over here.'

She moved to one side and I hoisted myself onto the bed and lay beside her. She pillowed her head on my arm.

'Now what was all that about and why the obvious excitement?'

'I had just finished reading the report and was coming in to see you, when the girl downstairs came up and told me Adams was on the phone and wanted a word.'

I then went on to tell her and repeated exactly what Adams had said to me.

'That's great and I bet Eddie will be really pleased when he finds out. Let's hope he gets something worthwhile from it.'

She picked up her copy of the report and waving it casually in the air said, 'Neat but cruel in the way they work, aren't they? Lean on one and then the other; twist the truth; frustrate them; harass them and work them into a corner; emotional blackmail; threats and promises. Promises: the snidest technique of them all, if you ask me. But still, you name it and they use it and all so damned effectively.'

'They obviously have their tried and tested methods, as we do and as you say, you must admit they are very effective, but on the other hand, don't they guess and surmise a hell of lot as they go along? Almost as bad as some of our interrogation techniques and did you notice that when they find they have got something completely wrong, they ignore the fact and simply drop it and immediately adopt an entirely different approach? I noticed they did that on several occasions as they went along. They would be pursuing one line then, without warning, they simply dropped it and immediately adopt an entirely different track and did you notice how many times they hammered a point when it was obvious that it was getting nowhere. They did that more than once. Then when they were pursuing one line of enquiry with, I think it was with Whiting, they then, without warning, stopped, and you never heard anything about that particular subject again. At the same time and right out of the blue, along comes an entirely different question or subject and more often than not in the middle of something else. A confusion technique no doubt, or is it the investigating officer's inability to concentrate on one subject for any length of time? But whatever, they can't lose in the end, can they? Just, as long as they keep at it. They hammered poor old Johnson once they realised he was the weak link and didn't they go after Scampton once they caught him out? I bet after this lot Bridgett Raines, to select just one, is a nervous wreck.'

'So in the end it was Whiting,' sighed Fred, 'or the Fisherman as we called him, who went up to the cliff top on the, so-called, fateful night. The fateful night! When I say it like that it makes it all sound like a television drama: "Where were you Doctor Death, on that fateful night?" He must have bumped into Edison, the poor soul, either by accident, or if not by accident, perhaps when Edison confronted him intentionally, or maybe it was completely the other way round and Edison bumped into him accidentally. The police seem to think, that either way, it was intentional, as they believe Edison had discovered what they were up to. But did you notice they have no real proof of that and the whole theory is based on pure speculation. They found nothing, no records, no notes, and could not even guess at an acceptable motive for him going up there when he did. I agree with what they say though, he just didn't go there for no reason that night. He must have known something, either about the smuggling or his wife's affair. My guess is that it was the smuggling. Sad really and a pity he left no written evidence, especially when in the end it cost him his life.'

'You can say that again. I bet he didn't join the Coastguard to end up wrapped in plastic and buried in the woods without being consulted about it in the first place.'

'You're terrible, do you know that? The man is dead,' as she stabbed her elbow into my ribs.

'Alright, sorry.'

'But getting back, to this report, now. I notice also, that the Police propose to contact CSOS with a recording of Whiting's voice to see if it matches any of their previous VHF transmission recordings.'

'Yes. I saw that. It's amazing what they can do with these modern voice enhancers. These days the poor pervert who fancies the odd dirty phone call to get his kicks, has had it. With modern electronic wizardry they can nail him almost straight away. So unless the poor "perve" sticks to heavy breathing and then does that in a foreign accent, he has no chance of practising his peculiar line of perversion. Poor sods, I wonder what they will come up with to get round that one? Anyhow, I suppose that what the Police hope to gain from all-this voice enhancement and electronic wizardry is more valuable additional material and evidence to ensure final convictions. They seem pretty confident that it was Whiting who sent out the VHF message to abort that first stake out that came to nothing. Remember the "Big Boy, Little Boy" message we came across recorded in those print-outs that we got?'

'Don't I just? I certainly do and the time we spent ploughing through them and it all now seems a hell of a long time ago and wasn't it cold that night when we went out for nothing? They could have, at least, done us a favour and shown up when we first expected them. It might have saved a lot of time and a load of this subsequent hassle.'

'And deprived me of my holiday while waiting for their second trip. I'm glad, in a way, they didn't,' I replied.

'Yes, that was nice I must admit and I suppose we should be grateful for that.'

'Anyhow, back to reality young lady. I don't know about you, but I found it interesting how they tricked them all and confused everyone, until they discovered that Whiting was the one who went up to the cliff top on the night of Edison's death. By the way I never saw any reference, in this lot,' waving Fred's copy of the report in the air, 'as to whether there was any, supposed, activity on the night of Edison's death. If they were expecting anything to come in or if they believed Edison was out on his own personal stake out. There was no mention of anything like that.'

'No, your right. I didn't see anything either. But how would they know? Edison left no evidence and so unless someone confessed to knowing something was coming in on that occasion and had they done that, it would certainly have been somewhere in the report and we would have seen it, but there is nothing. That will probably remain an unanswered question, unless it perhaps comes out much later, at a trial or something.'

'Either way, they found out that Whiting then came back down and collected Scampton and then they both went back up, to return later with Edison's body between them and then how, it was Scampton who took the body away in

his Land Rover. All the cross-accusations, suggestions, speculations, innuendoes, and downright lies that they used to trap them amazed me. Scampton, despite his denials in the beginning, did contact Raines' wife direct and it was him who gave her details and locations of all the buried materials. She then passed this information on, but I found it strange that, so far, no one has established the real depth of her husband's involvement in it all. I just can't see, or accept, her working entirely independently of him, can you? They are, after all, husband and wife and damn it, they were living together.'

'I found it mildly amusing where one of the Investigating Officers, added the footnote, which said, that he would not be surprised if, eventually, they discovered that Scampton had had an intimate relationship with Raines' wife. Not a guy to miss an opportunity, Scampton, was he?' laughed Fred.

'He has certainly been active all the way round. He was the one who took final delivery of everything, carefully wrapping it all, including Edison then selected locations for it's burial and only passing the information on to Mrs Raines. Not about Edison of course. That was a separate issue, if you follow what I mean? Is Scampton an Irish name?'

'I don't know. Why?'

'I wonder if anyone will ever find out how he originally became involved in all this. Was he emotionally, politically or religiously involved or was he an opportunist, a modern day pirate, a gun runner and smuggler; only in it for the cold hard cash?'

'Who knows? But any doubts about the existence of modern day, large-scale smuggling has certainly been sorted out on this job and perhaps Eddie and his team may eventually throw some light on that. He has plenty to go on.'

'You can say that again. I wonder just how much of it is going on, at anyone time, around the entire coastline. It's mind boggling when you think about it and what will happen if ever they open the Channel ports to the Continent and do away completely with Customs Control. Or what ever else they propose to do under these Common Market agreements that we constantly hear being banded around by politicians, who live in cloud cuckoo land.'

'Do you think they ever will?' she said snuggling up closer.

'What? Do away with Customs Control entirely and open up the ports. I don't know, but I personally hope not. Too many Raines, Scampton's and Thornton's and the likes of them about these days and I have never entirely trusted the continentals.'

'Anyhow, back to the present. Did you see where the investigation into the origin of the polythene led nowhere?'

'Yes and despite the original desire to tie it back specifically to Scampton. They couldn't even tie it back to Thornton as an alternative. The whole lot, that from the builder's store, his garage, Johnson's house, Scampton's Land Rover, his cottage

and the Parks Department warehouse, all from the same batch. All manufactured by the same company and distributed through wholesalers nationally. They must really turn it out in vast quantities and it must, literally, get everywhere.'

'And how about the tape?' she added.

'Yes. That was about as bad. I bet those forensic boys were well pissed off when they painstakingly removed all that sealing tape from both the body and all those cases and then after all that, could not match up a torn end with that roll from Scampton's house.'

'Do you wonder? He had probably used the stuff more than once since it was used on the body and that last batch of cases. But that was not the only roll don't forget. Remember how much they found altogether? There was a roll in nearly every house they visited and nearly all bought from the local Post Office. Bit of a wasted effort, if you ask me, but they must not have thought so.'

'Obviously, otherwise they would not have gone to one hell of a lot of trouble to do it and then mention the fact, that it led to nothing, in a report. You tend, or I do, to diplomatically miss out the failures, unless to include them, prevents someone from enquiring later why you did not adopt that line of enquiry in the first place, or include it, in your investigation.'

'Why do you think they, or Scampton, or whoever it was, buried Edison's body, where they did, so close to that batch of cases? If a third party was to be responsible for retrieving the guns later, then they could have very easily have dug up Edison at the same time,' asked Fred.

'Panic, I should imagine, was what prompted them to do it, that and the time factor. They had not planned to kill him, but did, and had to dispose of him quickly, so I assume Scampton dumped him in one of his prepared holes. Anyhow, I should imagine that the type of people, who would eventually come and dig the stuff up, would not be too concerned if they came across a body in the process. They would probably just throw it back and leave it.'

'I noticed also that they propose to prove that Whiting was the contact man for incoming supplies and got his information through the port at Whitby.'

'Yes, I saw that,' I replied. 'But nothing about how Thornton got his information. There is no mention of a tie-up between the builder Thornton and Scampton, although the Police claim to have established that Scampton was a frequent visitor to both the wife's shop and her home, when Thornton was away. He could have been passing information to her, Mrs Thornton, the builder's wife, when stuff was due to arrive, so that she could pass it on to her husband, thus implicating her far more than she maintains or anyone has so far found out. But I doubt it because that implicates other people who are into different things and I can't see a Terrorist Cell doing that. So my guess is he visited her for entirely different reasons and in a roundabout way, it had nothing to do with this investigation.'

'For nookie? Some bloke, some girl,' sighed Fred.

'Yes. Nookie. I don't think she is all that deeply involved, to the extent of passing detailed information about drugs and the likes, if you know what I mean? So the question of Thornton getting his information may never be answered unless of course it comes out later.'

'Not Johnson then, who worked both teams and despite the fact that he was not an integrated member of the Cell set-up? But then he could still hardly be considered as a suitable messenger, could he? If they did need a contact I am sure they would have selected her first. She is sufficiently intelligent but was probably just not included, whereas Johnson was just too thick and too unreliable to pass messages of importance to be even considered. Too stupid and talkative by far, and even more so, when drunk, and we had a sample of that, if you remember, when he performed that night in the Pub. Come to think of it, I'm surprised he was used at all in any capacity. He must have been their weakest link and a constant threat to them all and he must have talked when on their so-called, fishing trips with the Builder.'

'That reminds me of something else that has just crossed my mind and doesn't seem to have been considered in the report. I wonder if the booze and cannabis were all actively encouraged as part of the total overall set-up, although they acted independently and despite what we have already been told and assumed were perhaps used as some sort of screen to cover the more sinister aspects of their activities. Remember, all the villagers knew something was going on, despite the fact that some of them emphatically denied it. After all it is nothing new and has probably been going on around there for generations. Even the local Bobby knew something about it and therefore everyone, one way or another, must have been aware of it to some lesser or greater extent and accepted it. That way no one took too much notice or interest, in the nocturnal activities, which included the regular use of motorised transport and people regularly going back and forth up and down to the beach from the village, and passing through it, and doing so at all hours of the night. The fact that they regularly came across illegal booze as it circulated in the village and maybe heard some hints of drugs satisfied their curiosity and kept them basically quiet.'

'If that was right and the two were closely linked, or one was, as you suggest, a possible cover for the other, then I am sure the Police would have gathered that and put two and two together by now, and it would have been mentioned in the report. They were probably still two separate operations. The only common factors being Johnson, who worked both and the fact that both activities involved smuggling,' decided Fred.

'I wonder if they will ever find out just how much useful information Raines' wife managed to extract from the Customs and Excise man and how much of it was actually used. I feel sorry for him, as he will, no doubt, go for the "Drop of York" and end up in jail or at the very least, end up as a Supermarket Security

Man somewhere. Also I would dearly like them to prove, beyond all doubt, that Scampton had a helping hand in the forest, because from the beginning I could just not see him doing that lot alone. Perhaps they will now they have tied in those two that were picked up in the van?'

'Do you think Eddie's team will make any special efforts to try and find out who would eventually have come to collect those boxes buried in the woods?' asked Fred, changing the subject slightly.

'It wouldn't surprise me if the anti-terrorist boys don't already know that, or at least have their suspicions and it wouldn't surprise me either, if they thought, for one moment, that no one knew the dump had been discovered, if they didn't go ahead and fill it in or rebury something and then stake it out, in an attempt to find out what happens next or where it might lead them. But you heard what Eddie said about them, the terrorists, that is. Abandoning sights at the slightest suspicion. No doubt Eddies lot will do whatever they think is best. They are after all a very bright bunch.'

I am glad they found out where Raines' wife got her information from, despite the fact that it resulted in our first stake out being called off and us having to spend a miserable night out in the open.'

'Why? What makes you say that,' I asked.

'Well, I hate to admit it, but at one time I thought that perhaps her Customs man had got his initial information from the one, I can't even remember his name, who came to the village and we sent packing.'

'Len, what was his name? He sat opposite you. Strange you should say that because the thought had crossed my mind. Damn it, what was his name? Hang on a minute. It will be here, somewhere in this report, at the beginning, under persons attended.'

'It doesn't matter, you know who I mean.'

'It's here, Jones. Len Jones, that's him and another thing; did it also cross your mind that it might have been Eddie who told him everything that was going on in the first place, before we put the block on it, and he, Jones that is, passed it on to their uniform branch?'

'Yes.'

'Don't worry. Thankfully it wasn't him. But I still feel rotten over it and must admit, that at the time, I thought about it quite a lot and there was no one more pleased than me, when it turned out to be completely untrue,' I confessed.

'Do you think we should mention any of that in our final report to Cruickshank?'

'What, about Eddie? No, I don't think so. It is not necessary and may have harmful repercussions. If the Old Man has any sort of vendetta going on with the Anti-terrorist boys, then who knows how he might use a snippet like that. Let him make and fire his own bullets. Anyhow I think this report here, will be good

enough for the basis, at least, of our final report and then if we stick a few extras bits in, here and there, to impress the Old Man it should be good enough and keep everyone happy. Me in particular.'

'Why you?'

'Because I hate writing reports, that's why. So if you happen to be a dab hand at it, then you do it and I will add my name to it with pleasure.'

'You lazy beggar.'

'No I am not. I'm just not cut out for the administration stuff that's all. If I have to think about and then write, a Birthday card it can leave me exhausted.'

She laughed as she hit me across the chest with her copy of the report.

'Ouch, that hurt.'

'Not half as much as it will if you come up with any more bright ideas where I end up doing all the work.'

'I know one thing you like very much, where you are quite happy to do all the work,' I teased, as I gently stroked the area where her legs met at the top.

'Bugger,' and the report crashed down for a second time, only this time much harder.

'I thought we were discussing this report, not beating me to death with it.'

'We are, but won't get very far if all you can do is play cleaver devil and make silly remarks. If you want to be serious and discuss it then be serious and don't snipe at me or touch me. Particularly touch me there.'

'Sorry dear, where were we? Serious now. The report: and no more touching. Well for the moment at least. Are you sure about that?'

'Am I sure about what?'

'The touching?'

'For now: yes. The report.'

'If you insist but can I touch later?

'For goodness sake.'

'Can I?'

'Not if you don't get on with it.'

'With what?' I said as I gently touched her once more in the same very sensitive spot.

'Not that,' she laughed, 'you silly sod. The report.'

'If we must! Where were we? Oh yes, the police. The Police seem confident that Whiting killed Edison and will prove it, but there is no mention of how they reacted or what they did when Scampton changed his story and claimed that they had found Edison already dead at the top of the cliff when they got there and had removed his body so that it would not be found until they were well clear of the area. Secondly, with no body, he claimed that they believed, the Police would treat

him simply as a missing person and file the information away and not go sniffing around too much, thus leaving them free to get on with their dirty work.'

'I should imagine there was little or no reaction because of the simple fact they are confident of a conviction in any case. They have Whiting and a charge of murder, even as an accessory, or of terrorism, levelled at him and Scampton and both carry a similar penalty. So either way they have him and he will go down for a long time. Anyhow if it were true and they had found Edison dead and simply decided to remove him, then their assumption from that, that he would be treated as a missing person, with no fuss and then forgotten, did not work out, did it, for if you recall, there resulted from his reported disappearance, several unsuccessful searches and they were very extensive and spread over a fair period of time and covered a very wide area.'

'Yes, I suppose you're right and, as you said before, I doubt also if anyone will ever find out what Edison knew, discovered or suspected, that made him turn out that night. Unless of course, later on, the Police turn up some written or documentary evidence which shows he knew something but I should imagine they went after that right at the beginning and if they failed to turn up anything then I can't see them doing so now. Unless it comes out and they find out later, that he discussed it with someone else.'

'Who, a superior?'

'No. Not a superior or anyone associated with the Coastguard otherwise it would have been on record or in a report and we would have come across that. No I suspect that if there is someone, it will be someone not directly involved and who is a little reluctant to come forward at the moment because of the seriousness of the whole affair. I don't know who and I can't even begin to imagine anyone it might possibly be. It could be anyone. We don't know who his friends and confidants were. Again, something which may come out sometime in the future.'

'Have you given anymore thought to the dog?'

I turned my head and looked at her, 'The dog?'

'Yes: Edison's dog. Don't tell me you have forgotten about that. Remember it turned up back at his home on the night he disappeared and no one could understand why. Everyone said it would have stayed with him and probably stood it's ground and barked, or fought.'

'Maybe it did. Just think it through for a moment. If Edison took the dog with him, as his excuse to go out and the dog barked when Whiting got close to their hiding place, then it was the dog who simply blew their cover. Whiting is a big bloke. You saw him close too, yourself, in Whitby, that time. He may well then have kicked Edison, from what we know, or have been lead to believe concerning the damage done to his body, in the side of the head and possibly did so as the result of Edison being laid down at the time, hiding in the long grass. A quick, single, blow knocking him unconscious or even killing him outright. He may then

have turned and kicked out at the dog, who may have been barking and aggressive at the time, or on the other hand, he may simply have shouted at it and the threat was sufficient to make the dog run away. So either way hurt or frightened, it might have decided enough was enough and slunk off home. Who knows what a dog might do in those circumstances. I for one don't know very much about dogs, or their behaviour patterns in any given set of circumstances, let alone that particular dog or what it might do when it's master comes under attack. Come to think of it, we are already agreed that we know nothing of the circumstances surrounding anything that happened up there that night, so how can we start to assume what might have happened to the dog. All we know is Edison died from a single blow to the side of the head, consistent with a blow from a heavy boot and there were no signs of a weapon, if indeed one was used.'

'I guess your right, but it still strikes me as odd, unless in reality, the dog was as much her dog as it was his and it ran back home, frightened, to its mistress. Edison may only have thought that it was his and taken it around with him, but if she was the one who always fed it, then that might be another story.'

'Anyhow I think the dog and in particular what it did, or did not do that night, is irrelevant, don't you?'

'Yes. Thinking about it, I suppose so. But it was something that crossed my mind and I was curious about it.'

'Good god! Is that the time? Let me get up from here. It is time we moved our-selves and thought about something to eat. We haven't had much today and I wondered why my guts were rumbling. I think we should go out and eat tonight. That little restaurant we passed on our way back from the Police station, almost opposite Boots, looked very inviting. What do you think?'

'That will suit me fine.'

'Can I have a quick touch first?'

'No.'

* * *

Some short time later when I was in my room and getting ready to go out for the evening, Fred came in. She had a broad, cheeky grin spread across her face.

'You have to ring the Old Man right away.'

'I have to ring the Old Man, now? How do you know?'

'Because, I have just rung him! Now before I came in. I know just how much you dislike doing it, so, as I was feeling rather generous, following your offer to take me out for dinner tonight, I did it for you, but he still wants to speak to you and is expecting you to ring straight back. It is nothing confidential so you can use the phone downstairs.'

'Better go do it now, I suppose, and get it over with. At least if I do it straight away, I will have time to settle back down and then it might not spoil the rest of my evening too much. I won't be long and when I get back, I will be almost ready to go out.'

I went downstairs and across to the public phone by the reception desk. The telephone, at the other end, after I dialled, was answered almost straight away.

'Grundy here Sir.'

'Ah… Grundy. Yes. I am pleased with what I have been hearing. The report I got from Huntington, a short while ago, made a very pleasant change from some of the other reports that have recently been finding their way onto my desk. Reports from some of our other operatives none of who seem to be doing very well at the moment. In fact the department is heading for a near disaster if things don't improve tremendously and very quickly. But that is no concern of yours. But what is, and what I want an answer to, here and now, is since when did you think you can get another agent to obtain personal information on your behalf?'

I had no idea what he was talking about. 'I am sorry Sir, but I am afraid I don't follow.'

'Don't you? Well Huntington gave me a lengthy report and then added that you had specifically requested her to establish how much leave was due to you. She knows full well that I don't have that kind of routine information at my fingertips, but she said that you had specifically asked her, to ask me, to find out and that you required an answer as soon as possible. Immediately, in fact, was the impression I got. What the hell are you two up to now, is what I want to know? Out with it man! What is your game? You know damned well that I don't handle that type of routine information and we have been through this scenario before and I thought then that I had made my position on the subject very clear. You have no right and a damned impudence to ask for it and for that matter any other information of that nature, through me. I have far more important matters to attend to than to concern myself with staff entitlements.'

'I don't know anything about it Sir, but I will take the matter up straight away, with Huntington.'

'You had better and at the same time, tell her, for her information, that it is twenty-eight days, and in future to make her enquiries through the correct channels and not to request that type of information through me.'

'I will Sir,' was all I managed to say before the line went dead. You prat, I thought. Don't concern yourself with staff leave and entitlements. You made enough noise and were very much concerned over it all last year, when faced with a departmental request for a review of annual leave and possible salary increases.

I went back into my room to find Fred sat on the edge of the bed, thumbing through the report.

'What have you been up to now?' I demanded as I closed the door behind me. She looked up and just grinned.

'The Old Man is freaking out. What the hell have you been doing asking him about leave due to me? I have just had a lecture on procedure and the various sources from which not to obtain personal information and who it is not available to and all that rubbish.'

'He is our contact at HQ, just ask him, when we are out in the field and is always insisting that everything goes through him and that he is always to be kept fully informed. Well I asked in order that he is fully informed and I can plan and work out our next move. For what we do next and where we go from here, is going to be very important.'

'And have you worked it all out, now that you have successfully managed to get my ear chewed off?'

'Yes I have. First of all, you take me out to dinner tonight as you promised. Then tomorrow we settle our account here and take the camper back to the hire company. Then we collect the other car, go home, and report. Deposit what needs to be returned to stores and file our expenses and take all leave that is owing to us. Then with the camping gear, that I have decided to keep, we come back this way in my car and have a genuine holiday makers look at this lovely place and the surrounding countryside.'

'You really fancy roughing it in a tent after all?'

'Yes I do. Don't you. Or don't you want to come with me?'

'Don't be daft. Of course I do, but why in a tent?'

'Because what I have planned for you in a sleeping bag and under canvas, would embarrass hotel guests, even the most broad minded of the North Yorkshire people.'

'Shall I start packing now?'

'Not until you have taken me out and wined and dined me tonight.'

* * *

I have always hated those short strip lights that Hotels always believe to be essential equipment and therefore strategically place over the mirrors in bathrooms and all other washbasins. Granted they light up your face, but at the same time, the damned things blind you and always seem to be at their brightest and cause the most inconvenience, first thing in the morning. Who wants a strip light less than a foot away from your face first thing in the morning? I screwed my eyes up against the glare whilst at the same time I tried to focus on the razor nick that had appeared on my face and assess the damage I had just done. The surface water already on my face did nothing to help and the trickle of blood, suitably thinned was beginning to run down my neck.

'Fred: you there? Have we any tissues around here?'

There was no response and the blood continued to flow and spread even further and was now on my fingers and the face cloth. I stepped out into the bedroom to find it empty. I found a box of tissues on the dressing table and having grabbed a large wad retreated to the bathroom. When I finally stemmed the flow and re-emerged with a nasty nick on my face the room was still deserted.

The door opened and in walked Fred. She held a brown envelope down to her side and was reading from an open sheet of paper held in her other hand. She said nothing and, standing in the middle of the room, carried on reading.

'Where were you when I was bleeding to death and needed immediate medical assistance?'

'Shh,' was all I got in reply.

'Fan mail! It must be important if cutting my throat with a brand new safety razor is not important. I nearly died in there just now.'

'Shut up will you. This is important. Pat Edison is dead.'

I instantly felt numb and a strange feeling ran through me, 'Dead. How? Why?'

'Look. If you don't shut up and let me read this we will never find out, will we?'

I moved over and stood behind her, planning to try and read over her shoulder. She twisted her body and moved away.

'Go away. You can have it as soon as I have finished. Now move out of the way and let me read.'

The hand holding the sheet fell to her side before, without looking up, she slowly offered it to me. As I took it she said, 'Pat Edison has jumped off the cliff, or they think she has.'

I took the single sheet of paper with the Police Badge embossed on the top left hand corner and the word, 'Confidential' stamped in red along the top.

'How come?'

'Read and you will find out. Poor woman.'

I sat on the edge of the bed and read it through. Fred placed the empty envelope on the bedside table and stood looking out of the window. I notice how pale and dejected she looked and how, suddenly, she looked so tired and all in. This latest piece of information had obviously had a very profound effect on her.

'Where did you get this?'

She pulled herself together and seemed to brighten up a little. 'They handed it to me when I went down stairs. I got there just about the same time as a Policeman came into the foyer to deliver it. What do you make of it?'

'Sad. A bloody tragedy. What the hell made her go do that?'

'It tells you in there.'

'Does it? It tells you what they think happened.'

'It must be true, she left a damned note according to them.'

I continued to quietly re-read through the lengthy typewritten sheet.

'Despite what it says here and I am not disputing it, she had no need to go topping herself. In fact that's the last thing I expected she would do. Just goes to show you never know what goes through people's minds. But why did she have to get all worked up over that bastard Scampton?'

'Look, you've read what it says and sadly women have been known to do silly things like that over men.'

'Yes, but why if it was necessary to do something as drastic as that has it taken her so long? He had been bothering with Jenny for months, as far as we gathered.'

'More recent events I should imagine. The loss and finding of her husband and the ordeal of being dragged into that Police Station and the possible implications that might arise from that, all were probably too much for her. Who knows? All her long term plans and aspirations shattered. Lost her lover. God knows.'

'Exactly, but I am still staggered and find it hard to believe. She obviously thought long and hard about it, hence the note saying where she was going and what she proposed to do when she got there. Then she calmly goes and does it. Could you sit down and write a lengthy note, almost an explanation to justify it and then walk all that way to where Edison's stuff was found and then simply throw yourself off the cliff to land on those rocks below?'

'No I couldn't, but who knows what people will do when they finally make up their minds and are desperate?'

'Desperate, just because her lover left her and went chasing her daughter and then refused to come back after her husband disappeared. That's enough to go nose dive off the cliff?'

'She apparently thought so. The poor, poor woman,' said Fred.

'She bloody did and I'm amazed. According to that report she obviously calmly sat down and wrote down a detailed explanation of how she had told Scampton about the possible Insurance money and the few thousand already in the bank, that Edison's father had left him a few years back, and how if he came back to her he could have it all to start his Market Garden, and they would work it together, and he apparently said no and stayed with the daughter, Jenny. She then puts it in an envelope, addresses it to the Police, and puts it in the Pub letterbox as she passes on the way up to the cliff top where she goes hand gliding without wings. She had either a lot of guts or was, sadly, very sick.'

'Either way she has done it and if she was sick, which is always the first excuse trotted out when someone decides enough is enough, then someone made her that way, someone drove her to it and now it is too late and there is nothing anyone can do about it. I only hope that all the shit heads involved in this nasty business realise just what misery they can cause and how often things like this drag

in and seriously affect perfectly innocent people. Bastards everyone of them and I hope they all rot in hell.'

I stood up and as I did so Fred lunged at me, snatched the document out of my hand and angrily threw it onto the floor. She then flung her arms round my neck and buried her head into my shoulder. 'Fuck, fuck, fuck,' she sobbed.

I held her close and all I could think of, and all I was able to say, under the circumstances, was, 'Gentle now. I know it should not have happened but it did and we, sadly, were not in a position to do anything about it.'

* * *

The following day, after we had sorted everything out and as we left Humber on the journey South, I noticed the placards outside all the local Newsagent shops; they read, "COASTGUARD DEATH - SUICIDE VERDICT." "INQUEST TO BE HELD ON WIFE."

THE END

Printed in the United Kingdom
by Lightning Source UK Ltd.
106606UKS00002B/36